I0773203

BOOK FOUR OF THE

FERAL FLAME

JOAQUÍN BALDWIN

Copyright © 2025 by Joaquín Baldwin.
Written by Joaquín Baldwin.
Edited by Andrew Corvin.
Proofread by Shiloh Skye.
Cover illustration by Ilse Gort.
Book design and layout by Joaquín Baldwin.
Illustrations and maps by Joaquín Baldwin.
Author's Photograph by Timothy Dahlum.
Typeset in: *Concourse*, by Matthew Butterick; *Cinzel*, by Natanael Gama; *Inknut Antiqua*, by Claus Eggers Sørensen. *ETbb*, by Dmitry Krasny, Bonnie Scranton, Edward Tufte, David J. Perry, Daniel Benjamin Miller, & Michael Sharpe.

Library of Congress Control Number: 2025921274
ISBN: 978-1-961076-12-9 (e-book)
ISBN: 978-1-961076-13-6 (paperback)
ISBN: 978-1-961076-14-3 (hardcover)
ISBN: 978-1-961076-15-0 (audiobook)

First Edition, 2025.
Los Angeles, California.
NS4-P1.05

"Such distortion tells me nothing of him, and is only
terrifying because so much is unknown of myself."

— Samuel R. Delany, *Dhalgren*

UNTHAWING OCEAN
Elanúbril
KHAAR DU TRIBES
TESLURKATH
Baysea Beyenaar
Tesz Bay
FJORDSULF
STELM NEDROSS
Spine Bay
FJORDLANDS
Needlecove
STELM
Koroberg
Isdinnklad Sea
Zovaria
Isdinnklad Lake
Moordusk
ZOVARIAN UNION
Nebush
Muskeg
STELM CA'ÉLI
VARANUS
Old Karst
New Karst
Klemes
Klad Senet
Fel Varanus
FREE TRIBELANDS
Fel Baulos
QUESCENT OCEAN
Yanan
STELM ANKROV
Allathanathar
BRASHA'IN SCABLANDS
Sajal Crater
UKHRELA RANGE
STELM SAJAL
Dunewaar
YENWU
MOUNT LOOR
Yenmai
Lhambor Di
UNCLAIMED TERRITORIES
Esduss Sea
Aksas Di
YENWU STATE
AZUREAN
Navar Mat
KINGDOM OF BAURAM
Kizad
Bay of Hashmun
Bauresht Sea
Gulf of Erjilm
ASHEN
Taring
Ngau Tor
Nisos
Normouth
REPUBLIC OF LEREV
NISOS
CAPRICIOUS
Loorian Continent
Denjan Continent

NOSS

Khaar Du Wastes
Khaarkadesh
Ash Sea
Dathereol Princedom
Therimark
Falbagrish Range
Loorian Continent
Jerjan Continent
Unclaimed Territories
Bergsulf
Da'Aju Caldera
Stelm Khull
Brimstowne
Fractured Range
Wujann
Anglass
Megian Empire
Lequa
Lequa Sea
Withervale
Anglass
Shaderift
Wyrmwash
Ophidian Sea
Hestfell
Bayanhong Tribes
Heartpine
Thornridge
Ultad
Farjall
Kayamur
Montano
Stelm Rilgékeo
Caerlye
Kalford
Brinelaar
Bighorn
On Khurderen
Sharzi
Dorhond Tribes
Stelm Tai-Du
Stelm Rilganesh
Oskirin
White Desert
Bay of Negórmea
Using Empire
Tarpits
Archstone
Elmaren Queendom
Azash
Hashan
Shusnukran
Moonrise
Shash
Stelm Mokvo
Nargara
Graalman Horde
Doralghon
Sharr Helm
Tumultuous Ocean
Alommo Sea
Tharma Federation
Scoria
Mount Alvforg
Sundhollow
Korolok
Cape Artok
Kingdom of Afhora
Ocean
Illenev
Druhal
Austral Sea
Wastyr Triumvirate
Farkhalum
Seafaring
0   100   200   300   400   500   Distance in Miles   1000

Bay of Hashmun
Sentirya
ENDFALL TRENCHES
TUNIRIO RUINS
LONGFLAV EXPANSE
Salúmna
ASHEN DOM
TROMMODROLOM
Jubiet
SHARDBOW HINTERLANDS
CHASEN COULOIR
Northden
Phuoccong
BLIGHTWOOD COASTS
ASH KEEP
Using Empire
SORROWFIELD BARROWS
NIGHTWELL
Jova
FAULTCRAGS
RUMPLE FELL
Cherville
Thurv
HUM-O-TARY LURESS
Thuan
FA-HOL RUINS
SILVUR'S CREST
Shuled
Oberes
CRYSTAL CAVES
LAAJA KRISSI
Shun-Ji
Tsogri
Gulf of Erjilm
Astaoth
Tegon
COLOSSUS OF THYKA
SIPHON KEEP
Quar
GRENGLE WILDLANDS
ENTORBA
Sinsimbo
Flyyra
VOLCANIC FORGE
LAAJA LOVAD
Biiro
Bracutir
LAAJA VERELIA
Taerim
FRONVELL
Guyo
Raraq
Gar-Ji
Iglit
LAAJA ASH
Ngau Tor
Nudoroth
SUNKEN TEMPLES
Phalax
OMÃO DESERT
Nannúr
ESRES PASTURES
Tetra
Anbi
Jema
Fargo
Esres
Güer
URROST REMNANTS
TWIN VIE
CHALICE
BRAMBLE MESA
Vaurvon
Rummo
SANDVEIL
Millwell
Silkru
Silkari
NOVOK GATE
Shin-Par
Ewut
CONRA
SENTIRO
Arbergo
Kimor
Capricious Ocean
0   10   20   30
DISTANCE IN MILES

Perifall
Dathereol Princedom
Foen's Tomb
Lixallen Peninsula
Thimbell
Voresea
Shatter Harv
Dismal Shores
Alla Vei
Grasius Isle
Pelesh Quinesh
El No
LEQUA DOME
KROSTDROLOM
Er Isle
Lequa Sea
Cossta
Tib's Tower
Pel Eru
Quagro
Pel Shixen
Tunfss
Isdinn Kimen
Almoth Bay
Bay
Eskis
Suil Drenith
Bramble Bay
Ushwen Krost
Kruss
Apáni
Kelbus Ngth
Shiorelc Forest
Lith-Leo
eaborr
Aldávi
Loompool
Shallu Forest
Munn
Fexr-Nol Ruins
Khanotámba
Stelm Midir
Durg Namba
Ferne Goror
Dier
Calbor
Yango
enshire
Jiannu
Ifen
Klad Jilo
Cowomu
Lamy Stein
Khai
Ruins of Lixaon
Stelm Oath
Trod Bumeroi
Ommuv
Erath
Stelm Astar
Orjusa Forest
Fort Hio
Bayanhong Tribes
Si-Chi
Tunhau
Tonhond
Birka Forest
Dejian
Klad Luvo
Mount Nox
Spire Falls
Mireinfield
Shaderift Aqueduct
Shaderift
Naysayer's Crypts
Amáho-Dierr
Negian Empire
Vezza Bay
Wyrmwash
Pel Adden
Angin
Wyrm Core
Ophidian Sea
Haulf's Covenant
Zerren
0   10   20   30   40
DISTANCE IN MILES

ICHOR WELL
DOMINION WILDERNESS
LAAJA HUÄMBAR
STONELEAF MESA
TANUS RETREAT
NETHERPOINT
FROSTFORGE GLACIER
VENOM TIP
KLAD GOLLOM
MONFARE FOREST
SOLANTE
SULFIL
MOUNT VELLUS
HEXAIR
PARSI RUINS
STELM RILGÉREO
DRIFT FOREST
FORRATH
NORTH MARR
UNAUR'S TRENCHE
GURROCK
BIGHORN DOME
RILGDROLOM
SLAIN PASS
UNAUR'S OUTLOOK
DARHELM
KI FORD
Caerlye
GWIN FOREST
KHEH GLACIER
Bayanhon Tribes
POTASH MINES
RILLEN
YAVISA
AJACAD
PORAS
ENHELM
ERU TIH
UV TIH
Degian Empire
SEGIO
EWAW FOREST
On Khurde
FEL TIH
Uinin
SJOB
MANKAR DUOL
WAGRAVE JUNGLE
STISS OVEH
MOUNT RASHUR
HONYA
Brinelaar
Runa
JI TIH
VODUR
MANKARREN
MIDIR
NU'EV
GASESH
SALT MINES
NEF TIH
MAFARG FOREST
OOLAR
KLAD RUUN
PUMICH
MANKAR ENOS
LOOJAD
TURU GOLM
SHRIIN
JUSSMOR JUNGLE
YAVVER LOOKOUT
BATR
DUR
MORAINE CABIN
ORJUSS
NAMIV
JERJA GLACIER
NIR TIH
AR TIH
ALLITH GLACIER
Dorhond Tribes
GALVANUM VEINS
LAAJA JERJA
ELEVATION: 38,264 FEET
NAMBRO GLACIER
ELDARA CATACOMBS
NAMOOR DEPTHS
FROSTREACH EXPANSE
STELM RILGANESH
Namoor
SHARDMERE GLACIER
HOARFOREST
JANUDETH MARR
RUX GAT
SERAC CANYON
THE WITNESS
YLIA MARR
SUNDD ALTAR
IGNIMORR
WITHERED FORUM
WINDERA FOREST
FANTUR RUINS
AZURA GLACIER
LAAJA NEVIENN
NEVI ATH GLACIER
NEVI UR GLACIER
ECHO ALTAR
TOMBS
0   10   20   30   40
DISTANCE IN MILES
SCAR TENUA

Regent
Olgerbunn
Honfur
Kelabek Trenches
Scera
Terem
Norté Desert
Malady Spring
Kurtkara Crater
Ceras Cape
Eolian Bluffs
Portello
Fenrye
Lone Wolf Cape
Pandu
Engolbar
Drossmuur
Bandit's Hideout
Chaamu Tago
Onyx Monolith
Razuura
Ommo Khurassash
Crumbling Altars
Zahi'ne Ruins
Gremin
Temba
Iaaja Wentaresham
Stelm Nibral
Erot Glacier
Maashu
Cedar-Liv
Quas Omin
Hirg Glacier
Taifad Glacier
Magnus Maar
Bialu
Tharma Federation
Sulfide Mine
Garlot
Fehenstelm
Gravelands
Taga Srascas
Nebat
Freeti
Aurnuo
Tombol the Boiled
Liga Deadlands
Ennvii
Byron's Quarry
Ommo
Tartarus
Vesicant Fumaroles
Laaja Dustfenn
Maw of Roen
Ather Dai
Khestduur
RigChes
Trod Ingot
Stelm Summ
Enholm
Miregalf
Gomatolite Reef
Bullion
Maw of Caen
Trod Mory
Gayan Shore
Slagg
Blindriver Valley
Argyria
Sansor Crypts
Fel Strata
Fel Galvanum
Galza
Gerkan
Tratpop
Coatlan
Fel Onett
Fel Ringcreo
Fel Keldura
Falos Remains
Hunnu Crater
SCORIA DOME
BALASTDROLOM
Kingdom of Athora
Fallen Urth
Suras Vin
Sundhollow
Fairlion
0 10 20 30 40
DISTANCE IN MILES
Trothiz Tumuli
Vault of Arrazu

Table of Contents

Author's Note

Hello reader; I'm glad you made it to Book 4 of the *Noss Saga*! This volume has quite a change of pace—I hope you'll enjoy how different it is from the others. As with the previous installments, I have a few recommendations before you get started:

Maps and illustrations

There are several new maps for this book. To properly read all the details on the maps, I recommend you view them at full resolution and in color. Visit the link below to find all the maps, illustrations, and other goodies.

Guides & glossary

Characters, locations, and common Miscamish words can be found in the appendices at the end of this book. Previous guides, such as the pronunciation guide that was included in Book 1, or the guide to the Eighteen Clades from Book 2, are not printed in this installment, but they are available on the link below alongside even more extras.

Supplemental Materials

Follow this link to access all the Supplemental Materials, including the color illustrations, maps, glossaries, lists of characters, locations, and more.

JoaquinBaldwin.com/book4extras

THE STORY SO FAR

The *Noss Saga* is a complex tale. It's easy even for me to forget all that happened in previous books. While I try to remind the readers of the preceding events along the way, I recognize the need for a full-on refresher.

The following is not a comprehensive synopsis, so it will not make much sense unless you've read the previous books in this series (you should not be here if you haven't read them yet, either way).

Thank you for joining me for the next part of this queer and epic journey. I hope you enjoy your return to Noss.

May the moon light your path,

— Joaquín Baldwin

BOOK 1 - WOLF OF WITHERVALE

Lago Vaari is entrusted with Agnargsilv—the mask of canids—by a shapeshifting elderly woman named Sontai, who asks him to take the mask to her grandson, Bonmei. Lago tricks Chief Arbalister Fjorna Daro of the Negian Empire, who had been hunting Sontai to acquire the mask. Fearful of the mask and the soldiers pursuing it, Lago and his best friend Alaia hide it away in a coal mine. After his father kicks him out of his home, Lago gets a job at the Mesa Monastery, delivering packages for the Havengall monks and helping Professor Crysta Holt with the monastery's telescope. He falls in love with the stars, the planets, and the moon. A dire wolf, a species thought extinct, is killed near Withervale. The creature is much larger than any in fossil records, and the recent collapse of the Heartpine Dome's roof seems to be related to the giant's appearance.

Six years later, Withervale is attacked by Fjorna Daro and General Alvis Hallow. Lago escapes through the coal mine and retrieves Agnargsilv, aided by a scout from the Free Tribelands named Ockam Radiartis, who considers Bonmei his adopted son. Alaia and Lago's pet dog Bear join them. Lago learns how to see the threads of life with Agnargsilv but knows there are more powers the mask is hiding. Shortly after they arrive at the Thornridge Lookout, Fjorna's squad attacks them, killing Bonmei. Lago defeats Fjorna's soldiers by using Agnargsilv's powers, which let him see in the pure dark and foresee the attacks of his enemies. Platoon Commander Jiara Ascura also joins their party, and the five of them flee by using Agnargsilv to penetrate the wall of vines that surround the Heartpine Dome, hoping that taking the mask away from the Free Tribelands will avert a potential war.

After being imprisoned for some time with a handful of survivors from her squad, Fjorna and her team escape to warn Alvis Hallow. When they find him, Alvis is already in possession of the mask of cervids, which he stole from the Anglass Dome. With Artificer Urcai's aid, Alvis finds his elk half-form. As the Red Stag, he kills the weak Emperor Uvon dus Grei and takes the throne of the Negian Empire under the title of Monarch Hallow.

Inside the Heartpine Dome, Lago and his friends discover that the Negians exterminated the Southern Wutash tribe who lived there. They find strange quaar artifacts at a broken lattice located in a temple at the dome's trunk, and also encounter Safís, a white wolf shapeshifter who is the spirit of canids. They help her escape the dome and then head north, searching for the Firefalls—also known as Minnelvad—where they hope they might find the surviving "cousins" of the Wutash.

After a steamy visit through Brimstowne, they venture up the hot creeks of the Firefalls, where they are struck by a blizzard. Lago is caught in an avalanche and overcome by the toxic fumes of the falls. He hallucinates a huge golden bear coming to save him. He wakes up in a cabin and meets a corpulent giant named Banook, who rescued him and his friends. Lago quickly grows fond of the mountain of a man.

Banook, who is the spirit of ursids, tells the wayfarers the story of the Downfall, and how the domes were grown to protect the eighteen chosen clades from the cataclysm. He reveals that the dome of ursids was never grown, causing the demise of the Northern Wutash tribe. Banook also teaches them about the Nu'irgesh—animal spirits of each major clade—and tells them that the mask of ursids, Urnaadisilv, lays buried under the icy caldera that engulfed the city of Da'áju. He promises to take them there once Winter is over.

With Banook's aid, Lago finds his timber wolf half-form and is gifted with the name of Sterjall, as well as with a dagger named Leif, which Banook and Ockam crafted from a lattice segment and dire wolf fang that Lago took from the Heartpine Dome. Lago-Sterjall and Banook fall in love but are fearful of their future because Banook will not be able to join them—he can only travel where other bears reside, and the bears only live in the mountains of the north.

During an excursion into Brimstowne, Banook sees that Negians are searching for the mask Lago-Sterjall wields. He meets with a ranger named Ardof, who tells him that the Red Stag may be readying to attack Withervale.

The Red Stag has ransacked the Anglass Dome and reshaped the Negian Empire's politics. He captures and mindlocks Sovath, the cervid Nu'irg, forcing her to join his army of enslaved cervids, including the megaloceroses (giant elk) and cervalces (giant moose). The Red Stag ventures to the Lequa Dome. With the aid of Fjorna, he acquires Krostsilv, the mask of musteloids, and gifts it to General Jaxon Remon. He also gifts him with caged jarv wolverines—vicious, bear-sized creatures he captured in the Lequa Dome.

Throughout Winter, Lago and his friends train with Jiara, preparing to journey into Da'áju. Once the Thawing season arrives, they leave Bear in the cabin with two bears who will take care of the mutt, and venture into the Da'áju Caldera. They find the ice-buried temple of ursids and rescue Urnaadisilv from its forsaken depths. Ockam becomes the wearer of Urnaadisilv, although he is not yet able to shapeshift. From a rock-carved map, they learn that there was once another dome in a volcanic desert known as the Brasha'in Scablands; they do not know why it is no longer there. They decide they should travel west, to the Moordusk Dome, in hopes of finding a Miscam tribe who might know why the domes have not opened as they were meant to open, and who might know how to defeat the Red Stag.

Upon exiting the glacier, they spot an orange glow in the distance: Withervale is on fire. Lago-Sterjall needs to help Crysta and his other friends in the city. Banook tries to follow them to Withervale, but once he is too far from his bears, the Nu'irg withers and turns feeble. Unable to follow any longer, he kisses his precious cub goodbye.

Book 2 – Masks of the Miscam

After leaving Banook, the wayfarers hurry to Withervale to save their friends, but the Red Stag breaches through the ramparts with his megaloceroses and conquers the city with his army of cervids. Lago-Sterjall is attacked by General Jaxon Remon, a wolverine general wearing Krostsilv, who kills Khopto and breaks Sterjall's arm. During the Winter months, the Red Stag had traveled east to the Lequa Dome, where he enslaved the local tribe and took the mask of musteloids for his general; he now faces Sterjall, flanked by Fjorna's arbalister squad.

Taking a feral bear form, Ockam saves Sterjall, but dies from his wounds aboard the catamaran sailing them toward the capital. Jiara becomes the steward of Urnaadisilv.

After Ockam's funeral, they travel to Zovaria to meet with Balstei Woodslav, an artificer who studies the aetheric elements. Kedra (a scout who has been helping Crysta) betrays them and calls for her uncle, Admiral Grinn, to seize the masks. Balstei helps them escape Zovaria. They journey through the bogs and enter the Moordusk Dome, where the Laatu Miscam live. They meet Khuron Aio-Kulak, Nelv (the felid Nu'irg, a clouded leopard), and Blu (Aio's smilodon companion). During a Laatu council, they decide they need answers and determine that Mamóru, the proboscidean Nu'irg, might have them—if he is still alive.

To prepare for their adventure, they train with an allgender shaman named Sunu, who has an azure-hooded jay herald named Olo. They learn about hot crystals of aetheric sulphur named *brime* and scout the perimeter of the dome to prepare for the threats they may encounter. Sterjall takes Kulak outside the dome to see the stars, and Kulak takes Sterjall to see fireflies. They begin to develop feelings for one another, fearful of being caught by the strict Laatu.

The wayfarers venture out of the dome to the Brasha'in Scablands to locate Mamóru. Jiara finds her bear half-form while climbing among redwoods; she receives the name of Kitjári. In the volcanic desert they find Mamóru, who tells them the true story of the Silvesh, that Noss themself is truly conscious, and that the Silvesh were used to speak to Noss in times before the Downfall. He recounts the story of Jiu Zezi, who discovered the comet that would later cause the Downfall. Mamóru's entire story is written upon the walls of lava tubes, a story he intends to preserve for the future. He explains that the threads the mask-wearers see with the Silvesh are consciousness, and that the masks control the force of empathy itself. Mamóru helps them retrieve the proboscidean mask from the collapsed temple, for which he himself will be the wielder.

They battle their way back into the Moordusk Dome, with Mamóru taking the form of a mammoth. At a council they decide to open the Moordusk Dome and agree that their new goal is to gather six Silvesh, the minimum needed to speak to Noss, who may have the answers that Mamóru is unable to provide. While Balstei travels with the Laatu and felid migrations with the intent of transcribing Mamóru's petroglyphs, the rest of the wayfarers sail west to the Fjordlands Dome aboard a ship named *Drolvisdinn*.

Through Olo, Lago sends a message to Crysta, asking her to travel to the Moordusk Dome before it fully opens. Crysta replies that Banook is now with

Safís, the canid Nu'irg. The white wolf has claimed that the Anglass Dome is slowly growing out of shape, causing them to fear for its future. Crysta rushes to the Moordusk Dome accompanied by Hefra Boarmane, her naturalist friend. After exploring the Laatu lands for some months, Crysta and Hefra decide to follow in Balstei's footsteps. They reunite with him in the new Laatu colony hundreds of miles away, south of the scablands.

The Red Stag is amassing an army of cervids, planning to strike the Jerjan Continent. Crescu Valaran, second-in-command of Fjorna's squad, is promoted to general and given the title of Silv-Thaar Valaran, taking over Jaxon's legion. He finds his half-form of a raccoon, but a rift forms between him and his old arbalister squad. The Red Stag crosses the Ophidian Sea and breaches the Bighorn Dome, using giant pipe segments to keep the vines open, enabling his entire army to flood into the dome. Two Ikhel Miscam factions inside Bighorn are at war with each other. Luhásu, chief of the Western Ikhel Miscam, helps the Red Stag defeat the Eastern Ikhel, and as a reward is granted Rilgsilv, the mask of caprids, becoming Silv-Thaar Markhor. With the aid of a caprid army, the Negians take the Bayanhong capital of On Khurderen. The Red Stag decides to split his efforts, sending Silv-Thaar Valaran and the arbalisters to take the Moonrise Dome while he secures the Archstone Dome.

To the far west, the wayfarers sail into the Fjordlands Dome, land of the Puqua Miscam, where they recruit Prikka-Nalaníri (a skilled chef, wielder of Nagrasilv) and Captain Siffo. Nalaníri sets the dome to open and boards *Drolvisdinn* to sail away with the wayfarers, followed by *Fjummomurr*, Siffo's vessel. They are attacked at sea by Admiral Grinn and Kedra, but defeat their enemies and enter the Varanus Dome, where the Mo'óto Miscam once lived, though they have all died from a terrible disease.

From a sunken palace the wayfarers retrieve Kruwensilv (the mask of reptilians) and befriend the Nu'irg, Ishke'ísuk, whose primal form is that of a double-crested basilisk. Sterjall sets the Varanus Dome to open. Ishke'ísuk wants Sunu to become the wielder of Kruwensilv, and although under Laatu Miscam law allgenders are denied such honors, Aio-Kulak vows to change the laws. The prince also openly declares his love for Lago-Sterjall, causing his Laatu followers to desert him. While Sterjall cares deeply for Kulak, and they finally have a moment of passionate if somewhat disconnected sex, the wolf remains hesitant to reciprocate the prince's feelings, haunted by the greater love he feels for Banook.

With six Silvesh in their possession, the wayfarers initiate an audience with the Noss consciousness. The planet tells them that the Noss of old is dead, and that only a patchy memory of those times past remains. Noss also claims that many more memories reside in the domes that are still sealed, urging the way-farers to travel on, some toward the southern domes, others to return east and open the domes the Red Stag ransacked, before they begin to collapse in the way Heartpine has. Noss teaches the Silvfröash how to take their feral forms and encourages them to seek the aid of the Nu'irgesh to aid them in the war that is certain to come.

Mamóru dies, using the last of his energy to tell Noss as much of the history of the last hundred thousand years as he can recall. Momsúndosilv turns inert.

Kitjári and Nalaníri choose to venture toward the Negian Empire aboard *Drolvisdinn*. Sterjall, Kulak, Sunu, and Alaia choose to go south aboard *Fjummomurr*. Before parting ways, Sterjall writes a letter to Banook and asks Kitjári to deliver it to him.

The two ships sail their separate ways.

BOOK 3 – RELINQUISHED REALMS

Lago-Sterjall's party sails out of the Varanus Dome and is chased by Zovarian ships, led by Admiral Grinn. After a battle at sea, during which Alaia kills Kedra (Grinn's niece), they sail south toward the Kingdom of Bauram. Siffo and his crew hide *Fjummomurr* in a canyon while Sterjall's party crosses the Cobalt Desert toward the Azurean Dome.

During an encounter with a pack of spotted wild dogs, Sterjall figures out how to mindspeak with canids. As the party traverses the desert, they encounter ruins buried in the sands. While exploring the ruins, Sterjall and Kulak secretly trade masks, finding their mountain lion and jackal half-forms. Separately, Sunu finds their half-form of a varanus dragon and receives the name of Lummukem.

Lost in the badlands, with no water remaining, they encounter a wanderer named Serdein. They promise him a pharolith lantern if he will lead them out of the desert. Serdein instead knocks them out with poison and locks them in an underground chamber, stealing their bags, their weapons, and their Silvesh. The wayfarers escape, reaching the city of Navar Mat. There they meet with Duchess Hilid Kei, who has captured Serdein but has been unable to make him reveal the location of his stolen treasures. The wayfarers trick the duchess, rescuing Serdein and forcing him to return their belongings. The party is attacked by moa riders, one of whom severs Alaia's left thumb. They escape into the Azurean Dome, home of the Ji Miscam and the clade of marsupials.

While they recover from their escape, Sterjall paints Aio's scalp with dots representing the constellations. He finally tells the prince that he loves him, and that he feels guilty and afraid, loving both Aio and Banook in very different ways.

Inside the Azurean Dome, they encounter Mio, a farmer with a strange bump on his head: a trepanation hole, which the Ji Miscam fill with soot to ease communication with other species. They meet Hud Ulésse, the old wombat Quajufröa, and Ëalcor, the thylacine Nu'irg. Ulésse shows them how the Ji use soot to read the connections between the plants in their vast gardens, similar to how the members of the Havengall Congregation read the connections between the threads. Ulésse explains the different levels of awareness and consciousness, and how their tribe decides which kinds of animals or plants to eat.

The Ji agree to open their dome, but Ulésse declines to join the wayfarers, as she is too old for combat. Since there are no marsupials left in the rest of the New World, she instead stays behind with the Ji to focus on reintroducing the clade across the great island of Fel Baubór.

Sailing in the opposite direction, Kitjári and Nalaníri return to the Fjordlands Dome, which is now far along in the process of opening. They find Probo (the suid Nu'irg, a javelina) and recruit him for their mission, beginning their journey east through frozen lands. Along the way, Kitjári asks the ursids they encounter to spread a request for bears to migrate south and east, which will allow Banook to finally travel beyond the mountains.

Past a frozen lake, the trio enters the senstregalv mines of Laaja Khem, abandoned long ago by the disappeared Dorvauros tribe. Inside a crypt, Kitjári finds and takes the legendary quaar bow Dunokh Sull, along with a massive senstregalv glaive. They travel east to the Emen Ruins, the hot springs in which Banook and Sterjall first kissed. Kitjári begins to make a move on Nalaníri, but she falters, and their relationship becomes strained.

They continue south and reunite with Banook, Bear, and Safîs. The women join Banook in his cabin and tell him they seek his help to open the domes ransacked by the Red Stag. Kitjári delivers a letter from Lago-Sterjall, and through it Banook finds out about Aio-Kulak. He also learns that Kitjári wants to "suckle on Nalaníri's twelve teats," and agrees to secretly find out if Nalaníri would be interested.

While they travel down the path of the Firefalls, Banook sneakily sets Kitjári and Nalaníri up on a date, and the women finally kiss. Once in Brimstowne, they find Ardof, tell the ranger their secrets, and recruit him for help entering the Anglass Dome. Together, the small party infiltrates the temple at Anglass and sets the dome to open. They rescue as many Teldebran Miscam slaves as they can, travel through the canyons of the Fractured Range, then venture inside the Lequa Dome—land of the Jojek Miscam and the clade of musteloids. They find a honey badger named Muri, the Nu'irg ust Krost. During the Day of the Lost, the Nu'irgesh and the enslaved Jojek start a revolt to distract the Negians, while Kitjári and Nalaníri set the dome to open. Kitjári, Nalaníri, Probo, and Muri escape the dome by water, while Banook, Ardof, Bear, and Safís choose to stay behind and fight the remaining Negians.

The Red Stag arrives at the Archstone Dome, the dome of perissodactyls and the Alampaari Miscam. He and his troops, having been decimated while crossing the White Desert, venture into the dome to search for respite, finding ancient giant species roaming the plains inside. They are attacked by the Alampaari, who nearly destroy the Red Stag's troops with the help of Estriéggo (the woolly rhinoceros Nu'irg) and the enormous behemoths. As they escape, General Gino Baneras kills the Alampaari chief. He is granted control of Almelsilv, finds his half-form of a steppe wild horse, and is named Silv-Thaar Baneras.

While the Red Stag fights his way into the Archstone Dome, his second army, led by Silv-Thaar Valaran and Fjorna Daro's squad of arbalisters, heads east. Making use of the Negian fleet, Valaran's legions take control of the Elmaren Queendom, exterminating the pacifistic Khardok Miscam tribe living in the Moonrise Dome. Däo-Varjak (the pinniped Nu'irg, a ribbon seal) jumps off a cliff to prevent herself from being enslaved. All other Nu'irgesh feel Däo-Varjak's death.

Shea (one of Fjorna's arbalisters) murders Silv-Thaar Valaran, then is killed in return. Fjorna Daro and Aurélien Knivlar (the squad's shaman) decide to break away from the Red Stag with their army and ships, for they believe he is obsessed with the Silvesh, and that he no longer has the wellbeing of his people in mind. Now leading the army they brought with them, Fjorna inherits Krostsilv, becoming Silv-Thaar Daro and finding her half-form of an ermine. Aurélien inherits Gwonlesilv, becoming Silv-Thaar Knivlar, a deadly leopard seal. Together they sail their fleet southwest under a new banner and name, calling themselves the Cabal.

Lago-Sterjall's party leaves the Azurean Dome and, with the help of giant marsupials, defeats a troop of moa riders while hurrying to board *Fjummomurr*. They sail south toward the Nisos Dome, where the Sehján Miscam live alongside the clade of glires (rodents and lagomorphs). They are intercepted by Admiral Grinn's fleet, and their vessel is boarded. While being questioned by Grinn, a Lerevi fleet arrives, led by Fleet Admiral Theggo Saurfall. The Lerevi, being worshippers of Noss and their animal spirits, and seeing that the wayfarers are being aided by Ishke'ísuk, agree to help their cause.

After docking on the island of Nisos, the wayfarers and their Lerevi rescuers meet with Princeps Vordeno and other representatives of the Republic of Lerev. The princeps agrees to aid the wayfarers' journey into the Nisos Dome. The scrollsingers (leaders of the Lavra Faithful) are not happy with letting the Sehján Miscam out of the dome to migrate into their lands.

Theggo and a troop of kudu-mounted dragoons accompany the wayfarers into the Nisos Dome. They find that the Sehján have lost Okrisilv (the mask of glires) to the Oxruk, an underground-dwelling tribe. The Sehján have been living upon floating islands, helped by giant beavers (castoroides), always fearing that the Oxruk might appear from underground to kill them. With the help of the wayfarers, the Sehján try to negotiate with the Oxruk, but mistrust and betrayal result in a war, a hostage situation, and a suicidal rescue mission. Ierun Jessha (the Sehján queen) kills the Oxruk leader and reclaims Okrisilv, but she succumbs to her own wounds. Before dying, she gives the mask to Puuja and Pol, her twin children.

With the help of the Nu'irg ust Okri (a hazel dormouse named Gwit), the twins find their way to the temple of glires. Both Pol and Puuja learn to wield the mask, and together set the Nisos Dome to open.

After a battle to escape the collapsing underground city of the Oxruk, the wayfarers begin their journey out of the Nisos Dome. Sunu-Lummukem is very fond of the orphaned twins, becoming their language and battle instructor.

Once the wayfarers and the Lerevi dragoons exit the dome, they are joined by Lerevi infantry and learn that the scrollsingers have killed Princeps Vordeno and taken over the Republic of Lerev, now calling it the Theocracy of Lerev. Infantry General Seera Ashbend demands that the Silvesh be turned over to the care of the scrollsingers. Surrounded, the wayfarers choose to fight.

FERAL FLAME

AGNARGFRÖA

CHAPTER ONE

DAY OF RENEWAL

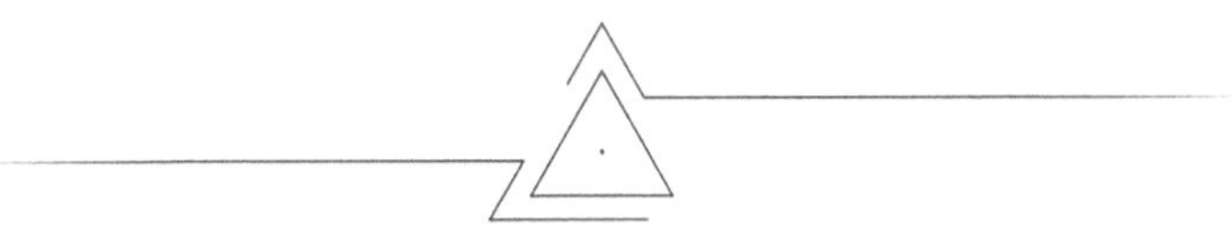

They were surrounded, outnumbered. Betrayed.

Sterjall clamped his footpaws against Blu's saddle and held tightly to Kulak's back. He looked wearily at the Lerevi soldiers encroaching on them: there were over a hundred, and more were arriving with each slamming heartbeat.

Atop Pichi's saddle, Alaia quickly assembled her quaar blowgun, but Lummukem warned her to tuck the weapon away for the time being. Puuja and Pol held fast to both of them, fear tightening their freckled faces.

"What is happening?" Puuja asked Tsei, who rode with one of the nearby dragoons, but the Sehján warrior seemed as confused as the twins.

Admiral Theggo Saurfall held tight to Tinnomeg's reins; his giant eland was agitated, but Theggo kept his expression cold and hard as north-facing granite. Princeps Vordeno was dead. The Republic of Lerev was dead. The new Theocracy of Lerev was spreading like a dark fog across Fel Nisos, where Holy Princeps Brovon now ruled with a mandate to uphold the sacred laws of the Lavra Faithful. His voice, his faith, had been given ultimate authority.

"Dragoon Leader!" Infantry General Seera Ashbend called out. "Do as I have ordered. Secure the prisoners and confiscate their masks."

Rapier in hand, Dragoon Leader Seshéni directed her kudu-mounted soldiers to advance toward the smilodons and their riders, toward Theggo himself. When the dragoons were close enough to strike, they halted.

"Dragoon Leader, stop wasting time!" Seera Ashbend's copper-and-yellow armor sparkled in the morning light. A valknut had recently been embossed onto her breastplate; the three interlocking triangles were painted in copper, matching the new flags that flew over the city of Normouth.

With a quick command, Seshéni turned her mount around, her dragoons following her lead. The mounted soldiers surrounded the wayfarers, but now did so protectively, their blades facing the Lerevi infantry.

"Insubordination will cost you more than your rank, Dragoon Leader," Seera warned.

"We were sent with the fleet admiral as witnesses, as protectors," Seshéni replied. "Our orders came from Cavalry General Garvall Ferwillow. As far as we know, we are still under his command. We do not answer to the infantry. Stand back, General, and let us through."

"Ferwillow has been relieved of his duties," Seera said. "For the time being, I command both the cavalry and infantry. So you better start by—"

Both Gwit and Ishke'ísuk jumped down from Pichi's saddle and shapeshifted in midair, becoming a giant beaver and an enormous saltwater crocodile. The compacted ground shook with the impact of their landing. The infantry line broke; some soldiers retreated, while others fell to their knees in adoration.

"Do not be fooled by their tricks!" the general shouted. "They are mind-locking the spirits just as the Red Stag does to the Spirit of Urg. They are enslavers!" Most of the kneeling soldiers rose again, albeit hesitantly. With a quick gesture, the general ordered all the forces on the front line to unsheathe their weapons.

Lummukem reached back toward Puuja and asked for her mask, then shapeshifted into Sunu, holding the masks of glires and reptilians high in their hands. Olo fluttered right above the two dark shapes while the shaman spoke. "Gwit, the Spirit of Okri, is acting of his own volition, and so is Ishke'ísuk, the Spirit of Kruwen. If you wish to fight us, the spirits themselves you will also fight, as they are our allies." Returning to their half-form, they added, "Noss themself set us upon this mission, and the spirits will see us through it."

Theggo brought Tinnomeg closer to Lummukem and added, "If you are so eager to kill our own gods—assuming you do not first die by their teeth and claws—that is your choice, warriors of Lerev. You can believe the spirits you worship, or believe your general, but may your choice be marked in history and forever remembered, whether in songs of valor, or songs of betrayal."

Some soldiers at the back defected, but most stood on guard, having already been warned by Seera of this possible outcome. They were ready, and they were by far the majority.

"Theggo, Seshéni, this will not go well for you. We are many to your few," Seera said. "Surrender now, or you will force me to vanquish you. We will spare the spirits and free them from your influence, as they are not guilty of what you've done to them."

Pol began to whimper, holding on to Lummukem's back. The dragoons held their protective formation and tried to guide the smilodons with them, hoping the wall of soldiers would make way.

The soldiers did not budge.

The first line of infantry charged.

Ishke'ísuk bolted in front of them and swung his tail like a scythe. The soldiers toppled over, some with shattered legs, the rest stunned. The crocodile roared, displaying rows of teeth.

"Do not kill them," Lummukem voiced for all to hear. "Let them face the shame of their own sins for the rest of their lives."

The general issued a command, and two more squads attacked from the flanks. Ishke'ísuk bared his sharp teeth in front of one squad, making them stop, while Gwit stood like a furred wall in front of the other group, protecting the dragoons behind him. An officer pushed forward to lead his unit, slicing his rapier toward the giant rodent.

Gwit dodged swiftly, swinging his tail at the officer and hurling him over the assembled army, then rolled like a giant log to crush the rest of the squad. The giants held unyielding as dams while two more waves attacked. But the charges had only been a diversion to keep the Nu'irgesh occupied. Another unit breached through to the center, where the dragoons barely held them at bay, unable to take advantage of their speed in such tight confines. Their kudus felt trapped and began bumping into one another.

"There are too many!" Sterjall cried out. "We can't hold them back!"

If not for the Lerevi's hesitation to strike the Nu'irgesh—their very gods—the wayfarers would all have been skewered by now. Mounds of broken Lerevi were piling at the edges of the tight battlefield, but there were hundreds more ready to attack.

"Hold together!" Theggo cried out. "Slowly advance toward the gates!"

The city gates were a mere stone's throw away down the road. What advantage crossing the threshold would gain them, Theggo did not know, but it seemed preferable over waiting to be disemboweled.

The dragoons and the Nu'irgesh slowly pushed toward the gate, stomping over fallen soldiers. Two of the kudus fell, and their riders were taken down with them.

"Stop this madness, Theggo!" Seera implored him. "Tell your people to surrender! This is pointless bloodshed. Make them stop, now!"

"Keep moving to the gates!" Theggo bellowed in defiance.

As they neared the enormous archway, Theggo's heart sank; reinforcements flowed through the gates like grains of sand through an hourglass, marking the last heartbeats before their doom.

Another dragoon fell, then another.

Theggo pulled hard on Tinnomeg's reins, making him rear. An axe-wielding infantrywoman sensed an opportunity and lunged toward the eland's exposed belly, but Tinnomeg dropped quickly and swung his screw-shaped horns at his attacker. He sank one horn into her jaw but took a hit on the other, which was sliced clean off. Theggo was bathed by sprays of blood from his eland's severed horn, but he restrained the buckling animal as he deflected yet another soldier's swing.

The new wave of soldiers positioned itself in front of the gate, blocking it completely. The odds of escape were now entirely extinguished.

"Hold! Stop!" Theggo called. "General Ashbend, we surrender. Hold your units at bay!"

Seera lifted a hand and whistled loudly.

"Once we are captured," Kulak said to Sterjall, "do not let them take your mask, no matter what they do to me."

"I won't let them hurt you," Sterjall replied, his hope draining.

"Children, do not leave our side," Lummukem said in Miscamish, holding protectively to Pol, while Alaia held Puuja.

For a brief moment, the battle halted. Then a battlecry echoed from beyond the gates.

The newly arrived soldiers barely had time to turn before they were trampled by the hooves of an armored troop of kudu riders led by Cavalry General Garvall Ferwillow. The kudus sliced a wedge through the infantry while constantly shifting formation, opening a clear path for the wayfarers and their allies to escape.

"Seshéni! Escort them to the ports!" Garvall ordered. "Make haste!"

Seshéni and her remaining dragoons led the smilodons through the protective tunnel of kudu riders. The infantry tried to push in, but Garvall's troops slammed into them, letting none through.

Ishke'ísuk and Gwit shifted back to their basilisk and dormouse primal forms and rejoined Lummukem, then the smilodons kicked up a cloud of silt and followed Theggo and Seshéni through the cleared path. Instead of engaging further, the cavalry who rescued them retained control of the gate. Once the smilodons were a safe enough distance away, the cavalry feigned an attack, then turned around to follow the giant cats, leaving the infantry in the dust.

The wayfarers and their allies galloped quickly around the rampart that encircled the palace of Normouth. Alarm bells rang throughout the city. Many Lerevi reinforcements took up arms, but with no mounts, they could do little else than loose a few aimless arrows or leap out of the way to avoid being trampled.

Garvall Ferwillow caught up to Theggo, who was struggling to wrap a cloth around Tinnomeg's severed horn. "We hear your song of truth!" Garvall said, galloping at nearly full speed. "Fleet Admiral, you must hasten to the port. Your flotilla is still loyal to you, although I cannot vouch for the rest of the navy. Once the vines began moving, I alerted them to your imminent return. They will be ready to sail."

"And the black-sailed ship?" Theggo asked.

"The pig sailors are ready and eager. And hopefully not drunk."

They exited the city gates and entered mile eighteen of the Esplanade of the Spirits, the one dedicated to the Spirit of Hoombu, or primates. With no pursuers nearby, they slowed their gait to a soft trot.

The smilodons panted. The eland and kudus grunted through strained breaths.

"What in the name of the Old Kings happened here, Garvall?" Theggo asked the general.

"The scrollsingers is what happened. They saw their chance to finally take power. Brovon convinced the people that this mission into the dome would bring the Miscam out to conquer their lands, that they would use the same sinful strategies the Red Stag is using. Many did not listen to his profane words, but most of the faithful followed blindly."

"What will become of the Republic?"

"The Republic is no more, Admiral, at least for now. But we will be steadfast and hold our ground. We have allies in Welmouth and Aran. Normouth is hopelessly in the control of the Theocracy, and Nisos is still split. You should take your flotilla to the east. Do not wait for the other admirals, as you can't know which ones will be eager to stab you in the back."

"What of the Tsing Empire? What is Empress Pian-Thi's stance?"

"We have not heard from the empress directly, but my heart tells me that the Tsing will support our cause. The scrollsingers' power grab aims to compete with the might of the Tsing Empire itself—it violates our treaties. They will not condone such acts."

"Thank you, Garvall, you are an honorable man. I owe you my life, as do we all. But what fate awaits you? Our flotilla cannot carry the entire cavalry with us."

"We will stay here and fight back against the scrollsingers. We have moved our barracks to Welmouth for the time being."

They traveled past the stupa of Kruwen, entering the mile dedicated to Trommo.

Sterjall had been listening intently, trying not to interrupt. He jumped in now, saying, "The Sehján will be leaving the dome any day now. There is a large group moving west. Another waits to exit north, close to where we emerged. You should form an alliance with them. If they know we trust you, they will trust you as well."

"How can we gain the trust of your Miscam friends if you will not be there to speak to them?" General Ferwillow asked. "The scrollsingers will try to exploit the situation and persuade the Miscam to their side. They can spout lies as easily as we can speak truths."

Sterjall did not have an answer. He signaled to one of the dragoons, who rode in closer with Tsei holding to his back. He tried to explain the crisis to her, but too much had happened, involving complex politics the Sehján had no knowledge of.

Tsei understood enough of the direness of their situation to know she could help. With a determined look toward Pol and Puuja, she said, "I must part with you, Ierun and Khuron, that I must do. I will need to follow their general and find our friends traveling north and west, to warn them of the betrayal, to tell them who they may or may not trust. I must help the word spread."

"But Tsei!" Puuja said. "We need you!"

"You do not. You have Lummukem. You have Sterjall, Kulak, Alaia, Theggo. You have Gwit, who will always be there for you. And most importantly, you have each other."

General Ferwillow was glad that Tsei offered her help; he did not believe the Sehján would trust his soldiers otherwise. Although he could not yet properly communicate with Tsei, the general knew of several scholars in Welmouth who spoke the Miscamish tongue and could facilitate communication with the Sehján.

They rode through mile fifteen of the esplanade, dedicated to the Spirit of Okri. The sculptures of glires had been adorned with thousands upon thousands of flowers, flags, fruits, and other colorful offerings. A throng of devout followers was promenading around the stupa, chanting hymns in honor of the spirit.

"Mile fifteen has never been busier," Theggo observed.

The cavalry general agreed. "Once the people found out the very Spirit of Okri was living on our great island, they came from all over to seek his guidance. We had to block off roads to control the flow."

Gwit groomed his tail while perched on Pol's shoulder, uninterested in the tributes or songs of the Lerevi.

They rode by the stupas of Quaju, Almel, and Rilg. Soldiers spotted them, but seeing the powerful kudus and smilodons, they did not try to stop them.

Mindrel, Agnarg, Krost, Nagra, and Momsúndo were followed by Urg, Balast, Urnaadi, and Kroowin. Once they reached the mile of Gwonle, Theggo had the unpleasant job of informing the general about the death of the pinniped spirit, Däo-Varjak.

"I don't understand. How can you be certain?" General Ferwillow asked.

"The spirits can all sense each other, in their own manner. They felt it as it happened. All of them. The sorrow they expressed was heartbreaking."

"Noss forgive us all. We had heard that the Moonrise Dome had fallen to the Negians, but had no idea their cruelty could reach such despicable levels. We *must* stop them, no matter the cost."

Mile one, dedicated to the cetacean Spirit of Amá'a, came last. Past it sprawled the port city of Nisos. A troop of soldiers blocked the road, wielding shields and pikes. The kudus slowed to a stop. The general waited for his cavalry to take up formation, facing the enemy ahead.

"Fleet Admiral Theggo Saurfall, it has been my honor," the general said. "We'll open the way for you. Take it, and flee this cursed island. Sail east, and prove to this wretched theocracy that their hearts have been seduced by evil. We will protect the true patriots, and we will fight with and for the Miscam. For the spirits. For Noss."

"Your honor will live in canticles that will outlast even the oldest of scrolls," Theggo replied solemnly. "Let this Day of Renewal be celebrated in history as the day you made your stand—from now until the Endfall takes us all."

The general ordered his troop to gallop in a wedge, carving a path for the others to hurry through. Between the clashing rapiers and shields, they made their escape. Seshéni and her surviving dragoons followed the small group through the curved streets of Nisos until they reached the port.

A scuffle had broken out at the docks. Siffo and his Puqua crew were holding their ground against a dozen soldiers attempting to seize their ship. Theggo's flagship, *Silverweave*, was docked right next to *Fjummomurr*, and its crew was also trying to prevent the infantry from boarding. The rest of the flotilla waited at sea.

"Cap'n Siffo!" Sterjall bellowed as Blu rode toward the battle. "Board the ship! We need to get out of here!"

Reinforcements were marching toward them. The soldiers in the lead had their rapiers out, while those farther behind were readying their bows.

"Weigh anchor before they arrive!" Theggo yelled to the sailors of his ship, rushing to the pier.

Seshéni and her dragoons broke through the ranks of the Lerevi soldiers attempting to board *Fjummomurr*, allowing the Puqua sailors to return to their duties. The kudus left the scraps of the battle to the smilodons and continued tearing forward, aiding *Silverweave*'s crew.

"Sweet time ye took!" Siffo berated the wayfarers as the smilodons climbed the ramp. "Hurry aboard now! All of ye!" He then sang a command, which was answered fervently by his crew.

> Up ye go hogs pigs and boars.   *–Board!*
>
> *Light-ho d'kenzir stone.*
>
> Haul them foresheets, stow them oars.   *–Board!*
>
> *Bright-glow as cold as bone.*

"I will rejoin you at sea!" Theggo hollered, riding Tinnomeg toward his vessel.

The dragoons did a quick loop back toward *Fjummomurr*. "We will escort Tsei back to safety," Dragoon Leader Seshéni said. "Go now, guardians of the spirits. Restore balance to our realms. For the land is our cradle, and we are merely seeds upon it."

Before Sterjall could thank them, Seshéni, Tsei, and the dragoons were gone.

CHAPTER TWO

TWIN SECRETS

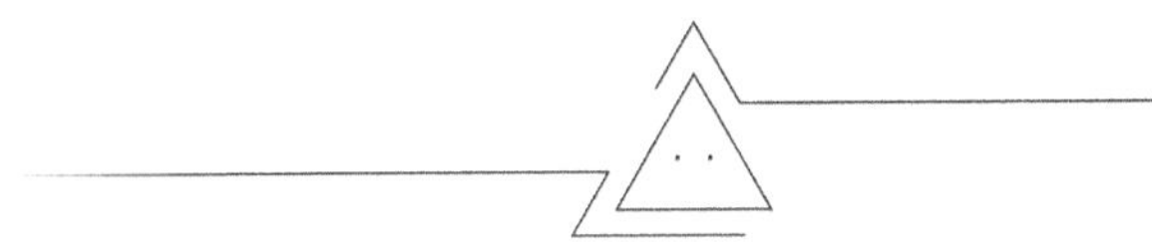

Fjummomurr's black sails swelled with the taut Winter winds, pulling the ship away from the incoming barrage of arrows. The Puqua ship followed right behind the excessively numerous sails of *Silverweave* as both vessels rushed to meet the rest of the flotilla.

"Ne'er been happier t'see yer furry faces!" Siffo bawled, then lifted Sterjall in a powerful embrace, nearly crushing the wolf's ribs. He rubbed his warthog nose to Sterjall's, scrunching the wolf's muzzle back so forcefully that Sterjall looked as if he was snarling.

"Happy to see you too, Cap'n," Sterjall gasped, refilling his mistreated lungs.

The warthog bounced his eyes between Alaia's ochre elytra armor and Sterjall's blues. "Fancy armor ye two are wearing," he said, then crushed Alaia before going for Kulak and Lummukem, who were tending to Pichi's wounds.

Pol and Puuja hovered near Lummukem, gawking at the strange ship, at its huge sails and countless lines. Captain Siffo tried to greet the strangers in his customary Puqua way, but the children recoiled from his snout. Pol shied away behind his sister, though he seemed intrigued by Siffo's pharolith-decorated tusks.

"Why'd ye bring children with ye?" Siffo asked. He then noticed Okrisilv tucked under Puuja's arm. "Where are them parents?" he asked. "Where is d'Okrifröa? Did them end up aboard Theggo's ship?"

Lummukem placed a claw on Puuja's red hair. "Your eyes are staring at the Okrifröa, Captain. This is Puuja, and her twin brother, Pollomekh. But your words they will not understand, for they only speak Miscamish."

"Her? D'tiny red-capped warbler? What's d'toddler's age, six?"

"She is eleven," Lummukem replied. "And it is a long story."

"N'did ye find d'Nu'irg ust Okri?"

"He's also right in front of you," Sterjall said.

Siffo looked down and noticed the golden-brown dormouse on Pol's shoulder.

"As small as them children, but d'baby rodent'll do." He then addressed the dormouse directly. "Welcome t'*Fjummomurr*, Lorr Gwit. I hope yer mour be-haved than old Probo—that javelina can be a pest."

Gwit understood none of the words, though he did seem to lightly twitch when Probo's name was mentioned.

"Can we sit down to rest and talk?" Sterjall pleaded. "In your comfortable quarters, perhaps?"

Siffo grunted affirmatively.

The returned wayfarers were too tired to recount their full story. Though it was bright in the New World, it was past midnight for them. The day had been long, exhausting, and stressful, and it was showing in their slumped shoulders and heavy lids.

After they had recapped the basics of their exploits with Siffo, the captain asked his crew to pull closer to Theggo's flagship to coordinate the route they would take overnight. The wayfarers made their way to their bunks and collapsed into slumber even before the sun had set.

Lummukem and the twins were the first to rise, before Sunnokh showed his face. The twins were upset about missing their first sunset, so Lummukem had promised they'd show the children a sunrise.

The three of them waited at *Fjummomurr*'s bow. Pol and Puuja had climbed atop the ship's precarious narwhal figurehead; Gwit was enjoying the ocean breeze at the tip of the twisting, silver-painted tusk that protruded from the sculpted figure, dangerously close to sliding off the end.

"Narvwald. Is Pol correct?" Pol asked in his basic but quickly improving Common.

"Narwhal," Lummukem spoke slowly, emphasizing the pronunciation. "You are correct, Pol."

Lummukem gestured to various sights while saying their names aloud: sky, water, ship, waves, gull, sails, wind. They would try to explain the concept of sunrise once the twins had seen it happen.

Siffo came by, drinking from a steaming mug. "Lerr Lummukem, would ye be kind enough t'finish a-telling me d'full story uf yer journey? We can sit in mine quarters where it's warmer."

"After sunrise," Lummukem said. "The twins need to see the beauty."

"There's coffee a-brewing," the captain taunted.

"After sunrise."

Siffo snorted and left them alone.

Puuja hopped back onto the deck. "Siffo ugly," she said, eyeing the captain and getting the Common pronunciation quite right.

Lummukem frowned. "He is not ugly, only different, like we are different. Siffo is a good man. But look, Sunnokh rises."

"There he is!" Pol cried out. "Making Lakemother glow!"

The twins stared with newly born awe.

Gwit held to the spiraling tusk and watched silently, rebirthing a thousand memories.

It was an hour past sunrise when they gathered in the captain's quarters. The twins were ecstatic after witnessing their first sunrise, but Sterjall, Kulak, and Alaia were still groggy and trying to adjust. Theggo joined them, as did Captain Dedric and Captain Mareesha, who had commanded the flotilla during Theggo's absence.

After catching the three captains up with their story, they planned for the journey ahead. Captain Siffo consulted a calendar. "D'next time d'beacon uf Ilaadrid shines shell be in two n'a half weeks. We shell have enough time t'make it to d'Taring Peninsula by then, t'pick up d'kitty."

Kulak's ears flicked as he squinted at Siffo. "Nelv will be waiting at the headland, my scalp hopes," he said, "if Kenondok delivered the message in time."

"And perhaps Crysta will be there too!" Sterjall said. "And maybe we could take her to the Yenwu Dome and see the observatory together, if it's still there."

"What is this observatory you speak of?" Theggo asked.

"It's where Jiu Zezi, an old cosmologist from the Equilibrium Epoch, first saw the comet that would cause the Downfall. Mamóru told us about her, said that the observatory she made her discoveries from might still be there, waiting for us inside the dome."

"Before Kroowindrolom, to Trommodrolom we must go," Lummukem said. "The Ashen Dome. Why is it the New World calls it so?"

"Because of the smoking clouds that billow from its top," Theggo answered. "It should be easy for us to access, either by sea or by land."

"It is a strange sight to behold," Captain Dedric, who had been to the Tsing Empire many times before, added. "The Ashen Dome fumes like a volcano, covering its snowcap with streaks of gray. When the clouds clear, one can see the smoke above, like black columns that turn red with the sunset."

"Let's hope it's not burning un d'inside," Siffo half-joked, then refilled their enamel mugs with more coffee.

"Is there news from the Red Stag?" Kulak asked.

"Yes," Captain Mareesha answered. "As we had suspected, the Moonrise Dome has been taken, so it seems likely that it was by Negian blades that the Spirit of Gwonle perished. The Elmaren Queendom is under their control, where most of their fleet was stationed."

"Should we be wary of their fleet coming to meet us?" Sterjall asked.

"Not at all," she answered. "We will be traveling through the Gulf of Erjilm. The Negian fleet will likely focus on attacking or allying with the Tharma Federation or the Kingdom of Afhora. Perhaps they'll enter the Alommo Sea and try to take the Scoria Dome from there. If they do come this way, aiming to get to the Ashen Dome, they wouldn't sail past the Kilkarag Peninsula. They would remain on the east side. Either way, it would take them too long—the old realms are far to the east."

"The largest portion of the Red Stag's forces were marching toward the Archstone Dome," Captain Dedric offered, "but our contacts in the Graalman Horde have gone silent, and we have received no more updates. The other curious bit of news is that the Fogdale Citadel, way up in the Anglass Dome, has fallen."

"Anglass? Near Brimstowne?" Sterjall asked, earnestly surprised. "Who attacked the citadel?"

"No one did," Mareesha answered. "It was built around vines, as a means of protection. Apparently, the vines have begun to retreat, and they brought the entire citadel down. Even the walls around the fortress have collapsed."

"Jiara made it!" Sterjall belted out in joy and relief.

Kulak kicked him under the table. Only then did Sterjall realize he had said too much.

"Jiara Ascura, the old scout commander who once traveled with you?" Theggo said, seemingly unsurprised. "We supposed she was behind this. I'm sorry, Sterjall, I don't mean to pry. You are free to keep your secrets, as we once discussed. Whatever is going on there, I'm glad it's working out."

"Yes, sorry, and I won't tell you more. Not because I don't trust you, it's simply a matter of safety. Their safety." Sterjall said the words earnestly, but he could not help sharing excited smiles with Alaia and Kulak.

"This is all we know about the east," Mareesha continued. "Hestfell has been keeping busy during your absence."

"What is our next destination?" Kulak asked. "Are we sailing to find Nelv?"

"No," Theggo said. "We still have time before the Ilaadrid Shard shines again. There is a Lerevi outpost in Orhumbelen, only a few days' voyage from the tip of the Taring Peninsula. My flotilla had to set sail in a hurry, so we'll need to stop there to resupply and hope the maritime town is allied with us instead of with the Lavra traitors. If there are any more Lerevi flotillas in the area, they'll likely be smaller than ours, and I'll try to recruit them for this mission."

"Do you think they'll listen to you?" Sterjall asked.

"The Spirits of Kruwen and Okri will be very persuasive in that situation. And if we tell them we are on the way to ally ourselves with the Spirit of Mindrel, there won't be a single sailor who does not heed our call."

The voyage was dreadfully cold as they sailed toward the port of Orhumbelen. The unforgiving winds of Frostburn hit the ships hard; icicles sprouted from mast, line, and hull alike. The voyagers stayed belowdecks to keep warm, except for Lummukem, who spent their time above board teaching the twins about this new world, challenging them with language and fighting lessons. Both Pol and Puuja were highly skilled for their age when it came to handling the quarterstaffs; they had been well trained since they were four years old, learning that they should always be ready for an Oxruk ambush.

"We have a present for you today," Lummukem told the twins one morning, before their practice on *Fjummomurr*'s deck began. "We have asked our Lerevi friends for some help with this, and they have done an exemplary job." From behind the mainmast they pulled out the twins' quarterstaffs, which had been capped with steel tips.

The kids lunged toward their upgraded weapons, but the dragon held them out of reach. "Not yet, not yet," Lummukem said. "First, you must promise us you will be careful with them."

"Sure, promise," Puuja said. Pol simply nodded eagerly.

"Good. And now, stay right where you are and watch, for we will show you something else."

The twins stood still, eyes wide open. Lummukem spun the two quarterstaffs, weaving them through each other in a hypnotic dance. Although they were not bladed, with such speed, with such control, the bludgeoning weapons were most deadly. In a climactic flourish, Lummukem lowered the two poles and let them spin so close to the deck that their iron caps scratched the surface—but the caps were more than just iron, having been fitted with brime cubes at the tips. The aetheric sulphur flashed fiercely, sending up twin streaks of overheated sparks.

"Yes!" both kids yelled.

"What in d'cursed seas uf Urrúnot d'ye think ye are doing?!" Siffo belted out, rushing to stomp out the fiery sparks.

After an awkward apology and a sworn oath to Siffo to never again shoot brime sparks while aboard *Fjummomurr*, Lummukem at last handed the quarterstaffs to the twins.

"Like Lago's bracer," Puuja said, mimicking the posture Lago-Sterjall took before using his Brime Strike.

"Yes," Lummukem said, "but you must not stand the same way he stands. You follow your training. And you make sure to never strike the caps of your quarterstaffs while on this ship, unless you want Captain Siffo to feed us to the sharks. He vowed he would, and we believe him."

The kids promised, then continued with their training. Puuja was exceptionally versatile when wearing the mask, able to anticipate most of Lummukem's moves. She was stronger than Pol, but the boy was more limber. Although Pol normally kept a contorted and uncomfortable posture, his back straightened out during battle. Yet, despite his dedication, Pol began to lag behind, not only in the fighting lessons but also in the language ones.

The three of them were deep in the hold of the Puqua ship, covering themselves with wool blankets. The crate-filled space felt cold as pink moonlight. Lummukem spoke in Miscamish so that their complex thoughts would not be lost to the children. They were teaching the siblings how to focus to achieve their half-forms. It was, unfortunately, a very subjective process, and one that even Lummukem themself did not entirely understand, but they were able to guide the children's minds in the right direction.

"There is one ability the Silvesh grants us that we still have not had a chance to use," Lummukem said to the twins.

"You mean opening the dome like Pol did?" Puuja asked.

"We did it together, in a way," Pol quietly said, hiding his expression behind the mask of glires. Only when they could get privacy aboard *Fjummomurr*—which was not very often—did he dare to wear Okrisilv.

"Well, two abilities," Lummukem corrected themself. "Opening a dome is one we have not had a chance to perform, as we were not as fast to reach the temple in Kissumar as you two scurrying mice. The other ability, the one we were referring to, is another way of shapeshifting—one that is dangerous to attempt in some situations."

Lummukem explained to the twins that Noss had taught the mask-wearers how to take their feral forms. He told them of the time they joined Kulak, Sterjall, Kitjári, and Nalaníri in a stupa in the Varanus Dome, and how the other four had turned into their full, feral selves.

"Why is it dangerous?" Pol asked. When they were alone, Pol was nearly as talkative with Lummukem as he was with Puuja. He still held his posture tight as a ship's rope and avoided eye contact, but at least he spoke more often.

"It is a dangerous form because some who undertake the change are unable to return from it. However, Noss also taught us the secret to prevent this outcome, so that our human minds remain in control and we do not slip entirely into our feral selves."

"What is the secret?" Puuja asked.

"The key is to seek the presence of people you trust, of those you love. Retaining awareness and remembering your loved ones helps one not to lose themself."

"And you saw the others become full animals?" Puuja asked.

"Yes. You should have seen Khuron Kulak as a caracal. He looked like a toy next to Sterjall, the black-faced timber wolf."

"We want to see the small cat!" Pol said.

"Perhaps they will show you someday. Only Jiara-Kitjári had a bit of trouble returning from her form, but she controlled it in the end, as we were all there to support her. They all experienced their feral forms, but we did not."

"Why? Why did you not do it?" Puuja asked.

"Because we were only Sunu then, not yet Lummukem. We did not yet know we were a varanus dragon."

"You should try it now!" Pol yelled excitedly. "We want to see a real varanus dragon!"

"We are a real varanus dragon."

"Yes, but we mean a *real* one. Down on four legs, like Ishke'ísuk." The boy lowered his body over bent arms and hissed at the crates around them.

"It is something we fear, as we are never certain of our own skills, especially of one we have never attempted before."

"How are you going to learn if you never try?" Puuja inquired.

"We are here with you," Pol added. "You said the people who love you can help you."

Lummukem smiled.

"And then you can teach us how to do it," the boy added.

Lummukem shook their scaled head. "We do not think we can teach you. It was Noss who placed the memories in our heads."

"We'll learn, somehow," Puuja said. "But for now, will you show us?"

"Please?" they pleaded together.

Lummukem considered, knowing they'd gotten themself into this situation in the first place, and feeling the kids were too eager. And they had to admit to themself that they too were eager but had never mustered the courage or the motivation to attempt the final transformation.

"Fine," they said, and the children squealed with excitement. "But remember to stay with us and to talk to us, so that we may find our way back. We will listen to your sweet voices and let them guide us."

Lummukem withdrew toward the hold's staircase to make sure the hatch was still closed, then returned to where the three of them had been hiding behind the crates. They dropped their wool blanket and accepted the sting of the cold. Next they removed their necklaces, their long-sleeved shodog, and their belt. As they dropped their tailcoat kilt, the nearly invisible slit upon their crotch was revealed.

The only light to see by came from a swaying pharolith that could use a fresh knapping. Lummukem closed their eyes and focused. They did not ask for the change: they welcomed it, letting the essence of the varanus dragon become them, giving in to Kruwensilv's impulses.

While they were still standing on two feet, their torso grew, their limbs shortened, their neck elongated. Soon enough, they were unable to hold their stance and fell to the floorboards, continuing to grow until they were a scaled beast twenty feet in length, barely fitting in the confined spaces between the crates.

The dragon studied the surrounding tightness, slithering through the labyrinth of crates, tasting the air with their bifurcated tongue. Though they could see the threads no longer, they could feel their presence tingling their scales like a discharge of static electricity. They wobbled forward, dragging their belly on the floorboards, and found themself surprised at how natural that felt. Their limbs at first seemed too short to be useful, but they were powerful and deadly, although not nearly as deadly as their long, whip-like tail.

"—tand us?"

They heard a noise nearby. They turned by curling their long body into a horseshoe shape, looking back.

"Can you understand us?" Puuja said.

The twins. They knew the twins. How could they forget? The dragon tried to say *yes*, but only a spattering hiss came out.

"Nod if you can understand us," Pol said, fearful of having attempted something too risky and it having gone wrong. He cowered behind his sister.

The varanus dragon nodded clumsily. They felt sure of themself now; they understood they were many, and this was just one of the many forms they took. They approached the siblings and lovingly rubbed their scaled head against them; the purple patterns the twins had splattered over their scalp were still noticeable even in their feral form.

The dragon hissed, expressing their affection through wet pink gums. The children did not understand, but they did not seem afraid.

"You are bigger than we thought you'd be," Puuja said.

Lummukem grunted, trying to comprehend the enormity of their body.

"Are you feeling well? Is it scary?" Pol asked.

Lummukem did not know how to reply, so they simply blinked and swished their tail.

"Maybe it's time to turn back," Puuja suggested. "Maybe you aren't scared, but we are getting a bit scared. We don't want you to get stuck in there, that we do not."

The dragon blinked once more, then ambled to the spot where they'd dropped their clothes, and under the cold pharolith light began to shapeshift back. Their torso and neck shrunk, while their limbs stretched out. The form held for a bit in the smoke-like state, somewhere between a half-form and a feral form. Lummukem felt the pull of the mask, the eagerness to fall back into the feral form, and had to fight against it. They took a deep breath and shapeshifted all the way to their human shape in such a quick burst that Kruwensilv fell off their face.

Sunu kneeled on the ground, breathing harshly.

"Are you alright?" Pol asked, afraid to approach.

Sunu saw the fear in the boy's eyes and rearranged their expression into a smile. "We are fine. We apologize if we scared you." As they stood up, Sunu covered their slitted penis, trying to avoid further confusing or scaring the twins. But the twins glimpsed it.

"Are you boy and girl down there too?" Pol asked.

"Yes, we are," Sunu answered, a bit flustered. "We share two bodies in one."

"You don't need to cover yourself up," Puuja said. "You are just like us. Like both of us at the same time."

"But it is cold," Pol added. "Maybe they should cover up."

Sunu extended a warm smile and reached for their clothes, for it was truly cold in the cargo hold. "Let us go now, children," they said. "This was an exciting night for Sunu-Lummukem, but it has left us tired. We thank you for your help, and we hope that someday you will learn to do what we just showed you."

CHAPTER THREE

THE ANCIENT LIGHTHOUSE

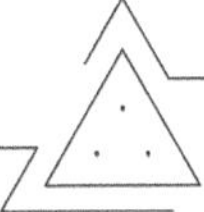

"This better be the night," Crysta complained to Hefra as they followed Nelv over the remote headlands of the Taring Peninsula. "I'm too anxious. We can't keep doing this twice every month."

"Twice *every* month?" Hefra grumbled. "It hasn't yet been two months since we started this!"

"Sure, but waiting all night nearly killed me last time! Just to sit there for so many hours, and for nothing, not a ship on the horizon. I can't rest from all the anxiety. And this… cat… gives me the goose pimples. I think at any moment she could claw our heads off."

"Not in that form she won't. She's like a baby jaguar."

Nelv strolled ahead in her clouded leopard primal form, neither understanding nor caring to understand the words of the mildly annoying women. Her sharp shoulder blades swung up and down. Her pace was steady, determined.

"And she's taking her sweet time today!" Crysta protested. "We're already late. The Daystar has been shining since noon!"

"Love, you need to relax. Kenondok said we were supposed to meet them there at night, not at just any moment the shard shines. We still got a few more hours till sunset."

"And it's already cold as the nethervoids," Crysta whined, tightening her fur-lined hood. "The sea breeze will be the death of us."

Crysta and Hefra had been camping near the southeastern end of the peninsula for the past six weeks. They had followed Nelv there with a group of shamans who had protected them during the cold, treacherous journey. At least they had been allowed to ride on smilodons this time. The large cats terrified Crysta, but it was much better to hold on to their saddles while they jumped over chasms than to try jumping them herself.

One of the larger smilodons, of nearly Pichi's size, had hauled the supplies for the entire group. The majority of the weight was Hefra's naturalist gear, including her specimen samples and notebooks—she wasn't about to part with them, not after all the sweat she had dripped while collecting samples in the Moordusk Dome.

The shamans had dropped them off at the ruins of the pre-Downfall city of Taring, then left without once coming back to check on them. The nearest inhabited town was Klesh, over thirty miles away. Next closest was the port of Orhumbelen, nearly a hundred miles on a raven's wing. Any suitable destination was much too far away to take trips back and forth from, so their only hope was to stay at the ruins, camp away from the frigid onshore winds, and wait. Every time the Ilaadrid Shard was ready to shine, they ventured out following Nelv, carrying the entirety of their over-encumbering gear.

During their days waiting, when her hands weren't shivering too violently to hold a pen, Hefra kept herself busy taking notes on Nelv's behavior, her different forms, and her attitude, which always verged between noble and entitled. There were plenty of other species to study upon these remote shores, but those studies could be managed by any naturalist at any other time—Nelv became Hefra's passion.

Sceres was high in the sky when they arrived at the edge of the headland; she was shining pink with subtle hints of green, like a slice of watermelon. As usual, Nelv headed straight to the old lighthouse, an ancient tower that was only half standing. The ruined structure was mossy, slippery with ice, and teetering on old stone bricks that could easily topple over.

High above them, Nelv perched and waited, her sight locked southward. She took the form of a snow leopard this time, to feel more comfortable under the icy winds. Hefra took note, jotting it all down.

"I'm running low on notebooks, sweet plum," she said. "I've never had to write in such tiny print before. I hope your friends come equipped with plenty of paper to spare."

They sat down on their usual not-too-uncomfortable rock, not too far from the lighthouse. They had Nelv in their view, and a clear vista of the Esduss Sea to the south and southwest, where they believed the black-sailed ship would most likely appear.

Sunnokh was setting, turning the sea a fiery orange. Nelv was up high, inhaling her last breath of sunlight, but Crysta and Hefra were already in the dark, feeling the cold stone chilling their thighs.

Hefra lit a fire in the ring of rocks they had built their first time here. During their last visit, the winds had been too strong, forcing them to give up and spend the night with no comforts. This time, the wind blew from behind them, and it seemed like the fire was going to hold.

"There we have it," Hefra said. "Stay sputtering this time, you fidgety flames." She sat next to Crysta and covered both their laps with a thick blanket. After pulling a log from the fire, she dug a hooked barb into a burrow in the hard wood.

"What are you doing?" Crysta asked, worried she'd get burned.

Hefra pulled the barb out, and with it came a toasty, steaming grub.

"They are much better when baked inside the wood. The sap and smoke make them sweeter."

She popped the grub into her mouth with a juicy crunch. "Want one?" she asked, digging into another burrow.

"No thanks, you can have them all."

Hefra devoured a handful more of the grubs, all perfectly cooked, then kicked the log back into the fire and looked toward the remains of the lighthouse.

"This is what I don't quite understand about Nelv," she began, watching the Nu'irg's silhouette over the gloaming sky. "She's a snow leopard now, but when she's not, shouldn't she be freezing up there? It's like it doesn't bother her. She's made of the same stuff you and I and any felid are made of, but somehow she's able to withstand so much more. That day she hunted the ox and got kicked in the chest, I thought she'd die. She must've had ten broken ribs! Yet she healed fast as a tiger beetle runs, all back to normal in a couple of days. I don't understand the forces at play here, Crysta. It's something beyond what we are used to studying." Hefra glanced up toward Nelv, whose long tail switched like an irate pendulum, longer and fluffier than any tail should be allowed to be.

"It is rather peculiar," Crysta observed, trying to sound smart even though this was not her field of study. "I like to try comparing it to other natural processes. Those transformations, they seem so effortless to her, but from what the shamans told us, they are only able to shapeshift so often, lest they get fatigued. And they need to eat more in their larger forms, but where does that food go when they shapeshift back? There is an exchange of energy happening somewhere in that process."

Hefra shrugged. "If you want to get all spiritual, which I don't, you could say the energy comes from all felids. And perhaps from the Silvesh, like with Mamóru's case. How that works, well, it beats me." She adjusted her bum on the rock, easing the numbness, then continued, "I don't get it. I'm used to taking samples, writing down data, proving or disproving my hypotheses based on observations or experiments. Here, there's nothing I can do but speculate. And now I know better than to try to get my hands close to that animal—even the Laatu are terrified of her."

"I did get you that fur sample though, from when she rubbed against the sycamore."

"It just sparked more questions, not answers. Looked exactly like lynx fur, the form she was in at the time. And then, when she shifted into a tiger of completely different coloration, the hairs you collected remained the same. What does that tell us? *I don't have a fucking clue*, Crysta, that's what it tells us."

They paused for a moment, the flames nearly licking their outstretched hands. Luckily, no snow was forthcoming that evening. The sharp light of the Ilaadrid Shard felt cold to their eyes, but it held a comforting fringe of warm pinks thanks to the half-moon that held up the beacon.

Crysta tried to keep her eyes on the horizon, but her neck tired. She looked to the ground, where the moonlight cast surreally sharp shadows, while the fire created ghostly, shifting shades with no clear edges. Her eyes drifted over the flickering forms, making her feel sleepy.

Hefra was heavy-eyed too, but she leaned back to watch Nelv atop the broken lighthouse. The snow leopard's long fur coat glistened as if covered in sparkling dew. She had been chewing on her tail, but suddenly let go of it. She stirred, then stood up, swishing her tail to-and-fro.

"Something's happening," Hefra murmured. She looked to her side— Crysta was dead asleep.

"Hey!" She punched her friend in the arm. "No sleeping! We are here to keep watch. Look, Nelv is acting strange."

Crysta forced her eyes to open. Her lids felt heavy, as if they were trying to lift Hefra's abominable backpack. She gazed toward Nelv and saw her shapeshift into a dinofelis—a felid like a small smilodon, with an ashen coat that looked even more pale in the twilight. Nelv growled at the sea, at the stars.

Crysta and Hefra followed her gaze. Nothing. Only a darkening horizon.

"There's nothing there, puss!" Hefra yelled.

"Wait… she's on higher ground. Maybe she sees something over the curve of the horizon."

"Do you ever stop thinking like a cosmologist?" Hefra protested.

They stood on their cold stone bench, hoping the added height would make a difference. The unsteady fire in front of them was not helping their eyes adjust, so they moved away from it and climbed onto the base of the shattered lighthouse, careful not to slip on the ice growing between the stones.

Grrouw-grruuom, came the strange vocalizations of the dinofelis above them.

"There! Lodestar guide me, I see something!" Crysta shouted.

Far on the southwestern horizon, over the curved edge of the sea, a tiny white dot was visible—a sail, like light glinting off the tip of a wave and freezing in place. The little dot grew, and all around it, more and more dots appeared.

Nelv groaned a strained meow.

"There's more of them," Hefra said. "That's disappointing."

"Why?"

"Look at that. They keep coming. Must be hundreds of them. We are looking for a black-sailed ship, not a thousand ships with white sails. Aren't those frigates Lerevi?"

"Lago might be with them, maybe."

"Love, don't be delusional." Hefra kept staring at the approaching dots. They were clear now, sharp as moonlight.

"You know what? I don't care what you think, Hefra," Crysta said. "I will hold on to my hope."

She walked back to the fire, grabbed a bundle of firewood, and tossed it into the pyre.

"Hey! That's meant to last us all night!"

"Now it doesn't need to. Lago will be here before then. I'd prefer it if he can see us. It's not as fancy as a lighthouse, but Nelv can stay up there and be pretty and useless while we make some light for Lago to spot us."

Hefra tried to retrieve some logs from the bonfire, but Crysta pulled at her arm.

"Don't you dare," she said. "If I'm wrong, you can have my blankets later."

They both returned to the base of the lighthouse, which now glowed bright orange on one side, as did Nelv.

Grouww-gruouom the dinofelis implored from above.

Suddenly, between all the white sails, they noticed something peculiar: another ship was there, white as bone, but seemingly sailless. The ghostly ship began to brighten with points of light, like fallen stars swimming in the Esduss Sea. Aided by the cold lights, they finally discerned a dark shape hanging over the spectral ship—black sails.

"Lago!" Crysta bellowed. "Lago, up here! May the moon light your path! Lago, it's me!"

Nelv roared, shaking the very foundations of the ruins.

CHAPTER FOUR

ALL ABOARD

Sterjall paced the deck anxiously, binoculars in hand. The west gleamed with the afterglow of sunset. The Ilaadrid Shard beamed straight above *Fjummomurr*, glowing fiercely within Sceres's Tourmaline half-face.

"I hope she's there, I hope she's there," he implored in a mumble.

"She will be there," Kulak assured him. "Nelv will not fail us."

"Not Nelv, Crysta. I mean, Nelv too, but I hope Crysta also made it."

"You always speak kindly of Crysta," Kulak said. "My heart will be very happy to meet her at last." The caracal looked up at the pink moon, having to squint at the brightness of her white shard. "She is most beautiful when in pink," he added, voice hushed in awe. "My eyes have seen her now wearing five dresses. Only one more she has yet to show me."

Fjummomurr's sails blended with the darkening skies, in striking contrast to the kuba bone hull and deck, which shimmered like snow under the moonlight. The Puqua ship was being escorted by Theggo's fleet, which had increased its numbers considerably, having been joined by multiple flotillas who had heard of the admiral's recent escape.

Once they reached the port of Orhumbelen, they spent a week sealing new alliances, solidifying oaths to fight for the return of the Republic, and strengthening their resolve. After fully resupplying their vessels, their fleet took to the wind like a flock of gulls.

A herald had flown ahead of them, carrying a letter to notify the Tsing Empire of their approach. The Tsing were a cautious people, sending the herald back with instructions for the Lerevi fleet to meet them at Fel Duyenhai, so that from there they could be escorted through the gulf. But their first destination was the tip of the Taring Peninsula.

Sterjall was unable to keep still. He stood next to Theggo, who had boarded *Fjummomurr* for this part of the journey. "How is Tinnomeg doing?" he asked.

"No longer in pain, I think," Theggo answered. "But I wonder if he's upset at losing his horn—he seems dejected. I would love to thank him for his friendship, for his efforts, for keeping me safe. I wish I could speak with him the way you can speak with canids. Perhaps the wielder of the bovid mask will be kind enough to say a few words to Tinnomeg in my name."

"I am certain they would not mind doing so." Sterjall tiptoed forward and craned his neck, as if gaining a few more fingerbreadths would allow him to see farther. He aimed his binoculars past the narwhal figurehead and kept fidgeting with the focus knob.

Theggo's long hair of gold and silver flapped in the wind. He observed Sterjall with curiosity. "You've been so focused on finding the headlands that you haven't even noticed the Ashen Dome."

"The dome? But we aren't even in the gulf yet."

"Look to starboard, Lorr Vaari."

Sterjall turned his head. Directly east, over the vast Gulf of Erjilm, when the skies were clear like today, one could see hints of the distant Ashen Dome. The wolf rested his binoculars on his muzzle and strained his eyes, but he saw nothing more than a hazy flattened cloud, nearly imperceptible from over two hundred miles away.

"Perhaps you won't see the dome's gray snowcap yet," Theggo said, "but those are the ashen clouds that rise from its smoking top."

"It frightens me to think that the inside of the dome might be nothing but a pit of lava. Perhaps we won't find anything in there."

"If that's the case, it's been that way for fifteen centuries. The smoke is more noticeable in Umbra and Winter, but the fumes have always been there. And the dome has not grown out of shape, which is a good sign."

Sterjall bounced on his footpaws impatiently, tail flicking with his irritation. "How much farther?" he asked Theggo. "I haven't seen land for a while. I'm getting anxious."

"Land should be visible soon. Be patient."

Not even a wick after Sterjall asked the question, a call resounded from the crow's nest of a nearby ship. "The Dark Watcher approaches!"

"The Dark Watcher? What does that mean?" Sterjall asked.

"It's an old lighthouse from before the Downfall, one that shines no more. You'll see its dark silhouette soon."

Sterjall searched with his binoculars. "Come on, come on," he mumbled. As if invoking the Loorian Continent into being, he at last spotted a few distant jagged peaks. He followed the saw-toothed edges in and out of the water until he found the form of the broken lighthouse. But the Dark Watcher was no dark silhouette, as Theggo had claimed—it was an orange streak of light, beaming on the horizon, reflected clearly against the Esduss Sea.

"The Dark Watcher doesn't look so dark to me," Sterjall said.

Theggo looked toward the ruin with his spyglass, letting his knees bend to counter the motion of the ship. "Well, it never does shine, except for tonight, I guess. A bonfire burns near it. I see people moving on the headland."

"Crysta!" Sterjall cried out, wagging his tail so hard it smacked against Theggo's calves. "Cap'n Siffo! Let the lights of the kenzir stones shine!"

"Like it shines within us all!" the captain replied, then issued commands to his crew.

One by one, dozens of pharoliths lit up the black-sailed ship. Awash in the cold glow, Sterjall stood with hopeful eyes and a sparkling grin.

The headlands drew nearer. The Dark Watcher shone brighter, closer. Most of the fleet kept to its course farther east, making room for *Fjummomurr* and *Silverweave* to approach the rocky, icy shore.

Sterjall spotted a figure jumping in front of a fire. *No, two.* He focused his binoculars once more, aiming them at a larger form perched at the tip of the lighthouse. He heard a distant roar.

"It is Nelv!" Kulak yelled from behind him.

"Lago!" came a diminutive voice in the distance. "Lago!"

"Crysta! I'm here! We are coming!"

Once they were directly beside the towering headland, Sterjall heard a clearer call. "Meet us farther down the shore, where the cliff drops! We are coming down!"

Fjummomurr arrived first and docked at a derelict pier from times long gone. The Puqua sailors lowered ramps and waited on the bright, glowing ship.

Nelv was the first to arrive, dashing speedily as a dinofelis. Theggo fell to his knees as soon as he saw her, clutching his silver triskelion pendant as if in prayer.

Nelv cared not for the ramps or for the supplicant stranger. She launched herself from the pier directly aboard the ship, flying over Theggo's bent figure and landing behind him as a clouded leopard. She hurried toward Kulak and slowed in front of him, regaining her composure. Kulak lowered a handpaw, and Nelv walked into it, allowing him to softly caress her back and lightly pet her tail. Nelv even allowed herself the luxury of releasing a soft purr, which struck Kulak's heart, as he had never witnessed the Nu'irg express herself so openly.

"My heart missed you too, fearsome Ierun of all Mindrel," Kulak said.

"Is this kitty d'lovely Nu'irg ust Mindrel?" Siffo asked, stepping closer to pet the spotted cat. "Great t'meet ye, mine name—"

Kulak nearly tackled the captain to the ground. "Do not," he simply said. "Do not, ever. Not with Nelv."

Nelv began to explore the skeletal hull of the ship, and Kulak followed, telling her all that had happened since they last saw each other.

A moment later, two more figures came trudging down to the shore, hauling enormous backpacks. Crysta climbed up the ramp first, panting from exertion. She was followed by Hefra, whose bags were at least twice as burdensome.

"Lago!" Crysta croaked, trying to sound excited but lacking the breath. She dropped her heavy bag on the deck and embraced her old student. "Lago, I'm so happy to—sorry, Sterjall, I'm so happy to see you, so happy." She kissed his muzzle on the left, then the right, then kissed between his pointed ears.

"Very happy to see you too," Sterjall murmured, a bit embarrassed but earnestly joyful.

"What is all of this? This ship? You brought an entire fleet? What is making those strange lights? Are those people all wearing pig masks?"

"There's a lot to explain—"

A heavy thud reverberated, followed by glassy clinks and clanks, as Hefra dropped her monstrous bag onto the deck.

Crysta pointed a delicate hand toward her friend. "Sterjall, I would like you to meet Hefra."

Sterjall raised a handpaw. The short, stout woman took it and shook it with bone-crunching power. The wolf winced in pain. "Nice to… meet—"

"The world-famous Lago-Sterjall Vaari of Withervale?" she said, measuring Sterjall's expression while trying to not look too interested.

"Hefra? As in Hefra Boarmane?" Alaia asked, stepping closer after sharing a friendly hug with Crysta.

"Do I know you, gal?" Hefra responded, smelling her own hand to study Sterjall's scent.

"No, but I love your books! My favorite is the *Field Guide to Birds of the Loorian Continent*. Those illustrations you did are simply exquisite!"

Hefra crushed Alaia's metacarpals and said, "Well, I don't know you, but I like you already."

Sterjall introduced Crysta to Theggo, then to Pol, Puuja, and Lummukem, who Crysta was extremely uncertain of how to greet, but she felt more comfortable after she saw Hefra shake the dragon's claws like it was the most routine of pleasantries.

"Hefra Boarmane," she said to Lummukem, then moved around to examine their long tail. Lummukem did not know how to respond.

"Boarmane is yer name? Then ye are welcome aboard mine ship!" Siffo happily grunted. "I'm Cap'n Siffo. Let me a-show ye 'round *Fjummomurr*, Lurr Boarmane."

Sterjall watched them go and spotted Kulak coming back from speaking with Nelv. "And this here is Kulak, the Mindrelfröa," he said to Crysta. Kulak was giddy and could not hide it, having heard countless stories of Sterjall's old mentor.

"Khuron Aio-Kulak," Crysta said. "Balstei told me a lot about you. A true pleasure."

Kulak's whiskers lifted in a shy smile. "My scalp is… You, too," he fumbled, flicking his ear tufts and nodding awkwardly.

"Crysta! Come here!" Hefra called from somewhere farther down the ship. "You have to see Cap'n Siffo's ship! And these glowing stones they have!"

The night was as young as it was cold. There were a lot of frigid limbs, and a lot of stories to be told.

Sterjall pleaded with Siffo to let his friends gather in the captain's quarters, as the cabin was the warmest and most comfortable room on the ship. Siffo reluctantly agreed, resigning himself to getting no rest that evening as the wayfarers convened to chat, reminisce, and enjoy their mutual company by the warmth of the iron stove.

Pol and Puuja were lightly snoring in Siffo's bed, thick blankets pulled up to their necks. The twins had only had a few weeks of Common lessons so far, and had not understood much of what the newcomers had said, so they had promptly passed out.

"You are telling me that the dormouse sleeping with the twins is another one of the spirits?" Hefra asked, glancing at Gwit, who was curled into a perfect ball of fluff atop Puuja's red hair.

Lummukem nodded.

Hefra snorted and smirked. "Neither the basilisk nor the cute dormouse are quite as terrifying as Nelv, let me tell you. I almost lost my head once, when I dared toss her scraps from my meal."

Kulak's eyes widened. He slowly shook his head in dismay.

"Which reminds me," Hefra said, reaching across the table toward Sterjall.

"Ow!" Sterjall yipped, rubbing at his arm.

"Just a little fur sample. Don't mind me, whiskers."

"Hefra, please," Crysta said. "You'll have enough time to… *study* my old student. Control yourself."

"Here's one fur ya," Siffo said, handing Hefra a wiry tangle he plucked from his chest.

"Thank you, Cap'n," Hefra beamed, "that's mighty helpful of you. How come you are a warthog, if you say you aren't the one wearing the suid mask?"

"Unly quarter hog, at most. It's d'way we've done it in Nagradrolom fur centuries. D'Nagrafröash breed d'traits uf them half-forms, n'since each uf them takes a different suid species, we Puqua end up with boars, javelinas, kubas, bushpigs, n'a few uthers, such as warthogs, like yers truly. Ye'll find a healthy mix among mine crew."

"Where is the Nagrafröa, by the way?" Crysta asked. She looked to Sterjall. "And that reminds me, where is Jiara? Didn't one of your letters say I'd get to see her in her new bear form? Balstei told me so much about her! What was her new name again?"

"Kitjári," Sterjall answered. "They… Umm…"

"We have chosen not to speak of the Nagrafröa or Urnaadifröa," Theggo interjected, "for their own protection. Not even I know what their mission entails, as my friends believe they require utmost secrecy."

"Thank you, Theggo," Sterjall said, then looked apologetically to Crysta. "I can't say much more, but I do hope you'll get to meet them both. I'm just… I'm really glad you made it here. I was afraid you wouldn't be able to leave the institute in time to see the Moordusk Dome open."

"It was the most wonderful experience of my life," Crysta said. "We were probably the very first ones to venture in, as soon as the vines began to part. We met Hud Quoda and saw the Laatu fleet sail off into the Isdinnklad, like leaves carried in the current. Then we met Queen Alúma, who treated us very kindly."

"Kindly? She wouldn't let us borrow a couple of smilodons!" Hefra complained.

"But other than that," Crysta continued, looking at Kulak. "Khuron Kulak, your mother, she wanted us to tell you how the Laatu migration is faring."

Kulak nodded expectantly.

"Zovaria hasn't been the kindest to them," she said, "but tempers have cooled off a lot. The Union is cooperating, at least in some territories. Wuovad Kladesh, the Laatu settlement south of the Sajal Crater, is holding strong. The process of transforming the volcanic lands has been a struggle, but they are making good headway."

"It might take decades, even centuries," Hefra added, "that's what Lerr Fingrenn told me. It's a hard terrain, covered in hot lakes, too acidic for most plants to thrive, but the Laatu seemed confident they could make it work. They have the aid of most companion felids there, and the roads provide them with a constant supply of munnji from the dome. Well, what is left of the dome."

"How… how does Mindreldrolom look now?" Kulak hesitantly asked.

"Like an obstinate spiderweb in the sky," Hefra replied. "A patchwork of holes, of light and dark. The trunk and the columns are still all there. My guess is that it will be a long time before it all shrivels away, decomposing like a mushroom after releasing its spores."

"And then there is Birsulf Allastirg," Crysta said, "the settlement in the Udarbans Forest. The new homeland is flourishing, but isolated. It is deep in a jungle, far from any cities, so the Laatu have found no opposition. That's where we went to after visiting Arjum."

"Why did you go there instead of staying in the dome?" Sterjall asked.

"We went there following in Balstei's footsteps. Since no one really knew where you had gone to, we were hoping maybe we'd find you with him, at the Laatu colony. And if we didn't find you there, I thought maybe we'd help Balstei with his work transcribing Mamóru's petroglyphs. We had lost hope of seeing you again, when that big fellow, Kenondok, came by with your letter and the message for Nelv."

Crysta paused. "Your letter…" Her eyes turned glossy and distant. "Your letter was beautiful. And persuasive. And… Do you really think we could see the Stelm Yenwu Observatory? You weren't joking about that?"

Sterjall made a gesture somewhere between a nod and a shrug. "I really hope so, if it's still inside the Yenwu Dome."

"Telescopes are nice and all," Alaia said, "but I'm more interested in seeing the billions of birds that live in the dome."

"That's exactly what I told Crysta, Oldrin gal!" Hefra said, slamming a hand on Alaia's shoulder. She looked toward Kulak. "No offense, Lorr Mindrel—your dome was outstandingly beautiful, but it was not the most diverse when it came to avians."

"His name is Kulak," Crysta quietly reminded her friend before turning back to Sterjall. "I do wonder how advanced those old telescopes were. The ones we were able to reconstruct—at least those that were not too far damaged—were already better than the ones we can build today. But we know there were others, ones able to glimpse much farther, far beyond what our optics of today can handle."

Puuja unstuck her matted hair from Siffo's bedding, then dragged her feet toward the group. She hugged Lummukem's side. Lummukem lifted her up and placed her on their lap. "We should learn from the children," they said, "who need their rest as much as we do."

Theggo was the first to stand. "I will head back to *Silverweave*. We will spend the night docked on these shores, and in the morning sail east to meet with the Tsing ambassador."

"Come fullow d'cap'n, gentle maidens," Siffo said to Hefra and Crysta. "I shell show ye to yer quarters."

CHAPTER FIVE

AS ABOVE, SO BELOW

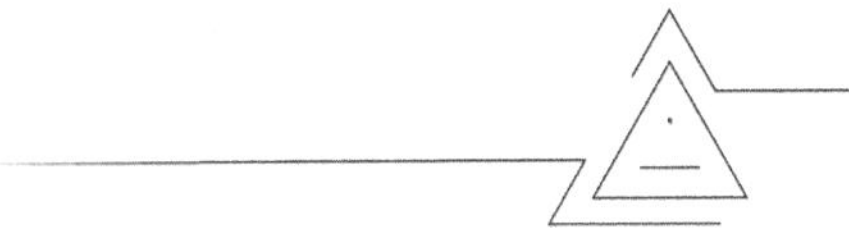

Fjummomurr was sailing east alongside *Silverweave*, taking point among the enormous fleet. Fel Duyenhai was visible to starboard, its craggy shores growing into inaccessible peaks where flocks of shorebirds had whitened the rocks with centuries of droppings and feathers.

"This thing is remarkable," Crysta murmured.

"What is it made of?" Hefra asked, tapping on the metallic-blue plates. "Some kind of aphid resin?"

"How did you know?" Sterjall asked. He was sitting between Kulak and Crysta on the bench encircling the mainmast, showing off the pauldron of his elytra armor. He hadn't worn the armor for the past week, as they did not expect any trouble while under the protection of the Lerevi fleet.

Hefra stood in front of the three, spinning the pauldron in her hands, letting the scales tinkle against one another. She looked at Kulak. "And where is your armor?"

"Laatu fare better with no armor," the caracal replied. "Too restrictive." Other than his oilskin coat, Kulak was wearing his knit cap to protect his head from the wind, with his tufted ears poking through the holes.

Hefra handed the pauldron back to Sterjall. "It is gorgeous. But are you going to let me take a look at your mask today, or what?"

"Hefra…" Crysta warned.

"He said he would."

"It's fine," Sterjall said. "Just be careful with it. Don't get it near your face, and watch the wind—it's so light it'd blow away if—"

"I'll be careful, whiskers." She extended a demanding hand, then watched carefully as the wolf's figure turned to the solid, refractive smoke and the mask formed on the young man's face. Lago handed over his mask, cold hands trembling with hesitation.

Hefra traced her stubby fingers across Agnargsilv's elaborate contours and patterns. "Fascinatingly complex," she said. "And I can't tell what species it's meant to be. It's like the perfect blend between canid species, neither here nor there, vague in its specificity. The quaar filigree is exquisite."

"Do you also study quaar, like Balstei?" Lago asked.

"Nah, I'm no artificer, but I am good at finding connections, and I do think soot is involved in all of this. I have some ideas I've been wanting to test, but I don't have the equipment to do so."

Lago was intrigued. "What sorts of ideas?"

"Well, unfortunately I did not get to discuss this with Balstei, since he might've offered some insight... But the fur specimens I've been collecting, I want to measure if they have a higher concentration of aetheric carbon than regular fur might. But I'd need expensive tools and reagents to dissolve, purify, and isolate the soot to see if that holds true."

"You think that even me, when I'm Sterjall, would have quaar in my fur?"

"Soot, not quaar. Just the particles, not the crystalline form. I'm not sure about you, but I have a hunch that the Nu'irgesh might follow that pattern. Puuja procured me a sample from Gwit already—he didn't seem to mind. I still need to get some from Ishke'ísuk. Does he shed his skin often?"

Lago didn't know, and Lummukem was not around to ask.

"I've been telling Hefra that we should find a way to visit Professor Lai-Nu at the Yenmai Institute," Crysta said to Lago, changing the subject. "Balstei mentioned that Lai-Nu has developed a theory on the origins of soot, one that is so groundbreaking that Empress Pian-Thi herself has ordered it be kept a secret."

"Why keep it a secret?" Lago asked.

"Because soot equals power. It means fast communication in a world where being first gives one the best chance of exploiting riches. Knowing the origins of soot might indicate where one is likely to find more. Or it might point to different types, different ways to use it, or even ways to manufacture it. We don't know, but the Tsing Empire keeps tight hold of their knowledge because they know it gives them an advantage against other realms. Their secrecy is how they've managed to outgrow everyone else and leave us in the dust."

"We should speak to this professor," Kulak said. "We will be going toward Yenmai, eventually. It is next to Kroowindrolom. The woman you speak of may be secretive, but good secrets we have to trade. Even their empress might wish us to know what she knows."

"I'm more interested in studying the Yenwu Dome," Hefra said. "If I could gather samples from its internal structure, I would have something to compare to the Moordusk Dome specimens."

"You have plenty of samples already," Crysta said. "You can't possibly go around carrying more."

Kulak's ears perked up. "Samples from Mindreldrolom?"

"Indeed," Hefra answered. "Lots of specimens of the filtering vines, thorns, root systems, and countless vials of white sap from the differentiated organs."

"Organs? What organs?" the prince asked. He tightened his oilskin coat to block the wind.

"The different types of vines serve different functions," Hefra said. "Did you not know this?"

Kulak shook his head, making his ear tufts wiggle. "We were not allowed close to the vines," he said. "We kept away. Well, sometimes." He paused for a moment before adding, "Sometimes we also broke the rules."

"No better reason to have rules than to break them, tufts," she said, stealing a smile from the caracal.

"What did you learn from Mindreldrolom?" he asked.

"Plenty. Some vines seem to regulate temperature, some act as filtering mechanisms, some cross internally as a vascular system to distribute the sap better. Most are there merely as a structural barrier, as protection. Well, at least those are my hypotheses. There must be more. Probably advanced immune systems, moisture regulation, energy storage, wind generation, even a nervous system might reside in there, who knows? I only got to study a small sample as we ventured into the wall. I couldn't climb up to see what the miles-high vines were up to, nor could I dig below the ground."

Hefra handed Agnargsilv back to Lago and scrutinized him as he turned back into his timber wolf half-form. She then gestured to Kulak. "Lemme see yours, tufts."

Aio handed Mindrelsilv to her, laughing as he retrieved his knit cap, which had gotten stuck on the mask's ears. While Aio placed his hat back on, Crysta shot a curious glance at him, noticing a pattern of dots on his hairless scalp.

"Is that… Were those?"

Sterjall noticed her gaze and hesitation. He pulled Aio's head covering off, revealing the pattern of constellations he had lovingly painted during a green-lit night on the outskirts of the Azurean Dome, not long after they had fled from a troop of moa-mounted soldiers. The pigments were fading by now, but Crysta recognized the dim pattern immediately.

"Your head, it's a star map!" she cried out, her voice pitched up with excitement.

"Sterjall painted it for me," Aio murmured self-consciously, leaning his head forward for Crysta to get a better look.

"How beautiful! I see Kerja right on top, Jawsplitter over here, Dunokh Sull way on the back, the Glires Nebula, Shiffrigan, the Beggar, the Tailless Scorpion, and you even have your friend Lummukem over here."

"To protect me," Aio said, straightening up.

"And the Sword of Zeiheim, with Pellámbri as luminous as your teal eyes," Crysta added.

"Lodestar guide me," Aio intoned with a sharp smile.

Crysta wanted to squish his sweet, soft cheeks, but felt the gesture might go a bit too far—she had only just met the Laatu prince the previous night. She cocked her head. "But wait a moment…" she mumbled, taking a better look at the young man's scalp. "Sterjall painted this?"

"He did."

"Sterjall, why is the Sword of Zeiheim pointed in this direction? If Kerja is right above, the sword should be tilted counterclockwise."

"Of course you'd be the one to notice that," he complained.

"Well?"

"I thought it'd look better pointing straight up, otherwise it'd be crooked."

"You can't just change the stars to follow your whims. This map could lead this poor prince astray."

"You might be overthinking things a bit."

"Crysta, I have to agree with your student," Hefra chimed in. "You are always overthinking things." She handed Mindrelsilv back to Aio. "Would you mind showing me how you mindspeak to your sweet cats? Not Nelv, I've had enough of her, but the two big kitties I'm very curious about."

"Uh, sure?" Aio said, glancing at Sterjall for support, but the wolf simply shrugged.

"Come with me, star prince," Hefra demanded.

Crysta and Sterjall were left alone, sitting before the mast.

"You know I was just kidding, right?" Crysta said. "Do you think he's mad I mentioned that your star map is wrong?"

"It's not wrong, it's… customized. And no, I told him I straightened up the sword a bit. Aio is fine."

"Fine indeed. He's a good-looking fellow, and seems quite smart." Crysta leaned in conspiratorially, and through the corner of her mouth whispered, "And is it true? About the two of you?"

"What? I mean, yes? But where did you—"

"Balstei told me about you two."

"Balstei? He knew?"

"Of course he knew, he's not blind. I mean, even if he hadn't told me, the way you look at him made it quite clear."

"We aren't hiding it anymore," Sterjall said. "I mean, mostly. I just hadn't had a chance to bring it up yet. But Balstei? We were so careful back then."

"Please. People who love you will know."

"And... Was he okay with it?"

"Bal? Well, it's certainly not something the Doctrine of Takh is very approving of. But let's just say Bal isn't as strict in his following of the Takh Codex as he once was. He's changed, quite a lot. When I met up with him, he wasn't even wearing his pendant. First time in ages I looked at his chest and didn't see it there."

"I believe that. You must've looked at his chest quite a bit."

"Excuse me?"

Sterjall smirked. "I've only seen you two in the same place once, at his lab in Zovaria. But I noticed how you looked at his—"

"You shut that muzzle, boy. Don't you—"

"Oh, so it is true then?" Sterjall grinned.

Crysta's face flushed beet red. "How did you even—I didn't do anything weird, did I?"

"No, you were fine. I saw you touch his arm, and it looked like there was something there. Like you said, people who love you will know."

"It's... Noss, this is embarrassing. We had a fling, years back. Nothing more. I'm a married woman, and he's a, well... The Laatu called him a 'mighty warrior,' which made me laugh, but he's... He's got an attractive physique, that's all." Crysta hurriedly changed the subject. "Either way, I like Aio," she said, her voice cracking a bit. "I think he's much better for you. Closer to your age—and to your size—than, you know..."

Sterjall's eyes opened wide. "Wait, you know about that too?"

"About you and Banook? Of course. Balstei told me that as well. I just didn't consider that was appropriate, you know. He's not even a real... I mean." She became aware of the sudden blitheness in her words, and quickly concluded, "I'm glad you found someone more fit for you this time around."

Sterjall's ears flattened. "Why does Banook being different, or being bigger, mean he's less fit for me?"

Crysta sighed and looked up to a flock of birds for answers, finding none. "It's just… I don't know how to explain it. Isn't it obvious?"

"Not to me. I love him."

"But I heard he's nine feet tall, and wider than a barrel, and don't get me started about his age, it's just—"

"I love him," Sterjall insisted, rising to his feet without realizing it. "And I think he is beautiful, not despite his size, but *because* of it. I know that's hard for some people to understand, but it's the truth, it's the way I've always felt about men. And Banook is the loveliest man I've ever met. The kindest, most tender and selfless. And his age should be a reason to trust him, not doubt him."

Crysta tried to find a more direct way to express her worries. "But he's… he's a bear!" she finally said.

"And I'm a wolf."

"No, you're a kid. A young man, I mean, even if—"

"But I am also a wolf. And what difference does that make? We love each other. And we are still together, Banook and I. Even though we are far apart." He turned his back toward her, crossing his arms.

"What do you mean? He's out in the mountains, and you've found a new man for yourself now."

"I'm with both of them. I love them both, each in a different way."

Crysta stood, shuffling closer to him. "Lago… Sterjall, that is not fair to them. What are you doing? Do they even—"

"They both know. I talk to Aio about Banook, sometimes. And I sent a letter to Banook explaining it all. He will understand, he's old enough to know that relationships can be complicated."

"I agree with *that* part," she said, rubbing the bridge of her nose. "With him being old, I mean. Too old."

"What difference does that make? Why does it matter that he's a bear, that he's bigger, that he's older? Explain it to me, tell me exactly why that is wrong."

Crysta held her breath. Resignedly, she said, "I don't know how to explain it. This whole thing, it just doesn't seem right. You can't be cheating on them with—"

"It's not cheating!" Sterjall snapped. "It's following my own heart. It's what *you* taught me, long ago. *You will only face true regret by not following the path your heart says is right for you.*"

"Those words were about something else, dear. They are still true, but which path are you choosing?"

"I don't know." Sterjall sighed and looked away, toward the sea. "Perhaps there is more than one path for me."

A fleet of yellow-sailed ships waited on the eastern shores of Fel Duyenhai, shimmering like streaks of sunlight. The bright sails were emblazoned with a hollow black square to represent a Lode: the most basic, lowest denomination of the Qupi, the building block of several major economies. Yellow and black, simple and unmistakable was the banner of the Tsing.

"Gilded sunsets and silver twilights!" a familiar, high-pitched voice greeted them from *Canvasback*, the most extravagant of the ships. It was Vor-Vor, ambassador to the Tsing Empire for Lerev, the old eunuch they had met at the Normouth Palace before the Republic was overturned. The Jabrak-Tsing dignitary had been delighted to learn that Theggo had rescued the Silvfröash and Nu'irgesh from the hands of the scrollsingers.

Canvasback, *Fjummomurr*, and *Silverweave* docked at a long stone pier, where the ambassador asked the group to join him under the shade of a thatch-roofed bungalow. After being briefed on recent events, Ambassador Vor-Vor said, "We have agreed to escort the Lerevi fleet to the port of Ngau Tor. Empress Pian-Thi is aware of your plans to enter the Ashen Dome, and offers her support." Even under the current circumstances, the Tsing Empire considered itself a strong ally to the defunct Republic of Lerev; the Lavra Faithful had always been an impediment to their negotiations, as the teachings of the Lavra Scrolls were incompatible with those of the Hi-Than-Mi Codices the Tsing promulgated.

"We offer our thanks, Ambassador," Theggo said.

"How many ships will your party need to escort you into the dome?" Vor-Vor asked. He was dressed in flamboyant yellows. His single Lode earring bobbed left and right as he spoke.

"Our masks can only spread the vines so wide," Sterjall said. "I believe we'll only need one ship. Siffo's will do."

Vor-Vor understood and agreed. He mentioned that the empress wanted to meet with the wayfarers, but there was no time to waste, not with the Red Stag moving by land and sea with such speed. The trip to meet the empress at the Tsing capital of Hashan would have to wait.

The fleet followed the incomprehensibly opulent *Canvasback* past Fel Duyenhai, through the strait between the island and the Kilkarag Peninsula, at the far southwestern tip of the Jerjan Continent.

Sterjall saw Crysta leaning on the starboard side of *Fjummomurr*. He approached hesitantly. They hadn't exchanged a word since their recent confrontation, and the wolf did not want to feel the pressure of the silence any longer. "I've never been to the Jerjan Continent before," he offered quietly.

Crysta glanced back with a comforting smile. "I have been, but nowhere close to here." She rubbed her hands for warmth. "I visited the Yenwu Peninsula long ago. It's covered in amazing mountains, thin like daggers that shoot up to the sky."

Sterjall peered through his binoculars, hoping to catch a glimpse of the southeastern continent. The Ashen Dome was unmissable, straight ahead. He studied the structure, which looked like a flattened blister with a billowing, smoky top. Its snowcap was streaked with gray.

"You need to take better care of that, it's not a toy," Crysta grumbled, noticing the scratches on the binoculars' front lenses.

"Sorry. They've been through the nethervoids and back. I'm surprised they still work at all."

"They've even been underwater once," Alaia offered, ambling by with Puuja by her side, and with Pol scurrying like a shadow not too far behind—she had been teaching the twins a few Common words to allow Lummukem a break. "Binoculars," she said.

Puuja looked up at the instrument. "Imocublars," she said, her lips moving invisibly behind Okrisilv, which she seemed to be wearing very comfortably now. "Can we see?" she asked.

"May I see," Sterjall corrected.

"You saw already. Can we see now?"

He sighed and handed her the binoculars.

With Okrisilv on her face, Puuja could not get the device to line up or focus properly.

"You need to take off the mask," Sterjall said.

"No!"

Crysta kneeled next to her. "Here, darling." She adjusted the binoculars so that the eye spacing matched Puuja's, and so that the focus could work with the added distance from her eyes.

"Lakemother shelter you," Puuja thanked her.

"Just don't break them," Sterjall implored, seeing her slam the eyepieces to her mask.

"There's not much more breaking she can do to them," Crysta noted. She rubbed the girl's red hair in a motherly gesture so instinctive that she didn't even notice she was doing it.

Sterjall felt utterly at odds; to him, any interaction with the children was forced, transactional, as if he had to carefully plan what to say and how to react to all the unknowns they brought with them.

Crysta scratched her nose and said, "*Hmm*, that's a lovely fragrance. What is it?"

"It's vanilla," Sterjall answered, used to the child's sweet smell by now.

"No," Puuja said, shaking her head. "No vahneela. Okruwom juice."

Sterjall furrowed his dark brow, not sure whether the girl understood what they were talking about.

"What's an okruwom?" Crysta asked.

The girl produced a tiny green bottle of sparkling glass, uncapped it, and put a drop on her index finger. She rubbed it on her neck.

Sterjall immediately smelled the strong, enticing scent.

"Put?" Puuja offered her finger.

Both Crysta and Sterjall let Puuja place a drop of the sticky liquid on their necks—she had to dig deeply to get through Sterjall's long neck fur.

"Oh hey, is that what I think it is?" Hefra asked as she strode over to them, lured in by the vanilla scent. She sniffed at Crysta's neck. "Beautiful fragrance. Pure extract from a beaver's castor sacs."

Sterjall's amber eyes lit up. "Castor... sacs?"

"A set of glands down by the beaver's asses," Hefra elaborated. "They secrete it and mix it with urine to mark their territories." She took the bottle, tapped her finger on the wet tip, and licked it. "Yep, indeed. Stronger castoreum than any I've tasted before. This would sell for a fortune in the Khaar Du markets."

Crysta placed a hand over her mouth. She wanted to rub the sticky substance off her neck, but also did not want to touch it, or insult Puuja. "I'll be right back," she said briskly, heading off to search for a washcloth.

Puuja kept playing with the binoculars, learning how to focus the apparatus by herself.

"*Kroovieth burdrolvesh!*" she said, aiming the glass toward the horizon.

Alaia overheard the words—the Miscamish name for *emerald starlings*. Intrigued, she gazed into the distance. "Emerald starlings? Like the ones we saw in Okridrolom?"

"Nuh-uh," Hefra said. "Those two are jade stealers, not starlings."

"How can you tell without binoculars?" Alaia asked, having a hard time even seeing the distant birds.

"Flapping pattern. And stealers tend to travel in pairs, though I don't think I've ever seen them so far from Wastyr before. They could be heralds."

"Are those the same kind we saw a while back?" Sterjall asked Alaia. He leaned over the railings, trying to get a better view of the two birds. "Remember, by Knife Point? When we first approached the Heartpine Dome with Ockam, there were two—"

Splash! Sterjall looked down and saw an explosion of water. Wide-open jaws with sharp teeth lunged toward him. He had no time to react. The jaws bit into his shoulder and pulled him down with the force of a sledgehammer.

Sterjall tumbled over the ship's railings. He felt a pull on his left footpaw, then a scratch as whoever had tried to hold him lost their grip. He saw the bone-white hull of *Fjummomurr* flash by his side, then crashed hard into the water.

The dual pains of the bite and the impact were immediately forgotten, subsumed by the shocking agony of the freezing water. He tried to swim for air, but knew not which way was up. His oilskin coat tangled with his limbs, and his limbs tangled with themselves, as he struggled without yet knowing what had happened.

Through the blood-tinted water, a pack of maroon-colored seals began to circle menacingly, their long, reptilian-like faces snarling. They surrounded him and bit his arms and legs with their enormous maws—not hard, simply to hold him down and prevent him from struggling.

Air. I need to breathe. I need—

Another figure materialized in front of him, of a different yet similar species, glowing with an aura that had the synesthetic color of rippling sea foam, cold and evanescent. She was smaller than the other seals, but with longer arms and legs, paddling her delicate, webbed hands and feet. Her short, glossy fur was a mixture of grays and whites, like that of a snow leopard. Swirling bumps covered her smooth coat, tracing scarified galaxies over her body. She looked beautiful, like a mermaid from ancient spritetales.

Sterjall felt the last bubbles of air leave his lungs. The sharp-toothed seals let go of his limbs. As he tried to swim to the surface, he realized his handpaws had been tied together, as were his footpaws. He swung his bound arms up and down like useless fins, pumping water to nowhere.

Air. Don't breathe. Don't, not until you—

He felt the dense fur of a seal rub against his chest. The pinniped forced Sterjall to wrap his tied arms around his thick neck, then propelled him upward, dragging him by the arms.

Out they came, breaking through the whitecapped sea. The wolf tried to exhale, but no air was left within him. He swallowed a shattered, forceful breath, and in a moment of weightlessness saw the worried faces of his friends on the deck of *Fjummomurr*.

"Sterjall! Hold—"

His head hit the water sideways, muzzle twisting back, making his neck feel like it was about to snap. He lost the air in his lungs once more and panicked, but a tug jolted his stomach, and once again he found himself in midair, inhaling hurriedly.

He glanced back. The ship was farther away now.

Weightlessness.

Before he hit the water, this time Sterjall flattened his chin against the seal's head so they dove in as one, the water smoothly gliding around them.

Air. Breathe. Dive.

So… cold…

More seals followed alongside him. At the center of the pod swam the woman with the sea foam-colored aura, watching him with intense eyes.

Weightless once more.

The ships, all the ships were so far behind.

During the next leap, Sterjall took a quick look around. No ships anywhere, only water and sky.

Chin down. Dive.

It's so cold. I will die like this. There is no land, nothing. I will die, frozen.

His only respite was the warmth of the maroon seal who was carrying him. The densely packed fur insulated his chest and arms against the draining cold, but his back felt like it was being pierced by ice needles.

Up, then down again.

The wolf considered strangling the seal; his arms were around the pinniped's neck already. *But they don't need to breathe as often. Can they even be strangled? Maybe I can bite.* He reconsidered. *What will that accomplish? There are dozens more around.*

More air, another hopeless breath.

They were moving so fast. Though it had only been a handful of heartbeats, it seemed like hours. Sterjall could not even shiver. The pull of the water over his body was too intense.

I… warm. I can't…

Air. Water.

Can't feel. Too cold. I'd… I'd rather drown…

He thought about breathing the water in, to let go of the intense pain from the cold. The only thing stopping him was the fear of being filled with cold water, of freezing from the inside.

The seals around him wove in strange patterns, their threads and the sea foam aura of Gwonlesilv braiding as one. Like afterimages, they lingered even when he closed his eyes, as he began to hallucinate under the cold and pain.

Let me die already, he begged.

Air. Breathe. Cold.

Please. It hurts. It is too cold, let me…

Air. Choke. Smoke?

He thought he saw a cloud flowing out of the water. Another hallucination, perhaps.

Air. Weightlessness. Fire?

The salty water pushed so hard against him that his eyes compressed in their sockets, making him see explosions of light that were not there.

I will die, he thought again. *I will die and I will never see you again.*

Flashes of pink, of green, of gold. Rumbling pressure that his ears could not block.

Air. Fire. Smoke. Rocks.

I lend an ear, the granite speaks… I hear… I hear the… the mountain… song.

Sterjall stopped struggling. His eyes closed.

CHAPTER SIX

WHITE AND BLACK

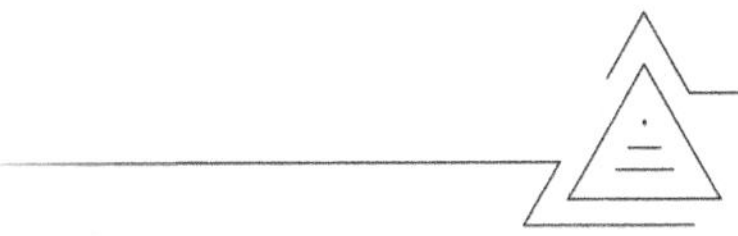

Sterjall opened his eyes.

A fire crackled in front of him.

He was rolled up in a bundle of furs, tied so tightly around him that he could not move. He wouldn't have had the energy to do so anyway.

His head hurt. His body hurt. His arms were numb, and he could not feel his toes or fingers. His shoulder hurt the most now, pulsing with agony where the seal had bitten him. His throat and eyes felt raw, and though he welcomed the fire in front of him, it was nearly singeing his whiskers, and it made his wet nose sting.

At least there was some warmth. He had given up hope of ever feeling warmth again.

In front of him was only the fire and a rising rocky prominence. And then there was the sky.

He heard a creak behind him, obscured by the slapping of waves. Wet footsteps were followed by cold drops falling on his neck. Someone grabbed the cocoon of furs and hoisted him up. His head dragged down limply. He saw gray and white webbed feet leaving strangely shaped prints on the rocks.

Sea foam.

He remembered then that he could see with Agnargsilv; his mind had been so unfocused that he had barely noticed the threads around him. He glimpsed the sea foam-colored aura of the leopard seal carrying him. His mind was too shattered to perceive more.

Barnacles. Wooden planks.

He—the bundle—was tossed into the bow of a narrow skiff. At the stern, the leopard seal sat naked, beautiful, merciless. Her form was streamlined, her torso flowing almost seamlessly into her head. When closed, her legs nearly merged, looking more like a tail than two separate limbs. Other than at the bumps of her spiraling scars, the seal looked smooth and rubbery, yet she was coated with short, tightly packed fur.

Two green birds flew down to perch on the seal's nearly nonexistent shoulders, sinking their claws into the dense coat. The woman caressed the creatures with her webbed hands.

Sterjall heard strange trills, like a metallic purring from below the water. He felt a jolt, and the skiff began to move. He could see the island now, and the fire, and the column of smoke rising from it: nothing more than a few sad rocks jutting out in the middle of an endless ocean. The islet vanished quickly, too quickly. The boat, oarless and sailless, moved at an impossible speed. He tried to focus his mind and followed the threads. He saw enormous seals swimming. He saw ropes.

The vessel raced over the water faster than any vessel should have been able to move. It skipped over short waves, letting Sterjall feel the weightlessness once more, making him nauseated as he remembered those torturous moments with his arms tied to the seal.

"Where…" he dared speak. "Where…"

"We'll be there soon," a graceful voice said. "Don't die on me. Not yet, wolf boy."

Sterjall closed his eyes and tried to ignore the lurches as the skiff hopped over the remorseless sea.

He was lifted again, jolting his mind partially awake.

He could smell a forest, hear voices nearby.

Creaking wood. A stone pier inside a hidden cove.

He saw a wooden ramp, and then he was moving over the deck of a ship. He looked to the sides and saw ratlines, barrels, a gray flag with a yellow-green sigil on it—an anchor. No, a crossbow. No, the sigil upon the flag was both an anchor and a crossbow blended into the same shape.

A hatch opened, and he was carried down into the lamplit belly of the ship.

A frenzied roar made his fur bristle. To his right, trapped in a cage, was a rabid-looking jarv wolverine, large as a grizzly bear, angrily spitting out his discomfort at being confined.

Sterjall heard footsteps to his left and turned his head.

A middle-aged man with an athletic build was sitting on a crate. He seemed distantly familiar. He glared at Sterjall, rubbing at his long nose.

"Trevin, help me with this sack of shit," the leopard seal woman said.

Trevin stood up. "Nice catch. No trouble?"

"None. But it's been hard to keep him alive. He's warm now, but still in shock."

Another roar, then a jolt as the jarv wolverine slammed his head against the cage.

"Khest!" the man named Trevin swore. "Can't you do something to keep him under control?"

"Not with her so far away," the woman answered. "He'll calm down when she arrives. The cage will hold."

"Fine. Let's go collar our new pet."

He was at Thornridge, Sterjall remembered, seeing the man's face up close now. *He was part of Fjorna's arbalister squad.*

Trevin helped remove the furs wrapped around Sterjall's body. The wolf had lost his oilskin coat, and his tunic and trousers were shredded and still wet.

Leif! he remembered. He wanted to reach down to his waist, but his arms were too numb. *Where is Leif?!* His belt was gone, his dagger nowhere to be seen. He couldn't have done much with the weapon either way, not in his current condition, but it hurt his very soul to have lost the dagger gifted to him by Banook.

"What shall we do with him?" Trevin asked.

"Keep him in one piece, at least till she returns."

Sterjall didn't try to resist them. He let the two lift his limp body and lock heavy iron shackles around his wrists, spreading his arms wide. He was forced to either stand with his arms spread open, or dangle from his wrists. He chose to rest on his legs until their strength was exhausted.

The man and the leopard seal withdrew from the chamber, locking the hatch behind them.

Sterjall took a moment to study his surroundings. He was inside a relatively small ship, likely one built for speed. The hull was nearly empty, with only a handful of hammocks dangling by a few barrels and crates. Opposite him, toward what he guessed was the prow of the ship, sat the thick-barred cage holding the jarv wolverine. The beast was quieter now that their captors had left, but still snarled pointlessly.

Three short crates were arranged in front of Sterjall, almost like benches, and the floorboards beneath him were clean; he guessed the place must not always have been that way, as there were many more shackles on the walls to his left and right.

It took an exhausting, conscious effort to do so, but Sterjall focused Agnargsilv's sight to perceive beyond the ribs of the vessel. He sensed life in the water, and barnacles that covered the outside of the hull. He felt a stone pier scraping lightly over the port side of the vessel.

He could see no 'tween deck; the stairs led to a wide hatch that exited straight onto the main deck. There were quarters at the forecastle, above the wolverine's cage, where fewer than a dozen people sat. He could sense their threads mingling with one another, and could barely hear their chatter as a low rumble on the floorboards.

They are sitting around a table. They must be eating. I'm so hungry. He diverted his attention and focused directly above him. In a room that must've been the captain's quarters, he saw it.

Leif! It's still here! He clearly sensed the familiar directional pattern of the threads flowing through his dagger's quaar hilt. *I didn't lose it. I didn't lose you.* He could not see the blade itself, but he was certain it was up there hanging on a wall, scabbard still attached to his belt. A man was in the room, standing by a table. *Is he drawing? Maybe measuring something.* He guessed the man was Trevin. It felt like him; the threads had the same flavor. *Maybe he's looking at a map.*

Another figure entered the room above him—the leopard seal woman again.

"—are lucky he's still alive," said the muffled voice of the leopard seal. "He almost gave in to the cold." Sterjall's eavesdropper ears immediately perked up and oriented themselves toward the sound.

"It was a good plan," Trevin said. "She'll have a wonderful surprise when she returns."

They don't know I can hear them, Sterjall realized. *They don't know my ears are this sensitive.*

"And Muriel will be happy too. But we need to keep her away from him—she'd slice his throat without giving it a moment's thought."

"Silv-Thaar Daro wouldn't let her. But the two of them better hurry back from the dome. The Lerevi fleet will come searching for the Zovarian maggot."

Daro? Fjorna Daro in the Ashen Dome already? Sterjall felt defeated. *We are too late. There is no hope now.*

"We'll be fine," the leopard seal said. "They won't find us in this cove. They'll be looking for the Cabal fleet, not just one small ship."

We must be close to the Ashen Dome, Sterjall thought. *If Fjorna has gone in, we must be on the eastern side of the Kilkarag Peninsula.* He did his best to rationalize everything, to recall the maps he had studied. If there was any chance of escaping, he would need to know where to escape to. *If I follow the shoreline, maybe I'll spot Fjummomurr and the fleet. That is, if I ever get out of this mess…*

Footsteps. The two figures above him walked out of the room.

"Who do you think will get his—" the voices dimmed, too far away to hear now. They joined the group of sailors at the forecastle.

Sterjall was left alone with his thoughts, alone with the growls and whines of the mindlocked musteloid.

Hours passed. His belly grumbled.

He did not want to fall asleep, but his body was too tired. He tried to use his legs to reach a crate, so he could maybe sit or kneel on it, but the crates were just a smidge out of reach. He gave in to exhaustion and dangled from his shackles, like a cut of meat at a butcher's shop.

Birds. Waves on the shore. A hint of light filtering through cracks in the deck. *It must be morning,* he thought. *No, later. Midday at least.*

Sliding metal sounds. The locking bars were removed, and the hatch creaked open with a blinding light. The hatch closed. Down came the leopard seal woman.

"Quiet!" she yelled at the wolverine, tossing him a dead eel, which he promptly devoured. She was carrying a bowl of gruel and a cup of water. She held the bowl in front of Sterjall.

He was starving. He ate, like a dog.

She pulled the bowl away before Sterjall could lick up the last bits of the foul meal, then offered the cup to him, letting him lap at the water. "Good puppy," she taunted, pulling it away before he could drink even half of it.

The seal sat on a crate in front of him, somehow both menacing and gentle. She was naked, her scarified patterns barely visible in the faint light. She placed a seductive hand over her curved hips.

Those scars, Sterjall thought. He recognized her now, despite her new form. She had also been in Fjorna's group. He had beaten her quite badly and disabled her. The Free Tribesfolk had tied her up by the gates of the Thornridge Lookout, next to Fjorna and the other survivors.

"So, you remember me now," she said.

"I remember all of you."

"Back then I was only Aurélien. Now I am also Silv-Thaar Knivlar." She pulled down the tatters of Sterjall's tunic to inspect his shoulder. The wound from the seal bite had not bled much. "I am familiar with the Miscam traditions," she continued, "and you seem quite fond of their misguided kind. What do they call you now, Lago Vaari? What name did they give you?"

"You can call me *Famuthuk Oset Khar.*"

She kicked him in the balls. Sterjall contorted in pain.

"Funny. Eat it yourself, if you can reach down that far like the dog you are. I can't wait for her to rip that fucking mask off your face. We chased after it for so long."

"Alvis Hallow will never have Agnargsilv. I won't—"

She laughed heartily, shaking her head. "You are utterly clueless, aren't you? She'll be here soon, don't worry."

She swayed away, a perfect feminine form weaving through the shadows. She unlatched the hatch.

"Silv-Thaar Knivlar, tell me something," Sterjall said, making her pause. She turned, eyeing him impatiently.

"I understand you kill your enemies. You fight for the Empire, but—" The leopard seal snorted, but let him keep talking.

"—but how could you… You wear Gwonlesilv. You must know the pain. How could you kill Däo-Varjak, the Nu'irg ust Gwonle? How could you be so heartless as to kill your own kind?"

A flash of anger clouded Knivlar's otherwise impassive face. The wolverine growled behind her, but she did not acknowledge the sound. She looked away, stomped up the hatch, and locked it tight.

Sterjall blacked out again. He awoke to the sound of whistling.

It was dark around him, though he could see hints of a cold light filtering between the planks of the deck.

"Chief Daro is almost here. Fetch us some drinks," he heard Trevin say, followed by footsteps receding.

He sensed the now-familiar aura of Silv-Thaar Knivlar sitting in front of Trevin.

"I can't wait to see her face," Knivlar's muffled voice said, followed by a clinking sound. "What a surprise it'll be." Another metallic clink. "Take that! Your Horn is mine."

"Not so fast," Trevin said, moving his hand toward the table between them. Three more clinks. "You fell for it!" he cackled.

"You can't move the Hex like that, you sleazebag!" Knivlar complained.

"Khest… Hold on, hold on," Trevin said, then went quiet for a while.

They are playing Qu, Sterjall realized, although he could not see the chips or the game board. *Maybe while they are distracted I could—*

"Do you think she'll have Trommosilv with her already?" Trevin abruptly asked, recapturing Sterjall's attention.

"Nah, she's merely scouting," the leopard seal replied. "I doubt the savages in there will be as easy to dispatch as those in the Moonrise Dome. I heard legends about their race." Another clink. "I got you know!" Knivlar cried.

"You cunt," Trevin groaned. "I'm not letting you—"

The vessel tipped ever so slightly. Someone had stepped on board. Sterjall focused his sight and felt two figures, one of which glowed with an aura of tawny ochres striated with hazel.

I remember this aura, he thought, *the same color the one-armed wolverine had. Krostsilv.* He remembered a letter Crysta wrote to him, mentioning that a new general was wielding the mask. *What was his name again? Crescu. Crescu Valaran.*

Hurried footsteps from a sailor. "Silv-Thaar Daro, they are waiting for you in the cabin."

Fjorna! Sterjall suddenly realized. *The person wearing Krostsilv is not Crescu, it's Fjorna!*

Silv-Thaar Daro entered the captain's quarters, followed by the other newcomer. Trevin and Knivlar stopped their game and turned to face them.

"Braaw? What's the occasion?" Daro's familiar voice asked.

"Oh, we have a nice surprise for you," Trevin teased from his seat. "A celebration is in order. You'll see in a moment."

"By the Shade of Yza, put some fucking clothes on, Knivlar," Daro said.

"It's pointless," came the voice of the leopard seal. "I dive in and out of the ocean all the time, and I'm already coated in fur. You better get used to it."

Daro sat down and gulped her drink. Sterjall could see Krostsilv's aura extending down her body, shaping into a slender tail that reached the ground. She had claws and a pointed snout, but that was as much detail as Agnargsilv could show him.

"So, are you going to tell me what your devilish smirks are all about?" Daro asked.

"I'm beating his ass at Qu again," Knivlar said, "but that's not the only reason I'm smiling. We'll tell you in a moment, but you go first. How did you fare in there?"

"Not so well, but as expected, I would say. The Miscam of the Ashen Dome are well armed *and* well armored. We will not be able to take their dome by force, not even if we ask Osef to bring in the entire Cabal fleet."

"We need him out in the Alommo Sea anyway," the new woman said, taking a seat next to Daro. "It'd be pointless to bring our fleet this far—the Tsing would crush us."

"Muriel is right," Daro concurred. "This is but a quick detour. We can't risk staying here for long."

"So… Then what?" Trevin asked. "What do we do if we can't fight them?"

"We do what Alvis did at Anglass—we charm the wearer of Trommosilv and say we will show them the outside world. Once we drag them out, we take the mask. Let the rest of the Miscam inside the dome wonder what happened. Maybe we'll come back for their riches at some later time, but the mask is all that matters right now."

"No offense, but do you think you can handle that?" Trevin asked. "As charming as you are, you are not as persuasive as Alvis Hallow."

"I think I'll manage. They speak Common, not Miscamish, from the little I overheard. I couldn't get too close without risking being seen. They have an enormous rampart I couldn't climb, but I heard their soldiers speaking at a gate. And these people, by Yza and Yaumenn combined, let me tell you, it would not be wise to try to fight them. If you think you've… Actually, no, it's your turn. What is going on with you two?"

Knivlar rose to her feet. She walked to a wall and picked up Leif, still dangling from Sterjall's belt. She dropped it on the table, making the Qu board bounce.

"What is this?" Daro asked. "Why are the threads moving like…" She unsheathed the blade. "Is this quaar? And this blade… Dorvauros style?"

"Like the relics from the temples, and made with real senstregalv," the leopard seal answered.

"Where did you get this?" Daro asked reverentially.

"I took a detour of my own while you were exploring the dome. Islav and Aness spotted the Lerevi fleet, who were coming to meet the Tsing. I took my pinniped babies with me and snatched a little prize from one of their ships."

"And quite a beautiful prize it is," Daro said, examining the blade. "But that's risky, just for a—"

Silv-Thaar Knivlar took the dagger from her and slammed it into the table. It pierced through the wood as if through butter.

"This toy here is not the prize, Chief. Feel, with your mask. Look around you."

Silv-Thaar Daro focused Krostsilv's sight, scanning left and right, feeling nothing. Then she tilted her head down.

"By Khest! Who? What is—?"

"Follow us and you'll see."

The hatch opened.

The light of a lantern cast long, shifting shadows as Silv-Thaar Knivlar stepped into the hold, followed by Trevin, then Muriel, and then Silv-Thaar

Daro. The caged wolverine growled, but was quickly subdued with no more than a thought from Daro, curling into a ball against a corner of his cage.

"I… I can't believe it…" Daro whispered.

"Is that? Is that what I—" Muriel could barely contain her excitement. She unsheathed her knife as she ran forward. Daro grabbed her arm, stopping her.

"It is," Knivlar answered. "Lago Vaari, in the fur and flesh, and not yet too mangled."

The white ermine smiled grotesquely. "My, my. This… This I was not expecting. What an incredible—" She turned to Knivlar. "Did anyone follow you?"

"Not a soul. I don't think their slow ships could even guess at what direction we took. We lost them before they even knew their dog was missing."

"Please," Muriel begged, clutching her knife between white knuckles. Sterjall recognized her too; she still had the same short, spiky black hair. "For Waldomar, let me just—"

"You'll have your chance, Muriel," Daro assured her. "We need to think this through."

The four of them stood right in front of Sterjall. He looked at the ground, defeated, but not wanting to give them the satisfaction of seeing the fear in his eyes.

Daro pulled up a crate and sat in front of him, adjusting the beautiful crossbow she carried on a strap around her shoulder. She placed a white-furred handpaw under the prisoner's muzzle and lifted it, forcing him to look at her. Daro's ermine fur was white as snow. Her unshapely face was fractured and distorted, the scars tracing furless gulches. Both her irises were steel gray, but one eye was bloodshot and dangled lower than the other.

"Lago Vaari," she mocked, smiling through crooked lips. "We had given up on chasing after you. Instead, you came to us. Do you know who I am?"

"Of course I know," Sterjall snarled, looking into her cold eyes. "I knew the instant I saw that bloated, rotten thing you call a face. Not even Krostsilv could fix your mangled—"

Daro slashed her sharp claws over Sterjall's right cheek, tearing his skin in four deep gashes, some cutting as deep as his gums.

"*Nnggh!*" Sterjall contained a cry.

"Now your face isn't so pretty either."

Sterjall sucked on his torn lips and spat, spraying red over her white fur.

"Yours is still uglier, you elk-felching—"

She punched him in the stomach, quieting him.

"Let me cut his balls off," Muriel urged. "Just let me—"

"Back off, Muriel," Daro said, standing up. "We need to strategize exactly what to do with him. This is not the time to act impulsively."

She pulled on Sterjall's ear, lifting his bloodied face. "We'll be right back," she said, then let the wolf's head drop.

The hatch latched tightly again.

Fuckers are going to kill me, Sterjall thought, his breaths nearly as fast as his heartbeat. He looked around for anything to aid him. They had left the lantern hanging from a beam, but it was far out of his reach. *I need to get out. I need to—*

"—get his mask and be done with this shit," he heard Muriel's voice above him. "That dog and those mucks killed my brother. Leave him to me, please, *please,* Chief."

"We need to get more information out of him first," Daro said. "And Trevin deserves to have some fun with him as well. And Knivlar too, if she hasn't yet had enough. Then, I promise you Muriel, he's all yours. You can gouge out his eyes, rip his teeth out, chop off his tail, as long as you keep him alive—we could use him in the future, to lure more masks toward us."

"And what of *his* mask?" Trevin asked.

"We will come to a decision on that soon, but not yet. There should be no enmity among you. One of you will get the canid mask, the other will get the one from the Ashen Dome."

"Either way, we should hurry," Knivlar said. "The Lerevi fleet was headed to Ngau Tor, but with their dog missing, they'll probably be looking for us first."

"They won't find us in this cove," Daro said. "We'll get to Trommosilv before them, don't worry. Allow me some time with the boy. I'll pull more out of him."

Muriel tensed up. "Don't—"

"I won't kill him, Muriel. He'll die by your blades alone, once we are done using him. I won't kill him, but I *will* see him suffer."

The hatch opened once more. Sterjall kept his eyes on the ground, watching blood drip from his muzzle.

"I'll make this simple," Silv-Thaar Daro said. She stood in front of the hanging lantern, casting a hard shadow upon the wolf. No one had followed her this time. "I will ask you questions, and you will tell me exactly what I want to know."

"Why in the fuck would I tell you anything?" he mumbled.

"Because the more you delay it, the more I'll make you suffer for it. Understood?"

Sterjall tried not to tremble. His dark face was matted with blackened blood that was oozing into a puddle by his footpaws. He had pissed himself, he now noticed, and he couldn't even remember when it had happened. He felt sick and embarrassed, yet still tried to pretend to be brave.

Daro unsheathed a white-hilted dagger and placed the silvery tip on Sterjall's dripping nose. She pressed lightly until it pierced through, and a drop of blood rolled down the twisting blade.

Sterjall suddenly lunged around the blade, biting hard, but he merely bit the air. Daro had sensed his move and pulled back just enough to leave him dangling in front of her.

She slapped him over the four cuts on his cheek, splattering blood into his right ear and eye, reopening the coagulating wounds.

"Bad puppy," she said, then her face tightened. "I want to know where to find the missing masks. We know Kruwensilv and Mindrelsilv travel with your friends, but we have not had news of the others yet. We know you have this information."

"The scrollsingers took the other masks from us," Sterjall said. "That is why we fled Lerev. The Republic is dead."

"Hard to believe that, though our spies have informed us of the troubles the Lavra Faithful have caused. We know some of the masks never made it to Lerev. Your lies will not do."

She kicked his stomach.

Sterjall twisted, chains loudly clinking by his sides. He tried to snarl, but the cuts on his cheek hurt too much.

"I'd ask you again, but you already know the question. Tell me now, Zovarian maggot, or—"

The hatch creaked open. Trevin poked his head in. "A cormorant just landed. Urgent message from Osef."

The ermine wiped her dagger on Sterjall's tattered tunic.

"Don't go anywhere, dog. We will tell you when it's time to take a walk."

She followed Trevin and locked the hatch behind her.

I'm so fucked, Sterjall thought. *But maybe, maybe if I try to—*

Footsteps above him. The arbalisters were all back in the captain's quarters.

"Well?" Daro asked.

"We haven't read it yet, but the wax color is—"

"Hand me that," Daro said. Sterjall heard a wax seal being broken, then the sound of unrolling paper. It all went quiet while Daro read.

"Scorch their flesh sixteenfold!" she hissed.

"What is happening?" Muriel asked.

"It's Hallow. His army made it to the Scoria Dome before Osef could even enter the Alommo Sea. Osef made it to the strait, but the Tsing are blocking his passage."

"How in Khest did Hallow get past the Graalman Horde so quickly?" Knivlar asked.

"They joined him. The cowards joined him. The Horde wants to take the Tsing Empire down, and they saw an opportunity. They have thousands upon thousands of horses on those plains. Now Hallow controls them, too. He will get to the chiropteran mask before we do."

Sterjall's eyes opened wide. *Fjorna is not working with the Negian Empire?*

"We needed that fucking mask!" Daro protested. "We need to move by air, and the avian mask is not within our grasp. We can't match the Negian numbers, not now that they have the Horde on their side. Bats, wings, that would've been our only advantage."

"But we'll still have the same number of masks," Knivlar said. "Once we take the bovid one, and the one from the dog."

"I say we are still ahead," Muriel declared. "We have more opportunities here. Afhora and the Federation are with us—more so if the Graalman have taken the Red Stag's side. We could have Wastyr as our ally if we spend some time convincing them."

Daro paced around. "That would take months. Wastyr is too far out of the way, and so is the Seafaring Dome. Hallow will find his way to the next mask somehow, I know it. This is a race now, and we need to get to the Tarpits Dome before he does."

"The Nargara Bastion will stop him *and* the Horde from breaching into the Tsing Empire," Trevin said. "They don't have a fleet. The Horde only knows how to handle their horses, nothing else. Even if Hallow finds a way through the bastion, it will require a long campaign."

"But with the mask of bats, he could send someone flying," Muriel said. "Then no bastion, rampart, or fortress could stop him from getting to Hoombusilv."

"Who cares about Hoombusilv?" Knivlar retorted. "The primate mask is weak. It cannot mindlock. It's written all over the Miscam stories—it was the first, a prototype, it did not have the same powers as the other seventeen."

"Maybe," Daro granted, "but we know he will want them all in the end. Whether or not Hoombusilv can control the primates, it can still provide an advantage in war. Either way, it is far out of our reach. For now, we need to secure Trommosilv before Lago's friends warn the tribe. Follow me, we need to inform the sailors."

"And the dog?" Muriel asked.

"Trevin, you go play with him, but don't break him too much. After you are done, I'll go back and get some information out of him. If he doesn't speak, he's all yours, Muriel."

"Then you better fucking hurry, Trevin," Muriel growled, hand already feeling the grip of her knife.

The hatch unlocked. Sterjall heard Silv-Thaar Daro projecting her voice, making sure he heard her. "Your turn, Trevin. Make him hurt."

Trevin walked down the steps, holding a wooden cudgel.

He left the hatch open, Sterjall noticed. He stared at the bright opening from the corner of his eye, hoping his interest in it wasn't obvious.

"Now it's just you and me, wolf boy," Trevin said.

"You look familiar," the wolf baited. "Aren't you one of the jackasses we beat up at Thornridge? I remember you tied up by the gates, crying for—"

Trevin slammed the cudgel against Sterjall's chest.

Sterjall wheezed and contorted, struggling to take a breath, his ribcage throbbing.

Trevin picked up the hanging lantern and held it close to Sterjall's face. "We've been waiting so long for this. Every single one of us." He pushed the lantern closer, pressing the hot glass right onto the wolf's lacerated cheek.

Sterjall first smelled his fur smoking, then felt his cuts burning.

He snapped, biting at the lantern and making Trevin drop it. He hoped that perhaps it'd cause a fire, but it simply left them in the dark.

"You rabid mongrel!" Trevin cursed, then beat Sterjall repeatedly with his cudgel. Once he stopped the beating, a bit out of breath, Trevin picked up the fallen lantern. It was shattered beyond repair. He shoved the bludgeon into Sterjall's ribs and said, "I want to see your eyes as I bash the teeth out of your filthy muzzle, as I make you turn back to a hopeless little boy and rip off that mask you stole from us." He looked around for another source of light, but could see nothing save for the light coming from the still-open hatch.

Do not lose yourself, Sterjall thought, preparing himself. *Do not give in all the way.*

Trevin paced toward the hatch, tapping his club against his hand. "Thinking about it, it's not even from us that you stole that mask," he said. He stopped at the steps and looked toward Sterjall, seeing nothing but darkness and two reflecting retinas, like amber drops in a void. "You stole it from that bloodskin witch, who you abandoned to rot in a cave. You stole it from her and from the little maggot she protected. Did you know it was my arrow that caught him in the back? I still remember the way that kid wailed, it was—"

The amber eyes moved closer in a flash, and suddenly Trevin's throat was crushed by heavy, sharp jaws. The wolf bit down hard, collapsing Trevin's trachea and spine into one mutilated mess.

The wolf had let himself sink into his rage, surrendering entirely to the impulses of Agnargsilv. In an instant, Sterjall's body had changed into his feral form, letting his now-wristless paws easily slide through the metal shackles.

The wolf shook Trevin's limp body by the neck, tearing into him with glee. He looked to the side, still holding on to the gurgling flesh, and made eye contact with the wolverine. The beast was still subdued, tamed by Daro's coercive command.

"What was that?" he heard from above.

He could barely recognize the words now. Words were human things, and he was not human. He was a caged animal who needed to escape.

A shadow appeared over the open hatch. He stared up, amber eyes scintillating within the blackness of his fur. His nose curled up in a snarl to reveal his gums and teeth. The cuts on his cheek parted like bloodied gills.

"Trevin? Shit, close the—!"

He charged, fangs first, biting into the screaming woman's arm and falling on top of her. He shook his maw left and right, tearing through the skin, ripping tendons and shattering bones.

To his left side he saw the white-furred ermine.

"Open the cage!" she commanded.

A man ran down the steps while five more humans took positions behind the ermine, who was readying her crossbow.

In front of the wolf were the deck's railings, and beyond them a sandy beach leading to the freedom of a dense forest.

The white-furred woman loaded her crossbow while the others charged.

Freedom, the timber wolf thought with a feeling that was not a word. But something called to him, something to his right side. A door, a room; a song.

Instead of leaping over the railings, he raced to the captain's quarters. Upon a wooden table, obsidian tip buried in the grain, was a dagger of white and black.

L... Le...if... the wolf thought.

A blade swung behind him, cutting through the long fur of his tail. He barely dodged the sword, and in the same move jumped to the familiar dagger, chomping down on its quaar grip while in midair. The table flipped with the pull, scattering Qupi chips and shattering glasses across the floor. The wolf landed behind the table as a heavy crossbow bolt slammed into the wood and sent splinters spraying around him.

Enclosed space, unknown, dangerous.

The only exit was blocked by the white-furred creature, who was reloading her crossbow, her white-hilted dagger clutched in her mouth. He wanted to finish her off. He wanted to disembowel her and bathe in her blood, then piss on her carcass. He snarled, holding the dark dagger in his dripping muzzle.

The woman spoke things, words; he did not care.

More humans at the door. No exit.

The wolf looked around him, behind him, then saw the pink light of Sceres shining through a window.

The white ermine lifted her weapon.

The wolf turned and jumped, crashing through the glass. The crossbow released the bolt. It grazed him, cutting the skin of his back as he tumbled from the ship.

He fell.

Weightlessness, again.

Water. Freezing cold. A memory so recent and so distant.

The blade slipped from his jaws. He saw it sinking under the pink moonlight.

No, I need you.

The wolf dove down.

I can't lose you, he thought, using the last words his feral mind could muster.

He bit into the coldness and found the grip.

He swam toward the rocks, toward freedom.

The salt stung his wounds.

From the water came a metallic trill, a call—maroon seals, swimming as fast as a falcon dives.

The wolf scratched his claws over a barnacled boulder, then jumped onto the sand as the enormous pinnipeds crashed into the rocks.

Moonlight. Pink and green. Safety, a forest.

Run, his instincts urged him. *Run.*

It was a simple request.

All he needed to do was run. All he needed to do was live.

He heard the trampling of heavy claws on a wooden deck, then the growl of a giant beast.

His body ached, yet he ran. He ran for his life.

CHAPTER SEVEN

WOUNDED WOLF

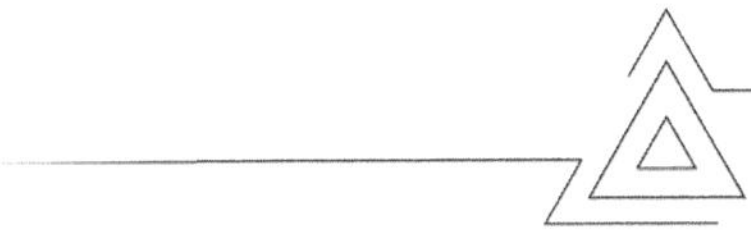

The black wolf fled through the forest, his paws heavy like boulders, his gait forceful as if fighting a storm. He plodded beneath icy rocks and pushed his broken body behind a toppled tree.

Thwump. Thwump. Thwack! Three arrows narrowly missed their target, lodging themselves into the snow and the gnarled bark. The wolf stumbled out and pushed on. Uphill he sped toward the darkness, hearing the growls of the wolverine behind him and the *tchtchtchwick* of the crossbow reloading. The salty scent from the nearby shores reminded him of something distant that he needed to seek. With his heart shriveled and weak, he dejectedly pressed forward.

Fwip. Fwip. Thud! Two arrows missed, but the third sliced through the skin by his ribs, spraying a warm stream of blood. Despite the tearing pain, he tried not to slow.

The smell of iron choked his muzzle. The cries of the humans and the ripping claws of the musteloid drew nearer. Unless the wolf found the energy to escape them, he would run out of hope, out of sense. Out of blood.

Whap! Another arrow exploded against a rock, spraying splinters onto his fur. He yowled in fear, his heart faltering. He remembered those he loved, seeing the light of their eyes in his mind. *I cannot forget them, my task is too important to fail.* While his human mind threatened to slip away, he held on tightly to a memory, to a dagger, to a song.

He felt the energy of the forest around him, like electricity tingling his black and dusky-gray fur. His eyes were matted with coagulating blood, but he could hear his pursuers closing in. The rocky path ahead was jagged and exposed—he could see no shelter or chance to escape—yet every cell in his body urged him uphill.

Up a snowcapped cliff rumbled a cold waterfall. The black wolf sensed a shadow closing in behind him. The beast. He jumped away from the claws, leaving a red trail behind him.

The cold wind howled.

CHAPTER EIGHT

VOICE OF THE CANIDS

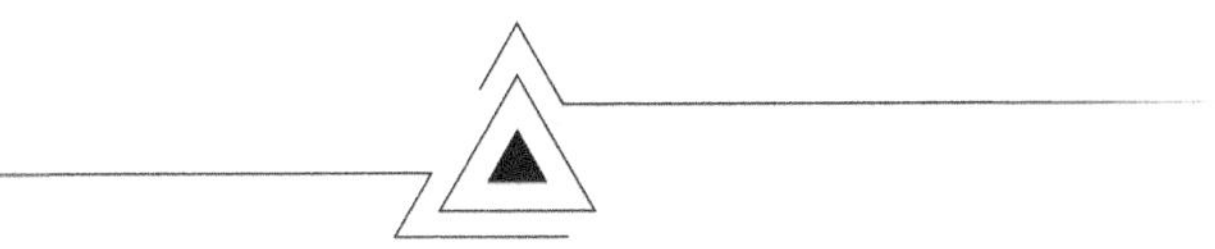

So cold…

The wolf lay shivering on the nightly shore. The mounds of snow around him were painted pink by the Tourmaline moon setting in the west.

The waterfall he had jumped into was nowhere in sight; not even a distant rumble remained. Beyond the creek that had carried him, the Ashen Dome rose like a wall. It seemed so close, yet it was miles away.

The wolf vaguely remembered the fall, the howling wind, a black-and-white dagger tumbling to his side. He remembered diving for the blade, barely catching it, and holding it tight as the foaming water dragged him away. He had let the will of the river carry his limp form, succumbing to its gelid embrace.

Leif! he thought, lifting his head.

It was there, by his side, half-buried in the sand and ice.

He forced himself to stand and saw the redness he had imprinted on the snow. His jaws closed around the black grip of the dagger. He… Sterjall. *Sterjall*, he remembered. *That is who I am.* He began to limp alongside the widening creek, hoping that it would eventually empty out at sea. *Follow the shoreline,* he told himself, though he could not remember why.

He carried his dagger away, weaving in and out of forests, chasms, and streams. He smelled something rotten and followed the scent. A dead gannet. His fangs pulled on the feathers and tore through the soft bones. Not enough. He needed energy, sustenance.

The forest thickened, swallowing the stream and darkening the undergrowth where little snow had piled up. He felt safer in this darkness, like he belonged. He lumbered about for hours until he felt the top of the canopy sparkle.

Sun. Warmth. He found a clearing and waited atop a rock for Sunnokh to greet him, then dropped tiredly, basking in his rays.

Sterjall, he thought. *Mustn't forget. I am Sterjall…* The wolf lost consciousness.

Growling. A threat.

The black wolf shook awake. Snarling muzzles flashed their sharp fangs at him.

Wolves. A pack.

He cowered, but there was nowhere to run; he was on top of a rock, in plain daylight.

«Who are you?» the eldest seemed to ask. «Intruder. Our territory.» She stood defensively in front of her pups.

The dark-furred wolf nearly heard the concepts in his head, as if the wolf mother was speaking to him. *Sterjall*, he remembered, and communicated the concept to the wolves. They did not understand. They bit at the air around him, their snarls so intense that he could see nothing but pink gums and yellowed teeth.

A word, one of those obscure concepts, came to his mind. «Agnargfröa.» He said it to himself, but also said it to the pack of wolves. He rose on trembling legs and repeated the word in his and their minds. «Agnargfröa.» He could barely understand what he was saying, but the pack quieted down, pacing uncomfortably around him. One of the wolves began to whine, pushing his head down.

The black wolf mindspoke again. «Agnargfröa.» He tasted the word. «What does it mean?» He faced the pack and willed himself to think more clearly. «I am hungry,» was the most immediate thought that surfaced.

«Follow,» the wolf mother communicated with a stare. «Follow.»

The pack led him to the carcass of an ox. The meat was mostly gone, but he still managed to rip out some cartilage and find sweet marrow in the remaining bones. The four cuts on his cheek bled as he ate. He lapped at his own blood, unable to risk losing any more of himself.

He regarded the pack. «Thank you,» he mindspoke. He picked his dagger back up, eliciting a curious look from all the others. The wolf mother stepped closer and studied his foreign scents, the severity of his wounds. She was worried.

«Sea. Shore. Ships,» he tried to communicate, but he could not remember why.

She understood the first two concepts, but was unfamiliar with the last one.

«No,» she urged. «Rest.»

«Sea. Shore,» the black wolf insisted, then walked away.

The pack followed.

Sunnokh vanished. The sky was clouded with smoke from the billowing dome, but a dim, pink glow still dared to break through it. They walked through a forest of leafless oaks, with the occasional evergreen holding on to a thin coating of snow.

The view opened onto a flat horizon.

«Sea.» The wolf hurried, limping.

A male wolf trotted next to him and dropped a squirrel by his feet. The dark wolf devoured it hastily, then continued his lame hobble as quickly as his blistered paws could carry him.

He reached the rocky shore. The sea breeze was biting cold. Choppy waves flashed their white crowns before slamming down on the rocks next to him. He backed off to where it was dry again.

«Why am I here?» he wondered. «What am I looking for?» He felt the quaar grip drying his tongue and remembered two words. «Leif. Sterjall.» He remembered them, but no longer knew what they meant. The words ate him up from the inside, screaming to come out, but they had lost all meaning.

«*Agnargfröa*. That I can remember. That I know. That I am.»

He carried onward, following the shoreline while searching for something unknown on the twilight-blue horizon.

His legs numbed as the night turned colder. His knees buckled and betrayed his step.

The wolf collapsed.

A tongue, pulling on his whiskers, lapping at his teeth and gums. He cracked open his eyes. The wolf mother was urging him to wake up. She seemed nervous. «Danger. We must go.» The rest of the pack was waiting at the edge of the forest, their expectant eyes filled with fear.

«Danger. Move, Agnargfröa, we will protect you. You are one of us now. You are one of our pack.»

And he felt it. He felt the kinship. This pack was who he was meant to be with. A wolf, that was who he was.

The strong pack I am not, the wolf thought, but didn't know where the words had come from. *A frail wolf I am, the strong pack I am not. Yet… yet pack and wolf are of one heart.*

The words made no sense to him, they only upset him.

He lifted his head. «Where is the danger?» he asked.

The wolf mother looked toward the sea.

The dark wolf saw strange floating shapes with white wings atop. He was afraid of them, but he also felt attracted to them.

The wolf mother trotted toward her pack.

The dark wolf felt fear rise in his throat. *Humans*, he knew, and he knew them to be trouble.

He forced his legs to straighten, barely able to hold his weight. He limped, then toppled to his side again. He struggled up once more and dragged a few heavy steps toward the pack. He was already exhausted from the effort. He lifted a paw and stopped—he had nearly forgotten.

Leif!

He turned his body and saw the sharp object resting on a rock. It sparked a memory within him. His gaze drifted from the dagger to the sea, where he saw among those white shapes one crowned by dark wings. Dark and bright. Black and white. Like the dagger. *Dagger. Leif. Ships.*

He picked up the dagger once more, the grip cold against his tongue.

His head throbbed, trying to formulate concepts that were not meant to fit within his wolf mind.

«I am Sterjall. I am Agnargfröa,» he said to the wolves, struggling to understand himself. «I am Sterjall.»

The ships were moving away, too far from the shore to see him.

«I am Lago, Lago-Sterjall,» he recalled. «My friends, my friends are there.»

The wolf mother let out a shallow bark, warning him. «Come with us, and live.» It was a simple concept, and it made sense.

He looked at her. «I am Sterjall, I am Lago.» She did not understand. And he didn't understand either. *The ships,* he thought. *Why go back to that painful life? Why not follow the pack? Live free in the forest?* Wolves were his true kind, after all. The temptation was warm as a den, sweet as fresh venison.

«Come with us, wounded wolf,» she urged him. «We will feed you, protect you until you heal. Come with us before the humans see you and hurl sharp sticks at you. Be one with our pack. Run with us in the fresh snow.»

He had no more strength to stand. He sat heavily, facing the sea.

As his jaw slackened, the dagger fell away, clinking mutedly against a rock.

He, Sterjall, turned his head again. The black-winged ship was now covered in stars, cold and alluring. Above it were the real stars, some green, some golden, drawing shapes that seemed eternal. Two sounds came to his mind. *Banook… Kulak…* And though they were more than mere sounds, they still made no sense.

Banook… Kulak…

He began to remember.

He looked down at the dagger.

He looked up at the ships, at the stars, then howled.

His weak howl came out as shattered as his lungs. He tried again, inhaling deeply despite the pain in his ribs. This time he let out a louder cry, deep and resonant, but it did not last long.

He tried again and nearly vomited from the effort.

«Help me,» he said, turning his head toward the wolf mother, toward the pack. «Help me.»

They did not understand what he asked of them, but they knew he was their voice, somehow.

«Help me. My friends. My pack. I am Sterjall, Lago, Agnargfröa. I need your help.»

He tried howling again, but only gurgled out a whimper.

«Help me,» he pleaded. His body slumped over the rocks. He whined faintly, the strength leaving his body in a cold breath. «Help me, please.»

The wolf mother craned her head toward the pinkness of the smoke-veiled moon, then let out a piercing, heart-wrenching howl. The sound stretched like black wings over the waves. More voices joined the chorus as the entire pack cried out as one.

The dark wolf listened to the melancholy-filled voices and added a soft whimper to the echoes. He laid his head over the dagger, then closed his eyes.

«Thank you.»

PART TWO
SPLIT MOUNTAIN

CHAPTER NINE

OPHIDIAN JOURNEY

The fires of Eskis receded as Nalaníri and Kitjári pulled away from the shore, leaving Banook, Ardof, Bear, and Safís behind. Hundreds of ships, big and small, floated quietly into the safety of their contained pocket of the Lequa Sea.

Upon the now-distant docks, a naked giant swung his glaive, hurling a dozen Negian soldiers into the air like dandelion seeds. The sounds of their smashed armor reached the ships a heartbeat later.

"Them'll be alright, m'dear," Nalaníri said. "Banook shell make a long Negian skewer with them." She tried to place an arm on Kitjári's shoulder but flinched at the pain from her chest wound.

They had boarded a medium-sized vessel, filled to the brim with Jojek Miscam rebels. A few arrows tried to reach them as they sailed away, but the Jojek warriors on land kept the Negian soldiers busy, blessing the escapees with a safe departure.

In a nearby canoe, Kitjári spotted Macúsca, the Jojek slave who had led them to Muri's cave and helped organize the revolt in the Lequa Dome. Macúsca waved at them while a young man cleaned the wounds she had accumulated during the battle; she seemed very proud of her injuries.

Kitjári turned to face Nalaníri. "Let me get a better look at that now." She shapeshifted into Jiara so that her sensitive fingertips could more safely handle the delicate work she was about to perform. She removed Nalaníri's vest and shirt and cleaned the large cut on her torso with a damp rag.

They had fought bravely at Ommo ust Krost. Now that the dome was opening, it was only a matter of time until the Jojek could sail through the walls and make their escape. In the meantime, they'd have to take care of each other, as there were many wounded, and many more would join them in the coming days.

One of the shamans who had been hiding in Muri's cave was in the same ship as the wayfarers: an old, scrawny woman named Irólven. She made Nalaníri swallow two drops of vernuus sap, which tasted horribly bitter, but would help with the pain while Jiara sutured her ghastly gash.

"Careful, m'dear," Nalaníri hissed through her small tusks. "It stings like d'spotted stingrays uf Atêmmo."

Once finished, Jiara attempted to aid Probo, who as a kuba had been the target of dozens of arrows and pikes and was now covered in scores of small cuts. The javelina strutted away, seemingly unconcerned.

"M'boy says he'll be a-healing fast, not t'worry too much," Nalaníri interpreted. "He's jis' tired frum all d'shapeshifting."

"Tell him to let me clean his wounds, at least."

Once they were all patched up and could sit down to rest, everyone aboard the ship assembled on the deck to figure out what was to come next. Jiara did most of the talking, as few of the Jojek knew enough Common, and Nalaníri was still struggling to learn Miscamish.

"We should get to the edge of the dome before morning," she said, "but the vines will open slowly. It will take some time, perhaps weeks, before a ship this size is able to find a path through. You'll need to live on the ships for a while, and help each other until you're able to sail north to the Fjarmallen Peninsula."

"What if the Negians set a trap and wait for us on the other side of the vines?" Irólven asked.

"It is unlikely. Their fleet has sailed far from here, following the Red Stag. At most, they'll have a handful of warships available at Seaborr, but they cannot compete with the numbers you have here. I don't believe they will know what is happening for a long while, and by then it will be too late to recall ships from elsewhere. You will need to avoid the Negian outposts when you reach Fjarmallen, and find a new home until the war is over. Maybe then you will be able to return to your own lands."

The Jojek wanted to know what fate had befallen Krostsilv, and though Jiara didn't know for certain, she told them all she knew about Crescu Valaran, the general who had inherited the musteloid mask. She explained the mask was now in the Jerjan Continent, across the Ophidian Sea.

"There are other domes that need our help," Jiara said, "and we need to hasten to them. We cannot stay with you until Krostdrolom fully opens. We'll have to leave as soon as we're rested."

"How will you sail so far, child of Urnaadi?" Irólven asked.

Jiara looked to Muri. The honey badger grunted an affirmation, even though he understood none of their words—they had already settled their strategy before the revolt started.

"We will not be sailing," Jiara said. "Muri will help us. Muri, and his giant otters. We will need a smaller boat, a canoe perhaps, and ropes. The otters will swim for us, faster than any sailing ship could follow."

"We will find a canoe for you," a Jojek hunter said, "and we'll have our best warriors travel with you."

"We thank you, but we need to travel alone for this mission. If we are spotted, if we get into a fight early on, then we'll have already lost." Jiara put a hand on the hunter's shoulder. "But don't worry about us. Probo and Muri will protect us. You saw them fight, and you know we'll be safe with them. Stay here and protect your tribe. They will need you more than we will."

As the cold of night sank in, they spread blankets onto the deck to rest. Kitjári snuggled up next to Nalaníri, who had her eyes closed and brow tightened.

"How are you feeling?" Kitjári asked, caressing her lover's tusks.

"I'll live, m'dear. It's been a rough day. I'll miss that man who is a bear, that Bear who is a dog, n'that brave arsehole who jumped uff our ship at d'last moment. N'maybe I'll miss that arrogant lady wulf as well—I was beginning t'like her."

"They'll be alright. But I hope Banook finds a way to have his bears cross the Ophidian later on. Can bears even swim that far? It's dozens of miles wide."

"Yer a bear, ye should know."

"Haven't been one for too long," she said, trying to sound cheerful.

"I say them'll be fine. With Banook t'guide them, them'll probably build floating log cabins n'be singing songs to d'mountains by d'time we meet them next."

"I'd like to see that."

She gave Nalaníri a soft kiss on her heart-shaped nose, extinguishing for a heartbeat the light of the boar's nosering.

They passed out next to each other, utterly spent.

The arudinn were brightening at the trunk, but they were not yet lit at the far horizon of the dome. More boats had arrived overnight, and still more were coming.

"Will this do?" Nalaníri asked Muri, showing him what seemed like a noose to hang him with, but with a knot that would not tighten when pulled.

The honey badger chewed lightly on the rope, rubbed his anal glands on it, and grunted approvingly.

They tied three ropes to the prow of a small canoe, whose passengers were very happy to trade for a spot on the larger ship. Five megalenhydris otters waited patiently in the water, paddling between the boats and the wall of vines. The wayfarers loaded their canoe with enough supplies for their journey and hopped aboard.

"You are looking much better already," Kitjári said to Probo as she examined his wounds—they were still visible, but had sealed up extraordinarily fast.

"He's a tough yam," Nalaníri said. "N'a sweet one too. Probo, m'boy, can ye ask our friend if he's ready?"

Probo did. Muri responded by leaping off the canoe, shapeshifting into a giant otter and masterfully piercing the water with nary a splash. They fitted the rope hoops around Muri's neck as well as the necks of two of the other otters.

Kitjári and Nalaníri bid farewell to the Jojek Miscam, and to the Lequa Dome, which would be no more if they ever returned to these lands. Together, they used their empathic focus to spread open a tunnel within the vines, then ventured inside.

The very moment they breached to the outside world, the unforgiving cold of Frostburn slapped them. The interior of the Lequa Dome had been much warmer, feeling more like Umbra than Winter, but here they had to contend with biting-cold winds as well as icebergs and ice sheets littering the edges of the dome.

"Probo says t'get ready, it'll get windier now," Nalaníri warned, wrapping their thickest blanket around the two of them, flattening their ears beneath it.

"Windier how—"

The canoe jolted forward. The otters sped ahead, dragging the vessel at a speed that not even the finest Afhoran pontoons could match. Three more otters followed at their sides, diving in and out of the water like dolphins, waiting to relieve their friends once they tired. A white wake trailed behind them as they raced over the Lequa Sea, circling the periphery of the dome.

They stopped to rest, eat, and warm up every evening. It took seven days for them to travel around the dome, southwest into the Ophidian, and onto the shores of the Jerjan Continent. They stopped a few miles north of the Negian settlement of Ultad. There were too many ships nearby, likely patrols or merchants traveling from Wyrmwash to Kayamur. In a hidden nook overgrown with mangroves, they hid their canoe. Muri mindspoke to the giant otters, seeming to thank them before they swam away.

The wayfarers slung their bags over their shoulders and looked toward the southeast, spying the Bighorn Dome cradled between the imposing grandeur of the Stelm Rilgéreo and the Stelm Rilganesh.

"It'll be a hard hike up," Kitjári cautioned Nalaníri. "There are plenty of Negian roads connecting to the mines by the dome, but we certainly can't risk those paths. We'll have to make our own way." She regarded the foreign landscape. There was no snow at sea level, but the whiteness piled up quickly as soon as the mountains began to rise.

"I think d'snow will help a bit," Nalaníri said. "It makes crossing rocky grounds like these a bit easier sometimes."

"I hope so. It's so strange… I've been to many faraway places before, especially when I was training as a scout, but I've never set foot on the Jerjan Continent."

"I've never set hooves anywhere but un mine tiny little domed home, so don't ye get all nostalgic un me. Let's go n'explore these treacherous mountains."

East of Ultad, before the steeper climb began, they found a road that predated the Downfall. It must have been vast and wide once, but was now overgrown from disuse.

"Old mining road, perhaps," Kitjári said.

"Glad t'see no tracks in d'snow," Nalaníri noted. "Ye think this'll take us far enough?"

Kitjári pulled out their map, which covered too great an area to provide useful detail. "An abandoned road probably isn't on a map like this one," she said, but still tried to find her bearings. She pointed to a row of jagged pinnacles. "This will probably get us to those peaks over there, but from there we'll have to find our own way through."

Chapter Ten

Twelve Temptations

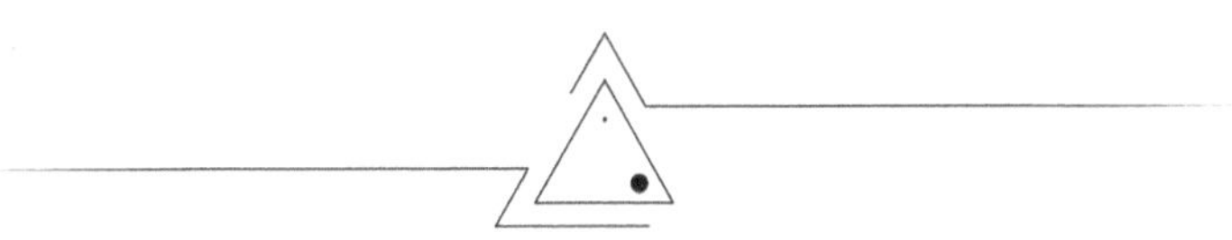

Probo and Muri led the way. The Nu'irgesh stopped constantly to wait for Kitjári and Nalaníri, attempting to hurry them while understanding that it was much harder for two legs to cross the snow than four.

Muri had taken the form of a marbled polecat, slinking over the snow like it was solid rock, hopping playfully ahead of them. His grouchy demeanor had entirely vanished in his new form.

Nalaníri stopped to catch her breath. "Probo's a-telling me he can carry us as a kuba."

"It's too dangerous," Kitjári said. "I can see wagons on the lower roads. If we can see them, they'd spot an enormous boar walking up the mountain."

"Kubanochoeruses aren't boars!"

"Warthogs?"

"Now yer seriously insulting them."

"What are they, then?"

"Them are kubas. That's what them are. It's like me calling ye a, umm… what were them black n'white fluffs we saw in d'Stelm Nedross?"

"Giant pan—"

"Pandas. It's like me calling ye a panda."

"Well, I didn't know the difference."

"It's alright, it's not like them are much different. Kubas are unly as big as a house, have a horn in them foreheads, n'look nothing like any uther suids out there. N'also them sounds are less like grunts n'more like whale calls."

"Fine, fine, I apologize!"

"Probo's asking what we're arguing 'bout. I can't tell him d'truth. I'm a-telling him ye were finding his bouncing balls too distracting."

"Please don't—"

"Too late, m'dear. Believe me, it's better than if I had told him what ye actually said."

Probo shook his wiry mane in a dismissive shrug and bounced ahead of them, making sure his balls rebounded picturesquely.

The following morning, as they packed up their camp, Kitjári did some quick calculations using their map.

"We aren't traveling fast enough. At this rate, it will take us a month to get to the dome."

"Probo's got an idea," Nalaníri said. "He says we could fullow in our feral forms. We'd be able to catch up to them that way."

"That's… clever, actually. And as long as we keep together, it shouldn't be dangerous."

They asked Probo to help with their bags, and he did not mind. He took the form of a celebochoerus, with tusks extending sideways like shovels. At this intermediate size, he could carry their gear without sacrificing speed and without being as conspicuous as a kuba.

Kitjári took off her clothes without complaint, as she was completely covered in fur and did not feel the bite of the cold. It was not the same for Nalaníri, however, as she was mostly smooth on her chest and belly. She shivered as she removed her garments.

"Once we start trotting, you won't feel cold at all," Kitjári said as she stuffed her clothes into her bag, which was already tied to Probo's back. "And when we stop, I'll keep you warm."

"Fine, fine," Nalaníri said through teeth that were starting to chatter, hopping up and down to warm up. Her rows of nipples bounced, as did her triangular ears. She huffed, breath forming into dense clouds. "Ye ready?"

Kitjári nodded, then dropped to all fours, taking her feral form nearly instantly. Nalaníri followed her lead. They resumed their uphill climb, now at a much faster pace.

The road they had been following was lost beneath the snow at higher elevations. Muri, still a marbled polecat, kept ahead of them, scanning the landscape for the best paths. Probo was behind him, plowing a path with his wide tusks. Nalaníri followed the celebochoerus, ignoring his hypnotic testes. Kitjári was at the tail end. To her, the strenuous climb felt relaxing and natural, even at their hurried pace. And she had a really tempting view ahead—one that made her feel constantly aroused.

She paid special attention to smells, sniffing the environment around her as if she was tasting everything. She could still sense the threads, like a soft tingle on her skin, but she could no longer see them as she could in her half-form. And plenty of life there was around them, hiding among the leafless aspen and snow-weighted pines, beneath cold boulders, and alongside creeks that had not yet frozen.

After a long day of working their way up the mountain, they stopped to examine tailings from an ancient mine shaft. Darker than the surrounding rock, the debris melted the snow, looking like a discarded trash heap, and the cleared area would offer a good place to set camp. A wide chamber was accessible very close to the entrance, which seemed unlikely to topple over anytime soon.

Kitjári was the first to come out of her feral form; it was easy for her, as she had been very aware of herself and her friends throughout the journey.

Nalaníri followed soon after. "Mine teats!" she yelped, rubbing her frigid and furiously pink nipples. "They've been dragging un d'snow fur hours. It felt like them were a-going t'freeze n'shatter, n'I wouldn't know I'd dropped them behind us. Could ye make us a fire? I need t'warm them up."

Kitjári thought about suggesting something more erotic to warm them up, but with Probo and Muri around, it felt a bit improper. "Here, rub this on them," she said instead, handing Nalaníri a cube of hot brime. "I think we are far enough from the other roads by now. It should be safe to light a small fire."

They gathered firewood, struck their brime cubes to set it alight, and huddled by the comfort of the crackling flames.

When morning arrived, they realized that the snow would be there to stay for the entirety of their journey to the Bighorn Dome. They once more hoisted their gear onto Probo's back and, after returning to their feral forms, continued onward.

Kitjári remembered what Nalaníri had said the previous evening, about how her nipples dragged frigidly over the snow. She trotted next to her lover and peeked beneath her, seeing the twelve bouncing buttons lightly scraping the snow wherever Probo had failed to properly flatten the path.

The bear teased her by ducking her muzzle under the boar and extending her long tongue to lick at the flushed nipples. The boar could say nothing back, but she snorted and made an expression that the bear read as appalled, though with an air of playfulness to it.

The cinnamon-colored bear kept teasing. Her keen nose detected that, despite the rebuttals, the boar was becoming aroused by her advances. It had been a long while since they'd had any time alone together.

The bear felt oddly at ease with being secluded in her own mind and having no means of proper communication. It was liberating. She could be herself, truly herself, and not worry about what she said to others or what they thought of her. She was a bear, and she need only worry about bearish things. She did not lose touch with her conscious mind, as the goal ahead of them was always latent, and her friends were there to constantly remind her of who she was. Yet she felt such a release of tension exploring the world in this form.

This is the truest way to experience the mountains, she thought in bearish concepts alone. *This is the freedom of being, of existing as we are meant to be.* Her mind drifted between smells of pine and soil and sap, between sounds of wind and rock and bird, in the brightness of the snow and the fullness of the skies.

They took a break in the midafternoon, resting in a dense forest of tall pines that had dropped wide circles of brown needles, where the snow did not care to meddle. Probo went away to dig for tubers, while Muri tried to find hidden caches of nuts that squirrels might've buried nearby.

Kitjári, as a bear, approached her friend, her lover, who after the long walk had simply dropped to her ample, boarish side, sighing a grunt of relief as she lay atop the sharp-scented pine needles.

The bear sniffed playfully. She used her muzzle to push at one of the boar's legs so that she had to roll onto her back. It was an awkward position for a boar; she wobbled before settling. The bear straddled her and sat on her belly. She tenderly licked the boar's snout, flipping her nosering to make the pharolith beads point up, then down, then up again. She stared into those kind and joyful eyes.

I am a bear, and she is a boar, her bearish mind contemplated. *We are so different, and yet the same.*

She again recalled Nalaníri's remarks about her nipples feeling cold, so she pushed the weight of her warm buttocks upon them.

Nalaníri grunted with pleasure.

The bear shifted her legs, bent down, and began to softly lick at the higher rows of nipples. The boar squirmed, tickled and uncomfortable, but did not fight back. The bear looked at the plump lips between the boar's legs and wondered what she would taste like in this form.

A loud snort shattered the moment.

The boar quickly shook and turned, sending the bear toppling to her side. Probo was standing there, holding two wild yams in his snout. The suid dropped the yams and turned, visibly upset. He stomped away on furious hooves.

Nalaníri swiftly shifted into her half-form and reached into her bag for her parka. Kitjári did the same, concerned by Nalaníri's agitated expression. "What is it?" she asked.

"I… Well… In a way, I'm kind uf glad Probo interrupted us. I was a-feeling a little uncomfortable there."

"Sorry. I was a bit eager, we haven't—"

"I don't know how t'feel about this," Nalaníri interrupted. "I've been fine in mine half-form, n'I'm slowly learning t'be comfortable in mine human form. But them feral forms, I had not even considered them before. Not like that. Ye took me by surprise."

"I should've been more considerate. I feel… Maybe I was a bit impulsive. Since we can't talk in those forms, I just let my instincts guide me. And well… My instincts draw me to you, in each and every form you take."

Nalaníri seemed to blush, though it was hard to tell, given that the parts of her that were pink were already pink enough.

Kitjári's embarrassment rose like heat, making her itch under her fur. She tried to change the subject. "I think… I think Probo is mad at me."

"Oh, he is mighty upset."

"I didn't take him to be a prude."

"It's not that. He's a ladies' suid, he is much possessive. He sees me as one uf his own when I'm in mine feral form, n'ye are d'competition."

"Are you serious?"

"I am. Why d'ye think he's got such big balls? It's fur all them boar ladies. But don't ye worry, he's not mine type. He'll have to resign himself to screwing all d'uther millions uf suids out there instead. I think he'll overcome his struggles."

Chapter Eleven

Ikhel Survivors

It took the wayfarers two weeks to reach the Bighorn Dome. The ancient road they had been following ended at an elevated overlook on the northwestern perimeter, near the town of Caerlye. From there, they could see the artificially terraced mountains and the extensive tailings left by the mines. The landscape was covered in striations of pink, brown, and cream, with filthy, dark-green lakes at the bottom.

"By d'light uf d'kenzir, them mines are enormous!" Nalaníri gasped. "Mine eyes had never seen a mountain cut to pieces like it was a cake. What are them digging fur?"

"Potash. It's to fertilize their crops, make soap, glass, a bunch of things. Without these mines, many of the Empire's farms would be nearly useless."

"Them fertilize plants with rocks? Yer world is truly out uf balance. Our plants n'animals work t'make d'ground fertile. D'unly time we cut open mountains is fur metals, or fur kenzir stones."

"The domes were grown in the most fertile lands, and you have knowledge we don't. Not all the lands can be equally fertile." Kitjári peered more closely at the mines. "It's odd that there are no tracks in the snow. It looks like the mines are closed."

"Because uf Winter?"

"I don't think so. They'd still be working in Winter, here and at the salt mines farther south, which they need to keep the roads clear of snow."

"Them roads farther that way don't seem empty."

Kitjári took out the spyglass they had long ago stolen from Admiral Grinn and aimed it toward Caerlye. The mining town was active and lively. A bit east of the town, a series of roads were clearly being put to use: enormous wagons moved on them, coming in and out of monumental warehouses.

"What are those wagons carrying?" Kitjári asked.

Nalaníri borrowed the spyglass. "I think them curved shapes are segments fur pipes. Like d'ones frum Krostdrolom."

"They are making more of them in Caerlye? Maybe that's why the mines are so quiet. That operation is enormous. Look at how massive those warehouses are."

"D'Red Stag must be planning to install d'same kind uf pipes in d'uther domes. There's probably pipes in this one already."

"It's the easiest way for him to keep the resources inside the dome under control. But not for long, Alvis Hallow, not for long…"

"Let's go tear them plans t'pieces, m'dear."

Seeing no tracks on the snow, they were not too concerned about being spotted. The four of them hiked down the terraced mountain and hurried past the many open shafts.

Kitjári took notice of all the machinery that lay dormant. From their state of disuse, it did not seem as if the mines had been abandoned for long—less than a year, she guessed.

"The Negian states must be livid about this. If they don't get their potash, their crops will fail. The ministers will not support Hestfell if the capital isn't helping their economy stay afloat."

As they neared the edge of the dome, the sterile cliffs gave way to a lush forest of mountain hemlocks. Not long after entering the greenery, they arrived at the vines.

"I guess any old place will do to cross," Kitjári said, eyeing the thorny wall.

The vines parted at the behest of the Silvesh, unleashing a small avalanche peppered with hemlock needles and cones. As they quietly ventured in, Kitjári noticed a sweet scent emanating from the vines. Each one of the domes possessed a particular smell that she had come to recognize, like remembering the face of a friend. All the domes shared the acrid tinge of the white sap, but there was a particularity to each of them that she, and perhaps only she, could discern. This one reminded her of the smell of fresh mushrooms picked from a rotting log.

Walking through the wall presented an unexpected challenge, given that much of the Bighorn Dome's perimeter sank into the mountains themselves. As they opened their path, they found chasms, dislodged rocks, holes left by the vines, and nearly impassable walls. They had to trudge about blindly, hoping the next turn would lead them to a traversable passage.

Nalaníri held up a dim pharolith; its outer layer had begun to exhaust its light, and it needed to be knapped or sanded down to bring it back to life.

"It's a good thing we have a compass," Kitjári said, looking down at the brass instrument. "Southeast is right behind this boulder."

Behind the boulder was a tall wall of rock. They found themselves stuck at the base of a cliff, unable to see what lay beyond. Kitjári stared up at the wall, clenching her claws. Probo followed her gaze, his expression a bit skeptical, but Muri seemed confident that the obstacle would not stop them. For the first time in a while, Kitjári had to make use of her climbing skills. She lowered her bag to take out her ropes, pitons, and harnesses.

"Mine arse is not gonna be supported by them little spikes," Nalaníri said.

"You'll be fine. We used this same gear to help Banook climb in the ice."

"Banook? A-climbing? That's a sight mine eyes would love t'see. Yet still, I unly know how t'climb hoodoos. Ye can't wrap a rope around these stone walls."

"I'll teach you how to do it. Just pay attention while I set it all up, and keep the vines open. Then all you'll need to do is climb up the same path and try not to fall too often. If you fall, I'll belay you and help you get back on your hooves. Or, actually, it'd be better if you climbed as Prikka. Your hooves would not do so well with these types of holds."

"So ye want t'embarrass me too. Is that d'plan?"

"I think you would look, er, exceedingly attractive while pulling yourself up. But don't mind me, I'm very biased."

The climb was quite easy for Kitjári. While she set up the anchors for the ropes, Nalaníri sat carefully knapping at the dying pharolith. She had detached the kenzir stone from the metallic petals that encased it, and was using a rock to carefully chip small bits from it. With every dislodged fragment, a bright dot of pristine, cold light appeared on the surface of the stone. Tiny glowing fragments piled up by Nalaníri's cloven hooves, as if she was standing on a nebula that she had birthed, bringing new stars to life with each careful hit of rock upon rock.

"Hey! The vines?" Kitjári called from above. "I told you to pay attention!"

"Sorry!"

Nalaníri was finding it hard to keep focused on two jobs at once, and had let the vines close up on them. She used her empathic focus to push them open again.

Kitjári finished setting up the ropes, then masterfully helped herself back down. "Whoa, that's much brighter than I expected," she said, squinting at the freshly knapped pharolith.

"Ye shell see them when them come fresh out uf d'mines. Well, maybe not, it'd pain ye if ye did, miners need t'wear veils so them don't go stone-blind." She secured the kenzir stone back in the wire armature and closed the lamp's petals, leaving them standing upon a galaxy of glowing kenzir fragments.

"It's so beautiful," Kitjári said. "Like we are standing in our own universe, with nothing but the nethervoids around us, and the stars at our feet."

"Nothing but us, our stars, n'them awkwardly staring Nu'irgesh," Nalaníri corrected her. "Probo's not very happy t'be sitting in d'dark, with so many a vine closing in un his hairy arse." She gave Kitjári a soft kiss and twisted the lamp open again. "If I'm to climb this treacherous wall, then it's yer turn t'keep them vines open, m'dear. Get to it, n'show me how to wrap this dreadful quaar rope around mine belly."

After changing forms, Prikka stuffed Nagrasilv into her backpack.

Before Kitjári had finished securing the harness around Prikka's waist, Muri had already climbed the wall, looking down at them with a red and white face while waving a long, striped tail.

"What kind uf animal did Muri turn himself into?" Prikka asked.

"Oh!" Kitjári exclaimed, staring up with a smile. "Look at him! He looks adorable. I've never seen him take the form of a red panda."

"Aren't pandas bears? What's he doing as an ursid?"

"I guess not this kind of panda? Either way, giant pandas or red pandas, they are all lovely."

"I hope he's not as useless as them giant pandas. Help me get up there, I want t'see him up close."

Prikka took a few tumbles as she attempted to ascend the rocks, protesting that climbing in this manner—with those sausage-like human fingers—was not her forte.

"Don't fumble with the rope like that!" Kitjári yelled. "Keep your limbs clear, or you'll tie yourself into a knot!"

"I'm a-trying!"

Another fall. Kitjári held Prikka up and helped her get back on the holds. "I can only take so many falls before you snap my spine!" she complained.

"Then stop a-yelling at me n'let me work!"

Prikka struggled her way up the wall, trying to ignore Kitjári's discouraging comments. Once she made it to the top, she pulled up the bags—one of them holding Probo as a pygmy hog—put her mask back on, and kept the vines open while Kitjári made her own way up again.

As her lover reached the top, Nalaníri slumped against a rock, tired and upset. She tried to pet the red panda, but as friendly as Muri looked, he could still growl menacingly in that form.

"See? Not too bad," Kitjári said once she crested the final slope. She began to pull up the ropes.

"Not too bad? I nearly cracked mine skull twice. N'I believe one mour fall would've snapped even d'quaar rope. I'm not as skinny as I look."

"You don't look skinny."

"Precisely. N'yer not a good teacher, all ye do is yell at me."

"Not a good teacher? You made it up on your first try! I was helping to keep you motivated." Although the words were meant to be comforting, Kitjári delivered them in a nearly imperious manner.

"Ye were not, m'dear. N'watch yer tone. I hope we never have t'climb again, fur that was not an enjoyable experience. Get yer stuff, we need t'get out uf here."

"Fine, suit yourself," Kitjári said, arms up in defeat. She began to stow her gear rather than arguing further.

They could see nothing once they breached the dome, not only because it was still an hour before dawn, but because they emerged in the middle of the mountains, where the many snowy peaks in front of them blocked their view.

They guessed at which ridge would offer them the clearest vantage point and began to hike in its direction. One of the supporting columns peeked above the mountaintops about a dozen miles away, slightly to their left, and after a long trek uphill they felt the glow of the trunk directly ahead of them.

It was that magical hour in which radial shadows streaked away from the dome's brightening central trunk. Each peak around them cast a tenuous dark twin on the vines, until soon enough the growing light melted the sharp shadows away. By the time they crested the ridge, the trunk was fully lit and the arudinn were brightening toward the enclosed horizon, reaching out like tendrils from an anemone of light.

The mountains of the Bighorn Dome were of a scale unmatched by those of the other domes they had visited. They were already so far up in the Stelm Rilgéreo that the dome's wall did not rise perpendicular to the ground, but instead emerged at a shallow angle, creating an illusion of perspective where the vines seemed to dramatically push into the distance.

From the south, the Stelm Rilganesh flanked a vast, lake-sprinkled basin. At the dome's center was a ring-shaped lake from which a gargantuan peak of volcanic breccia grew like a black pyramid, with walls too steep to hold much snow.

"By the Crone of Ukhagar's saggy tits, that mountain… It's so imposing, so vertical." Kitjári extended the spyglass and peered at the distant summit; so tall it was that its peak encroached on the trunk's vines at the point where it began to branch out, piercing the hollow spaces between the forking tendrils.

"Looks as steep as a hoodoo, n'much taller than Stelm Shäerath," Nalaníri said, referring to the Tricolored Mountain at the center of the Fjordlands Dome. "Don't ye be thinking 'bout climbing it, m'dear, we got uther things t'do."

"We might have to climb some of it. Wouldn't the temple be up there? At the top of the trunk?"

"Let's hope not!"

They hiked to a slightly higher viewpoint to assess their surroundings.

"D'dome's still mostly in good shape," Nalaníri noted, "but there be forests a-burning far in d'east, plenty uf them. That must be d'Negians' doing."

"We should try to find a member of the Miscam tribe before anything else. It'll be the best way to get some answers."

Peering through the spyglass, they spotted multiple small villages, the nearest of them at least a day's walk over the mountains. The dome had not fully lit up yet, so they chose to wait until the pastel-white lights evened out the landscape. They huddled quietly atop a rock, watching the mountainous dome brighten.

At this high elevation the surrounding peaks were treeless, but far from lifeless. Mountain goats traversed the nearly vertical walls as if unaware of concepts such as gravity, friction, or fear, feeding on mosses and lichens that blossomed on the rocks.

"They didn't draft all the caprids to war, it seems," Kitjári observed.

"Too inaccessible a place t'recruit them all," Nalaníri said.

Kitjári inhaled the variety of scents. She could clearly smell the smoke, the silt, the moss, the goats' musk, and another animal scent which she had a hard time discerning. She stopped observing with her eyes and instead brought the threads into her perception, to watch how these organisms connected to one another. With her eyes closed, she narrowed her focus to perceive a bit farther while slowly shifting her gaze around. Beneath her, she sensed something unexpected. She opened her eyes and froze.

Nalaníri had been watching her intently and noticed her reaction. "What is—"

The bear put a claw on Nalaníri's snout. She pointed and mimed for her lover to take a look. Nalaníri sensed the threads and quickly spotted shapes huddled about fifty feet below them. Under an outcrop, crouching to remain concealed, were five human forms: one child and four adults, holding tightly to each other. One of the adults was covering the child's mouth with her hands.

Nalaníri whispered, "If them have a kid, them couldn't be Negian, could them? D'ye think them are Miscam?"

"I can feel their fear," Kitjári whispered back. "They must've heard us. Maybe they think we are Negians? We should approach them."

"Ye should do d'talking, as them are mour likely t'speak Miscamish than Cummon. D'ye think our half-forms might startle them?"

"Maybe, but I don't want to risk an ambush. I'd rather see all the threads around me and be able to fight back if needed."

Nalaníri agreed. "Let's go down, but let them hear we're a-coming." She explained to Probo what was happening, and he in turn informed Muri, who had been sniffing about for insect larvae. They climbed down a side crag, making enough noise to avoid surprising anyone. They kept their Silvesh's sights on the trembling figures and stopped before reaching the outcrop.

Kitjári projected her voice, speaking in Miscamish. "Please, don't be afraid. We saw you hiding down here. We aren't looking to hurt you. We come from—"

"*Aaaaugghh!*" a scrawny man screamed, rushing toward Kitjári while wielding a mining pick. Urnaadisilv warned her of the man's strike, and she easily dodged the blow, letting him swing past her. The man clumsily recovered, turned, and locked his bewildered hazel eyes on her. He then noticed Nalaníri, who had flattened against a rock to stay out of his path.

"More of you? What else could you want to take from us?!" the man roared in Miscamish.

"Get them, Tupiel!" a woman shouted, poking her head out. "Take their Silvesh. It's our only chance to escape!"

The man swung again, but he was weak and obviously not a trained warrior. Kitjári sidestepped and pushed the man away, careful not to hurt him with her claws.

"We are not looking to hurt you!" she repeated. "Please stop attacking—"

He swung once more, but this time Muri dropped from above; as he landed, he shapeshifted into a jarv wolverine, snarling viciously. The man faltered, dropping his weapon as he backed off in terror.

"Nu'irg! Please, don't," he supplicated.

"Tell Muri to stop!" Nalaníri yelled to Probo.

Probo came trotting from behind her and stood next to the wolverine, who slowly covered his teeth.

"Father, no*hmph*—" they heard a young voice being muffled.

Kitjári had not drawn a weapon, though she had ten at her fingertips. She lifted her handpaws in a sign of surrender and said, "Please, stop attacking us.

We are not looking to hurt you. We came from outside Rilgdrolom, and are looking for—"

"Rilgsilv is no longer here," the man said. "The others of your kind already stole it. Leave us alone, there is nothing more you can take from us."

"We are not here for Rilgsilv."

"Take some Western Ikhel if you wish, there are plenty of them alive," the man begged. "We are no good as slaves, please, the invaders already took the strong ones. We would only become a burden to you, even if—"

"We are not looking to turn you into slaves, either. Would you please let me speak? My name is Kitjári, I am the Urnaadifröa, and this is Nalaníri, the Nagrafröa. Your name is Tupiel, did I hear that correctly?"

The man quieted, faintly sobbing. He held an arm up protectively, but let Kitjári speak. She quickly explained that they were not there searching for the mask, and that they were enemies of the Red Stag—enemies of the Negian Empire.

"What are you doing in the land of the Ikhel Miscam, in the land of your enemies, if not searching for their masks?" Tupiel asked. His family was still hiding behind the rock, too fearful to do more than peek out.

"It's a long story. But since you are here hiding in the mountains, I believe we might be able to help you escape."

"Don't believe a word she says, Tupiel!" a male voice demanded from behind the rocks.

"He's right," Kitjári agreed, "you should be careful and not believe everything a stranger says. But I'd have you hear our story, and we'd hear yours in turn. Then you can make up your minds. We are not going to hurt any of you, and neither will the Nu'irgesh." She nodded to Probo and Muri.

"He… he is one of them too?" the man asked of the javelina. "Probo? Nu'irg ust Nagra?"

Probo did a little prance and grunted twice.

Tupiel's shoulders lost some tension, but he still kept his guard up. "We… we will listen to you, but you must keep your distance from my family. They are afraid."

"That is fair. We will sit here and move no closer, if that will be agreeable to you."

Kitjári spoke at length with Tupiel, pausing to interpret for Nalaníri when the boar became too confused. Tupiel's family eventually came out of hiding; though they kept their distance, they sometimes shyly answered Kitjári's questions. Tupiel's wife, daughter, and two cousins—one male and one female— were there with him.

After Kitjári related the reason for their visit, Tupiel told her that the Ikhel Miscam were a split tribe. The Western Ikhel had joined forces with the Red Stag, and together they had overthrown the Eastern Ikhel to capture Rilgsilv. The Western Ikhel had been at war with them for centuries, wanting to seize the mask so that they could open Rilgdrolom, as they did not want to wait five hundred more years to venture outside the dome.

When the Red Stag arrived with news from the New World, it not only validated the views of the Western Ikhel, but drove them to fervent loyalty toward the Urgfröa, particularly once their chief, Luhásu of Uinin, was offered Rilgsilv as a reward for helping the Negians take over the dome.

"We had been fighting against our siblings for centuries," Tupiel brooded, "trying to prevent them from opening Rilgdrolom. And now that the Western Ikhel have taken over, the dome remains yet closed. In a change of fate, it is *us* who want the dome to open now, so that we may escape."

"Then our goals align after all," Kitjári said. She scratched her round ears, thinking. "But I'm confused. Are the Western Ikhel not slaves of the Negians?"

"No. They work for them willingly, even though they are treated as inferiors. Even the lowliest of Negian soldiers outranks them. They can't see that they are, in a sense, slaves as well. They do not want to believe it."

"Do the Eastern Ikhel have warriors left? If it came to that, could you fight with us?"

"By Beiféren's horns, I wish we did… But no, most of my kin are dead. The few of us who live now hide in the mountains or work dreadful lives as slaves. We are not enough to make a difference."

"Shit," Kitjári muttered in Common, then clarified the situation to Nalaníri.

"We can't start a revolt like we did at Krostdrolom, m'dear," Nalaníri said. "Nor can we simply attack d'temple like we did at Urgdrolom. We don't have Banook, or Safís, or even Ardof t'fight with us. We don't even have Bear with us, that's how bad our situation is."

"Let me ask him more about the temple. There must be a way to get to it safely," Kitjári said, then asked Tupiel for more details.

"Our capital, Runa, sits at the center of Mount Rashúr," he explained. "That is where you will find the entrance to Ommo ust Rilg."

"You mean we'd have to climb the mountain to get to it?"

"Not so. Mount Rashúr is split, the capital is cradled between the peaks. You can only see the split from the north or south." He kneeled down, and on the sand sketched two half-circles that nearly touched, with a smaller circle wedged at the center, representing the trunk. "The mountain has a gap from which the trunk was grown. The north end of the gap houses the Caprid

Shrines, but there is no access to the temple from there. The south gap is our capital, Runa, where the old palaces still stand, and the entrance to Ommo ust Rilg awaits."

"How hard would it be to get into Runa?"

Tupiel scratched his chapped nose as he considered the question. "It'd be impossible to go unnoticed. It's full of Western Ikhel now, they think they own our city. There are plenty of Eastern Ikhel slaves there too, and the dark-skinned ones they call *spurs*. But Runa is truly commanded by Negians, who boss all the others around. Most of the Negians left with the Red Stag, but those who remain are here to give orders to the Ikhel, to protect the piped exits, and to keep watch around the temple."

Kitjári stared at the crude drawing of the split mountain. "I'll have to give this some thought. The odds are against us, but maybe there's a way."

CHAPTER TWELVE

THE ABANDONED SILOS

The wayfarers took a day to reset their bodies to the abrupt swap of day and night. Tupiel and his family let them sleep in a secluded rhyolite canyon, where they shared meals while learning from one another. The Ikhel family now trusted that the strange visitors meant well, but more importantly, their presence offered a glimmer of hope.

The Eastern Ikhel who had not yet been captured made no long-term camps. They traveled in small groups to avoid detection, mostly keeping out of sight by remaining at the highest elevations and staying close to the vines, where scouting parties searching for fresh slaves were less frequent. Their Western Ikhel enemies refused to venture close to the vines unless Negian soldiers were whipping them to do so, yet the Eastern Ikhel had learned to overcome their taboos in order to survive.

"How can they tell if you are Eastern or Western?" Kitjári asked Tupiel as they sat for dinner, sharing a sticky soup of mashed moss and roots.

It was his wife, Siro, who answered, "By our clothing, and by the color of our eyes. We have darker yellow eyes. The Western Ikhel's eyes are bright yellow, like the bitter fruit of the jassumaur trees." She then gestured to her tunic, which was a complex tangle of leather belts, furs, and dangling bones; it looked beautiful, though not very comfortable. "The Western Ikhel wear similar clothes, but their bones do not dangle, they do not sing in the winds. They are bound by metal plates, like cages."

At trunk's first light the next day, while his family anxiously waited in the canyon, Tupiel led the wayfarers down the mountain to the nearest Negian encampment, which was in the Western Ikhel town of Ajacad, tucked next to a supporting column. An enormous, ring-shaped building encircled the column, connected to the vines by raised pipelines that had once fed white sap into the processing pools where munnji used to be prepared.

"Are you sure no one will be in the processing plant?" Kitjári asked Tupiel.

"Most certain. It's been abandoned since the giant caprids left for war. Any soldiers will be at the village. They don't like the acrid smell of the sap."

"Perfect," Kitjári said. "Let's go."

As they made their way toward the silos, Kitjári readied her bow, removing the cloth cover she'd sewn back at Banook's cabin to veil it from curious eyes while traveling. Tupiel stopped abruptly, emitting a loud, choking gasp.

"What is wrong?" Nalaníri asked, halting mid-stride.

Tupiel lifted a shaking finger toward the weapon. "A quaar bow?" he asked with devotion. "With a quaar string? It cannot be…"

Kitjári half-shrugged. "I… Well…"

"It looks like the legendary bow from the myths!" Tupiel continued. "Dunokh Sull. They say that Beiféren took inspiration from the bow's perfect curves when shaping his horns, and that was how the clade of caprids came to be. I heard that the aetheric elements were born from the vibrations of its bowstring, and that it did not shoot arrows, but lightning bolts made of pure aether."

"It might not be the one you are thinking of, then," Kitjári said. "Just a plain old quaar bow, this one is. Shoots plain old arrows."

Tupiel was disappointed. "It is still beautiful," he said. "For a moment, I believed the old legends were true." His eyes kept darting back toward the weapon, but he continued down toward their destination.

They snuck into the ring of silos, which did indeed reek strongly. The structures were beginning to grow weeds and ivies from the lack of maintenance. Inside, massive pipes lay forgotten, from which waterfalls of white sap had once spilled. Tupiel led them along overgrown trellises and elevated walkways, reaching rows of additional cracked pipes that dangled long vitreous stalactites of sap, like brittle, bitter daggers.

Dozens of feet down in the silos, pools of sap had crystallized to yellow, dust-covered crusts. Some of the deep pits held rotten clumps of ashborn beans, juniper ashes, taloncyst fungi, and other ingredients key to the preparation of the nutritious munnji paste.

The architecture repeated itself every few hundred feet. After reaching the southern end of the column, they spied the town of Ajacad from behind a fern-adorned window.

Not much appeared to be happening. A few miners ambled quietly; farm workers worked up a sweat. Near the outskirts of the town, soldiers performed routine inspections, making sure the eyes of the Ikhel were the brighter yellow of the Western people. In reality, the inspections were simply a display of power—a way to make the Ikhel used to answering to the Negian authority.

"Are ye ready, Probo?" Nalaníri asked, ducking back behind the window.

Probo grunted twice.

"Then get yer arse a-going. We'll be right here."

Probo shapeshifted into a domestic pig and trotted out through an arched doorway. He approached the village candidly and waited for a Negian soldier to be left alone. "Women only," Nalaníri had said. Although Probo didn't understand the reason for such specificity, he complied with the odd request.

A lone soldier at last spotted the pig. Probo played innocent, rubbing his nose in the grass, pretending to search for food.

"Aren't you a fat one?" the soldier said as she approached. "How d'ye get out?"

Probo slowly stepped away from her, dragging her closer to the archway he had emerged from.

"Oh, don't go in there, filthy hog. It stinks."

Probo crossed under the archway and waited.

The soldier walked in.

Clank! A metal pipe struck the soldier's metal helm. Nalaníri had swung fiercely but missed the neck. Despite the faulty aim, the brutish slam did its job; the soldier toppled like a wet sack of grain.

"Pellámbri weeps!" Kitjári swore, inspecting the woman, who had nearly been mortally wounded. "You almost tore her head off!"

"I'm sorry! I got carried away. I can wear d'bent one if ye'd like. Probo, we'll need one mour. Can ye find us anuther fine lady?"

Probo grunted happily and trotted away.

"She's still breathing," Kitjári observed as she began to hastily undress the woman.

"What shell we do with her?" Nalaníri asked.

"Don't know what you're thinking, but she's too young for me," the bear joked, then felt guilty, seeing that the woman's head was gushing blood. "She might not make it for much longer."

"Them are evil lowlifes, killers, enslavers, them don't deserve our mercy. I wish I had hit her harder so we could be done with it."

"She didn't see us. I can patch her up before she bleeds out, then we can leave her at the far end of the silos all tied up."

"Them'll come looking fur her eventually."

"Yes, but they'll think it was an Eastern Ikhel who hit her, stole all her stuff, and abandoned her."

"Why go through so much trouble? We'll have t'kill plenty uf them sooner or later."

"Because… I simply can't do it, not like this. I try to block what Urnaadisilv shows me, but I can't fully disconnect from it."

Nalaníri placed a hand on Kitjári's shoulder. "I'm not indifferent to yer pain, m'dear. I understand, n'I feel it as well. But we can't take d'time, can't take d'risk." She sighed, then conceded, "Jis' wrap her head with a cloth n'maybe she'll—"

A squeal outside interrupted their conversation.

Kitjári scrambled up and peeked through the window—Probo was being chased by five soldiers, one of them twirling a lasso.

"Shit, get ready," Kitjári said. "Tupiel, drag this woman out of sight, and stay hidden." She climbed up on a stone platform and readied an arrow. Nalaníri positioned herself behind the archway from which she had surprised the other soldier.

Probo squealed a warning as he trampled in, pulling hard on the lasso that had wrapped itself around his neck. His body twisted, but he kept on struggling.

"Easy, pig!" a soldier said. Three of them came in, pulling the rope taut. "Where did this big-balled one come from? Have the goat lickers been hiding animals from us?"

Nalaníri was about to strike, but Kitjári gestured for her to wait.

Probo pulled harder, dragging the soldiers deeper into the building.

"Is this… blood?" the leading soldier asked, crouching down.

As soon as the last of the soldiers stepped through the threshold, Nalaníri buried her axe in the one at the back of the group, while Kitjári shot an arrow directly into the forehead of another. Probo quickly shifted into a pygmy hog to escape from the tightening rope, then into a celebochoerus, and slammed his tusks into two of the Negians.

The soldier Nalaníri had struck managed to turn and jump on top of her, axe sticking out from his metal cuirass.

"Get uff me!" Nalaníri yelled, digging her hoofed fingertips into the man's eyes, then shifting her weight around, making them roll sideways. She pushed away just as Probo's hoof stomped hard on the man's chest, driving the axe all the way in.

Kitjári heard the last remaining soldier yell for help, but before she could bury an arrow in him, Muri had taken care of him, shredding his throat with his jarv wolverine claws.

"Damn these reckless smeglappers," Kitjári complained. "Make sure no one heard anything. Move the bodies out of here, fast."

They dragged the five soldiers behind the curved wall of one of the deep pools, where Tupiel was hiding with the soldier they had disabled earlier.

"What did you do?" Kitjári asked, as she found Tupiel waiting not next to an unconscious soldier, but a dead one, her neck sliced wide open. Tupiel shrugged, holding a bloody knife, not a drop of guilt on his face; his expression reminded Kitjári of Ardof, and of how quick the ranger had been to take the life of a captured Negian in the Lequa Dome.

"Let d'man be," Nalaníri said. "We have mour important things to worry about."

They undressed the dead soldiers and selected as many pieces of non-bloodied clothing and armor as they could salvage, stuffing their loot into a burlap sack. They had to mix a few of the male garments into the pile, which fit Nalaníri better due to her broad waist.

"Help me with this one, he's heavy," Kitjári said to the other two.

Tupiel and Nalaníri helped lift the limp body, dragging it over the short wall of the silo and dropping it into the crystallized pit. The man's skull cracked with a wet crunch as it hit the dried pool of sap.

They tossed in the remaining bodies and pieces of armor, then did their best to conceal the blood by the archway.

"Let's get the Khest out of here before anyone comes looking for them," Kitjári said.

Once they reached Tupiel's family in the safety of the canyon, they selected the best garments and cleaned up as much of the blood as they could.

Jiara dressed first. Her cleavage was a bit tight under the plate armor, but other than that it was a good fit. She kept her own boots, as they looked quite similar to the Negian-issued ones, but were more comfortable.

"Ye can't let yer hair loose like that," Nalaníri observed. "Them Negian soldiers had them hair tied in small braids."

"It's been a while since I've braided it," Jiara realized. "I only know how to make a single braid. Would you help me?" Nalaníri gladly lent her assistance, twirling a dozen ash-blonde braids and letting them spill down Jiara's shoulders before helping her don her helm.

"I can't hear a thing through this much metal," Jiara complained. "How do they even fight with these things on?" She glanced toward the Ikhel family. "Would you mind giving us a bit of privacy?" she asked, foreseeing that Nalaníri would be quite uncomfortable being half-naked as Prikka in front of a crowd.

Tupiel nodded and led his family around a bend.

Jiara helped Prikka get dressed.

"D'previous owner had one too many onions fur lunch," Prikka protested, her nose tightly wrinkled.

"Your nosering, dear," Jiara pointed out.

"I always furget." Prikka smiled. "Ye never called me dear before, m'dear. I like a-hearing sweet words coming out yer filthy mouth."

Jiara laughed. "I will try to offer more, when time permits. Why do you still wear that anyway? It was Odask who gave it to you. Doesn't it bring bad memories?"

"It's not about him," Prikka said. "We exchanged them during wedlock, but t'me, them two lights represent mine children, not their father."

Jiara shrugged, then placed a helm over Prikka's head. "There you go. You look absolutely… hideous. Exactly like a Negian soldier."

"Thank ye, likewise. Though I do like yer new braids."

"All done, you can come back now!" Jiara said, projecting her voice.

The Ikhel family returned and inspected them. "Look, Mother, they look just like Negians!" the young girl said to Siro.

"They even smell like them," her mother added.

"Thank you," Jiara added, "that's comforting."

Tupiel's two cousins thoroughly scrutinized the disguises, helping wipe off a few more smears of blood they'd missed before.

"While you were dressing, my cousins and I had an idea," Tupiel said. "We would like to help you infiltrate the city of Runa."

"You could fit in the uniforms," Jiara said, "but you'd never look Negian enough. Your faces—"

"Not in that way. We will go as your slaves. You can make us carry your gear. The three of us have been to the capital many times before. We can guide you, so you don't look lost."

The young girl hugged her mother, distraught at the thought of their father leaving them. Siro looked worried as well, but her pride and determination overpowered her apprehension.

"It's very likely we'll have to fight, sooner or later," Jiara cautioned. "And the odds are definitely not in our favor."

"Then we will help you fight," Tupiel said.

"You will not convince Tupiel otherwise," Siro warned. "Once his mind is set, there is no way to stop him. This is the best chance we have. For our people. For our little girl."

MOUNT RASHÚR

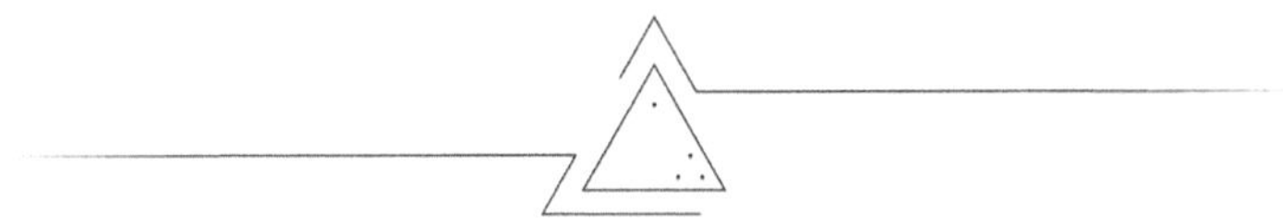

Tupiel and his cousins fixed their clothing so they'd look more like the slaves they had seen from afar. Tupiel's male cousin was named Thorodic; he was a bony youth, merely in his twenties. The woman was named Olústri; she was somewhere in her forties, like Tupiel, and always wore a cheerful face. They did not look at all alike, making Kitjári wonder what the meaning of *cousin* was for the Ikhel.

The three Ikhel dutifully hauled Jiara's and Prikka's backpacks, which luckily didn't look entirely out of place, as the Negians didn't have a particular style to their traveling gear like they did with their uniforms. Probo and Muri hid within one of the bags, both in their smallest forms. The Nu'irgesh weren't exactly comfortable, and Muri was a bit bitey at times, but they could breathe well enough through the unclasped flap.

The city of Runa was far away. Plenty of Negian officers and soldiers traveled the wide roads to the capital, typically followed by Eastern Ikhel slaves, so the infiltrators did not look suspicious. Western Ikhel squads patrolled the path, always keeping their distance, sneering at the sight of their Eastern siblings.

"Keep your eyes open for any wagons that only have Ikhel drivers," Jiara said to the others. "I don't want to have to talk to Negian soldiers if I can help it." So far, the vehicles they had seen pass by were either too full, too small, or driven by Negians. They played it safe and kept walking, eyes on the road.

A few days into their trip, they finally spotted a wagon large enough to fit them all, with two Western Ikhel drivers and no Negians. The wagon was pulled by a single, enormous bootherium—a thought-extinct caprid resembling a muskox but of much larger stature, with thick horns that nearly formed a helm over their skulls. Few bootheriums remained in the Bighorn Dome; most had left with the Red Stag's army, under the control of Silv-Thaar Markhor.

Jiara flagged the wagon, signaling for them to stop.

"Don't say a word if you can help it," she told Prikka. "If they hear your accent, they'll get suspicious."

"Mine accent? What d'ye mean? Mine accent's perfectly fine, m'dear."

"Proving my point. Mouth closed, please. I'll handle this."

The wagon crawled to a stop. The yellow-eyed drivers stared at the two women, their eyes fearful.

"Where is this wagon headed?" Jiara asked, emphasizing the roughness in her voice. "Do either of you speak Common?"

"To Vodur," the younger of the two said. "No Common, Lurr. *Etoss uth lakho.*"

Jiara pretended to search for something in her bag while she quietly asked Olústri where Vodur was located.

"It is on the path to Runa," Olústri whispered. "But it would only take us halfway there."

"It will have to do."

Jiara faced the drivers again. "We have slaves we need to take to Runa. Your wagon is empty, and our feet are tired, so you will take us there."

"No Common, *lakho,*" the yellow-eyed youth repeated.

Surprising the two drivers, Jiara next spoke in Miscamish, though she mixed up words and tweaked her accent to make herself sound less familiar with the language. "I spoke you take we to Runa. Slaves to carry, take to Runa. Wagon for rest to our tired feet. Do not ask me repeat words, I do not like dirtying my mouth with your filthy tongue."

"Yes, Lurr," the young man subserviently answered, but the older driver did not enjoy being treated so poorly. He eyed the five of them carefully as they hopped into the wagon.

Even while pulled by the powerful, untiring bootherium, it still took two more days to get to Runa. Luckily, the Western Ikhel drivers kept to themselves. Their larger group, with such a heavy beast of burden and such a diverse mix of passengers, must have seemed to be on important business—no one on the road bothered them.

They arrived at the base of Mount Rashúr in the early afternoon. As they climbed higher and higher, they at last saw the enormous crack that split the volcanic mountain in half. It was as if a giant axe had struck down from the heavens, cleaving the mountain with a perfectly vertical, mile-wide cut. In that cut grew the Bighorn Dome's trunk, framed by blackness on both sides.

The trunk was dark green at the bottom, but it brightened smoothly with a sprinkle of arudinn as it climbed. It seemed as if the two halves of the mountain were separated by a bright sky, but it was vines lit with arudinn that hung between them instead. The sight was unsettling.

"Don't stare like that, you look daft," Thorodic murmured to Jiara.

"Sorry," she said, lowering her eyes. "I've never seen a mountain like this. I'm in awe."

"Our capital was much more beautiful before the Urgfröa took it from us. The streets are filthy now. Noisy. This was a sacred place—now it is but a monument to their cruelty."

The outskirts of the city of Runa were teeming with activity, Negian and Ikhel alike. Jiara noticed the increasing number of slaves. She found them easier to spot now, telling them apart not so much by their clothing, which was relatively similar to that of the Western Ikhel, nor even by their eyes, which she often could not see, but by their posture. The Eastern Ikhel carried themselves sorrowfully, with bent bodies, eyes to the ground, faces stripped of hope. The Western Ikhel walked with tension in their shoulders and suspicion in their eyes, but chests held up as they tried to aggrandize their presence.

The wagon reached a deep chasm crossed by five stone bridges, with the core of Runa sprawling on the opposite side. The bootherium pulled their vehicle across the central bridge, following slowly behind a large caravan.

"You need to tell them where to go now," Tupiel said to Jiara. "There is a place where they keep slaves, but I do not know its name. Tell them to take you there."

Jiara leaned over the drivers and in Miscamish said, "We need you take us to the… the… I do not know word. Where they keep Eastern Ikhel goat lickers." The older driver nodded, seeming to understand.

Guards stood at the end of the long bridge, but they did not stop the wagon, which rolled over a road lined with cobbles as it entered the capital.

At last the true city of Runa revealed itself, cradled between the black halves of the split mountain. The walls were so flat that they had an almost mirror-like sheen to them, and although there was room aplenty between them, the Ikhel had carved the lower levels into concave shelters, deep enough to house entire city blocks under their shade. Multiple levels of buildings filled the indentations, and many more sprawled in the mile-wide gap. A garden blossomed at the center, replete with fountains and sculptures; four temples rose at its corners, each crowned by split minarets that dared not even dream of competing with the split mountain.

The wagon turned left at the garden and followed the road into an open plaza where hundreds of slaves were gathered: some sleeping, some sitting, some simply standing not knowing what to do. The slaves weren't shackled; they were free to run if they wished, but they knew they would not get very far.

Jiara noticed guards handing out metallic pins to the wagons ahead of them, which were in turn traded for the slaves their vehicles carried.

"I hope ye know what t'say now," Prikka murmured through the corner of her mouth. "Because I have no idea how we're getting out uf this one."

"Don't worry, I'll take care of it." She nodded to Tupiel and his cousins and quietly said, "I guess this is where we get down. Thank you for helping us get this far. We'll try to help you all in return."

"You do what you need to do," Tupiel replied. "We will inform our enslaved tribe of what is happening. If a time comes in which you are in need, perhaps we'll be able to aid you."

The wagon stopped next to two Negian guards. The drivers said nothing.

"Numbers?" a guard inquired.

"Sorry?" Jiara answered.

"Their numbers. For the ledger."

"Oh, they are new. We captured them up north. They are weak, we worked them too hard during our travel. Don't send them out yet, keep them for later."

"Good catch, Chief," the guard said, eyeing her up and down with a curious expression. Jiara couldn't tell what the guard had spotted, but it made her nervous.

"We'll take care of them," he said at last, handing her a pin for each of her slaves. "I'll fetch fresh ones to carry your gear."

"Thank you, but we'll handle it."

Prikka and Jiara hopped off the wagon and shot one last glance toward Tupiel, Thorodic, and Olústri as they were rolled away into the slave encampment, then the two women ambled down a busy street, their bags on their shoulders.

"I just realized what happened," Jiara said once they were far from any soldiers. "Why that guard looked at me so weirdly. I didn't even think of it, I'm a numbskull. The helm I'm wearing has chrome rivets, it must've been from the leader of that squad. But my cuirass has iron rivets—it doesn't match the rank of the helm."

"Will this get us in trouble?"

"I hope not. Maybe no one else will notice. Stay close to me. If we seem busy with one another, they are less likely to bother us."

They approached the temple's entrance, feeling safer among the multitudes. As they neared the enormous trunk, its scale felt entirely off: the vines seemed larger than the mountain when taking up so much of their field of view, but once they looked to the sides, they felt the pressure of the black rocks once more.

A black parabola of rock wrapped across the base of the trunk, forming a too-perfect curve that dipped at its center. The temple's archway waited under it, while above it loomed the rock-carved caprid glyph—it was enormous, a triangle of nearly a lodgepole in height, a sharp portent of shadows hollowing an already dark frame.

"Don't stare too much," Jiara reminded Prikka, then studied the threats by the trunk. "Two guards, one at each side of the archway."

Many more Negians patrolled the area, seeming bored but attentive. Not all soldiers were at work; many were leisurely strolling by, issuing orders to the Ikhel or simply resting their feet and backs.

Jiara signaled for Prikka to follow her to a bench that had an inconspicuous view of the temple's entrance. They took their helms off so they did not look like they were meant to be on patrol, then ate a late lunch.

"Here ye go," Prikka said, pushing a hand into her backpack. Probo and Muri devoured the stale bread she handed them. "Quiet!" she whispered, leaning over her bag. "N'don't make d'bag shake!"

While they pretended to be busy with their food, they studied the movements of the soldiers, their ranks, numbers, and body language.

"Check their rotations," Jiara said. "See those two headed to the archway? They'll relieve the others."

Two wooden belltowers framed the temple's entrance, incongruous with the Ikhel architecture—Negian-built, purely functional with no ornamentation. Sentinels watched from the belfries, keeping an eye on everything that happened below. Jiara noticed the large clocks mounted to each tower; at the moment the two soldiers arrived at the archway, the hour hands snapped into place and the bells tolled.

"Exactly as the hour rings," she said. "They are punctual."

"Thinking what I'm a-thinking?" Prikka asked.

"Unfortunately."

"But what about our bags? Them look mighty suspicious. I don't see no soldiers a-carrying gear like we carry."

"I'll think up an excuse, we have time."

Three Negian soldiers had gathered under a nearby tree; they were obviously on break, not worrying about their posture, their demeanor, or their loud voices. Jiara overheard a few key words and shuffled to the edge of the bench to eavesdrop.

"—imagine? The Graalman Horde, working with the Empire. We'll be unstoppable."

"How far has he gotten?"

"All the way to the Scoria Dome, the one with the bats."

"Khest. He's going to take those flying rats to war, give them all the glory, and leave his soldiers behind to guard their guano-filled holes. Just like he left us here to take care of these lazy goat herders."

A guard noticed Jiara watching them. He eyed her up and down, but mostly down. He made an excusing gesture toward his friends and made his way to her.

He extended a hand. "Astien, Fifth Legion, lancer."

Jiara wasn't sure what was polite in these circumstances, so she shook his hand and didn't say a word.

Astien smiled. "Like I guessed, definitely not from around here. What sort of shake was that?" He took Jiara's arm and shook it by the elbow. "That's how we do it," he said, holding a strong grip. "From Mireinfield? Or Loompool perhaps?"

Jiara played along, "Mireinfield. Sorry, we… I just got transferred here."

"I can see from your bags," Astien said, taking a seat next to her. Luckily, he didn't sit between them, letting Prikka have a bit of privacy on the far side of the bench—she chewed on a dry piece of jerky as unappealingly as possible, noticing the man was hungry for something else.

Astien scooted closer to Jiara. "Is it true what they said about up there?"

"What they say about what?"

"That the dome by the Lequa Sea is opening up too. Some uprising or something. Didn't you come from Mireinfield?"

"It's true. That's why I got transferred here."

Astien smirked. "Well, I'm glad you did. Lorrs abound but not many Lurrs in these regions." The man was now staring straight at her chest, as if trying to use his eyes to pry open the armored plate.

Jiara crossed her arms. "I heard you talking about stuff down south. We never received news where I was stationed. What is happening down there?"

"I can show you what is happening down *here*," Astien said, putting his hand on Jiara's leg. He abruptly stopped looking at her too-concealed breasts, noticing the helm by Jiara's hip. "Shit! I… I'm… I did not know you were a chief! Lurr, I apologize for my behavior. I didn't see your helm. But… your armor—"

"Sorry, they are mismatched," Jiara said with a rough but playful voice. "Got most of it stolen by some goat lickers and haven't found a replacement that will fit these breasts." More tenderly, she added, "You can be at ease, Astien. You aren't in my squad, I'm not going to report you. But I do want to know what is happening with the Red Stag's army. It's been a while since we heard anything."

"All manner of things happening, Lurr," Astien said, squaring his shoulders. "I think I should—"

"No, stay, I want to know. And maybe later you can show me more."

Prikka shot a dirty stare in her direction, which Jiara did not catch.

"Well, if you put it like that." He relaxed a bit. "I was just telling my friends that after Chief Daro stole the mask, she and the deserters allied with the Tharma Federation, and now with Afhora, too. They call themselves the 'Cabal,' those boil-brained insurrectionists. Couldn't even come up with a less traitorous name."

Jiara's surprise at Fjorna Daro's betrayal made her stumble. "Fjo… Fjorna? Yeah, what a piece of, um—what is that scoundrel trying to accomplish anyway?"

"Isn't it obvious? She wants to get to the masks before the Red Stag does. But we'll get them, then hang her ugly face and all her arbalisters as well. Hallow is ahead anyway, he's already done with the Archstone Dome. I hear very few of the soldiers who went there survived, but somehow they beat the savages in the end. And now the Graalman Horde has finally come to their senses and allied with us."

"The Horde? What do they want in this?"

"To take down the Tsing, is my guess. Hey, if you want to talk more privately, we could—"

"Later, Astien, tell me more. I heard rumors that the Moonrise Dome was opened, like the domes in the north. Is that true?"

"That's old news, Lurr. But at Archstone—by the way, I did not catch your name."

"Janielle," Jiara said, putting a hand on Astien's leg, "but you can call me Jani." She licked her lips. "And what happened at Archstone?"

"That's the news I was coming to tell my friends. It's opening too, like the Moonrise, Lequa, and other domes."

The report gave Jiara a glimmer of hope, but also disconcerted her. "I fail to see why the Red Stag would do that. Doesn't he want to keep his resources locked down, like here?"

"They say he couldn't get enough of the damn pipes. Too many of his soldiers and beasts died in the desert, and a lot of the pipe segments were buried there. But either way, his pipes weren't going to be big enough."

"Big enough for what?"

"For the giant beasts they found there, the behemoths. Much bigger than the elk he brought from Anglass. I'm guessing that in order to leave Archstone with those giants, his only choice was to let the damn blister pop and be done with it. He's more focused on his pretty pets than on his Negian-born soldiers nowadays."

"That egomaniacal curdguzzler…" Jiara mumbled.

"Careful, Lurr," he whispered. "Most of us hate him, but it's better if some don't hear you say those words." He pointed his eyes toward his group of friends.

"So, what is he planning to do next?"

"I hear he's at the Scoria Dome right now. You know, for the… keenoperants?"

"Chiropterans," she corrected him.

"That one. He's been there for a while, not sure what's taking them so long. But his army, and the Horde, they want to get to the Tsing dome already."

"The Tarpits Dome?"

"That one. Mask of monkeys, they say. I don't know what he'll do with a bunch of monkeys, he already treats us like monkeys anyhow. That's where the big war will take place. Bunch of monkeys fighting alongside deer and goats and flying rats. What's Noss come to, I ask you… Either way, that's the last dome to take, since the Seafaring Dome is much too far away for him to bother with."

"I don't know how he plans to fight the Tsing," Jiara said. "There's the bastion, and the Tsing fleet, and their weaponry is decades ahead of everyone else's."

"Dunno, Lurr. But he'll lure the Tsing and their petty allies into a war. If he's got the Horde supporting him, and all the damn goats he stole from here, the Red Stain—excuse me—might just be able to make it." Astien made himself more comfortable, rubbing his leg against Jiara's. "But I've done plenty of talking, Lurr, and I don't want to get my tongue too tired yet, you know? Why don't we go to your barracks, and we can talk some more?"

"I can't right now. The rest of my squad is meeting me here soon. I tell you what, Astien, why don't you come meet me here once the last light of the trunk fades."

"The trunk?"

Jiara pointed at it.

"You mean the axis?" Astien said.

"Sorry. The axis. Some people in Mireinfield call it the trunk."

"That's still too many hours away, Lurr."

"I'll make it worth the wait." She dragged a hand between his legs, cupping a tight bulge, then pulled back and looked away. "Leave us, now, before my squad members come back and I start regretting my offer."

"Yes Lurr," Astien said. He covered his crotch and walked away.

Prikka was fuming. Without looking directly at Jiara, she said, "Was that all necessary? Whose head shell I bash in first, yers or his?"

"Please, I hated that more than you did. I need to wash my hand now."

"Hard t'believe, m'dear. Next time, at least find a female soldier fur yer advances. Now tell me everything that disgusting man said, except fur them filthy parts. I don't want t'hear 'bout them."

CHAPTER FOURTEEN

CRIMSON NIGHT

Jiara and Prikka approached the temple's entrance, walking as naturally as they could while hauling their backpacks. Six columns barred the portal like a cage, with two guards standing in front of the central ones. Jiara saluted the guards in the same way she had seen the previous ones do so, by slamming two closed fists to her chest.

"Excuse me, you are?" the guard standing to the left asked.

"You are relieved, soldiers."

"It's three wicks till. Where are Brandun and Fedri?"

"They got lucky. We just got here and got put straight to guard duty. Haven't even dropped our shit in the barracks yet."

"They should've given that to a slave to deal with, did they—"

"They didn't give us fuck. Honestly, it'll be a relief to just lean back against this wall for a bit, we've been traveling all day on foot. You may go. It's early, but we'll take it from here."

"Yes… s-umm… Chief?"

Jiara saluted the men again, who began to walk away.

One of them turned. "Why…"—he obviously felt embarrassed asking the question—"why are you carrying a sword and bow, not a lance? They should've given you—"

"Like I said, we haven't had a chance to stop by the barracks yet. This sword will do just fine, all we are doing is standing like statues anyway."

The guards shrugged uncomfortably and left the area, whispering to each other as they went.

The two infiltrators dropped their backpacks behind the thick columns and stood at attention in front of them.

Jiara stared at the clock on the wooden belltower and through the corner of her mouth said, "We don't have long before the next shift gets here. Once no one is paying attention, we rush in." She was glad her helm covered not only her anxious expression, but her dripping sweat as well. "Almost clear on my end," she forewarned. "Make sure your side is clear as well."

A moment passed, stretching like an hour. The clock's hands ticked menacingly.

Prikka nodded her signal.

Jiara waited for a soldier to clear her line of sight. "Fuck, let's go," she said, rushing back around the column. She grabbed her bag and bolted into the long tunnel, Prikka following behind her.

Once they were far enough from the entrance, in an area where the light of the few, sporadic sconces did not reach, they stopped to breathe.

"Do ye think them'll come looking fur us?" Prikka asked.

"I think they'll look elsewhere instead. Two defecting guards would not be trying to escape *into* the temple. I'm more concerned with the trouble we'll find at the far end. Let's get ready."

"Out ye go now," Prikka said, freeing Probo and Muri. The Nu'irgesh remained in their smallest forms, stretching their legs and shaking their fur. The women took out their Silvesh and stowed the Negian helms in their stead, then shapeshifted into their half-forms and readied their weapons.

The end of the vaulted tunnel differed from the previous ones they had encountered. Mirroring the tunnel's entrance, it widened significantly, with six columns separating the hallway from the circular chamber beyond. Using the focused sight of their Silvesh, they scanned the room ahead.

"How many d'ye see?" Nalaníri asked.

"Ten," Kitjári whispered. "One behind each of the columns, plus four more deeper in the temple. From their stances, they look like they are heavily armored. Make sure Muri knows our strategy."

"He's un it, don't ye worry."

They snuck toward the six columns. The chamber beyond was well lit by lamps circling the temple's periphery, but the hallway remained perfectly dark, hiding their approach. Kitjári caught a glimpse of the guards deeper inside, who were pacing around the marble throne at the dais.

Shit, crimson guardians, all of them, she thought, unwilling to risk saying the words out loud. *Those dungholes are tough.* She nodded to Nalaníri.

"Yer turn, boys," Nalaníri whispered.

The pygmy hog and least weasel trotted toward the temple, hugging opposite walls. They moved unseen at the edge of the shadows until they'd made it halfway into the central chamber, but then one of the red-armored knights spotted them. "Did you see—are those rats?" his muffled voice asked.

The Nu'irgesh began to move toward the center, approaching the four knights at the dais.

"Hey, Gillem, look at that thing, it looks like a tiny—"

The small animals swiftly grew.

Two crimson guardians fell immediately, one torn apart by Muri's jarv wolverine jaws, the other hurled into a thorny vine by Probo's celebochoerus tusks. The remaining eight knights drew their longswords.

"It's the monsters that attacked the Lequa Dome!" one of the men by the columns screamed. "I told you they'd—shit, we must sound the alarm!" He bolted down the hallway—Nalaníri smashed the back of his neck with her glowing axe.

Kitjári had Dunokh Sull ready; as a second guardian ran into the hallway, she loosed a senstregalv arrow, fitting it right through the slit of their visor.

The two infiltrators rushed in to help the Nu'irgesh. While Probo parried a longsword with his tusks, another knight rushed him from behind. Kitjári released another arrow, but even the senstregalv tip did not pierce all the way through the strong armor; it merely lodged itself in the crimson guardian's pauldron, making him stumble. Muri took advantage of the knight's loose footing and ripped him apart.

In heartbeats, half of the crimson guardians had been disabled or killed, but the five who remained were now attentive and ready to fight.

Muri snarled at two knights who rushed him in a coordinated attack. He leapt to dodge the first longsword, but as he tried to slash downward at the attacker, a second blade followed more violently. The Nu'irg instinctively deflected the blow, but not without incurring a cost: his front right paw was chopped in half. He roared in pain as he rolled onto the ground, then lunged at his assailant, slashing with his left paw and with the meaty stump that remained of his right. The knight wailed as his red armor was torn and splashed with more red.

"Muri, watch out!" Nalaníri yelled, noticing that the other knight was about to swing at him again. She reacted quickly, hurling her axe. The powerful throw dented the guardian's chest plate and shoved him right within

Probo's reach. The giant suid swatted the knight with a swing of his tusks and hurled him into the marble throne, shattering the delicately carved seat.

Only two knights remained standing. *Wait, there should be three of them,* Kitjári realized. *One of them escaped!* She was about to warn Nalaníri, but an enemy was running at full speed toward her, his longsword pointed forward like a lance. She lifted her bow just in time to deflect the blow, feeling a sudden guilt at sacrificing her weapon to save herself, but the quaar limbs deflected the strike while taking no damage. As she reached to unsheathe her sword, she received a hard kick to her stomach. The bear hit her head on the stone wall and collapsed face down.

"Kitjári!" Nalaníri cried as she tried to make her way toward her lover. Another knight stood in her way, but he was suddenly lifted, a tusk piercing his thigh as Probo hurled him away. Muri caught the man in his fangs and crunched down on him.

Nalaníri sprinted through the spray of blood toward the last crimson guardian, who was swinging his sword down toward the fallen bear.

"Keep yer hands uff her!"

She jumped onto his back, grabbing his shoulders and uselessly battering at his helm. Probo wanted to help, but the two were grappled together; he knew not how to strike without hurting them both.

The guardian ran backward and pushed into one of the vine columns, the sharp thorns piercing all the way through Nalaníri's stolen plate armor and into her back. She wailed as she let go of her enemy, falling to her knees with her back dripping blood and white sap. The crimson guardian had defeated her, but Probo and Muri now charged at him together, stomping and tearing until his screams ceased.

"It… It burns," Nalaníri gasped, trying to regain her balance. Probo helped hoist her up with his tusks. "Mine back, it's full uf… Kitjári, where is Kitjári?"

Flat on the ground in a pool of blood, Kitjári lay motionless. Her dark-mahogany eyes were wide open, but they seemed to be staring at nothing.

"Kitjári! Don't ye give up un me now," Nalaníri pleaded, propping the bear's head onto her thighs. "Don't ye give up, m'dear. Please! I need ye, please, show me yer with me." She caressed the bear's round ears and felt blood on her fingertips.

"Ye'll be alright, m'dear, jis' gotta get ye out uf here. Can ye hear me? Can ye stand?"

Kitjári moaned.

"Where did they… Are they—what is happening?" the bear asked.

"M'dear, ye hit yer head. Are ye hurt elsewhere?"

Kitjári didn't answer. Her eyes locked on the quaar lattice above them as she recalled what they were meant to do. She tried to stand but could not quite tell where the ground was. "Go, finish this! I'll be fine, open the dome while I recover. Go. Go!"

Nalaníri helped her sit up straight against the wall, then hurried to the shattered throne at the center of the temple. She brushed off a few pieces of marble and sat, immediately feeling a shocking pain; the thorns, still lodged into her back, had pushed themselves deeper. White sap seeped acidly into the punctures. She had no time to remove her armor and clean her wounds, so she swallowed the pain and focused on the lattice.

A bit more slowly than when she had done this in the Fjordlands Dome, the lattice began to collapse. The tubular conduits and geodesic spheres snapped into new tessellated configurations, wrapping themselves around the smooth, glossy core vine. A long, tedious moment passed as the quaar structure sank below ground, dragging the core vine with it. The hole left behind filled with white sap, eager to crystallize.

A deep tremor vibrated through the temple, punctuated by smaller jolts, as if the mountain's stomach was rumbling.

Kitjári had managed to stand up. As she searched for her dropped gear, she recalled something. "There was a guardian who escaped. He must be far ahead of us by now."

"Them'll come to us no matter what," Nalaníri replied. "But we need t'take care uf him before he loses too much blood."

Kitjári followed Nalaníri's gaze, finding a limping jarv wolverine. Muri was bleeding profusely from his severed paw, and his sides were covered with an array of dire wounds. When Kitjári approached, Muri growled, not letting her get close.

"He'll keep un battling," Nalaníri said. "He refuses to stop now."

"Fine. It is your turn, then," the bear said, helping Nalaníri remove her armor, then plucking sticky thorns out of her back. The puncture wounds would need proper cleaning later, but at least the sharp prickles would no longer be digging into her. Kitjári quickly wiped the sap off the boar's back so that the white hives would not settle upon her, then reattached the cuirass.

A mighty jolt shook the split mountain and beyond.

"Let's go," Kitjári said. "If that didn't alert the Negians, nothing will."

But their enemy had already been alerted. In the corridor they could see the crimson guardian who had escaped, now returning with a reinforcement of dozens more soldiers.

"Takh smite them, more are coming!" Kitjári swore. She stood straight, sword in hand, but still off balance from her concussion.

Nalaníri held the bear's elbow to keep her from falling sideways. "Them are almost here. What do we do?"

They looked to Probo, who was scratching the stone floor with his forefeet and shaking his enormous tusks in defiance.

A rumble of hurried, armored feet clinked down the tunnel. Commands were called out, and dozens of voices replied in unison. In the shadows behind the six columns, a wall of soldiers formed, taking position with lances and shields at the front while more gathered behind.

"Tell Probo to trample as many as possible," Kitjári suggested. "Maybe we can run past them."

"He can't fight them all," Nalaníri said. "He's tired, n'them are too many! N'ye can barely stand straight!"

"Drop your weapons and your masks, demons of the nethervoids!" a crimson guardian ordered.

Probo grunted, spit dangling from his long snout. He stood in front of his friends like a wall of tusks.

"Quell the ire of your monsters," the guardian said, pulling his red visor down. "You have nowhere to run to. We will let the beasts live, but only if they do not fight back and allow us to tie them down."

Kitjári glanced hopelessly to Nalaníri; she noticed the boar had a spark in her eyes and could tell she was mindspeaking to Probo. Probo, in turn, was looking at Muri, who was limping toward the opposite end of the chamber—they had a plan, one that Kitjári could not guess at, which made her terribly anxious.

"Fullow our lead," Nalaníri whispered, unable to say more. She faced their enemies and stowed her glowing axe in its scabbard, extinguishing its lights. She held her arms up. "We surrender! Probo, stand back!"

Probo shuffled away toward the perimeter of the temple, opposite Muri, doing his best to portray an attitude of defeat by keeping his head low, tusks nearly dragging on the ground.

The Negians tightened their grips on their weapons and cautiously marched in.

Probo charged, not toward the soldiers, but toward the walls of the temple. The suid ran with his head tilted at an odd angle, tusks dragging on the walls to butt against the hanging lamps. Sudden bursts of brightness were followed by the light dimming. On the far side, Muri limped as fast as he could, swatting lamps then stomping down the fire.

"Stop them!" the crimson guardian called out. "Charge!"

Smash! The room darkened further.

Nalaníri pulled on Kitjári's elbow, dragging her behind one of the thorny vines for cover.

Crash! Shards of glass impacted the ground. The gloom became oppressive.

The Negian soldiers burst into the vast chamber.

Probo kept dragging his tusks over the wall, shattering the few remaining sources of light. He stomped the last of the fires out; pure darkness followed.

"Flint! Torches! Now!" someone ordered.

"Don't let 'em light d'fire," Nalaníri whispered in Kitjári's ear. Both of them could clearly see the threads of their enemies, trembling in the gloom like hesitant, blind worms.

Kitjári spotted a soldier crouching down, lowering a bag to the ground.

"I see him," she murmured, pulling an arrow from her quiver.

"Hurry!" someone called out. "Light that fuckin—" *Slam!*

Probo had raced toward the sound at full speed. The soldier was flung up into the void and soon came crashing down, armor ringing like funeral bells.

A spark. The room was briefly streaked by sharp shadows.

Kitjári pulled on Dunokh Sull's bowstring, struggling to keep her aim.

Another spark, but she needed no light to see. She released her arrow, but in her shaken state, her aim faltered. The arrow stabbed the flint striker's heel. Though he screamed in agony, the soldier struck the flint once more, setting his torch alight.

"Over there!" a voice called out as they spotted Kitjári and Nalaníri. Five soldiers rushed toward them.

A weasel had snuck up on the torch wielder, following the sparks. Muri stood beneath the limping man and looked up at him. The man looked down at the tiny creature with curiosity and surprise. The weasel grew, and his maw closed around the man's groin, chomping down.

"He's right here!" someone warned.

Muri slashed with his good paw, and once he saw the torch land on the floor, he jumped on it, extinguishing the fire with his belly.

The acrid stench of burnt fur filled the darkness. Soldiers wailed, not knowing where their enemies were.

Fwhip! A soldier fell silent with an arrow through his head.

"*Aaaaugh!*" another screeched, ribs crunched by Nalaníri's axe, which glowed only for a moment before vanishing back into her scabbard.

They worked quietly in the dark. Nalaníri became Probo's eyes, telling him when to charge, when to retreat. Muri worked on his own, waiting until he could smell a soldier in front of him, then slashing before retreating to safety.

Kitjári was regaining her balance. She had a dozen senstregalv arrows left, and she made each count, releasing them with such power that the impossibly sharp obsidian tips sometimes stabbed clean through one soldier and took down another.

More sparks of flint. For a frozen moment, the room existed, then vanished. Another flash of light, revealing only monsters in the dark.

Kitjári pulled on the bowstring and released. The soldier striking the flint fell backward with an arrow through his ear. One last spark brightened the room as his helm hit the ground.

The six columns suddenly brightened from behind—a guard had hastened to retrieve one of the hanging lamps farther down the tunnel. Kitjári watched as the shadows of the six columns spread apart. The guard stood at the center, reflected in a pool of blood, mouth gaping at the massacre. Four injured Negians fled past him, slipping on the gore as they hurried out of the tunnel. The poor guard with the lamp heard a growl and looked to his side to find Muri, his sliced paw still bleeding profusely, his muzzle soaked in red.

He dropped the lamp and ran. There was the sound of a goresome tear in the darkness, followed by a muffled, wet scream, and then all went quiet.

"Find your gear. Let's get the Khest out of here," Kitjári said.

Muri was nearly unconscious from blood loss and exhaustion. In one final effort, he shapeshifted into a weasel before passing out, allowing Kitjári to quickly bandage his wound and place him inside her backpack.

They sprinted down the half-mile vaulted tunnel. Strangely, no more soldiers came at them.

"It must be a trap," Kitjári fretted. "There were hundreds more in this area. They must be waiting for us at the exit."

"Trap or not, we have t'keep going."

They saw the light of the exit ahead of them. It was too bright outside for their eyes to resolve what lay beyond, but what they heard took them by surprise: screaming, shouted commands, structures collapsing, swords and shields slamming. The city of Runa was a battlefield.

At the end of the tunnel, they found a barrier of Eastern Ikhel slaves protecting the portal.

"Watch out!" Kitjári called, pulling Nalaníri back under the archway. One of the Negian belltowers collapsed in front of them, splintering over bodies dead and alive, the bell tolling one final time. The other tower burned like a fiery lighthouse. Soldiers jumped from the belfry, preferring to die by the hands of the Ikhel slaves—or from the impact—than be consumed by flames.

The wayfarers climbed over the wreckage and hurried into the plaza. Among the battling Ikhel, Kitjári spotted Tupiel pinned beneath the shield of a Negian spearman. She reached for her quiver and found she had only one arrow left—she let it fly into the Negian's chest.

Tupiel shakily rose to his feet, only then noticing Kitjári coming to meet him. A hopeful grin spread over his face.

"Tupiel, it's done! The dome, it's opening!"

"We thank Noss for your blessing!" he said with proud tears in his eyes. "You've saved us, even those of us who will die today. Go now! Save yourselves while you still can."

"Come with us," Kitjári offered.

Tupiel shook his head. "Some of us will die so some of us may live. Perhaps we'll see each other again, at another time, or in another life. Take the western path through the city, it will be safer for you until you reach the bridges." He rejoined the battle and hollered a battlecry. "Rilgdrolom is opening! Leave, to the walls! Rilgdrolom is opening! We are free!"

The voice was echoed by all the slaves, causing confusion among the Western Ikhel, who had once dreamed of this moment but were now uncertain of what it meant for their own futures. The throngs of slaves dispersed, scattering throughout the city to make it harder for the Negians to capture or kill them.

Kitjári and Nalaníri opened their own path through the streets of Runa, following Probo's trampling hooves. They broke into a marketplace that was also engulfed in chaos, but that was not as tightly defended as the thoroughfare they had come through earlier.

"To the walls! Rilgdrolom is opening!" came the calls all around them.

Slaves ran, fought, trampled, killed, and died. Merchants tried to hide their wares, but it was not their goods that the slaves were after.

"Fullow me here!" Nalaníri called out, turning into a tight side alley. She asked Probo to hop into her bag as a pygmy hog, then kicked open a random door. A family of Western Ikhel were taking shelter in the building, children hiding behind the adults.

"Don't scream," Kitjári ordered, pointing her sword at them and feeling guilty at the fear she saw in the children's eyes. "Keep quiet."

They lowered their bags, turned back to their human selves, and traded their Silvesh for the Negian helms.

"Thank you for staying quiet," Jiara said to the family. "Stay inside, it's not safe out there."

Back under their disguises, they exited the small home and hurried through the streets once more. They found it easy to remain invisible with all that was happening around them. Eastern Ikhel slaves ran free, some fighting, some rousing for more to follow them out of the city. The Negians still were too numerous and powerful to defeat, but inevitably some of the Ikhel would make it out, one way or another.

The wayfarers wove their way down the streets, guided by the unmissable magnitude of the two black mountain walls, which felt more and more like a titanic vise about to bite down upon them.

Past the core of the capital, they reached the chasm with the five bridges. Some Ikhel slaves were taking their chances at battling their way across the bridges, while others attempted to climb down the steep chasm. There was barely a trickle of water at the bottom; those who fell did so to their deaths. Rows of crimson guardians protected the five bridges, as well as mounted soldiers and an infantry wall of pikes, shields, and swords. Archers shot indiscriminately at any Ikhel who ran toward the bridges, sparing no time to check the color of their eyes.

"Which bridge?" Jiara asked.

"Makes no difference, m'dear. Work yer charms un them."

They picked the rightmost bridge, being the closest, and strode to it with an attitude of self-importance and purpose. They easily walked around the shielded infantry, who paid no attention to them, and even past a row of crimson guardians. As soon as they stepped onto the bridge, however, a mounted knight stopped them.

"Hold! Soldier, officer, where do you think you are going? The battle is ongoing." His black gelding stomped, flicking his tail.

"We have an important delivery to, er, Uinin, Lorr," Jiara said, lifting the straps of her backpack to show him they were carrying something.

"What kind of delivery could be so important? Go back into the city. You may finish your errands once the slaves are subdued and the infiltrators are captured."

"Lorr, this is important. It needs to reach Hestfell at once."

"Who is your superior? Whose orders are you responding to?"

"General Behler Broadleaf," Jiara answered, using the name of the only high-ranking officer she could recall.

"From Shaderift? Who in the—" His eyes narrowed. He looked up at Jiara's helm, then down at her armor.

"Chief, your plate. Your helm. Why are they not matched in rank?" he unsheathed his sword.

Before Jiara could think of what to say, Prikka barked, "Probo!"

Probo hopped out of her bag, ran underneath the soldier's horse, and quickly transformed into a kubanochoerus, sending the horse and knight flying into the air only to crash onto the next bridge over. The mammoth-sized Nu'irg bowed down, flattening his heavy chin onto the cobblestones.

As the stunned soldiers around them readied their weapons, Prikka took Jiara's hand and helped her onto Probo's tusks, then they climbed onto his platform-like cheekbones while holding on to his fur-covered horn.

"Hurry, m'boy! Take us out uf here!" Prikka said.

The bridge shook under Probo's hooves. His single horn pointed directly ahead, toward the end of the bridge. He trampled over the soldiers in his path, splattering some into red smears, sending others into the chasm to crash like languid puppets at the bottom. He grunted a deafening, whale-like oscillation, doubly frightening the horses in his path. On the other four bridges, mounted soldiers spotted the enormous suid and galloped parallel to his path.

Jiara and Prikka considered it pointless to try to hide now, riding atop a kuba, so they traded their Negian helms for their Silvesh.

While Nalaníri tried to swing her backpack onto her shoulders, a mounted soldier in their path chose to jump atop the kuba instead of being tossed over the bridge. The horse was hurled into the chasm, but the soldier landed on a protruding cheekbone right next to Nalaníri. As he tried to find a safe way off the kuba, the soldier kicked at Nalaníri's chest, shoving her toward the abyss. The boar swung her axe to hook it around Probo's velvety horn, then tried to grab a hold of anything with her other hand, clenching on to the Negian's pauldron. The man was tossed toward the pit, but at the last moment he clutched Nalaníri's backpack, snapping one of the straps off. Nalaníri was pulled down by the shoulder, dangling off balance.

"Help me!" she implored, swinging like a pendulum from Probo's horn, both hands now tightly gripping her axe's handle. Probo kept running; he could not stop with so many horses chasing after him, and trying to shake the soldier off would also send Nalaníri over the edge of the bridge.

Kitjári hopped around the kuba's head to Nalaníri's side and grabbed her arm while also holding tightly to Probo's horn. She tried pulling Nalaníri up, but the added weight of the soldier made it impossible.

"Let your other arm go!" Kitjári said.

"But mine backpack—"

"Now!"

Nalaníri released her grip from her axe. Her arm lowered, and the single strap of her backpack slid down, pulled by the soldier's weight. There was a scream, then a metallic, wet crack far below.

"Mine bag…" Nalaníri complained as she pulled herself up and retrieved her axe. "Mine cooking gear, mine clothes…"

"We have other things to worry abou—shit, get down!"

A hailstorm of arrows streaked through the sky. The women crouched behind Probo's head; most of the projectiles snagged into his wiry fur, while many others pierced through his thick hide. As he reached the end of the bridge, Probo slammed into the few soldiers daring to block his exit, then turned left onto the main road. Horses galloped behind them.

"Will he mind if we grab some of those?" Kitjári asked, nodding toward the arrows as she readied Dunokh Sull.

"I'll get ye some," Nalaníri said, climbing over Probo's forehead to pull arrows out of his thick fur and hide. "Sorry, m'boy, them'll have t'come out sooner or later." She handed the arrows to Kitjári, one at a time.

"Get back here and hold on," Kitjári warned, eyeing the horse riders, who were encroaching on them from every side.

Probo did his best to keep his head steady while Kitjári took aim. She loosed one arrow, quickly followed by another, taking care of the mounted archers first. Though she felt pained about it, she aimed at the easiest targets: the horses, making them either limp to a stop or sending them crashing over their riders.

Six horses fell, but a dozen more were approaching.

"Shit, I'm out of arrows!" Kitjári said.

"Probo, get us up onto d'rocks!" Nalaníri said as they headed straight toward a switchback road that climbed a long cliff.

More arrows flew by. Speeding horses surrounded the runaways, some taking positions in front of them. Probo was fleet of hoof, but the horses had more stamina and would eventually wear him down. Mounted soldiers tightened positions next to them, raising their swords to swipe at Probo's legs.

"Get yerself ready!" Nalaníri cried out.

While Kitjári tried to retrieve more arrows, she felt a jolt pulling her down, followed by weightlessness. Probo leapt up, skipping a segment of the switchback as he hurtled directly onto a higher level. He landed ungracefully, dislodging boulders that rolled onto the cavalry below. The kuba crawled up, breathing heavily, until he reached flat ground. Eyeing the next cliff, he kicked his hooves, snorted, and rushed at it, again leaping up onto a higher level. He slid halfway down but held tight and dragged himself back up.

Farther up the road was a tower, rising next to a tall stone wall and a wide gateway that led to the mountains. Probo hurried toward it, hearing the guards atop the tower already sounding the alarm.

Kitjári heard an arrow whistle right by her face, just before it landed in Probo's shoulder. She spotted an archer in the tower.

"Here," Nalaníri said, extracting the arrow and handing it over. Kitjári dodged the next projectile, then took the archer down before he could nock a third arrow.

Four soldiers blocked the passage by the tower, pulling on heavy wooden doors. The doors slammed closed, but Probo arrived before they could be barred, and slammed through. The doors crushed the soldiers behind them as they broke off their iron hinges.

Probo paused to look back; the horses had taken the long way around the switchback but were catching up again. An arrow fired from above landed in his forehead. Angered by the painful wound, Probo positioned himself by the tower, then bucked like a mule, kicking at the stones and weakening the structure. He repositioned his hind and bucked once more, and again three more times until with a strained roar the tower collapsed, blocking the mountain pass.

"Great job, m'boy!" Nalaníri said. "Into d'forest. We need t'find cover."

Probo hollered his low-rumbling tremolos, shook his wiry mane, and carried them away.

CHAPTER FIFTEEN

GENTLE TUSKS

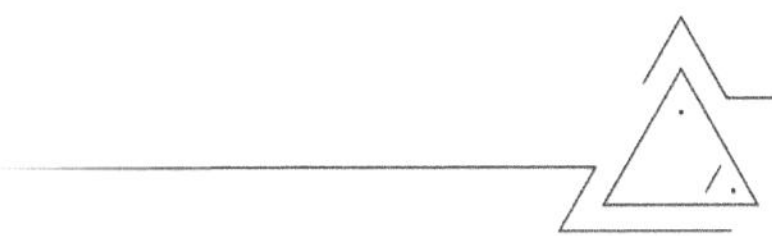

"Careful, m'dear," Prikka said.

"I have to get the tips out, stay still," Jiara replied as she slid small tweezers into a puncture on Prikka's back and pulled out yet another broken thorn. As the wound began to bleed, she used a water-soaked rag to wipe the sap and blood away before moving on to the next thorn.

It was dark out.

They were sitting by a rumbling creek, somewhere in the safety of a forested mountain.

After Probo had collapsed the towers and blocked the mountain pass, soldiers had tried to follow them, but they quickly lost their quarry. The wayfarers finally stopped fleeing many hours later, leaving Probo utterly exhausted.

"The wounds aren't deep or wide enough to need packing," Jiara said. She held a single pharolith lamp between them, only ever-so-slightly opened, providing a thin streak of light to see by. Prikka's back was a puzzle of pink and black, prickled by dozens of red spots that looked purple under the dim light.

"Them itch like Probo's fleas," Prikka complained.

"You have a bunch of blisters, but I don't think you'll get the hives. That Negian armor saved you, otherwise the thorns would've dug into your lungs."

Jiara turned around and aimed the pharolith behind them. Both Muri and Probo were deep asleep. At some point, while Jiara was taking care of Prikka, Muri had shifted into his primal form, and his small bandages had detached from his severed paw.

Jiara crawled on her knees to him, carrying the light. Muri's closed lids tightened while he lightly snored.

"He's passed out cold," Jiara said.

"Probo is too. We're asking them to do too much uf d'heavy lifting fur us. I feel guilty anytime them have t'save us, when them are hurt because uf us."

"They aren't doing this for you or me, but for all of us, for Noss." She took a closer look at Muri's maimed paw; only two out of five claws remained, loosely attached, but the wound was already scabbing over. "These Nu'irgesh heal as fast as a Puqua downs a pint of braaw. Do you think they'll grow back?"

"Ain't ever seen it happen, but I heard stories uf Probo a-losing his tail to a shark, then a-growing it back. I don't know if it's true, but I'll ask him in d'morrow. It's one uf them stories we tell our piglets so them stay out uf dangerous waters."

"The Puqua call their babies piglets?"

"What else would we call them?"

"Babies?"

"Absurd! But ya, I think Muri'll be alright. Them Nu'irgesh are tough potatoes."

"Yet still, the Negians managed to kill the pinniped one," Jiara muttered.

Prikka nodded absently. She slid back into her shirt, then put the Negian arming doublet on over it. After losing her bag to the abyss, it was all she had left to wear, other than the plated armor. She hooked her glowing nosering back on, donned her mask, and with a satisfied sigh returned to her boar half-form.

She sniffed at the clothing and winced dejectedly. "All I have left is mine axe n'these stinking Negian clothes. Mine bag is gone, mine parka, vest, spices. All mine cooking supplies. N'mine mum's chef's knife! N'even mine hot brime crystal."

"I'm so sorry. But I'll keep you warm tonight, don't worry. And for now, you can have my brime." Jiara reached into her bag, pulled out her cube of aetheric sulphur, and handed it to her lover.

Nalaníri grunted softly, then shivered.

Jiara placed her cloak over her. "We need to get you more Winter clothing if we are to travel through the mountains. And after all we learned, we need to strategize what to do next."

"Ye mean what *ye* learned, when ye were a-flirting with yer new boyfriend. I hope he's being stomped un by a swarm of angry Ikhel."

"You really got jealous, didn't you?"

Nalaníri didn't answer.

"I'm sorry? I was getting information. Believe me, I felt as dirty as the looks you gave me."

"Am I enough fur ye, Jiara?" Nalaníri asked, head turned away.

"What? Where is this coming from?"

"Am I?"

"Of course you are. You are more than that."

"Ye seemed like ye enjoyed that man. Seemed like ye had practice with this sort uf thing, I mean."

"I was merely acting! Men are gross. Been with a couple before, in my twenties, and swiftly discovered I'm as lurrkin as they come. Not my thing, you don't have to worry about that."

Nalaníri compressed her hoofed hands between her thighs, shoulders tense. "N'with women? I know I'm not yer first. But ye were… ye are mine first."

"I've been with other women, but that was nothing like what we have."

"How… how many?"

Jiara chewed on her cheeks, unsure of how to answer. "Why do you want to know? It'll only upset you."

"I jis' do."

"But that's not going to change anything—"

"I jis' do, alright?"

Jiara looked around the dark forest as if searching for an answer. "It's hard to explain," she said, then paused before adding, more quietly, "It's in the triple digits."

"Three uthers? What are them names?"

"No, dear, *triple digits*, as in somewhere between one hundred and nine hundred ninety-nine. Although not on the high end of that range… I think."

Nalaníri's eyes widened in shock. "How… Why so many? How did—"

"I've been active since I was quite young, with the Tribelands Scouts."

"Hundreds?"

"It's not like I dated them, rarely had a chance for that. I could have fun with a dozen women one night, nothing the next."

The explanation didn't seem to offer any relief for Nalaníri.

"Look," Jiara continued, "if it's any consolation, I've had my fun. I've tried it all, and nothing's ever been good enough for me. The only time I've felt anything emotionally satisfying has been with you."

She scooted closer to the boar, facing the creek, and put an arm over her shoulder. Nalaníri winced and sucked air through the gap her tusks made.

"Sorry," Jiara said "I have to be careful with—but why are you asking me this? What makes you think you aren't enough?"

Nalaníri's silence was masked by the gurgling water. After a long pause, she answered, "I've always been less than uthers around me. D'only reason I got this mask is because uf that, because them thought me less complete. Cooking has been a place fur me t'hide, to be better than them expect me t'be. But even mine sense uf taste is better because uf d'mask, while I'm jis'… I'm no warrior, no ierun, no chief. And now I'm not even a chef no longer. I hold ye back."

"Dear, you saved me countless times. We couldn't have been here without you. I couldn't have done *any* of this without you."

Nalaníri wiped her wet snout and tightly shut her eyes. "Will ye still do things with me once… once this journey uf ours is over?"

Jiara leaned in, trying to see into Nalaníri's eyes, but they were sunken in shadows. She reached for her snout and made the boar face her, then caressed her small tusks.

"If you'll have me, I'll be with you till the Endfall and the unspoken times beyond," she said, then planted a soft kiss on each tusk. "I love you. I couldn't see myself doing this with anyone else. Or living any kind of normal life after this, not with anyone else. We've both changed, together, and I see you as part of me."

"Do ye really?"

"Yes, like a part of me had been miss—"

"Love me, I mean. No one's ever said that t'me, no one uther than mine mum, n'Probo, though his way uf saying it is much different."

"Yes. I love you, 'gentle tusks.' I mean it."

Nalaníri's lips, perpetually raised by her tiny tusks, rose a tad higher. She leaned her head on Jiara's shoulder.

"I love ye too, m'dear. N'it scares me. I've never a-felt like this before."

Jiara kissed the top of her snout.

They sat in silence, listening to the flow of the water and the song of the nightly forest. Jiara made their bed and invited Nalaníri to join her, keeping her warm throughout the night.

"What in d'twelve fjords!" Nalaníri screeched as she awoke.

The dim morning light revealed a pile of fuzzy creatures crawling in a twitching lump as big as Nalaníri and Kitjári combined, like a roiling mass of giant maggots.

Kitjári opened her eyes. "Scorch them filthy—what are they?!" she bellowed, pushing back on her bedroll.

The mass seemed frightened by the loudness. In an even more terrifying motion, the spasming lump began to pull apart and slink away.

Ferrets, martens, and weasels—dozens of them—had been piled in a mound. The mustelids fled to the trees, hopped behind rocks, and some even took the quicker route down into the fast-flowing creek, leaving behind the awakening body of the groggy honey badger they had been crowded over.

"What was that about?" Kitjári asked, arms up, watching the last of the animals scramble away.

Muri had his head up, vividly alert, with a snarl questioning why they must bother him so with all the noise.

"What were those creatures doing?" Kitjári asked. "They could've suffocated the poor thing."

"I need t'ask Probo 'bout this. M'boy! Where'd ye go?!"

Probo came trotting back to camp; he had been on patrol and had found no threats nearby.

Nalaníri described the horrifying orgy she had witnessed. "Probo says that them slinky fellas were a-helping Muri heal. Them very presence is a balm to his broken body. D'closer n'd'mour uf them there are, d'faster he can heal." She stepped closer to the honey badger. "N'look. Muri's a–growing new claws."

"Huh, tiny ones," Kitjári observed, "but claws nonetheless."

Muri had indeed regrown his sliced paw. All the digits were back in place, with tiny, pink claws beginning to grow at the tips. The new paw was furless, moist-looking, like an embryo.

"This is great for Muri," Kitjári said, "but it makes me worry a bit now. For Banook, I mean. We left him there wounded, with no bears near him. Do you think—"

"He'll be alright, m'dear, he's got at least one Bear t'protect him."

They ate a cold meal, unwilling to let smoke give away their location, then sat by the creek to plan what could come next.

"I was thinking about this all night," Kitjári said, "I could barely get any sleep. Noss asked us to help with opening the domes, and we've done that so far. But now Fjorna and her army have opened the Moonrise Dome on their own, and it seems Hallow did the same in Archstone. They might open up Scoria as well, might not, but there's no way for us to know. Either way, his entire army is there now, not just the tailings he leaves behind after their ransacking is done."

"What do ye think we shell do, then?"

Kitjári spread open a map of the continents, which used to belong to Ardof but had been in her bag when they split up. It had his notes scribbled on it, and the path they had guessed they would be taking on their way to the Bighorn

Dome. They hadn't known what route the Red Stag would take next, so they hadn't had a chance to plan beyond Bighorn.

"I think…" she began to say, tracing a claw, imagining where everyone would be headed. Her claw landed on a large island labeled as the *Republic of Lerev.* "I think by now, if everything is going well with Lago, they might've made it this far already." Her claw moved over capricious waters and veered into the great Gulf of Erjilm. "And if they've hurried, maybe they're already in the Ashen Dome. We can't know, but even if they've made it that far, they have a long way to go." Her claw slid further, following a crescent-shaped range, and stopped on a dome cradled beneath snowy peaks.

"Hoombudrolom," Nalaníri whispered.

"Everyone will eventually converge here. At the Tarpits Dome, where the original Acoapóshi tribe settled. That has to be Hallow's next goal. If he wants to take down the Tsing, he will have to break through the Nargara Bastion, and only then will his army reach the City of Bridges."

"D'City uf Bridges?"

"It's what they call Hashan, the capital of the Tsing Empire, which is a few miles south of the Tarpits Dome. It's the largest city in all the realms, sixteen-fold bigger than Zovaria, they say, though that's probably an exaggeration. The whole thing is made of black pillars of basalt. Their city blocks have canals between them, connected by bridges. Hundreds of bridges. Lago might make it there before Hallow, but that is very unlikely."

Kitjári lifted her claw and regarded Nalaníri. "But I think we should try to beat them all there. We can get to the dome of primates and warn the Acoapóshi before the Red Stag has a chance to take Hoombusilv."

"But it's such a long way away."

"Not as far as the Scoria Dome, which would be the only other destination for us to attempt. Hallow moves with an enormous army. He needs to keep them supplied, and that slows him down. The four of us alone can travel much faster. If we hurry, we could arrive before he does."

She pondered for a moment, digging into old memories. "Before we met you, back when we first spoke to Mamóru in his cave of petroglyphs, he said something about Hoombusilv… He said that the mask of primates was the least powerful of all Silvesh because it could not mindlock its kind like our Silvesh can. Yet Hoombusilv kept the Acoapóshi in power for millennia. There must be something to it."

"We must stop d'Red Stag from a-getting to it, either way."

Kitjári drummed her claws on the map as she studied it once more.

"If we exit west out of this dome instead of continuing east, we could follow the road out of Kalford, toward Sharzi. We could take the Ravine Road south from there, but that is Graalman territory, and they are now allied with the Negians. But the Stelm Tai-Du… That would be the most direct route to the dome."

Nalaníri squinted at the map. "How would we get over them endless sierras? I don't see no roads."

"The mountain passes from before the Downfall. They are steep, and no one uses them anymore, but we could cut through them. Otherwise, we'd have to venture into enemy territory and make our trip much longer."

"Do ye know them trails? I thought ye'd never been to this continent before."

"I haven't. And I don't know the trails, other than from stories. But we have two Nu'irgesh who might."

Nalaníri asked Probo and Muri to come closer. She did her best to explain the situation, trying to translate abstract concepts such as distances and maps into suid thoughts that would make sense to Probo.

The javelina understood, in his own way. He knew what the Stelm Tai-Du were, although he had not been through them before, only around them. He spent some time interpreting for Muri, his prismatic pink aura blending with the ochre and hazel striations of the honey badger.

"Probo says Muri knows d'sierras quite well," she said at length. "He lived there mostly as a pine marten fur a few thousand years. He does not believe most trails will be in good shape—too long has passed since d'Dorvauros tribe were cast out frum those lands."

"Dorvauros? The same from the ruins we rescued my bow from?"

"D'Stelm Tai-Du was them homeland, before d'Acoapóshi banished them to d'north. But trail or no trail, Muri says he can guide us through them sierras quicker than through unknown lands."

Probo snorted and shook his wiry mane.

"What's wrong, m'boy?" Nalaníri asked. Her brow tightened as she listened to the suid. "Probo says that Banook once took that path. He almost perished, 'cause d'sierras were too vast n'no bears lived there."

"Lago told me about that once. What does Banook have to do—"

"D'problem is not unly about bears. Probo does not believe any suids live in such high mountains either. Too far frum his own kind, he'd be. Muri would be fine, there'd be plenty a marten n'badger around, but Probo would suffer greatly." Nalaníri paused, stroking the javelina's prickly mane. "He could die," she added softly.

"He wouldn't die, not if Nagrasilv is with us," Kitjári said. "In the same way Mamóru survived in the scablands, thanks to Momsúndosilv. There were no proboscideans left, but the mask kept him alive for centuries."

"Barely alive," the boar noted, remembering Mamóru's feeble constitution. "N'we don't know if Probo will be as strong as d'old mammoth."

"That's true… We can't force him to do something like that, it sounds too painful. Maybe there's another way."

Nalaníri silently conversed with the Nu'irg. "M'boy says that, like Banook, he knows his limitations. He says we shell take that trail, n'he'll go with us as far as he can. If he has t'turn back, at least we'll be much closer to our goal by then."

Kitjári scrutinized the javelina; his eyes were downcast. "It's his decision. But whatever we do, we need to get moving now. We have to leave this dome before we are found."

CHAPTER SIXTEEN

FOLLOW THE WHITE WOLF

Another earthquake.

Bear whined.

"It's okay, boy," Banook consoled him, "it's just Krostdrolom telling us it's opening."

They were waiting in the depths of Ushwen Krost, the cave in which Muri had hidden with the Jojek shamans when the Lequa Dome had been taken by the Negians. Muri was gone. The shamans were gone too—some dead, some lucky enough to have escaped in the boats. The cave was echoing the rumble of the crashing waves, but all was quiet otherwise.

Banook flinched. "That one stings," he warned.

"I have to finish cleaning your wounds," Ardof said, holding a pharolith as he worked on Banook's back. "I'm worn down to the bone, but I'll rest after I patch you up. Why is Safis not back yet?"

"She must still be battling at the lakes," Banook wearily answered. "There were many more boats there, and escorting them downriver must be taking some time."

"Maybe we should go help her then, eh?"

"I can't travel farther east, I am too far from my bears already," the bulky man said. His beard was almost fully white, and his gaunt face was tightened against an internal pain. "We agreed to meet here, and so here we'll wait for her return. Right, Bear?"

Rrrwouf! Bear said.

By the time the trunk began to brighten, as Ardof was finishing treating Banook's wounds, Bear suddenly scrambled to his feet, his ears perked.

A shadow blocked the dim light at the cave's mouth.

"Safís!" Banook called. "Oh, proud lady of sharp teeth!"

The enormous white dire wolf lumbered in, covered in blood, arrows, lances, pikes, and even an axe stuck in her ribs. She collapsed in a pool of her own blood. Bear crawled next to her and whined, licking at her paw.

"Hold still, mistress of moonlight," Banook implored, plucking an arrow from her side. "Do not yet change forms. I will remove these intruding sticks from your body, and then Ardof will take care of your wounds."

A week after the Jojek revolt, after Safís's wounds had mostly healed up, the four ventured out of the cave to see if the vines of the Lequa Dome had opened enough for them to make their exit. Banook had not been able to heal as promptly as he normally would, as no ursids could be found anywhere near them.

They made good progress over the course of a few days, nearing the western wall of the dome. They could see no holes in it from afar, but they had noticed a lot of wisps during the night, indicating that the openings were widening, and doing so quickly.

"I feel them already," Banook murmured. "Bearkind is near."

He looked at his scabs intently, as if he could see them closing while they walked; he could not, but he did feel rejuvenated, and his beard and skin were picking up warm hues once more.

Only silence permeated the forest now that the war had subsided. Most of the Negian soldiers were focused on securing the port towns and pointlessly protecting the piped entrance to the southwest; very few bothered trying to find Jojek rebels in the forests—most had either died or taken to sea by now.

"So, have you decided on our course of action, pal?" Ardof asked. "Did you consider my proposal?"

"I did. And I'm uncertain. Walking into a Negian fortress is the last thing on my mind right now."

"Farjall will be filled to the brim with Negians, that is unavoidable. But we'll need to cross the Ophidian, and for that we'll need a smuggler we can trust. My contact there should be able to secure enough ships, for the right price."

"And the kenzir stone will be enough to buy her favor?"

"That or nothing will. Can't think of anything quite as valuable, maybe with one exception." He eyed Banook's senstregalv glaive.

"Don't you smear your dirty eyes on my weapon."

"I'm just saying, it's likely worth a fortune."

"Not for sale. Either way, it is not like a skiff rental will suffice. Your contact will need to help us smuggle hundreds, thousands of bears across the sea. Ursids need to move first and spread on their own before I can follow. The journey will be treacherous—Farjall is too far away."

"The farther the better! The longer we walk, the more bears we'll find. And I know just the path we could take." He rummaged through his side bag as they walked, then grumbled. "Where in Khest did I leave that map? Either way, Farjall has plenty of merchant ships coming in and out of the Topaz Beck. My contact could bribe some downriver, away from the Negian base. Perhaps."

"Sounds farfetched."

Ardof shrugged. "It's our best shot, unless you and your bears *really* like swimming. You gotta start herding them, big buddy."

Banook huffed. "It won't be easy to go about unseen, not while packing a few thousand bears with us."

"The Negians have seen them migrate through their lands for months now, and they don't dare mess with them. Oh, here we are."

Out of nowhere, in the middle of the dense forest, the wall of vines appeared. It wasn't much of a wall anymore; a series of tunnels now wove between the larger vines.

"Let's hope it's opened up enough for us to meander through," Banook said, and headed in.

They soon became lost in the labyrinth of new tunnels, so they camped inside the wall while waiting for the vines to further recede; two days later, they finally saw light on the other side.

"By Wawumána's three teats, it's cold!" Ardof complained.

It was the middle of Frostburn, and the Lequa Sea was blowing the northern winds right into Ardof's chattering teeth. The rocks and trees were armored in ice from a recent freezing rain; the ground crunched under each of their footsteps.

Ardof looked haggard, face blue and brittle from the cold, while Banook was the opposite; having recovered his youth, he now looked plump, flushed, and joyful. Though he saw no bears around, the Nu'irg could feel their presence nearby, filling him with energy.

"Come on, friends, we have a long way to go," Banook said, then heard a whine and looked down. Bear was shivering, leaning against his boot. He picked Bear up and wiped the snow off the mutt's paws, cradling him in his arms. He then noticed that Ardof was shivering just as intensely, but the ranger was too self-conscious to lean against the big man for warmth. Banook took off his bearskin cape and wrapped it around Ardof.

They were near the spot where they had entered the dome, close to the port town of Seaborr. They followed the perimeter of the dome due south, finding cover behind mounds of snow and frozen trees.

Safís scouted ahead of them, following a trail as invisible and white as herself. She suddenly stopped atop a rock, her pristine fur blowing in the wind. Her head turned, and she sniffed the air.

"What has your keen nose picked up on?" Banook asked.

Safís hopped from one boulder to the next, following the scent.

"No, we do not!" Banook complained, following the white wolf.

"What? What is she saying?" Ardof asked, tightening the bearskin around his neck.

"She says bears smell like rotten skunks. She's picked up bear scents, and not from me, I hope." Banook projected his voice toward the wolf. "It's not even mating season! I'll have you smell a ripe bear in the month of Lustbloom, see how it compares."

Safís's muzzle contorted in a gagging gesture entirely out of place for her flawless form. She shook the image off and walked ahead. As the others made their way past the boulders, they saw the wolf treading warily toward the mouth of a cave; if there had been any tracks in front of it, they were now covered by fresh ice and snow.

Banook walked into the cave and peered about. "It's them two again!" he said, aiming a pharolith toward two nestling brown bears.

"The bears we met before entering the dome?" Ardof asked, peeking in. "The lost brothers from the *Barlum Saga*?"

"Wadrook and Cashe, the same ones. And sleeping as soundly as the Snoring Mountain."

"Well, it is mid-Winter…"

Banook packed a substantial handful of snow and hurled it at the bears.

"No time to hibernate!" he yelled as the two bears jerked up in confusion. "We must travel to the south and to the west! There is a war to be fought, and you and all other bears we find must join us. Up on your paws! Up you go, lazy brothers!" The two bears had no clue what Banook was going on about. They tried to doze off again, but Banook pulled them up and out by the thick skin of their necks.

"Let's go, my boys, you are merely the first two of many. Onward we march, toward the fortress of Farjall. Onward, into the lands of the Heartpine Dome."

CHAPTER SEVENTEEN

DARK WINGS

The Negian army marched relentlessly.

The Red Stag had lost many soldiers, caprids, and cervids in the White Desert, then nearly lost it all against the Alampaari Miscam in the Archstone Dome. With more luck than skill, he had managed to take Almelsilv, granting his army the power of the perissodactyls—the advantage they needed to defeat their enemies. Then came the battle against the Graalman Horde, in which he was victorious in part thanks to the Horde's own horses, which Silv-Thaar Baneras had savagely mindlocked.

Rather than surrender, Suux, head chief of the Horde, had asked for an alliance of convenience. She agreed to let the Red Stag pass through her territories, to supply provisions to his army, and to later provide the aid of her cavalry to at last take over the lands of the Tsing. The alliance had proven fruitful; after only a few weeks' march, the Negian army had arrived at the cratered lands of the Scoria Dome.

Sunnokh was about to sink in the west, so the battalions stopped to set camp inside a vast crater of black rock, where the rim would block some of the icy winds. As the pavilions were being raised, a Graalman falconer was assigned to scout for the best points of entry into the dome.

"Tomorrow, we begin our incursion," the Red Stag said to Silv-Thaar Baneras. He paced around the encampment, studying the morale of his legions. His soldiers seemed to have improved their mood, having found good rapport with the Graalman riders who accompanied them.

Baneras removed his zebra-striped helm and shook out his mane. "Have there been any sightings of the Tharman army?"

"None. The barracks at Drossmuur were deserted. All their forces have retreated to Sharr Helm. The Federation does not want to risk us striking them next. And we won't, we have no time to waste with them." He stopped, looking up the columnar legs of a behemoth who stood solemnly with blank eyes. "Make sure your beasts stay close to one another this evening. A cold spell is coming."

"I will, Monarch Hallow. Although I will be reassigning their chain of command in the morning. Now that I've gotten to know them better, I believe the elasmotheriums will be more suited to lead the units." The steppe wild horse general tilted his long head toward a heavy rhinoceros with a single thick horn, so large it could serve as a siege weapon on its own. "Their natural armor will allow them to wedge a path through the enemy's infantry, and their large horns are easy to spot for the other hoofed soldiers—even more so once we paint them red."

Like the Red Stag and Silv-Thaar Markhor had done before him, Silv-Thaar Baneras had splattered red paint over the hides of certain members of his mindlocked legion, assigning them to act as leading officers. Those officers could be sent charging against enemies, leading platoons of other animals who would trample anything that the red-painted officers trampled. It was a strategy that had worked well at the attack on Withervale, and in the battle against the Bayani at On Khurderen.

"And what of the anisodons?" the Red Stag inquired. "I thought you were growing fond of them."

"I thought their dexterity in climbing would make them suitable to lead, but they can reach places the others cannot. And they are not as fast as the rhinos, and not nearly as tough-skinned."

While battling the Alampaari tribe in the Archstone Dome, Baneras had amassed a legion even more powerful than that of the Red Stag's cervids. In addition to the countless horses, tapirs, and rhinoceroses, Baneras had captured three new companion species, of which the anisodons were the smartest. The long-armed creatures walked with a nearly simian gait and demeanor, and they had grown to three times the height of the Alampaari who had bred them into a sapient species. A particular breed of horses, too, had been bred to enormous proportions—the garrison horses; the bulky creatures inspired reverence from all Graalman who laid eyes upon them, facilitating the alliance between the Empire and the Horde. But Baneras's greatest prize was the gargantuan, hornless, long-necked and thick-skinned paraceratheriums, also known as behemoths; the giants seemed to move slowly due to their scale, yet they matched the pace of the horses with one step for each dozen of theirs.

"I will get the elasmotheriums painted at first light," Baneras said. "They are not as smart as the companion species, but I think that makes them better for this role. All I'll need them to do is trample their way into the enemy's battalions."

The following afternoon, the Negian army reached the northern perimeter of the Scoria Dome, only to find the vines inaccessible. The hard Winter gales of the Jerjan lands blew to the west and to the south, creating a slope of snow and ice that climbed up the side of the dome. Only the rims of glass-sharp craters were exposed around the volcanic lands; the rest was white.

The Red Stag sneered at the obstacle. He called for Silv-Thaar Baneras and said to him, "If we try to open the vines where they meet the snowpack, we will encounter a drop into an abyss. We must open them at the place where they meet rock."

"Your male megaloceroses could plow a path for us," Baneras suggested.

"And they shall. But command Estriéggo to break the crust first, then my giants will take care of the rest."

Baneras ordered the Nu'irg ust Almel to relinquish his woolly rhinoceros primal form so that in the form of a behemoth he could break the snow loose. The Nu'irg complied unwillingly, although this task was much easier to perform than the acts of savagery he had been forced to commit within the Archstone Dome. The megaloceroses finished the job by scooping snow out of the way with their shovel-like antlers.

The icy canyon the giants had cleared was large enough to serve as an encampment. Colossi gathered all the pipe segments the army had available, waiting with them next to the vines. As the Red Stag had foreseen, they did not have enough segments to create a full pipeline into the Scoria Dome. But Viceroy Urcai, all the way from Hestfell, had recommended an alternative.

"The Horde is arriving with the materials Urcai requested," Silv-Thaar Baneras informed his monarch. "Do you really think wooden stave pipes will work? I'm afraid the vines might simply pierce their way through them."

"The Graalman use only the hardest of woods for their irrigation systems, and they say they resist roots and rot as long as they are kept soaked."

"Which we won't be able to do."

"No, but Urcai thinks we will have some weeks of durability before they collapse. I trust his judgment."

For several days, while the Red Stag and his Silv-Thaars kept the vines open, the Graalman assembled the wooden pipes, banding them tightly with iron hoops. The wooden portion of the tunnel was not as wide as its ceramic counterpart, barely providing enough room for human soldiers to crouch through. Small caprids could be herded in for food, but the Negians could not bring any mounts with them.

They took a conservative approach and brought in only a small force to avoid portraying themselves as a threat to the Bikhéne Miscam. In case he needed protection, the Red Stag chose to bring in Sovath, the Nu'irg ust Urg, in her nonintimidating primal form of a chital.

Once the workers finished tightening the final wooden pipe segment, the Red Stag stepped deeper into the Scoria Dome and gazed at the immensity before him. *This land will be nearly impossible to conquer*, he pondered. *How does the local tribe navigate such a terrain?*

The vast landscape was a chaotic jumble of peaks overgrown by impenetrable jungles. There was no path for an army to march on, no respite from the density of the vegetation or the steepness of the crags. And there were also caves everywhere, hiding in the foliage like the dark bowels of the mountains themselves.

It did not take them long to find the first of the Bikhéne Miscam clans—one of only a few hundred members, living in an isolated, bracken-embellished cave. Unlike the excavated tunnels of the Anglass mines, the Bikhéne's caves were almost entirely natural. They lived where the bats lived, in the same guano-coated tunnels. The tribe did not mind being in complete darkness, as they could move about easily by clicking their tongues or lips and listening to their echoes. Even their archaic Miscamish had developed clicks and other peculiar sounds.

Silv-Thaar Markhor was placed in charge of communicating with the clan. After long introductions, she at last asked how they could gain an audience with the Balastfröa.

"Our tribe is split into many clans," an old Bikhéne sage told her. Her hair was long and white, partially from age and partially from guano. "We do not see our siblings often, as the mountains are steep and wild. Some clans have caves connecting their lands, but others like ours live mostly in isolation, taking care of our small districts. Although we do not travel far, our chief does. Hud Thallam flies to see us all. Her dark wings are one with the sky. If speaking with her is what you seek, we would be honored to send a night herald to summon her."

Once the meeting concluded, a Bikhéne shaman sent a noctule bat to call for the Balastfröa.

This is perhaps too easy, the Red Stag thought as they exited the clan's cave. He leaned toward Silv-Thaar Baneras and whispered, "Who would've thought? Their leader will fly to us and deliver her mask straight into our hands. And there is not even an army here that could protect her."

"The mask will be ours soon enough," Baneras agreed, "but the resources of the dome will remain unreachable, unless we wish to spend months cutting through mountains and tearing down jungles."

"There is only one valuable resource I care about in this dome, other than the mask. And we'll be able to extract it."

The Bikhéne performed a smoke cleansing ritual on the newcomers as they waited for their chief to arrive, trying the Red Stag's patience. But soon the dome began to darken, evidenced not just by the dimming of the arudinn, but by the countless clouds of bats which took flight to feed and breed and savor the crepuscular air. Between the flocks of blackness, a larger silhouette approached, beating her membranous wings to hover above the Red Stag, his generals, and Sovath.

Hud Thallam, in her fringed myotis half-form, landed at the edge of a cliff. She wrapped her wings around her slender body and kneeled in front of the invaders. "Servants of Noss, you have summoned me," she said, though only Silv-Thaar Markhor and the Bikhéne clan members understood her words. "I wish to hear the wisdom that you carry from the world beyond. Is it true, what the night herald said? That we are to at last leave our secluded world and once again fly beneath the dome that is of turquoise blue?"

Hud Thallam looked up with her beady eyes, aiming her expansive black ears at them. Her aura was dusky and branching, like purple lightning in a wispy fog.

The Red Stag requested a translation, and Markhor provided a rough approximation. As he was about to speak his answer, he noticed a change in Hud Thallam's face, as well as a tightening in her threads. The myotis straightened abruptly, taking two terrified steps back.

"What is wrong?" the Red Stag quietly inquired, but Markhor had no answer.

The monarch then saw a minuscule, white-and-yellow dot on the Balastfröa's shoulder, and promptly realized his mistake. Fuuriseth, the Nu'irg ust Balast, was mindspeaking to Hud Thallam, warning her that she had been lured into a trap. The white leaf-nosed bat had been wary ever since feeling the deaths of Mamóru and Däo-Varjak. She sank her tiny claws into Thallam's shoulder and told her that her old chital friend, Sovath, who was standing behind the group of newcomers, was dead-eyed. A parasite was clutching Sovath's mind, Fuuriseth explained; she was mindlocked to Urgsilv.

Hud Thallam heeded the mindspoken warning, her eyes widening in horror. In one hastened swoop of her wings, she took flight.

"Take her! Before she flees!" the Red Stag screamed. Those equipped with bows quickly responded and shot holes through Thallam's wings, slowing her retreat but not stopping her.

In a moment of rage and defiance, the Red Stag hurled his replica of the Spear of Undoing. The quaar spear flew true, lodging its obsidian blade into the giant bat's hips. Hud Thallam wailed, then fell down the cliff in a tangle of membrane-wrapped bones, draping her bleeding body over jagged rocks.

The clan who had sent the night herald scrambled to find weapons, but they were not ready. The Red Stag ordered Sovath to trample the Bikhéne with her heavy megaloceros hooves, then looked down the cliff at the fallen leader. "Hurry down before they get to her!" he commanded his troops.

General Korten dus Fer, who was to inherit the next captured Silv, was already descending before the monarch issued his command. He slid and tumbled dangerously down the steep precipice, his determination and ambition making him uncaring of the risk.

Fuuriseth crawled over Hud Thallam's agonized face, tinting her white-and-yellow body with streaks of red. She shapeshifted into the largest of chiropteran companion species, a desmodus giant vampire bat, and with her claws gripping Thallam tried to fly her away. Though the vampire bat was enormous for their particularly small clade, the species was not much bigger than a glaive eagle. Her beating wings were only strong enough to drag Thallam's broken body over more rocks.

Hud Thallam held on to a gnarled root, begging the Nu'irg to stop her pointless struggle. With her breath tremulous and weak, she told her old friend, "Save yourself. Carry Balastsilv away from here. Escape these monsters or they will have you trapped." She shapeshifted into her human form and held the mask up for Fuuriseth to take.

The giant vampire bat grabbed on to the weightless mask and flapped away, but Korten dus Fer's sword had swung behind her. The blade cut through both of Fuuriseth's short legs, dropping the mask with bloodied claws still clenching it. The general lodged his sword into the Bikhéne chief's chest, then grabbed on to the dark visage and lifted it in defiance.

Fuuriseth flew away, defeated and hopeless, bleeding from her amputated legs.

Ropes were cast down to help Korten climb back up the scarp. It took some time to hoist the general up the hill; by the time he arrived, the entire Bikhéne Miscam clan had been exterminated.

"Stupendous work, Korten," the Red Stag congratulated him as he reclaimed his quaar-shafted spear from the general's hand. "Or should I say, Silv-Thaar dus Fer."

Korten began to smile, but his smile was interrupted by a rising screech. A deafening sound soon enveloped them. Unseen in the darkness of the dome's night, an enormous cloud of bats encroached on the invaders. Inside the tenebrous cloud, Fuuriseth hid, like a weakly pulsing star in a twilight sky.

"Take cover!" the Red Stag said as he and his followers jumped out of the way and flattened to the ground. A few bats collided with them, but most flowed steadily above them, with only one destination in mind: the wooden stave pipe.

The bats flowed through the pipe like a river of tar.

"Stop them!" the Red Stag howled. "Block the pipe!" But no one could hear him over the screeches and clicks of the chiropterans.

Thousands of bats escaped with each heartbeat. The Red Stag tried to reach the pipe, using his quaar shield to keep himself from being pummeled by the ebony wings, but the compounded force of the impacts swept him aside.

Through the torrent of bats he saw a once innocent and pure figure: a spotted deer, her white markings shining like a starlit sunset upon her orange fur. Sovath was shambling slowly, as if struggling against a current, headed toward the pipe as well. Her body trembled, desperation and confusion clouding her thoughts.

The Red Stag tried to mindspeak to the Nu'irg to stop, but he was losing his grasp on her. He stopped suddenly, sensing a purple aura like a tiny cloud of lightning. *No*, he thought, *it's that damnable Nu'irg.* He spotted a dot of bright yellow holding on to the chital's forehead. Fuuriseth, able to mindspeak to her Nu'irg sister, was imploring Sovath to flee, to leave the dome and escape the hold Urgsilv had on her—and it was working. The small bat forced the chital to listen to her voice, making her inch slowly toward freedom.

"Sovath!" the Red Stag spat. "Do not pay attention to that creature! Stay where you are, not one step more!"

But Sovath was not listening to him, or was trying not to listen.

I can't lose my most precious weapon, the Red Stag mourned. *I* won't *lose you.* He bolted right into the torrent of bats, shielding himself while being pushed toward the wall of vines. He exited on the other side covered in viscera and ripped wings. He hurried toward Sovath, and with one heartless, backhanded slap, tossed the white bat off her head.

Fuuriseth slammed into the grass, wings and ribs shattered, still legless and bleeding, all energy drained from her.

You will be mine now, and regret what you did, the elk thought as he rolled under the stream of wings and snatched the bright-colored Nu'irg in his hooves. "Sovath, stop them!" he ordered at once, giving precise instructions to the once-again-subdued Nu'irg.

Sovath listened without wanting to and obeyed as she had before. She shapeshifted into a megaloceros and stepped straight into the torrent of bats, dropping her enormous body in front of the pipe.

The free-flowing cloud suddenly shifted, unable to reach the tunnel, with the exception of a few stragglers that pushed through Sovath's fur and crawled slowly out. The dark shroud of bats hovered like an uncertain hurricane, with no exit readily available to them, then flew higher and dissipated, becoming one with the dark-blue void of the dome.

Sovath's heavy body held still beside a pile of twitching, broken bats.

"Don't you dare move," the Red Stag hissed at her. He then faced his generals. "Korten, rally the Graalman workers. Have them construct a doorway that can close the pipe. Markhor, set up a perimeter. Baneras, hasten outside to inform the troops of what happened, then bring reinforcements."

"At once, Monarch Hallow," Baneras said. Then, more tentatively, he added, "Lorr, your antlers."

The Red Stag felt blood dripping onto his forehead. He glanced up to see bats skewered on his antlers like macabre offerings. He shook them off and stomped away.

The pipe was blocked by a hastily constructed door.

Monarch Hallow's officers gathered near the closed portal, surrounded by shield-bearing lancers and archers.

"We lost countless battalions of them," the Red Stag complained to his generals, still wiping clotted blood from his brow. He cringed as he imagined the mess upon his face—real blood never looked quite as vibrant and striking as the red paint he usually wore.

"There are millions more bats still inside," Korten offered. "That cloud was enormous, and there have to be more of them who were not warned, still sleeping in the caves." He held on to the chiropteran Silv, studying its shapes under the light of a bonfire. The upturned nose, the large ears with too many folds—it looked mangled yet somehow perfect.

A courier returned through the pipe, bringing an item requested by his monarch: a magnium-reinforced cage, with bars spaced closely enough that no small creature could escape from it.

The monarch tossed Fuuriseth in the cage and locked it tightly. The Nu'irg was still unconscious, her wings still shattered, but she had stopped bleeding.

"She'll wake up and heal," the Red Stag said. "General dus Fer, once this area is secured, we'll set our camp here to train you and the shamans with Balastsilv." He held up the cage with the injured Nu'irg. "This new winged toy will help you practice."

Korten had once objected to the Red Stag's strategy that would force him to share his mask with the shamans. He was about to object once more, but the Red Stag pointed a finger at him. "Not a word, Korten. The mask will be yours alone when the time comes, but you and the shamans will train as one. Once all of you learn to control it, you will gather as many of these winged rats as you can, then we will move on. The Tsing Empire is waiting for us, and I'm ready to bring a cloud of winged death to their doorstep."

PART THREE
THE FOUR BLESSINGS

CHAPTER EIGHTEEN

FERAL

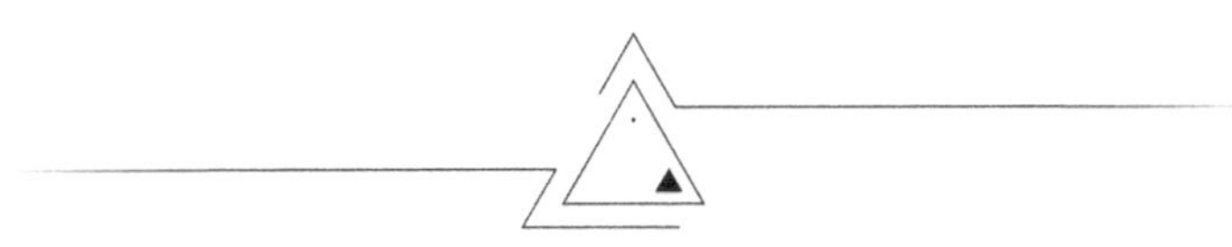

"—be alright?"

"—lost a lot—we need to—"

Throbbing. Swaying. The wolf felt lulled by the oscillating pulls of the ship.

He sensed presences around him, yet he could not open his eyes to see them. As if whiskers were caressing his fur, he felt the threads of consciousness permeating through him, making his pores tingle with the sensation.

An intrusive hand lifted his muzzle, wiping a wet rag on his wounds, gently cleaning off the dried blood that held his eyes shut. For a brief heartbeat, he saw a red-tinted figure covered in scales. He tried to bite at it, but was too weak and slow. Then guilt settled within him, recognizing the figure but unable to recall their name.

He felt a cold light, but also a warm one. Fire. The wolf heard it dully crackling inside a metal cage. His body was sprawled on a carpet of furs. He felt as if he was resting atop an enormous wolf. Dire wolf. *Leif*, he suddenly remembered, but could not tell why, nor could he recall what *Leif* was.

"—him wake up, we have—"

"Please, you must let me—"

"—is he doing?"

Hours. Perhaps days. He heard the voices cradling him. He felt his tongue lapping at something. The fire burned; the ship swayed. He kept his eyes closed, but felt the shadows of those around him. He felt them wait by him, sleep alongside him, feed him, wash him, talk to him. Strange sounds they made, those shadows—senseless, meaningless.

The darkness was comforting.

The wolf awoke.

The room was silent as a starlit meadow.

He forced his crusty eyes to finally open, and looked around. The space seemed familiar to him. *Ship*, he thought, almost understanding the meaning of the word.

He tried to stand, but his frail legs failed him, dropping him back onto the fur rug. The morning light washed in distortedly through thick glass panes, falling onto a figure asleep in the bed. Two others, covered in blankets, dozed in nearby chairs.

The wolf forced his legs to support him; one trembling step at a time, he shambled toward the bed. A bald head poked out from under the blankets. A young man. The wolf knew his scent. He could almost remember his name; he nearly had it.

The young man opened his eyes and sat up quickly.

Frightened, the wolf tumbled backward, bumping against a wall as he lost his balance. The two figures in the chairs stood up. It was only then that he realized he was snarling. His muzzle stung with the effort.

"—okay Sterjall. It is me, do not—"

The wolf barked and growled, retreating into a corner of the room.

A door opened. Silhouettes. He saw daylight, freedom. He tried running to it but merely tripped on his paws.

"—close it, now!"

The door slammed shut. Threatened, caged. Shapes on two feet stood tall around him: the hairless boy, a scaled creature, a fat one with tusks that glowed coldly, a woman with auburn hair, a girl of dark skin and sad eyes, two young-lings who were one.

"—move back, don't scare him, let's—"

The wolf cowered. He could snarl no more; it hurt too much. Ears flat-tened, he whined.

"—doesn't remember us…"

"Sterjall. It is me—" the boy said, but the wolf was too scared of the sounds.

"—it'll help him—if we try to—"

The bald-headed boy put a dark mask on. He vanished. In his stead there stood a new creature with brown and cream fur.

The wolf tried to avoid looking at him.

"—me, Kulak."

The wolf hesitated. His eyes darted around ashamedly.

The dark-skinned girl kept uttering sounds. "—bring it, it'll help him—"

The furred creature turned and walked away. He soon returned and placed something sharp on the ground. Something white and black.

Leif, the wolf thought. He had been carrying the object with him. *Leif.* He tried to remember what the word meant. He recalled running away from humans, but it hadn't been from these humans. Why had he been carrying that sharp object? What did it mean?

"—wish Mamóru were here…"

He recognized more of the sounds. He kept staring at the object. White bone blade with black crystal edges. *Dire wolf. Obsidian.* A dark hilt. *Quaar. Dagger.* A white pommel, carved into a figure, an animal. *A bear, a wolf.*

He was confused. He let out a resigned growl as he dropped his weight like a stone to the ground.

The dark-skinned girl sat next to him. He wanted to protest but had no energy to spend. He watched her as she placed a hand upon his shoulder blades. He snapped, biting the air.

"—okay, it's okay."

She put her hand down again, gently.

"—have to remember, Sterjall, come back to—"

The wolf did not want to fight, he just wanted it to be over. He closed his eyes to make the world vanish.

The girl began to make a strange sound. It vibrated through her, down her arms, into his fur. He couldn't tell what she was doing.

"—calls forth where I belong. I lend an ear, the granite speaks, I hear—"

Those sounds, they echoed through his mind like a rumbling creek.

"—for fish I'll leap and full I'll sleep behind clear waterfalls. In mounts so high—"

He knew these words. He knew not their meaning, but he knew how they made him feel. They were… She was… *singing.*

"—wind caress my fur, sharp claws resound along. The spruce and pine, and cones of fir all join the mountain song."

Mountain song. I hear…

"—reach the Wujann peaks and climb their steep gray walls. Fresh trout and berries we shall—"

… seek amongst these hallowed halls. The melody flowed through his memory like wind through a canyon. *I know this… this song. I remember.*

"—where paws were then now two feet stand and home I am at last."

The wolf whined softly, as if to sing along. His brow furrowed and his heart ached. He gave in to the oscillations of the song, and they brought back memories of a warm cabin, of a broad, welcoming chest, of a beard like redwoods and pine sap. He could almost smell the lemongrass.

"—wolf cub thaws through fevered dreams and lifts my heart with joy."

He felt a presence by his side. A large, benevolent, loving presence.

Banook, he remembered. *Banook.*

"I hope he knows that we can be together all along—"

When far apart he thinks of me and hears the mountain song.

The wolf let out a weak howl, so small and sorrowful that it tore the heart of the girl who sang.

Sterjall. I am Sterjall.

The wolf embraced his fears. He battled against the strong instinct driving him and took control. Filled with sorrow and warmth, he willed his body to slowly change. As he became something else, his memories came rushing back into him, his very sense of self. He looked at his handpaws and still felt uneasy. He pushed further as if birthing himself anew, cocooned in a refractive mist until his fur was gone.

Lago scratched the mask off his face. Its absence left behind a sobbing, naked young man.

CHAPTER NINETEEN

INTO THE DOME OF ASHES

Lago was carried to a comfortable chair beside the iron stove. His friends wrapped a blanket over him.

"How… how did I get here?" Lago asked, recognizing Siffo's quarters.

Lummukem handed him a glass of water. "We sent Olo after you. He led us to a small island and then toward the peninsula. We sailed along the coast, hoping to find more clues."

"We were so worried about you," Alaia said, holding his hand. "I thought for a moment… I thought that…" Her voice caught in her throat, and after a moment Kulak spoke in her stead.

"We searched during the day, moved to new areas at night," the prince continued. "My eyes cried for you, every day, every night. We were sailing near the coast when Blu heard the wolves calling and warned me about it."

"Wolves… the pack…" Lago murmured, barely remembering. "They saved me…"

"We followed the howls and found you near the shore. The wolves were watching over you. You were unconscious, matted in dry blood, resting on Leif."

Lago glanced toward a side table; his dagger rested there, a streak of red still smeared along the bone at its core.

Lummukem squatted next to Lago and checked the cuts on his cheek and lips. "We were not able to stitch your wounds. The injuries had fused and dried up by the time we found you, and you would not let our hands touch you. But while you slept, we applied a bit of velvet knifewood, which is helping your healing. You were not easy to deal with."

"Sorry…" Lago said, wincing as he felt the cuts with his tongue. He had four deep gashes that ran diagonally from his upper cheek all the way to his lips.

"The wounds are closing," Lummukem assured him, "but do not force them. They will leave scars. Perhaps the scars will help you remember not to take your feral form while none of us are around."

"I… I had to," Lago quietly said. He readjusted himself on the chair, feeling the sharp pain of the cuts on his back and chest. He had bruises on his ribs, on his face, on his wrists. His right shoulder had a necklace of red punctures from where the seal had bitten him to pull him overboard.

"I'm remembering some things," he mumbled. "I was trapped in a ship. I realized that in my feral form my paws would slide through the shackles, so I had to do it, to escape. It's so hard to remember. I'm only getting glimpses of it."

Everyone had gathered around him by now. Lummukem sat on the ground with the twins whispering to them over their shoulders. Siffo had pulled up chairs for Crysta and Hefra. Alaia and Kulak stood leaning against a wall. Even Theggo, his captains, and the Tsing ambassador had come.

"Our scalps understand you are tired," Kulak said, "but anything you can tell us would be of value."

"I'm… I'm trying to recall. It feels so distant now, and at the same time so present, like all of my memories are coming back at the same time."

"Start from the beginning," Crysta said. "You were next to me when this… thing, pulled you—"

"It was a Negórmea seal," Hefra offered, "easy to tell from their maroon coats. Though they don't grow so big in the bay, that I can tell ya—must've come from within the Moonrise Dome."

Lago forced himself to recall. The pain on his shoulder. Falling into the sea. The cold splash. He shivered.

He told them how he was dragged through water, and then warmed by a fire and placed on a skiff pulled by seals.

"The one wearing Gwonlesilv traveled in the boat with me," Lago said. "She calls herself Silv-Thaar Knivlar. She's one of Fjorna's arbalisters, the one with red hair and pretty scars all over."

"I remember her," Alaia said, sucking at her teeth.

"She's some kind of seal now. She took me to a cove. I… I don't know where, but it was very close to the dome."

"There are not too many locations where that could be," Captain Mareesha said, more to Theggo than to Lago. "Not on the eastern side of the Kilkarag Peninsula. But we've sailed far from there by now."

"Lago, can you tell us more?" Theggo asked. "This might be critically important for the safety of all of us."

"I'm trying. I didn't see much at first. They shackled me inside a ship's hull, and then Fjorna came. She… It was *her* wearing Krostsilv, not that other general. She was an ermine. An ermine with a mangled mess of a face."

"Last we heard of Crescu Valaran," Ambassador Vor-Vor said, "the general who had been wearing that Silv, he'd been sent to Azash by the Red Stag. Do you think Fjorna betrayed him?"

"I'm not sure about Valaran, but Fjorna has definitely betrayed the Red Stag."

The Tsing ambassador narrowed his eyes. "How so, Lorr Vaari?" he asked, his high-pitched voice rising even higher.

"I overheard them talking. They defected from the Negian army and are trying to be first to get to the remaining masks."

"And they have control of the Negian fleet," Vor-Vor said, nervously brushing his tufted tail back and forth. "I wonder if Afhora, or perhaps the Federation, will now ally with them."

"And it gets worse," Lago said. "The Red Stag now has the support of the Graalman Horde. He is already at the Scoria Dome. Fjorna was trying to get there first, but I heard them say that it's too late—her fleet is just now entering the Alommo Sea."

"If their interest was in the Scoria Dome, why come to the Ashen Dome?" Theggo asked.

Lago thought for a moment. He wiped his dripping nose with the blanket before saying, "Fjorna can travel faster without the other ships, using those seals. She hurried this way so they could steal Trommosilv before anyone else entered the dome." His voice took on an urgent tone. "We need to hurry and warn the Tjardur Miscam not to trust her! Where are we now? How far are we from the Ashen Dome?"

"We're un our way to Ngau Tor," Siffo said. "Been sailing fur a day n'some since we found ye. We shell arrive t'morrow evening. But yer in no condition t'venture out yet."

"I don't care. Fjorna said she'd try to convince the Trommofröa to follow her out of the dome. Once outside, Fjorna will kill them and take the mask. We need to stop her! Take me back to where you found me. Maybe I'll be able to spot the cove they were hiding in."

Siffo snorted. "We're too far, wulf Lorr. It'd take us a few days t'sail all d'way back, then many mour t'properly scout."

"Ngau Tor is closer to us now," Vor-Vor said, "and right next to the dome, although on the west side of it. We could enter there and warn the locals."

"Then that's the way we are going," Lago pointedly said.

"What sort of enemy are we fighting?" Lummukem asked. "How many of them should we expect?"

"Fjorna and Aurélien, plus at least two more of the arbalisters. No, wait, only one. I… ripped one's throat out, and I think I injured the other. And there are about ten more who I believe were sailors. They only have a small ship. They came in a hurry, with the single goal of stealing the mask."

"A small crew then," Theggo said. "While you venture in from the west, I could take *Silverweave* the long way around the peninsula. My fast vessel can carry enough soldiers to overpower them. If you are too late by land, at least we might be able to intercept them by sea."

"I shall go with you, Fleet Admiral." Vor-Vor tucked his tail over his belt, then added, "If you will welcome me aboard your mighty frigate."

Theggo nodded.

"Thank you, Theggo," Lago said. "You should get going, you have a long way back. We'll keep sailing toward Ngau Tor, then ride into the dome as soon as we dock."

"You need to rest," Lummukem said to Lago.

"I'll rest until we arrive. That will need to be enough."

"Ye could stay with mine crew in *Fjummomurr* n'let d'uthers go," Siffo suggested.

"No," Lago said. "I'm going. I don't care that I'm injured. I will be able to hold on to Blu."

Lago waited anxiously, resting in Siffo's bed. He closed his eyes briefly, hoping to take a short nap.

"We are almost there," Kulak said as he entered the cabin.

Lago sat up with a jolt. He had fallen deeply asleep, missing part of the night and most of the next day. The warmth of an approaching sunset tinted the glass panes over the bed.

He was ravenous. Kulak brought him some food, then helped him to his feet. Lago's legs were working again, at least well enough that he wouldn't stumble.

After Lummukem changed Lago's bandages, Alaia walked into the room wearing her elytra armor full of ochres, shimmering crimsons, and yellow accents. She held her quaar helm under one arm and a bundle under the other.

"You aren't leaving without me this time."

"This will be too dangerous," Lago protested, "we can't—"

"Shush. I may not be as fierce as you all—actually, you don't look fierce at the moment, you look more like a beaten-up, scabby stray—but I can help, and I will not slow you down."

"I don't think—"

"Shut that muzzle," she said, dropping the bundle onto the bed; it was Lago's own elytra armor. "I'll help you with these," she added, with her eyes focused on Kulak and Lummukem, who quietly exited the cabin. Alaia helped him put on his padded chausses and arming doublet, then the lamellar skirt, cuirass, greaves, and bracers.

Lago winced as Alaia finished tightening the armor's belts and drawstrings, then sat on the bed. The two of them were alone in the room. They could hear the sailors laughing on the deck.

"You're sweating," Alaia said, wiping a drop off Lago's forehead.

"The armor is quite warm," he demurred.

Alaia was clad the same, yet her forehead was dry. "It's actually quite cold today," she said. "You might have a fever, maybe we should—"

"I'm fine," Lago interrupted, reaching for his mask. "I have to do this."

"You don't have to do anything. You can take a break, you know?"

"But I can't!" he barked, then closed his eyes. "I'm sorry. I didn't mean to yell at you. It's just… sometimes… I don't understand why so much was placed on my shoulders. Why me? I'm just… I'm not cut out for this, but I just can't let them… I… I can't—" He began to sob.

Alaia scooted closer to him, her head leaning on his shoulder, an arm reaching across his back. "Gwoli, not everything is your responsibility to fix. Some things will always be beyond our control."

"Some things, but not all things. When I can make a difference, I have a duty to try. But some days I'm just so tired of it all. Some days I want to go back to Banook's cabin and sit there, and watch the fireplace with him, and do nothing else. Nothing else."

"And that day will come. You are allowed to feel this way, but you are also allowed to rest."

"I know. Thank you. And I might take it easier, but not today. This is too important. But I'll have you with me, as always—I truly can't do this alone."

"Of course, Gwoli. We'll all be with you."

Lago sniffled, wiped his nose and cheeks, then reached toward the nightstand for his dagger. "Shit…" he said, looking down at his waist. "I just realized, my belt, it was in Fjorna's ship… Leif's scabbard, it's gone."

"We can find a replacement, don't worry."

"But you don't und—"

"Of course I understand, Gwoli. But you still have Leif. And you can ask Banook to make you a new scabbard when you see him again." She measured his expression while holding his gaze.

"You are right," he said. "I'm overreacting. To everything. Would you… Would you be able to find a scabbard that will fit?"

"That I can do. I'll go ask Siffo if he has one." She left to search for a replacement.

Lago stood. He reluctantly reached for his mask and put it on his face, a latent fear suddenly tightening around his throat. *It will be fine,* he told himself. *Just don't let yourself go too far.* He groaned from the pain as he shapeshifted into Sterjall, then fixed up his greaves and limped out to the deck.

The Ashen Dome was a wall of black in the twilight; a darker, flattened cloud floated above it. The port of Ngau Tor came into view, reflecting the firelight of the overwater bungalows that sprinkled its shallow reefs.

Sterjall was exhausted, but he forced his eyes to remain open, wanting to see this new land. The citizens of the quaint and lively village seemed happy and welcoming, having been informed of the wayfarers' approach by heralds Vor-Vor had sent before they parted ways. As *Fjummomurr* drifted closer to the docks, he noticed that a sizable proportion of the villagers were Jabrak-Tsing, perhaps even half of them. They proudly displayed their tufted tails, decorated with rings, ribbons, and braids. He remembered Penli, his old classmate from Birth-Light School, and hoped he was still with his girlfriend Kara, and that they had escaped Withervale. He then recalled the tailed man he had met in Brimstowne, who had very tenderly made love to him. He hoped all Jabrak-Tsing were as kind as Penli and as the man whose name he had never learned.

"Are you sure you want to do this?" Kulak asked, tightening the belt on Blu's saddle as he watched Sterjall approach. "You do not have to go. You can rest."

"I'm sure. Help me up."

"Do not strain yourself," Lummukem warned, helping hoist Sterjall up. "If there are battles to come, you hold on to Blu and let us do the fighting."

Fjummomurr docked in a deep bay, guided by a Jabrak-Tsing woman who waved fiery torches. The two smilodons immediately hopped off the ship and hurried toward the dome. Nelv led the way as a cheetah, rushing in a blur of gold and spotted blacks. Sterjall held tightly to Kulak's chest, their legs clutched around Blu's saddle. Pichi carried Lummukem, with Ishke'ísuk and Olo on their shoulders and Alaia right behind. Also riding on Pichi was Gwit, sitting alone in a pocket of the saddlebag. The twins had complained mightily when told they would have to stay aboard *Fjummomurr*, but Lummukem had been inflexible; they did not deem it wise to bring two children on such a hurried mission.

The dome was right up the coast from the village. As they raced toward it, Lummukem and Kulak aimed their quaar conduits so that they could create an opening, traveling faster through the wall of vines than they ever had before.

Once they breached the wall, they were ready to gallop at full speed again, but found themselves stopped by another wall, one made of dangling plants that would not obey their Silvesh. Lummukem twirled their halberd to slice through the lianas and ivies, clearing the spiderweb of vegetation to reveal an ancient yew forest. The gnarled trees leaned their contorted branches into the ground, as if supplicating humbly both to the dome above and to the soil below.

It was too warm inside the dome, feeling closer to Spring than Winter. The forest was rough terrain to traverse, but Nelv and the smilodons were used to such density of foliage and could find their way on the ground as well as across branches. They'd made it barely a mile into the forest before another barrier stopped them. Rising up past the branches of the gnarled yews was a rampart of gray stone, one of inconceivable height and might.

"Why put a wall next to a wall?" Sterjall asked while looking up, but the dense canopy obscured most of his view. "It's so tall." With Agnargsilv he could feel the threads of the mosses and lichens blossoming over the fortification, but was unable to estimate its height.

The yews had been planted parallel to the rampart, leaving the space next to it clear, at least on the ground. The passage was covered in hoof prints and other animal tracks. The wayfarers trotted southeast under the vaulted branches.

"How are we going to get across this?" Alaia asked after they'd followed the tunnel for a couple of miles.

"Where there are walls, there are doors," Lummukem answered.

Not much farther ahead, the forest ended in a grassy meadow. Half-sunken into the rampart, two enormous columns framed a double gate cast in steel plates, of a scale seemingly meant for titans. The barbican above the gates was crenelated by triangular merlons, like sharp stone teeth.

They dismounted the smilodons to explore the entrance, finding recent hoof prints in the soil. Halfway up the gate was a symbol of a bull's head with four horns, all pointed up. Atop each of the horns was a triangular glyph: the leftmost had sinuous curves like the forms of water, the next seemed to be some sort of blade, the third had a hexagonal pattern, and the last was flame-like in appearance.

The gates had no handle to pull, no keyhole, but there was an oversized knocker on the right panel, shaped like dangling testicles.

"I guess we should knock?" Sterjall said, looking toward Kulak.

The caracal took hold of the metal gonads. He lifted them up high, then let them drop.

The knock resounded through the steel like an explosion, making Blu and Pichi jump back hissing. The clang reverberated for a long moment; once it subsided, a different sound could be heard from behind the double gate: a voice.

"Mindrelsilv sees someone," Kulak said. "A man comes."

"A man?" Sterjall said. "But he has horns like—"

Something heavy unlatched. The metal doors slowly swung inward. The crack widened, revealing an athletic man in his half-form of a common eland, similar to Tinnomeg, Theggo's trusted mount, but standing on two hoofed feet. He was wearing partial armor of plated steel. Even his spiraling horns were plated with colorful metal rings. He wore an expression between reverence and joy, but mostly just looked confused. The eland bowed deeply, pointing his horns at them, letting his long-haired dewlap dangle till it scraped the ground.

"*Hurff*. Head strong! More Silvfröash come to further bless Jels Urosh!" he said with a rhythmical Common accented by grunts. "Speros of the Eland bows before you, Lerrs from lands far and away. Have you also come searching for Servant Lune?"

"You have seen others like us?" Sterjall asked.

"Have I? I have not!" Speros answered. "Your friends came not through Nannúr, but through Lawu, southeast of here. I believe Servant Lune is with them at this time."

"Servant Lune?" Lummukem asked. "Is that the name of the Trommofröa?"

"*Hurff*, one of her names."

"We are too late!" Sterjall lamented, and he was about to explain himself when he noticed a dozen more people approaching. Having heard the loud clang, villagers from up the road had made their way to the gate. They were not partially half-formed like Siffo and the Puqua, but fully half-formed bovids with human proportions, as if they each were wearing a Silv. Most of them were bison, while three were kudus, and the others a cow, a yak, and two prominently humped zebus. Other than the eland and the kudus, the bodies of the bovids were thick, particularly their chests and backs, rippling with muscles beneath their short and long fur. A few of them wore simple togas, but most were clad in steel-plated armor.

Sterjall stepped closer to the eland. "The Trommofröa is in danger, we need to warn her!" he pleaded. "The others that came, they are not our friends. We must hurry. They want to take Trommosilv from her. They want to kill her!"

Speros cocked his head in confusion. He glanced at Sterjall's cut cheek; the wounds were reopening due to the wolf's exertion, tinting his black fur with four crimson streaks. The eland instinctively lowered his longbow from his shoulders and twisted his back so that he could reach his quiver.

"Where were they seen?" Sterjall demanded. "You need to take us immediately!"

Kulak stepped in front of the wolf. "It is a matter of utmost urgency," he added, his own voice calm but tight with tension. "Time is of the essence."

"If Silvfröash are not to be trusted, how do we know to trust you?" one of the zebu citizens inquired, shaking his ears.

"You cannot, you should not," Kulak said. "You may lock us up later if you wish, but if you do not act now, the Fröa ust Trommo might not live to see another day."

"But Felid Lorr," Speros objected, "could we not bring this matter to our clan leaders first?"

"There is no time," Kulak said. "If you do not trust us, then trust the Nu'irgesh." Nelv suddenly shapeshifted into a powerful dinofelis and roared in notes so low that the half-bovids felt it more in their marrow than in their ears, filling them with a sense of dread and unease. Ishke'ísuk and Gwit both followed her lead, the basilisk turning into a frill-necked lizard and hissing, frills fully extended; the dormouse hopping out of the saddlebag and in midair shapeshifting into a castoroides, slamming his tail down with the power of an armorer's mallet.

"Spirits of old!" Speros cried, falling to his knees.

"Please, take us, our scalps beg of you," Kulak insisted. "We will explain while we are on the way, but we must hasten."

Speros exchanged looks with the citizens, who had all tipped their horns in reverence. "*Hurff,* I will take you, Lerrs, but you must explain as we travel. Fifteen miles down the Nudoroth Rampart we must ride, to the gates of Lawu. Servant Lune's presence was requested there. I know not if she has yet arrived."

"Show us the way," Sterjall said.

Speros regarded an allgender yak, who had three oxpeckers perched on their curved horns and matted crown, with a few more crawling up their long-furred chest. The colorfully beaked birds stared with blood-red eyes. "Hefferen, send an oxpecker to Lawu, another to the citadel. Servant Lune is to return to Bra'uur at once. In grave danger she is. Tell them the Silvfröash who requested her presence must not be trusted. Urge them to lock the gates. *Hurff!* At once you must warn them!"

Hefferen nodded their matted head.

Speros eyed the dinofelis before him. "Your felids seem faster than our hooves. May I ride with you?"

"Not on Nelv," Kulak warned. "But Pichi can carry you."

Lummukem helped Speros up onto the enormous smilodon, climbed up after him and Alaia, then said, "Lead us, Speros, guardian of the steel gates."

CHAPTER TWENTY

HEAD STRONG

Speros pointed the way up the rampart, leading them to the expansive barbican. At the top of the fortified gateway was a massive horn several strides long, twisting in a soft vortex decorated by delicate ridges.

"Wait here," Speros said, hopping off Pichi. He rotated the horn upon its heavy platform, aiming it down the rampart's path, then inhaled deeply and blew into it. The rumble that erupted cut through the air like thunder. The sound was deep but piercing, oscillating in cavernous fundamentals and trilling with sparkling overtones.

Speros climbed back onto the saddle without missing a beat. They galloped southeast, following the crenelated parapet. The fortification was wide enough for the two smilodons and Nelv—once more as a cheetah—to travel abreast, with plenty more room to spare.

A horn blast with a unique pattern and intonation met them from the direction in which they traveled.

"They have received my warning!" Speros yelled so the others could hear. Though the cats' paws were silent, they were moving at full speed, and the wind made it hard for them to communicate. "Please, now you must tell me more!"

Since Alaia was sitting in front of Speros, she was the one to catch him up. She began with introductions, something they had glossed over in their haste, and then briefly explained the situation.

Another horn blast resounded from farther down the rampart, then a third one from farther still.

"That is the Latifrons Horn of Lawu," Speros said to the wayfarers, though only Alaia could hear him clearly. The eland held a glimmer of hope in his black eyes.

Alaia told Speros about the wars of the New World and the coming of the Red Stag. She was interrupted by a *tsik-tsik!* call from their side. It was one of Hefferen's oxpeckers, who hovered aloft next to Pichi. Speros responded with a nearly perfect mimicry of the sound. The oxpecker hurried in front of them, quickly overtaking them.

"*Hurff*, the guards at Lawu will be fully informed before we arrive," Speros said. "The gates will be locked. Pray to Pamúnn that Servant Lune receives the message before it is too late."

Alaia resumed her story, explaining how Silv-Thaar Daro was hoping to trick the Trommofröa into leaving the dome, intending to steal her mask.

A barbican ahead of them held another massive horn like the one Speros had blown. A dozen armored half-bovids had spotted the approaching creatures and stood at attention with weapons ready. Speros stood up on Pichi's back, waving his longbow in the air while holding on to the top of Alaia's quaar helm for balance.

"Head strong!" Speros bellowed. "Make way! Head strong!"

The guards were clearly confused, but they recognized one of their own and moved out of the way. "Head strong!" a few of them replied as Nelv and the smilodons flashed by.

Speros sat back down, then tapped his hoofed fingers on Alaia's helm. "Head strong indeed you are, Lurr of dark helms. A beauty beyond compare."

"Thank you," she replied with a smile.

"The helm is what I meant. Not to say you aren't a beauty as well, *hurff*, but I would dare not speak so bluntly to a princess of the New World."

Alaia laughed, intrigued by the forward nature of the horned stranger. She clarified that she was not much of a princess before continuing her tale.

Sterjall could barely hear Alaia and Speros's conversation, but he was glad it was his friend doing the explaining, as he was growing too weary to say much. He stared at the strange bovid, studying his figure. Speros had wide-set diamond-shaped ears, silky orange fur, and a darker nose bridge. Except for his forehead and crown, where his fur was spiky and a bit longer, his rusty coat was short, highlighting thick veins underneath.

Sterjall's eyes drifted toward the landscape. The Ashen Dome was unique, in the way that every dome was unique, so he was not taken by surprise. The

Nudoroth Rampart they were riding atop ran parallel to the dome's wall, about a mile away to their right. The yew forest was compressed between them, overgrown and inscrutable. To their left was an extensive landscape of grasslands and dense forests. Enormous bovid herds lumbered through the distant terrains, gathering more densely around the nearest supporting column. As if sucked in by a maelstrom, the herds circled the base of the column in a spiral.

There must be millions of them, Sterjall thought. *Some of them are enormous.* Even from this distance, it was clear that a few of the species on the prairies were as big as mammoths. He spotted a few of the giant bovids up close, right beneath the rampart; they looked like the Bergsulf bison that pulled wagons around the Withervale Mesa, but preternaturally overgrown, and with horns that poked sideways like those of longhorn highlanders.

The wolf's gaze shifted to the central trunk, which sprouted from an elevated plateau under the watch of four prominent volcanoes. Despite it being deep Winter, the mountainous summits were the only places where any snow accumulated. Each of the peaks fumed; three of them exhaling black clouds, while the shortest one let out white steam. The fumes billowed up to the top of the dome where they seeped through the vines, glowing as eerie rings where they came into contact with the bright arudinn.

Jels Urosh, Sterjall thought, recalling words Speros had spoken earlier. *Four Blessings.* He thought he could see another tall rampart at the base of the four volcanoes; it was too distant and dim to clearly make out.

"Head strong!" Sterjall heard someone call. He looked to the side and saw another of the great horns flash by them, and more guards making room for them to pass.

The exhaustion rose in Sterjall's chest like an unstoppable tide. All that had happened in the last few days bubbled within him, from his abduction by seals, to his near-death experience in the cold sea, to facing Knivlar and Daro, to barely escaping down a half-frozen waterfall, to being rescued by wolves and found by his friends. The tiredness soaked through his fur, to his muscles, to his bones, saturating every cell of his body. His head sagged, his energy waning with every step of Blu's quick paws.

"—ling well?"

He jolted his head up. "Huh?"

"Are you feeling well?" Kulak repeated. "My back feels your muzzle drifting upon it."

He wiped off a streak of blood his lips had left on Kulak's shodog. "I fell asleep. I'm fine."

"Speros says we are almost there."

Ahead and to their left was Lawu, a town of stone buildings circularly arranged over a series of hillocks. Directly ahead, the rampart widened into another barbican, this one crowned by the Latifrons Horn of Lawu. Guards patrolled the battlements, keeping watch through the embrasures. Sterjall could not see it, but he knew that a giant metal gate was tightly locked right below the barbican.

"Down the steps," Speros directed.

Nelv, Blu, and Pichi hurried down and stopped, panting at the base of the steps. Dozens of half-bovids were waiting for them, all heavily armored and armed. The largest of the group stomped to the front. She was in her half-form of a gaur, with deeply curved horns and a back so thick and muscular that it seemed as if she was carrying an unwieldy backpack beneath her cuirass. Her steel armor was decorated in golden trims, denoting her higher rank.

"Speros! Head strong!" she called out, lifting her oversized mace in a defensive stance.

Speros dismounted Pichi. "Ogóre, do not fear these strangers, they are the ones who warned us of the betrayal. We must stop Servant Lune from meeting with the others. Has she arrived at Lawu yet?"

"*Hurmf!* Too late came your warning," the armored gaur said in a deeply rumbling voice. "Nearly by two hours. That is when Servant Lune left the Lawu gate. To Pamúnn she should have listened—he refused to leave with them."

"Who was with them?" Sterjall asked impatiently. "Did any guards travel with her?"

"Diduk of the Yak, one of her husbands," Ogóre said. "He accompanied Servant Lune. Five scouts went as well, who joined them to the wall and have only now returned." Ogóre nodded to the five kudu scouts who stood behind her, all sharing looks of deep concern on their slender, striped faces.

"Through the vines themselves we saw them walk," one of the kudus said. "The vines shaped to their will, like white smoke and green flame."

"Who came for them? How many?" Lummukem asked.

"*Hurmf,* two came in, four went out," Ogóre said. "An ermine with fur as white as the clouds of Laaja Ash, Silv-Thaar Daro she said her name was. And a spotted sea creature with swirling scars on her naked body, who called herself Silv-Thaar Knivlar."

"We are not too far from where Lune and Diduk exited," the kudu scout added.

"Take us there," Kulak requested. "We might still have time to save them."

"Unlatch the gates!" the wide-bodied gaur roared. Something heavy and mechanical resounded from within the columns that framed the portal.

Speros climbed back on top of Pichi as two zebu guards pulled the gates open.

"Follow my hooves!" Ogóre said, already trotting through the threshold, heavy armor clinking as each heavy hoof landed.

Ogóre of the Gaur moved like a boulder rolling down a mountain, easily keeping up with the speed of the smilodons, leading them down a nearly straight tunnel of branches formed by draping yews. The soil below was moist, and clear tracks could be seen upon it, but Ogóre needed not look down at her hooves—she kept her eyes straight ahead.

Lummukem and Kulak once again used their quaar conduits to open a passageway from a distance, seeing the vines at the end of the tunnel.

"Ogóre, track their hoof prints," Speros said. "Show us where they went through."

The gaur entered the tunnel of vines, still unsure of all that was going on, but feeling the urgency to act instead of question. They reduced their speed to a striding march, with Ogóre scouting ahead of them, trying to make sense of the prints on the ground.

Sterjall and Alaia provided cold pharolith light for all to see by. Ogóre did not question where the impossible light was shining from, too focused on her task. "*Hurmf!* Too broken are the tracks, holes grow everywhere," she complained.

"Just keep moving straight ahead from this point," Sterjall said, "we'll soon exit on the other side."

When they reached the nighttime cold of the exterior world, they found themselves in a pine forest. Sterjall could smell the salty shore, hear the crash of waves. As the path descended, the pines took more angled forms, with windswept needles pushing away from the shoreline. Everything was gilded by sharp brushstrokes of pink moonlight.

"There! I recognize that clearing!" Sterjall said. "The cove is down that way!"

The trees abruptly gave way to a white beach with black rocks rising to the left and right, circling the hidden cove. Daro's ship was at the far end, next to a stone pier, upon which four figures were walking.

Ogóre bellowed as she ran, casting a shadow much larger than herself in front of her. "Lune, Diduk, it's a trap! Arm yourselves! Escape! Head strong! *Hurmf!*"

But the figures were already stepping onto the deck.

"Nelv, go!" Kulak shouted.

The felid Nu'irg sped as a cheetah toward the stone pier, flashing by Ogóre and leaving them all behind. Ishke'ísuk pushed his claws through the white sand as a perentie, bolting toward the clear waters. Gwit followed the lizard as an agile long-legged mara.

The yak who had accompanied Servant Lune was the first to react to the warning, unsheathing a sword and stepping in front of his wife, who drew an inconveniently heavy war hammer.

Silv-Thaar Daro and Silv-Thaar Knivlar drew their own weapons, and the rest of their crew did as well, moving to surround and overpower the two bovids.

Nelv was a bolt of yellow lightning, running faster than any felid could.

In the darkness, Sterjall saw the ship move. The sails were reefed, but the vessel still jolted forward, extending a white wake in front of it. Sparks and metallic twangs of battle exploded on the deck.

Nelv reached the stone pier, but the ship was far from it already, accelerating too fast. She climbed onto the black rocks at the edge of the cove, following alongside the vessel from above. From an overhang of rock, the cheetah leapt, shifting into her clouded leopard form so that her leap could carry her farther. She barely reached the stern of the ship, slamming hard against it. Her claws ripped through wood and lines, pulling her up onto the quarterdeck.

A sailor charged, swinging his sword. Without hesitation, Nelv jumped at his face, biting part of his jawbone off before kicking the man overboard. She spotted Silv-Thaar Knivlar right in front of her, keenly aware that the leopard seal was in some way responsible for the death of her Nu'irg friend, Däo-Varjak. Knivlar's eyes filled with terror at the sight of the felid. She ran down the deck clumsily, tripping on her webbed feet.

Nelv growled, the sound small but petrifying. She ignored all others to give chase to the impostor who had stolen Gwonlesilv. She vaulted over an armored yak, pushing out her retractable claws, hovering in the air as she flashed her fangs toward the spotted coat of the fleeing leopard seal.

Tchk-clang!

Nelv was suddenly propelled sideways in the air, her own momentum added to that of a heavy bolt that had struck her chest. Silv-Thaar Daro watched from behind her crossbow as the felid Nu'irg's trajectory shifted, sending her flopping over the side of the vessel.

Nelv splashed into the cold water.

Kulak screamed, still atop Blu as the smilodon struggled to close the distance toward the fleeing Negians. It had all happened too fast.

They heard a deep-voiced man howl wretchedly at the ship.

"Diduk! No!" a husky female voice wailed in response.

Swords and shields slammed, armored plates sparked, crossbows ejected bolts mercilessly. A rumbling voice bellowed, then the water splashed.

Ishke'ísuk had just reached the shore. He shapeshifted into his saltwater crocodile form while Gwit took his giant beaver shape. Both swam as rapidly as possible toward the location of the splash.

"Send the seals!" came Daro's voice from the departing vessel. "Kill her! Take the mask!"

Crossbow bolts and arrows pierced the water like the sharp beaks of egrets.

"Veer southeast! War frigate incoming!" called a receding voice.

Ishke'ísuk kept on swimming, bridging the distance to the figure that had splashed into the pink-tinted sea. Servant Lune was struggling underwater in her half-form of a water buffalo, weighed down by her heavy armor. She managed to remove her metal helm, then tried to pull her steel cuirass off, all while trying to kick off her greaves. A dozen maroon-colored seals approached her. One bit her single, crescent-shaped horn, another chewed on her bracers. Her pauldrons were ripped away by sharp fangs, and more teeth sank into her thick shoulders. As she struggled, her lungs emptied. She told herself not to inhale, but the exertion from the fight against the seals forced her to take an unwelcome gulp of salty water. Her green eyes closed. Her sight darkened.

Ishke'ísuk arrived jaws first, tearing two of the seals apart in one bite. Gwit followed closely behind. Seeing Lune unconscious, the castoroides grabbed her by the horn with his enormous incisors, then beat his tail down to smack at the seals. He swam away, kicking up a turbid plume of sand. The seals gave chase, biting at Gwit's legs and tail, but the crocodile came to his aid and chewed off the pinnipeds' back ends, then took a defensive position beneath Gwit, whipping his tail at any pursuers.

Curses could be heard as the ship exited the cove. A few last arrows and bolts were loosed in the dark, impacting harmlessly in the sand and water. Speros returned a few hopeless shots with his longbow, unable to see where his arrows landed.

Gwit reached the shore and hauled out the Trommofröa, hoping to hear a gasp from her, but the buffalo's saltwater-filled lungs drew no breaths.

Ogóre was the first to arrive to aid her. The gaur pushed on Servant Lune's chest, compressing rhythmically until the buffalo threw up all the water she'd swallowed, inhaled deeply, then dropped sideways onto the sand.

At the distant stone pier, Blu was still running.

"Wait, what are you—" Sterjall began to ask as Kulak rose to his feet on the smilodon's shoulders. Before Sterjall could finish his question, Kulak used Blu's forehead as a diving board, launching himself into the freezing water without hesitation.

The prince swam toward a floating mound of fur. He found Nelv afloat sideways, gurgling as she tried to paddle to shore with one front leg. A heavy crossbow bolt was lodged in her ribs, right under one armpit. She weakly hissed at Kulak, but he ignored her fierceness, carefully placed her over his neck, and swam back to the pier. He was shivering as he pulled himself out, but he had not yet noticed. "Hold tight, fierce lady," he said, as Sterjall helped them both onto Blu's saddle. They hurried toward the others, who were gathered around a dark figure on the beach.

Lummukem saw them approach. They placed a blanket over the sand and to Kulak said, "Lower her here, Khuron. She will bleed a lot once the bolt comes out, but it must come out."

Kulak placed Nelv down and said to her, "My heart can feel it hurts, and my scalp knows you are tired. But take a larger form for us, so that Lummukem may safely remove the bolt. Can you do that for me, spotted beauty of Humenath?"

The clouded leopard growled. The bolt was substantial, not letting much blood spill out. She slowly shifted forms, taking the shape of a lioness. Now the bolt looked more like an oversized nail, and Lummukem easily extracted it. Blood sprayed out freely.

Kulak kept a handpaw on Nelv's shoulders. "Good. Now turn back, so that they may treat you."

Using her last bit of energy, Nelv shifted back into her primal form before passing out. Lummukem pressed down on the wound to staunch the bleeding, then asked Kulak for aid while suturing the wound.

Sterjall shuffled toward the others. Speros and Ogóre were tending to Servant Lune, while Ishke'ísuk and Gwit kept watch. Gwit's giant beaver tail was still bleeding, but his wounds were minor in comparison, so he stood guard attentively.

Ogóre helped Servant Lune remove what was left of her heavy armor. The bloodied sand beneath the water buffalo was a red darker than black, shimmering with pink highlights from the Tourmaline moonlight.

Despite her grievous state, Sterjall thought Lune looked beautiful. She was thick, tall, and muscular, with a heavy, solid head holding only one horn on her right side, shaped like a crescent moon. The single horn was armored with a steel cap and adorned by colorful metal rings. Her missing left horn was nothing more than a textured bump on her thick skull. Lune's graphite-gray fur was glossy and velvety. For a moment, Sterjall felt entranced, but then he felt foolish and useless, and he dropped exhaustedly to the ground.

Ogóre hurried to dry the buffalo, both to warm her up and to better access her wounds. Sterjall watched, uncertain of what to do. Lune looked up at him with her green eyes, and they saw each other; she glimpsed deeply into his fathomless indigo aura, while he gazed in a trance at her aura of a green so sparkling and rich that it seemed like the first sprouts of Spring rimmed by silver tendrils of starlight. She seemed to want to say something, but she merely coughed, expelling more salty water from her irritated lungs. With each coughing exertion, blood squirted out from her chest and belly punctures.

"*Hurmf,*" Ogóre grunted. "Too many wounds. Too many arrows and cuts."

Servant Lune coughed again. "I… Di… Diduk…" she grunted, staring at the bloodied sand but seeing the image of her husband being slayed. "What happened? *Khumm…* Og-Ogóre, who are these… p-people? Safety, we must…"

Ogóre did not answer, too busy treating the injuries. Speros answered in her stead. "Fear not, Servant Lune. These friends warned us of the dangers, of the betrayal of the two who lured you out of Trommodrolom."

Sterjall crawled a bit closer to Lune. "I am Sterjall. There is much we need to tell you, but you have to save your energy now. Let Ogóre heal you."

She extended a bloodied, hoofed hand. Sterjall held it tenderly, and with his empathic focus he took some of Lune's pain away, sinking it into himself until his entire body throbbed. He was so tired that the pain paled in comparison to how heavy his eyelids felt, which seemed as if they were cast in lead and weighed by anchors. He struggled to remain conscious.

He heard Alaia yelling something and looked up. She was spying out the tapered mouth of the cove with binoculars, toward a distant ship. "It's *Silverweave!*" she called. "It's Theggo!"

"Do you think he'll catch them?" Sterjall asked, his voice frayed by exhaustion.

"He's following them, but it doesn't look like it. Fjorna's ship sails faster than the wind."

"It's not sailing. It's being pulled by those monstrous seals."

"I'll make sure Theggo can see us, before *Silverweave* ventures too far away." She hurried over the sand and up the rocky cliff that bordered the cove, waving a pharolith lamp as she ran.

Another pharolith illuminated the wounds Ogóre was tending to. They were deep and ghastly.

Lune looked down at her broken body. From her wide nostrils, more red dripped. "Home…" she mumbled. "Take me home… It is cold…" Her green eyes closed, and she toppled backward.

"We cannot keep our servant in this state," Ogóre said. "We need help from Bra'uur's chirurgeons."

"Our friends are in the ship Alaia spotted," Sterjall told her. "They have good medicine, and can take care of—"

"*Hurmf!* No!" the gaur interjected. "To Trommodrolom we must return. We thank you for your help, but it is important we keep our Trommofröa safe, in our own home. We cannot trust this outside world. It is cold, it is dark, it is unknown to us. Down we let our guard, only once, and suffered for it. We will not do so again."

"You cannot reenter on your own," Lummukem gently reminded them. "Only the Silvesh can open the path." The dragon looked to their friends and added, "We will go with them. Pichi can carry Servant Lune. We have velvet knifewood to help her heal, once she stops bleeding." They looked toward Kulak. "We will leave some leaves with you, for Nelv."

"Thank you, Lummukem," Kulak said.

Sterjall put a handpaw on Lune's forearm. "Take care of her," he said to Lummukem while keeping his eyes on the buffalo. "We will meet with you later. We need to warn Siffo, Theggo, and the Tsing ambassador. How will we find you?"

"We will be in Bra'uur, at the Taur Citadel," Ogóre answered, "where the dome sprouts between the Four Blessings." She finished packing a wound, then looked up. "Speros, could you travel with them, and through our lands guide them?"

"*Hurff*, yes Gaur Lurr," Speros answered.

"Then all of you, help me move our dear servant."

Together they bundled Lune in a blanket and carefully placed her atop Pichi's back.

"We will be waiting," Lummukem said, hopping onto the smilodon. "Ishke'ísuk has explained all to Gwit, has told him he should follow you and protect you."

Ishke'ísuk turned back to his primal form and climbed atop Lummukem's shoulder, opposite Olo. Lummukem had Pichi carefully trot back up toward the pine forest, making sure she did not shake the wounded buffalo too much. Ogóre followed by their side.

Sterjall watched them leave, then turned back toward Nelv. "How is she doing?" he asked Kulak. "Shit, you're shivering. You must be freezing. Hold on…" He quickly rummaged through one of their bags for a dry blanket. "Turn back into Aio, to dry up."

Kulak complied, teeth chattering. "My s-scalp understands n-now, h-how cold you were when you f-fell into the sea. But I c-cannot feel cold now, I have t-to stay s-strong, for Nelv."

"She will be fine," Sterjall said, helping Aio dry off. "Lummukem did a good job. We just need to get her to the ship. She'll recover. The Nu'irgesh heal very fast."

"If these are the Nu'irgesh of your clades," Speros said, "the spotted cat I can understand, but... *Hurff*, why is yours a giant rat?"

"Gwit is not..." Sterjall began to explain. "The Okrifröa is also with us. She stayed behind, on our ship. The Nu'irg ust Agnarg is far away, someplace else."

"If a war is blowing in with the Thawing breeze, I am glad to see them by our side," Speros said, then he grunted. "*Hurff*, Trommodrolom will remain strong, no matter how big an army attacks. Never will our ramparts be breached. For centuries we've prepared. They will not bring war to us, we will bring war to them!"

"I believe you," Sterjall said, dropping his weight on the sand. "I just... I need to..." he lay down and lost consciousness.

Kulak kneeled next to Sterjall, caressing his pointed ears.

"Does the Canid Lorr need aid?" Speros asked.

"He has had too much in too short a time. What he needs is rest."

Alaia hurried back from the cliffs. "I'm quite certain the sailors saw me. They waved a pharolith back," she said, panting, then looked around in confusion. "Hey, where's Pichi? Where did everyone go?"

CHAPTER TWENTY-ONE

SPEROS OF THE ELAND

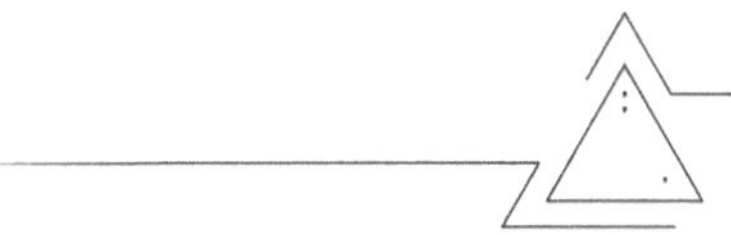

Silverweave picked up the wayfarers stranded at the cove. Admiral Theggo Saurfall had given chase to Fjorna's ship, but the enemy vessel ultimately outpaced them despite not having spread its sails. After a short, frustrating pursuit, Theggo had ordered his frigate to turn back, to investigate the pharolith light he'd seen signaling at the cove.

"It will take us at least a few days to get back to Ngau Tor," Theggo said once Lago finally woke up and joined the others upon the deck. "We need to circle around the entire peninsula." Aio-Kulak and Alaia had caught Theggo up on what had happened while Lago slept.

"How is Nelv?" Lago asked Aio, raising a hand to feel at his scarred cheek. The reopened wounds had dried up but were quite sensitive to any motion.

It was Theggo who answered. "She is stable. My medic is tending after her. Well, sort of. He has been providing instructions so that Aio can tend after her. The Nu'irg won't let anyone else near her."

"And Speros?"

"He is doing what all of us do our first time outside our domes," Aio said, amusement creeping into his voice as he pointed up.

Above them was Speros, leaning precariously over the crow's nest, right beneath the black flag with the silver triskelion. His long snout was stretched into an uncontainable smile.

"His eyes are watching the blue sky," Aio continued, "trying to comprehend the boundless horizon. He will come out of it, sometime."

Ambassador Vor-Vor approached from the stern, holding up his sunrise-colored robes so that the expensive fabrics would not drag upon the deck. "I have dispatched cormorants to our fortresses at the Alommo Sea," he said. "Our fleets will be on the lookout for the Negian ship that sails with no sails. But, given the speed at which the ship moved, I doubt they will be able to intercept it."

"Thank you, Ambassador," Lago said. "Last night, when we saw Daro's ship moving away, I remembered what she called her group. *The Cabal*, I heard them say, when I was shackled in their hull. That flag, the yellow crossbow that looks like an anchor, you must tell your allies to be on the lookout for it."

"I will keep my people informed. Thank you, Lorr Vaari. In a way, I am glad for their presence. The Cabal's, I mean, if that is what they've named themselves. They are weakening the Red Stag's influence, splintering his forces. We may have an easier chance at fighting them separately."

Lago felt a shadow blocking the sunlight. Speros was clumsily descending, uncertain of how to line his split hooves over the ratlines. He jumped down the last six feet and shook himself, making his long dewlap slap around in waves.

"*Hurff!* Too big it all is. How can your eyes adjust to such distances? I try to look at the sky, and there is no detail, nothing for my eyes to fix to, and then I begin to cry."

"My scalp understands you, Speros," Aio sympathized. "There is much more your eyes still need to see, so much more."

"Head strong!" Speros said to Aio. "I don't believe we've met."

"It is me, Kulak, but I am also Aio," Aio said, and then realized Speros had also not yet met Lago. After another awkward reintroduction, Speros looked toward Vor-Vor. He shook his wide ears and cocked his head.

"Is this possible? How did I not see before?" he exclaimed, staring at Vor-Vor's tail. "A descendant of Umar-Vaor!" He had briefly met Vor-Vor the previous night, but in the dark, and with too much else to worry about, he had failed to notice the ambassador's tail. "*Hurff,* our clans will be happy to know Umar-Vaor's aurochs blood still runs strong!"

"Wh-who is Umar-Vaor?" Vor-Vor asked, utterly confused.

Speros looked even more puzzled. "You are not familiar with the son of Bum-Vaor?"

"Nor with the father," the ambassador confessed.

"Bum-Vaor was one of our eight prophets, a Trommofröa of old. He was the one who dared defy the senseless laws of the Acoapóshi. He shared his aurochs blood with the Jaburask tribe. Mighty statues of Bum-Vaor rise on

Bra'uur, on Phala, on Shun-Ji, and on Taerám. Our values, our ideals, all derive from his teachings."

"I am afraid I have not heard his story before," Vor-Vor said, "though the name *Jaburask* sounds eerily similar to that of my race, the Jabrak, or Jabrak-Tsing."

"*Herm-hurff!* You are worthy of our praise then, Vor-Vor of the Jaburask-Tsing!"

"Banook once told me about this," Lago interjected. "He said Bum-Vaor had a child while in his half-form, with his wife, Walu—"

"Head strong! Walu be praised!" Speros excitedly voiced. "Apologies. Continue, Canid Lorr."

"He said their child had a tufted tail like yours, Vor-Vor, but the Acoapóshi had been strict that they did not want any of the Silvfröash to conceive while wearing the Silvesh."

"Tyrants they were!" Speros interjected once more. "They wanted all of us to be the same, to be like *them!*"

"It seems like most Miscam tribes followed their teachings," Lago said, "at least in that regard. Banook said that Walu had to run away and hide their son so that they wouldn't be killed. They both disappeared, never to be seen again."

"*Hurff!* Not so! That is what was told to others, to safeguard Walu and her child. She came under the protection of the Jaburask, who took care of Umar-Vaor, the tuft-tailed prince, high up in the peaks of Mount Alvforg. Bum-Vaor took secret pilgrimages to visit his son and wife. While at Mount Alvforg, he inscribed his teachings in the Trommo Hides, teachings which our eight clans follow to this day."

"So it is true…" Vor-Vor muttered. "We Jabrak-Tsing have plentiful legends about our beginnings, some similar to the ones you tell us, Speros, although the names have been lost to time, or perhaps purposefully disguised. I would very much like to learn more about our progenitors."

"Then I shall teach you all I can about our prophets, our tenets, our clans. We are many, but we are all Tjardur. Some old fools still say *Tjardur Miscam*, but most just say *Tjardur*. I am Speros of the Eland. Some of you have met Ogóre of the Gaur, and Lune of the Water Buffalo. Many more of us there are. We are one family, sharing many kinds."

That evening, Sterjall and Kulak were sitting at the quarterdeck, gazing up at the nearly full Tourmaline face of Sceres. Everything sparkled in pink around them, and though the mid-Winter breeze was sinking into their bones, the flushed color of the moonlight somehow made them feel as if it was not too cold out after all.

Kulak turned to face Sterjall and carefully pulled at his whiskers, parting the fur on his muzzle.

"Careful…" Sterjall said through sharp, gritted teeth.

"The wounds heal well. But like Lummukem says, it will leave big scars." He kissed Sterjall's scabbed muzzle and combed the fur back down. "My scalp thinks you will look fearless, dangerous. The scars will suit you well, as our lives are full of scars, and some we must wear on our skin so that Noss may know we too suffer with them."

"It's not too bad, but it stings when I drink." Sterjall used his long tongue to feel at the inside of his lips, dragging it over the cuts that had sliced all the way through. He sighed, then added, "I'm more concerned about Nelv. How is she?"

"Better today. Nu'irgesh are tough. Her skin is already scabbed over and her broken ribs will mend. She will heal faster once we are on land, closer to more of our kind."

"I just wish… I wish I had done more. Even Nelv took the initiative to go after them. If I had thought things through, maybe I could've killed Fjorna, taken her mask. I could've done something other than just get beaten up."

"You escaped. You survived and kept Agnargsilv safe. That is good enough." He leaned his head on Sterjall's shoulder and held on to his handpaw. "You are not Nelv, she is tougher. We are also strong, but strong together. You were alone."

The floorboards creaked. Through the corner of his eye, Sterjall saw Speros approach. He quickly straightened himself, not sure how the eland might react to seeing him and Kulak in this way. He still felt guilty whenever his self-conscious reflexes got the best of him.

Speros had a thick wool blanket over his body. He exhaled a puff of pink breath into the frigid air. "*Hurff-hemm,* cold is this world. How do you manage to stay alive?"

"It's not too cold tonight," Sterjall said. "And we are far south. You should see what it's like up north this time of year—your dewlap would turn to icicles, then shatter to pieces."

"Would it truly?" the eland asked, tucking himself deeper into his blanket.

"He jests," Kulak said. "But it is colder in the north."

The heavy armor underneath Speros's blanket clinked loudly when he sat next to Kulak.

"We are safe here, Speros," Kulak assured him. "You need not wear armor. It must be cold, uncomfortable."

"Cold it is! But one must always be ready."

Sterjall turned toward him. Though Speros was covered with the blanket, Agnargsilv could see through it. Strangely enough, the image felt fuzzy. He could still see Speros's threads, but there was an odd ripple to them, like a heat haze, though the subtle distortion did not manifest itself around the eland's head or hooves.

"Speros, may I see one of your armor pieces?"

Speros squinted curiously, then detached an arm bracer and handed it over. It was masterfully forged, delicately embossed with the four-horned symbol they had seen displayed at the steel gates of Nannúr.

"Do you see what I'm seeing?" he asked Kulak, holding the bracer over his arm.

"I do… Waves in the threads, as if seeing underwater…"

Sterjall looked back up. "Speros, what is this material?"

"Bra'uur steel, of course! Best steel there is, forged in Laaja Ëovad, with iron from Laaja Kriss and soot from Laaja Trell."

"With soot? Is it quaar then?"

Speros laughed, making his dewlap oscillate. "Nothing that fancy, Canid Lorr! The only quaar armor my eyes have yet seen is the helm of your dark princess."

"Then what does soot have to do with it? How was this made?"

"I'm merely a lowly gate guard, not a blacksmith. You should ask Servant Lune, she'd be delighted to tell you all about it. She works with the smiths at the forge. I believe Chawól, our chief armorer, is the one who crafted this particular piece."

"Lune is a blacksmith?" Sterjall asked.

"As are all the Trommofröash before her, of course!"

"I noticed most of you were wearing plated armor. Were you expecting trouble?"

"Trouble? No trouble. Our gates are strong, our horns are strong, our cities are strong! Why does armor speak trouble to you?"

"I mean… Why wear armor if you aren't going to be fighting?"

"It's what the Tjardur wear. It's tradition. Heavy steel makes the body strong, prepares us for jousting tournaments, for working the fields. We are strong, head strong, *hurff,* our attire must reflect that."

Speros latched his bracer back on, looking brave and mighty. Then he tucked himself to his neck in his blanket, looking more like a shivering child. He leaned back and stared at the moon.

"We heard many tales of Sceres," he said. His breath escaped like a misty sprite, dancing pinkly and vanishing on the wind. "I did not think she would be so round. I thought she would be shaped like a horn."

"It depends on her phases," Sterjall explained. "She's full right now. In a few weeks, she will look like a crescent again."

"Good. I believe Servant Lune will be glad to learn her horn still looks like Sceres, at least sometimes. That was her second given name, *Lune*, like the shape of the lady of six dresses. *Hurm.*"

"Why do you call her *Servant* Lune?" Sterjall asked. "Wouldn't she be Ierun Lune, or at least Hud, or Lurr?"

"*Hurrumf!* That would be disrespectful!" Speros frowned.

"How so?"

"What is more important, more honorable, than being a servant to the people? She is proud of her title, of her calling. She is Servant Lune of the Water Buffalo, and she is a good servant, for she truly cares and treats all equally. I wish I could properly serve my people, like Servant Lune does. But as I said before, I'm just a lowly guard."

"My scalp wonders about something, Speros," Kulak said. "Why does Trommodrolom have a wall of stone next to its wall of vines?"

"The Nudoroth Rampart is only one of the three great ramparts. We have it there for protection, of course."

"Protection from what?"

"*Harhurff,* from whatever may come, when the time for Trommodrolom to open arrives."

"That may be happening soon," Sterjall commented quietly.

"Good it is then that the ramparts were built. They will preserve our ways, they will preserve our mighty kind."

CHAPTER TWENTY-TWO

WAY OF THE TJARDUR

"By the nethervoids, we were so worried about you!" Crysta gave Sterjall a fierce hug. "What happened? Why did you come back with Theggo?"

Silverweave had just docked next to *Fjummomurr*, near the overwater bungalows of Ngau Tor. The wayfarers began to gather at the pier.

Puuja and Pol came running to join the others, then looked around in confusion. "Where Sunu? Where Lummukem?" Puuja asked.

Kulak began to answer, "They had to stay in the dome, to help—"

"No!" Puuja yelled. "Bring them back!"

"It's okay," Crysta told her. "We are going to go see them." She looked to Sterjall. "We are, aren't we?"

"That's the plan. There's much we need to tell you."

Siffo came trotting down the pier, a bit behind the others. He stopped in front of Speros and tried to greet him by rubbing noses, but Speros misunderstood the gesture and returned the greeting by leaning his head forward and bumping his forehead and horns.

They shared an awkward moment of mutual hesitation. Siffo cleared his throat and said, "Welcome to d'beautiful town of Ngau Tor, honored Trommofröa. We did not expect ye t'arrive with our friends, but we're glad t'have ye."

"*Hurff*, Trommofröa I am not, honored Nagrafröa."

Siffo laughed. "Me? Nagrafröa? I'm jis' a simple cap'n."

Speros looked confused. Siffo looked confused.

"Let's all gather in Siffo's quarters," Sterjall interrupted. "We'll explain everything."

They regrouped around Siffo's oval table, where a map of the southwestern Tsing Empire was spread open; the circle of the Ashen Dome served as a cartographic cartouche, displaying the compass rose, legend, scales, and everything except what hid within the dome itself.

"Speros, you've told us we'd be better off entering the dome by sea," Theggo began. "Do you mind showing us where that would be?"

"*Hurff*, I do not! May I draw upon your map?"

Siffo nodded and handed Speros a pencil.

The eland scribbled noncommittally at first. "If this strange arrow points to where the magnium seams search for their lost souls, then our two great bays, the Keldris Troméia and Keldris Tromaag, would be located around here." It was not hard to guess, as he could see the coastline from the New World, and the border of the water matched with his knowledge of the dome's interior. He then indicated the Tjardur's three defensive walls: the Nudoroth Rampart to the southwest, atop which they had hastened from Nannúr to Lawu; the Tsogi Rampart, which ran close to the perimeter from the southeast to the northwest, covering the majority of the dome's area; and the Jels Urosh Rampart, which rose from the center in a somewhat circular shape, wrapped around the four volcanoes he labeled as Laaja Ash, Laaja Ëovad, Laaja Kriss, and Laaja Trell.

"If we are here," he said, tapping the tip of the pencil on Ngau Tor, then drawing a thin line, "then this—*hummmf*—is where I think we should go. The port of Sinsimbo. Into the Jels Urosh Rampart it will take us, directly by water. Not far from Bra'uur we will be. There we will find Servant Lune, hopefully in good health, and the Dragon Lerr."

"Cap'n Siffo, when can we depart?" Sterjall asked.

"Anytime yer whiskers want t'feel d'breeze!"

"Shall I have *Silverweave* follow behind you?" Theggo asked.

"Fleet Admiral," the Tsing ambassador began, "your flagship might be more needed out here, in Tsing waters, in case trouble returns to this peninsula. Would you be willing to hold at this location?"

"A prudent request," Theggo agreed. "As much as I'd like to explore this new world, I will stay behind to support our vessels. But *you* should go with them, Ambassador, as there will be much to discuss with the Tjardur regarding the opening of their dome. They will soon be migrating to your lands."

"That is, if we choose to join your cause," Speros said. "Head strong we are, sometimes too much so. But it will be good to have you, *hurrf,* Vor-Vor of the Jaburask. I believe my people will listen to a descendant of Bum-Vaor and Umar-Vaor."

"I will leave a delegate with you, Admiral," Vor-Vor said, "who will help you handle the dealings with the Tsing. After hearing of your mission in the Nisos Dome, I well know how involved these adventures can get, so I will not expect to return so promptly."

"A good assumption that is," Siffo said, "but we'll be a-doing our best t'get back out in time. Shell I get mine crew ready?"

"Yes, the sooner the better," Sterjall said. "If we could, I'd like to leave before dark."

Siffo nodded. As he left his quarters, his deep voice bellowed, "Grind yer tusks n'stow that tail!"

The vociferous sailors replied, "*Weigh!* Light-ho d'kenzir stone!"

Not long after, the Puqua ship began sailing to the Ashen Dome.

"No, no, like this," Sterjall said to Puuja. He held a quaar conduit in front of him, almost like a sword, and pointed it at the vines.

Puuja took the conduit, her brother watching over her shoulder. "Like this," she said, putting it to her eye to stare through it.

"It's not a spyglass."

"But they are opening," Kulak informed them. "It works just the same."

"Fine, use it however works for you," the wolf said to the girl. "But just make sure there is enough room for the mast to fit, okay? Do you know what a mast is?"

"Stick," she said.

"Close enough."

"I'll stay with her," Crysta said, squatting next to Puuja and scaring Pol away. "You go do what you must." She placed a hand on Puuja's head and said, "That's a beautiful spyglass! Show me how you use it."

Sterjall rolled his eyes. He took the steps up to the quarterdeck, from where he was tasked with making sure the vines did not close upon their rudder. From the forecastle, Kulak opened the path forward. The Puqua uncovered the ship's pharolith sconces and pulled out their oars as *Fjummomurr* slowly made its way into the wall.

Speros lingered at the stern with Sterjall, trying to catch one last glimpse of Sunnokh before returning to the confined immensity of his home. Once the last breath of sunlight was swallowed by the closing vines, he sauntered around the bone-white ship, admiring the patterns of shadows cast by the pharoliths. He reached the forecastle and stood next to Kulak.

"Mindreldrolom is no more, then?" Speros asked as he approached the caracal.

"No. Not like it once was." Kulak smiled politely, but a nostalgic light reflected in his eyes. "My scalp knows not what it looks like today, for I have not returned to my home since Mother asked our dome to open."

"*Hurff*. I fear you will find hardship in Trommodrolom. It won't be easy to convince our eight clans to surrender the safety of the dome's walls."

"My scalp is still confused as to how you are eight clans, not just one."

"One tribe, eight clans. One for each of the primordial kinds. The Spiral-Horned Clan is my own, that of kudus, nyalas, balboks, and many others. But there are also the Four-Horned, like the sacred tetracerans, as well as the Pelorovis, Aurochs, Buffalo, Gaur, Yak, and Wisent clans. *Hurmmmff-horr,* eight we are, one we are."

Siffo paced nearby, overhearing the conversation. He had been using a push pole to collect samples of the inside of the dome's wall for Hefra, who had persuaded several Puqua sailors, as well as Alaia, to help in her endeavors.

Siffo retrieved a sample of tangled fibers; it dripped white sap onto the bone-white deck of his ship, making him cringe. He extended the sample toward Hefra, who quickly stuffed it into a glass vial and pointed with a well-aimed pharolith at a new location to probe.

"I'm much curious," Siffo projected his voice toward Speros, "how d'ye manage t'take yer full half-forms in such short a time? D'Puqua have been attempting d'same since Nagradrolom sealed us into our fjordesh. N'look at me—despite mine beautiful warthog face, mine four great tusks, n'mine hoofed fingertips, most uf mine body is still plain-skinned."

"*Hurff,* your four tusks look mighty, and holy. Four is the sacred number, so proud you should be, Warthog Lorr. Hard have us bovids worked since Trommodrolom closed, like suidkind must've. The Trommo Hides demanded of us, *You must find all aspects of your true selves,* and so we did."

"But how? There hasn't been enough generations since them domes aclosed. We suids got about d'same number uf species, but only a handful uf new piglets are born fur each generation. Mayhap mour if d'Nagrafröa is male n'takes after Probo, turning a bit promiscuous. Yet that hasn't been enough fur us t'change as much as ye have."

Hefra was now listening intently, taking notes in her head.

Speros seemed perplexed by what Siffo was telling him. "Your Nagrafröa may have only a handful of *hurff*... piglets. But what of the rest of your clans? Do they not make use of Nagrasilv's blessing?"

Now Kulak's attention was also caught.

"Make use? What d'ye mean? Unly d'Nagrafröa wears Nagrasilv."

Speros shook his head and dewlap while snorting, utterly baffled. "*Hurrmm-hauff,* no, my Warthog Lorr, the Silvesh were made to be of use to the tribes. The Silvfröash provide a service, the Silvesh facilitate it." Though he seemed careful not to divulge some sensitive subjects, Speros explained that Trommo-silv was indeed assigned to one Trommofröa at a time, but the Trommofröa would lend it to couples looking to breed, particularly those from clans that still had too many plain-skinned traits.

"Every Nossday this service is offered, *hurff,* and servants like Lune are there to mentor us, and to help us bovids overcome the pain of wearing the mask, and the greater pain of having to part with it after. That is how we bring the future generations closer to their true half-forms."

Siffo seemed incredulous. "Them half-forms can take weeks, sometimes months t'be found by d'wielders uf d'masks. How can them a-find it in unly one Nossday?"

"We all find out who we are when we reach four times the sacred age," Speros said, "as by then we have explored all of our desires, and breathed in the—" He stopped himself, realizing he had said too much. Changing his tone, he continued, "I am Speros of the Eland, *hurff,* and though I have never worn Trommosilv, if I were given the honor, I would have children as Speros of the Anoa. *Haurrrf-hurff!* That is my second calling, and I know it like I know each curve of my horns. Our forms may look complete, but not all Tjardur are entirely in their half-forms yet. Some families are more plain-skinned than others, particularly among the tetracerans, who are rare and sacred, who teach us the values of altruism and holiness."

"Wait, wait, wait a moment," Hefra said, unable to hold her tongue any longer. "I hear what you are saying, mooncake, but if you are out there lending the mask to the first passionate couple that knocks on your door on any given Nossday, wouldn't the mask be, say, unavailable for a long period of time after that, if the person wearing it was a woman?" She squished a sample of fibers in her wooden press, then continued, "If she got pregnant while wearing it, she couldn't just change back, could she? Not with a different species' fetus inside."

"You are smart, Plain-skins Lurr, for that is the case. Most times, the mask is lent to the men, as if our women did wear it, they could lose their children when they returned to their first forms. Unless both their forms were of the same clan, such as a kudu whose second calling was that of a nyala. Oftentimes, our second callings are from different clans than our first, so this does not happen frequently."

Hefra considered further implications. "And what if your half-forms or your regular forms—which I guess are also half-forms, but you know—do not match with those of your partners? Does that disqualify you from this honor?"

"Not at all," Speros said. "We have servants for that reason, of every sex, of every clan. When necessary, they lend their seed, or in rarer cases their wombs. And hybrids across clans are possible, although very rare, and often infertile."

"Fascinating," Hefra said. "That makes me wonder… Since you are all half-formed, like the Trommofröa… can you also mindspeak with one another?"

"Hey, I asked Nalaníri that exact question once!" Alaia interjected, handing a sample of dome fibers to Hefra. "She laughed at me like I was a fool."

"Not a foolish question at all, Dark Princess," Speros said, "not one hair. It is not the half-form that allows mindspeech, but the Silvesh, which restore something within their wielders that was lost long ago, acting as a bridge with their clades. The Trommofröa can mindspeak to the feral bovids, thanks to Trommosilv, but we cannot. *Hurff!*"

"There is a tale in the Codex of Absent Parables," Ambassador Vor-Vor said from nearby, "that speaks of the time humans lost their voice. Or rather, hominids, as our ancestors were called. If and when we make it to Hashan, I suggest you procure a translated copy, as it might be of interest to you, even if purely academic."

"I would like to read such stories, *hurff!*" Speros said. "From stories we learn truths. They teach us the right paths and show us how to be true to ourselves."

"Well, I like ye, Speros," Siffo said. "Ye n'yer people seem t'have it all figured out much better than we have. I often wunder why d'Acoapóshi were so damn strict. I hope suidkind n'bovidkind get t'meet in greater numbers someday. Ye would love our fjordesh n'our Tricolored Mountain, uf that I'm certain."

"Our Four Blessings will welcome your kind, Siffo of the Warthog, and any who seek to be as authentic as yourselves, for authenticity is one of our virtues, and from it derives one of our core tenets."

THE FOUR BLESSINGS

Fjummomurr made its way into the Keldris Troméia before the first glimmers of dawn. The crew could not see very far due to the darkness, but also due to the mists that blanketed the great bay. They cut through the low layer of vapors, following the coastline northeast. The thick fog covered the bottoms of the shores and most of the trees that rose beyond them. The tall grayness of the Nudoroth Rampart rose above the mist and snaked away, losing itself on the soft horizon like an enormous eel floating in clouds.

Speros warned them not to follow the wall too closely, as it was built near a rocky shoreline. He directed Siffo on their course, confident of the waters he asked him to sail through, as he was fond of fishing in these areas.

The domed sky turned green and highly textured with the trunk's first light. Each of the supporting columns cast enormous curtains of shadow that extended all the way to the dome's perimeter and crawled up to the brightening sky. The warmth of the arudinn spread and soon scared the mists away, luring in the fishing knarrs of the Tjardur. The long and shallow vessels had stemposts that split into four horn-like shapes: sometimes pointing to the sky, sometimes curving downward, and at other times spiraling gracefully in every direction. The fisherfolk rowed their vessels toward the newcomers, entranced by the beauty and mystery of the white ship with black sails. But the knarrs were much too slow compared to *Fjummomurr*, which sailed past them and left the fisherfolk wondering if the apparition had been real after all, or merely a foggy daydream.

"Sinsimbo's harbor is up ahead!" Speros told them. "Sail your mighty ship through the Horns of Valor. *Hurrrf!*"

The bay funneled two opposing walls toward a single passage, framed by two curved horns twice as tall as the monumental ramparts that held them. The horns were carved of rock and covered in elaborate steel plates streaked with pelican droppings. They sparkled dully under the pastel-whites of the vines above.

Despite Speros's assurances, *Fjummomurr* was not simply granted passage between the Horns of Valor. A dozen warships blocked its path, alerted by the resounding calls of latifrons horns; their sails were wide and rectangular, striped in the colors of the Tjardur: white, gray, black, and red.

"Head strong!" Speros called as *Fjummomurr* slowed to a halt. "Head strong! Speros of the Eland requests safe passage into Sinsimbo! Servant Lune's saviors have returned, those who alerted us to the betrayal, who helped Ogóre of the Gaur and myself protect our Trommofröa!"

The recent events had made the Tjardur more skeptical and vigilant. A bulky bison questioned them from the safety of her warship. Once she confirmed Speros's identity, she boarded *Fjummomurr*, greeting the eland with a quick strike of her voluminous head to his slender horns.

"Head strong, Speros of the Eland," she said with a voice as thick as the woolly tangle of her fur. "I am Admiral Brannoa of the Wisent. We heard of you, Speros. Ogóre of the Gaur sent heralds to inform Sinsimbo and Güer, guessing you would make your return through either of the ports. All rampart gates are also on the lookout for you." Admiral Brannoa stood alert. Her matted fur poked out from between plates of her bronze-streaked armor. Her longer chin fur was braided, adorned with metal rings of all colors, like the ones she wore around her short, spiky horns.

"Head strong, Brannoa of the Wisent," Speros said. "*Hurff,* we must know, we must ask—how is Servant Lune faring? We left her in dire condition. We hope she reached Bra'uur in time."

"*Grommph,* despite the severity of her wounds, her body is well. It is her soul that needs healing. The loss of Diduk of the Yak has made her heart shrivel. She has requested you meet her at the Taur Citadel, where she waits with the Dragon Lerr."

"Could you take us there, Brannoa?" Sterjall asked, then self-consciously backtracked. "Sorry, my name is Sterjall, I am—"

"Head strong, Sterjall," Brannoa interrupted as she leaned down to bump heads with the wolf. It was a gesture much like that of the Laatu, although more frontal and much harsher.

"Head… strong," Sterjall continued, rubbing his impacted forehead. "We would like to speak with Servant Lune. There is much she needs to be informed about."

"*Groumm,* I can take you to her. But I believe your scale-skinned friend has been telling her much already. Rumors I heard, that they want our dome to open. Is this true?"

"It is. That is what Noss asked of us, and the reason we came this way."

"Many will not be pleased, not now that the acrid stench of war has wafted in through the vine walls. But I will take you and your friends, Sterjall of the Wolf. Have your skeletal vessel follow my own, *grommph!*"

The port of Sinsimbo was extravagant, displaying the full majesty of the Tjardur. Their architecture was grand and opulent, constructed of serpentine green marble mixed with black calcite marble, and always embellished with wrought steel ornaments.

The wayfarers left *Fjummomurr* and its crew at the port, though Siffo decided to join them this time around. They were taken to a train of open-top carriages, all attached to one another with flexible joints and pulled by a single enormous pelorovis: a bovid species long-extinct outside of the Ashen Dome, which here had grown large as mammoths, with horns as wide as their bodies were long. The giant looked like he should be entirely off balance lifting such massive, curved horns, yet he seemed unbothered and traversed the streets without bumping his horns into the framing colonnades.

Brannoa was sharing a carriage with Sterjall, Kulak, Alaia, and Vor-Vor. Behind them were Crysta, Siffo, Pol, Puuja—with Gwit—and Hefra, accompanied by Speros. The third carriage carried Blu, who looked a bit bored, and Nelv, who had mostly healed, though she still limped a bit and hissed more frequently than usual.

The city of Sinsimbo was vibrant and full of life, teeming with half-bovids of mixed clans—although most belonged to the Wisent Clan, that of Admiral Brannoa. Pelorovis-pulled trains were not uncommon in the city, and the passage of the newcomers went mostly unnoticed.

Though Sinsimbo was dense and built up like the center of a sprawling city, it ended abruptly. The train exited onto a country road, crossing wide-open fields where herds upon herds of feral bovids grazed.

"Our herds are strong!" Brannoa proudly voiced.

"Strong!" Speros concurred from the next carriage.

"Thanks to our companions, our herds listen to us," the admiral continued. "They help us, the same way we help them. And so we are many clans, many species, but always one."

Up ahead, an enormous statue stood in their path.

"We approach Thyra," Brannoa informed them, "the sacred city where Bum-Vaor once lived. Behold! The Colossus of Thyra greets you all!"

The statue of the old prophet Bum-Vaor grew as they drew nearer, towering over them, tall as the rampart walls they had left behind. The likeness was that of a man in his half-form of an aurochs—a primordial bull—with legs spread open in a defensive stance, holding a war hammer in one hand, and in the other a rune-covered scroll that unfolded to the ground. The colossus was carved out of black marble naturally streaked with golden filaments, and wore its own suit of Bra'uur steel armor, forged at an unimaginable size.

"Those are the Trommo Hides our prophet is holding," Brannoa told them. "Forged of steel plates."

"Steel?" Alaia gaped at the statue. "It flows so smoothly, like leather."

"*Grommph!*" Brannoa grunted affirmatively. "The Trommo Hides are the keystone that holds our civilization together. Although this one here is made of Bra'uur steel, the real ones are made of the hides of Bum-Vaor's own parents. Underground the original hides are preserved, in the Vaults of Thyra. There, the histories of our ancestors will live on for epochs untold."

Brannoa regarded the Tsing ambassador and said, "I hope your hides too are inscribed with long and meaningful stories one day, descendant of Umar-Vaor, after the tetraceran spirit comes to take you past the veil."

Vor-Vor smiled awkwardly.

The pelorovis-pulled train passed underneath the statue, right between the legs of black-and-gold marble. They all looked up, staring at the enormous testicles that dangled precariously above them.

"Let's hope those don't break off," Alaia said. "It would be an embarrassing way to die."

"Worry not, for his balls are strong!" Brannoa said. "Like our heads, like our horns."

"Head strong!" Speros called from the back.

The city of Thyra was built on the slopes of one of the volcanoes, but stopped short of the snowcapped peak, which was spewing a thick black cloud over them. Somehow, the smoke rose straight up, the ashes rarely tarnishing the city.

"Laaja Ëovad rises above your hornless heads," Brannoa told them. "Ëovad is one of our Four Blessings. We are always thankful for its presence."

"Could you tell us more about the Four Blessings?" Sterjall asked.

"Certainly!" the bison said with a bit too much enthusiasm. "The four volcanoes are our blessings, as they—"

"Hey Brannoa!" Hefra howled from the next carriage. "Speak up, muffin, we want to hear this too."

"*Grommph!* I will, stout Lurr!" Brannoa projected her voice. "The four volcanoes are our blessings, as they gift our lands with all we need to be head strong Tjardur, to remain mighty, proud, authentic. The one above our heads, our fire mountain, is the site of our Volcanic Forge, where Bra'uur steel is forged. *Grommph,* mightiest steel of all!" The bison slammed her bracers against her small horns, making them spark against the steel caps.

Brannoa pointed toward a volcano to the northeast. That mountain was also snowcapped and fuming, with the areas not covered in snow or vegetation taking a rust-veined gray color. "That beauty is Laaja Kriss, our iron mountain, where we mine the ore for our precious steel. Not normal iron, no it is not, but iron that burns hotter in our furnaces and smelts like a dream. Endless ores can be found at Laaja Kriss's core—though venture not too deep, *grommph,* or its heated heart will burn you to ashes."

As they continued down the road, they entered a grass-covered valley between the Four Blessings. Brannoa pointed to the next volcano, straight east of them: a dark peak with a skirt of dense greens.

"There rises Laaja Trell, our black mountain, where we mine our soot. We remove the graphite, break it down, and purify it. Deeper than the Bra'uur Catacombs themselves do our endless dark tunnels meander, and just as endless is the amount of soot we can mine from it."

"What is a catacombs?" Puuja loudly asked from the other carriage. She had been trying to guess at the meaning using Okrisilv's aid, but it was a slippery concept.

"The catacombs are where we keep all the skulls of our ancestors," Brannoa explained, "and where I hope my own skull will one day reside. Filled to the brim with skulls the tunnels are, with horns of all kinds and sizes. Most dreary place. Most beautiful in its gruesomeness."

Pol and Puuja smiled at each other, savoring the prospect of seeing such a place.

The pelorovis turned a corner around a sharp cliff, slowly revealing the fourth volcano, which partially hid behind the trunk. This fuming mountain was lower than the rest, though still of admirable height. Its top was flat and fervently steamy, as if it had just been sliced with a hot knife. It billowed white instead of black.

"And the last of the blessings," the bison admiral said, "is Laaja Ash, our white mountain, where the sacred Pink Caldera is located. Those are our Four Blessings, the core of Trommodrolom, our pride and glory. *Grommph!*"

"Wait," Alaia said, "what's special about Laaja Ash? What is the Pink Caldera?"

Brannoa looked to the carriage behind them. Speros made eye contact and shook his head. Brannoa faced Alaia again and said, "Some Tjardur things are only for the Tjardur to know. Perhaps Servant Lune will tell you more, but it is not my place to speak further, as I am not a servant of the same kind."

CHAPTER TWENTY-FOUR

THE EIGHT TENETS

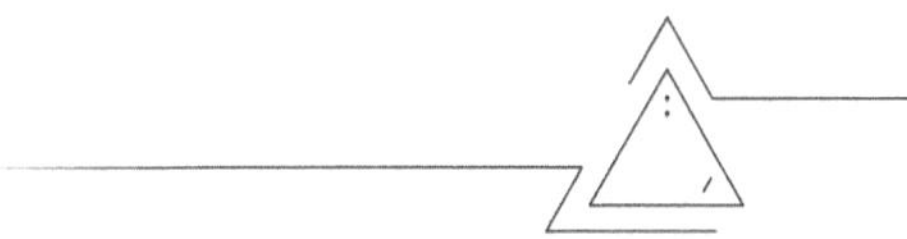

The capital city of Bra'uur was located on the steep highlands between Laaja Ëovad and Laaja Ash. The tireless pelorovis pulled their carriages along a wide road that followed a cliff's edge, giving the passengers an expansive view toward the southwest, where the Klad Pumme shimmered with yellow-colored waters and the Jels Urosh Rampart drew an internal, lower horizon that split the dome into an inner circle.

The Ashen Dome's trunk grew from the core of the capital, which, like Sinsimbo, was once again a marvel of green and black marbles, with opulent statues pledging allegiance to nearly every street corner.

As the carriage stopped, Brannoa bid the others farewell and told them they could find her in Sinsimbo, where she would make sure the Puqua sailors were well cared for.

The wayfarers hopped off the carriages and followed Speros up the marble steps of the Taur Citadel. The wide rectangular ziggurat was terraced in compound, receding levels, with the top one holding the entrance to Ommo ust Trommo. Even when seen from the bottom of the citadel, the temple's entrance was imposing, opening beneath four enormous steel horns, all pointed up, with green flames burning at their tips.

Speros led them to the bottom level of the citadel, and they soon entered a lush, terraced garden where they spotted Sunu-Lummukem walking alongside Pichi.

"Sunu!" Puuja screamed. She and Pol ran to embrace the shaman.

Servant Lune was shuffling slowly ahead of Sunu, with the aid of a chrome-handled cane. The Trommofröa was draped in spotless robes of white and green embroidered in silver filigrees. Her single crescent horn was ornamented with twisting metal chains that dangled down to connect to the septum ring on her wide buffalo nose. She wore many silver earrings on her diamond-shaped ears, and a gorget of steel that covered her jugular notch. The colors she was dressed in—lime-green and sparkling silver—blended seamlessly with Trommosilv's aura.

Servant Lune was clearly in pain, but just as clearly wanted to force her body to move and heal. Her thick and muscular form was bandaged in many places, and though her energy seemed low, she received them with an energetic smile. "Head strong. *Khumm.* Sterjall, Kulak, Alaia. It brings my heart joy to see you once more." Her voice was mellow. Throaty, yet sensual. She stopped in front of Sterjall, and the wolf gazed up at her; Lune seemed even taller and burlier than on the night they had seen her bleeding upon the sandy beach.

She looks beautiful, he thought, *like a broken goddess.*

"Who are these kind visitors from beyond who accompany you?" the buffalo asked.

After a round of introductions, Lune walked her guests through the garden. "Sunu-Lummukem has told me all about your adventures," she said. "They told me of the peril we all face, and the reasons for your visit. *Khurmm…* I must again thank you for coming to my aid. Sad is my heart, as I lost my dear husband to our now common enemies."

"We are sorry we couldn't get to you sooner," Sterjall said. "We should've—"

Lune put a hoofed hand on Sterjall's shoulder and simply shook her head. "My fault this was. Mine alone is the burden to bear. I should have listened to Pamúnn… He told me he felt uneasy about leaving the dome, that we should call for a council before rushing into decisions. *Khumm…* Right, he was. I almost lost it all, for myself, for my people." Her ears jerked, jingling her earrings as she flicked a fly away from her green eyes. "I have given thought to the troubles we face and called a meeting with the eight clan leaders. They have agreed to meet in Bra'uur the day after tomorrow, at the Loth Amphitheater. In the meantime, I would like to learn more from all of you, and I would like to answer questions you may have about us."

As they strode through the aromatic gardens, they told Lune of themselves and their goals. It was a pleasant walk, punctuated by flickering flocks of birds and the occasional pine marten scurrying around the trunks of old trees.

Nelv had been limping next to Kulak in the form of a lioness. She suddenly stopped, turned, and rumbled a deep grunt. Kulak followed her gaze. Half-hidden under a wisteria's canopy strode a most colorful, exuberantly coated creature.

"Nu'irg ust Trommo…" Kulak whispered.

Pamúnn, in his nyala primal form, was a beauty to behold. The Nu'irg's brown body was striped by twelve bands of black and white. His orange socks were as luminously vibrant as the orange fur on his forehead. Black were his neck and head, adorned by subtly spiraling horns tipped in translucent orange. The white dots between his eyes were complemented by two more at either cheek, like pockets of the last snows of Thawing that stubbornly refused to melt. He wore a spiked-up mane that rose over his spine like serrated, snow-capped sierras.

The gallant Nu'irg silently stepped forward, dipped his head to salute Nelv and Gwit, then stood at a safe distance, observing the newcomers with regal curiosity and open distrust.

Sterjall tipped his head, entranced by the beauty of the bovid antelope. His lime-green aura shimmered distantly, cautiously.

"The cow is green," Puuja said.

"He's not a cow," Sterjall began to say, "he is a—"

"Pamúnn welcomes you," Servant Lune interjected, "and thanks you."

"He is astoundingly elegant," Crysta observed.

"That he is, *khumm*. Forgive his guardedness, he might eventually choose to come closer. For centuries he has kept watch on our bovids, making sure their habitats are in the best conditions. Healthy is our dome, but our ramparts create impediments for certain species, so, well guided they need to be. Pamúnn is the best guide of all."

A long-horned man with a bullish face hurried down the steps of the ziggurat. "Head strong!" he called to the group.

Sterjall looked to the man, and then back to Pamúnn, but the elusive Nu'irg was already gone.

The man approached them. He was wearing white and green robes like Lune, but with the strange addition of steel pauldrons and a belt from which steel tassets dangled. He gave Lune a peck on the mouth and introduced himself as Cort of the Pelorovis.

"The accommodations for the new guests are ready," he said, bowing while making sure his impractically wide horns did not bump any of those present. "But feel not the need to hurry."

Cort said Pichi and Blu should follow him, as he had special rooms and meals reserved for the smilodons. He then regarded all the newcomers, and with tender earnestness said, "Thank you. My dear wife would have been lost if it hadn't been for your courage." He bowed once more and took his leave.

Before Sterjall could ask an improper question, Sunu answered. "Servant Lune has six husbands and nine wives. We have met most of them, though not yet all. You will see them around the Taur Citadel. They are all as kind and respectful as Cort."

"If you will follow me," Servant Lune said, "I will show you around the citadel before the arudinn go to rest. And rest is something my wounded body will soon need as well."

They approached the colonnade that bordered the garden. On the lush grass, covered in tendrils of moss, was a full-sized pelorovis skull. The enormous cranium rested atop a trapdoor fastened with a rusty lock.

"What's down in—" Sterjall started to ask, but Lune's answer interrupted him.

"One of the many entrances to the Bra'uur Catacombs," she said. "A sacred place of morbid beauty. We will not be venturing there." She led them past the enormous skull and leisurely walked into a gallery that burrowed deeper into the terraced building. Frescoes and friezes on the gallery's walls illustrated legends and heroes of the Tjardur, mostly dealing with the great Bum-Vaor, who had been clearly embellished into myth. The long hallway was illuminated by candles that burned green, wafting a white smoke with a pleasant, sweet smell.

"Sunu-Lummukem asked me about our history," Servant Lune said, "and told me you would be equally curious to learn about it. That is why I bring you through these galleries."

She moved slowly, aided by her cane, giving them time to appreciate the art painted on the walls and sculpted on the vaulted ceiling. She told them that the artwork recounted the history of the Tjardur during the Unification and Equilibrium epochs, times during which the eighteen masks were created by the Acoapóshi and gifted to the chosen tribes. It was then that the expansion and rebalancing of the animal clades took place. A parallel gallery dealt with the Segregation Epoch, from the discovery of the comet by Jiu Zezi until the closing of Trommodrolom. There were other galleries, which showcased legends of the times before the advent of the Miscam tribes, during the Expansion and Revelation epochs, as well as galleries that covered the succession of Trommosilv's wielders through the nearly fifteen centuries since the dome's closing.

They promenaded by a series of panels that depicted scenes of Bum-Vaor's predecessors fighting against invaders from a kingdom Lune called the Rashi, who'd come from the sea to overtake the lands of the Tjardur and the Bikhéne.

"The Rashi were too numerous," she explained. "The Acoapóshi, who lived in the sierras farther inland, knew the Rashi would come for them sooner or later. We were not on good terms with the Acoapóshi, as our cultures differed too greatly in ways that were difficult to reconcile. They were not a culture of war, they knew not how to defend themselves from invaders of that ilk. But we were ready for their attacks, and we held strong, head strong, *khumm*."

They stopped next to a painting of Trommosilv being passed to a knight in shining armor by a one-eyed king wearing purple robes.

"The Acoapóshi offered us a truce. If we helped them fight the invading Rashi hordes, and helped them build bulwarks in their homeland of Eba, they would gift us Trommosilv and welcome us into their quickly growing Miscam tribes. They showed us how Trommosilv could be of help to us, not just in war, but in finding the equilibrium needed in our broken lands. We accepted."

Lune caressed the long bridge of her nose, as if feeling the mask's presence, although the mask was not there, not in that way. "It took decades, but we helped the Acoapóshi raise powerful walls around their sacred Ommo ust Enwenn, around their fertile lands, and all the while helped fight the invaders. When at last the Rashi were defeated, we joined the Acoapóshi as one of the Miscam tribes and learned about the true mission they hoped to accomplish."

"We noticed you hold an enmity toward the Acoapóshi," Sterjall said. Although it wasn't a question, Lune answered.

"Their goal was an honorable one, and one we also believed in, as we too worshipped Noss. But their methods were not always righteous. They were a coercive tribe. Noss wanted the Acoapóshi to pick cultures different from their own to form the Miscam tribes, so that in diversity there would be strength. The Acoapóshi saw that as a means to assimilate disparate cultures and turn others closer to their own image. They valued some differences, but many they fervently rejected and sought to quash."

The next several panels showed a figure they were now familiar with: that of a half-man, half-aurochs.

"Over thousands of years, we slowly lost ourselves. More and more like the Acoapóshi each generation turned, forgetting our ancient rites, leaving behind parts of our culture that were once intrinsic to our ways of being. But Bum-Vaor changed that, *khumm*. He was the first Trommofröa who rebelled against the Acoapóshi and praised our differences as our only path toward authenticity, one of our most cherished virtues."

Lune stopped by a concave niche with an arched top that held a fresco with an image nearly identical to that of the Colossus of Thyra, of Bum-Vaor holding his war hammer in one hand, and the Trommo Hides draping from the other. Hovering above Bum-Vaor's head was an octagonal halo of lime-green color, shimmering with silver highlights. Unlike the monumental statue, which emphasized physical might and power, this painting gave Bum-Vaor a weightless, prophetic, nearly god-like appearance. The old prophet stood atop the serrated peak of Mount Alvforg, bathed in golden light. The rendition of the sun was peculiar, as it resembled the halo over Bum-Vaor's head, in the sense that Sunnokh was merely the outline of a yellow-colored circle, with the interior being a blue as dark as the twilight indigo used to paint the sky. Sterjall assumed it was a literal interpretation of what a yellow circle shining in a blue sky would mean to an artist who had never seen the sky outside of their sequestering dome.

Lune regarded Ambassador Vor-Vor, lowering a hoofed hand upon his shoulder. "You must be proud of your heritage, descendant of Umar-Vaor. I am glad Bum-Vaor's seed held strong in the world beyond."

The next painting portrayed Bum-Vaor standing proudly atop the Jels Urosh Rampart, lifting his heavy war hammer to the dark-blue sky.

"The Jels Urosh Rampart was built long before Bum-Vaor's time, but it was not until he came to power that the rampart's gates were fully closed, forbidding any Acoapóshi from entering our sacred lands. With that decree in place, our culture was free to develop without their influence once more, at least within the confines of our Four Blessings."

"I'm guessing the Acoapóshi were not very happy with that," Alaia said.

"Not in the least, *khumph,* but they were also still dependent on our might, for these lands were heavily contested. Up until the final days in which Trommodrolom closed, we considered ourselves Tjardur Miscam. But after that point, once we had a chance to fully return to our values, we began to see ourselves as properly Tjardur once more, no longer keeping the Miscam title among our eight clans."

Siffo leaned in close and squinted his eyes, trying to read the minuscule Miscamish runes in the scroll Bum-Vaor held—runes that must've been painted with a brush no wider than a hair. "I'm much a-curious, dear Lune," he said, "what are them inscriptions upon d'hides? What are them teachings Ieron Bum-Vaor professed to them peoples?"

"Ieren titles we do not use among bovidkind," Servant Lune said. "Simple are the eight tenets, though into further hides they were later expanded, by

Bum-Vaor and his disciples. With one of our eight sacred virtues each tenet deals. Follow me this way, so I may show you."

Servant Lune took a turn into a different gallery. She led them to a decagonal rotunda in which two opposing walls served as the entrances, while the remaining eight walls held depictions of the prophets of their eight clans, each embodying one of the virtues inscribed in the Trommo Hides. Each of the prophets had a green-and-silver octagonal halo hovering over their heads.

Lune stood straight, seeming yet taller than before. Her green eyes towered nearly seven feet up, with her single horn reaching even higher. Sterjall was afraid her horn might bump into the candled chandelier above them.

"This will be our last stop before I take my leave for the evening," Lune said, "as my body grows weary, *khumm*. But more I will teach you in the coming days."

She pointed her cane toward the panel directly left of the entrance they'd taken, one that depicted a half-form of a tetracerus, a deer-like bovid named after the four small pointy horns atop their heads. Yet this tetracerus had no horns, for she was a woman. Her slender head glowed faintly due to the light of her green halo. The woman was naked on a snowy field, wrapping her cloak around a dying woman who would take her last breath of life feeling warmth. The prophet held the woman's baby boy down by her udders, sharing her sweet milk with him.

"The first of our eight tenets speaks of the virtue of altruism, which the Four-Horned Clan have adopted as their core virtue," Servant Lune said. "Bum-Vaor wrote that we should strive to be of service to others, not because of what we may gain in return, but because being of service is the worthiest goal unto itself."

Crysta squatted next to the panel and noticed Miscamish runes inscribed at the bottom. "That's almost word for word what the panel says," she observed, slowly reading. "It's written in Common, not in Miscamish, but it's using Miscamish runes."

"You speak truth, *khumm*," Lune said. "The Tjardur rejected the Miscamish tongue, returning to our Common roots. Bum-Vaor's Trommo Hides were inscribed in the same manner. A great sin, in the minds of the Acoapóshi. They wanted the hides burned, but the hides were—and still are—safely kept within our rampart walls, in the vaults of the city of Thyra."

Lune stepped toward the next panel, which showed a prophet who reminded Sterjall of Hefferen, the yak who had sent the oxpecker heralds to notify the other gates of their arrival. The yak in this mural was naked, though their fur was thicker than any clothing Sterjall could imagine, keeping their sex obscured. They had their arms spread wide in a welcoming gesture, hands cupping seeds that fed squirrels and birds. Small creatures of all sorts crawled into their matted fur, some to make nests, some to keep warm, some to hide from a circling fox on the hunt. A flock of minute bushtits swarmed by the yak's halo and curved horns. Their head was bleeding, their eyes were closed. Perched on their cheeks and neck were dozens of oxpeckers, drinking their blood and pecking at the gashes opening in their skin. Despite the yak's painful state, they held a smile on their face, seemingly grateful for all the creatures who took comfort from their fur, from their blood.

"*Khummmm.* Our second virtue, that of empathy, is embodied by the Yak Clan. The tenet asks us to strive to feel as others feel, to understand circumstances from differing points of view, so that we may be one and be many. We must be grateful for not just our wellbeing, but for the wellbeing of others."

"As the Silvesh teach us," Lummukem said. "And soot, before it."

"Indeed. And although many do not wish to acknowledge it, it was the Acoapóshi who brought this influence to our culture. We owe much to them, despite our disagreements."

The half-form in the next panel was that of a gaur, like Ogóre, but of an even stockier build, rippling with so many muscles that the anatomy became grotesque. He was wearing only a loincloth, and to his curved horns were attached chains, which he was using to pull a plow ten times his own size. Though he pulled his burden over a barren wasteland, the path he carved behind him was verdant and fertile.

"The Gaur Clan represents the virtue of might. Their kind are mighty indeed, composed of not just gaurs, but also bantengs, koupreys, and gayals. Their tenet tells us to strive to take forms as mighty as the bovids of old, to protect our culture, to defend those weaker than us, to build for our future, to uphold our oaths to Noss."

"Ye seem t'be doing well in that regard," Siffo remarked, eyeing Lune's bulging neck and arm muscles. She placidly smiled back at the captain.

The fourth and last panel on that side of the decagonal rotunda illustrated the half-form of an anoa, a species very similar to that of Lune, though with horns that pointed upward instead of curving into crescents. The prophet, of indistinct sex or gender, was bathing in pink waters, with pink mists lifting from their wet, thick shoulders. They seemed to be meditating, with one hand up by their face, the other down, holding their crotch. The ghostly plume of vapors exuding from their wide nostrils twirled above their head, and under the green light of their halo took the form of eight figures, their bodies tangled in an orgy of steam, penetrating body parts, soundless orgasms, and pink-green lust.

"Our fourth virtue is that of cleanliness, manifested in the Buffalo Clan—the clan of anoas, tamaraws, and different species of buffalo, like myself. *Khummm.*" Servant Lune bowed to the pink-bathed figure. "Our citadel is clean, our temples are clean, but Bum-Vaor also wrote that we must strive to keep a clear mind and a clean body. He urged us to look for our true selves within the pink mists."

"What are the pink mists?" Alaia asked. "Admiral Brannoa mentioned something about the Pink Caldera to us, but she would say no more about it."

"*Khummph.* With the other clans I may have to discuss this topic, as it is not one I'm free to speak of, not to those who are not of our own tribe. I apologize."

Alaia nodded her disappointment. Lune directed them to the other side of the rotunda. The first panel on this side depicted an aurochs half-form. The primordial bull was wearing his halo as a blindfold while holding up two bleeding, torn horns, one in each outstretched hand. In front of him was a supplicant young aurochs, bleeding profusely from where his horns had been severed. The boy was covering his ashamed eyes. Behind the two stood a naked tetraceran girl, also covering her face, but doing so with a different kind of shame.

"The fifth tenet deals with the virtue of justice," Lune said. "Bum-Vaor told us to strive for fairness. To punish those who deserve it, but to do so with compassion. The Aurochs Clan, which also includes zebus and the taurines—what the Acoapóshi used to refer to as *cattle*—represent the virtue of justice."

"Is the aurochs in this painting Bum-Vaor once more?" Sterjall asked, by now easily recognizing the figure, even if the prophet was blindfolded by his halo in this depiction.

"*Khummm,* indeed, Canid Lorr. Bum-Vaor he is. And the aurochs boy being punished is none other than Umar-Vaor himself."

"His own son?" Ambassador Vor-Vor gasped.

"Justice must be dealt impartially, even when it pains us to do so. And once dealt, debts can be considered repaid, and so Umar-Vaor was absolved of his sins."

"Are all the prophets in these paintings based on once-living Tjardur leaders?" Vor-Vor asked.

"They are indeed legendary Trommofröash of old. Rumah, Au'óro, Drurum, Naj'al'alás, Bum-Vaor. And also Gweléshi, Ejokk, and Seitho-Dovár, who I will get to next."

She moved on to the following panel, which was dark except for a silver-green halo near the center. The dim image was hard to see under the faint light. As Sterjall moved closer to inspect the image, the room seemed to brighten. He turned to look behind him and squinted at the green candles on the chandelier. *Were those flames smaller a moment ago?* he wondered, but Lune spoke before he could ask any questions.

"Cast your eyes upon this panel, which represents our sixth virtue, that of perseverance, which is embodied by the Pelorovis Clan."

In the panel was rendered a stormy scene upon a mountaintop. The summit was cracked in half, and stuck between the two halves was the half-form of a pelorovis with horns so wide that they formed a bridge between the two sides. She dangled while her clothes were torn to pieces by the hailstorm, yet she held a peaceful expression upon her drenched face. A group of pilgrims crouched protectively as they crossed the chasm, using the prophet's horns as a bridge.

"Like the Four-Horned Clan, the Pelorovis Clan have only one species in their midst. Gweléshi of the Pelorovis is who you see in this image. Of perseverance, Bum-Vaor told us, *Strive to be steadfast in your goals and the goals of the tribe. Work not for yourself, but for the generations to come. Persist with dedication, with mindfulness.* And so we follow his teaching."

Only two more panels remained. Next to the pelorovis was a painting of a steppe wisent—a bovid with horns more akin to thick, majestic scythes. The half-form was a pensive male sitting cross-legged, watching his own reflection in a silvery pond. He had one hoofed finger sunken in the crystalline water, but there were no waves rippling from it, as if he had either placed the finger down impossibly slowly or had waited a long time after submerging it. His halo was only visible in the reflection, in which the steppe wisent was nothing but a yellowed-out skeleton.

"The Wisent Clan represents the virtue of prescience, which Ejokk of the Steppe Wisent here embodies," Servant Lune said. "The seventh tenet says that we should strive to have the foresight to anticipate the consequences of our own actions. It asks us to be cautious, to be ready for those outcomes hidden from our sight. Bum-Vaor told us to trust our intuition, but with skepticism, for we must trust the truth above all else."

"This virtue I very much like," Hefra said, "although I don't understand what is going on in the painting."

"That is for the viewer to decide," Lune demurred.

They had reached the last panel, which was next to the entrance they had come in through. The scene depicted a nyala, the same species as Pamúnn, the Nu'irg ust Trommo. It was a female half-form, however, wearing a male nyala skull over her head, clad in its spiraling horns. Her fur was decorated with paints of bright whites and deep blacks, mimicking the more colorful patterns of a male nyala. Her curvaceous body was fully exposed, displaying her mixture of bovid udders as well as human-like breasts. She was the epitome of sensual beauty, posing seductively with one hand on the flushed udders by her belly, and another spreading her labia.

Sterjall stared at the male-ornamented nyala and felt the image looked familiar somehow, but could not figure out why. He found himself suddenly aroused and tried to clear the thoughts from his mind. *She is nothing like what I normally find appealing*, he told himself. *Why does her body make me feel this way?*

His wandering thoughts were interrupted by Lune's monologue.

"This luscious figure is Seitho-Dovár of the Nyala. She represents the Spiral-Horned Clan, one of beautiful bovid antelopes like the kudus, elands, bushbucks, bongos, and sitatungas. She and all of her kind embody the virtue of authenticity. The eighth tenet asks us to strive to explore all aspects of our true selves, to be closer to who we truly are, and not to the person others expect us to be."

"She's truly a beauty," Siffo said. "A goddess, perfection personified. Thank ye, Lune, fur a-showing us yer eight virtues, fur telling us uf yer eight tenets."

"*Khummm.* Most welcome you are, Siffo of the Warthog."

Speros had remained quiet the entire time, feeling a bit out of place on such sacred grounds. He spoke now, a bit shyly. "*Hurff,* this depiction of her I had never had the pleasure of seeing. The paintings of Seitho-Dovár at Nannúr and Sinsimbo do not do justice to her true beauty. *Hurfff-hmmm.*"

"A truth you speak," Lune agreed. "Though not even this painting does her justice—nothing but her own presence in our dreams can attain her perfection. Will you stay with us as well, Speros of the Eland? We hope you do, for you are as honorable a guest as all those you travel with."

Speros bowed, surprised. "*Arrf-hurff,* umm, yes, I'd be honored," he awkwardly mumbled.

Lune looked around the room, leaning on her cane. "My body tires, and our dormitories are not too far away. Tomorrow you may explore the Taur Citadel at your leisure, where there is much more you can discover. Sunu-Lummukem can show you where I may be found. I asked them to watch over me, and their medicine and knowledge has kept me well these last few days."

Sunu nodded, offered a freckled arm to hold Servant Lune's, and helped her walk toward the dormitories.

"Follow us now," Lune said. "Let us wash ourselves, then sleep. Sleep and dream of our virtues. But be wary, for once you have laid your eyes upon her, Seitho-Dovár likes to find her way into your dreams. *Khummm...* Be wary, but accept her, as there will be nothing for you but to do her bidding. You will find her irresistible."

CHAPTER TWENTY-FIVE

CONJURER OF FLAMES

The wayfarers' bags were waiting for them on a long table lining the hallway that opened to the showers and dormitories. Lune insisted they wash themselves before entering the rooms, and that they also wash themselves every morning.

"We must uphold the virtue of cleanliness, that of prophet Naj'al'alás of the Mountain Anoa," she said, making sure they understood this was not a request, but a requirement.

After their showers and a communal dinner, they each picked up their bags, chose their partners and rooms, and settled in for the night.

Sunu stepped into their room, followed by Pol and Puuja. Despite the opulence of the Taur Citadel, the dormitories were humble: simple rooms with no luxuries other than two or three beds, a small side table, and a green-flamed candle burning in a glass lamp. In a corner of each room was a washbasin filled with water, next to a stack of fresh towels of pristine-white cotton hemmed in green. Olo had been waiting there, perching patiently at the rim of the washbasin, which had a pair of downy blue feathers floating in it. He greeted the twins with an *eihnk-eihnk!*

As soon as their door closed, Puuja took off Okrisilv and handed it to Pol, who put it on immediately.

Pol was still upset that Sunu had not let them join the first hurried excursion into the Ashen Dome, and even more upset that Sunu had stayed to care for Servant Lune instead of returning with the others. He had not said a word since, not even when the three of them had reunited earlier in the day. "Where is Gwit?" the boy finally asked.

"Gwit is with the other Nu'irgesh," Sunu answered. They picked up their Silv, which had been sitting on the table in their dormitory, and put it on. As Lummukem they sat on one bed and wrapped their tail around their crossed legs. The azure-hooded jay hurried to roost on their scaled shoulder. The twins sat on the opposite bed, which was small, but would suffice for their smaller bodies.

"Why you leave us?" Pol shyly asked, eyes on the cold marble floor.

"You are too young to face certain situations. Sometimes we cannot know in advance what dangers we will encounter, so we must be cautious."

"But we fight good, that you said, that we are," Puuja retorted, taking her brother's side. "We practicing even alone, every day."

Lummukem regarded them with pride.

Both the twins had been improving their use of Common with astounding speed, and their handling of their quarterstaffs was improving as well. Now that they were no longer aboard *Fjummomurr*, they'd be able to practice with the brime-and-steel capped quarterstaffs Lummukem had gifted them, free to scrape them on the ground and shoot fiery sparks—although they would first need to inquire with Lune regarding safe locations where they could do so.

"Your skills are admirable. Every day, more you learn," Lummukem said. "But you still do not fully control the power of Okrisilv. And only one of you can wear it at a time, while the other is left at a disadvantage."

Pol shook his head, picking up the meanings of Lummukem's words with much more ease now that he was wearing the mask. "Not disadvantage to have each other, we can protect Puuja and Pol."

The dragon blinked in acknowledgement, then reached for their bone halberd and leaned it on their crossed legs. They pricked a finger to the halberd's tip so they could feed blood to the bloodmoss they had planted in its carved, bladed end.

"Can I give as well?" Puuja inquired.

"No, the blood must be our own. This way, the moss will be attuned to our threads. This way, we will someday sense the halberd's presence as clearly as that of our tail. But Hud Ulésse warned us that the process might take years, so we will feed the moss our blood until the time the moss decides we are worthy of their gift." They sucked on their finger, tucked the halberd under the bed, then placed a pillow between their back and the cold marble wall. "Have your scalps given more consideration to the nature of your half-forms?"

"Of course… Every day," Puuja said. "But there are many. Can we be all?"

"No, you cannot. Only one form you will take. Well, two, in your case, unless you both choose the same form."

"We think a new okri every time," Pol said. "Tomorrow we think different. We do not know how to choose."

"That is well. There is no hurry. Whichever forms you choose, you could never be uglier than Lummukem, so you must not fear." The dragon opened their pink maw and hissed at them.

Pol wanted to remain upset, but he also wanted to not be upset any longer. He pretended to be frightened and hid behind Puuja, then poked his head out and hissed back.

Siffo looked around his empty, modest room. He was not used to such minimalism and found it a bit distasteful. So did Vor-Vor, who, as an important dignitary, was accustomed to all manner of luxuries. Speros, on the other hand, seemed earnestly ecstatic about the humble accommodations.

"Well, at least it's clean, that's fur certain," Siffo half-complained. "Never seen marble shine this much."

Siffo and Speros sat on beds opposite each other, while Vor-Vor took the one in the far corner. The ambassador immediately dropped onto his bed and passed out; the exhaustion caused by the time shift within the dome was too much to bear for the old eunuch.

Siffo unpacked his few belongings on a side table while Speros dropped his longbow and quiver to the ground, removed his armor, and took off the quilted garments he wore below them. He made himself nakedly comfortable, without a hint of embarrassment.

While averting his eyes, Siffo said, "Much grateful we are to Servant Lune, but she could've given us a room with a window. It's d'least she could've done."

"*Hurff,* these are servant rooms," Speros said. "Greatest of privileges this is. Same as the room of Servant Lune herself."

"She a-sleeps in an empty box like this one? Them should offer her better perks fur her job."

"Her job is to serve, and serve she does. It is most honorable to be of service."

"Be uf service? Mine tusks would prefer t'be *serviced*, n'I can picture jis' by whom. Oh, what a beauty is Seitho-Dovár uf d'Nyala. I think I might've fallen in love a-seeing that last painting. All she's a-missing is a tusk or two, then she'd be perfect."

"Perfect she already is, *hurff*." Speros lay on the bed, propping himself up on one elbow, exposing himself to Siffo without noticing the warthog's discomfort. He sighed, and with perhaps a hint of self-consciousness added, "But as much as Seitho-Dovár is gorgeous, Speros of the Eland thinks that plain-skinned women are more attractive."

"Plain-skinned?" Siffo snorted twice. "No, mine friend, ye must be mistaken. Plain-skinned women are plain. What's in them to love? No tusks, no fur, no tails, n'unly what, two teats at most? Not nearly enough, I say."

Speros caressed his dewlap, which draped onto the mattress like a meaty, long-furred scarf. He then turned around in bed and began to picture exactly what Siffo had described.

Siffo could hear the motions of the eland pleasuring himself and felt utterly ill-at-ease. He extinguished the green flame so that he would not have to witness whatever Speros was doing, then snorted as he lay on his bed still clothed. He covered himself with the thin blanket and tried to ignore the grunts he heard near him.

When Siffo woke up the next morning, his cock was painfully hard. There was an arousing image in his mind, but it was quickly fading. He tried to recall who he had been dreaming of, and though he could not remember, he knew for certain that the presence in his dream had not been Seitho-Dovár.

Crysta, Hefra, and Alaia picked a room that was luxurious in comparison to the others, for it had not one, but two side tables.

"Please, put that thing on the ground," Crysta said, rolling her eyes. Hefra had placed her monstrous backpack on one of the tables and was unloading its contents onto her bed, readying to take notes before succumbing to sleep.

Alaia sat by the other table. She took a whiff of the white smoke wafting from the green-flamed candle and said, "They smell really nice, but they look a bit too eerie." She blew out the candle and replaced it with a pharolith lamp. On one of its metallic petals, she placed her Pliwe figurine, letting the goddess cast a long shadow on the wall.

"The wax must be made of sap, if it burns green," she said, placing the glass chimney back over the extinguished candle. "How do they make it burn so cleanly? And without the usual stench?"

"It's bad luck to burn green flames indoors," Crysta said.

Alaia cocked an eyebrow. "Oh, are you a Free Tribeswoman now? That is what Jiara used to say."

"It's just… creepy looking. And those kenzir stones too, their light is so cold."

"Love, you are getting a bit picky here," Hefra mumbled, holding a quill in her lips while uncapping her inkwell. She then produced a bundle of brown, tangled hairs.

"What is that specimen from?" Crysta asked.

"Fur from our admiral friend, Brannoa."

"When did you even—"

"When she helped me down from the carriage. Don't worry, sweet plum, she didn't notice. Now, the sample I really wish to acquire will be a tough one. That lovely nyala, what's his name, Pamúnn? I'd like to get just a few hairs from that Nu'irg. What a treasure that would be."

"Please… please don't," Crysta pleaded.

"I'll fetch you some!" Alaia said, thrilled by the challenge. "But it'll cost you."

"Name your price, peach."

"I want to help you with your research," she replied without a moment of hesitation.

Hefra was stunned. "You what?"

Even Alaia looked stunned by her own words. She regained her composure and found a way to reply. "I… I like your books. I like what you do, especially anything to do with birds. An Oldrin like myself would never get an opportunity to work on something official, to have her name published."

"That's… Nubbins, that's not up to me. There are no Oldrin scholars. The institutes won't allow it."

"Perhaps, but you have a lot of influence. I'm sorry, I didn't mean to—I was just joking, anyway." Alaia seemed suddenly mortified. She turned around and pretended to be fixing her bed.

While Alaia was focused on becoming invisible, Crysta shot a judgmental glare at Hefra.

Hefra responded with a cringe and an uncomfortable shrug.

Crysta rose a threatening finger.

Hefra rubbed her temples and sighed.

"Well, Pamúnn's fur would be a start," Hefra half-mumbled. "But if you want to help me with true research, there's a lot more you'd need to learn, sweet gal."

"What… what do you mean?" Alaia asked, turning around.

"I mean, you can't be a proper naturalist without knowing how to properly gather, store, and classify specimens. And how are your note-taking skills?"

Alaia beamed from ear to ear.

Hefra put on her serious face. "And I'm not looking for a machine," she said. "If I am to take an apprentice under my wing, I need someone with initiative, someone who can discover stuff on her own."

Alaia pointedly nodded. "Understood."

"But don't get too excited, gal. First, get me some of that nyala's fur."

"Fancy," Sterjall observed dryly as he and Kulak entered their little room.

"What sort of hospitality is this?" Kulak complained. "They should have the best rooms for guests, not a box with a candle. And green flames, at that. Very disrespectful."

"They smell good though, unlike the green torches you had at Mindreldrolom."

They threw their bags on one bed, then stripped off their clothing and hopped naked onto the other one. Kulak immediately pushed himself to kiss Sterjall.

"Watch it… your rough tongue, take it easy…"

"Sorry. It has been too long."

"I know… but I'm just. So tired…"

Sterjall placed a soft kiss on Kulak's cheek, then threw his head onto the pillow, staring up at the polished, green marble ceiling. The candle was perfectly reflected above them while their own bodies over the white sheets looked like shadows frozen within the cold stone.

"It's the change from daytime to night," Sterjall said apologetically. "It always tires me out every time we enter or exit a dome."

"My scalp thinks it is more than that," Kulak said. "Your body is still broken. It has not had enough time to heal."

Sterjall absently played with Kulak's small balls, almost like he was twiddling his thumbs.

"It is okay," Kulak said. "You can rest. You let me do the work, and just relax."

"You don't have to—" but Kulak's fingers and mouth were already exploring Sterjall's sheath. The wolf lost himself in the moment. He let his erection grow and fully relaxed his body, closing his eyes. He soon began snoring, without having had any release.

Kulak propped himself up and stared at the tired, beaten-up wolf, feeling somewhat guilty. He draped the sheet over both of them and fell asleep with an arm over his lover's chest.

"My scalp remembers you saying you were too tired for it," Kulak joked the next morning. "What a mess you have made."

"I'm so sorry, I had a… It was just a wet dream."

Sterjall tried to wipe the drying cum from his sheath and thighs, and from Kulak's short tail. He wasn't sure if someone would come to change the sheets for them, but he already felt embarrassed by the prospect.

Kulak shapeshifted into Aio, wetted a towel in the washbasin, and used it to wipe his smooth body. Sterjall followed suit as Lago.

"And such a large amount," Aio said with a sparkling grin. "Impressive."

At least he's laughing, Lago thought, blushing awkwardly while cleaning himself.

"And you are still hard." Aio poked at Lago's cock. "You have to tell me who you dreamed of. Was it me? Or someone else?"

Lago pulled up his trousers. "It was… I… I can't remember anymore," he said unconvincingly. "It was one of those dreams that vanish when you wake up."

"Too bad. My scalp guesses it was Banook, because I have never seen you unload so much with me." The prince mentioned Banook without any hint of malice—he was simply curious, and a bit excited himself. He laughed at his own joke and kissed Lago's scarred lips.

Lago smiled and changed the subject. "How late do you think it is?"

"Impossible to tell here, with no windows."

"Let's go find out. I'd like to shower, and it'd be 'required' we do so anyway."

"Why is Lune so obsessed with that?"

"I guess because it was written in the hides."

"Let us not upset the old hides then. We go to the bathing chambers."

After cleaning themselves and drying off, the two of them put on their masks and went exploring. They had gone to bed soon after the dome went dark; being deep Winter, the nights were still as long as the Ophidian, so they had risen before the arudinn brought forth the new day. The wax of the candles along the hallways had dripped puddles into the bowls below, but the flames were still burning bright and green.

The citadel was eerily quiet.

"I think they are all still asleep," Sterjall whispered.

"It is fine," Kulak replied. "Lune said we are free to look around."

They walked past a gallery they had seen the previous evening and followed the hallway until they reached a cloister with an open garth. It reminded Sterjall of the enclosure at the Mesa Monastery, except that this one was rectangular instead of hexagonal, and instead of a garden full of plants, the garth was carpeted by short grass. At its center stretched a long marble table, topped with countless delicacies that waited for their hungry stomachs.

It was dark in the garth, with the only light being that of the dimly blue arudinn against the rectangular patch of sky, but they only needed their noses to know what awaited at that table. They both salivated, stepping onto the grass.

Sterjall saw a shadow moving across the table from them, placing down more savory and sweet treats. Though the shadow was dim, he recognized the form, as it had only one horn curving over it.

"Good morning, Servant Lune," Sterjall said.

"*Khummm.* Head strong, Sterjall of the Wolf and Kulak of the Caracal," the one-horned shadow replied with a throaty and sensual voice that seemed lower-pitched than they remembered. "Mind me not, as I am merely preparing your breakfast, which will be ready promptly."

"Shouldn't you be resting? We can—"

"No need for help. I thank you for your kindness, but I am a servant. It is my honor to serve, it is my calling."

The shadowed form placed one last plate down and then lit four candles on a candelabra. The green light clearly revealed the servant, who looked somewhat like Lune, but not exactly.

At that moment, Sterjall realized that the bovid mask was resting on the table, and that the figure setting up the table did not have the lime-green glow of Trommosilv. The buffalo in front of them was not a water buffalo, but a savannah buffalo. The servant's single horn was curved more prominently, growing more to the side rather than upward, fusing into a continuous shield over the rounder, thicker skull. The buffalo's fur was black as soot, unlike Lune's graphite grays.

But something else seemed different to Sterjall, something about the proportions, the posture, the voice. "Lune?" he asked, then swallowed.

Kulak held on to Sterjall's arm. "That is not… She is not…"

"*Khumm.* It is I," the thick voice said. "But my name is not Servant Lune at this moment, but Servant Rud."

"Are you a… Your voice, am I mistaken or—" Sterjall mumbled, and then he understood. "You are not a—"

"I am a man, in this form," the buffalo affirmed, "if that is what bewilders you. As Lune, I am a woman. As Rud, a man."

Servant Rud picked Trommosilv up. The mask was wider and more powerful-looking than most Silvesh, shimmering in a filigree of dark upon dark. Two ears extended sideways from it, and two curved horns rose from its crown, although not as prominently as Rud's single horn. The buffalo slowly brought Trommosilv to his face.

Sterjall had always thought that the masks had been crafted to fit human faces, but now he began to question that assumption. The Silvesh were hollow, after all, and had to reshape their internal structure when placed upon a human face so that they could sit comfortably on human foreheads and noses. Now that he saw the bovid mask settle upon a bovid visage, it seemed much more in place, as if it truly belonged there.

For a moment, Servant Rud had two horns on one side of his head, and one horn on the other. He shapeshifted slowly, letting the horns on the right blend into a single cloud of refractive smoke, while the horn on the left, which belonged to Trommosilv alone, slowly vanished. The proportions of the savannah buffalo changed slightly, replaced by those of a water buffalo. Rud's yellow eyes turned translucent; once they re-coalesced, they had returned to green. Lune's familiar face materialized.

"If this form makes you more comfortable," the softer voice said, "then I do not mind being Lune."

"It's not… I wasn't uncomfortable," the wolf said. "I was just… surprised."

"My scalp was, is, also very surprised," Kulak admitted.

"*Khumm.* Why did my two forms surprise you?" Servant Lune asked. "Does your friend Sunu-Lummukem not have two forms which are one?"

"They do," Sterjall said, "but they are both man and woman at the same time. How… I didn't know the Silvesh could do this."

"It is not very common. I know of two other Trommofröash who were soulshifters, though both were female-born and took male half-forms. One of them lived only two generations ago. The other lived before the times of Bum-

Vaor, when such changes were seen as improper, and so Trommosilv was taken from him, from her, and a new Trommofröa was chosen."

"But I… I don't understand. I thought the masks only changed one's species. Did your… you know, your whole anatomy—"

"It did, *khumph*. My entire body changed. Male and female genitalia are more similar to one another than a man and a buffalo are. It is not a big change to make, relatively speaking."

Servant Lune pointed at the four candles that burned between them. With a flick of her finger, the flames began to move, dancing as if caught by a playful breeze, stretching upward.

Sterjall and Kulak were confounded, unsure of what trickery of light or wind they were witnessing. The four flames grew larger, taller than the candelabra itself. They slowly wove together and reshaped, taking the form of a penis and testicles, glowing green on the outside, brighter yellow and cyan toward the inside.

Am I really seeing this? Sterjall wondered. *What is happening? How can—*

Lune twirled her hoofed fingers as if directing the flame, and the flame obeyed, slowly shifting positions in the air. The fiery testicles rose and opened like a flower, merging with the sheathed penis. For a moment, the conjured images took an intersex form, but soon they reshaped into a clitoris and the supple folds of labia.

Sterjall craned his neck left and right, seeing through the dimensional form of the sculpted flame. Even the ovaries and other internal structures were visible. The white smoke seemed to form a bubble around the flaming illustration, giving it diffused edges.

Lune closed her fingers into a fist, and the green image settled back into four small flames, sputtering a bit more excitedly than before. The white smoke dissipated.

"What just happened?" Kulak asked, and Sterjall was glad he did, as knowing he hadn't been the only one witnessing the magic made him feel a bit more sane.

"I was merely illustrating," Lune said. "Weaving the pathways for you to see."

"Weaving what?" Sterjall asked.

"The pathways, Canid Lorr, *khummmph*. Cheap conjurer's tricks, nothing else."

"My scalp does not understand," Kulak admitted. "Was that… magic?"

Lune exhaled a soft chuckle. "Magic? Nonsense." Then she took heed of their expressions and understood that they really were clueless young men. "You really do not know how to weave the pathways?" she asked, tenderly cocking her head. Sensing no forthcoming reply, she added, "I will explain to you." She picked up the candelabra and brought it closer between the three of them. "Look at these flames and tell me what you see."

"Only green flames," Sterjall said.

"But look at my threads behind them," she added. "Not with your eyes, but with Agnargsilv's and Mindrelsilv's eyes."

"Mindrelsilv sees it," Kulak said. "The threads past the flames, past the wax, they shimmer. They are distorted, like Speros's body was behind his armor."

"They are!" Sterjall said, noticing the subtle effect. "What does that mean?"

Lune smiled. "Speros's armor was forged with Bra'uur steel. Did he tell you how our steel is made?"

"No, he said he isn't a blacksmith, but that you are," Sterjall answered.

Lune caressed Sterjall's whiskers, careful not to touch the four parallel scabs, and said, "These candles are made from munnji fat. We not only eat the munnji cakes, but we make wax from the fats, which are long-lasting and have pleasant smells."

"What does munnji have to do with steel? With smoke magic and—"

"It is not magic, Canid Lorr, it is simple manipulation, like the kind the Acoapóshi performed to create the very mask you wear. *Khumm,* yet they aimed to keep that a secret. But we, the Tjardur, know their secret. Well, partially."

"Now you *have* to tell us," Sterjall said excitedly. "Can you teach us? What is the secret?"

Footsteps.

"Smells so good!" an approaching voice called.

Crysta, Alaia, and Hefra walked into the garth. Trommodrolom's trunk was just beginning to light up now, casting a soft, directional shadow on one side of the cloister.

"And I will tell you," Lune said to the couple, "but our other guests are awake, and I have not yet finished preparing breakfast for you all. If you will excuse me, I need to boil water for tea."

Lune left them.

"Alaia! You won't believe this!" Sterjall said, running to her with his tail wagging behind him. Alaia was already stuffing her face with pastries.

"It's Lune, she's like… She's also a buffalo in her other form, but she—I mean he—she's also a he. Balls and everything. And he can make the candles, the flames I mean, dance and take forms like as if drawing with fire, like smoke magic, she's—"

"Is he alright?" Alaia asked Kulak, not even listening anymore. "Is there something funny in these pastries?"

VOLCANIC FORGE

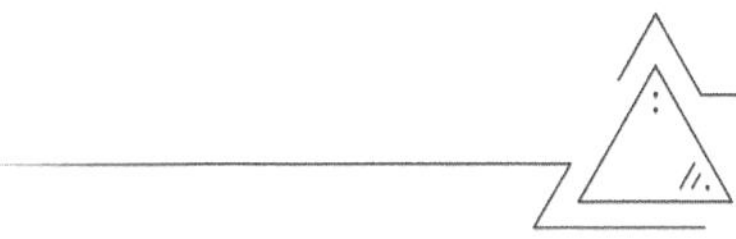

Sterjall and Kulak did their best to explain what they had learned from Servant Lune—and Servant Rud—but they did a poor job of it. By the time all the others had joined them at the table, they had needed to repeat the entire story, a bit more concisely this time, yet still mangled by blabbering incoherence.

"I'm not quite following," Crysta said. "Maybe you two didn't get enough sleep?"

Lune returned with four kinds of fresh-steeped tea and additional delicacies that she placed on the marble table.

"Lune, my sweet peach," Hefra said, "could you explain what these two imbeciles are trying to tell us? They seem a bit… well, a bit unwell."

Lune smiled pleasantly. She sat with them—though she did not partake in the feast—and showed them her other form, as Rud. Then she demonstrated with the candelabra, making the flames dance once more, this time breaking them apart into the shape of a four-horned bovid skull, like the symbol on the gates of Nannúr. The four flames licked the air, seeping tendrils of white smoke. Lune focused, holding her breath and squinting at the smoke, making each of the four tendrils knot themselves into smaller patterns, forming triangular glyphs of smoke over the flaming horns. She then exhaled loudly, letting the green flames return to normal.

Hefra had been torn between staying put to observe and running to get paper to take notes. She decided to stay and stare.

"You have to explain more about this fire… smoke thing," Sterjall said. "And what does it have to do with steel?"

"*Khumm.* I would prefer to show you in person, instead of simply telling you. There is no better excuse to show you the Volcanic Forge. I am still weak, mind you, so I will not be doing the smithing, but I can manage the explaining."

"Please, our scalps would love to learn more," Kulak said.

Ogóre of the Gaur, dressed in her thick gold-rimmed armor, met them inside the Taur Citadel. She introduced herself to those she had not yet met, thanked Sterjall, Kulak, and Alaia for so promptly returning, and ushered them down the steps, where two linked carriages waited for them at the base of the ziggurat. These carriages were not being pulled by a pelorovis, but by an even larger bovid: a longhorn bison, with fur thicker than that of a steppe mammoth. The giant pulled the carriages through the city of Bra'uur, toward Laaja Ëovad, the volcano not too far to the northwest.

"I'm so curious," Sterjall said. "Can't you tell us more now?"

Lune shook her head. "Patience is not one of our eight virtues, *khummm,* but a virtue it is."

Lummukem leaned in. "We are happy to learn the Silvesh can change one to a sex they feel more comfortable with," they said to Lune. "At one point, we would have wished to take advantage of this. At one point, we were dissatisfied with ourselves, thinking that being a man, or being a woman, was bound by only two choices. But we are glad to know ourselves better. We are both, in both forms, because that way we are most true to ourselves, to an aspect of ourselves we were once afraid of."

"Seitho-Dovár would be proud of you, Lummukem of the Dragon," Servant Lune said. "Authenticity above all. Truthfulness begins within one's own soul. The Silvesh know this, and will only allow a wielder to take their half-form if they know themselves and accept themselves as they are."

Pol and Puuja listened intently to her words.

"When I found my other self," Lune continued, "I understood I was also a woman. I am still a man when I am Rud, but I am a woman as Lune, and I am happier that way, being two and being one." She looked toward Sterjall and Kulak. "You are two as well, Lago-Sterjall, and Aio-Kulak, even if both of your half-forms are male."

"What I'd like t'know," Siffo said from the other linked carriage, "mour than them Silvesh or flame tricks, is how ye made them pastries n'cheeses so delicious. Mine good friend Nalaníri needs to a-try them sometime. Them were utter perfection."

"Thank you, Siffo of the Warthog," Servant Lune said, projecting her voice. "They are made with buffalo milk. My own." She put a hand to her belly, where her udders rested beneath her robes. "It is my honor to be of service."

Siffo nodded his four tusks politely and tried to avoid overthinking the matter.

After a winding climb up the side of the volcano, they followed a road framed by obsidian columns. The pillars were sharp, like blackened teeth, and pointed the way straight into the mountain. Carved there was an archway so vast that two longhorn bison could easily enter abreast, with room enough to spare for their wide horns.

"Welcome to the Volcanic Forge, *khumm*," Lune said, pointing to the top of the enormous arch, where the four-horned Tjardur sigil was carved. Among the four runes of the sigil, the one that resembled a flickering flame was most prominent, illuminated from within.

They entered a short, dark tunnel with an alluring glow at the far end. Once past the dark vault, they found themselves in an enormous chamber dug into the very heart of the mountain, illuminated by flowing rivers of tightly controlled magma. A waterfall of molten rock rumbled right at the center, draining into a pit deep inside Laaja Ëovad's bowels.

Sweat-streaked bovids worked enormous crucibles, where they smelted iron ores and alloyed them with other elements. The sounds of slamming, shearing, bubbling, and hammering permeated everything. Molten metal spilled freely from the heavy machinery, filling molds for the simplest implements such as nails, hinges, and doorknobs, to enormous hulls that would be used to fortify warships, or angular plates that would be used to strengthen their rampart walls.

They exited their carriages. Aided by her cane, Lune slowly led them beside an open trench that flowed with fresh magma. The heat nearly singed Sterjall's fur; he had to keep away from it and could not even directly look at the glowing liquid. He was surprised, however, by how well-ventilated the space was.

"Cold air from the snowy peaks is pumped downward," Ogóre informed them, as they were all struck by a sudden cold wind. "It freshens our lungs and cools our horns. *Grommph.* For thousands of years this forge has been running, for thousands more the mountain has served us."

As she led them deeper into the forge, Lune picked up a piece of iron ore from a cart and passed it around. "The iron from Laaja Kriss is exceptional," she said. "Something in its composition makes it burn hotter when smelted.

This makes the steel more durable, it purifies more cleanly, and makes it much more malleable when still hot. But that is not all there is to Bra'uur steel, that is not the secret I wish to share with you."

The magma channel split in two, and Lune followed the leftward trail once more, directing them to the armory. Smaller crucibles were being put to use in this space, as well as more commonplace instruments like anvils and mallets. The walls of the armory displayed suits of armor, shields, axes, war hammers, swords, and other instruments of battle.

"All you see in this room is crafted with Bra'uur steel," Lune said. She picked up a bovid-shaped helm and placed it atop an anvil. "It is the strongest steel of all. The perfect alloy of iron and carbon, a flawless matrix. It does not buckle, it does not dent."

Lune looked to Ogóre. "Would you be so kind?" she asked the gaur, nodding toward the helm.

Ogóre picked up a war hammer from the wall and swung it down fiercely. Her back muscles rippled like an earthquake as the hammer impacted the helm, making the Bra'uur steel spark and clang beneath her might.

Servant Lune picked up the helm. "Like I said, it does not buckle, it does not—"

"There's a dent in it," Alaia pointed out.

Lune inspected the helm, then shot a displeased look at Ogóre, who offered a shrug in return.

"*Khumm,* maybe it *can* dent, but that is Ogóre's fault, not that of the blacksmiths. Either way, it is the strongest steel there is." She dropped the lightly dented helm and walked to a shelf where hundreds of flasks were piled up, all filled with a black powder. She picked one up, removed the cap, and lifted the container for all to see.

"These are all filled with soot?" Ambassador Vor-Vor guessed, who had remained quiet until that moment. On those shelves, his mind's eye was not seeing mere flasks of black dust, but of gold, gemstones, of treasures beyond imagining, of wealth defying measure.

"They are," Lune answered, picking up a large pinch between her hoofed fingertips and spilling it onto the ground in a gesture that the Tsing ambassador thought of as wasteful. "We need plenty for our alloys, as I will soon show you, but we don't store much of it in here. Pay attention now, especially those of you wearing the Silvesh. What I am about to reveal is one of the secrets the Acoapóshi wanted to keep from us. The core of this concept we discovered before the domes closed, but we did not know how to use that knowledge.

We experimented here for centuries, in the safety of our forge, until we learned how to control this power, *khumm*."

Lune focused her attention on the flask, squinting at it as she had to the green flame earlier that morning. A shimmer formed above the flask, as if a thin gas was escaping and refracting the air, like a spiderweb in a heat haze. Those wearing the Silvesh also saw that the threads that normally spread chaotically over the soot were more organized, arranging themselves into parallel filaments.

"Did you see it?" Lune asked, losing her focus, making the effect cease.

"Yes," Puuja was the first to answer. "We liked green fire more." She distractedly looked around the forge for something more interesting to play with. Pol followed her.

"It looked like a thin curtain of smoke?" Alaia asked uncertainly. "Kind of?"

"We saw threads taking ordered forms," Lummukem said.

"Is that… Are you moving the particles of soot with your mind?" Sterjall asked.

"Not exactly," Lune answered, "but you have begun to comprehend the idea, somewhat. Do you find what you see hard to believe, Sterjall of the Wolf?"

"Well, it's the first time I've seen anything like it."

"But you have done the same yourself many times before, *khumm*, if the stories you've told me are true."

"I'm confused."

Lune gestured toward Ogóre again while putting on a leather apron. Ogóre fetched a metal ingot mold, as well as a small crucible filled with molten iron. She placed the mold atop an anvil and carefully inched the crucible to it.

Puuja and Pol rushed to see the demonstration, hoping something would spill, burn, or turn exciting in some way.

At the same time as Ogóre carefully poured the liquid iron into the mold, Lune tossed a cloud of soot onto the white-hot metal. "Observe it carefully," she said, focusing her attention on the falling dust.

The Silvfröash saw the particles of soot slowly drifting within the liquid that was to become a solid. Without any stirring or physical intervention, the particles aligned into long, parallel filaments. The structure was not perfect; many of the filaments still seemed broken or slightly misaligned, but overall they arranged themselves into a cohesive, ordered form.

"Mind you," Lune said apologetically, "we would not be mixing soot and iron in this manner, this is only to demonstrate. We'd place them both in a clay crucible, then sink them into blast furnaces to allow the soot to migrate evenly into the iron, before continuing with the process of alignment. We'd pound the metal, hammering it and folding it to further enhance its toughness. Carbon is always used in moderation to create steel alloys. But we, the Tjardur, do not use common carbon, but only the finest soot from the graphite mines of Laaja Trell. We do not smelt common iron ores, but only the finest ores from Laaja Kriss."

Sterjall pondered for a moment. "I'm trying to put on Balstei's hat," he said, confusing some of those present. "What I mean is, I'm trying to understand if what you are doing is crafting quaar. Aren't those filaments you weave into the steel thin strands of quaar?"

"I am afraid not, Canid Lorr," Lune answered. "They are neatly arranged strands of soot, but not nearly of the same makeup as those of quaar. Despite all the secrets from the Acoapóshi we have discovered, we are yet to understand how they were able to weave the intricate crystals of quaar. We have tried everything, for generations, but have not had any success."

"I see what you are doing with it, but I still don't understand it," Sterjall said. "You said I've done this before, but I haven't made Bra'uur steel. I haven't even been inside a forge before. I don't understand how you move the particles."

"You have not worked at a forge, but you have used the empathic focus in the same manner. When you open the vines, how do you do it? Do you speak to plants? Do they speak back to you? For Agnargsilv is not the Silv of vines, it is the Silv of canids."

"But that's different, they respond because… because…"

"Because there is soot in their sap," Alaia deduced.

Lune nodded and blinked slowly. She lifted a hand as if to point through the mountain. "These domes were grown not only near sources where we could mine soot from, *khummmph,* but where their roots could be fed by the soot that lies beneath. All life is filled with carbon, and also with small amounts of the wavering elements, but the white blood vines are filled with more soot than any other form of life. Perhaps also with more oxygen, nitrogen, and other elements of the wavering kind, but we do not know that for sure. That is how they can grow so large, and so strong."

"Maybe it is not specifically the sap," Hefra hypothesized out loud, all the while quickly scribbling in a notebook. "Maybe it is soot itself that has something to do with your companion species growing so large and so smart."

Lune nodded. "The white blood coming from the core vine is different from the rest. How different, I do not know, but there is something special about it."

"The vines are full of soot then…" Sterjall said, almost to himself. "So, when I make the vines part, I'm moving the particles of aetheric carbon in them?"

"Not quite," Lune said, again too cryptically. "But you are inching yet closer."

"You are enjoying this too much."

Lune smiled cunningly. "We cannot move particles with our minds, no matter how small, not even with the empathic focus. But the empathic focus can carve channels through which soot can move. Channels through which the threads of consciousness themselves move. *Khumm.* That is how you connect your empathy to that of others. You do not pull their threads to you—you open a pathway through which they may reach you. Like scoring the sand on a beach and letting the water flow through it to fill a pond on the other side."

"I've... never seen these channels," Sterjall admitted.

"Before Agnargsilv, you also had never seen the threads, yet there they were. Whenever you held someone's hand, spoke words of comfort, or even when you discharged your ire or felt hurt, those empathic channels were manipulated by you, and those who you were closest to at the time felt the change. You can do the same to a greater degree thanks to Agnargsilv, but in the same way the threads were always there, so was your own empathic focus there all along."

"What about the flame, though? And the smoke. Why do they react to you?"

"What is a flame?" Lune asked. "What is it made of?"

Crysta was proud to jump in. "A flame is carbon and oxygen, working together to create heat. It's just a glowing gas, with carbon as part of the fuel. Or soot, in this case."

"Good. And the smoke above it?"

"Depends on the type of fire," Crysta said, "but mostly made of the same. It's just the area where no combustion is happening."

"Made of carbon, and lighter than a feather," Lune said. "And hence why they are easy to control, for those wearing the Silvesh. *Khummm.* Smoke, flame, a cloud of soot, they all react similarly to the pathways of empathy. Like learning to draw, I trained myself to shape the pathways with my mind, learning to respect them, for otherwise they turn capricious. Long I trained, like all Trommofröash before me, so that I may serve our eight clans at the forge."

"And her work is like none other! *Grommmph!*" Ogóre said. "If you think my swing was mighty, you should see Servant Lune slamming her sledgehammer down. Power like only the legendary Drurum of the Gaur could muster."

Lune waved her off. "*Khummm,* I'm not nearly as skilled as my predecessors. I have been reckless, ever since I was a young buffalo. That dreaded machine over there"—she pointed to a set of enormous shears slamming into each other to cleanly cut plates of steel—"is where I lost my left horn. I was an apprentice here, and was loading sheets of steel into the shears. The pincers I wore on my overalls fell to my hooves, and I carelessly bent over to pick them up."

Lune rubbed the textured bump where her left horn used to be. "I was lucky. The shears only took my horn. They could've taken my head."

"How is the forge still working while you aren't around?" Sterjall asked. "Don't they need you to be here to… pull the pathways for soot, I guess?"

"Oftentimes I lend Trommosilv to the other smiths, such as Chawól, or Var-Lummet. But once the filaments are set in the steel, it can be worked without them being destroyed, simply by reheating the metal to a specific temperature, then hammering it in the right angles. We have enough stores of Bra'uur sheets at our disposal, so my presence for that purpose is rarely needed."

Servant Lune hung her leather overalls on the wall. "But that is enough of the forge for one day. I will return here once my wounds heal. I lost parts of my precious suit of armor in the cold waters of the New World, as well as my favorite war hammer, and new ones I wish to forge. Let us return to the Taur Citadel, friends of the Tjardur, where I can further be of service to you all."

CHAPTER TWENTY-SEVEN

ALAIA'S STORY

Crysta and Hefra were getting ready for bed, but Alaia simply sat in the humble room, leaning her back against a pillow. She stared at the reflections her pharolith lamp summoned on the polished walls.

A soft knock at the door, then Servant Lune stepped in, bringing fresh towels. She placed them next to the washbasin. As she was about to leave, she stopped and stared toward the wall. Alaia's Pliwe figurine was casting a still shadow on the marble, her three horns drafting an ominous triple crescent.

Intrigued, Lune stepped closer. "Three horns? I know no bovid or caprid species that are triple-horned, *khumm*."

"She's not a bovid. It's Pliwe, one of the Oldrin deities," Alaia explained.

"One of your prophets?" Lune asked, picking up the statuette.

"Something like that. I don't know too much of the Oldrin religion, to be honest, but I still love keeping Pliwe around. She's my most treasured possession. I've had her for so long."

"She looks like a very old carving," Hefra said from under her bedsheet. "Taamir style, I believe. Where did you get it?"

"Well, it's a bit of a story," Alaia said to excuse herself, which only further piqued Lune's curiosity. The buffalo sat heavily next to Alaia, handed the figurine back to her, and waited attentively. Even Crysta turned around in anticipation, head on her pillow.

"Well," Alaia said, nerves making her skin feel warm. "Do you really want to—"

"Yes," Lune said. "I have told you of our eight prophets, and I would like to hear about yours as well."

Alaia smiled. She fidgeted with the figurine in her four-fingered hand, then began, "Beyond six lands, beneath six seas, I was—" she interrupted herself. "No, wait, maybe I shouldn't start it like that. I'm not some princess in a spritetale." She began anew, "When I was very young, I think five, or six years old? That's when I got the figurine, back in Withervale. Oldrin are treated a bit better in Withervale than elsewhere in the Union, but we are still looked down upon. We are expected to cover up our spurs, to never show them in public because idiots are repulsed by them. I didn't know that yet. I was always at the mines where it's mostly Oldrin workers, and we don't treat each other that way. Or maybe they warned me, but I just didn't understand it."

She placed the tiny figure down on the table, then continued. "One day I heard people talking about how there was gonna be a faire at the Alban Bazaar. They said it would be filled with merchants arriving from all over Noss. I knew where the bazaar was—I had been there with Bahimir before, one of the mine supervisors. That blonde turd Fjorna killed him." She clenched a fist, distracted for a moment. "Anyway, the bazaar, it's right by the southwest gates of Withervale proper, and easy to get to. I could walk there on my own, so I did.

"I left the mines, walked the farm roads, slipped under the gate, and entered the marketplace. I got happily lost in the narrow streets, seeing all the wonders the vendors brought from Yenwu, from Lerev, and even from Dathereol. It was all so exotic. I was enjoying myself so much, but then I noticed that people were staring at me. Staring at my nub." Alaia scratched it. "And then this mean-ass couple… I mean, the lady had a baby in her arms, how could she be so vile? This couple stared at me in disgust, and the lady said, *You filthy spur, cover that wart on your head before you spread it around.* And her butt-ugly husband spat at my feet, then they stomped away. And all of that from just my nub. They hadn't even seen my thirteen sisters."

Alaia pursed her lips and shook her head. She briefly closed her eyes, then continued. "I cried, and I ran, trying to find somewhere safe, but there were people everywhere, and they were all staring at me even more now that I was being so loud and obnoxious. I crawled underneath one of the merchants' tables, hiding under the fabrics, and that's when Umiimi found me.

"She was Oldrin too. Traveled with a caravan for months, she said, and was headed to the Yamazu Market in Zovaria. She was such a pretty woman—in her sixties, I gather—and the thing that immediately struck me was that her spurs were not only not covered up, but they were carved and painted. They grew from her cheekbones. The right one was bigger and curved down in a peculiar way, but the manner in which she had them decorated made them look beautiful.

"Umiimi pulled me from under the table and placed me on her lap, and I was all shy, covering my nub and still crying. I didn't want her to see my ugly spur and get mad at me. She gently pulled my hand away and said, *What a beautiful nub you have! I wish I could have one like that, but mine only grow on my cheeks. Yours is breathtaking!* And she stroked it, and then played with my hair, and told me that what I *should* do is make sure my hair showed just how beautiful my nub was, so that everyone could see and be as envious as she was. She braided my hair as I sat on her lap, and made it so that all the braids pointed toward my spur, kind of like I have it now. She showed me in a mirror, and I smiled so wide. I had never seen myself as pretty before, but I looked damn gorgeous.

"Umiimi told me that she came from Dorhond, where the Oldrin race originated, and that people there find ways to make their spurs look as fine as they can. I asked her what Dorhond was like, and she told me about the White Desert, a place where they build their temples right in the sand. She said the sands stretch so far, and the dunes are so white and sparkling, that it's like an ocean of sugar, only sweeter. *Brighter than snow!* she told me. And she told me that at night the dunes look different every time Sceres changes seasons—gold during Sulphur, green as a jungle in Jade, each of the six seasons giving the desert new life. She said I should spend at least a year there to see all the possible colors the sand can take on."

Alaia picked the Pliwe figurine back up, rolling it in her dark hands.

"Umiimi said she taught me of those places so I could dream about them, so that I wouldn't forget our homeland. And then she handed me this little statuette, told me Pliwe would protect me and guide me, and that I should take her back home to Dorhond when I go there myself one day. I promised her I would.

"And that's why I carry it with me. I don't know if we'll go that way during this weird journey, but whether we do or not, someday I'll take Pliwe back home and let her see the white sands again."

Lune smiled broadly, pulled Alaia closer, and kissed her nub. "Your authenticity shines like a beacon in the fog," she said. "Seitho-Dovár would be proud, *khummm*. Your prophet has already taught you much about yourself. I can see it within you. You know who you are, Alaia of the Oldrin, and you must be proud to know yourself."

Chapter Twenty-Eight

Green Nebula

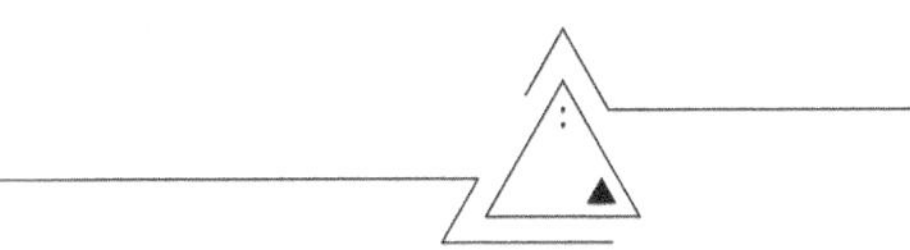

"I think I've almost got it," Sterjall said to Kulak. They were back in their modest dormitory after a long day exploring the city of Bra'uur and meeting the friendly—and oftentimes vociferous—locals. The two sat naked at the edges of opposite beds, the small table between them topped by a green-flamed candle.

Sterjall squinted, trying to mimic Servant Lune's expression when she had shaped the flames. The green light flickered a bit, but he could not tell if it was due to his mental efforts, from his own breathing, or from impurities in the wick or wax.

"Your face strains too much," Kulak said. "Lune did it while relaxed. Let me try."

Sterjall leaned back, frustrated.

Kulak's teal eyes shone brightly under the green flame. The pupils narrowed to thin slits. His whiskers bent forward, as if probing.

"Don't burn your—"

"I am careful. Let me focus." He concentrated, but was unable to affect the flame. After a long moment, he pulled away. "My scalp just realized something. Perhaps the Laatu have been doing this all along. Shaping in this manner, but not with flames."

"What do you mean?"

"At home, in Mindreldrolom, shamans ask the roots of the banyan trees to grow in certain ways, to make bridges, to make ships, to make walls. Like the hull of *Drolvisdinn*, like the staircase of roots that lead to mother's room. But only banyan trees that grow near the trunk will listen to the voices of the shamans."

"You think those trees also have more soot in them?"

"My scalp thinks so. They live longer than the trees of the same kind in other areas, and grow bigger too. Shamans must shape the pathways, and the trees follow them like saplings attracted to light. I wish I had learned those arts. Perhaps if I had, I would be able to paint with flames now."

Kulak stared at the flame again, brow tensed. He decided to try something different, and as he concentrated once more, he blinked pointedly, and the flame sputtered weakly.

"Did you do that?" Sterjall asked.

"My scalp thinks so? But be quiet. Perhaps I understand." He focused again, and this time the flame suddenly shot upward, becoming three times taller, and a bit thinner.

"There!" Sterjall yelped. "How did you do it?"

Kulak allowed the flame to return to normal, letting out a self-satisfied sigh. "It is not the flame, but the space above it that my scalp focused on. Ignore the flame. Tell the air to let the flame through. Like carving a path for a root to grow through. Try it."

Sterjall gave it another shot. Quickly, he found a way to make the flame taller. He focused higher, picturing a pocket in the air, like a void. The white smoke that wafted from the candle fell to the attraction of the invisible spot, filling it, creating a white bubble as wide as a few fingerbreadths. It was not particularly symmetrical or interesting, but it was something. The wolf strained to make the bubble bigger, but could not figure out how.

Kulak extended a claw and poked at the hovering globule. Most of the smoke dissipated, though some tendrils were pulled back into a weak vortex.

Sterjall loudly exhaled. The bubble was dispelled.

"Were you holding your breath?" Kulak asked.

"I… I guess I was. But it works! I don't know how Lune manages to draw complex shapes, or how she separates the flame from the smoke, but at least I can make a… whatever that was."

"It was much uglier than her magic. Very uninspired."

Sterjall playfully growled, then his ears perked up. "Hey, I just thought of something." He reached under the bed for the war belt of his elytra armor. He unsheathed Leif from the temporary scabbard Alaia had procured for him, and moved the dagger toward the candle.

Once Leif's quaar conduit lined up with the flame, the fire found the invisible channel and aligned itself to it. Leif did not exactly push the carbon particles through, but created an attractive void for them to fill, thinly extending the flame for a length matching that of the blade itself. The channel was so thin that the fire did not have much space to burn into, so it sputtered languidly, but the smoke followed the pathway a bit farther.

"Interesting, but not very useful," Kulak observed. He tried with his quaar blowgun, attaching all four conduits in a row. It had the same effect, with the smoke extending farther this time, but the flame was quickly choked out in the narrow pathway.

"Well, not much to that either," Sterjall said. "I was hoping Leif would turn into some sort of, I don't know, like a flaming dagger? Something magical and terrifying."

"Or blowgun that shoots darts of fire."

Kulak played with the flame and conduits for a bit longer, then remembered something. "What about the spheres we picked up? The joints of the lattice."

Sterjall bolted to his feet, reaching for his tunic. "Alaia has them in her bag."

Hefra and Crysta were already asleep, but Alaia was just sitting in her bed, writing in a notebook, with the Pliwe figurine keeping her company. Quietly, Sterjall knocked, then entered.

"Hey… What are you doing?" he whispered.

"Just taking notes."

"Notes? Since when do you 'take notes'?"

"Just learning a bit from Hefra, that's all."

"Learning about wh—"

"Did you find them?" Kulak interrupted, reaching the doorway while wiggling his way into his kilt.

"What are you two scheming?" she asked.

"The joints from the lattice. Do you still have them?" Kulak asked.

"Yeah, in my haversack." She closed her notebook, too curious now.

"Come with us," Sterjall said, "and bring a few of the spheres with you."

They hurried to the other room and sat around the candle, showing Alaia how the quaar conduits affected the green flame. Kulak then picked up one of the spheres. The faceted, geodesic design was hollow, with a hole leading from each face down into the center. He looked at the flame through the sphere, then moved it over the candle.

"Ow!" he yapped, dropping the artifact. The sphere had shot out smaller flames all around it, burning the pads on his handpaws.

"Be careful, nubhead," Alaia said, picking the sphere back up. She pushed a conduit toward it, which attached as if pulled by a magnet. She then snapped more conduits to the first, assembling a long handle. As if aiming to cook a skewer over a campfire, she lowered the sphere to the candle.

Her face lit up, both with light and astonishment.

"Whoa. Now *this* is amazing," she said.

Through each and every orifice of the spherical joint, thin verdant flames sprouted, looping and knotting through the holes beside them. A complex architecture of invisible pathways was revealed, woven in fire. White smoke exuded around the green flames, becoming trapped in a tenuous, spiky bubble, like a bright apparition shrouded in sweet-smelling mists.

"This is the most beautiful lamp I've ever seen," Alaia said, eyes unable to gaze away from the geometric, flickering magic. "It will look great in my plain dormitory—there's not much to look at in there."

"It is truly beautiful," Sterjall said. "Like a green nebula birthing dozens of stars."

They all fell quiet. For a moment, the three of them were children once more, not worried about the oncoming war or thinking of the days ahead. They stared in awe, marveling at something simple, something new, something beautiful they could treasure.

"But what is it good for?" Kulak asked, shattering the spell. "What can we do with it?"

"Exactly what we are doing," Alaia said. "We can look at it. It's good because it's beautiful, because it makes us smile. It needs no more than that to be glorious."

CHAPTER TWENTY-NINE

TJARDUR COUNCIL

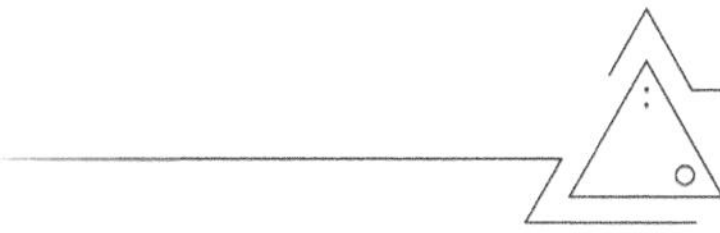

It was early morning on Iskimday, the twenty-eighth day of Frostburn of the year 1456 after the Downfall—the day on which the Tjardur Council was to convene. As they shared breakfast before departing for the proceedings, Alaia, Sterjall, and Kulak surprised Servant Lune with a candleholder rigged to dangle one of the spherical joints over the flame. It was a rushed job, using wire and silverware to concoct it, but it served its purpose. When they lit the candle and the sphere burst into myriad looping green knots, Lune's smile stretched from ear to ear.

"You made one for her too?" Crysta asked, approaching the group.

"And lovely it is," Lune said. "The fire dances in circles, weaves like a loom of flame."

Crysta shook her head, her eyes directed toward Sterjall. "So, you go around robbing sacred artifacts just so you can make, what, lamps with them?"

"We didn't rob the conduits," Sterjall barked. "Mamóru told us it was fine to—"

"I'm joking, calm down. These lamps *are* beautiful. I'd like one myself, if you have more of those things to spare. Actually, Balstei would die for something like this, especially once you tell him how soot is involved." She gulped down the last of her tea and regarded Servant Lune. "How formal is this gathering? I am afraid I don't have any dressy shirts or blouses left."

"We do not impose a particular kind of vestment," Lune said, "or any vestment at all, so you should not worry, Crysta of the Holt. But let us get ready now, *khummm*. The clan leaders will soon arrive. It is time we decide the fate of Trommodrolom."

The Loth Amphitheater was a half-circle split into eight radial segments pointing toward a central staging area. Though the space could hold thousands of spectators, only one person sat at the very lowest tier of each segment, with at most a couple of advisors hovering behind them. Sterjall, Kulak, Lummukem, Puuja, and Servant Lune sat in front of a table that had been set upon the central platform, as if they were being judged. Puuja held on to Lummukem's arm, feeling uneasy, as the Tjardur had asked Pol to wait with the others, observing from a waiting area behind the proscenium without participating. Even Olo had been required to wait there, perching confusedly upon an unlit candelabra, leaving only the Silvfröash at the center.

Servant Lune's single horn was adorned in red, black, white, and grayish-purple flowers, and her body was wrapped in a simple yellow toga. Though her wounds were still healing, she was not using her cane today, and looked as powerful as she looked beautiful.

The eight clan leaders introduced themselves, beginning on the far left of the half-circle from the perspective of the Silvfröash. Representing the Four-Horned Clan was Maon-Javána of the Tetracerus. The allgender was the most plain-skinned of the leaders, with the body of an androgynous human and the slender face of the deer-like tetracerans. They had four pointy horns atop their crown and spoke in soft tones, without the grunting interjections most Tjardur let slip in their speech.

Seven more clan leaders followed Maon-Javána. For the Yak Clan stood Mia-Mei of the Domestic Yak, wearing no clothing other than her own draping fur, which dangled to the ground and was braided with precious stones that sparkled like sequins.

Dirvauk of the Gayal stood next, to represent the Gaur Clan. He was clad in cumbersome plates of armor that could withstand a mountain falling over them. Dirvauk displayed a habit of constantly leaning his heavy head down, pointing his forward-facing horns at those he spoke to.

Ar of the Dwarf Buffalo was there for the Buffalo Clan. His short stature and even shorter legs, together with his potbelly, were deceiving, as he was perhaps the strongest clan leader present. He had won the onyx horn at the jousting tournament four times, and likely still had it in him to win again.

Once Ar finished his introduction, Buulin of the Zebu snorted and stood up. She was the leader of the Aurochs Clan. Her enormous hump seemed as though it must be uncomfortable, but Buulin was obviously very proud of it, letting it wiggle every time she turned to face in a different direction.

Suháve of the Pelorovis introduced herself next. Six metal censers dangled from her inconveniently wide horns. The Pelorovis Clan leader did not need to swat flies with her ears or tail, as they would not approach her thanks to her perfumed incense barrier.

Seudi of the Wood Bison rose next, for the Wisent Clan. Though his short horns did not seem threatening, his voice certainly was. After the briefest of introductions, he bellowed a grunt of dominance and sat back down, letting his long-braided goatee drape down to his belly.

The last of the leaders to stand was Topú'a of the Bongo, representing the Spiral-Horned Clan. Her horns were smaller than those of a male bongo, but still prominent. When her introduction concluded, Topú'a extended her hoofed hands in a rehearsed gesture, tossed her striped robes over her body, and resumed her seat.

A high-ranking servant brought forth a horn filled with a fermented drink. One by one, the eight clan leaders took the liquid into their mouths, then spat it back into the horn without swallowing. The horn was then passed to the guests at the center. Lune swished the fermented drink in her mouth before spitting it back out.

"As our servants, we must spit the bitterbroth back into the Horn of Phalas," Lune informed the others, handing the horn to Lummukem. "But you have the honor of drinking from it. Drink, and we will listen."

Lummukem seemed unfazed. They took a large gulp, then handed the horn to Kulak.

Kulak twitched. He held his breath and took a not-so-large swallow, quickly passing the horn to Sterjall.

Sterjall's brow creased as if asking for help; he flattened his ears like a beaten puppy.

"It is not so bad," Kulak croaked. His half-comforting words did not match his discomforted expression. "It only tasted like the spit of a dozen buffalos. Try it."

Sterjall mustered his courage and drank. *It tastes like Blu's breath in the morning,* he thought. After the liquid fully permeated his mouth, the foul taste faded slightly, leaving only a fizzy tingle of halitosis.

He passed the horn to Puuja. The girl cleverly placed the horn under her rodent mask, hiding it beneath the hollow area below the muzzle, then leaned her head back, pretending to drink. "Mmmmmm!" she said, handing the horn back to the servant.

The Tjardur Council began by recapping all that Servant Lune had told the clan leaders when they'd called for this meeting, with more detailed information layered in by the other Silvfröash.

"I mean not to sound disrespectful, *grummm,*" Suháve of the Pelorovis said from within her cloud of incense, "but the one thing we know for certain is that we must be cautious. The last time we chose to trust strangers, our dear servant lost a husband and nearly lost herself."

"What you ask of us could mean the collapse of our culture, what we so fervently have protected for centuries," Dirvauk of the Gayal added, accusatively pointing his horns toward the foreigners.

Ar of the Dwarf Buffalo stood on his short legs, and in his low, nasal voice said, "*Khuff,* yet this is why we built the Tsogi and Nudoroth Ramparts. The plan always was for Trommodrolom to open at one point or another."

"But we expected it to happen five hundred years from now," Dirvauk retorted, "and to exit in peace, on our own terms, not into a war of someone else's making."

Sterjall felt ill-at-ease, unable to jump into the conversation. The clan leaders were too loud, too busy arguing with each other.

"Noss could've talked to us at any moment and asked us directly," Topú'a of the Bongo said.

"Noss did ask for this," Lummukem said, jumping in. "We bring not our own request, but that of Noss themself. We have explained this."

"But how can we know this to be true?" Mia-Mei of the Domestic Yak inquired. "Servant Lune, was that not the same argument the treacherous ermine used?"

Lune nodded her flower-draped horn. "Similar, yes. Yet the one who calls herself Silv-Thaar Daro kept her threads hidden from me, unlike our guests at this table who speak openly. Trommosilv cannot know if they speak truth, but it can sense they mean well."

"Most who fight on the wrong side earnestly believe they are in the right," Suháve of the Pelorovis said matter-of-factly. She waited for a reaction within her curtain of smoke.

"True this is," Lune resignedly agreed. "Yet Silv-Thaar Daro and Silv-Thaar Knivlar are not the same as our guests. They are thieves, having taken their Silvesh by force. Those masks do not belong to them."

Seudi of the Wood Bison had remained mostly quiet. He now stood up, letting his braided goatee swing like a pendulum. In his gravelly voice, he said, "Other than Servant Lune of the Water Buffalo and Kulak of the Caracal, I do not see these Silvesh being wielded by proper representatives. I see a wolf who is not of the clan of wolves, a dragon who belongs to the clan of felids, and a sweet child who is the true heir, but is too young to bear the burden."

Mia-Mei tried to break into the conversation, but Seudi stopped her. "Just like the ones from the ermine and the water creature who attacked our servant, these Silvesh are misplaced. *Khrommph.* Placing trust upon them would be the same as the mistake Lune made in trusting the other two."

"We *saved* her!" Sterjall blurted out, not caring to hear any more of the bison's assumptions. "If we had wanted her mask, like those monsters, we wouldn't have brought her back to you. What you are saying is insulting."

Lune placed a calming hand on Sterjall's back. "There are similarities in the situation," she said, to Sterjall's surprise, "but not in the way you phrase it, Seudi of the Wood Bison. It is true that some of these Silvesh landed in hands other than those we might have expected, but it is not up to the Tjardur to judge the laws of the Miscam tribes or realms of the New World. Trommosilv was the mask entrusted to us, and for it alone will we answer."

Buulin of the Zebu shook her head to get their attention, sending ripples across her massive hump. "Servant Lune, did you not mention that this New World is cold and frozen? Have we not tried this once before, and thought it unwise? *Hummm.*"

"This is something our guests are unaware of," Lune said to the leaders, then regarded the confused faces around her table before continuing. "Two hundred and seventeen years after the Downfall, Rocan of the Sitatunga decided to explore outside Trommodrolom. He was told by our clan leaders that Trommosilv should only be used in that manner two thousand years after the great closure, but he chose not to listen and took the risk sooner. *Khummm...*" Lune paused briefly, looking up at the columns that rose in a half-circle around the amphitheater.

"Rocan took with him dozens of kudu and bongo scouts. The lands he found outside the dome were frozen and deadly. They were trapped in an ice storm. Most of the scouts perished, and Rocan himself lost his life. One of the scouts, Jurhek of the Kudu, recovered the mask and learned to wield it. She returned to Trommodrolom months later, with only two surviving scouts."

"But that was during the Reconstitution Epoch!" Sterjall complained. Realizing he'd sounded a bit whiny, he cleared his throat before continuing. "It wasn't until hundreds of years later that the temperatures returned to normal. It's a bit cold outside now, since we are in the middle of Winter, but the world is not frozen anymore. Your dome is simply warmer than others, maybe because of all the volcanoes."

"Yet we will need to adapt to the new temperatures," Topú'a of the Bongo said. "We nearly lost it all due to Rocan's recklessness. One careless excursion was all it took."

"And careless it was," Dirvauk of the Gayal added, "just like Servant Lune's excursion was careless. She should have listened to Pamúnn, who was distrustful of the strangers."

"Pamúnn is distrustful of everyone," Ar noted, hoofed fingers drumming on his tight belly.

As if summoned, Pamúnn suddenly chose to make himself visible. He had been standing behind the exterior colonnade, holding still to remain inconspicuous. The Nu'irg walked slowly toward the center of the amphitheater. From the sidelines, both Hefra and Alaia kept their eyes tightly focused on the beautiful coat of browns, oranges, blacks, and whites.

After a long pause, during which Pamúnn returned to his statuesque immobility, Servant Lune said, "I explained to Pamúnn what was just said about him, as he heard his name, and was curious."

"What is the Nu'irg ust Trommo's opinion?" Buulin of the Zebu inquired.

"He said he was distrustful of the ermine and the leopard of the seas. He is also distrustful of the wolf, the caracal, the human girl, and the dragon."

Sterjall and Kulak glanced to each other with concern, while Puuja scowled under her mask, holding on to Lummukem's arm.

Seudi of the Wood Bison grunted three times. "We should listen to the Nu'irg, as he is wiser than any of us."

Lune nodded her agreement. "Pamúnn is wiser indeed. He also says that even though he distrusts the Lerrs from lands far and away, he trusts Nelv, Gwit, and Ishke'ísuk, the other wise Nu'irgesh. Ishke'ísuk himself was there when six Silvesh were used to call an audience with Noss. The Nu'irg ust Momsúndo was there as well, who gave his life for this cause which Noss and our guests find so pressing."

Pamúnn stepped closer. He stood right in front of the table, so close that Sterjall could smell the silty and grassy scents of his luxurious fur.

Servant Lune continued interpreting. "Our Nu'irg says that human matters are for humans to decide, and though we may be close to our half-forms, humans we still are. He has no vote in our council, but wishes us to consider that, if and when the dome opens, it remains our duty to care for bovidkind as much as it is his own duty."

"Before Trommodrolom closed," Ar of the Dwarf Buffalo began, "the other kingdoms showed no respect for our kind. Is that still the case in the

New World? Do they still butcher bovids for meat and leather? Do they still punish them for pleasure? Breed them into slavery?"

Servant Lune looked to Sterjall, who was the only true representative for the New World at the table. The wolf uncomfortably fixed his tail in his seat and, already regretting his honesty, answered, "Not everywhere, but in many places."

The eight clan leaders grunted their displeasure.

Pamúnn himself stared at Sterjall, making him feel guilty for the crimes of others, which had been at times his own crimes as well.

"But it happens in all realms, with many kinds of animals," Sterjall added, trying to avoid Pamúnn's measuring gaze, who slowly walked away while holding his stare. "I've seen you wear rabbit fur, which I'm sure the Sehján would not be pleased with. And I've been served pheasant and deer while hosted at the Taur Citadel, which I presume the Teldebran and Murtégo Miscam might not be happy with either."

"Do atrocities against bovidkind take place in the lands that directly surround Trommodrolom?" Seudi of the Wood Bison inquired. "Those of the ones you call the Tsing?"

Sterjall looked over his shoulder for Ambassador Vor-Vor's help, but it was Hefra who spoke from behind the proscenium. "The Tsing do indeed keep domestic cattle in the manner you eight are concerned about, though not as much in the southern lands, where the Jabrak-Tsing are more numerous. The Jabrak eat horsemeat, however, and hunt whales. But in the northern Jerjan lands, the Tsing ranches keep dairy shorthorns, Tai-Du grays, and Hashan spotted breeds, though they also breed longhorn highlanders in the northern regions, and hybrid bison in the Yenwu sovereign territories."

The clan leaders seemed appalled, particularly Seudi of the Wood Bison.

Vor-Vor rubbed the bridge of his nose, looking as if he was trying to disappear, and Sterjall wished he hadn't looked around for help.

"*Phummph!* We would be sending our bovids to a slaughterhouse!" Seudi spat. "Even if we were to trust the newcomers, how can we pretend to trust this empire that rules the lands around ours?"

"This empire is the only thing holding the power of the Red Stag at bay," Sterjall said. "If the Tsing fall, the Red Stag's army will come this way. You need not agree with their ways, as I am sure they would not agree with yours, but this is not about the Tsing. This is about helping Noss, and about stopping the advance of the Negian army before it is too late."

"The Tjardur still have a part to play," Lummukem added. "Whether Trommodrolom opens today, or in five hundred years, your oath was to safeguard the bovid species—which you have done exceedingly well—so that they may once more roam all lands. The ramparts you have constructed can protect your culture, but they are a prison to the feral bovids and the other species you are entrusted with. Sooner or later, the great gates will need to be unfastened."

"I am Dirvauk of the Gayal!" Dirvauk said, banging a fist on his cuirass. "I am Tjardur! Perhaps we were once Miscam, but that is no more. Our union with the eighteen tribes was one of convenience, and one that ended when the domes closed upon us. We are free of our bonds now, free to choose our own path. Ancient oaths to the Acoapóshi do not bind us."

"Our oath was not to the Acoapóshi," Maon-Javána of the Tetracerus countered. Other than during their introductions, the allgender tetraceran had not yet spoken. They stood slowly. The others quieted. With their cervid-like head and human body, Maon-Javána looked more like a plain-skinned human wearing a deer mask. "Our oath was not even to Noss themself," they continued. "It was to our culture, to bovidkind. That is what we sought to protect. Yet Noss knew better. They knew that our clades need balance, that they need room to grow, adapt, and change with time. Only through the health of Noss can we bring back health to ourselves, to all bovids."

"But how can we trust that our bovids will not be enslaved? That our lands will not be taken from us?" Topú'a of the Bongo asked. "We will spread once more, but is this the right time?"

Ambassador Vor-Vor stood at the waiting area behind the stage. In his high-pitched voice, the old eunuch said, "As the representative for the Tsing Empire, and a descendant of Umar-Vaor, I will gladly negotiate a treaty with Empress Pian-Thi, making sure your requirements are met."

Maon-Javána of the Tetracerus gestured for Vor-Vor to come forward and stand by the Silvfröash. "Do you command such power as to make decisions for your kingdom?" they asked the ambassador.

"For my empire. And not directly, but I have enough influence, and I am a good negotiator."

"*Grummm.* Why would your empire agree to our demands, Vor-Vor, descendant of Umar-Vaor?" Suháve of the Pelorovis asked from within her cloud.

"Because a war is coming," Vor-Vor answered. "A war is coming to our lands, and if we lose, it will soon reach yours as well. The odds do not look good, and we will need all the help we can get to protect ourselves from the Red Stag. Just as you joined forces with the Acoapóshi long ago to fight against the Rashi, the Tsing now need your help to battle the Negians. Heed our call, and we'll both prosper."

"But what can your empire offer to us in turn?" Topú'a of the Bongo asked. "Why should we sacrifice our warriors for a war that is not ours?"

Vor-Vor understood that in order to capture the Tjardur's attention, he'd need to continue speaking with the Tjardur in mind, and he had already devised a potential plan. "We can offer you the lands upon which the sacred hides were inscribed," he said. All ears focused on him now. "Mount Alvforg, where my ancestor, Umar-Vaor himself, once lived. The mountain and the peninsula are part of our empire, and they encompass an area greater than all of Trommodrolom. I can secure it for you, as long as you let the Tsing Empire keep jurisdiction over the Alvforg Strait, to control the passage of ships in and out of the Alommo Sea."

The sacred mountain was of great interest to all the Tjardur present. Their history, their legacy, had grown from there as much as from the Four Blessings.

"In exchange, we'd ask that you help us in the coming war," Vor-Vor added. "I cannot promise the empress will agree, but I am confident in my skills and in our needs. Your clans are powerful, and your steel surpasses in strength any from the two continents. We will need your strength, your metals, your might, your determination."

"Head strong! We might as well fight!" Speros bellowed, standing at the back between Siffo and Hefra. The unsanctioned outburst from beyond the stage unleashed grunts of disapproval among the clan leaders, but Maon-Javána allowed the eland to speak.

"Bra'uur steel protects us, our strength protects us," Speros continued. "We have values and tenets that make us head strong! We can persevere through adversity, we trust our intuition, we are mighty, we are just. We keep a clean body and mind, and know ourselves better than anyone. We care for the wellbeing of others, for we feel as they feel." He looked straight to Maon-Javána as he finished his speech by reciting the tenet embodied by the tetraceran kind. "And we strive to be of service to others, not because of what we may gain in return, but because being of service is the worthiest of goals!"

"Speros of the Eland speaks wise words," Maon-Javána said, "for he speaks the words of Bum-Vaor himself. Yet heed the warnings. If the descendant of Umar-Vaor is to negotiate for us, we need to be certain that our demands will be met. I believe there is more we would seek in return."

"Name your demands, and I will see they are given a fair consideration," Vor-Vor said.

"Then let us discuss our options, *khuff!*" Ar of the Dwarf Buffalo said. "We will deliberate promptly."

The clan leaders stood and gathered in a tight circle at the far end of the amphitheater. They discussed amongst themselves in private, away from the ears of Vor-Vor and the Silvfröash.

"How come they don't invite you to make these decisions?" Sterjall quietly asked Lune. "Shouldn't you be up there with them?"

"It is not my calling. I am a servant. What they choose, I will help with, but it is up to the clan leaders to make the decisions. Ar of the Dwarf Buffalo is there representing my clan. He and I see eye to eye, despite our height differences. I trust that my best interests are being voiced by him."

Lummukem walked over to Vor-Vor. In private, they asked him, "How certain are you that the empress will agree to the promises you are making?"

"The mountain has no critical resources we need," he answered, "though its position is of strategic importance due to the proximity to the strait. There will be pushback from some inhabitants, but I feel it's a trade the empress will be happy to agree to—or at least will *have* to agree to."

Sterjall and Kulak secretly held each other's handpaws under the table, nervously waiting for the leaders to come to an agreement.

Lune leaned toward Sterjall and whispered in his ear, "You need not hide yourselves. I see you, through Trommosilv. Not just your entwined handpaws, but I see your hesitation. *Khumm.* Follow Seitho-Dovár's teachings, Lago-Sterjall of the Wolf, and shun away your fears. You will be more respected by all others present if you embody her tenet."

Sterjall nodded to Lune, then pulled Kulak closer, relaxing a bit more.

After a long discussion, the clan leaders were ready to deliberate. They took their seats once more.

Maon-Javána of the Tetracerus remained standing to speak. "We have chosen a path of action. Because we do not agree in all matters, we have leaned toward prudence. We, the eight Tjardur clans, believe that if the descendant of Umar-Vaor can negotiate as promised, then we would be willing to help the Tsing in the oncoming war. But demands we do have. Firstly, if and when Trommodrolom opens, the Tsing Empire will provide ample space for the bovids to migrate, as per Noss's request. We will not ask for the Tsing Empire to change their ways, as we understand their lands are expansive and harbor dozens of different cultures, but we will demand that none of our bovids be captured by any of their territories. We, the Tjardur, may be issued restrictions, but the feral bovids will be given permission to roam free, wherever they please."

Vor-Vor bowed. "Understood," he said.

"Secondly, in order to help our bovids begin their migration, we will need to be assured safety as we travel. We will be given new lands on the southern shores, including Mount Alvforg, the site upon which Bum-Vaor first inscribed the Trommo Hides. The locations of other new lands will need further discussion, but they must add up to at least twice the area of Trommodrolom."

"Many southern lands are populated," Vor-Vor said, "though not extensively. I shall bring your demands to the empress and come to an agreement."

"An agreement we could reach for the other lands, although our rule of Mount Alvforg is not to be negotiated," Maon-Javána continued. "Thirdly, as a way of solidifying our mutual commitment, we will offer to the Tsing our strength in the coming war. Stopping the Urgfröa from taking more lands is in our common interest. Bra'uur steel we have aplenty, and we will work tirelessly to craft more weapons and armor with it, to serve not only us but our allies. Although we, the Tjardur, vow to help in the oncoming war, our feral bovids shall not be forced to make such a commitment. Unlike the Urgfröa, we do not coerce our own kind. We will ask only our companion species—the pelorovis, longhorn bison, and bongos—individually if they wish to commit to this war, but the choice will be theirs alone. If they choose to join, only a portion of them will do so, as others will need to aid the migrations to populate distant lands."

"A fair request and a generous offer," Vor-Vor granted.

"Fourthly," Maon-Javána continued, "we will not open the dome until we are assured that our demands are accepted by the empress. We will inscribe these demands upon the hides of an ancestral tetracerus, and we will ask the descendant of Umar-Vaor to carry these hides to his ruler and ask her to inscribe them with her sacred sigils. If any of these demands is not met, then Trommodrolom will remain closed, and we will negotiate once more in five hundred and forty-four years, with whatever empire, realm, kingdom, or barren wasteland we find outside our walls at that time."

"Clan Leader," Vor-Vor said, unsure of what honorific to use, "Empress Pian-Thi resides far away, in the capital city of Hashan. Journeying there and back might take weeks by sea and river. I could perhaps send a written notification via herald to grant her acknowledgment—it would be more expedient."

"We will need certainty of the empress's commitment, of her word. No herald we know of can carry hides as large and heavy as will be needed, nor could they negotiate directly as you might. We do not mind waiting for your return, but the hides will need to be inscribed properly. That is the way of our laws. Fifthly," they continued, surprising Vor-Vor with more demands, "Speros of the Eland, would you please stand?"

Speros was startled to hear his name called. He awkwardly stood, fixing up his armor as he did so.

"Speros of the Eland, you have bravely fought to protect Servant Lune, and have once ventured out into the New World. We would like to name you Servant Speros, as we would ask you to be of service to the Tjardur by accompanying the ambassador. You must present the hides to his empress and stand as witness as she agrees with our demands. Would you accept the title of servant?"

"*Hurff!* With honor and pride toward myself, my family, and my clan! Head strong!"

"Head strong, Servant Speros. These are our demands, and fair we consider them to be," Maon-Javána concluded.

The Tsing ambassador bowed and said, "Although not a servant in the same manner, I'm honored to be of service for this negotiation."

"I hope our guests agree that this is a cautious and proper path of action," Servant Lune said, nodding her head toward the others at the table, letting a few petals fall from her horn.

"Our scalps are in agreement," Kulak said.

"Yup," Puuja added distractedly.

"I think they are fair demands," Sterjall agreed. "This will delay us a bit, but I believe Vor-Vor might be able to request help from Theggo, who has a ship that can move faster than the gulls who chase after it."

"If the fleet admiral offers his frigate, I will not object," Vor-Vor said. "I will ask him once we regroup."

"We agree that this is prudent and fair," Lummukem said. "We can help the ambassador and servant exit Trommodrolom. When are they to depart?"

Buulin of the Zebu answered, "In two days, on Sunnday. That should give us enough time to prepare the hides. We will meet again upon the descendant of Umar-Vaor's return, and if all goes well, we'll set the dome to open that very day. And now we need to speak to Servant Lune and Servant Speros in private. The Tjardur Council is dismissed."

CHAPTER THIRTY

DOUBLE INCENTIVE

Two days later, the clan leaders met the visitors from the realms beyond at the port of Sinsimbo. Two copies of the hide treaties were given to Vor-Vor and Speros, with the Tjardur demands inscribed with utmost care upon the supple leather of ancient albino tetraceruses.

"Ambassador, I have an odd request…" Sterjall began, right before Vor-Vor boarded Siffo's ship.

"Yes, Lorr Vaari, what may I help with?" the elderly Jabrak-Tsing asked.

"Since you'll be in communication with Empress Pian-Thi… Crysta believes it might be of use to visit Professor Lai-Nu at the Yenmai Institute. Later, that is, once we leave the Ashen Dome. We heard of her studies on soot and quaar, and we think her knowledge might be of help to us."

"The 'studies' you have heard of, you should not have heard of. Her work is confidential, and of great importance to the Empire. Your request might prove hard to accommodate. Soot is too valuable to us. It is one of our main exports, and a key tool in trade and war."

"I know soot is of great value to the Empire, as it is to all realms. But soon enough, it won't be."

"And why do you think soot will no longer be of value?" Vor-Vor asked.

"It's not that it won't be of value, not exactly… but its rarity will decrease, and its cost will drop. You've seen how much soot they have available here— they toss it casually in their iron to make things as simple as nails and bolts. I've seen someone swat at a fly with a Bra'uur steel spatula."

"Hmm." Vor-Vor fidgeted with the tufted end of his tail as he pondered. "My nature is to be cautious with matters of a sacred nature. I know one must tread lightly when dealing with different cultures and customs, so I dared not ask much of the Tjardur regarding their sources and stocks of the black powder."

"Soot is sacred in all domes," Kulak said, walking into the conversation. "But in Trommodrolom it is much more common than in Mindreldrolom. Sacred, but commonplace."

"We think that meeting Lai-Nu might offer important insight," Sterjall added. "We need to understand how the masks work if we are to defeat the Red Stag. She might know something we do not."

Vor-Vor nodded, his Lode earring swaying. "This quandary you present about soot's value and abundance might be useful in my negotiations with the empress. Do you think we might be able to provide a sample as an 'incentive'?"

Sterjall saw where this was headed and went to Lune to ask for help. She mentioned that there was a glass foundry in Sinsimbo, where the sacred powder was used for improving the resilience of their glass. She sent a young bull to fetch samples for the ambassador.

"So, will you get us an audience with Lai-Nu?" Sterjall insisted. "We will be heading to Yenwu eventually. We could speak with her before we enter the dome."

"I will inquire with the empress."

Shortly thereafter, the young bull returned with a sizable crate and dropped it at Vor-Vor's feet.

"For the descendant of Umar-Vaor," he said. "I hope it's enough. The foundry was running low, so I apologize." He stretched his tired arm muscles and hurried away, a bit embarrassed.

The ambassador stared in disbelief. The crate was filled with pure soot separated into sixteen glass jars. Each of those jars alone would be worth the price of a mighty Tsing carrack.

"This... this will do just fine," Vor-Vor said with a cracked voice. "Kulak, would you please help me by carrying this aboard?"

Kulak's ears perked up, surprised to be asked. He picked up the heavy crate and followed the ambassador up the gangplank, taking the soot to Siffo's quarters.

"Khuron Kulak," Vor-Vor said before Kulak could exit the room. "I have a favor to ask of you."

"Ambassador?"

"Just as we have made dealings with the Tjardur, I believe it will be important to ensure the aid of the Laatu. And of the felids."

"They are not on the same continent, Ambassador, but far from here. And my scalp does not rule them. They make their own choices."

"I understand, but we have means to bring them to our lands, if need arises. And their might we may soon need."

"There is enough threat of war with the Zovarians for them to deal with."

"The Zovarians are becoming more concerned with their long-term survival at this point, worried that if we lose the war on the Jerjan Continent, the Loorian Continent will fall soon thereafter. They have been keeping their hands off your people, mostly."

Despite the relief Kulak felt at the reassuring words, he kept his face impassive as he regarded the ambassador.

"I am not asking for your commitment, Khuron, only for your consideration. Once I meet Empress Pian-Thi, if you will allow me, I will mention the possibility of our alliance, and I'll ask for a token of our appreciation to be prepared, for you, for your help. Will you consider it?"

"My scalp will have to think about this," Kulak answered. "And I will have to speak with Nelv and the others. It is not a decision I can make, but one my people need to make for themselves, and one the felids need to make without my influence."

"Your consideration is appreciated, Khuron Kulak. There is still time to prepare. I will mention to the empress that there is a possibility."

Kulak nodded and withdrew from the room.

Sunu-Lummukem helped open a passage to escort Vor-Vor and Speros out of the Ashen Dome. Once in Ngau Tor, the ambassador and servant boarded Silverweave. Theggo had offered to help the ambassador after all, as he also wanted to discuss the complicated politics of his torn republic with the empress. Vor-Vor gladly accepted the offer, knowing that even though Theggo's ship was not as luxurious as Canvasback, the fast frigate would greatly expedite their journey.

"And now what?" Sterjall asked once they were all back at the citadel. "We have plenty of time before they return."

"I'd like to learn more from the locals," Hefra suggested. "Particularly their shamans."

"Or we could see the other cities?" Kulak added. "Or visit their temples."

"I'd like to see the soot mines if at all possible," Alaia said, her pleading eyes looking up at Servant Lune.

"I will ask my husbands and wives to help entertain you," Lune said, "and to show you to any sights in Trommodrolom that you wish to see."

Sterjall's ears perked up. "What about the Pink Cal—"

"Except the Pink Caldera. We will plan something for each day of this coming week. But tomorrow, you should rest. And tonight, I should rest, for the day has been long and my body is still healing."

CHAPTER THIRTY-ONE

MOONDAY

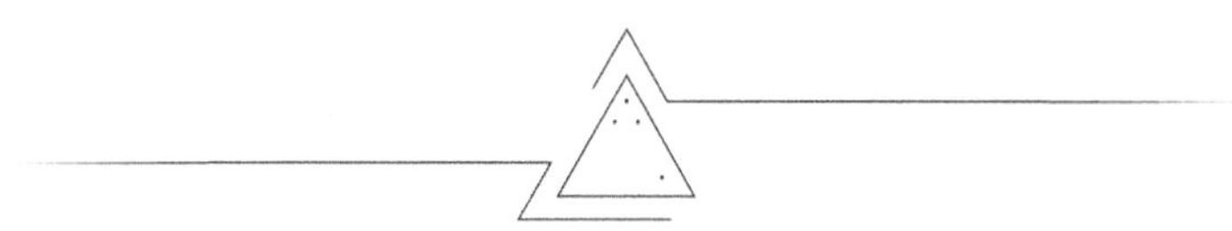

On Moonday, the first day of Mudfront, Servant Lune excused herself. She needed to spend the day at Ommo ust Trommo—as she did once every month—to work with the lattice and make sure the dome was growing healthily. She left her guests in the company of her nine wives and six husbands, who were all as thankful as Cort had been for them saving Lune's life, and were equally mournful about the death of their husband, Diduk.

"But are they all married to each other, or only married to Lune?" Sterjall wondered out loud later that day. He was leaning against the banisters at the cliffside that separated Bra'uur from a verdant valley to the southwest.

"It's more complex than that," Hefra said, facing the opposite way while leaning on her elbows, observing the crowd that moved along the busy street. "I talked to Cort yesterday, and he explained the intricacies of it all. They are all married to Lune, though some married her when she was Rud, and refer to her as their husband instead of wife, no matter which form she or he takes. And not all sixteen of them are married to one another, as there are mixes of lorrkins and lurrkins among the majority of lerrkins. There are four core subgroups among them. Some members are sexual, some coparenting, some asexual—it's a complicated mix. And two of the wives are allgender, but they don't have a separate word for that role, so they assign them the title of wives based on their physiological sex. Those two are the ones who primarily take care of the children."

"She's never mentioned having any children," Sterjall said.

"She does and she doesn't. Only one subset of the group takes on the breeding role. But she said she's lent her seed for other partnerships, as Rud. So, I guess that means she does have children, but they just aren't part of their family."

"That's fascinating," Alaia said.

"I think it's jis' weird," Siffo opined.

"Nothing weird about polygamy, truffle bun," Hefra said. "Many primates like ourselves have been doing it for millennia, but other species tend to be much better at it."

"It makes my scalp wonder," Kulak said, "what would Mindreldrolom have been like if we had not stuck so strictly to the Miscam traditions? How was Laatu culture different before we joined the eighteen tribes?"

Alaia shrugged. "Well, for one thing, I really wish Kenondok was here to experience this. The veins on his scalp would be pulsing like rabid eels by now."

CHAPTER THIRTY-TWO

KHUDAY

The group split up on Khuday. Lummukem and the twins ventured off to explore the crystal caves of Shun-Ji. Crysta, Hefra, and Siffo got to bathe in the warm and sulphurous waters of the Klad Pumme. Alaia, Sterjall, and Kulak took a trip to Laaja Trell, from where the Tjardur acquired the graphite that they purified into soot. Ogóre of the Gaur acted as their guide.

Instead of taking a carriage, the three young wayfarers and their guide rode on Blu and Pichi, who were happy to get out to explore this land a bit more. Ogóre felt uneasy climbing onto Pichi, thinking her weight would be too much for the smilodon to handle, but Pichi proved her wrong and seemed not to feel her at all—not even with all the heavy armor the gaur was wearing.

Though Sterjall and Kulak were not too impressed by the soot mines—they were, after all, very similar to other mines they had seen—Alaia was better at discerning the dissimilarities from the Withervale mines she was so used to. She enjoyed learning the ways in which their techniques for mining differed, particularly how cleverly they had solved the problem of air circulation, how safe their shafts were, and how laid-back their shifts. The workers were mostly tamaraws from the Gaur Clan, who were not only happy to work there, but proud to be of service to their community.

"It's very strange, how the shafts are distributed," Alaia noted as they made their way back to Bra'uur. She was petting Pichi's lifting and lowering shoulder blades while trying to visualize all the tunnels they had explored, mapping them in her head.

"What is strange about them?" Ogóre asked, sitting like an oversized boulder behind her.

"I don't know, it just doesn't make sense. They are not distributed on a plane, they don't follow seams like the coal mines I used to work at. You'd normally find a flat layer to dig through."

"Our soot does not grow in that way," Ogóre said. "The graphite from our mines is not a blanket of rocks laid softly upon our lands, to be covered by more rocks through time. Our graphite comes from the heart of Noss themself, from underground. The mountains grew and brought out a source most ancient, most pure. Under great pressures, under great stress, did our graphite form. Strong it is, like us. Head strong!"

"Yeah, yeah, head strong," Alaia muttered.

"You have much more soot here than we have in Mindreldrolom," Kulak said. "Many times more. And you do not seem to need to purify it as much as we do."

"You are observant, Felid Khuron," Ogóre said. "I think it is one of the reasons the Acoapóshi did not want us to cut them off from these lands. They showed us the value of soot, but did not want us to keep it all to ourselves. It is not like they did not already have enough from their own mines at Ommo ust Enwenn, *gromph!* Selfish they were, a most selfish kind."

They traversed a stone bridge, greeting fisherfolk as they passed.

"Have you seen the Nu'irgesh lately?" Sterjall asked from behind Kulak. "It's like they disappeared."

"Old friends, catching up," Kulak said. "They have much to talk about."

"They come back every evening," Alaia said confidently. "They all follow Pamúnn and stay mostly around the terraced gardens. If you get up early enough, you'll see them walking on the western trails."

"Sounds like you've been up quite early," Sterjall said.

"Just the last few days. By the way, I might need your help with something. Both of you."

"My nose smells trouble," Kulak prophetically intoned.

"Shush," Alaia said. "Anyway, would either of you help me with getting a little, you know, fur specimen from Pamúnn?"

"*Grommph!* What madness do you speak?" Ogóre questioned.

"I'm with Ogóre on this one," Sterjall said. "What is this about? Are you turning mad like poor Hefra all of a sudden?"

"Not quite as mad, not yet." Alaia sighed. "Remember those notes you saw me taking the other night? Well, I'm kind of... I'm going to become Hefra's apprentice. I'm helping her with her research. I mean, that's my goal. She hasn't fully accepted my offer yet, but her first request is for me to get a sample of Pamúnn's fur. Well, more like *I* offered to get a sample, and asked for her to take me in as my reward."

Ogóre grunted her displeasure again, but she was ignored.

"Are you sure about this?" Sterjall asked. "What are you aiming to do? You know scholars, they wouldn't—"

"I know, but... I don't know. Maybe one of the institutes will take an Oldrin girl?"

"Maybe, but we're a bit in the middle of something else right now."

"In the middle of what? Exploring mines? Volcanic forges? We have some downtime. I want to make the most of it."

Sterjall shook his head. "I mean we are in the middle of a war. It's so hard to know what will happen once all the domes are opened, when the Red Stag brings his army."

"Things *are* changing, I'm aware of that," Alaia replied, a bit flustered. "That's precisely why I think that maybe, just maybe, there will be an opportunity for me once this is all over." She let out a remorseful sigh and looked away, toward the distant rampart walls.

"Remember that time up at the Ninn Tago?" she asked. "When we were talking about you going to Zovaria to study. When we saw the giant teratorns fly by."

"Of course I do."

"Well... I was so happy for you that day, Gwoli. And it hurts me to admit it, but I had *never* been more envious in my life. You were getting this wonderful chance at making a life for yourself, a chance at choosing your own path, while I knew for certain that I'd live the rest of my life working at the mines. And now... Maybe now that things are changing so much, maybe I'll get my chance, you know? Hefra could open some doors for me. We're doing her a huge favor after all by bringing her with us on this trip. It's her dream come true. We might as well ask for a bit in return."

"Just..." Sterjall thought about how to phrase his concerns, but he knew not the best way. "I don't want you to be hurt, that's all, if things don't pan out."

"I will help you," Kulak said firmly. "My scalp does not care what Zovaria or anyone else says about the Oldrin. We will make it work."

Sterjall lowered his head. "I'm sorry," he whimpered in shame. "I didn't mean to sound like I don't support you. I do. We will help you, if that's what you want to do, who you want to be. We'll be there for you."

Kulak pointedly nodded. "And we will help you steal Nu'irgesh fur, as many times as you want."

Ogóre scowled and shook her head.

CHAPTER THIRTY-THREE

NOSSDAY

Alaia, Kulak, and Sterjall rose very early on Nossday. They found one of Lune's wives preparing the breakfast table, who told them that Lune had risen even earlier and would not be available today, as she was performing her services elsewhere.

"Where do you think she went?" Alaia asked Sterjall as they walked out to the gardens on the first level of the ziggurat.

"It must have something to do with that Pink Caldera. She's very open about so many things, and so secretive about that."

It was nearly dawn when they arrived at the fern garden. Alaia pointed at a trellis, under which a basket of fresh greens was placed for Pamúnn every morning.

"I don't think this will work," Sterjall said, approaching the basket.

"Let's just try it," she insisted. "But better hurry, he'll be coming around any moment now."

"Might be easier to try and tackle him," Sterjall teased.

Kulak widened his eyes in horror.

"I'm kidding," Sterjall clarified. "But why don't you just ask Lune?"

Alaia shook her head. "I fear it might be insulting. You saw Ogóre's reaction when we spoke of this."

"And rigging a contraption over Pamúnn's breakfast isn't insulting?"

"Not if Lune doesn't find out about it. Also, maybe Pamúnn will like it? Okay, you hold them up, I'll tie them together."

The three of them worked to attach a row of metal brushes right over the food basket, to force the nyala to rub his neck along them as he reached for his food. It wasn't a very stable structure, but all they needed was a small sample of fur. With the deed done, they hurried up to the next level of the ziggurat and waited.

"Here he comes," Alaia whispered, spying with the binoculars.

Pamúnn approached the basket, but unexpectedly stopped a few steps back from it. He stared at it for a moment, sniffed at the strange device, then snorted. His long neck turned, aiming his head up, straight at the three of them. He did not seem pleased.

The nyala shapeshifted into the smaller shape of a tetracerus and leapt into the ferns, to be seen no more that day.

"Shit," Alaia grumbled. "How did he even spot us? At this rate, Vor–Vor will be back before I gather the fur, and we'll be on to the next thing."

"Maybe Pamúnn will join us aboard Siffo's ship?" Sterjall said.

"Does not sound like a thing Pamúnn would like doing," Kulak said. "Too proud, too skittish."

Sterjall stood and walked toward the steps. "Let's remove that stupid brush trap before one of Lune's spouses finds it."

Later that day, the three of them climbed to the top of the ziggurat, to watch Lummukem and the twins spar near the entrance of Ommo ust Trommo. Ogóre was helping Lummukem with their battle lessons. She demonstrated techniques to deflect heavier blows, stances that worked with slower-moving weapons, and ways of spinning heavy maces. Despite her size and the weight of her weapon, Ogóre was nearly as fast with her mace as Lummukem was with their halberd.

The twins were particularly fond of slamming their quarterstaffs against Ogóre's heavy armor, making their brime tips spark fiercely to disorient her, then finding ways to attack together to distract the heavy gaur. Ogóre played along, letting her guard down from time to time to motivate the twins.

Content after a hard day of training, the four sparrers sat with their friends at the edge of the ziggurat and watched as the light of the arudinn faded on the horizon.

Alaia was suddenly distracted by an odd change in the light, and she looked to her left, toward the shortest of the four volcanoes. She noticed something peculiar on the snowy mountain. "Hey… Look. The fumes on Laaja Ash. It is steaming pink, not white."

"I see it," Sterjall said, standing up. "What is that?" he asked.

Ogóre pretended not to hear Sterjall's question.

"Does this have something to do with the Pink Caldera?" he insisted, leaning in so that Ogóre could not ignore him.

"Hurmf…" was all the gaur answered.

Sterjall stared at the rising pink clouds. It's almost like the steam is being scraped by the last rays of sunset, he thought, and suddenly missed the warm palettes of Sunnokh.

CHAPTER THIRTY-FOUR

ISKIMDAY

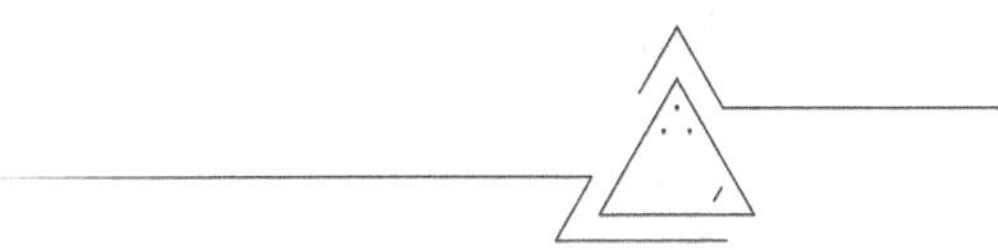

On Iskimday, Lune and Ogóre brought the visitors back to the Volcanic Forge. Lune explained that they would move ahead with the assumption that Vor-Vor and Speros would succeed in their mission, and thus the Tjardur would prepare themselves for the impending opening of the dome.

Production at the Volcanic Forge was now focused entirely on weapons and armor. Their war vessels would soon be retrofitted, as most ships had been used as fishing vessels since the dome closed. Their warriors would be instructed where to assemble if the Tjardur joined the war effort. As a civilization depending on their power to survive, the Tjardur had not lost their skill for battle; they had continued training with wargames through the centuries, making a sport out of them, even though they had been at peace.

"The smiths are working on a new set of armor for me," Servant Lune said. "I wish I could hammer it myself, but my wounds are begging me not to. I brought you here so we could take measurements of you all, so that we may craft Bra'uur armor fitted to your bodies."

"That is very kind of you," Sterjall said, "but I don't think I'd have the strength to haul those thick plates. My elytra armor is so much lighter."

"I get a hernia whenever I see Ogóre," Alaia added. "Are you sure heavy plates would be a good choice for us?"

"It is not a requirement, of course," Lune answered. "Your colorful armor is indeed exceptional already. But what about you two?" She eyed Lummukem and Kulak.

The two Laatu exchanged a glance. Their tribe simply did not care for anything impeding their movements, happy with their open-chested shodogs and their wind-welcoming kilts.

Before they could answer, Puuja spoke up. "We want one armor. Pol too. Two armor. We like them."

Lune smiled at the twins. "Armor of your sizes should be easy enough to find among the ones we give to our children to practice jousting." She then directed her attention to the others again. "To the rest of you, if full armor you do not want, let us at least outfit you with helms, *khummm*. Alaia has a helm more functional and lighter than we could ever hope to craft, but the rest of you need protection for your hornless heads."

They reluctantly agreed to try that. They weren't convinced they'd be comfortable wearing helms, but Lune was adamant, and they did not want to be disrespectful by refusing her altogether. Only Crysta and Hefra entirely refused, as they had no intention of finding themselves in combat.

The chief armorer arrived to take their measurements. She was a longhorn highlander cow named Chawól, who was wearing an armored leather apron crafted from leather scales reinforced with steel trimming. She had measuring implements and other tools dangling from her horns, and she could pick and hang them back up without having to look.

Chawól took measurements while admiring Sterjall's and Alaia's lamellar suits. Sterjall wondered how she could see anything she was doing with all that long tawny fur draped over her eyes.

"More durable than they seem, *grrmmmph*," the old cow said. "Now I understand why you wish not to replace them. This is fine, strong leather, with even stronger resins. However, some additions could improve them without adding much weight. Allow me to work on some upgrades."

"I would trust Chawól's judgment on anything regarding armor," Lune counseled.

Sterjall and Alaia hesitated, but gave in and took off their lamellar armor, handing the pieces to Chawól. The cow continued measuring their bodies, paying special attention to Alaia's thirteen sisters, carefully jotting down notes and measuring the distances between each of the spurs that protruded from the Oldrin's spine.

"Now you two," the armorer said, smiling at the twins. "Aunt Chawól will be able to customize smaller sets for you. I know just the ones."

The long-horned armorer said the upgrades and new helms would be ready within a week or two, then let them all go.

CHAPTER THIRTY-FIVE

ONGUDAY

The wayfarers were shown to the Vaults of Thyra on Onguday. The cold tunnels dug deep into the eastern slopes of Laaja Ëovad, far away from the hot core of the mountain. They comprised numerous, carefully curated chambers where the hides of Tjardur ancestors were preserved.

No Silvesh were allowed into the vaults, so the masks were left behind with the gaur guards. Why this rule existed, Servant Rud-Lune either did not know or was not allowed to reveal.

"Please remove footwear, if you have any," Rud instructed the others as he wiped his hooves on a mat. Once barefoot, they followed behind the savannah buffalo. "I have summoned you here so that you may witness the underground archives of Thyra. This is where the hides of our ancestors are stored. Here we safeguard our history."

He moved to one side, making way for an archivist walking in the opposite direction, who carried a roll under their arm. "When Tjardur die," he continued, "it is up to their children to skin, flesh, tan, and inscribe their parents' hides with the stories of their lives. That way, each generation may reminisce about the accomplishments of the prior one, safe in the knowledge that their memories will be preserved."

Crysta's face contorted with revulsion, but she flattened her expression before asking, "Y-you skin your own parents?"

"Khumm. A good friend will also do, for those who have left no children behind. A great honor it is, to inscribe the runes upon their supple leather. Not all Tjardur send their hides to the vaults, or their skulls to the catacombs. Some keep them in their homes, to tell their family history to their guests. Some do not remove the fur during the tanning process, keeping the furred hides as capes, so that their predecessors may keep them warm during their pilgrimages to the tops of each of the Four Blessings."

Most of the tunnels they traversed were carved from a pristine-white marble polished like pearl, although from time to time they passed by intrusions of volcanic rock which had been left raw and unpolished. There were no lights within the tunnels; each Tjardur they passed by carried their own oil lantern, lit by orange flames.

Rud approached a wall that was carved into diamond-shaped shelves. Rolls of hides were stacked and organized with a numerical system that took into account the clan and generation of each piece of leather. He pulled one out and carefully unrolled it, letting it dangle from one arm. The hide was wide, silky-looking, pinkish in color, and inscribed with hundreds of delicate lines of Miscamish runes.

"Frabben of the Bushbuck, these runes recall," Rud read. "Three hundred years old this hide is, quite recent. I do not know their story, but perhaps I will read it one day." Frabben's hide had been inscribed with care, using a hot pen to burn one rune at a time. Rud placed the hide on a table and rerolled it carefully before depositing it back onto its shelf.

"My own parents' hides are in a different tunnel of the vaults. My siblings and I took great care to accurately write their stories."

Servant Rud led them around a corner. They found themselves in a much taller vault where the higher shelves were only accessible by ladders. Rows of tables were in the center, also of white marble, where archivists worked under dim lantern light. At one table, an archivist was carefully cleaning an old roll of hide. At another, an archivist transcribed a leathery roll that had been too decomposed by time, as the tanning process had not been done with enough skill to properly preserve the material.

"He's making a copy?" Hefra asked. "Who volunteers to give their skins for such a thing?"

"The transcriptions are done on hides from feral bovids of the same species. Worry not, they all died from natural causes."

"Then where do you write their stories?" Alaia questioned. "Don't the feral bovids deserve the same reverence?"

Lago was about to elbow her to stop, but he held back, now wondering the same thing.

"They don't have tales to pass down the generations," Rud answered with a tinge of insecurity in his voice. "They live simple lives, and their way of communicating is not one easily transcribed to runes. It is a privilege for them to have their hides used in this manner."

"Sounds unfair to me," Alaia added. "I think they all deserve the same chances."

"Khummmmm…" Rud paused, inspecting Alaia and finding no mockery in her expression. "Your arrival heralds a time of overdue change. Perhaps this will inspire us to seek further wisdom in these practices." He pondered quietly for another moment, then asked them to follow him once more.

Many more tables filled the splitting hallways, with dozens of workers carefully caring for the hides. Farther in, the vault narrowed to an arched gateway protected by six gaur guards wielding sharp battle axes.

"Head strong," they called out as they let Servant Rud and his guests pass.

The chamber behind the guards was decagonal, like the rotunda at the Taur Citadel with the paintings of the eight prophets. Instead of paintings, this room had eight freestanding panels displaying hides that were spread open and flattened between glass panes encased in solid steel armatures. The panels were placed throughout the chamber, letting the group walk around to examine their fronts and backs.

Lago approached the hide to his immediate right, using a pharolith to illuminate the long text, but was unable to read the triangular runes. He circled the panel to examine the leathery skin from the other side. "It looks almost like human skin," he remarked, a bit creeped out.

"It is. All the hides in this room are, of course," Servant Rud told them matter-of-factly. "These hides date back to before Trommodrolom closed. Back then, we had not yet transitioned away from our plain-skinned selves. The hide your eyes landed upon is none other than Seitho-Dovár's."

"The nyala goddess?" he whispered.

"Khummmm… Yes, Canid Lorr, though she is no goddess, despite what her beauty might tell you. She was a prophet."

"So, all of these—"

"Are the hides from our eight prophets," Rud completed the sentence. He pointed at the glass panels, one at a time. "Seitho-Dovár of the Nyala, Ejokk of the Steppe Wisent, Gweléshi of the Pelorovis, Bum-Vaor of the Aurochs"— he continued on the other side of the room—"Naj'al'alás of the Mountain Anoa, Drurum of the Gaur, Au'óro of the Grassland Yak, and Rumah of the Tetracerus. We so wish we could have had their furred hides, the way they were when in their precious half-forms, but Trommosilv returned them to their human forms when they perished, and so only their human skins we have left."

"Well, at least you'll still be a buffalo," Alaia noted.

"Both of my buffalo bodies are my own, and I am proud of them."

Lago inspected the hide that belonged to Bum-Vaor himself. It just looked like a dark-tanned leather, with even darker inscriptions. He admired how carefully the glass and steel construction had been assembled to protect it.

"You cannot see it without Agnargsilv," Servant Rud said from behind the glass panel, "but this glass is constructed in the same manner as our Bra'uur steel. There are filaments of soot woven throughout it, making it nearly indestructible."

"Like senstregalv," Lago said.

"Precisely!" Rud exclaimed. "Perhaps not as strong as senstregalv, as our glass foundry cannot compete with the pressures that exist within the bowels of mountains, but our glass is strong and mighty, like Drurum of the Gaur. Follow me farther, if you will."

Rud exited on the opposite side of the decagonal room, which led to a much larger circular chamber. The white-marbled hall held a series of thirty-two hides around the periphery, each of them encased in glass and steel. Instead of being displayed vertically, these were nearly horizontal, at a slight angle to facilitate viewing. One more hide was exhibited in the same manner at the center of the room, secured in a steel case of opulent, audacious design.

"The Trommo Hides…" Lago whispered in awe.

Rud nodded his single, sickle-shaped horn. "Head strong. The original tenets are at the center. The other hides were inscribed by Bum-Vaor in the decades that followed, expanding on his core ideas."

"You did an outstanding job at preserving all these laws through the centuries," Hefra commented.

"Laws they are not, Hefra of the Boarmane," Rud said. "The tenets ask us to strive for certain ideals. To do our best, to aim to be worthy of following the eight virtues and exemplify them with how we live our lives. This way of life, these hides that hold our beliefs, this is what our ramparts truly protect."

"But they have not needed protection for centuries," Aio noted.

"No, but in the past, the ramparts protected us from many threats. From the Rashi, from the Tneruaga, from the Aejur, but mainly from the Acoapóshi, khum. Even before the Trommo Hides were inscribed, the Acoapóshi found our way of preserving history distasteful, sinful. Many hides they burned. Millennia of history they stole from us. But the Vaults of Thyra survived, and with them survives the core of our culture."

"Such assholes," Alaia muttered. "I'm not liking them so much anymore."

"Yet without the Acoapóshi, all of us, all of this, all of our history would've been destroyed. We are thankful to them."

"Aren't you afraid of storing all these precious items right next to a fire-spitting volcano?" Hefra asked.

"It is a stable mountain. When the domes were grown, the locations were selected for many reasons. Noss thought it safe, telling our predecessors that Laaja Ëovad would not turn vengeful for at least ten thousand years, and that the other blessings would remain dormant even longer. We are safe here for at least eight thousand years more. The dome is safe, our people are safe, our history is safe."

Rud turned slowly around, admiring the complex vaulted ceiling of the white marble room. With pensive yellow eyes, he said, "I brought you here so you could see, so you could understand, khummm. Soon the Tjardur Council will reconvene. I want you to be prepared."

He looked back down at the group. "We are obstinate bovids. We have persevered through time, steadfast in our goals, like Gweléshi of the Pelorovis taught us we should. We are comfortable where we stand and prefer to remain in safety. Be ready, as it is possible that the clan leaders may choose not to open Trommodrolom."

"And what do you believe?" Lago asked. "Whose side will you take?"

"I am a servant, Lago-Sterjall of the Wolf. I aim to serve. I am not the one who will make that decision, so what I believe is not important. The responsibility to choose what is best for the Tjardur is entrusted to the clan leaders. I will follow their mandate."

Chapter Thirty-Six

Sunnday

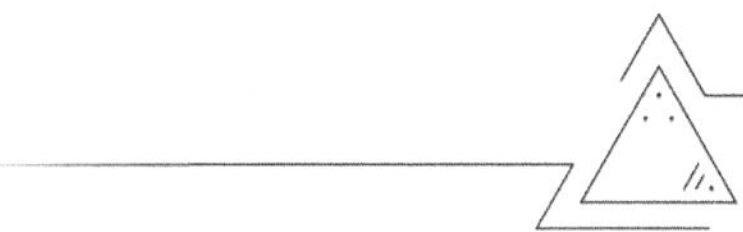

Sunnday was a day for sport. Servant Rud, who preferred his male form for the occasion, was excited to show the others the jousting battles that took place at the Bra'uur Arena, a triangular field that could seat thousands of spectators.

Jousting was a raucous and unruly affair. At the blow of a latifrons horn, three heavily armored contestants rushed from the corners of the triangular field straight to the center, heads down, to smash their thick skulls against one another. The goal was to either make the opponents fall to the ground, or to push them beyond a foul line using only their horns.

A longhorn bison contestant was the first to fall. Despite the threatening appearance of his horns, they were easy for his opponents to manipulate to the bison's disadvantage. They used his own momentum and pulled on his horns to direct him past the lines. The two remaining contestants, a buffalo and a kudu, clashed again, head-to-head.

"*Khummm,* in times before the Great Reformation, we used to wear no helms," Rud told them while watching the match. A powerful grunt erupted from the arena as the buffalo jouster tripped and rolled onto the floor, leaving a long wake of sand behind him.

"Helms or not, it doesn't look very safe," Crysta remarked, partially covering her eyes. "Is he bleeding?" The buffalo tried to stand but toppled over with blood dripping from under his helm. Servants hurried to drag him out.

"It's nothing, he will be fine," Rud told her.

The smaller of the three contestants, an agile yet still prominently muscular kudu, took off her horned helm and waved it in celebration. The crowd roared.

Sterjall's muzzle gaped open in confusion. "Wait, she took off her horns?"

"Female kudus have no horns, like female nyalas have no horns. So, they wear them on their helms. In times long past they could not compete because of that issue, but the games are fairer now."

"The horns aren't for safety, then," Crysta observed rhetorically.

The matches were short. Now that the kudu had won, servants came forward to change parts of her armor, trading her greaves for ones that looked bulkier and less practical.

"After each match, the winner for each bracket wears heavier armor. Heavier and heavier they get, just you wait, *khummmph*."

Just as Rud had described, by the time the winners from each bracket were set to joust against the other finalists, they looked like over-encumbered, humpbacked tortoises. The added weight was proportional to the weight of the contestants, so that a fight between an eland and a gaur would not be unbalanced. The final matches were slower than the ones at the beginning, but more powerful. Whenever a contestant fell, they made the ground rumble with the weight of the muscle and armor that toppled over.

In the end, it was a midweight steppe wisent who claimed the onyx horn. He hauled his armored body to the center of the triangular arena, took off his helm to reveal a bloodied crown, and grunted loudly. Steam rose from his overheated lungs. He took a bow toward the newcomers, dripping blood in their direction, making it clear he had made a great spectacle in their honor.

"I don't know about this," Crysta said as they left the Bra'uur Arena. "It's too bloody, brutal, gratuitously violent."

"Exactly! Head strong we are!" Rud proudly proclaimed. He put on his mask and turned back into Lune.

CHAPTER THIRTY-SEVEN

A GAME OF PERSEVERANCE

"I have spoken to the clan leaders again," Servant Lune said to the wayfarers late one afternoon, as she brought them to the top level of the Taur Citadel. "They agreed that if the hides are signed by the empress, and we become allies with your realms, that we will allow you—but only you, Lerrs from lands far and away—to learn about the Pink Caldera and partake in our ritual." She stopped at a grand overlook of the city, with the flattened, steaming peak of Laaja Ash rising only a handful of miles to the south.

"What does the ritual involve?" Sterjall asked.

"Until the descendant of Umar-Vaor returns with a positive development, I will not be able to say more," Lune answered. "But I have good hopes he will be successful, *khumm…*"

Pamúnn and Nelv had joined them that day, walking at a safe distance. Alaia kept an eye on Pamúnn, hoping to see the nyala scratch his neck and drop a few clumps of hair. She wondered whether bovids even did that.

She pulled Kulak aside. "Hey, Nelv seems to be very friendly with Pamúnn. Do you think you could ask her if—"

"I already did," Kulak whispered back furtively. "She finds Hefra distasteful. Nelv does not like it when people try to understand her felid self. She told Pamúnn to stay away from you. Gwit and Ishke seem to want no involvement in this either."

"Shit…"

"My scalp does not know how to help you in this. But I think I know who you should ask."

✦

Alaia woke up hours before dawn. She packed up her field journal and a few specimen envelopes, then swung her cloak over her overalls.

"Hey gal…" Hefra said, rising up in her bed. "Where have you been running to so early every morning?"

"Just trying to get you what I promised."

"Made any headway?"

"Not much. Pamúnn is trying my patience. I need to get closer to him, but I don't want to get in his way."

"Feeding grounds?"

"Tried that, didn't work. Gonna attempt a new strategy this morning."

"Well, muffin, you better figure it out fast." Hefra threw the thin covers back over herself and curled up to doze off again.

Once Alaia left the room, Crysta spoke from her bed. "You have to give her a little break. There's no way she's going to get that fur. That Nu'irg doesn't like to be around people."

"Bah. She'll figure something out."

For the past week, Alaia had been rising early to wait by Pamúnn's feeding area. She had not attempted the demeaning trick with the brush contraption again, but instead had chosen to approach slowly. Every morning, she'd scoot a tiny bit closer, though if she made even the smallest sound, Pamúnn would vanish into the foliage. At least she'd been able to follow his tracks and figure out where his escape route took him through.

Today she had a new plan.

"Hurry, you two," she said to her assistants. Puuja and Pol groggily followed behind her in the still-dark hallways of the citadel.

"We did not agree to help you this early," Puuja complained. "Could we have breakfast first?"

"After we are done," Alaia said firmly, turning into the gallery of frescoes and friezes, then hurrying into a service passageway the twins had told her about the previous day. With a barely exposed pharolith, she illuminated a gloomy corridor that led them to an antechamber with benches set under an illustrated tapestry. The textile depicted a muscular bull hoisting up a squarish boulder the size of an ox as he helped build a massive rampart.

"That's the door, by the ugly painting," Puuja said. She put on her mask. "It should be unlocked."

Alaia tried the handle and the door creaked open. A breeze blew in, carrying a fresh scent of moist leaves. She peeked out and could barely see the outdoors. She let a tight beam of her pharolith shine out, revealing a vaulted tunnel of branches. The passage was a natural trail carved through the vegetation by trudging animals, but to Alaia it felt more like the entrance to a funnel-web spider's lair.

"Servants don't walk tunnel, only cows do," Puuja said, referring to feral bovids of any kind.

"We do too," Pol added with a smirk, keeping his eyes on the ground.

"And you are sure it connects to the spot I described?" Alaia asked, receiving a nod from Puuja as a reply. She closed the door and took a seat on one of the benches. "Then here we shall wait," she declared.

"Will you teach us while we wait?" Puuja asked. "You promised."

"I promised I'd teach you after you help me, and you haven't yet done your part." She then sighed, pretending defeat. "But that's fine, we can get started, as long as you keep watch with Okrisilv. Can you pay attention to two things at the same time?"

Puuja nodded emphatically, then pulled one of the benches closer, as well as a side table which she placed between them and Alaia. The twins took their seats.

Alaia rummaged through her haversack and pulled out a metallic board, which she lay on the table. She then reached into a leather pouch, from which she retrieved two Quggons. As she pried the two cubes apart, the metallic puzzles partially disassembled due to their pull on one another, but she quickly put them back together.

"This is a Quggon," she explained, holding one of the colorful cubes up to the kenzir stone's beam. It glittered like a jewel. "And this blue one we call a Hex," she added, removing the blue chip from the cube.

"Hex," Pol repeated.

"Worth sixty Qupi, or sixty points in this case." She let Pol hold the chevron-shaped chip. "This shiniest one is called a Hand, and it's—"

"It doesn't look like a hand," Puuja interrupted. "Why hand?"

"Because it's worth five points," Alaia explained, waving the fingers of her truncated left hand. "Wait, wrong one," she said, switching to her right hand. She then showed them the Horn, Cup, Qupis, and also a handful of Lodes that were rattling in her pouch. "In a game of Qu, each player starts with a full Quggon," she said. "Although my friends and I used to play with wooden chips, or with painted Qupis, since few of us had a whole block saved up." She placed a Qupi on the board, letting it stick to the surface with a satisfying click. "At the start of the game, each player places their pieces on the board, following the—"

"He's here!" Puuja interjected, much too loudly. She covered her mouth, and quietly repeated, "Pamúnn is here. I see his colors, outside, on the trail."

"I'll teach you more later, I promise," Alaia said, stowing the game board and chips away. "Puuja, you keep your sight on the Nu'irg and let Pol know when it's safe for him to go. Pol, you know what to do. I'll go meet Pamúnn at the fern garden."

Alaia hurried back the way they'd come, taking the dark corridor until she reached the terraced gardens, on a hillock close to Pamúnn's feeding spot. She had been waiting there every morning, on a chair which she moved closer and closer every day, trying to get the Nu'irg accustomed to her presence.

She saw the nyala approach, crossing the wooden bridge into the fern garden, walking under the trellis, straight toward the offerings in the food basket. Alaia waited for him to be halfway done with his meal before she nonchalantly stood up and meandered toward him. The trunk was already brightening by then, making the nyala's fur shimmer.

Pamúnn stopped chewing, the hairs on his striped back standing on end. His spiral-horned head lifted as he stared at her with an indecipherable expression.

"Look," Alaia quietly said, "I know you know what I'm up to. But it's not really what you think. Could you please just—" And in one leap, he was gone, down the exact animal trail she knew he'd make his exit through.

Alaia hurried back into the citadel, through the corridor, and found the twins in the antechamber. "Did it work?" she asked.

"We don't know," Puuja said. "But we saw his aura flash by a moment ago."

"Let's go check." Alaia opened the door and walked into the funneling trail, having to duck to fit through. It was bright enough for her to see her way around now, but she still had to depend on Pol's guidance. He showed her through the branching paths until they arrived at a spot where he had carefully lowered strategic branches, obstructing the way enough that the nyala would have to brush against the branches; Pol had coated them with a sticky, odorless resin.

Alaia pulled at the branches, searching for the precious hair on them, but found none.

"Fuck," she swore, then looked at Puuja. "Did you not see him go this way?"

"We did, Okrisilv saw him. Maybe he turned small like Gwit?"

"I don't think bovids have forms that small," Alaia murmured, measuring the spacing between the intruding branches; Pol had set them up properly, not leaving gaps for the Nu'irg to avoid touching them. She then pushed the branches away and examined the opposite side of the trail, finding Pamúnn's tracks there, with the last pair of hoof prints significantly more prominent than the rest. She looked up and saw that the vaulted tunnel did not close entirely.

"That bastard jumped!" she said. "How did he jump so high?"

"What is bastard?" Pol asked shyly.

"Uh, nothing. He must've spotted the trap. And now I'm certain he won't be taking this path any longer, he's too smart."

"Will you teach us more Qu now?" Puuja asked. "We can beat you, after you teach us. That we can."

Alaia smiled weakly, still scheming in her mind. "Fine," she said. "You did well. I'll teach you more over breakfast."

CHAPTER THIRTY-EIGHT

REQUEST FROM AN EMPRESS

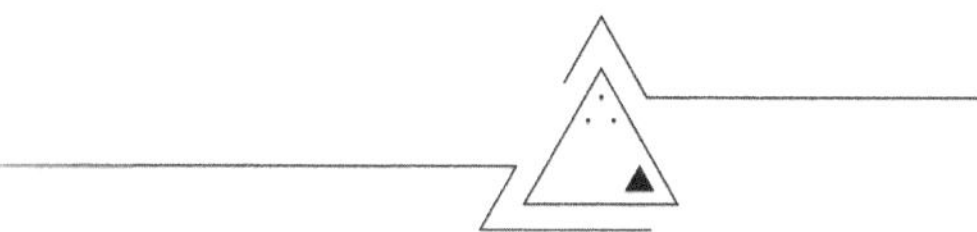

Two weeks after Vor-Vor and Speros departed, *Fjummomurr* once again sailed out of the Ashen Dome only to sail right back in, returning the ambassador and newly pronounced servant. On the day of their arrival, the Tjardur Council was called back into session. The congregation took place at the Loth Amphitheater once again, but this time all the thousands of seats were filled, with the throngs raucously awaiting the news.

The eight clan leaders took their seats at the lowest tiers of the half-circle, then stood up as Vor-Vor and Speros entered the staging area and sat at the table next to Lune. As soon as the two took their seats, the crowd quieted, with not even a whisper remaining. The other foreigners sat behind the proscenium this time, as it was not they who had been summoned for this council.

"We are all eager to learn of the outcome of your quest," Maon-Javána of the Tetracerus began. "Your placid smiles tell me perhaps things have gone well. What news do you bring to us, Servant Speros, and descendant of Umar-Vaor?"

The Tsing ambassador rose to his feet. He was wearing a surcoat of opulent fabrics mixing royal oranges with velvety blacks, with a bright-yellow capelet covering his left shoulder. His tail was draped over his belt, now braided with golden threads and sharp-cut topaz beads.

"Gilded sunsets and silver twilights," Vor-Vor greeted the assemblage. He unrolled a hide treaty, displaying the stamp of Empress Pian-Thi's personal sigil, and her blood signature beneath it. "I bring forth good tidings. The Tsing Empire has agreed to your demands."

The crowd cheered, but Maon-Javána lifted a hand and quieted them.

"A witness I was, *hurff!*" Speros said. "The empress signed both hides, keeping the other for their records. She has agreed with all the terms, though the Tsing do have a demand of their own that was not written upon the hide treaty."

"We said this was not up for negotiation!" Dirvauk of the Gayal belted out, slamming a gauntlet onto his cuirass.

"Let the servant speak," Ar of the Dwarf Buffalo said, standing at full stature, which did not amount to much. He looked to Speros and nodded.

"Empress Pian-Thi of the Tsing is requesting payment for the lands that are to be granted to us," Speros said. "She refuses to give them up for nothing in return."

"Nothing? We are offering our forces in the war that is to come!" Suháve of the Pelorovis said, shaking her long horns and casting a long waft of smoke from her censers. The spectators directly behind her craned their necks, trying to see over the cloud.

"What does the empress request?" Seudi of the Wood Bison asked. "We have already offered our weapons, our armor as well." The citizens behind him were getting riled up.

Vor-Vor lifted a hand to quiet the crowd. "Empress Pian-Thi wants the price of the lands in soot. For each fifty square miles of land, a full ingot of soot shall be repaid."

The crowd laughed, as did the clan leaders, except for Maon-Javána, who got to their feet. "You must've misspoken, descendant of Umar-Vaor. Do you not mean an ingot per each square mile of land, or per square bowshot? Or do ingots in the New World weigh as much as an anvil?"

"No, clan leader, I meant what I spoke. As Lago-Sterjall reminded me before we departed, soot could be very useful for negotiations with the New World. For an area twice the size of this dome—which shall include Mount Alvforg—the empress requests a total of two hundred ingots. That is one ton of soot, to be delivered directly to our capital, Hashan."

"Make it two tons!" Buulin of the Zebu joked, snorting all the while.

"I assume you will have no problem with this request then," Vor-Vor said. "And fret not, though we value soot this much, there was no trickery in my dealings with the empress. She wishes to make good use of the resource before its value across the New World drops. If you offer more, she will gladly take it. The empress also wishes to establish a permanent economic relationship with the Tjardur, asking for the trade of soot to remain strictly limited so as to keep control of its value during these critical times of war. These treaties are to be kept separate from our current dealing, as they would require further negotiations, but they will all lean heavily in your favor, as you will keep control of the source."

"Then I believe our preparations have not been for naught," Maon-Javána of the Tetracerus said. "Our armies are ready, our forge has been crafting weapons and armor like never before, and all of our companion bovids have been spoken with. Many have asked to join the battle, though the majority have chosen to leave human troubles to the humans alone, and will instead help repopulate the lands of the New World."

Servant Lune rose. "Then if it is so agreed, tonight I will set Trommodrolom to open, and in two weeks' time, our armies will march out toward Hashan, and to war!"

Not much more was discussed at the Tjardur Council, as all their plans had been agreed upon beforehand. The thousands of spectators quickly vacated the Loth Amphitheater and returned to their cities to make them ready for the dome's opening. The Tjardur and their companions would march out of the dome as soon as the vines receded, but the journey would take months, for the Tsing capital was far away.

Once the crowd cleared the amphitheater, Ambassador Vor-Vor signaled for Sterjall to come forward.

"I have more news for you, Lorr Vaari," the old ambassador said. "News that I did not find appropriate to mention in public. It's about your other friends. You know who."

"You mean Ji—" Sterjall stopped himself. "Wait, some of the others need to hear about this." He asked Kulak, Alaia, Siffo, and Lummukem to join them.

Vor-Vor regarded the five of them and said, "Our spies are becoming more unreliable as time goes by, but we have received reports from the domes the Red Stag recently conquered. You already knew that the fortress of Anglass had fallen, but soon after that, during the Day of the Lost, the Lequa Dome came under attack by a rebel force."

"A rebel force?" Alaia asked. "Who were they?"

"The Jojek Miscam who had been enslaved within," Vor-Vor answered, twirling his tail tauntingly. "But not without help from without. The Lequa Dome was set to open that very day, and is well on its way to being no more."

"They did it!" Sterjall said, his smile widening with joy.

"There is more. Not only have the Anglass and Lequa domes been set to open, but it seems the Bighorn Dome may be experiencing a similar fate. Once again, there has been a revolt from within."

"That is a relief for our ears to hear," Kulak said. "They have made it so far, so quickly. What else have you learned from your spies?"

"There is much confusion," the ambassador replied, "myths being born, too many exaggerations and hearsay. If it was your friends who were behind the Bighorn revolt, we hope they have made it out safely. But no more do my sources know."

"Thank you, Ambassador," Sterjall said as they began to walk out of the amphitheater. "And thank you for keeping this private."

"Discretion is in my nature, Lorr Vaari."

"Oh, one more thing," Sterjall said. "Did you speak to the empress about us meeting Lai-Nu?"

"I did. Your crateful of soot was persuasive enough. Professor Lai-Nu has been… reclusive, confined to her studies, ever since her discoveries were announced to the Yenmai Institute. I have permission from Empress Pian-Thi to escort you to her. We may go as soon as you are ready."

Before the arudinn dimmed, they were all back in the Taur Citadel, including the eight clan leaders, who had come to witness the ritual.

Servant Lune led them under the four great horns—their green fires perpetually lighting the entrance to Ommo ust Trommo—and walked up the shallow ramp into the temple.

"What if all the volcanoes erupt or something?" Alaia pondered. "You know, with the earthquakes and the vines going underground?"

Sterjall suddenly recalled the horrors they experienced at Oxmaaga, seeing the faces of the Oxruk who lost their lives in the cataclysm unleashed by the retreating vines. He was glad when Lune offered some comforting words.

"Noss themself made sure our sacred mountains were safe," she said, slowing her pace to walk next to Alaia. "They assured us that neither the growing nor the shriveling of our dome would cause our Four Blessings to betray us, *khummm*. The roots grew in such a way that they will not only not affect the volcanoes, but will make the land even more stable."

After stopping briefly in front of the dais and inhaling deeply, Servant Lune sat upon the four-horned throne at the center of the temple. Sconces cradling green flames illuminated the space, filling the circular room with a sweet smell.

"The smoke looks strange," Kulak said, eyes on the vaulted ceiling. The soot-saturated white smoke drifted there in unsettling, geometric forms, following the pull of the empathic channels the quaar lattice carved in the air. "I wish we had green flames inside Ommo ust Mindrel. Perhaps in the way the smoke moved we would have discovered more about the vines, the secrets of their white blood."

The eight clan leaders surrounded Servant Lune and kneeled. She placed her bulky forearms on the armrests and held tightly to the cold marble. With a clarity and purpose none of the other Silvfröash had commanded, she willed the lattice to collapse.

As the quaar conduits and joints began their mechanical, geometric reshaping, the white smoke above their heads began to take new forms. The lattice continued folding inward, wrapping itself around the smooth core vine that stood behind the throne, then quickly assembling into an armor not even Bra'uur steel could compete against.

The core vine lowered, trapped within its quaar cocoon. As it sank below ground, and the threads flowed faster and farther, the empathic pathways the lattice carved suddenly trapped the green flames from the sconces. The fire flowed inward from each of the fixtures, forming a fiery tornado in the place where the core vine had stood. The tendrils of green knotted with each other and rose, and in a burst of energy dissipated into geometric clouds of white.

The temple went fully dark.

"It is done, *khummm*," Servant Lune said. "Trommodrolom will soon be no more. From this day on, only our ramparts will keep our Four Blessings safe, as they did long ago."

PART FOUR
BRIDES OF DELIVERANCE

CHAPTER THIRTY-NINE

SALT

It had been four days since Kitjári and Nalaníri set the Bighorn Dome to open. After they made their escape from the city of Runa, they had joined a group of fleeing Eastern Ikhel who had taken shelter near the slowly retreating vines. The women helped the refugees exit the dome by speeding the parting of the vines, until all the Ikhel in their vicinity had escaped to the New World.

They exited on the western side of the dome, near the city of Brinelaar. There they had found a small group of Oldrin mine workers who had been inspired by the rebellion and wanted to join it. With their knowledge of the salt mines, the Oldrin thought they could guide the entire group to safety—but they knew their freedom would not be secured without a fight.

"Charge! Now!" Kitjári commanded.

Hundreds of Ikhel fugitives and Oldrin miners rushed toward the unsuspecting guards patrolling the entrance to the mines. Probo surprised the Negians as a kuba, trampling them from their flank. Muri struck from above, dropping from an archway in the shape of a jarv wolverine; the Nu'irg ust Krost had regrown his chopped-off claws by now, and they were just as deadly as before. Most of the guards dutifully fought back, while others hopelessly tried to flee. The rebels soon dispatched the threats at the entrance, but reinforcements were approaching from down the road.

"Quickly! Get yer arses in them mines!" Nalaníri hollered.

"Close the gate!" one of the miners called, but there were still too many people trying to press into the tunnels. "Close the gate!"

Mounted soldiers arrived in a thunder of hooves and slashed at the slaves trying to slide the heavy gate closed.

"Keep moving in!" Kitjári ordered, rushing back to the enormous entrance, following an Oldrin woman who had been key in organizing the rebellion. Eikra was the woman's name—a stringy miner with prominent spurs on her head. Half of her scalp was covered with frizzy hair, the other half with sharp bone protrusions that looked like mountain ranges. Eikra had supplied them with a map, a strategy, and best of all, she had sent word out regarding the arrival of the Silvfröash, providing the mine workers with the spark of hope they needed to break their chains.

The salt mining operations at Brinelaar had recently restarted now that the workers were no longer crafting pipes for the Red Stag. Salt and potash kept the Negian economy running. It provided for their farms; it helped feed their people, and for too long the entire enterprise had been halted to support the Red Stag's unstoppable conquests. Viceroy Urcai had ordered the operations to resume, and so the mines were once more filled with thousands of Oldrin slaves, as well as numerous—yet outnumbered—guards.

Kitjári and Nalaníri followed Eikra into the square-cut tunnel. It was vast, with lanes wide enough for multiple wagons to venture in and out at the same time. They hopped over the bodies of a dozen Negian guards and a few fallen miners; the rebellion had started hours before they had arrived.

"They've sent word down the shafts, Lurrs," Eikra said. "Not all the slaves dare support the rebellion, but thousands may be joining. They'll escort us through."

"Thank you, Eikra," Kitjári said, trying to keep the pace.

Ahead of them, the great shaft narrowed and split into multiple tunnels. Too many curious miners were waiting there, who might soon be trampled by the fleeing rebels if they did not step aside.

"Make room fur us!" Nalaníri bellowed. "Mour uf us are coming!"

With a loud whistle, Eikra directed the rebels into the proper tunnel, where they followed a gurgling water canal that fed the deeper shafts. The channel was overgrown with salt crystals that sparkled under the torches and lamps, sparkling even more fiercely with the light cast by the pharoliths that the boar and bear carried.

"Our saviors are here!" they heard a voice from deeper down the shaft. "The Brides of Deliverance have come to set us free!"

"Brides uf Deliverance?" Nalaníri inquired.

"Do they mean us?" Kitjári asked back.

"It is you," Eikra said. "You who have freed the Teldebran, the Jojek, the Ikhel, and now have come to free the Oldrin. For months we have prayed to Pliwe, asking her to send you our way, and our goddess kindly has answered. A better life for the Oldrin is coming, thanks to you."

Kitjári felt uncomfortable with the high expectations of their friends, but she said nothing, instead moving as fast as possible.

"Negians behind us!" someone called out. They could not hear the clinking armor over all the footsteps, but they did hear screams of battle.

"Keep moving!" Eikra ordered. "Down to the Rose Chamber!"

A fight broke out behind them, but there was no way for the Silvfröash to help; the tunnels at this level were too narrow, preventing them from doubling back past the other rebels to reach the enemy. Kitjári found herself morbidly hoping that the dead bodies left behind would obstruct the passages enough to slow the attackers.

"In! In! Quickly!" Eikra demanded, rushing through a doorway.

Once all the Oldrin and Ikhel were inside the Rose Chamber, the miners dropped a heavy floodgate. Two unlucky Negian soldiers made it halfway into the chamber as the gate descended; their bodies were crushed under the rusted teeth. The soldiers outside began battering at the wooden gate with their axes. The boards began to splinter.

"Heave! Heave!" called a troop of miners, slowly pushing a massive block of salt toward the shattering gate as one axe cut through, then another.

"Move out uf d'way!" Nalaníri warned those hauling the block as Probo took his kubanochoerus form and ran to push it with his forehead. Just as the gate broke open, Probo slammed the enormous slab of salt into it, blocking the entrance.

Oldrin shaftmen, muckers, and trammers lodged metal wedges under the block to prevent it from being pushed back, then used heavy ropes to tie it to the wall. For good measure, they piled metal and wooden beams on top of it. Only then did they take a breath, salty sweat streaking their faces.

"Get me the foreman!" a Negian officer growled from behind the blocked passage. "Find us another way in. Now!"

Kitjári finally had a chance to admire the enormous chamber, which fit hundreds of people at once, with room for many more. The walls were carved of pink salt cut in hard, even strokes, although portions had been sculpted to resemble round columns and even balustrades. The Rose Chamber was a gathering spot for the miners, where they could eat their meals before trading shifts and quietly complain about their Negian bosses.

"Most of our workers wait beyond the second traverse," Eikra said to get Kitjári's attention. She opened a dirty map in front of them. "That passage is deep, but we can cut through it, then head up to the Blue Shrine. From there, it'll be a long trek, but it should lead us out into the middle of the mountains."

"They'll be out there waiting for us," Kitjári cautioned.

"No doubt they will," Eikra agreed, "but they'll have to split their troops between dozens of shafts, some miles away from one another. If they are divided, we can take them, Lurr."

"Then lead the way."

The refugees descended salt-carved steps into a deeper tunnel. Many shafts opened to the left and right, leading into a dark yet sparkling labyrinth with ceilings blackened by years of smoke. They moved briskly past stacks of barrels—some empty, others filled with pink boulders of salt. Kitjári's attention was briefly caught as they scrambled past a niche with a carved figure illuminated by a wide candle; then she saw another of the strange carvings, and another. Eikra noticed her confounded face and explained, "They are salt carvings of Pliwe, Wawumána, and Raushamitt. Our Oldrin gods. You will see more of them at the Blue Shrine."

They continued for nearly an hour, past the first and second traverse, closing gates, blocking passages, and picking up more recruits along the way. They even enlisted a few sympathetic Negian miners—criminals sentenced to forced labor, subjected to nearly the same harsh treatment as the Oldrin.

"The Brides of Deliverance are here," Kitjári and Nalaníri kept hearing in hushed murmurs.

Occasionally they encountered Negian guards or supervisors. When the enemies fought, they were killed. If they smartly surrendered at the sight of the incoming masses, they were tied up and shoved aside, though sometimes even the yielding Negians were killed; the rebels were angry, their hearts pumping with vengeful blood, and in no mood to take unnecessary risks.

Their path climbed once more, past chambers narrow and broad, through the water pumps and the mills, until finally Eikra stopped at a closed gate of carved salt. Through a translucent, blue-tinted door, they could see the bright and welcoming flicker of firelight, refracted by the embossed figures of the Oldrin deities.

"I thought these mines would be drab and unwelcoming," Kitjári said, "but they can be quite beautiful."

"We made them our home," Eikra said, then banged a metal pole in a coded pattern that notified those beyond that it was safe to open the door. "The mines have provided salt for the Empire for nearly a thousand years," she said as they waited. "We have lived here for many generations. We are born here, we die here, and so we make it a place of our own, even if it will never be our Dorhond home."

The salt door to the Blue Shrine slid open. Six Oldrin priests waited beyond the portal, bowing lightly to the newcomers while casting fine grains of salt on the ground for them to walk upon. The shrine was carved of blue-tinted salt, and it was grander and more majestic than the Rose Chamber. Though the salt was contaminated with unwanted minerals, the Oldrin had worked hard during their little free time to make this a chamber of their own.

No cast bronze or carved marble could match the opulence of the salt sculptures within the Blue Shrine. In striking detail, the Oldrin had carved the beauty of the onyx temples of Oskirin, of the selenite shrines of the White Desert, and of the golden stupas of the Thirteen Peaks, all in one single chamber.

"The Brides of Deliverance!" many voices rejoiced, flooding the Blue Shrine with hope and excitement.

Once all of the rebels had entered, the salt gate was closed shut and workers secured the passage with twin iron portcullises. It seemed an unnecessary precaution, as many other gates had already been shut behind them; even an entire intersection had been collapsed to block any entry.

Kitjári and Nalaníri sat on fancifully carved salt benches, Probo and Muri panting at their feet, while Eikra spoke with the priests.

Kitjári looked up to a sculptural ceiling that disappeared into darkness. The blue of the chamber was striking, marbled with whites and turquoise smears, revealing its stripes and agate-like patterns in the smooth carvings. The architecture stunningly contrasted with the decorative statuary, which was all carved in pink. As the bear lowered her gaze, she took in the exhausted faces of the refugees; they had battled and fled for Takh knew how long, and they had not gotten more than an hour or two of sleep over the past few days.

"These mines feel larger than the ones at Laaja Khem," she said through an exaggerated yawn.

"Them do, although I doubt we'll a-find any senstregalv blades here. I could use a new paring knife, but a blade made uf salt would overseason all uf mine dishes."

"It'd overseason the Negians you stab, too."

Nalaníri chuckled tiredly. She moistened a hoofed finger, slid it across the blue salt of the bench, and brought it to her mouth; the salty taste was also slightly acidic.

Watching over her shoulder, Eikra noticed the gesture and approached them, leaving the six priests to wait for a moment. "A bit won't hurt," she said, "but do not eat the blue salt. It is poisonous. That is why the Negians let us carve this chamber, they do not want it."

"I'm surprised they let you build something like this," Kitjári said.

"It is harmless, and keeps us happy. Happy slaves work harder. But happy is a relative term, as we have just caught a taste of freedom, and no chamber of salt will ever again be enough for us—not today, not tomorrow, not till the Endfall buries us under the sands beyond time."

One of the priests shyly spoke something in the Oldrin tongue, getting Eikra's attention.

"The priests say we can spend the night here," she interpreted, "even though I believe it's already daytime by now. We need rest. It will take us all of tomorrow to get to the exit shafts. Perhaps longer, if we run into more trouble."

The priest bowed lightly and spoke once more, as if imploring. Eikra listened, then translated, "They want to know if you'd both offer your blessings. For their protection."

"Er, sure?" Kitjári said. "Though we don't know how."

"All you must do is kneel before the effigies and light a candle."

"Easy enough," Nalaníri said, getting to her feet.

Eikra spoke to the priests, who smiled widely before leading the way deeper into the chamber, sprinkling more salt to make a path for the Silvfrö-ash. Hundreds of miners began to follow them in a solemn procession, all eerily quiet.

"What's a-happening?" Nalaníri asked.

"Don't know. Just go with it," Kitjári murmured in response.

At the far end of the Blue Shrine was a fountain, flowing within a vaulted niche of blue salt that held three plinths, one for each of the major Oldrin deities. A pink statue of Pliwe was on top, her three horns wrapped around her like a triple crescent, spitting a constant stream of water from the mouth at her navel; Wawumána, to the left, offered three streams, one from each of her breasts; and Raushamitt, to the right, pissed a broken stream from his triple-split penis. Below the three deities was a triangular altar, sparkling with overgrown salt crystals as if the hoarfrosts of Umbra had settled upon it. Two life-sized pink salt statues stood upon the altar: one of a bear and one of a boar, both standing on two legs, side by side.

"Is that... us?" Kitjári had to ask, gawking at the depiction of herself. It was rather monstrous in appearance, a bit too gratuitous with the teeth and claws, although holding a certain charm in the calm posture.

"That may be ye, m'dear," Nalaníri whispered, "but that uther one can't be me. Them tusks are enormous."

Two unlit candles waited at the bases of the bear and boar statues. Eikra produced a braided length of hemp with a small flame at the tip and handed it to Nalaníri.

Nalaníri glanced at Eikra and the priests. "Shell I light mine own, or Kitjári's?" The priests seemed uncertain, not having any established protocol for this particular ritual.

"Never ye mind, I'll do Kitjári's," she said, kneeling in front of the bear statue and setting its candle aflame before handing the braid to Kitjári.

Kitjári kneeled as well, then lit the wick in front of the boar statue.

Reverential gasps echoed throughout the chamber.

The pink eyes of the two effigies looked down at the kneeling Silvfröash, shimmering with the reflected flames.

"The Brides of Deliverance have blessed us!" an anonymous voice called from a salt balcony. "We too shall be free!"

"To Dorhond! To freedom!" came a reply.

"To freedom!"

Nalaníri swallowed, then said, "Them are putting mighty pressure un us."

CHAPTER FORTY

STOWAWAYS

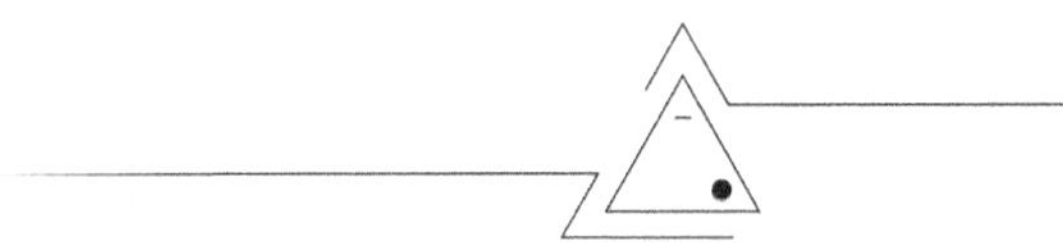

Kitjári and Nalaníri woke up in a small circular dormitory the Oldrin had set aside for them. The walls of salt glittered with the pharolith light, particularly on the ceiling, where the moisture had condensed and formed blobs of white crystals like spider eggs.

Kitjári pushed the door open, which made a scraping sound as it swung. "What is all this?" she asked Nalaníri, stepping out to find the ground in front of their chamber littered with small salt figurines. There were hundreds of them, shaped like bears and boars, some even shaped like badgers; some on four legs, more often on two.

"I think them are ufferings, fur us. Some fur d'Nu'irgesh even."

"That's… kind of them. But I'm not hauling a ton of rocks along with us. Let's find Eikra, it must be about time to move on."

After a quick meal a friendly miner offered them as they exited their quarters, the women reconvened with Eikra and the priests to solidify their strategy.

"We'll need the Nu'irgesh to help us fight our way out through these four shafts," Eikra said, pointing at the map. "The enemy will likely be waiting for us there, but we'll have a squad exit farther south as a diversion, then rush back in to draw their forces into a dead end. We'll flank them from these two shafts while our scouts rush up the hill to make sure there are no more incoming threats. Then we'll make our way out through the mountains, but that will take us months. Perhaps some of us will find a home there, while others might continue until they reach our homeland."

"You've given this much thought," Kitjári said approvingly. "And you read the land very well. Were you a soldier?"

"Captain for a Dorhond platoon, before we were captured and sold by the Negians. I do not wish to return to that life. It was full of death and uncertainty. I just want to roam free once again."

"Seems t'me that ye could've done this a long time ago," Nalaníri said. "Yer numbers are much greater than them Negians. Why haven't ye escaped through them mountains before?"

"A few have. The Negians punish the families of those who escape, as a deterrent, so not many ever attempt it. The rest of us just needed a nudge, a sign to join together and fight, so that we could all be free at the same time. We've been waiting, for you."

"Sorry we're a bit late," Nalaníri said. "We've been busy, ye could say."

"We will not be able to follow you through the mountain path," Kitjári added. "We need the Empire to lose our tracks, and we need to move west, not east or south, and as fast as possible."

Eikra considered for a moment, studying the map. "If you need to escape west, there is one way I could aid you. But it will depend on how nimble your bodies are."

For a day and a half, they sped through the mines. They didn't find many more Oldrin, as they were now passing through older tunnels, long exhausted or flooded, and abandoned for the richer, cleaner salts in the southern shafts. Their army had grown to nearly two thousand. Knowing the time to fight would soon come, the rebels picked up makeshift weapons while on the move.

"Stop licking your lips," Eikra warned Nalaníri, "it will just make them dry faster." The amount of air the large group displaced was lifting up clouds of salty dust which stuck to their lips and noses, making them feel as if they were traversing a desert.

The group arrived at an intersection where many old shafts connected. They broke through the wooden boards of abandoned tunnels and split their army across multiple shafts. Decoys were sent to the outside, who got the attention of the Negian patrols on the surface before hurrying back through tight shafts their foes would have a hard time entering.

As the Negian troops gathered to inspect the opening, miners flooded out like ants protecting their nest. Probo and Muri led the attack in their largest forms, taking down any mounted soldiers, while the Oldrin and Ikhel surrounded the infantry and slowly picked them apart.

"There are more coming over the hill!" a sentinel warned. "Two wicks till they get here!"

"Over the mountain pass, now! Do not slow down!" Eikra ordered, although she did not follow that path. "With me, quickly," she said to Kitjári and Nalaníri, "before they see us."

"Probo, Muri!" Nalaníri called. The Nu'irgesh returned to their primal forms and hurried to her.

After Eikra led them through a long, empty tunnel, they arrived at a chamber with a wheel in the center, with heavy spokes that were meant to be pushed by horses. The wheel was not for milling, but for lifting crates filled with salt up a vertical shaft, carrying them directly to the surface.

Eight Negian guards waited in the chamber, but they were all defectors who had helped the miners strategize since the start of the uprising. They saluted Eikra, then their leader told her, "They are ready to receive the goods."

Eikra approached the vertical shaft and whistled loudly. Another whistle answered her call, almost like an echo. "It is safe. Get in."

"Thank you," Kitjári said. "We are in your debt."

"It is we who are indebted to you, Brides of Deliverance."

"Please don't—"

"I am jesting. I know you hate the title. Hand me your gear, then get in the crates. We will plant offerings in your name to keep you safe. Go now, freedom awaits."

"Will the pig and raccoon mind sharing this crate?" one of the Negians asked, opening the lid and placing Kitjári's belongings in it, including her treasured bow.

"Javelina and honey badger!" Nalaníri corrected the man, then told Probo that he and Muri should take their smallest forms to fit among all the gear. Muri growled at this, but then shapeshifted into a least weasel and followed after the pygmy hog.

Nalaníri stepped into her own crate. "I'm not sure I'm gunna fit…" she complained, trying to negotiate how to contort herself within the cramped space.

Both Kitjári and Nalaníri barely fit inside their crates. Once the lids closed, they were sealed with rusty nails, making the two women feel as if they were being entombed in sarcophagi. The containers were loaded onto the lift alongside a set of identical boxes filled with pink salt blocks. One of these was marked with a red lid and had not just salt inside, but also a Qupi pouch stuffed with four Quggons, two silver Krujels, a precious topaz, and a vial of soot—a worthy bribe.

With Urnaadisilv's aid, Kitjári watched as the Negians pushed on the heavy spokes of the wheel, twisting the thick ropes and pulling the lift up the long shaft. They were quickly lost from her mask's sight.

"This damnable shaft is longer than a Puqua ballad," Nalaníri complained.

"Be quiet! We don't know if—"

"Eikra said d'men un top are people we can trust."

"They are being bribed," Kitjári said. "They think we are Oldrin slaves trying to escape. If they hear your accent, they'll know something else is going on."

A moment later, they felt sunlight breaking in through cracks between the planks. Kitjári observed the threads outside her crate, feeling the presence of four men and two bison ready to pull a wagon. One of the men used an axe to pry open the red-lidded crate, checking its contents. Satisfied with the payment, he ordered the others to load the cargo onto the wagon. The containers were tossed around with no care, tumbling and smashing against each other. Sore and cramping, Kitjári's only comfort was that Nalaníri's crate was right next to hers, the two of them bouncing up and down together while the wagon rolled down the road toward the city of Kalford.

Five torturous hours later, the wagon stopped. The crates were unloaded.

Kitjári was glad that this time they were at least placed in the proper orientation, resting on their backs. She could hear the sounds of workers at some sort of milling machinery, and could smell the foul, decaying flesh from a tannery, as well as the scents of cooking oils.

"What's a-happening?" Nalaníri whispered, noticing that the men had joined another group, far enough away that they would not hear her whispers.

"They're bribing the next group," Kitjári said. "Let's hope the payment was enough for all of them. At this point, it's in their best interest to get rid of us, because if they are found out, they'll also get in trouble."

"Mine arse can't tolerate this much longer."

"Well, I'm being cooked alive in here. I left my brime cube in my pocket, and it's boiling up this crate like a cauldron. It'll be a long while before we are out, so you better make your *arse* comfortable and think of what spices you'll season me with when you finally open my casket."

Their whispering was interrupted by an argument among the men. Voices were raised, fists were waved, but no blades were drawn. The men approached the containers and began to roll them away on dollies, down a path lined with cobbles, then up a wooden ramp onto the swaying deck of a merchant ship. Nalaníri anxiously watched for Muri's and Probo's auras as they drifted apart, but the Nu'irgesh's crate was placed not too far from her own.

"Probo says Muri's a stinker," Nalaníri remarked once there were no more threats within hearing range. "He says he's just as bad now that he's a weasel as when he chooses t'be a skunk."

"Please tell them to stay quiet in there…"

"He's holding his squeals, fur now, but can't promise t'do d'same with d'contents uf his stomach."

The ship jolted as it pulled away from the dock. The swaying motion was a comfort compared to the rattling of the wagon. They closed their eyes and tried to forget about time and their aching bodies, doing their best to relax as the ship sailed downriver.

The brightness and warmth of Sunnokh vanished soon after. Many hours later, when most of the sailors had gone to sleep, Nalaníri tapped lightly against the lid of her crate.

"*Pssst…* How many mour hours uf torture do we have left?"

"How should I know?"

"Are we close, at least?"

Kitjári rolled her eyes. "It's at least a hundred miles to the port of Duam, but we are helped by the Stiss Kikna's current. I'm guessing we might get there in the morning sometime."

"Then anuther bribe?"

"That's how things work. They'll leave the crates at the docks overnight, then we get out and run away. However, it's hard to trust these arsemunchers. Some of them will try to sell the slaves they 'rescue' back to other mines, far from Brinelaar."

They dozed off again, and later woke up to the tapping of raindrops on the tops of their containers.

Kitjári felt strange not being able to see the rain with her Silv, despite it being a fountain of life. The deck of the ship, the cargo, the lines, and the river beneath them were visible to her, covered by tenuous threads of consciousness, filled with life from all the microorganisms that inhabited every crevice. The rain, however, was only present to her by sound. But she was glad for its presence; the moisture seeped in and helped her cool off.

As the bear focused her sight around the ship, she noticed two sailors approaching. She recognized them, tasting a certain flavor through the Silvesh that she had sensed before: they were two of the men who had taken the bribe from the ones who had driven the wagon. The men seemed overly cautious, checking their surroundings as they approached the containers.

"—no no, on the other side. It's these three here."

They stopped. One of them squatted down and tapped on Kitjári's lid. "Hey little spur, I hope you are enjoying your cozy coffer. You better stay quiet now, you dirty mine scum."

"Which one is the odd one?"

"This here," the man said, standing by the crate that held Kitjári's backpack, weapons, and the two Nu'irgesh. "Crawfenn said it's another spur, but you can tell it's not, by the weight and how it balances. He's trying to deliver something valuable, otherwise he wouldn't have paid us so well for the job."

"What do you think it is?"

"Whatever those slaves were trying to steal from the salt mines, I guess. Why else would they be fleeing? Do you know if there's any gold in there? Magnium veins perhaps?"

"That'd be heavier than a spur."

"Yeah, maybe, might be something else. Whatever it is, it's worth something and then some, and that asshole is making us carry it for him and take all the risk. He should've told us the truth."

The man leaned over Kitjári's crate once more. "You keep your filthy mouth quiet, spur, or we'll rip off your teeth and nail them to your forehead." He straightened up and pulled out a crowbar. "Let's see what's in this treasure trove," he said, wedging one end of the crowbar under the lid of the crate that held the Nu'irgesh.

Crack!

"Fuuck—*aaaaagghh!*" came an agonizing scream.

Kitjári pushed up with her elbows, popping out of her crate to see a man with his face being slashed to shreds by an angry honey badger. Nalaníri freed herself as well, but immediately tipped over, her legs weakened and useless.

The other man saw the furred creatures and ran away screaming. "Stowaways!" he cried out. "It's the nether demons!"

"Get t'him, m'boy!" Nalaníri urged Probo.

The pygmy hog hopped out of the crate and gave chase, shapeshifting into a celebochoerus to trample the man, leaving him broken and moaning on the deck.

Kitjári inhaled the fresh air as she clung to the lines to regain her balance, relearning how to use her legs. She helped Nalaníri to her feet, then picked up her backpack and weapons. "We have to escape before they see us."

She unsheathed her sword, finished off the man with the torn face, then ran toward the one Probo had trampled. She hesitated for a moment, then self-consciously said, "Sorry," before slicing the man's neck. "Can't leave any witnesses."

"Who's there?" a voice called. A lantern cast shadows on the deck, moving closer.

"Where to?" Nalaníri asked.

"Just jump, we'll figure it out later. Jump!"

The four of them dove into the dark river.

They were shocked by the sudden cold; most of the Stiss Kikna was fed by glaciers or snowmelt from the mountains. They tried to ignore the feeling of frigid needles piercing their bodies and began swimming toward the shore.

It was miles away.

Light. Torches. The dead men had been found, and the sailors were seeking the stowaways who had murdered them.

"There's movement in the water!" a voice warned.

Kitjári felt something lifting her from below—it was Muri, in his mega-lenhydris form. She held on to the enormous otter as he swam fast to shore, carrying all of them, quickly leaving the ship behind.

CHAPTER FORTY-ONE

TRADING POST

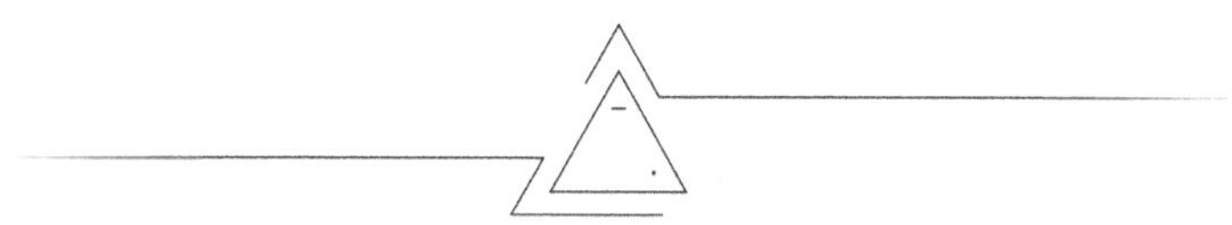

"Ye sure it's safe, m'dear?"

"I don't care if it's safe. Keep watch, we need to warm up."

Morning had not yet arrived. They had reached a silty shore, hopefully far enough away from any villages that they would not be noticed, although ships kept moving up and down the river.

Jiara took off her wet clothes and shook off the excess water before returning to her bear half-form. With her fur no longer wet, she began to light a fire with driftwood and dried dune grasses she found along the shore. The flames offered immediate comfort.

"Here, you can have my brime," she said to Nalaníri. "Keep it in your hands till they warm up."

Sitting close to each other, they warmed up by the fire before worrying about drying their clothes.

"It'll be fine once Sunnokh is out." Kitjári tried to sound comforting, but she knew full well that Winter still kept a hold of these lands, whether by day or night, and that Thawing would not arrive for two more weeks.

Probo curled up by Nalaníri's feet, still shivering. Muri, on the other hand, seemed perfectly fine, having taken the form of a red panda, insulating himself from the cold with his colorful fur.

Sunnokh rose, weakly offering a sliver of warmth.

They threw more wood onto the fire and hung their clothes to dry.

Kitjári pulled out their map and pointed with a claw. "I think we must be somewhere around here."

The paper was soaked and coming apart, the inks fading. Though the map had been kept in a waterproof pocket, it had not survived the long swim to shore.

Kitjári scanned their surroundings, memorizing landmarks. "That smoke south of us, I think that's Sharzi. It's a frontier town, part of the Tsing Empire, but it'll be filled with Negian soldiers and citizens. We'll have to be very careful."

A roadway cut through a deep valley toward the rising smoke. To its left were the Stelm Rilganesh: the tall mountains where the Bighorn Dome was now unmaking itself, although it was too far away for them to see it. To the right were the Stelm Tai-Du, white and unwelcoming, cradling the distant and invisible Tarpits Dome.

"N'that's where we're a-heading?" Nalaníri nearly gasped, eyes on the Tai-Du sierras. The mountains seemed impenetrable. They had hiked through more ice and snow in the Stelm Nedross and the Stelm Wujann than Nalaníri had seen in her entire life, but it seemed there was much more to come. She shivered at the thought.

Kitjári poked at the fire with a long branch. "I hope Muri knows his way, or we'll get lost in those peaks. Either way, we'll need more Winter clothes for you, and some supplies to help us across the mountains. I could buy what we need in Sharzi, while you hide somewhere outside of town."

"I'd like to pick mine own clothes."

"I wish you could come with me, but your spotted skin would draw too much attention. I can blend in better. It wouldn't be too strange for someone who looks like me to be traveling through here."

"Jis' make sure them aren't too tight fur me. And don't be a-getting into trouble."

Hours later, when their clothes seemed dry or at least warm enough to wear, they packed up, quickly scoured the nearby forest for nuts to eat, then headed south on an untrodden, snowy trail that ran close to the road to Sharzi.

"This will be a good place for you to hide," Jiara said as they neared the town, leading Nalaníri and the Nu'irgesh into a dense grove of trees bordering the western outskirts. "You can keep these," she added, wrapping her parka and cloak around Nalaníri's shoulders, all the while doing a little jogging dance to keep her own blood flowing. "I'll warm up while on the move."

"Do ye have enough money left?"

"Not much, but I still have one vial of soot I can trade." She wrapped her bright hair with a headscarf and left most of her belongings and weapons with Nalaníri.

"Ye sure ye don't want to take d'mask with ye?"

"It'd be too dangerous, someone might see it. And I'd rather not take my bag. I thought of an excuse so that I don't look too suspicious buying so many supplies at once." She tucked her Qupi pouch under her shirt, kissed the boar's snout, then took off down the road.

Sharzi was a quaint and welcoming mountain valley village. Although small and remote, it was well transited, as it stood in the crossroads between the Negian and Tsing empires and the lands of the Horde. Merchants from far and wide visited the village to trade goods; some sailing from the Ophidian, some all the way from the Alommo Sea, having to make their way through the Ravine Road, a great canyon that split the sierras.

Jiara's disheveled appearance did not seem entirely out of place among the mixed crowds. Still cold and shivering, she entered the largest store she could find: the Greywacke Trading Post.

A high-pitched metal bell rang above her as she entered the shop, but other than that, it was quiet inside. Disregarding the wares, she hurried toward the corner nearest the fireplace, warming herself while pretending to be interested in the boating equipment.

An old woman sat by the fire next to a younger woman who looked like her daughter. Both of them had their backs firmly planted against uncomfortable wicker chairs. The older woman had just lit a bundle of mistleaf in her much-too-lavish pipe.

"—escaped from Brinelaar, up the mountains," Jiara overheard. She sharpened her ears toward the conversation.

"Those Oldrin folk are so ungrateful…"

The older woman turned around, took a puff from her pipe and said, "May I help you, young Lurr?" Her demanding attitude suggested she was the trading post's owner.

"Oh. Sorry, didn't mean to eavesdrop," Jiara said. "I have a cousin who lives in Brinelaar. What happened?"

"The slaves escaped, helped by those monstrous Oldrin goddesses. They say they were summoned from the nethervoids, can you believe it? Not satisfied with ruining the other domes, they had to mess with Bighorn too, destroying our mines. How are we going to get salt next season? Huh? Who's going to provide for our farms?"

"That's terrible," Jiara said, then asked, "Goddesses?"

"The Brides of Devastation, that's what they call them."

"Brides of Desolation," the younger woman corrected.

"Right, that one. I found my two slaves praying to blasphemous figurines carved in their likenesses. I smashed them to pieces, that's what I did. Filthy spurs… Who knows where they got those horrible things?"

The old woman scrutinized Jiara, up and down then up again. "You have not heard of this? Have you been drinking, love?"

"Sorry, I just arrived in town. I was traveling up the canyon and… Someone stole my gear while I was hunting. Must've been those damn Oldrin fugitives."

The old woman struggled to relight her pipe, then faced Jiara again. "Unlikely, they aren't that far into the mountains yet. Have you reported the incident to Virrke? She's the head of the Sharzi rangers. You shouldn't let something like that go unreported."

"I'll do that as soon as I'm done here," Jiara answered.

The woman nodded, lips puckered into disgruntled wrinkles. "Just last week I saw a 'customer' stuff a potato in his pocket. I beat the sense and virtue back into his wretched self, and Virrke came right in and took the hoodlum away. For a potato. An unwashed, filthy potato. Can you believe it?"

"Sounds like he deserved it," Jiara said. "But please, don't beat me up if you see me stuff some things in a bag. My backpack was stolen too, so I'll have to carry things in one of the ones you sell here. I'll pay for it all, don't worry."

The old woman grumbled, shrugging dismissively, then got curious again. "You came all the way from Shusnukran, traveling alone?"

Jiara knew nothing of the Graalman city other than its name and that it was by the Alommo Sea. "Yes," she answered, offering no more details, then asked, "Have they captured those… demons? They are making me concerned for my uncle in Brinelaar."

"You mean your cousin?" the younger woman asked with a single eyebrow raised.

"Him too. Both of them, they are both in Brinelaar." Jiara swallowed, feeling a skeptical gaze settle on her.

The old woman puffed slowly, considering, and then said, "No, the demons escaped with the slaves. I hope they all freeze to death in the mountains. Would serve them right."

"Yeah, me too," Jiara replied, then moved away from the bitter women. She had warmed up enough and could make her fingers function properly again, so she began to browse for supplies.

Inside a new backpack, she packed a blanket, fire starting tools, a map, bags of dried meats, and a few pieces of survival and climbing gear, then went searching for clothes.

She tried on a heavy, oversized parka. "Don't worry, I'm paying for all of this," she reassured the old woman, who had left the wicker chair and was eyeing her curiously.

"Did they steal your clothes too?"

"I had left most of my belongings at my camp. But I never leave without my Qupi pouch." She jingled her pouch, which seemed to appease the shopkeeper.

Jiara tried to find practical garments in Nalaníri's size, but all the women's clothes were pointlessly fanciful dresses. In the men's area, she found canvas trousers and suspenders of the right size, as well as a good belt, heavier shirts, and other layers to wear.

She'll like this, Jiara thought, spotting a vest similar to the one Nalaníri used to wear, which had been lost to the chasm by the city of Runa. This leather vest was a tad heavier, but it included enough pockets for her lover's collection of spices.

Spices, she remembered. She picked a selection of condiments from among the meager choices, and also picked up better cooking supplies, including a collection of knives.

"Those are Graalman forged," the old woman said as she passed by the aisle. "They are quite pricy, just warning you."

"That'll be alright."

"Is there anything else you need? Where are you venturing to?"

"No, I think that'll be it, that's all that those thieves took from me. I'm headed to Brinelaar next, but I'll be wary of the escaped Oldrin, don't worry."

The old woman walked behind the counter and combed her long eyebrows, waiting. Jiara handed her the bag with all its contents. The old woman eyed Jiara carefully, eyes more on the Tribeswoman than on the items she was adding up in her head, calculating without aid of paper or abacus.

"That'll be two hundred and fifty-three Grunnels. Two fifty, to make it easier."

"I... Are you able to take Qupis?" Jiara asked.

"I thought you just came from Shusnukran. Shouldn't you be carrying Grunnels with you?"

Jiara was not familiar with the value of the Graalman coins, so instead of asking and looking like a bigger fool, she took out her Qupi pouch and spread her Quggon and change onto the table.

"That's not even half of it, dear," the woman said, sucking on her cheek.

"I can also trade you this." She took out her small vial of soot and placed it in the woman's hand.

The shopkeeper looked at the bottle while trying to keep her expression blank and cold as fresh snow. She swallowed, then candidly said, "You know, I can't take this much. I don't have enough Qupis, Krujels, or Grunnels with me for change at this time." She returned the vial of soot to Jiara, then began to hurriedly pull the items behind the counter. "Why don't you go to the bank and break this into something manageable, then come back and—"

"It's fine. You can keep the entire bottle."

"But it's too much for what you are buying, dear. You should come back later."

"It's real soot, I'm not trying to—"

The metal bell rang, and the woman glanced at the entrance of the store. Her daughter, who had left silently a bit earlier, came in, followed by a tall woman in leather armor.

"This is Virrke," the young woman said, "from the Sharzi rangers. I thought I'd bring her over, since I saw her down the street. You should tell her about that thief who took all your stuff."

The old woman at the counter eyed the ranger with urgency and fear.

The ranger glanced at Jiara, then at the trading post's owner, then back at Jiara. She put her hand on the pommel of her sword.

Nalaníri hummed as she tossed the hot cube of brime from one hand to the other. She was watching Muri hop around clumsily in the snow; as a red panda, he stood out vibrantly, looking entirely different from his more intimidating forms, and even less grumpy. Nalaníri was surprised at how even a creature as ancient and wise as a Nu'irg could rejoice in the simple pleasure of jumping in a mound of fresh white powder.

"We need to move! Now!" came a distant cry.

Nalaníri stood up. She could not see much from within the copse of trees.

"Nalaníri! Go! Run!"

Jiara broke into the grove, wearing an oversized parka and hauling a backpack full of supplies. "Where is Probo?" she panted. "We need him as a kuba."

"What's a-going—"

"Now! Grab our gear!"

Nalaníri called for Probo, who came tumbling through the snow. He quickly turned into his kubanochoerus form and let the two of them climb onto his back.

"In there! She went through those trees!" came a loud voice. Hooves of galloping horses echoed not much farther away.

"Go Probo! Move!" Jiara ordered.

Probo ran aimlessly, toppling down trees on his way out of their hiding spot.

"Muri! Here!" Nalaníri called, tapping on Probo's bristly shoulders. The red panda leapt toward Probo, grabbed on to his back leg, and climbed aboard.

The troop of rangers froze at the sight of the charging kuba, jumping out of the way to avoid being trampled by the enormous suid. Probo carved a path in the snow, uncertain of where to go.

"What in d'twelve fjords did ye do? Did ye steal all uf this?"

"I didn't steal anything, I left them a valuable vial of soot and all my Qupi. But I guess my lies weren't convincing enough. They got suspicious and—turn right! Here!"

The kuba turned sharply.

"We need to lose them in the mountains," Jiara said. "Can Muri help us?"

Nalaníri communicated with the Nu'irgesh as she rummaged through the backpack. While handing Urnaadisilv to Jiara, she said, "Muri's a-telling us t'enter that canyon. Might be our unly chance."

Jiara shapeshifted, standing atop the giant suid to get a better view; the canyon ahead narrowed too quickly, like a deadly trap. Behind them, the horse riders were catching up, some following Probo's tracks while others paralleled them on the roadway. Kitjári was suddenly jolted sideways as Probo turned toward the canyon, plowing through the tapered mouth and entering a wider, boulder-sprinkled labyrinth.

As a pine marten, Muri ran over Probo's back and launched himself from the tip of the kuba's forehead horn, landing in a poof of snow. Finding his way between logs and rocks, Muri directed them to higher ground.

Probo used his heavy legs to batter through rotten tree trunks, following the pine marten through a leafless, snowy forest.

"Over there! Up the hill!" echoed the calls from the soldiers, now joined by reinforcements from the village.

"Where is he taking us?" Kitjári asked.

"A shortcut," Nalaníri interpreted. "He says horses won't fullow this way."

Even Probo had a hard time following Muri. Despite his enormously long legs, the land was too uneven and too hard to read with so much snow obscuring the ground.

They ascended a terraced hill crowned by leafless birches. Muri kept on running ahead, leaping from tree to tree toward a flat wall of rock, while Probo pummeled his way through thin-limbed birches.

The wall drew closer and closer, yet Muri did not stop. Once at the base of the wall, he nimbly climbed a slender tree and jumped, easily reaching the top of the obstacle—but the top was nearly thirty feet up.

"You stupid, long rat!" Kitjári screamed. "We can't climb that!"

Their pursuers reached the terraced formations. "They are up here! Nock your arrows!"

Probo suddenly stood on his hind legs and stretched up, placing his chin on the rock wall.

Kitjári and Nalaníri barely held on to the wiry back fur, swaying left and right.

"Climb! Probo says t'climb!" Nalaníri managed to yell.

Thwack!

An arrow hit the rock wall. A dozen more followed.

"Hurry up!" Kitjári said, making her way toward Probo's ear. She assisted Nalaníri up to the kuba's horn, then boosted her higher until she reached the upper ledge of the wall. Nalaníri pulled herself up, then extended an arm down to help Kitjári, but the bear simply rushed up the suid's head, planted a solid footpaw onto the tip of his horn, and leapt, landing her elbows over the ledge.

More arrows rained down upon them, some flashing sparks against the wall, others sinking into the snow behind them.

"The rope! Hand me the quaar rope!" Kitjári shouted.

"Ye can't pull him—"

"Now! And tell Probo to turn into whatever is lightest."

Probo shapeshifted into a pygmy hog, disappearing into the snow just as more arrows impacted the wall where the kuba had been a heartbeat ago.

"Get them! Charge!" Soldiers galloped closer, following the clear path Probo had carved.

Kitjári made a lasso with the quaar rope and dropped it. "Tell him to stick his body in there."

Nalaníri did so, and Probo obeyed, but Kitjári pulled the lasso up too soon—it tightened around Probo's neck like a noose. The tiny hog squealed, then went silent from the pressure.

"Don't let them escape!" came a call from below.

Rather than pulling the rope one armful at a time, Kitjári ran away from the cliff, dragging Probo up at full speed. The suid bonked his head against the rocks, bounced over the cliff's edge, and landed in the snow.

"M'boy!" Nalaníri cried out, rushing to untie the rope from the Nu'irg's neck. "Mine poor boy, are ye alright?"

Probo shook himself to his feet and charged directly at Kitjári. He slammed into her at full force, although still only in his pygmy hog form. Kitjári fell on the snow, holding her bruised shin.

"Probo says ye deserve that one," Nalaníri said as she tightened the straps on her backpack. "Now let's get out uf here 'fore them find a way up. Muri! Show us d'way!"

CHAPTER FORTY-TWO

THE SIERRA PASS

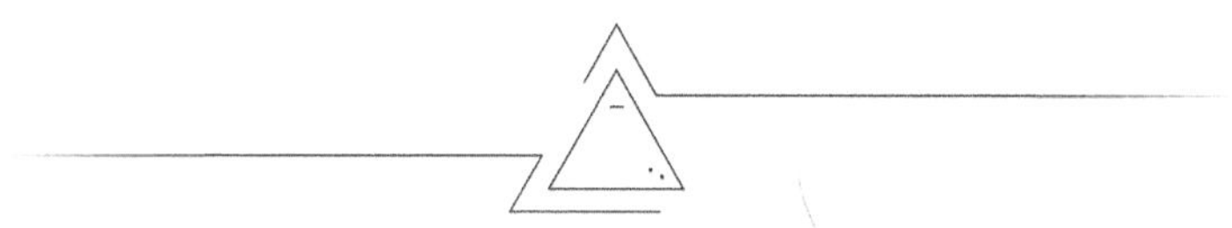

"Them fit me jis' right," Nalaníri said, trying on the new trousers, shirt, vest, and parka Kitjári had forcefully purchased at the trading post. "Never had t'wear one uf these. What's them called again?"

"Suspenders," Kitjári replied with an approving nod. "They look good on you, though you probably don't need them if you are wearing the belt."

"Them feel better, no pressure un mine belly."

They had nestled in a nearly unreachable crevice past a steep wall of rock. If any rangers dared follow behind them, they'd be able to hear them coming, and would have a clean and fast way out across a snowy slope. Nevertheless, Nalaníri kept staring upward, expecting someone to suddenly appear above them.

"Stop being so anxious," Kitjári said, picking out a few dried meats to lunch on. "Even if those soldiers were trained in the mountains, which by the looks of them most weren't, they'll have a hard time getting to us." She kept digging through the bag of goods. "Hey, I got you these, too."

Nalaníri picked up the leather bundle. Inside was the set of Graalman knives, including a chef's knife, a paring knife, a carving knife, a bread knife, a sharpener, and three other blades neither Kitjári nor Nalaníri knew the purposes for.

"Good steel," Nalaníri said. "Them'll do. Thank ye, m'dear."

"And these too." She handed her the few spices she had found at the trading post: pink peppercorns, cinnamon, oregano, thyme, powdered ginger, and nutmeg. "Not for cooking tonight, however. We'll be safe in this crevice, but making a fire would be asking for trouble."

Nalaníri smelled the spices. "A bit stale, but them'll do. No salt?"

"I… I didn't even think of it."

"Hmm… I didn't want it t'come t'this, but I may have t'use ye instead." She reached in her pocket and pulled out a bear-shaped figurine carved of pink salt.

"Hey! You kept one too?"

"Too?"

Kitjári searched in her bag and removed a pink boar.

Nalaníri laughed. "Never ye mind. I'm not a-cooking with our figures. I'd rather scrape d'salt frum mine sweaty brow instead. Them carvings are too precious."

Kitjári took both salt carvings and put them side by side on a rock, to watch over them.

"The Brides of Devastation will protect us tonight," she said.

"Wasn't it uf *deliverance*?"

"Depends on who you ask. Brides of Desolation too, apparently. That's what this shopkeeper called us. I have to tell you what happened there. It was a bit tense."

Muri quickly understood that a path fit for an ermine or badger was not necessarily one fit for human-shaped bodies or for Probo's cloven hooves. He found more suitable trails for them, often hidden, cutting through icy caves and chasms, guiding them deeper into the sierras.

Fortunately for the two women, Muri was an expert hunter, and even when Kitjári had no energy left to hunt, the honey badger would bring back something nutritious for them before Sunnokh dipped below the horizon. He would then wait patiently for Nalaníri to cook, grunting in anticipation.

The Stelm Tai-Du were inhospitable and hard to traverse. Without the Nu'irg's help, it would have taken many months to cut through the tall mountains. Muri had lived in these ranges for millennia, hunting for rodents, amphibians, hares, and birds. His favorite pastime had been stealing eggs from falcon nests and stealing cheese from the pantries of the Dorvauros folk who had lived among the peaks centuries ago.

A week into their journey, Muri recognized the first of the pre-Downfall trails, although it remained invisible to the others. He followed it, finding an abandoned underground passage, which led them into a snow-covered yet lively valley, with icy waterfalls beginning to cascade down the southern faces of the mountains—Thawing was near.

"This valley must look so colorful in Spring and Autumn," Kitjári said as they followed Muri and Probo. She kept count of all the different species of trees, all alive despite their leaflessness: with the cottonwoods, aspens, ashes, beeches and birches alone, the valley would look like a small paradise during any other season.

From the northern end of the valley, closest to the many waterfalls, they could peer over the summits to catch a glimpse of the Tarpits Dome, over a hundred miles to the southwest on a raven's wing. But ravens they were not, and their own path would prove much longer and windier.

"I wonder what the dome is like," Kitjári mused, gazing off into the distance. "I wonder what the Nu'irg is like, too. Banook once told us a bit about her. Did you know she can take the form of a woman?"

"Uf course," Nalaníri replied. "Buujik, Nu'irg ust Hoombu, d'red-shanked douc uf d'Sai-Salóm Forest. All Puqua learn about them Nu'irgesh when we are but furless piglets. We're told bedtime stories 'bout them."

"I wonder what she looks like… As a human, I mean."

Nalaníri eyed her skeptically. "Are ye thinking filthy thoughts 'bout a woman ye haven't even met? No, not a woman, a monkey. A Nu'irg monkey."

"I was just curious!"

"Keep them ideas out uf yer head, m'dear. We have a Nu'irg already with filthy enough thoughts fur all uf us."

Probo looked back at the women, then turned away and bounced his balls away, pretending to ignore them.

They dropped their bags by a shallow creek glittering with colorful, rounded pebbles. The gurgling of the flowing water made them eager to sit down and rest, as did the mid-afternoon sun, which contrasted soothingly with the chilling breeze.

"I'm glad the snow is finally beginning to melt," Jiara said, washing a bundle of wild beets and cattail shoots in the cold stream. She always took her human form when she helped Nalaníri cook—her human hands were better for it, and she didn't like getting her fur in the ingredients. "But we're going to be climbing higher each day," she added. "We'll likely travel through snow all the way till we get to the dome." She handed the beets and cattails to Nalaníri, who was preparing a grilled duck.

"Peel uff a few mour layers frum them, m'dear," Nalaníri said, handing back the cattail shoots. "Them are quite tender un d'inside. We can have them raw."

Jiara carefully trimmed the shoots while keeping her eyes on Probo. "How is he doing?" she asked.

Nalaníri took a quick glance toward Probo, who was sleeping at the base of a maple tree. He looked tired, despite being at rest. "He's beginning t'feel d'loneliness. There are no suids in this valley, or farther into d'mountains. Did ye notice d'gray hairs un his brow?"

Jiara walked over to Probo to take a closer look at him. She squatted down and petted the javelina's head. "Poor thing, I had not noticed. He does look weary. Maybe a bit skinnier than usual, but not by much."

"He'll tell me when he's feeling too distant," Nalaníri reassured her.

Probo lightly snorted in his sleep.

Jiara helped with the vegetables while Nalaníri prepared the duck. They tossed scraps to their sides, which were quickly devoured by a handful of pine martens, skunks, and raccoons who lived in the valley, and who had been eagerly following Muri around.

Nalaníri measuredly seasoned the meat. Despite having started with only the few spices that Jiara had picked up at the trading post, Nalaníri's collection had quickly grown. While hiking, she had picked up minty wintergreen leaves, spicy watercress, aromatic juniper berries, and tangles of reindeer moss, among many other delicacies that could enhance flavors and would not upset their stomachs if used sparingly.

The duck breast—marinated with thyme and black walnut syrup—was placed to slowly cook on the grill.

"Thank ye, Muri," Nalaníri said to the expectant honey badger. "This is a good bird. Nice and fatty fur a Winter catch." Muri grunted, pacing eagerly around the fire with two baby skunks following him.

Jiara sat next to Nalaníri to help her peel bark from birch branches, dropping the slivers onto a handkerchief. She let the flickering fire warm her skin as she emptied the cuts of birch bark into a pot of boiling water. "They better not make a mess of our camp," she said, eyeing the skunks.

"Them two are too young to spray, but we better not upset mum." Nalaníri kept watch for the mother skunk, who was hunting for water beetles in the stream.

The pink salt figurines of the bear and boar sat placidly on a leafless branch, facing the two of them. They had made it a sort of ritual to place the statuettes out to watch their camp while they cooked or slept.

"You know, these are still my favorite moments," Jiara said quietly, listening to the crackling fire, the bubbling pot, and the running stream. "Just sitting here with you, watching you work your magic hooves, then sharing a meal together."

Nalaníri flipped the duck breast over, then sat back down. "I feel most alive too, m'dear, in moments like this. I've served countless dishes at d'Guildhall uf Krûn, but it feels better t'cook smaller meals, jis' fur yerself n'd'one ye love."

"Don't forget about those hungry Nu'irgesh. They'll have to eat too."

"What, ye think I was a-talking 'bout ye? I meant Probo, uf course. Who couldn't love that sack uf fat n'snores?"

Probo lifted his head at the mention of his name, sniffed the air, and contentedly salivated.

After a long while waiting for their meal to slowly cook, Nalaníri pressed a finger on the meat to test it, and sensed the duck was ready. Well, almost ready—there was always a last bit of seasoning to be sprinkled, as well as garnishes to be added.

The baby skunks waddled closer to inspect the cooking area, standing dangerously close to the fire.

"Shush, ye stinkers!" Nalaníri scolded them. They lifted their harmless tails and smacked their front paws defensively. Their mother came to pick them up and guided them to safety.

"I wish we could keep doing this," Jiara said once she'd received a plate of food, tasting the duck and following it with a crunchy bite of a cattail shoot. "I mean, I wish we could slow down and enjoy the day instead of having to rush constantly."

Nalaníri poured the birch tea and mixed a bit of black walnut syrup in as a sweetener, the clinking sounds of the spoon against the enamel mug lowering in pitch as the syrup dissolved into the reddish brew.

"That time shell come, mine love," Nalaníri said, handing the mug to Jiara. "Fur now, at least we have each uther, n'moments like this."

As they moved deeper into the valley that afternoon, Probo grew more and more listless. By the next day, his fur had turned nearly fully gray, his usually plump body seemed slender, and his joyful trot had diminished to a dragging shuffle. He was still leading ahead of them, walking next to Muri, but their pace had slowed considerably.

"He looks like Banook did," Kitjári said, speaking quietly. "How he kept growing thinner, his hair whiter the farther we traveled from his bears."

"I'm so afraid," Nalaníri whispered back. "I don't want m'boy t'suffer. He's not looking good, d'poor thing."

They kept their eyes on Probo, never hurrying him. Before the end of the day, he began to stumble as if drunk. He stopped then, eyes clouded and unfocused, and dropped to the snow with a weak grunt.

"Mine poor boy!" Nalaníri said, sitting next to him and caressing his back. She looked up at Kitjári. "He can't keep a-going like this."

"We can't force him. It must be so painful for him. Do you think he can find his way back to safety?"

"I don't know, but he says he wants t'keep going. He doesn't want t'be left alone."

Probo's eyes drifted aimlessly. His legs trembled.

Kitjári crouched next to the Nu'irg, and to Nalaníri said, "Before he is too weak to do it, tell him to turn back to a pygmy hog. I'll carry him, but he has to tell us when to stop."

"No, m'dear, I shell be d'one t'carry him. He'll be better close t'me, close to Nagrasilv."

Probo strained to shapeshift, slowly turning smaller. In his weakened state, he weighed nearly nothing as a pygmy hog. Nalaníri took him in her arms and walked carefully, following behind the others.

The following day, after leaving many more miles behind, Probo weakly whined and shivered in Nalaníri's arms. The skeletal suid offered a dismal whimper, then convulsed as if trying to throw up, but with no energy to do so.

"He's not gunna make it like this," Nalaníri said, holding Probo delicately as she wiped away tears. "He's a-losing himself, a-losing his essence."

"I'll make a fire. You sit down and care for him," Kitjári said.

Nalaníri sat on a toppled tree and rocked back and forth, humming a melody to the small hog. Kitjári lit a stack of firewood in front of where Nalaníri sat. As the flames rose, Probo turned, stared at the sparks, and faintly squealed.

Nalaníri kept humming, and then began to sing a peaceful, quiet lullaby:

> Come un down mine piglet t'bed n'rest,
>
> Oh bring yer belly, tusks, n'tail,
>
> Fur yer mum's awaiting, d'blankets pressed,
>
> N'yer dreams are set t'sail.
>
>
> Hold mine hooves dear piglet n'shun d'night,
>
> Oh n'delight in thoughts uf morn,
>
> Fur shell soon d'arudinn set alight,
>
> N'a bright new day be born.

"It breaks my heart to see him like this," Kitjári said. "We are closer to the dome, but we still have much farther to go over the mountains."

"I thought I'd keep him safe," Nalaníri whimpered. "But now he's dying because uf me." She began to weep. Kitjári held her, desperately wishing she knew what to say.

Probo stared at the fire, a thin streak of his drool darkening Nalaníri's sleeves.

"I thought mine boy would be fine," Nalaníri continued, eyes clouded by tears. "He can't even mindspeak t'me no mour, he's gone silent. I thought he'd find strength with Nagrasilv near him… but it's not a-helping, he's not gunna make it."

Kitjári's brow furrowed as she considered something. "Why don't… Have you thought about taking off your mask? For Probo, I mean."

"He likes me better this way, n'ye know I prefer—"

"No, I mean, like Momsúndosilv fed Mamóru and kept him alive. Even if Mamóru remained weak, he never looked as bad as Probo looks right now. But you are using Nagrasilv yourself, you are taking the mask's energy into you as well. I mean, if that's how any of these things work."

"Ye might be unto something…" Nalaníri said. She wiped off her snot and shapeshifted into Prikka.

But that did not seem to ease the suid's pain.

Once Prikka pulled the mask off her face, however, it was as if a rejuvenating breeze blew into Probo's fur. He opened his eyes and inhaled deeply, like a newborn taking his first breath. He still looked old, nearly skeletal, but his eyes had a newfound sparkle, and his liveliness immediately returned.

"M'boy, yer back!" Prikka said. "I'm so sorry. It was me all along! I was selfishly taking frum ye." She hugged him a bit too tightly, making the pygmy hog let out a quiet squeal. "Don't worry, m'boy, I'll keep carrying ye, n'I'll keep ye warm. If ye feel too tired, we'll stop n'feed ye. N'if ye need us t'turn back, we will."

CHAPTER FORTY-THREE

FROZEN FALLS

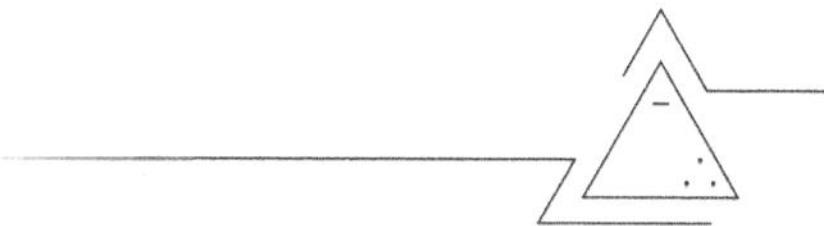

Muri stopped in front of a frozen waterfall, one of dozens that draped over a long, steep crag. They had been trekking all day through an ice field hidden in a bowl of volcanic rock, and now that they had reached this new impediment, the honey badger seemed flustered.

"I wish I could talk t'Probo, t'see what Muri's a-thinking," Prikka said. "He seems confused, like he's never seen this place before."

Muri searched the base of the frozen falls for a hint of the old path he remembered, but there was nothing left. It was as if an entire mountain had risen there, melting a glacier that had then refrozen over it. Traces of a relatively recent lava flow striated the otherwise icy wall, its edges eroded and crackled.

"Even mountains change given enough time," Kitjári said.

Muri set out to scout, moving faster on his own. He returned a few hours later with bad news. He did his best to communicate his thoughts; he first moved toward the side he had scouted and growled at it, shaking his body as if tearing something apart. He then repeated the gesture in the opposite direction. After that, he looked straight up at the falls and grunted lightly, blinking hard as if a snowflake had landed in his eye.

Above them was a saddle, tucked between two peaks, from which the tops of the frozen falls exhaled a constant oscillation of mist, like a ghostly blanket drying on a clothesline.

"Seems like d'only way is up?" Prikka guessed.

"Time for you to learn how to climb a waterfall," Kitjári said.

"I ain't a-doing no such thing! Ye've gone mad!"

"It's easier than it seems. A pick will provide a hold where there is none, and all you need to do is pull yourself up carefully. It'd be much more dangerous if there was water running behind the falls, but they are frozen solid."

"Last time ye tried to teach me, it was un rocks, not ice, n'it was bad enough. I don't want t'be doing this."

"And I taught you well. You made it up, didn't you?"

"Ye were terrible. Ye hurried me through it, n'gave me no chance t'rest."

Kitjári dropped her backpack, brushing the comment aside. "Let's rest here for the day. I'll teach you a few tricks, and we'll climb tomorrow."

"Ye'll teach me like ye taught Lago, Banook, n'Alaia?"

"That's the plan."

"Well, them took *months* t'learn, n'yer giving me half a day?"

"You'll be fine. I'll go first, place all the screws, pitons, and ropes, and will belay you up. We'll have to do it in perhaps four or five stages, stopping at each of the major breaks in the falls. Might take us all day, but it's better than wandering aimlessly around the mountains. It'll be much easier than last time, I promise."

Prikka snorted twice. "Last time d'wall wasn't icy cold. I have no hooves now, which means I'll have t'hold d'ice with these here meaty sausages."

"We have gloves. And I'll secure my crampons to your sexy Negian boots."

"I hate them stinking things," Prikka said, staring at her feet. She had gotten rid of her smelly Negian uniform but had kept the boots, which fit her human form well.

Kitjári began to unpack her bag. "Just stop bickering and listen, alright?"

Prikka stopped her arguing, but kept her posture tight and her temper boiling.

For the rest of the day, Kitjári showed Prikka the basic techniques she'd need to know, such as how to widen her stance for balance, how to keep her heels down, how to snap her wrist at the end of a swing with the ice axe, how to arch her back, and some basic rope handling to avoid tangling herself up. Prikka was practicing only a few feet above ground level, yet she felt utterly ill at ease with the experience.

"Not in the bulge," Kitjári explained. "Aim for the white spots, where the snow piles up."

"But that's snow! I'm a-trying to bury d'thing in d'ice, not d'snow!"

"The ice is stronger in the concave spots, that's where the snow gathers. Just do as I say and stop squabbling. Aim for the—watch it! You're going to cut the rope if you swing so carelessly!"

"Cut d'rope? I shell get a trophy if I'm able t'cut a quaar rope, with one swing or one thousand."

"It's not about the rope, it's about making sure your swings are purposeful."

"Them are purposeful. I'm a-trying t'murder this wretched waterfall before it murders me, that'll show it some purpose."

"You are too tense. Your calves are going to tire."

"*Ye* are too tense, I'm perfectly fine!"

Prikka swung hard, but hit the ice at an angle. The axe bounced off it with a sonorous wobble. She lost her grip on it and gave up, jumping down to the safety of the ice field.

"I *told* you, only let go of the pick once it's safely locked into the—"

"I know that! Do ye think I was jis' hurling it fur fun?"

"Don't get so defensive, you only have one day to—"

"Then don't get so bossy!" Prikka tossed the other axe to the ground. It lodged itself firmly into the ice. "M'dear, ye can be a pain in d'arse. I don't know how ye managed t'teach them uthers."

"Fine!" Kitjári snapped, picking up both axes. "We'll continue tomorrow, I guess."

Dinner was quiet. Both Probo and Muri seemed to be judging the lovers, sitting a bit farther away than usual and exchanging odd looks.

Prikka wiped her utensils and stowed them away, then sucked at the base of her thumb.

"Is that a blister?" Kitjári asked, craning her neck.

"It's nothing."

"It's probably from gripping too forcefully. I'll show you tomorrow how—"

"It's fine, them blisters were there before."

"I helped put your gloves on and I'm pretty sure that—"

"Them were there before!" Prikka snapped.

The quiet that followed seemed to rumble with tension.

An icicle slowly dripped. They had camped in a grotto beneath one of the many frozen falls, and the smoke from their fire was thickening like storm clouds above them.

"I'm sorry," Kitjári finally said, taking a sip of birch bark tea. It was unsweetened, as they had run out of syrup, and the few trees they'd recently passed had been too thin to tap for sap. "I was trying to be helpful." She kept her eyes on a wall of ice, suddenly realizing they had forgotten to place the bear and boar figurines out to watch over their camp. She felt too uncomfortable to bring it up.

"I'm sorry, I mean it."

"I was *a-trying* t'learn. But ye kept yelling at me. I'm useless like this. Like Prikka, I mean. I feel cold, I feel incompetent, incomplete, like a nuisance. It's been too long. I haven't been mineself fur such a long time." She tucked her cold fingers in her pockets. "I can't risk Probo dying, so I have to cope with it, cope with living torn in half. It's hard un me. I've never been apart frum Nagrasilv this long, not even when we were traveling with Banook. Back then I unly stopped wearing mine mask fur a handful uf days, n'even that much was unbearable."

"If it's becoming so hard for you, you could wear my mask for a bit," Kitjári said with a smile.

"I hope yer joking," Prikka said with an unamused, half-lidded stare.

"I'm kidding. I knew you were going through a tough time with this, but it seemed as if you were getting used to it. You weren't showing too much discomfort."

"Jis' a-hiding it. Didn't want Probo t'feel guilty. I feel weak. I feel ugly. N'I feel like ye love me less this way."

"What? Why would you ever think that?"

Prikka turned her head away and didn't answer.

The icicles caged them in their reflected, orange light.

Kitjári scooted a bit closer.

"We've talked about this, many times. You know I love you equally, whether you are Prikka or Nalaníri. You are both the same to me."

"Sometimes ye don't feel d'same t'me."

"What is that supposed to mean?" Kitjári asked, letting a domineering tone escape before she could stop herself.

"See? There it is. Sometimes yer voice, it jis' changes, n'ye turn a bit rough un me. Reminds me uf mine father, n'how he'd yell at me when I did something wrong. Like I have t'learn at yer pace, not at mine own."

Kitjári winced. "I... Shit. Shit, shit, shit!" she yelled, and covered her face. After a tense moment, she added, "I'm so sorry." She uncovered her eyes and looked around at the sparkling ice, seeing her distorted reflections surrounding her. With her cinnamon-colored fur, she looked nothing like the woman she used to know.

By Takh's two cocks, you are a fucking bear now, she admonished herself. *You are someone else, you are better, you aren't her. Don't become her.*

"I truly am. Sorry, I mean," the bear said, and scooted yet closer. "I'm not turning into your father, I swear. I'm turning into my fucking sister. Khest, that's depressing to admit."

"Yer sister?"

"I learned a lot from—no, I learned everything I know from her, alright? She's a force I could never contend with."

"Ye don't talk 'bout her at all. I've barely heard ye mention her. Don't even know her name."

"Sijma. The great Sijma Ascura. First female field marshal in the Free Tribelands. She taught me how to fight, how to climb, how to survive in the forest, how to work field medicine, how to command a platoon, how to do just about everything. And she was the most stringent oafwanker while doing it."

"What's a stringent oafwanker?"

"She was rough. She never let me do things my own way, pushing me to the limit until I'd break and start a fight with her, and then, of course, she'd beat me since she was bigger and stronger. And then she'd parade away with a smile, as if it had all just been another lesson, and she was proud of my struggle. I fucking hated her. And what I hate the most is that I wouldn't be here without her."

"I think yer perfectly capable un yer own."

"Maybe, but it's all because I wanted to prove myself to her. Even when I left Thornridge to follow Ockam, Lago, and Alaia, I did it with this stupid idea in the back of my head that she'd be so mad at me, but once I returned, I'd prove her wrong, show her what I'm capable of."

Kitjári broke an icicle off, crunched it in her claws, and tossed the pieces away. "And now that all of this has happened, I really don't care, you know?" She laughed with self-mockery, shaking her head. "I don't even care if I never see her again. Now that I finally made something of myself, it doesn't really matter. And to make it all worse, it seems that not only did I learn how to climb frozen waterfalls from her, but I also learned how to be an oafwanker toward the person I love most."

Kitjári felt embarrassed about the last words she'd spoken, not because of telling Nalaníri that she loved her—she had expressed that constantly and clearly enough—but because the words were an admission that her sister really did love her too, and that thought did not sit well in her mind.

"Yer not yer sister," Prikka quietly said. "Ye don't have t'be yer sister."

"I know, I know. I'm trying to learn things my own way now, and I should let you do the same. I'll try not to be such a pain. Will you forgive me? Can we start this over?"

Prikka stretched a hand out, taking Kitjári's handpaw. She locked her fingers with the bear's sharp claws.

"If ye'll forgive me as well. I wasn't being mine best self neither. We'll try again, in d'morrow."

Kitjári decided to allow more time for Prikka to learn, without imposing a deadline. Instead of forcing Prikka to follow her instructions, she first climbed by herself, doing her best to show all the basic techniques without placing a burden on the student.

As she ascended the frozen falls, she did so in her human form so she could more clearly demonstrate her approach. She placed ice screws and pitons in a few key locations and secured the rope on a wide ledge.

The following day, once Prikka felt comfortable enough to climb instead of practicing at the bottom, Jiara helped her into the harness, then took the rope to belay her.

"Take smaller steps on your way up," Jiara encouraged. "That's right, feels much easier when you push with your thighs. There you go." It was not a hard climb, though it was exhausting for Prikka, who needed to stress muscles she normally did not use.

"That wasn't too bad," Prikka said once she made it over the lowest ledge. She pulled on the rope to lift one backpack, then the next. Probo rested in the second pack, warmly bundled up between soft pieces of clothing.

Prikka dropped the rope down once more, this time with the ice axes tied at the end. Before Jiara could catch the rope, Muri grabbed on to it as an ermine and climbed expertly, reaching the top in mere heartbeats.

"Fine, not that I care, you slinky vermin," Jiara said. "I could go that fast if I wanted to." She retrieved her screws and pitons on the way up, then lodged her picks on the ledge and pulled her body onto it.

"That's one done out of, well, many," she said, looking up at the next wall of ice. At least the falls had clear breaks where they could rest. Jiara had already mapped out the route in her head, splitting it into manageable chunks.

"I think that's more than enough for today," she said, pretending to be out of breath. "Tomorrow we can climb three more segments, and if we feel daring, we can make it to the top. But this ledge has a nice view, and even a few dead trees to make a fire with."

The next day they repeated the process, with Jiara doing the heavy lifting by setting up the screws first, belaying next, and climbing up after that. They lifted bundles of firewood to the next few ledges, stopping not too far from the top of the cliff, under the blanket of mist that pushed over its edge.

"We have just enough for a good fire," Jiara said, untying the firewood.

"Don't need no fire yet," Prikka said, stopping her. "Let's try n'make it to d'top. We're almost there."

"Are you sure? That's a trickier pitch with the mist blowing over it."

Prikka looked up. The mist was twirling over their heads like spindrift from mighty ocean waves. "Ye'll catch me if I fall, like ye did d'first time we met."

"Then let's do it. I'll place the screws while you prep a snack. We'll cook a real dinner once we crest the final ledge."

Prikka had hot tea ready by the time Jiara returned, which was perfect for warming up her cold hands. The warmth quickly extended down to her tired toes.

"Alright, gentle tusks, your turn. Go easy on me. Last time you fell you nearly snapped my spine in half."

"How puny uf me. Hold un tight."

Two slips and falls but no injuries later, Prikka made it to the top ledge where, sunken in the blowing mist, she struggled to find purchase. Nearly blinded by the whiteness, she dug her picks deep and pulled her heavy body over the great slope of ice.

"I made it!" she yelled from the top, unable to see beneath her. "Send up d'bags!"

They once more lifted the gear, then Jiara climbed up without hesitation. Despite the complexity of the route for a beginner like Prikka, it was as easy as a walk down a cobblestone trail for a veteran like Jiara.

She entered the layer of mist, pulled herself up, and found Prikka sitting by the last anchor, breathing in the moisture.

"It's quite peaceful in d'mist," Prikka said. "Mine eyes couldn't see nothing. Mine ears could only hear d'breeze n'yer picks a-striking."

"We should find some shelter. We've done plenty for one day," Jiara said, putting her mask back on and growing the fur she had been sorely missing during the frigid climb.

They walked up a smooth hill of packed snow until they reached the top of the saddle, where the layer of mist no longer obscured their view. Prikka began to trek down the hill, but Kitjári caught her arm.

"Not so fast. Let's set our camp behind those rocks and watch the sunset. The view from up here is outstanding."

CHAPTER FORTY-FOUR

TOLLING THUNDER

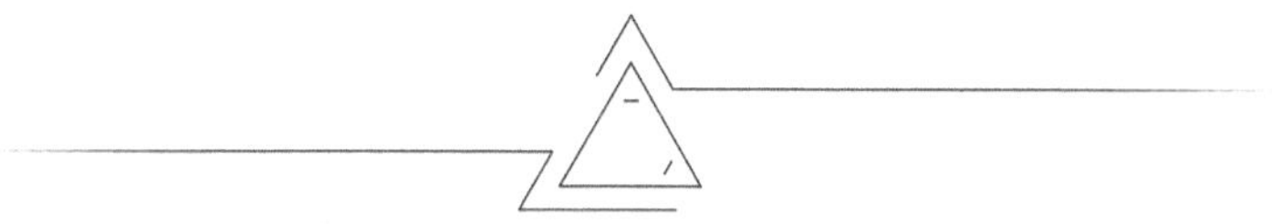

Banook and Ardof traveled west and traveled south. At first they followed Safis through the heavy snows until they reached the more temperate regions of the Great Steppes. Ursids they found aplenty among the plains, aided by Banook's keen nose and Ardof's tracking skills. Even Bear helped a little.

If the ursids they found were hibernating, they soon were no more, as Banook mercilessly shook them from their slumber and recruited them for their uncertain mission. Once the sleuth had grown to a few dozen, they let the bears themselves lead the way. The kiuon packs, helpful as always, hastened ahead of the group to recruit more ursids, to scout for Negian soldiers, and to survey trails that avoided populated or patrolled areas.

After trudging through reedy marshlands, hiding from bandits behind a frozen waterfall, camping among peaks of granite and caves of sandstone, and robbing one or two Negian convoys, they had amassed hundreds of brown bears, sun bears, spectacled bears, black bears, and kiuons. Even a few dozen polar bears had joined their ranks, who said they had grown sick of seal meat and preferred to try their luck farther south. Banook had warned them that Winter would soon end, but the ursid northerners hoped that perhaps among snowy mountains they could find a new home.

Ardof and Banook were certain that, by now, many surviving Negians from the Lequa Dome would have told their stories about the naked giant and the dire wolf who tore apart their legions. Though they brought with them an impossible-to-miss pack of ursids, they thought it prudent not to let spies see

Banook himself—while traveling, the Nu'irg ust Urnaadi had blended in by taking the form of a light-furred black bear, or a spirit bear, as the Khaar Du Tribes called them. His coat was not golden as in his primal form, but creamy in color, contrasting brightly with his pink nose.

"When will this merciless rain cease?" Ardof grumbled to Banook after a fortnight of unyielding storms. As if the clouds were dismayed by his comment, thunder cracked in the grayness above, making him flinch. The cold of Winter had not yet fully abated, yet Thawing was arriving early, bringing with it pillowy clouds eager to unleash their weight on the wayfarers.

The bears seemed unbothered, marching relentlessly. Even Banook, whose cream-colored fur took on a muddier tone when wet, trudged on without complaining.

"And my back is hurting once more," Ardof bickered. "This bear needs to learn not to sway so much when on the move." The ranger had taken to riding a polar bear, one who Banook assured him would not maul him so long as he did not dig his heels into her sides or try to issue her any orders. They had traveled fast in this manner, steadily and with few stops. "I would simply like to find a place to stop before dark," he added. "Somewhere I could open my bag without the contents getting drenched."

Sensing the displeasure in Ardof's tone, more than understanding the words, Banook shapeshifted to his human form. The big man shivered, suddenly aware of the cold rain splashing upon his bare skin. "Perhaps it's time we find a suitable camping spot, before it gets dark," he conceded. "The kiuon scouts cannot see far or scent for danger with so much rain." He looked toward Safís, who was walking with Bear following alongside her. "Dear lady, would you be so kind as to procure us a refuge in the forest yonder? Perhaps a place that will remain dry through the night?"

«I will find us shelter,» she communicated, then rushed away in a blur, leaving hovering droplets behind.

That night, they settled in the depths of a myrtle forest, sheltered beneath a steep overhang where the ground was covered by moist leaves, but with dry ones beneath, providing enough fuel to feed a sizable bonfire.

Banook and Ardof sat naked by the flames, drying their bodies and clothes. Even then, Ardof kept his arm wraps on, still unwilling to let Banook see his spurs. His copper skin glistened in nearly the same hues as the light-brown hairs of his beard, chest, and groin.

"You know, your kind used to inhabit these lands," Banook said.

"Humans had spread everywhere long before the Downfall," the ranger answered, uninterested. He stretched his feet toward the flames, letting the blisters on his toes dry.

"I do not mean humans," Banook added, chewing on walnuts his sun bears had found in the forest. "I meant the Oldrin race, who used to be known as the Vangu, or the Bone Golems."

Ardof reared back, crossing his arms. He was about to retort with a snappy comment but decided to keep quiet instead. After a prolonged pause, he reached for his bag and rummaged through it. He produced a map he had recently purchased from a wandering salesman, able to finally take it out of his bag now that it would not get wet.

"It's hard to figure out how far we've traveled," he said as he pored over the map. "After that encounter near Dimshaw, there have been few landmarks to guide us, and the side roads are nearly invisible with so much mud rushing over them."

"We have made good progress, but the lands of Heartpine are still far from us."

"And it's becoming ever riskier now. That caravan took us unawares, and that settlement in the canyon was completely hidden until we were nearly in their midst. We need to find a path that runs farther from the main road and—" The ranger stood up suddenly, head slightly cocked, eyes narrowed.

"What is it?" Banook asked, then quickly quieted, hearing a metallic, shrill tone in the distance.

The sound subsided, then it tolled again, clearer than before, then it did so again a breath later, and again without hurry, two dozen times in total.

"The bells of Umaagi," Ardof mumbled. "We must be much closer to the city than I expected. Dangerously close."

"Are they sounding the alarm?"

"No, they toll every fourth hour. They just marked the twenty-fourth hour, if I counted correctly. It is nothing to worry about, but we will need to find a safer path come morning."

"I will send a pack to find one as soon as it's bright enough for them to see," Banook said, then began to prepare a nook in which to rest.

Banook's sleep was restless. He kept turning over, always cautious of Bear, who liked to keep close to him for warmth and was scared of the storm.

He thought about Lago-Sterjall, wondering how far his lover's parallel journey had taken him, wondering how long it would be until they saw each other again. *I am coming for you. I will be with you soon enough.* The dripping sounds lulled him. *I am coming…* Just as he was about to succumb to his tiredness, a sharper sound shook him awake. The bells were tolling once more. *Three*—he took a long, slow breath—*four*. He counted the unhurried beats, the sounds distant yet clear. *Eighteen… Nineteen… How do people in that city ever sleep?* The final bell tolled to mark the twenty-eighth hour, but the sound extended eerily into yet another song, one more ominous and sorrowful—a howling. Soon the howls were answered by another—this one much closer.

"Safís!" Banook cried out, getting to his feet in an instant with Bear standing next to him, his hackles raised.

"What is the matter?" Ardof asked.

"A call of distress, we must hasten to—"

Safís rushed into the camp, fur wet yet somehow still looking pristine.

«Prisoners, they have them as prisoners,» she mindspoke in anguish.

"Who is imprisoned?" Banook asked. "Whose calls were those I heard a moment before yours?"

«Dire wolves,» she answered. «Their howling comes from the city of metal thunder. I know their voices, I know their faces. I must help them, I must—»

"Keep calm. It would be unwise to take rash actions."

Ardof loaded a smooth pebble into his sling. "Are we in trouble?" he inquired.

"No, not yet," Banook said. "Friends of Safís are captured in the nearby city." He gazed down at the wolf. "Are you able to find out more? Without alerting the captors?"

«I will. Wait for me here. Do not follow, Nu'irg ust Urnaadi.» She scurried away into the wet underbrush.

"Hold it there," Banook said to Bear, grabbing him by the loose skin of his neck. "She'll be back soon."

They waited impatiently, unable and unwilling to sleep any longer. Thankfully, they did not wait for long; only an hour later, Safís returned to their camp, her usually light footsteps now landing much more heavily. She was in the form of a dire wolf, and between her sharp teeth she carried something heavy and wet. As she dropped the bundle by the dying bonfire, it tried to squirm away.

"Takh! Have mercy!" it yelped. It was a Negian soldier, only lightly lacerated by the strong maw. "Keep that monster away from me!" he implored as he tripped on his own legs.

Ardof rushed to the man and wrapped the cords of his sling around his neck, pulling them tight. "Keep quiet and she will not eat you," he said. He pulled the soldier's hair to the side and studied his ranking insignia. "Nothing but a low-level guard. Why did she bring this filth into our camp?"

"For information," Banook swiftly answered, then squatted in front of the soldier. "Is it true you are keeping dire wolves captive?"

"Y-yes, anyone knows that," the man answered. "Who are you? Why did—"

Banook pinched two thick fingers over the man's blubbering lips. "Only answer what is asked of you. Where are the wolves located, and how might they be freed?"

"Freed? They would tear through our city!"

"Perhaps. But she will tear through you if you do not answer the questions."

"A-at the arena, of course," the man squawked, "right by the bell tower. But you can't set them free, that would be madness."

"Leave the madness to us and worry about keeping your head attached to your body," Ardof said, tracing his long dagger over the man's neck. "How did you come to capture such mighty creatures?"

The petrified soldier explained that the dire wolves had been captured months ago. Paw prints had been spotted around a pond only a few miles north of Umaagi, and Viceroy Urcai himself had requested that a poisonous concoction be spilled into the water—one that would put the giants to sleep when they sated their thirsts. Bound and only loosely conscious, the dire wolves had been locked in magnium-reinforced cages and brought to the Belfry Arena, where they were fed criminals, insubordinate slaves, or the losing gladiator at the weekly games.

"Urcai wanted us to use the games to train the beasts," the soldier said, "so that they may be tamed before being sent to Hestfell. But no chains would hold them, so we had to keep them in the cages. They proved impossible to train, b-but…" He became suddenly aware of Safis's piercing gaze. "But how did you manage to tame yours?"

"Keep your eyes and thoughts off her, if you want to live," Banook said. "The dire wolves, you were saying?"

"W-we were just about to give up on them, and considered selling their furs instead, and their bones. They say their bones are magsteel-tough, and that their blood can heal any ailment, and that they taste like—"

"Enough," Banook cut him off. "Tell us more about this arena, and do so with precision and without delay."

"I'm just one of the gate guards, nothing more. I was on my way to take my post when that netherbeast caught me." What the soldier told them next left them a bit disheartened, for the Belfry Arena served as a garrison and training ground for the army, and the only entrance was always guarded.

"If they are alerted, it would be like poking at a hornet's nest while inside it," Ardof said.

Banook pondered, studying the guard's expression. "The wolves are locked in cages," he said. "Do you happen to hold the keys to them?"

"Keys? Why would you need keys? The latches are beyond the reach of the beasts, and no one would be stupid enough to release them."

Banook patted the man's pockets just in case, finding nothing of use. "If you hold no keys, how were you going to take your post at the gate?"

"My friend has to unlock them for me. The locks are on the inside. M-maybe you could take me back, and I'll take my post, then let you through after my friend leaves."

Banook asked Safís to keep an eye on the guard while he took Ardof away for a private discussion.

"Hogshit," Ardof snorted. "As soon as he's through that gate, he'll sound the alarm."

"I don't trust him either, but he could at least get the gate unlocked for us. And I have a plan so that he doesn't lock us out."

"Is this worth all the trouble? There could be sentinels around, and hundreds of soldiers slumbering. Merely entering the structure will be risky."

"Safís will not abandon her siblings to die in such a manner. There are not many dire wolves left. Only about a dozen escaped Heartpine before the collapse sealed the exits. These might be the very last of them." He tightened his expression briefly, then continued, "I am keenly aware of the anguish that clutches one's heart when a species from your clade extinguishes its last candle, when that connection is severed forevermore, and you feel a part of you die with it. I know she knows the pain as well, for there were other giants inside Heartpine that did not manage to escape, who died of hunger or disease while she was still confined to that domed prison."

"You could ask the bears to trample through the city," Ardof suggested. "They could draw the soldiers out while we unlock the cages."

Banook consulted silently with Safís, but her answer was a conclusive no.

"She thinks it foolish to risk our own mission," Banook said. "If the bears are blamed for the deaths of Negian soldiers, attacking them while in the safety of their own city, Hestfell would send all their remaining battalions to hunt them down. She wants us to leave the bears out of this. She thinks it would be safest to infiltrate silent as mists."

CHAPTER FORTY-FIVE

THE BELLS OF UMAAGI

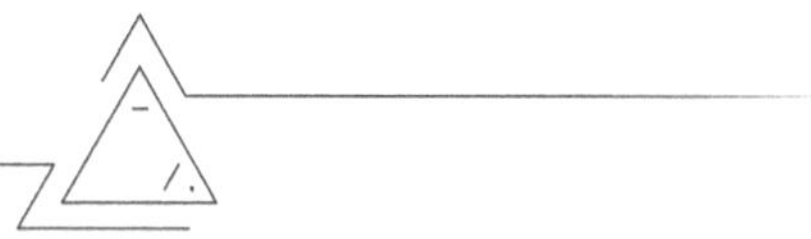

They discussed their plan quickly but carefully.

"I will take the form of a kiuon once we reach the city," Banook said, dropping his trousers. "If guards see me, they will think me just a weird dog."

"What about your glaive?" Ardof asked as he prepared his gear.

"I will pick up weapons if and when needed."

"It's her, isn't it?" the guard mumbled, his eyes locked on Safîs. "The monster who attacked the domes…" He then looked at Banook, eyes roaming up and down his nine feet of height, then at the many bears dozing around the camp. "A-and you…"

"We better get going," Ardof said, pushing their prisoner forward. "I won't tie you up, but if you call for help or try to run, she will chomp you in half."

Safîs squinted her yellow eyes, shapeshifted into her primal form, then darted away like a white lightning bolt. The guard reared back at seeing the transformation, but held his tongue.

"She says to hurry," Banook said, then looked down at Bear, who was trying hard not to whine. "And you, do as she told you. Stay here and guard our camp. Make sure no marauders touch our belongings. Will you do that for us?"

Rrgrouff! Bear said, staying put as he watched them leave.

It was dark as tar in the myrtle forest, but Safîs led the way undeterred, guided by her ears, nose, and rage, until they arrived at the outskirts of Umaagi. Few lights shone in the drenched city, the brightest one being the light at the bell tower, which hovered within a thin cloud like a devilish bog flame.

"No one should be bothering us this late at night, not with such a downpour," Banook said as they spied on the empty streets from a safe distance. "It's time we took smaller forms." He shapeshifted into a plump, pink-nosed kiuon, while Safis took the form of a fennec fox, momentarily making the guard think they had disappeared.

"This is what is going to happen," Ardof said to the guard. "You are going to carry this as you walk through the gate"—he held out a small satchel—"and *she* will be inside it. You make one false move, and she will be on your throat." He propped the bag open, and the tiny fox hopped inside it, letting a high-pitched growl escape.

The guard's hands trembled as he took the Nu'irg-filled satchel. He then felt Ardof's dagger poking his back.

"Move."

The two men walked side by side into the city, followed by the kiuon, as if it was perfectly normal to be out walking a pet during a thunderstorm.

The Belfry Arena sprawled at the center of the city, its stacked arches ending in sharp angles at the highest level, making it look like a giant bear trap. A vaulted colonnade circled the bottom level, but only one large gate connected to the interior, right beneath the bell tower. A warm light shone through the hinges of the heavy oak doors.

"The gate stays open behind you," Ardof warned, flattening his back against the wall. He pushed the guard toward the gate.

The man tried not to stare at the package he was carrying. He shivered, soaking wet and petrified with fear.

He knocked six times.

A panel slid open at eye level.

"Who goes th—Garb? You assgobbler, my shift was supposed to end hours ago!"

"S-sorry, I fell asleep," Garb said, then kept quiet.

"And?" the voice behind the door inquired. "Passcode?"

"I…" his eyes glanced sideways toward the concealed ranger, then back to the window. "Four strokes till the hollow hours."

A heavy latch unlocked, then the gate creaked open. Garb hesitated. He took one last look around, then hurled the satchel away and ran past the gate. "Lock it, lock it!"

Ardof rushed to the entrance and saw it slam in front of his face, but not before a tiny blur streaked past his feet and through the narrowing crack. There was a scream from behind the gate, cut short by a wet noise that blended perfectly with the water cascading down the gutters. Then there were the sounds of something crunching, something ripping, and then the gate creaked open once more.

Ardof glanced through the crack, then stepped inside. The dire wolf was standing there, her red maw foaming, shreds of cloth and flesh dangling from it.

"Do you think anyone heard that?" Banook asked from behind Ardof, spooking the ranger and nearly making him stab his dagger backward.

"I doubt it," he answered. "But we can't be certain."

They hid the dismembered sentries in the guard booth, making sure to leave the gate unlocked, then hurried through a long, wide tunnel following Safis, who was back in her primal form. With sconces illuminating the way forward, and wet tracks trailing behind them, there was nowhere to hide, so they marched purposefully and without delay. Paths branched left and right, with signs pointing the way to the dormitories, armory, bathing chambers, and refectory.

As they made their way deeper into the arena, Safis suddenly began to growl, her eyes focused forward, but her ears pointed back. Ardof was about to ask what was wrong when Banook spoke. "Safis says she can hear someone following us in the shadows," he whispered. "Do not look back! Pretend to be disinterested. Keep moving, then wait in hiding right past the archway."

They exited the tunnel into the lowest tier of the arena's sitting area. The long rows of benches were all wet and slippery. Banook flattened himself against the left side of the exit while Ardof took the right. Safis scrambled up and waited over the keystone, still as a gargoyle.

Banook saw Ardof unsheathing his dagger, felt Safis readying to pounce, glimpsed a shadow scurrying out of the tunnel, then hoarsely whispered, "Wait!"

"B-Bear?" Ardof gasped mid-swing.

Rrroouf, Bear said, rather quietly, then blinked awkwardly at the raindrops falling on him.

"Not again," Banook reproached, reaching down to pick the mutt up in his arms. "Did she not tell you to stay? Was she not clear with her instructions?"

Bear cowered in a tight curl, hiding his muzzle in Banook's elbow.

Safis stared down from the archway, offering an incisive growl. Bear recoiled further, scratching hard at Banook's arms as if trying to dig a hole to hide in. Safis snapped her teeth hard, the sound like a bone-snapping lash.

"You do not want to know what she just said to him," Banook told Ardof. "But she has placed fear in him that he will not soon forget." He placed Bear down upon the wet ground. "You will stay quiet now, won't you?"

Bear nearly barked his affirmation, but caught himself and simply looked at the ground, tail between his legs.

Safís hopped down, not wasting one more glance on the insubordinate dog, then hurried toward the balustrade ahead.

And there they were. At the opposite end of the arena's muddy grounds sprawled three enormous cages, barely visible as parallel glints of reflected orange light. The dire wolves inside were indistinct lumps of darkness. Safís hopped over the balusters and raced ahead before the others could react.

"Movement on the third level." Banook pushed Ardof away from the light spilling from the archway they'd emerged from. On the covered walkways behind the seating areas, where sconces shone brightly, several forms paced about.

"They could be guards," Ardof said, "or maybe just servants working the night shift."

"We'd be too exposed over the open field, even in such darkness" Banook fretted. "But we need to hurry before Safís is spotted. Circle the perimeter, and keep low. And Bear, you stay put this time."

Bear hid under a bench, seeming equally terrified and embarrassed.

They did not follow Safís's direct path, but circled the arena until they reached its opposite side, right above the three cages. The seating was substantially elevated above the floor of the arena, meant to keep fighters from escaping, but the cages were tall enough that Ardof and Banook managed to hop on top of the nearest one and slide down the bars until their feet splashed in the mud.

Banook's hand lightly rubbed a dire wolf's matted fur, but the creature didn't stir. The sight of the giants was both sad and gruesome. Each cage held only one wolf, but the enclosures had not been built for creatures of their size, leaving them unable to stand. A pile of bones—mostly human bones—rose by the wall, next to a pile of wet excrement.

The wolves' fur was patchy, revealing the bony shapes of their malnourished bodies. They could barely turn their heads. Their eyes followed Safís, who was pacing around the cages, whining helplessly and biting at the bars.

"They have been kept in this cruel state the entire time," Banook said, his words pained. "Safís says she knows them, that their furs used to blossom and flow in the wind like the seeds of cottonwoods, that their eyes once sparkled like starlight. We must hurry and set them free."

They found a heavy latch at the door of the nearest cage. Banook pulled on it, but the latch did not move. He pulled harder, but Ardof gestured for him to stop.

"Quiet, they'll hear the rattle!" He grabbed hold of a padlock, which was preventing the latch from rising. "Locked. That cuntwad lied to us." He looked around for something of use, then up at Banook. "Can you break it? Silently, I mean."

Banook wrapped a thick hand around the lock, then twisted mightily, holding back a groan as he exerted himself. There was a creak of metal, then a soft clank, but when he let go of the padlock it was still intact. He shook his hand, which was bleeding, his skin torn from his efforts.

"Keep watch while I handle this," Ardof said, pulling his hat down and removing a fishhook from it. He bent the metal to shape and began to probe at the keyhole.

"You better work faster," Banook said. "I see two people headed toward the entrance."

"I'm trying, I'm trying, I—"

"Who goes there?" a voice called from the seating area. A lantern rose above the balusters, dangling over the cages, followed by the smooth and wet face of a square-jawed woman. Her eyes widened in fear at once. "Shit, shit!" she cried, then took a deep breath as she lifted a horn to her mouth and blew hard. But her lips blew only on air, for something had pulled her arm and horn down and over the edge. She dropped her lantern as she was dragged forward, then slammed her hips on the balustrade and toppled over the edge.

There was a wet thud followed by a yip, then the lantern crashed and was extinguished. Banook hurried over and punched the guard in the face before she could make any more sounds, then moved her unconscious body to reveal Bear still holding tight to her arm, biting with all his might. "Bear!" he said, not as quietly as he had intended.

Bear let go of the arm and limped proudly away, teeth still bared.

"You stupid, heroic, disobedient child," Banook praised and scolded. As he kneeled to check on the mutt, he noticed something sparkling on the guard's belt: a massive ring with dozens of keys. "What would we have done without you?" he asked the dog, then ripped the keyring free and tossed it to Ardof. "Hurry now, before someone comes looking for her."

Ardof shuffled through the keys, struggling to tell any apart in the dark. He decided to try them one at a time without overthinking it.

«He must hurry,» Safís mindspoke. «Their pain is unbearable. I can't withstand one more heartbeat of their suffering.»

"He is working as fast as he can," Banook told her. "Ardof will—"

A blaring call stopped his words—a horn, blowing from the arena's entrance.

"They must've found the bodies," Ardof said, muttering a curse just as the key turned in his fingers. The padlock swung open. Ardof cast it away, flipped the latch up to unlock the cage, then rushed to the next one.

More horns blared, and shouts could be heard rushing toward the long entrance tunnel. Ardof struggled to find the key for the second lock. The dire wolf from the first cage began to crawl out into the mud.

«They are coming,» Safís warned.

A new sound struck them hard, forcing Ardof to cover his ears and drop the keys. The bells were ringing, marking the start of the thirty-second hour. The hollow hours had begun.

Banook tensed as Ardof dug through the mud to retrieve the keys. "To the voids with this," he muttered, then rushed to the wall and kicked at a column embedded in it, just as the second toll rang. By the third toll he was picking up a dislodged brick; by the fifth he was slamming it down to break the padlock, the sound barely noticeable amidst the chaos. The voices of the wolves joined the clanging of the bells. The sonorous ringing hurt their ears, and despite their tiredness, they bellowed out a dirge that prickled the hairs on Ardof's skin.

Two more tolls, and the third padlock had been shattered to splinters.

Sconces were being set alight all around the three levels of the Belfry Arena, and the light was reaching them clearly now.

"Don't let them see you!" Ardof urged Banook during a lull between tolls. He pulled his hood over his head and wrapped his black cape tighter around his body. Another toll, followed by a brief pause. "They won't recognize me, but they will certainly remember you if they spot you like this."

The bells kept calling, making the dire wolves flinch each time, but they abandoned their cages and forced themselves to stand on their weakened legs.

"Safís, we need you and the wolves to open a path for us," Banook said. He then looked down toward Bear, who limped toward him with a face that was half guilty, half smug.

«He is not hurt,» Safís communicated while glancing at the mutt, who quickly stopped his pretending and stood on four legs once more. «He was only begging for pity. Quickly now, Nu'irg ust Urnaadi. My wolves are tired, but they can still fight. Follow us.» She took the form of a dire wolf and hurried ahead.

Banook quickly shifted into a kiuon, then ran alongside Ardof and Bear.

"The dire wolves are esc—" a soldier began to scream, but his words were interrupted by the sixteenth tolling.

Safís was the first to reach the far end of the arena. By then the twentieth toll was ringing, and horns and screams resounded between each strike of the bells. She stretched her front legs to reach the balustrade and held her position like an icy ramp. Soldiers moved in front of her paws, too afraid to poke their lances at the wolf, but forming a barrier. Their line was demolished when the three muddied dire wolves came running over Safís's back and leapt at them, unleashing their long-sought vengeance.

"Climb, now!" Ardof said to Banook. They climbed onto Safís's back, then ran over her neck and muzzle and hopped into the pile of bodies the wolves had left behind.

They hastened into the exit tunnel, following the dire wolves and the screams pouring from the dormitories and armory. Safís guarded their back, tearing apart any who crossed her path.

The three wolves stopped suddenly, scratching and growling at the main gate, which had been closed once more. "Shit," Ardof gasped, clashing with two soldiers who had come down the side stairs. "The bar locks, lift the bar locks!" he called, all the while parrying the two enemies.

Ardof felt a blur by his side as the kiuon slashed the throat of one of his assailants, then saw the small ursid rush toward the gate.

More enemies were hurrying down the steps, pouring into the hallway in front of Ardof. He heard the loud clang of the bar locks unlatching. The soldiers between him and the gate suddenly hesitated, as if in fear of him, but it was not Ardof who they feared. As the ranger turned his gaze, he saw Safís galloping toward him.

The dire wolf lowered her muzzle as she ran, tossing Ardof up over her back in a quick motion. Ardof tumbled over her fur but failed to grab a hold, rolling as the beast hastened under him like white-capped rapids. With a final effort, he caught the dire wolf's tail between his hands and held on for dear life, hearing the last tolls of the bells receding behind them.

Far from the perimeter of the city, beyond the reach of the soldiers they had left behind, Ardof at last let go of Safís's tail and collapsed into the mud. Banook took his human form and hunkered down next to his friend. "Are you injured?"

"I'll live," Ardof said. "And you?"

"No major wounds that I can—oh, no, Bear! Where is Bear?!" Banook cried, the blood rushing to his head.

"He was following behind us," Ardof said, "but I lost sight of him at the gate."

"We have to go back, we can't let him—"

Schlop, came a wet sound of something dropping onto the mud next to them. Safís had opened her jaws and let the slobbered, terrified dog drop from her maw.

Rrgrouf! Bear barked, standing up excitedly while covered in wolf drool, with a slight erection poking from under his hindquarters.

"Oh, thank the Lodestar and all her sisters," Banook sighed, picking Bear up and checking the dog for injuries. "And thank you, Safís."

«No, thank you, Kerjaastórgnem,» she mindspoke, her eyes inspecting the three dire wolves beside her. «Thank you for aiding my children. I need to make sure they remain safe now.»

"They could join us, aid us in the battles to come," Banook suggested.

«Too few are the dire wolves who still live. I shan't risk their precious lives for a war they wish no part in. Cities can be rebuilt, but there is no return from extinction.»

"Then let us at least take care of them until they return to health. My bears will protect them."

«You think with your heart, not with your mind, Golden Claw. In this ruthless realm, their presence alone would be much too risky for you and your bears. I will lead them away so that their prints might be followed elsewhere, so that the enemy does not make a connection between their escape and your sleuth. I will show them freedom, and show them safety in nearby forests. Then I will return to you and help you find your cub.»

Safís and the dire wolves disappeared into a curtain of rain, leaving heavy paw prints in the mud.

Chapter Forty-Six

Dancing Wings

"I've had it with them!" General Korten dus Fer spat. "Enough of whatever nonsense the shamans have learned. Let me have the mask like you promised, so we can get the Khest out of this nethervoid."

"Five of them still lack the skill to control their kind," the Red Stag noted mildly.

"It's not *their* kind, it's *my* kind. Let them find their own damnable creatures."

The Red Stag strode over to Korten and stopped directly in front of him, forcing him to back into the pavilion's tarp wall. Without breaking eye contact, he said, "Watch your filthy mouth, General dus Fer. You will follow my strategy, and so will the shamans. Their skills will be needed, their expedience will be key to winning our battle."

"But… you don't understand. That mask is a part of me. It *is* me. I can't lead my legion while I'm being torn apart."

"Goodness, don't be so dramatic!" The Red Stag shoved Korten dismissively, still amused at his general's outburst, although beginning to lose his patience. "If anyone is suffering, it is the shamans, not you. They know they won't get to wear Balastsilv after this, yet I don't hear them whining about it. They agreed to this deal, just as you did."

"Those who haven't mastered it could learn later, if only—"

"They can't!" the Red Stag finally snapped. "I won't risk getting control of a new mask while unprepared. Once we seize them, we need our new Silv-

Thaars to take immediate command, or we forfeit our chance at capturing their animals."

Korten slumped his shoulders and looked away. "Five of them are taking too long. They should be whipped until they learn. The other seven have learned all there is to it, so their time with my mask could be granted back to me instead. I need to feel the wind carry—"

"Noted. Don't get sentimental on me or I will clip your wings for good. The seven who have mastered the skills will no longer be granted time with Balastsilv. Instead, they will focus on introspecting, until they know for certain what their half-forms will be if their time to wear other masks arrives."

The new rules were promptly delivered to the shamans. In the week that followed, three of the five shamans still in training learned how to mindspeak and mindlock the chiropterans, but the other two had yet to make any headway with those abilities.

One evening, after the unsuccessful shamans had finished their training for the night, Korten stomped toward the Red Stag's pavilion.

A soldier tried to stop him. "General dus Fer, no, the monarch is—"

Without missing a beat, Korten shapeshifted into his spectacled flying fox half-form and stretched his wings to shove the guard to the ground. "They are faking it. They are fucking faking it!" he yelled as he pushed his way through the tarp door.

"Silv-Thaar dus Fer!" the Red Stag barked. The Bikhéne woman underneath the naked elk flinched, covering her breasts. The Red Stag pulled out of her and stood in front of his general. His blood rushed to his head, making his cock turn flaccid.

"I'm… I apologize, I didn't—"

The Red Stag made a gesture of dismissal. Silv-Thaar dus Fer turned to leave.

"Not you, Silv-Thaar!" He glared at the woman he'd been fucking, who picked up her few clothes and ran out of the pavilion in despair. "You should know better than to interrupt me when I'm enjoying my well-deserved spoils, Silv-Thaar dus Fer."

The guard who the Silv-Thaar had forced his way past arrived to check on the Red Stag. "Monarch Hallow, he pushed past me, I—" The soldier stopped, seeing the confrontation between the two half-forms, one naked, the other wearing a tabard that let his wings easily expand to the sides.

The guard turned to leave at once.

"Soldier! Stay where you are!" the Red Stag commanded. "You are the sole witness, and witness you shall." He glared at the flying fox.

The Silv-Thaar's eyes were sunken in shame within the lighter-colored fur of his spectacles. His shoulders drooped, his wings wrapped around him protectively, making him look weak. He tried to look down but did not want to stare at the stag's wet sheath, so he looked to the side instead.

"What is it you wanted to say, dus Fer?" the Red Stag inquired with patently false courtesy. "What was so urgent that it required you to assault my guard and force me to pull my cock out before I had my release? Speak!"

"The… the two shamans, the ones who are still in training," he mumbled. "They are faking it, Monarch Hallow. They can control the bats, but they are pretending to still be learning. They don't want the mask taken from them, so they are dragging this out on purpose."

"Shaman Urmath and Shaman Danovan? Do you have any evidence to support your accusation?"

"I devised a trick, a clever one. Fuuriseth, she won't mindspeak back to me, she won't answer my questions. But she will obey commands of a physical nature. I ordered the Nu'irg to perch on the heads of the last two people who had her mindlocked, and she flew straight to them, right after their daily training was finished."

The elk huffed. "And this matter could not wait until morning?"

Silv-Thaar dus Fer remained quiet.

The Red Stag waited, then said, "Your mask, let me see it."

The bat hesitated. After a tense moment, his wings turned to a refractive smoke and shrunk down, turning into Korten's splayed fingers. He pulled off his mask and held it out.

The Red Stag took it and said, "Stop gazing down like a beaten puppy. If what you say is true, then I will have a chat with those shamans and have them suffer the proper punishment."

Korten nodded.

The elk drew closer. Intimately close, breathing warm air past Korten's ear. He wrapped Korten's left hand within his own and said, "And the same rule applies to you, Korten." With one quick motion, the Red Stag twisted Korten's left thumb, snapping the bones and cartilage with a wet crunch.

"Fuck!" Korten yelped as he curled his body down in agony. "Scorch you, why did—"

The Red Stag kicked the general to the ground.

"Be glad it was just a thumb. I could have broken your other fingers, and with that, taken away your wings. Don't ever enter my pavilion unannounced again. Begone now—I'll deal with your petty issues in the morning."

Korten held on to his shattered thumb and ran out past the shocked guard.

Once morning arrived inside the Scoria Dome, the Red Stag called for his officers to gather at the training grounds.

"You've been given enough time to learn," he said to the shamans. Silv-Thaar Baneras and Silv-Thaar Markhor flanked him, while General Korten dus Fer stood alongside the shamans, one hand holding his mask, the other wrapped with gauze.

The Red Stag continued, "Ten of you have mastered Balastsilv, but two are still lagging behind." He regarded the dozen shamans. The ten who were not being reprimanded seemed upset with the other two. The pair of laggards stood tall, trying to hide the trembling in their knees.

The Red Stag paced around, examining his subjects. "It is time we move on, for there are lands to conquer. We need to make use of our new power, of our new wings. And so it is that we come to the last day of our training, the last chance to prove yourselves worthy of wielding the masks we will soon have in our possession."

He nodded to Korten.

Korten handed the mask to one of the trembling shamans. A cage was placed in front of her, one holding a single white-and-yellow bat, hanging upside-down and wrapped like a cocoon within her translucent wings. Fuuriseth's legs had regrown, and her broken wings had mended, but her heart could not heal. She was not only a slave, but a tool for Korten and the shamans to practice with.

"Take your half-form, Shaman Urmath," the Red Stag commanded, with no inflection in his voice.

The petrified shaman put the mask on and shapeshifted into a hog-nosed bat.

"Speak to the Nu'irg, Shaman Urmath," the Red Stag continued. Then, with a mocking tone, he added, "Make her follow your will. Make her dance, make her sing, make her piss. I don't care what you do, but make it fast."

"Monarch Hallow, I have been trying," the shaman implored. "I have learned to take my half-form. It will not be long before I—"

"Korten claims you have both learned to control your kind already, but are pretending otherwise."

"That is not true. We have been—"

"Whether it's true or not, I may not be able to tell. But what I *can* tell is if you are being a waste of my time."

He unsheathed his wave-bladed longsword. It felt so much better in his hands, so much heavier than that ridiculous spear he was made to parade around with. So much deadlier. He extended the sword and placed its point at the shaman's throat, holding his arm perfectly horizontal, without flinching or dropping the sharp tip.

"Make her dance, Shaman Urmath, or you will lose more than your wings."

The shaman focused on the white bat. Urmath had already learned to mindspeak, but she had been unable to bind Fuuriseth to her will, to implant that sickly parasite into the Nu'irg's mind that would make her do whatever Urmath asked her to do.

"I can feel her, Monarch Hallow," she said, "I can. I just… I need a bit more time."

"Urmath is telling the truth," Shaman Danovan interjected. "We will both learn, it won't take us—"

"You will have your turn, Danovan," the Red Stag said, "very soon. By the time I count down from six. Six!"

"She hears me, I swear!" Shaman Urmath implored. "I've spoken to her! Her name is Fuuriseth, the winged beacon of Fel Mellanolv. I can speak to her!"

"Then waste not your words in pointless excuses. Five!"

"If only you'd let me—"

"Four! Make her dance, Urmath!"

The terror-struck shaman tried to kneel before the cage, but the blade was pressed too sharply under her chin. She tapped her wingtips on the cage, hoping Fuuriseth would move, hoping she would do anything.

"Three! Waste no more of my time!"

"Please, please Fuuriseth… dance, do it for me, please."

"Two!"

"I will, she is, I will, she can hear me, she can."

The Red Stag thrust his blade under the shaman's chin, penetrating the bat's trachea and dislocating her jaw. The blade poked out the other side, beneath her enormous ear. The hog-nosed bat fell convulsing to the ground.

"I dragged that out for far too long," the Red Stag said, spinning his blade to get rid of the blood. "Your turn, Shaman Danovan."

Urmath's strangled gurgles suddenly stopped. She twitched twice, then her wings vanished, and her soft ears were replaced by the hard quaar ears of Balastsilv, which rolled into the pool of blood.

"Hurry up, Danovan. I don't know if I feel like counting all the way down from six this time."

Shaman Danovan picked up the bloodied mask and shoved it to his face. He quickly took the form of a mouse-tailed bat and approached the cage.

"Five!" the Red Stag said, clinking his hoofed fingertips against the waves of his blade.

"But I wasn't—"

"Four!"

Shaman Danovan mindspoke his command to Fuuriseth. The bat did not understand what dancing meant, but the shaman forced her to pointlessly sway back and forth, opening and closing her wings.

"Three!"

"She's dancing, look at her, she is dancing!"

"You call that dancing? Pathetic! A limping spur could dance better than that! Two!"

The shaman picked up the cage with his membranous wings, asking the Nu'irg to fly in circles in the limited space, to screech, to bob up and down. He did so himself, swaying back and forth to an unheard, damnable rhythm that couldn't match his fast-beating heart.

"One!"

"She is dancing! She is!"

The Red Stag lowered his weapon. "I guess I can see that. She is a terrible dancer, just like you, Shaman Danovan. I should've started with you, then perhaps Urmath would not have delayed us and made such a spectacle of herself. Now put the cage down and kneel before it."

The mouse-tailed bat fell to his knees with a cold shiver. He lowered the cage to the ground, watching as Fuuriseth curled herself into the white discomfort of her wings.

The Red Stag let his sword swing like a pendulum in front of Danovan as he addressed the shamans. "Our training here is done!" he proclaimed. "All ten of you will eventually get a chance at your own mask, but that mask will not be Balastsilv, for it belongs to Silv-Thaar dus Fer, and no one else. He alone will be allowed to wear the mask of bats from this day forward." He lifted his sword, his dark eyes locked on Danovan's neck. "And to any who dare betray my trust, like this traitorous rodent here did, know that no insolence of this kind will be forgiven, that no—"

Danovan suddenly hopped forward, clashing with the Red Stag's hip and taking to the air. The elk slashed down with his blade, missing the fast-moving target by a hairbreadth. "Stop him!" he yelled. "Close the pipe!"

Shaman Danovan flapped his wings straight toward the gated pipe, which was usually kept open during the daytime so that supplies could be moved in and out.

Two soldiers heard the monarch's call and hurried to close the opening, but they were too far away, and their feet could not match the speed of the shaman's flight.

Shaman Danovan closed his wings over his body as he dove to freedom, like a falcon after a mouse. The shaman's ribcage crunched down suddenly, as an enormous horn slammed into him at full speed. Beiféren, under Markhor's control, had intercepted the flying shaman.

The bat's trajectory shifted, sending him in an aerial roll against the wall of vines. He slammed into them, his wings and bones pierced through by thorns. He hung upside-down in a smear of blood both white and red, his body slowly shifting back to a limp human form.

Balastsilv fell silently next to the open pipe, right at the feet of the woolly rhinoceros.

In her cage, Fuuriseth screeched mutedly, still wrapped in her thin, helpless wings.

CHAPTER FORTY-SEVEN

THE CRIMSON PRINCE

The Negians marched once more, onward to war.

The Red Stag assigned a platoon of Graalman falconers to guard the piped entrance to the dome, then his army set off north, away from the cinder cones and craters of the Scoria Dome. The monarch led his troops, riding proudly on Tremor, his Jartadi steed. Behind him, his army of caprids, cervids, and perissodactyls now marched under the flickering shadow of an ever-shifting cloud of bats.

Silv-Thaar dus Fer was swooping over the other generals when he heard the Red Stag whistle to summon him. Since the flying fox could not comfortably match Tremor's pace while flapping his wings, he instead perched atop the monstrous horn of an elasmotherium.

"Silv-Thaar, our heralds and spies have not been sufficient to gather information regarding the movements of the Cabal," the Red Stag began. "Now that we are out of that wretched dome, I need your wings. I need your spectacled eyes to spy upon them."

"I will gather all the information I can," the winged general said. "And if they lower their guard, perhaps I could snatch one of their masks for you."

"Do not take unnecessary risks—your mask is more valuable than any of theirs. The aerial advantage it grants us could win us the entire war."

"Understood. I would not attempt to fight them. I can barely swing a sword without shredding my own wings to tatters."

"Just bring me whatever information you can. But be careful—their forces comprise mostly archers. A single arrow can take you down. Try to remain unseen."

Dus Fer absentmindedly caressed a white-and-yellow patch on his shoulder; Fuuriseth perched there, now free from her cage yet chained to dus Fer's every command. "What about the Zovarian maggot, Monarch Hallow?"

"He may become your next target. We have word that a Lerevi fleet has gathered around the Ashen Dome. I suspect that little thief and his companions are now deep inside it, stealing the bovid mask from us. But there's nothing we can do about that. For now, get to Fjorna, then report to me. After that we will see how far along Lago Vaari is, and I might send you to him."

Silv-Thaar dus Fer nodded his long, pointed snout. He kicked off from the elasmotherium's horn and was soon lost among his cloud of bats.

The Red Stag kept riding Tremor due north, leading his army toward the Graalman capital of Doralghon, where he was to meet with Suux—the zealous head chief of the Horde—and join forces with yet more cavalry troops.

"Monarch Hallow, another herald!" Silv-Thaar Baneras yelled, making his mount trot to catch up with his leader.

"Please tell me there are no more troubles in Bighorn, Silv-Thaar," the Red Stag pleaded, already dreading the message to come. "The last news you brought was unsavory enough."

"Not from Bighorn, but from Hestfell," the horse general said. "And not bad news this time, but great news. News you have been expecting for quite some time now."

The Red Stag pulled on Tremor's reins, halting the thick-boned steed. "Go on!" he ordered, visibly eager in his impatience.

"The heir to the Empire, your son, he has come!" Baneras announced.

"My son?... I have a son? An heir! What does Urcai say about him, Baneras? Tell me. Is he... like me?"

"Urcai says he's got little hooves for feet, though his hands are normal. And he has bumps where his antlers may one day be. Perhaps they will grow when he is older."

"And he's healthy? How is Ulle?"

"She is at rest. The baby arrived early, and she's recovering. But Ulle is fine. They are both fine, they are both in good health."

"We stop here tonight!" the Red Stag bellowed. "This is reason to celebrate. The Negian Empire has an heir, one of my own making! We have an heir!"

The Red Stag hopped off Tremor. He was congratulated by his generals, shamans, and a long line of proud officers.

"Monarch Hallow," Silv-Thaar Baneras said once the commotion subsided, "Urcai wants me to send a response. Have you... Have you thought of a name?"

"I have," he said, letting a proud smile smear his long muzzle. "Buck. Buck Hallow. That will be my son's name."

PART FIVE
DESIRE

CHAPTER FORTY-EIGHT

THE FLAME OF DISCOVERY

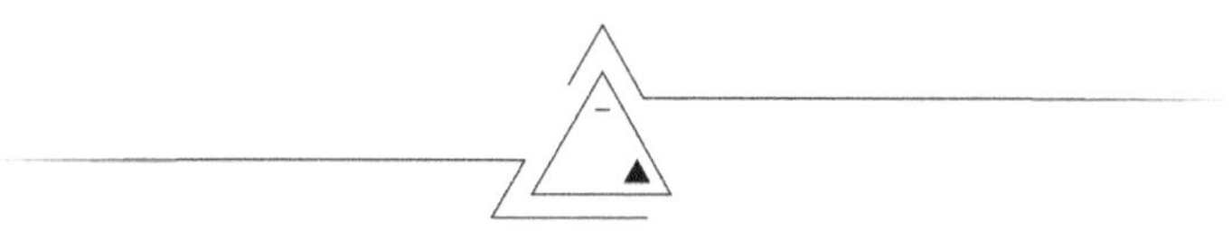

Alaia sat by herself at the highest level of the ziggurat, not too far from the entrance to Ommo ust Trommo. Her back was lit by the green flames from the four massive horns over the archway, while her face sank into shadows as the last of the arudinn went dark.

A subtle tremor shook the Taur Citadel, but Alaia barely registered it—she was getting used to them by now, as they happened several times each hour. Servant Lune had set Trommodrolom to open earlier that day, and the process was shifting things deep underground as the dome made room for its vines to retreat or shrivel away.

Alaia was writing in her notebook while consulting one of Hefra's, trying to learn how the naturalist organized her thoughts. Far below, the marble-carved city of Bra'uur reflected the dim blueness of the nighttime arudinn. A dozen miles away, the Jels Urosh Rampart that surrounded the Four Blessings shimmered like a necklace of verdant stars, lit by evenly spaced, green-flamed lanterns.

"This is my favorite view, *khumm*," Servant Lune abruptly spoke from behind her, almost causing Alaia to fling her notebook off the ziggurat.

"Khest! You scared me," Alaia blurted out.

Lune sat beside her. The ground shook around them, as if Lune's heavy form had caused the tremor. "I've seen you study every day. What is it your mind seeks?"

"I'm learning from Hefra. She studies the natural world, and I've always been interested in that, but never dared pursue it." Her face contorted with uncertainty. "I'm just starting, honestly, learning how to take field notes. I didn't see you come up the steps."

"*Khummm…* There are other ways around the back. I came to make sure the lattice is doing its work. And it is."

Alaia stowed the notebooks in her haversack.

Lune eyed her carefully. "The things you study… Do they have to do with your quest to brush Pamúnn's neck?"

"The what things of what?" Alaia stumbled over her words in surprise.

"Pamúnn told me that you have been watching him daily with your glass eye extensions. He said you constructed a strange contraption, which you thought he'd be stupid enough to fall into. Patiently you have waited for him each morning, for weeks, trying to get closer to him. That is what he said. What is it you seek from him?"

"Oh, by Wawumána's cooch, I'm so stupid, and I'm so sorry. I didn't mean to insult him, I just…"—she tried to bury her face in her hands—"I just wanted to get a fur sample from him, that's all."

"Worry not, Alaia of the Oldrin. *Khummph.* It merely sparked my curiosity. And he is not angry, only mildly irritated. It would take a lot more than that to make Pamúnn angry."

Lune looked quizzically at the young woman, but Alaia's face was still in hiding. "His fur is not magical," she continued. "It will not heal the wounded, make others fall in love with you, nor cast away demons."

"It's not for that. It's for research." She tapped a hand on her closed bag. "Hefra likes to gather specimens so that she can study them, and I wanted to impress her."

"I know not what you aim to discover by looking at simple hairs."

"I… had this idea, something I wanted to try, that I think will help us answer some questions. I haven't told anyone else about it, because I wanted to find out if my idea is any good before making a fool of myself." She paused for a moment before adding, "Well, I already made a fool of myself in front of you and Pamúnn, so I guess it doesn't matter any longer."

"A fool you are not, Alaia of the Oldrin. Tell me of this idea you had, and perhaps I will be able to help you with it. I yearn to be of service."

A bountiful dinner was served in the garth of the Taur Citadel that evening. As was typical, Lune sat with the guests but did not partake in the feast.

When does she even eat? Lago wondered. He helped himself to another serving of pheasant, then finished his glass of cider. "In how long will we be departing?" he asked.

"Three more days," Servant Lune replied. "We need a bit of time to prepare, say our farewells, and to show you one more thing." She paused through a smile, then continued, "Tomorrow, as it is Nossday, the clan leaders agreed I may grant you the honor of visiting the Pink Caldera."

"Finally," Alaia said with exaggerated relief. "So now you can tell us about it?"

"You will see, tomorrow. However, young Puuja and Pol will not be able to join us, as they are not yet four times the sacred age."

"But we want to go!" Puuja said. Pol nodded his head fervently next to her.

"It is something I cannot accommodate. I deeply apologize."

"Not fair! You treat us like children!" Puuja complained.

"You are children," Lummukem said. "We must respect the traditions of the Tjardur."

"Cort and my other spouses will take good care of you while we are gone," Lune assured the twins. Puuja and Pol pouted as they held each other, whispering curses in Miscamish.

"I have a question for you, Servant Speros of the Eland," Lune said, changing the subject.

"Yes, Servant Lune?" Speros asked, straightening his back. He was sitting at the table with the rest of them, but now that he was a servant himself, he had also refused to eat.

Lune continued, "As you have undertaken the rite of initiation before, you will not be able to join us in the same manner as our guests. But if you so choose, you may join us as servant, just as I will. Will you accept that honor?"

"*Hurfff!* Yes, Servant Lune, I would much enjoy serving, from this day until the Endfall itself."

Once dinner was over, the wayfarers were left at the table with their thoughts and the nebulous light of the quaar sphere lamp they had gifted to Lune.

Crysta leaned back in her chair, her eyes landing on Aio. "We have to do something about that head of yours," she told him.

"What did I do?" Aio asked, looking to Lago for help.

Crysta got up from her chair and walked behind the prince. "Your star map, it's fading. Lago, what did you use to paint these?"

"Grinesht. Comes from snails. Lummukem has some in their necklace pods."

"May I?" Crysta asked, her hands hovering over Aio's head. Aio nodded self-consciously. As Crysta examined the constellations Lago had painted on Aio's scalp, the prince's cheeks reddened.

"Well, let's get to it," the professor said to Lago without further ado. "Show me how it's done, and I'll help you repaint them. A bit more accurately this time."

"The only star map we have is back on Siffo's ship," Lago noted, trying to discourage whatever mood Crysta was falling into.

Crysta glared at him, pretending to be insulted. "You don't know all your stars by heart? Is that not your name, *Ster-jall*?"

"Like *you* do," Lago sniffed.

"Well, I take that as a challenge."

"Do I have any say in this?" Aio asked. "I believe it is my scalp we are—"

"You are leaving the Sword of Zeiheim where it is," Lago said to Crysta. "I like it pointing up like that." He asked Lummukem for some grinesht powder, then began to mix it with water while Lune brought them a variety of paintbrushes of different sizes. Aio resigned himself to being experimented upon. He only hoped it would not go as badly as it had for Sunu-Lummukem, the time the twins had vandalized their scalp.

Crysta studied the few markings that remained visible upon Aio's head, realizing Lago had done quite a good job, but still finding some mistakes in the star placements.

"Here's what we can do," she explained. "We keep the Sword of Zeiheim exactly like you had it, but we rotate the dome of stars to match its proper orientation, so that it's a more truthful representation."

"And you'll know what to place over his right ear once you do that?" Lago asked, with obvious doubt.

"Of course…" Crysta said, hesitating a bit. "Let's see… If Lummukem rotates this way and lands on top, then the Yellow-Eyed Ogre will move over his left ear—"

"That's not an ogre," Lago corrected her. "See? You don't know everything, *Professor*. The original constellation is Kerjaastórgnem, the ursid Nu'irg. That's Banook's constellation."

She leaned in to whisper in Lago's ear. "Is that appropriate?"

He shrugged.

"So, over Aio's right ear we should end up with the Thousand-Spot Cat," she continued more confidently.

"And that's Nelv's original constellation," Lago proudly added.

"Well, that's certainly appropriate," she declared. "Now get me those brushes and scoot that pretty lamp a bit closer."

Aio closed his eyes while Crysta worked, trying to visualize the stars each time he felt a poke prodding his scalp.

Crysta took special care with Banook's, Nelv's, and Lummukem's constellations, then continued with the others. She left the Sword of Zeiheim for last, which was kept upon Aio's forehead, point up, as Lago had demanded. The way she worked the hair-thin connecting lines between the stars of the sword was more jagged, to make the blade look like it was forged from lightning, as in the legends.

"Lummukem, do you have purple grinesht?" Crysta asked, without removing her eyes from her meticulous work. "The kind the twins smeared over your poor scalp."

"Gringralv, not grinesht," Lummukem corrected her, popping open a pod from their necklace.

"Aio likes the blue colors better," Lago said. "I don't think—"

Crysta waved him off. "It's for Pellámbri, the pink nebula. She would look better in purple, closer to her true colors."

"But purple is for allgenders, and he prefers—"

"I would love a purple nebula," Aio interrupted. "Why not mix some colors? My scalp thinks it is a good idea."

They prepared the smallest amount of gringralv, which Crysta used to place Pellámbri at the center of the Sword of Zeiheim, right where the crossguard met the blade and hilt. Using the finest of brushes, she painted purple streaks to make the nebula glow.

"That… looks really good, actually," Lago admitted.

Crysta added a few hair-thin lines to connect the other constellations, then paced to the left and right to check her work.

"And… we are done," she said. "Bright and blue, and with a purple accent. Much better, *and* more accurate."

"Does it look good?" Aio asked.

Servant Lune brought forth a mirror, letting Aio inspect his scalp. He grinned widely and nodded, seeming particularly fond of the new color added to the Lodestar.

"Thank you," Aio said. "My scalp will once again proudly wear the stars."

Alaia suddenly stood up and proclaimed, "Alright, if you are all done experimenting on the kitty's scalp, I have a little surprise I want to share with you. Wait here." She hurried away in the direction of their dormitories.

"What is it this time?" Aio asked Lago.

"No clue. But we better be ready."

Alaia soon returned with a porcelain bowl covered with a white-and-green cloth and placed it at the head of the marble table, opposite where Lune was sitting. The others moved in closer, but Alaia held a hand up to keep them away, asking them to remain by the table's sides. She held an orange-flamed candle in one hand to illuminate the covered bowl.

"Are you ready?" she asked, reaching for the cloth, anticipating the motion of pulling it back.

"I don't know," Lago said. "Is the bowl full of spiders?"

"I may try that next time. But no. This is even better."

"Do it!" Puuja yapped.

Alaia nodded, and with a theatrical flourish removed the cloth. The candle illuminated a clump of grayish-brown fluff that filled the bowl, like cobwebs and dust piled up in the corners of an unkempt room. It looked filthy, and the reaction was one of thinly muted disappointment.

"Amazing," Lago mocked. "Is that your collection of belly button fluff? Or is it just what piles up under your armpits?"

"Shush, you," she said. "What you see in front of you is a most rare specimen. The wondrous substance inside this bowl is fur from none other than Pamúnn himself. Heaps of it."

"What?" Hefra exclaimed. "How did you…" Then she saw Alaia doing the unthinkable. "What are you… No!"

But Alaia was already lowering the orange flame into the bowl. With a quick *fwhoomp* the fur caught on fire, but instead of burning orange, the hairs burned green, their tips turning black and clumpy as they curled upon themselves.

"Blasted girl, what are you doing?!" Hefra howled, shoving her way forward to stop the madness. But as she reached for the bowl, the flames rose in front of her, too bright, too tall, spiraling upward. Alaia cackled like a deranged witch, lifting her hands as if summoning a netherbeast while the growing fire reformed into a familiar shape—Pamúnn stood there now, made of green flames; regal, elusive, and untouchable as he had ever been. The flaming nyala's horns exuded a white smoke, branching into shapes that resembled the vines widening at the trunk above them.

The fire flickered, then brightened in a green flash, making them all avert their eyes.

When they could see again, the fiery Nu'irg was gone. They were left with an afterimage of the nyala that followed their sight wherever they looked, appearing in a complementary magenta every time they blinked. More than an afterimage had been left behind, however, as there was also the malodorous, sour stench of burnt fur.

"What just happened?" Hefra asked.

"How did you do that?" Lago joined in, blinking rapidly, recalling the image of the noble bovid.

"Again!" Puuja exclaimed.

Hefra leaned over to peer into the bowl; it was filled with nothing but ashes, still glowing with green tips. "Did you just… Are you *mad*, gal? Why would you burn—how did you—"

"Calm down!" Alaia said. "Yes, I burned the Khest out of it. But did you see what happened?"

"Of course I saw!"

"And what do you think that means?" Alaia asked with a smirk.

"I don't know, perhaps that your little nub is pressing hard into your brain? That I should never let you step close to my collections? Why would you burn such a specimen?"

"To prove a point. Don't worry, the fur isn't magical. It was Lune who made the figure with the flames."

They all looked to Lune, who was smirking placidly at the opposite end of the table.

Alaia paced around, as if giving a lecture. "But what this means is… If you were paying attention, I used a normal orange flame, not a green one. Yet the fur burned green, like sap would. And Lune was able to control it. This proves that Pamúnn's fur is replete with aetheric carbon. Perhaps each hair is a thread of quaar, I have no idea. But whatever makes Pamúnn who he is, it is not the normal carbon we are used to."

"That was so smart!" Aio said.

"That was senseless!" Hefra croaked. "You could've used a few hairs to demonstrate that, instead of a bowlful of them!"

With a cocky grin, Alaia reached into the front pocket of her overalls and pulled out a clump of fluff.

"Here, have at it," she said, casually tossing the fur onto the table. "Lune brushes Pamúnn every evening. He sheds clumps like this every time."

Hefra reverentially picked up the tangle of fur. "You are mad as a drunken gibbon," she said, shaking her head. "But that was… impressive, and quite smart of you."

Alaia nodded her agreement. "So, do we have a deal now? I can get you more than this. And I have a whole collection of fur from Sterjall in my bag."

Lago's eyes widened. "You what?"

"I'm just kidding, but I *can* get those anytime I want, you can't stop me." She looked back to Hefra. "So, will you let me be your apprentice? Or do I need to capture the Nu'irg ust Kroowin and set their feathers aflame as well?"

"I'll get you started right away, sweet gal," Hefra said. "But no more fiery tricks."

CHAPTER FORTY-NINE

MIRRORED DREAM

The twins lay in bed watching Sunu, who slept cross-legged in their own bed, their back separated from the cold wall by a thin pillow. Kruwensilv sat on the side table, facing toward the twins as if to keep an eye on them even while they slept. Olo perched atop the mask, watching nearly as intently.

"It's not fair," Pol whispered in Common, his voice muted by the mask of glires. Lately, both of them had taken to speaking in the foreign tongue, which they had learned much quicker than adults ever could. Every evening before bed, Sunu-Lummukem let Pol wear Okrisilv during their lessons, so that he could catch up to Puuja, who was free to wear the mask throughout the day.

"We want to go too," Puuja whispered back. "They already abandoned us once, and tomorrow they'll leave us with Cort and other strange cows."

Pol took the mask off and slid under the blanket. "We don't like Cort," he said with a scowl. "He smells like cabbage."

"We should show *them* what it's like to be abandoned. That's what we should do. That will teach them."

They both ruminated over that idea as they fell asleep.

Okrisilv rested serenely over Pol's chest. Puuja's red hair draped across their single pillow, blending with Pol's shorter hair, combining their forms into one. While Kruwensilv watched over them, Puuja and Pol dreamed the same dream.

"Where are we?" the twins asked.

They stood in a dim tunnel. The ceiling was illuminated by arudinn, following the shape of a branching root—it looked like frozen lightning captured in a narrow rift.

"It's too dark in here, we need to get out," they both said in unison.

The pale light was no comfort to them, so they walked forward, searching for an exit.

The walls were coated in yellow slime molds. The ground was moist and cold.

Their wandering feet found a pool of still water filling a perfectly circular hole in the ground. The slime mold gathered around the edges, streaking outward like a yellow iris. They both leaned forward and, without disturbing the glassy surface, looked at their reflection.

They were one.

The left half of their body was Puuja, long-haired, standing with confidence. The right side was Pol, short-haired, slouching and frowning, trying to avert his eye from the reflection. Their lips were streaked with a purple pigment, one vertical bar on either side. There was no midpoint between their freckled faces; the two figures merged seamlessly into one.

"We could escape through the water," they said with their single mouth. The water spoke of safety to them. Her cold, wet embrace would be reassuring.

They stepped onto the glassy pool, but their feet would not pass through it; they barely cast a ripple upon the surface. The water did not even feel wet. Like a polished black mirror, the surface was impenetrable.

They watched their distorted image ripple at their feet, silhouetted by the lightning-like arudinn. The distortion looked grotesque, and scared them, so they stepped away from the false water.

"Let's go," they said as one. "This is not the way."

Deeper in the tunnel, they saw a red light. Not fire red, but blood red. Ruby red. It gave them comfort. They ran together, synchronizing their split steps. Left. Right. Left. Right. Never faltering.

The red light was farther than they had expected, and it seemed to never get any closer.

Left.

Right.

After an eternity of running, with their breath nearly exhausted, one red light became two, slowly separating into a left light and a right one. They kept running toward the lights even as they spread farther apart, shimmering like the pupils of a nocturnal creature.

Their single body struggled. Pol wanted to run to the right, and Puuja to the left. Their legs fought against one another, nearly ripping them in two.

"Stop!" Puuja said singly, and they both stopped.

"We can't fight each other like this!" she said, speaking in Common and Miscamish at the same time. "We will tear each other apart!"

"But I want to go to that one," Pol's side said, pointing his right arm to the right light.

"We don't say that!"

"Say what?"

"We don't use that word."

"I don't know—"

"*That* word. The one that splits us apart. We are *we*, together, always."

Pol curled his side into itself, feeling threatened by the immutable concept.

"You treat me like a child, sometimes," he said, "just like they do. *I* can stand up for myself."

"Stop that! Don't say the word, don't—"

"I love you," Pol continued, "and I know you do this because you love me too, but you must let me be myself."

"But we are together!" Puuja wept. "We are not like them, we are like us."

"I want to be Pol," Pol said firmly, taking a step to the right.

"Stop!" Puuja screamed. "Please don't leave us."

But it was too late. Pol was standing on his own, next to her.

"Please don't leave me…" Puuja sobbed.

"I will never leave you, sister, that I won't do. We are one, but we are also our own. Walk with me."

Pol stood straighter and offered his left hand to her. Her right hand took his, and they walked together, each of them toward their own light.

They let the red warmth envelop them.

"What is wrong?" Sunu asked, shaking the twins' shoulders.

Pol and Puuja were crying in their sleep. They jolted upright in bed when Sunu finally managed to wake them.

"Why are you two crying?" Sunu asked.

"I… I don't know," Puuja said, catching her breath. "We had a dream… and I… can't remember it any longer."

Her own words sounded strange to her.

"I don't remember either," Pol said, tasting the threatening word on his tongue. The word felt good, though it carried sadness with it. He did not understand why.

"Dreams are sometimes doorways to understanding," Sunu said as they reached for their mask. Olo fluttered briefly to find a new perch on Sunu's shoulder—at that moment, Sunu had a glimpse of a giant nest, of a broken shell, of blue feathers strewn over a mossy ground, but the image evaporated as quickly as it had appeared. As they tried to rekindle the memory, they put their mask on, took their half-form, and quietly added, "Do not take your dreams for granted. Let them light the way."

CHAPTER FIFTY

CATACOMBS

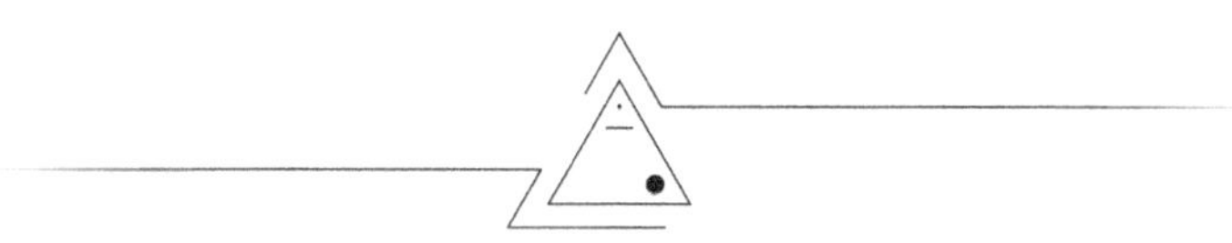

It was Nossday morning. Servant Lune asked her guests to clean themselves thoroughly and wear clothing suitable for cold weather, as she was going to take them up to the snowy summit of Laaja Ash, to at last reveal to them the mystery of the Pink Caldera.

All of them but Pol and Puuja.

"Why do they treat us like this? Fuck them," Puuja complained once the longhorn bison pulled the carriage away.

"That's a bad word," Pol reminded her, watching their friends leave.

"Alaia uses it all the time. Fuck them, that's what I say. Why do they have to leave us with… Cort." She turned to look over her shoulder, wearing a clearly fake smile.

Cort of the Pelorovis stood waiting past the bridge. He waved pleasantly at them.

The twins dragged their feet toward the long-horned man.

"Head strong!" Cort said to them, with a bit too much excitement. "We have a wonderful day planned for you two, *grummm*. My spouses will teach you the history of the eight prophets. You will learn about them while memorizing our sacred songs."

"Fuck *that*," Pol mumbled.

"What did you say, Son of the Sehján?"

"Nothing…" Pol curled into himself and hid behind his sister.

Servant Lune's many husbands and wives were waiting for them in the Taur Citadel. Cort told the twins that they needed to be clean before properly memorizing the songs, as only a clean body could host a clean mind.

"But we showered before breakfast, that we did!" Puuja complained.

"But you left the citadel," Cort declared, "so you must clean yourselves once more."

He ushered them to the showers and told them he'd be waiting with his spouses in the Ruminant Chamber, with the hides unrolled, ready to teach the children their sacred hymns.

"I hate it," Puuja said as she dried herself off. "They go out on adventures, and we stay here with the cows."

"Lummukem said they'll be back later tonight," Pol told her. "I don't want to learn songs. I want to see more. I'd even rather be back home, in our den."

"And why do we have to shower sixty-six times?" She put her outfit back on. Even their children's clothing they found disrespectful—they didn't get to wear elytra armor reinforced with colorful resins, but only the plain leather version of it.

"Why don't we just… leave?" Pol suggested. "Who cares what Cort thinks? We can be back tonight, just like the others will."

"And go where?"

"To the catacombs," Pol said with a devious smile. Puuja's face mirrored his.

They dressed up hurriedly and crawled out a small window.

"Should we get a pharolith first?" Pol suggested.

"Good idea." Puuja led the way, sneaking down a hallway toward their room. She looked around with the mask, searching for threads of anyone who could be nearby. She spotted a servant in their room, scrubbing the place clean. He was not one of Lune's spouses. They could not avoid being seen, so they walked in with purpose, hoping to avoid any questions.

"Head strong," the cleaning servant said. "Should you not be at the Ruminant Chamber?"

"Head strong," Puuja replied. "Cort wanted to, uhm, see one of our lamps." She grabbed a pharolith and scurried out like a rat.

"He will tell Cort," Pol noted, following his sister.

"Then we better hurry out before he does."

They entered the rotunda with the paintings of the eight prophets, then turned left at the gallery with the frescoes and friezes. At the end of the hallway that exited into the gardens, they could see the massive pelorovis skull guarding one of the trapdoors to the Bra'uur Catacombs. They checked left and right, then stepped into the grass.

The twins crouched next to the stone platform. It looked like an ancient well, with a wooden lid weighed down by the enormous skull. They were faced with two problems. First, there was a padlock; it was rusty, but still locked. Second, even if they both propped their necks under the massive, mossy horns, then pushed up with all their strength, they could not have lifted the trapdoor, as the skull was much too heavy.

Puuja tried to pick at the lock with her knife, but it was useless.

"Oxruk curse them!" Pol swore, kicking at the grass.

"Watch out, gardeners are coming," Puuja warned. They ducked behind greenery, watching the figures pass.

"Maybe Okrisilv can find another way in," Pol suggested.

Puuja focused to sense the spaces beneath the garden. It was hard to pick up on much, as the catacombs went deep, and there was little alive down there other than thin crusts of stubborn bacteria. She could feel the hollowness underground, but the feeling was too dim for her to visualize a path. She focused her sight farther, exploring the gardens, suddenly sensing a blend of colorful auras. Pamúnn was there, strolling through the fern forest. Next to him walked Nelv, Ishke'ísuk, and Gwit.

"It's the Nu'irgesh," she whispered. "Right there, behind the bushes."

Pamúnn stopped, sensing the twins' presence.

"I know what we can do," Pol said, poking his upper body out from the greenery. "Hey Gwit, come here!"

His voice made the skittish nyala bolt away. The other three Nu'irgesh stood there, seeming a bit miffed—they had been having a good time with their old friend until Pol scared him.

"Come quick, we need you!" Pol said before ducking back behind cover.

Gwit did not understand Pollomekh's words, other than his own name, but he sensed the boy's urgency. The hazel dormouse scurried forward and jumped into his cupped hand.

The twins snuck back toward the trapdoor, keeping their eyes peeled. While Pol held Gwit up in one hand, he grabbed the rusty lock with the other and pretended to chew on it. "Can you do that for us?" he asked Gwit, miming the chewing motion again.

Gwit seemed dubious, but he liked the siblings and was curious about what they were after. He hopped off Pol's hand and disappeared into the grass, then quickly reappeared as a castoroides. The giant beaver was hardly inconspicuous, but he worked fast. It took him only one bite to break through the padlock—or rather, to chew it free, as he sank his incisors behind it, removing chunks of wood where the latches had been attached. Gwit spit out the lock and splinters, then waited.

The twins tried to lift the trapdoor open by pushing the two horns up. With no lock to secure it, the trapdoor did rise, although only a mere fingerbreadth.

"Help?" Pol said.

Gwit cocked his head, then waddled toward the horn on Pol's side, ducked his bulky head beneath it, and straightened his body with a jolt. The entire skull lifted and rotated around the hinge of the trapdoor, rising so high that it flipped around, crashing down on the grass behind the opening.

The bones rumbled and cracked as they hit the ground. One horn flew off and tore through an azalea bush like an angry scythe. Gardeners all around turned their heads, spotting the giant beaver, yet failing to notice the two red-headed children who had already climbed down the damp steps. Gwit glanced around apologetically, then turned into a black rat and followed the twins.

"They'll be coming after us," Puuja said, spreading open the petals of the pharolith lamp.

Pol smiled, enjoying the rush of excitement. "Let's see how far we can get before they catch us."

They halted at the bottom of the steps. The long chamber that opened ahead of them was covered in skulls, like bricks lining an endless hallway. The craniums were positioned with their crowns forward, so that their horns poked out threateningly.

"—I don't know, I saw a—" came a voice from the top of the steps. One of the gardeners stared down, but the kids were already gone. She did, however, see a cold light receding down the tunnel.

"Thank you, Gwit," Puuja said while they ran, careful not to snag their clothes on the horns to either side of them. Water seeped through the walls, creating moldy patches of green, but the deeper they went, the browner and dustier the catacombs became.

"This place looks much better than the citadel," Pol said, once they stopped to catch their breath. "It is scary, and beautiful."

A twisting staircase had led them into a circular room that opened onto eight more paths. Like keystones, gold-painted skulls decorated the eight archways, each of a different kind of bovid.

"We're going to get lost in here," Pol fretted, sitting on the dusty ground. "Maybe we should go back?"

"Nonsense," Puuja said, walking around him. "We have Okrisilv. We have a pharolith. And we have Gwit. We escaped Oxmaaga while being chased by an army of Oxruk. Dead bones can't do anything to us."

"—down here—" they heard a voice from up the steps.

Puuja looked at her feet, then at the steps they had descended, and realized they had been leaving prints behind. The twins felt the glow of a green lantern above them and hurried away, picking one of the eight tunnels at random.

Unknowingly, they had chosen the tunnel decorated by a tetraceran skull. All the skulls in the subsequent hallway felt more disturbing than the ones they had seen before, as they were mostly human skulls, oftentimes crowned by four sharp but small horns.

The hallway was perfectly straight, evenly covered by bones, even up to the vaulted ceiling. Empty eye sockets looked upon them from above, with eerie, baby-like proportions. As they slowed down at a corner, they saw the green light far behind them, and knew their pursuers could see them as well. They pushed on until they found a more confounding set of tunnels, again of mixed species of bovids. All the skulls were green, kept moist and slippery from the water seeping through the walls.

"Gross," Puuja said, watching Pol unashamedly drink from a skull's dripping horn.

"It tastes fine. It's fresh. Even Gwit agrees." The black rat was washing off his dusty paws and tail under the thin stream.

Puuja's mouth was bone-dry. She closed her eyes and let the bovid skull drip freely into her mouth.

They kept walking through the green caverns, a bit more slowly now. For a moment, Puuja closed her pharolith to tease her brother in the darkness. "The pale men are coming for you, Pollomekh! They will rip off all your hair, then bathe you in bat dung until your skin turns pale like theirs."

"Stop!" Pol giggled.

She poked at him, tickling him, making scary Oxruk sounds.

"Stop!" Pol protested again. "They are going to hear us if you keep doing that."

Puuja stopped her teasing but kept the pharolith closed. "Here," she said, handing her brother the mask. "You should see what it truly looks like down here. The tunnels remind me of the Queen's Lodge."

Pol put Okrisilv on, and in the darkness saw the fabric of threads upon threads of moss and life. The even coating of moss made the skulls distinctive, down to the complex interiors of their craniums and the hollow curves of their horns.

"I wish we could both see like this, all the time," he whispered.

He grabbed his sister's hand and walked with her, traveling by the sight of Okrisilv alone.

He stopped, sensing a light ahead of them.

He felt an echo in his head, a remote feeling as if this had happened before, but he could not place it.

"They found us," Puuja whispered.

"No… It's not. It's not a flame."

They followed the glow, and found it was a beam of light landing sharply upon the spiraling horns of a kudu skull. A rusty ladder led up to a trapdoor, from which the light filtered through a crack in the wood.

"I guess we could exit here, before we get truly lost," Puuja said. She pulled herself up the ladder and pushed. The trapdoor was locked.

"Gwit?" she kindly asked.

Gwit happily complied, already a bit tired of this pointless pursuit, having realized that the kids were not after anything more substantial than getting into trouble. As a giant beaver, he pushed his head up, cracking the moist wood around the trapdoor's lock. He returned to his primal form and climbed out of the catacombs.

The three of them found themselves in a lush yew forest. This particular trapdoor seemed to be far from the city, in an area of overgrown, unused trails. They tried closing the trapdoor, but it was far too broken to seal shut. They shrugged it off and walked away under the gnarly branches.

"It smells so good," Pol said, rejoicing amidst the humid scents of rotting leaves, mushrooms, and lichens.

"I'm glad we did this," Puuja said. "I don't care if they get mad. What are they going to do? They can't do anything worse to us than make us learn songs with... Cort." She nearly gagged the name out.

A comforting sound found their ears. They instinctively followed it, discovering a cascading creek splashing through the forest, turning the greens yet more vibrant under its vitreous caress.

"What we need is a den of our own," Pol said. "Like we used to build back at home."

Puuja knew exactly what he meant.

They gathered dry branches from the yews, which were plentiful and easy to snap, and carried them to a flat rock in the middle of the wide creek. While Gwit watched them, the twins wove the branches together using lianas, tucking moss between them for padding. After a few hours of arduous work, they had built a dome they could both sit in comfortably. They secured their gnarly dome over the rock, adding more branches and rocks to hold it in place.

The only entrance to their den was by water, just like a proper beaver's lodge. Naked and laughing, they jumped into the creek and swam up into their dome, crawled onto the rock, and sat there, keeping the den alight with their pharolith.

Pol leaned against his sister's side, still wearing the mask. Puuja opened a tiny green bottle, and onto a finger dabbed the vanilla-scented secretion from the beavers of Okridrolom. She rubbed it on her neck.

"Lakemother shelter us," she whispered.

The smell of the Queen's Lodge—their true den in the floating city of Kisdik—quickly soaked through the entire structure.

"I miss home," Pol said.

"Me too."

"I miss Mom."

Puuja merely sighed.

The twins inhaled the scents of a distant land while listening to the droning sound of running water. They stared at the wavering reflections caused by the pharolith's cold light, as if hypnotized by the ever-shifting forms the water bounced into the branches of their mossy dome. They both held the memory of their mother, of their past, of their den, beating in their heads like distant drums. Both of them suddenly tensed up, lifting their heads.

"I know!" they said as they stared at one another.

Pol took the mask off and offered it to his sister. "You should try it first."

"I… Okay, are you sure?"

Pol nodded.

They scootched on their butts until they were face to face, sitting cross-legged. Puuja donned the mask and focused on the reflected lights bouncing off her brother's face. She now knew full well what her half-form would be—she had seen it in the reflections, in the smells, in the sounds. Without blinking, she concentrated on that form.

As she watched her brother's smile widen, Puuja felt something tickling her ears. She realized then that they had extended upward and were scratching the branches above them. She adjusted her posture, shifting on her nubby tail, as she could no longer cross her now-longer legs.

"A black-naped hare!" Pol exulted. "I knew it!" He jumped forward to hug his sister, pushing the hare against the wall of the den and nearly tearing the entire place down.

Puuja had first seen the hares during an excursion to the mainland, when she had briefly left the safety of her home island. She had been fascinated by their long leaps, and thought that if she could run as fast and jump as high as the hares, she too would never have to fear the Oxruk who lurked belowground.

While Puuja learned how to speak once more—which was particularly challenging due to her strange new teeth—Pol examined her curious, lanky body. Her fur was intricately textured in browns and grays, with the addition of a dark patch on the back of her neck, as if she was wearing a black neckerchief. Pol loved the feel of Puuja's handpaws, which, instead of having leathery pads like Sterjall's, were fully covered in soft fur.

Pol waved the pharolith around, watching as the red veins in Puuja's long ears became visible when the light shone from behind her. The purple pigments streaked over her lips were still there, now a bit hidden beneath her chevron-shaped nose.

Without warning, Puuja shifted back into her human self, letting her red hair fall to her shoulders. "You try next!" she said as she giggled, too curious about what her brother's half-form would be. "Do it!" She handed him the mask.

Pol focused in the same manner his sister had, with full confidence. He grew a much longer tail than the hare, and his snout became more pointed. The patterns on his fur coalesced into beautiful stripes of black, white, and orange-sprinkled grays.

"A long-eared chipmunk!" Puuja cried out with a big smile, hugging the adorable creature.

Despite the name, the long-eared chipmunk could never compete with the ears of a black-naped hare, but his long, bushy tail made up for what his ears lacked. Pol had once kept a long-eared chipmunk as a pet, and he had been heartbroken when the rodent died. His mother's explanation that chipmunks did not get to live for much longer than a handful of years had been of no consolation to him. He had always thought it unfair, and had wanted to kick the balls of whoever had made up such unjust rules.

"We should go out and see if you can climb a tree!" Puuja suggested.

"I vvant t'see how hi yeewv can jiump!"

It was getting dark already, and the siblings felt tired and hungry, but they did not care. They played in the forest, trading the mask and changing forms. Gwit watched them for a little while, but then grew tired of their strange behavior and scurried away.

Once their exhaustion got the best of them, the twins returned to the safety of their den, curled around each other, and slept.

CHAPTER FIFTY-ONE

THE PINK CALDERA

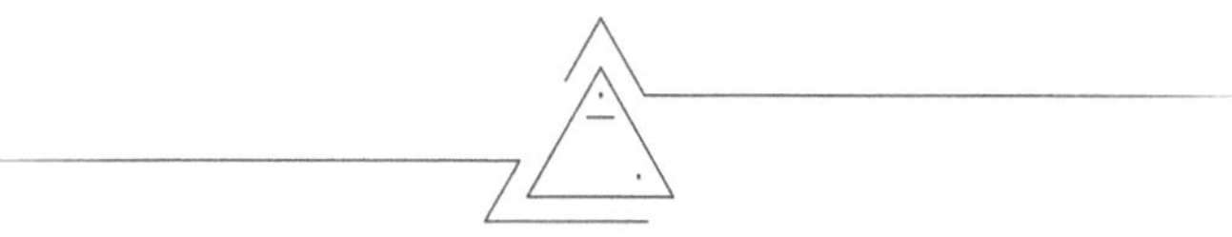

While Pol and Puuja ventured through the catacombs, the rest of the wayfarers were on their way to the Pink Caldera.

"This is normally a difficult pilgrimage our people undertake," Lune explained as they were dutifully pulled up a well-kept mountain road by a longhorn bison. "When we come of age, we must travel to all four peaks. First, we climb to the iron-streaked summit of Laaja Kriss, where we must break through rock to obtain an ore of iron. Then we venture into the mines at the top of Laaja Trell, where we are to procure a clump of graphite and carve it into a semblance of our current selves. Then we hike up the fiery crater of Laaja Ëovad, where we cast down the iron ore and the black idol to feed the mountain with our essence, and let it reconstruct ourselves."

Lune pointed to the white-steaming volcano in front of them. "And last, we climb the snowy trail of Laaja Ash, so that we may find ourselves in the waters of the caldera. The spiraling path could take several days to climb on your own. Since time is short, we chose to bring you through a more direct way that we servants take, *khum*."

Laaja Ash was the shortest of the four volcanoes, yet the climb to its top was still significant, even when using the shortcut. A few hours before dusk, as they finally neared the summit, they entered a dark tunnel. It was even colder in the tunnel than it had been out in the snow, so they tightened their parkas and watched as they approached the bright exit at the far end.

The longhorn bison pulled the carriages through the threshold and stopped.

Nothing could be seen—nothing but a dense fog. The steaming peak kept a perpetual cloud over itself, letting them glimpse only a few strides ahead at any given moment. They hopped off the carriages and followed Servant Lune, who walked next to Servant Speros on a marble path recently cleared of snow.

Sterjall spotted two women standing in the fog. *No, statues,* he realized, belatedly noticing the plinths they stood atop.

The marble carvings framed the path. On the left was a slender woman lifting a hand up to the skies. The figure on the right held the exact same pose, albeit mirrored, but she was in her half-form of a tetracerus, seeming yet more slender in her antelope-like form. A thin hoarfrost coated the nude statues, making them seem translucent.

"These are the two forms of Rumah of the Tetracerus," Lune informed them. "The same Trommofröa you saw depicted inside the Taur Citadel."

Not too far beyond Rumah was another pair of statues, of a man with arms outstretched and a yak in its mirrored pose.

"As you might've guessed, these are the two forms of Au'óro of the Grassland Yak, another of our eight prophets."

In the same order they had seen the paintings arrayed in the citadel's rotunda, more pairs of prophets materialized as they walked through the fog, all nude and proud of their bodies. Drurum of the Gaur was followed by Naj'al'alás of the Mountain Anoa, then by Bum-Vaor himself, in his human and aurochs forms. Gweléshi of the Pelorovis showed her long horns next, followed by Ejokk of the Steppe Wisent, who sat cross-legged upon his plinth.

Last came the sensual curves of Seitho-Dovár. Sterjall stopped there, entranced by the beauty of her half-form. Unlike at the painting in the rotunda, this nyala was not wearing the horns of a male, but was purely female and hornless. If she was meant to be painted with the colors of a male, there would be no way to know, for the prophet was embodied by white crystals upon white marble within white fog.

"You are making me a bit jealous," Kulak half-joked.

"Sorry. She is… There's something about her," Sterjall said. "I don't understand what it is—" He noticed everyone else was also entranced by the beauty of the carved likeness, each in their own ways.

"*Strive to explore all aspects of your true selves,*" Servant Lune recited, pulling them out of their trance, "*to be closer to who you truly are and not to the person others expect you to be.* Seitho-Dovár most strikingly represents the virtue of authenticity, as Bum-Vaor inscribed upon the Trommo Hides, *khummm.* But let us continue. The gates are near."

Sterjall took one last look at the seductive nyala, then tightened the hood around his cold neck and followed the others.

A monolithic double gate appeared in front of them, identical to the one they had found at Nannúr when first entering the Ashen Dome. The steel portal was lodged in a white marble wall just as tall as those of the Nudoroth Rampart. As with the rampart's gates, the knockers upon this one were shaped like bull testicles. Lune lifted them and let them drop, announcing their arrival with the all-pervading sound.

The gates creaked open. The interior of the marble structure was clouded in fog as well, though not as densely as the outside. A nude servant stood at either side of the entrance, apparently oblivious to the cold temperatures. "Head strong," they both respectfully whispered, bowing their horns to welcome the visitors in.

Once the gates closed behind the group, the cold breeze ceased tormenting them. A colonnade guided them to a long series of pools, all lined with white tiles. Orange flames allowed them to visualize the depth of the cavernous space. More servants were busy scrubbing the chamber, becoming uncertain silhouettes within the steam.

Lune pointed to the many pools, which were empty, sparkling clean, and bubbling softly. "You must leave all your clothes and any jewelry in this room. Then you must wash yourselves once more, and thoroughly scrub your bodies in any of the hot pools, alone or in groups—they all share the same warm temperature. Servant Speros and I will leave to undertake our own cleansing ceremony."

"I'm so ready to jump into a hot tub," Alaia said. "That walk in the cold froze my nub off."

"The Pink Caldera lies beyond that gate," Lune told them, her snout directed toward an archway much smaller than the one they had entered through. "When you are ready and washed, knock on it, *khumm,* and we will be waiting beyond." She lit a candle on a sconce scored with spaced markings—a candle clock. "You have three wicks at most, as the rite of initiation always begins on time." Lune and Speros left them, their three horns vanishing into the vapors.

The misty building had the quiet echoes of an abandoned temple, with only the bubbling sounds remaining constant. The wayfarers began to remove their Winter clothes and place them in diamond-shaped compartments carved into the walls.

Just as he was about to drop his trousers, Sterjall felt his old anxiety return. Too many people who had never seen him naked stood right beside him:

Crysta, Hefra, Siffo, Vor-Vor, and even the cleaning servants. His fear tightened around his neck like a noose.

"Hey," Alaia whispered to him. "No one can see through the fog. See?" She took a step back, partially disappearing.

Sterjall glanced around. Through the white, his friends were merely undefined silhouettes submerged in orange glows. He took a deep breath and continued undressing.

"You boys can find a pool away from the rest of us," Alaia suggested. "There are plenty to choose from. I think I'll find a big one just for myself." She vanished into the warm steam.

Sterjall and Kulak watched all their friends go before finding a more private pool for themselves. They sank their furry bodies into the water, rejoicing in the heat and the tickling of the rising bubbles. They found brushes at the side of the pool, as well as scentless bars of soap.

Sterjall elbowed Kulak. "See? I promised I'd show you hot springs someday."

"It was Servant Lune who brought us here, not you. You will still owe me after this. But this feels much better than a normal heated bath. Is this what your hot springs are like?"

"Not quite. This is too pristine and artificial. The hot springs Banook took us to were in the mountains, all naturally formed, though they were built up a bit after that, to keep the pools maintained."

"The heat feels soothing," Kulak said, wading closer. "Lean back, relax your body." He took a hold of Sterjall's legs, massaging them softly. Sterjall let himself float, his head anchoring him at the edge of the pool. He closed his eyes.

Kulak continued kneading, lower each time, until he reached the wolf's footpaws; he pulled them above water as he spread the digits apart, applying pressure between them.

Sterjall lightly moaned, his tired toes aching in delight. Then he felt something slimy and jolted upward, eyes wide open. "What are you doing?" he asked, eyes on Kulak, who had one of the wolf's toes in his mouth.

The caracal released the toe and said, "Only teasing." He then licked at the ball of the footpaw with his sandpapery tongue.

Sterjall twitched. "Why are you doing that?" He pulled his footpaws back and sunk into the pool all the way to his chin, hiding an emerging erection. His eyes followed a shadow—one of the servants glided nearby, like a specter of fog.

Kulak remained still, studying the wolf's flustered expression. Once the shadow passed, he said, "When we undressed, I felt your fear once more. Same as the time in Kruwendrolom when we were naked in front of Sunu, Kitjári, and Nalaníri. Why is it that nakedness frightens you?"

Sterjall's muscles tensed up. "It's… It's a long story. Insecurities. I find it uncomfortable when others see me naked, at least at first."

"Will you tell me this story as I clean your body? With the brush, not with my tongue."

Sterjall nodded and shifted into Lago, then let his mask float around the pool. While Kulak scrubbed every portion of his body, Lago told him the story he had once told Banook, about how as a small child he had tried to impress a couple of textile merchants by wearing the expensive mulberry silks his father was trying to sell, parading in front of them with a feminine strut. His father had forced Lago to drop his clothes in front of the tradesmen and stand there naked as punishment for embarrassing him.

"Your father was not a good man," Kulak said. "My scalp understands now. But we are not like him. There should be nothing for you to fear with us."

"It's not a rational thing," Lago explained. He dipped his head in the water, washed his curly hair, then repositioned himself to scrub the caracal's back. The fur turned smoky in his fingers as Kulak transformed into Aio. The prince took the felid mask off and let it bob up and down next to the canid one.

"It still bothers me, but I'm getting better at it," Lago continued. "I've never had much trouble being openly lorrkin, but being naked? That's always been complicated. Banook has helped me with it, and Alaia has always kept an eye on me to make sure I'm comfortable. And now you are helping me as well. Your confidence makes me feel more at ease."

He kept on scrubbing, using the soap and brushes, sliding his hands between Aio's slippery armpits, crotch, and neck. *He is so smooth,* Lago thought. The soap had made Aio's body even more sleek and soft. *Why does that feeling arouse me so much? Yet I feel equally aroused when he's covered in fur.*

"Why do you think the Tjardur are so fixated on cleanliness?" Aio asked, eyes closed while Lago rubbed his scalp.

Lago pondered the question while staring at the blue constellations Crysta had painted there—they looked black under the orange lamplight. "I'm not sure. There must be more to it than simply showing devotion to Bum-Vaor's writings."

"Perhaps their scalps read the hides too literally. But I do not mind—the water feels good, and so do your hands."

Lago nodded absently, looking around the room. "What do you think they do here? This whole place is so mysterious. They are so secretive about it."

Aio had no answer. He simply relaxed.

Lago tickled Aio's small testicles, signaling he was done with his scrubbing. Aio rinsed the soap off his head, then gazed at a line of shadows headed back to the room where they had dropped their clothes. "My eyes see our friends leaving their pools," he told Lago.

"We should get going as well then."

"Excuse me?" Crysta's voice called through the mists. "Someone? Could we get some towels?" Then, a moment later, she added, "Where are our clothes?"

The two lovers turned back into their half-forms and hurried to meet the others. Sterjall remained concealed in the fog, hiding behind Kulak. He checked the side compartments to find that their belongings had been removed. "Where did they place our things?" he asked.

"I'm sure our garments will be returned, Lorr Vaari," a high-pitched voice answered.

Sterjall turned, encountering Ambassador Vor-Vor. He couldn't help but notice the old eunuch's half-empty crotch, where his limp cock dangled with no balls underneath.

"This feels similar to some Jabrak traditions," the Tsing ambassador calmly added, "where we are to clean ourselves before practicing our rituals. We mustn't touch any soiled surfaces after our cleaning is done, or we'd have to wash all over again. Our dirty clothes were taken away so that this chamber, and we in turn, can remain pure. Even towels are seen as extraneous and unclean."

"So now what?" Alaia asked.

"We go knock with those knockers," Hefra answered, walking confidently toward the smaller set of steel gates. She lifted the steel testicles, then let them bang against the doors. The metallic rumble echoed pervasively, but was quickly softened by the steam.

The double doors opened, revealing the brightness of the outside once more, as well as the biting cold of the first day of Thawing.

"Head strong!" a nude Speros greeted them.

"*Khummmmm…*" Servant Lune hummed from beside him. "The Pink Caldera welcomes you." Her muscular body stretched to her full, formidable height. She wore no clothing or adornments, not even the smallest earring or horn cap. The scars from her recent wounds were healing well, and though they still looked pink and painful, she paid no mind to them. *She looks beautiful and imposing,* Sterjall thought, fascinated by the purity and strength of her figure.

The vast outdoor space comprised a new series of hot springs, with dozens of pools hiding in the steam beyond. Tjardur men, women, and allgenders were already bathing in the waters, which were ever-so-slightly pink in hue. Unlike the indoor pools, these were not artificially tiled, but had been grown from calcified minerals. The ground was uneven yet solid, with bulbous crystals coating every surface, and with stubborn pockets of snow and ice cradled in the uneven nooks.

Lune explained the next part of the rite of initiation. "You must saunter through the fog now, each of you, and find a pool to your liking that has servants in it. There may be many servants in a pool, but only one guest may be present in each, no more, *khum*. Submerge yourselves in the pink waters, and the servants within will explain what comes next."

Lune and Speros waited, their wet fur beginning to grow icy tips.

Vor-Vor was the first to step forward, with unabashed confidence. The others followed more hesitantly.

Sterjall and Kulak walked side by side. The walkways between the mineral pools were narrow, forcing the group to separate into their own paths, but the wolf and caracal kept together.

Sterjall clutched one handpaw over his chest for warmth, the other covering his crotch. "Look, geyser cones," he whispered to Kulak, pointing his muzzle toward one of many mineralized mounds that grew from the cratered landscape. The round-tipped cone reminded him of a termite mound, albeit one that was pink and bubbled lightly. "Keep your whiskers away," he warned, "they might shoot boiling-hot steam out." They continued deeper into the steaming labyrinth, watching the silhouettes of their friends become lost in water or fog.

The servants in the pools all nodded to them as they passed. Sterjall noticed they were all of different half-formed species and body types. He also noticed that each of the pools had a rectangular, flat platform at the center, flush with the level of the water.

The caldera was alluring and begged to be explored more deeply, but Sterjall's and Kulak's footpaws were freezing, and so were their ears. They spotted a pool with a group of Tjardur who were quietly chatting and seemed rather welcoming. They were about to step into the warmth, when Lune's voice stopped them.

"Only one in each pool, *khummm*," she reminded them.

Kulak had already dipped a toe in; he was told he could enter this pool, but Sterjall could not. Kulak awkwardly slipped into the water while Sterjall watched.

Servant Lune passed by Sterjall, leaving twirling mists behind her. She lowered her ample body into a pool near Kulak's. So as to not stray too far, Sterjall followed the buffalo. He dipped his footpaws in the same pool, settling across from her, separated by the central platform. Lune's figure relaxed at the edge of the pool, next to three other Tjardur servants: a portly dwarf buffalo man who reminded Sterjall of Ar, one of the clan leaders; an enormous gaur allgender with an amiable face; and a slender kudu woman whose spiral horns were sparkling with droplets.

"Moon… lights…" he shyly said to the group. "I'm Sterjall."

"Head strong," the allgender gaur said.

"Welcome, Canid Lorr. It will be our honor to serve you," the dwarf buffalo intoned.

The slender kudu simply nodded her horns.

None of the servants offered their names in return.

Sterjall glanced around nervously. His view of Kulak's pool was veiled by the steam. "What is going to happen now?" he asked Lune. "I have to admit, we are all quite confused."

"It's understandable, Sterjall of the Wolf. We keep the secrets of our Pink Caldera tightly guarded for a reason. But I will tell you a little of what to expect, in the same way our other servants will tell your friends, *khum*."

She pointed to the nearest geyser cone, which grew nearly at arm's length behind her. "Soon the pink mist will wash over us," she said, "always promptly, following the invisible clock of the crust. This is as it has been since before we moved into these blessed mountains. The pink mist will overpower you, Sterjall of the Wolf, but you mustn't fight it. Let yourself go and fall deeply into its arms."

"What does the pink mist do?"

"You will soon see. It won't be much longer."

A longhorn bison servant appeared through the fog. He lowered a silver tray next to Servant Lune, his long belly fur almost dipping into the water. The silver platter was topped with dozens of fruits of a kind Sterjall was unfamiliar with—red and vibrant like cherries, though more velvety, and a bit larger. Lune took one, thanked the bison servant, and chewed eagerly on the fruit, biting through the hard, bitter pit at the center. The bison offered his tray to the other Tjardur around the pool. When it was close enough for Sterjall to wade to, he reached up to take one of the fruits, but the bison pulled the tray away and left.

"The fruit of Themenn-Vaurvon is only for the servants to ingest," Lune explained. "It allows us to withstand the effects of the pink mist while we serve you. Besides, it tastes awful. You are not missing much." The other Tjardur puckered their wide lips and nodded in agreement, forcing themselves to swallow.

"Why is it that you only allow one of us in each pool?" Sterjall asked, feeling a bit more comfortable now, relaxed by the warm water and the chill air caressing his ears. He finally dared to uncover his crotch.

"Because we need to keep the pools pure," Lune said. "Servants undergo a much stricter cleansing ceremony, which is why several of us may join you and serve you. But the most important reason is that by being on your own, you will not feel pressured by your friends, by what they may think, and thus you may freely discover the truths of your hidden natures."

A hissing sound startled Sterjall. Behind Lune, the geyser cone was erupting in a cloud of pink steam. Nearby, hundreds of other geysers erupted, nearly at the same time, all billowing with the same flushed color. The rosy cloud began to twirl and soon flowed to Sterjall's face. He flinched when he first smelled it, as it had a metallic tinge that left an acidic flavor at the tip of his tongue.

"Do not fight it, Sterjall of the Wolf," Servant Lune advised. "Take a deep breath. Fill your lungs with the pink mist and let it release your inhibitions."

Sterjall hesitated for a long moment, then drew in a pink breath.

Chapter Fifty-Two

Uninhibited

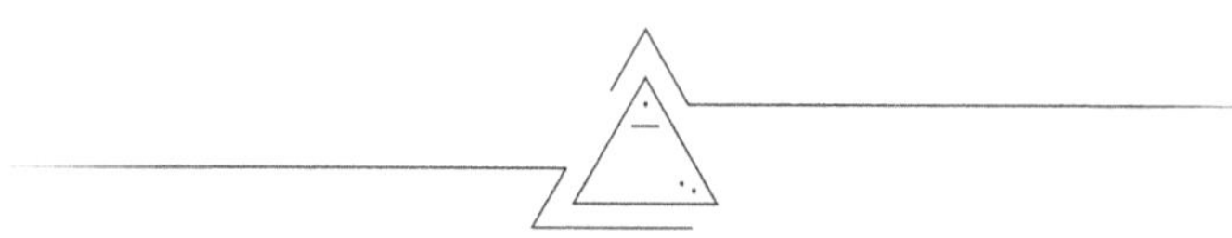

Sterjall thought he had passed out, that perhaps hours had gone by, though he distantly knew it had only been two heartbeats since he'd inhaled the pink mist. He felt lightheaded, but not drowsy. His senses were sharply focused, yet his muscles were loosening up. He did as the pink mist requested, floating on his back.

Above him he saw the silhouette of Lune, her crescent horn rising like Sceres in her Obsidian season. Her green eyes looked down tenderly at him, while her thick arms held his shoulders, allowing him to float without any worries. The other three Tjardur began to massage Sterjall's body, breaking through every knot in his muscles, releasing the built-up tension.

Why do I feel so relaxed? he wondered, suddenly very aware of his clarity of mind. He was fully conscious, well aware that three strangers and Lune were massaging his naked body, but not minding it at all. He opened his eyes again, and for a moment thought he saw Kulak above him, but it was just Lune.

"What is happening?" he asked the pink mist.

"Your inhibitions are melting away, like flurries fallen in a hot pool," Lune's distant voice said, though she had whispered right in his ear. "The pink mist will show you what you truly want. Let it guide you. Let it flow from your lungs and through your entire body, *khumm*."

Sterjall relaxed, but had a moment of panic when he realized he was fully erect. He began to breathe faster, and with his exertion drew in more of the pink mist, causing his shame to quickly subside. He let himself enjoy the moment and tried not to think about the throbbing between his legs.

I feel so at peace, and at the same time, so confused, he thought.

The four servants reached with their hoofed fingers under him, placing him on the platform at the center of the pool, which was mossy and pillowy, comfortably cradling his body. His arms dangled limply in the water.

The wolf looked around, baffled but never fearful. He realized that nearly a dozen more Tjardur had gathered around him. The naked bodies waded toward him, and he wanted them. He felt he needed them beside him, inside him, but he still hesitated, as if his mind should bury those thoughts and not let them surface.

The geysers erupted once more, but this time they did not stop, steaming in a constant flow.

"Breathe in deeply," Servant Lune encouraged him. Sterjall let his head droop back as the pink steam turned denser. He took another deep breath and let the mist overtake him.

"You are not losing yourself, but finding yourself," Lune whispered. "It is your choice as to what you will experience."

Sterjall began to hallucinate, yet knew he was hallucinating. Despite his mystified state, his rational mind was sharp as a senstregalv blade. He saw the figures around him change from bovid forms to more-human shapes he nearly recognized, only to be quickly lost to the mists like a foggy daydream. His heart beat louder, in his chest, in his head, thrumming in his cock.

He felt Lune lean in front of him but saw his own face instead of hers—a black wolf looking down at him. Lune's horn flickered within the vision, blending into the pinkness. The mirage vanished, and only Lune remained. She leaned down, and in his ear whispered, "What does your body desire, Sterjall of the Wolf?"

Sterjall's immediate reaction was to look to his side, trying to get a glimpse of Kulak in the nearby pool. He could tell Kulak had also been placed on a platform and was being surrounded by many figures. He thought he could hear the caracal moan.

The one-horned buffalo placed a hand on Sterjall's muzzle and made him look up at her. She said, "Not your heart. Your body. What does your body desire, Sterjall of the Wolf?" She leaned in, covering Sterjall's muzzle with a wide ear.

Sterjall felt a sudden compulsion, an urge to open his heart like a blooming lotus. He whispered what his body craved, what he was too scared to admit, what he wished he could say out loud but had to keep contained within himself. He revealed many truths, yet he still did not say it all.

The servant listened for a long while, taking heed of every word, every nuance. Once Sterjall quieted, she gazed at the bovids who surrounded them, letting Sterjall see them too. She whispered to the wolf, "And do you accept us to be the conduits to fulfill those desires?" She once more placed a diamond-shaped ear over Sterjall's muzzle.

"Yes, all the men and male-born allgenders," he whispered with a cracked, eager voice. "And you as well, as Rud."

Lune straightened back up and shapeshifted. "Then so we shall serve you, Sterjall of the Wolf," he said in Servant Rud's deeper voice, letting Trommo-silv float by his side.

Rud leaned down and kissed Sterjall as deeply as he had requested.

Once their mouths parted, he saw Rud rise to his full height and whisper to the other servants, one at a time. All the female-born servants left. As Rud returned to face the wolf, Sterjall's vision flickered once more, as if he was looking up at a mirror. Instead of a buffalo, there stood a wolf exactly like himself, except taller, but Sterjall knew it was Rud behind the canine face, behind the burning amber eyes. Rud straddled the narrow platform and sat directly on Sterjall's cock, letting him slide in.

Sterjall moaned, seeing himself sitting upon his own body—a wolf penetrating a wolf. He thought of Aio, and the dark-furred wolf riding him became a smooth and eager young man. In the blink of an eye it was Kulak who sat on him, and then strangely enough it was himself again, but as a human, curly hair dripping sweat.

He felt something wet in his muzzle, more in his handpaws. He felt tongues and body parts exploring his body, from the tips of his ears down to the claws of his toes. As the geysers kept hissing, the hallucinations became stronger. He let his mind accept what he wanted, changing the forms around him into what he desired at each moment. In his handpaw he felt and saw Banook's heavy cock, and he looked up to see the bear's belly looming over him, his wide smile above it. Banook transitioned between his bear and human shapes, abruptly settling into an aspect that only a Silv could've allowed him to take—a half-form. Gold-furred and pink-nosed, this new form blended all the kinds of beauty that the corpulent Nu'irg possessed.

The bear leaned down to kiss him, the enormous muzzle nearly swallowing the wolf's more slender one. Sterjall could smell lemongrass on the bear's breath and taste a hint of chocolate and cardamom. When the bear's wide lips pulled away, a cream-furred yak flickered into existence in his stead, who nodded and stepped back into the vapors. Sterjall noticed then that Rud was no longer riding him, but exploring his six nipples. The buffalo had taken the form of a dark-skinned Jabrak-Tsing man—the same one Lago had once shared a bed with in Brimstowne. The man's tufted tail caressed his belly, tickled his scrotum.

Sterjall felt something forceful in his mouth and welcomed it all the way in. As the long member pulled out of his throat, he saw it belonged to the dwarf buffalo who had been in the pool with them, yet instead of the servant, Sterjall briefly saw Deon, his schoolmate from Withervale. The contours shifted into Deon's father: older, but with the same features, the same soft paunch. He noticed that Trommosilv was being passed among the servants, allowing them to change forms in reality while they further changed in Sterjall's mind.

The husky allgender gaur took their place between Sterjall's legs, spreading them open. The wolf begged with his eyes, watching as the gaur's tapered cock probed his sphincter. "I always wanted the real you inside me," he moaned out loud, seeing Banook reappear instead of the gaur. Much as they had tried, Banook's human and primal forms had been too large for him to take, but this time the bear slid easily into the wolf. With each slow thrust, a wave of displaced water warmed Sterjall's back. With each slow thrust, the figure changed as Sterjall imagined—and felt—Banook shifting between his human form, primal form, and half-form. He clenched tighter around the gaur, around Banook, and saw that the other bovids surrounding him were taking new shapes, becoming all the men he had at one time or another desired, even if briefly.

Sterjall let his lust overpower him, surrounded by all of his fantasies at once. So strongly convincing was the illusion that he even saw himself change. At times, he was much younger or older, more muscular or fatter. He transitioned through new fur patterns and even different species. For a moment he was a mountain lion once again, feeling his back resting upon blue sands, with a jackal penetrating him. Each reverie that shuffled through his mind turned into an ephemeral reality, and he lost himself in ecstasy.

"What does your body desire?" said the mysterious voice right against Kulak's tufted ears. Kulak hesitated, unsure of how to answer.

He had been confused for a short while, but quickly his inhibitions had begun to melt away. He felt his small cock throbbing and heard the voice repeat the question in his ear.

"What my scalp wants…" he whispered back, "is for all of you to tell me what *you* want."

The servant paused, seeming a bit puzzled, then leaned down to listen carefully as Kulak described his particular desire in more detail.

Once Kulak was done, the servant asked, "And do you accept us to be the conduits to fulfill those desires?"

Kulak nodded urgently. The servant then stood and discussed the request with all the others.

One by one, the bovids approached the caracal and revealed their own desires. As the servants spoke, Kulak hallucinated his body changing form, taking the shapes the Tjardur had said they preferred, yet he did not see the servants themselves change—he saw them as they were. He knew somewhere deep within himself that he was merely hallucinating his own transformations, but he was uncertain whether the servants could see the same or were immune to the pink mist's power. He cared not, as the bovids seemed happy to comply, and they used Kulak's body in the manners their own bodies desired.

One by one, Kulak welcomed the diverse bodies, enjoying the servants being themselves, instead of whatever *he* wanted them to be.

Sated and exhausted, after having taken their turns with the caracal, the servants let their backs rest against the edge of the pool. A kouprey with a meaty dewlap stepped toward the central platform and asked, "Will that be all, prince of the Laatu?"

Kulak ran a handpaw over his sticky abdomen, considering the question. "Well… Maybe there is one more thing my scalp wants to try."

Lummukem shivered, splayed flat on the mossy platform, their thick tail trailing into the hot water. They felt anxious, tormented by the thought that any contact of this sort was strictly forbidden for their kind. Even though Khuron Aio-Kulak had vowed to change the Laatu laws, the same laws seemed carved in stone within their reptilian brain. They had even abstained from pleasuring themself throughout their life, with a few exceptions when curiosity had gotten the best of them—those moments lingered in the back of their mind, filling them with guilt.

They breathed in the pink mist, still unable to let go of their fear.

An allgender aurochs leaned down next to them and asked, "What does your body desire, Lerr Lummukem of the Dragon?"

"I… We… We want to feel wanted," they said. "We are many in one, yet we feel separate, and never whole. We want to feel loved, in every… every part of our body."

"And do you accept us to be the conduits to fulfill those desires?" the aurochs inquired.

The geysers gurgled more hot steam through their arteries, making Lummukem reel and breathe harder. "Yes. All of you," they said at length.

Though the allgender servant had a long penis and drooping balls, Lummukem saw them suddenly change, as if they too had both sexes at once. Looking around, they saw that where the other bovids had been now stood hairless men, women, and allgenders, all with blue- or purple-painted scalps. They approached the dragon, welcoming them to touch and explore their bodies.

The lead aurochs remained in their intersex bovid form, and reached within the dragon's slit to pull out the complex duality that Lummukem had kept hidden. Not one, but two penises sprouted out, alien in shape, blossoming like wild orchids. The aurochs straddled the dragon and rested his tapered cock between the two erect forms, then penetrated the slit.

Lummukem hissed out a moan, letting themself bask in the pleasure they had always denied themself.

Captain Siffo breathed in and out heavily, taking in too much of the pink mist too quickly. He looked down toward his belly, seeing how his wiry chest fur transitioned smoothly toward his unlikable, plain-skinned bottom half. Through most of his childhood, he'd been scared of showering with other piglets, feeling disgusted by his fat, sickeningly plain lower body.

A yak woman spoke the question in his ear, and Siffo responded hungrily, spewing out all of his desires a bit too hurriedly, as if it was important to get them all out at once.

"And do you accept us to be the conduits to fulfill those desires?" the yak woman asked.

The captain looked around at the bovids who surrounded him. In the yak's ears, he answered, "D'women, yes. I want all uf them, all uf ye."

The yak dismissed all but the women from her group, then stood tall next to Siffo.

The warthog felt a deep urge boil within him. He looked back down toward his gut and hallucinated his lower body sprouting dense orange fur, his feet turning to hooves, his cock growing thin and long and twirling in a spiral. He even realized what half-form he would have taken if he had been the one chosen to wear Nagrasilv. He knew, for he could see a velvety horn growing from his forehead.

He darted his confused eyes to either side. The naked forms wading around him had turned to suid women, all in their perfect half-forms of warthogs, babirusas, pigs, and every other kind of suid, all stout and hairy as he'd always said he liked them. As the many women approached and let him fondle their bodies, he shook his head and closed his eyes.

He opened them again and saw a boar, then a yak woman, and then a boar again, sitting on his corkscrew cock. He moaned with pleasure, but his muscles were too tense, and he was trapped in a sense of unease.

The yak, the boar, leaned down and whispered, "You are not being true to yourself. There is nothing to fear. We are here to serve you, Siffo of the Warthog. Tell us what your body truly wants, and your body will have it."

A dense cloud of pink wafted by.

Siffo trembled. He opened his tusked mouth and spoke his true desires, hoping the boar, the yak, would hear.

The yak straightened back up, tightening around him.

Siffo suddenly saw her and all the other suid women changing. Their snouts shortened, their fur shrank, their tusks vanished, and in their stead were left plain-skinned women of all colors, all short and stocky, all willing to serve him. For a moment he felt a jolt of guilt—a horrible pain from acknowledging that those grotesque plain-skins were what he had always preferred. He gulped dense breaths of pink mist, and his disapproving thoughts eased.

He looked at the woman sitting on him—no longer a yak or a boar. He recognized her.

"Hefra…" he grunted, then exploded within her.

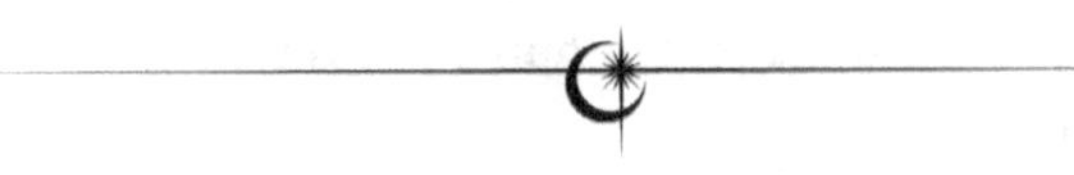

Hefra's fantasies were much more colorful and convoluted. She pictured herself as wearing each and every Silv there ever was, and a panoply of others that never were, taking a different half-form from each clade. She was a polar bear, a manul cat, a cayman. Then she was an anisodon, a pink dolphin, a pangolin, a saddle-billed stork. Her mind drifted to outlandish places as she turned into a crab, a newt, an earthworm, a fungus releasing spores. The bovids around her were all male, though she was distantly aware that there had been women among the group that had approached her; somehow they had changed sexes, and she minded not. The species of the servants soon changed as well, mirroring the feral forms of each creature Hefra's wild imagination concocted. She let them all inside her, requesting all her orifices be used at the same time.

As her body was filled by her servants, Hefra's mind wandered into realms not only of carnal desires, but of trying to understand the motivations and feelings of each unique organism that manifested in front of her. She took notes in her head, for later, but soon felt the effort too tiresome and loosened her body to the pleasures she was being gifted with.

Crysta at first was terrified. If she had been more courageous, she would've run away the moment she saw the creepy, naked bovids in those pools. She found them disgusting, monstrous even, at least when it came to their physical appearance.

Yet once the pink vapors filled her lungs, she found herself soothed. She still thought of the bovids as gross and unclean, despite them being much cleaner than she was, but as they placed her on the narrow platform, she stopped thinking about them in that way. She saw them as they truly were, as kind and loving beings who were there to help her. Their strange bodies were nothing more than vessels for their kindred souls.

When a cordial cow whispered the question in her ear, she spoke her desires out loud, with no shame. The cow asked if Crysta would accept all of them to take part in her fantasies, and she requested only the more muscular of the men to stay, but also asked the cow to keep her company. The Tjardur servants complied with her request.

The brawny servants around her began to change, most of them turning into scholars from the Zovarian Academic Institute. The youngest of the servants, a nearly plain-skinned tetracerus, took the form of Crysta's husband, Rowan Holt, looking as he had when he'd been only nineteen and she'd fallen for him. His presence at first made her feel uncomfortable, given all the other men around her, but then she saw that Rowan was not judging her, that he was happy to see her opening up. Watching her young husband's approving eyes, and holding on to the cow's hoofed hand, Crysta let her thighs unclench.

She felt herself penetrated. She tightly closed her eyes, for a moment afraid she'd see one of those bulls probing her, but when she opened them it was not a bull standing between her legs, but a gray-bearded man with thick arm muscles. He pushed deeply into her.

"Oh, Bal…" she moaned.

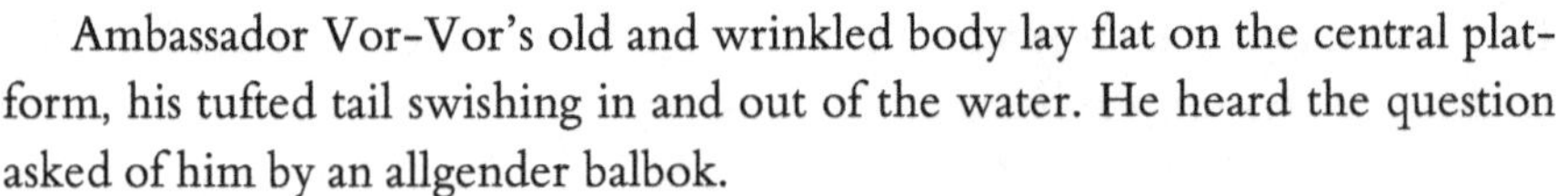

Ambassador Vor-Vor's old and wrinkled body lay flat on the central platform, his tufted tail swishing in and out of the water. He heard the question asked of him by an allgender balbok.

He considered the question, thinking all the way back to his childhood for answers. Vor-Vor had been castrated at ten years old. His parents had granted him life as a eunuch as a kind of endowment, to ensure that he would command a position of great political power and influence in the Tsing Empire—a Jabrak-Tsing could otherwise never climb so high up the complex ladders the Empire carefully controlled.

The Tsing's lust for eunuchs, and their trust toward them, was immeasurable, invaluable. Vor-Vor recalled how he had been used for all manner of sexual payments, bribes, coercions, and investments. His sexual life had been a tool, a most powerful one, particularly during his early youth. Now that he was being granted the chance to fulfill any sexual fantasy, he realized he had perhaps already tried everything, sometimes willingly, most times not.

"I do not know what my body desires," he confessed to the balbok. "I'm nearly seventy years old, and I still do not know. Perhaps my body has never desired anything. I've only been fueled by ambitions from my mind, and used my body to meet those goals."

"Your body may be aged," the balbok replied, "but it can still want. Breathe in deeply, and you will see."

Vor-Vor inhaled a lungful of pink mist and felt his erection rise.

He called for the bodies near him to come close and said, "What I want is for you to pleasure yourselves while I watch. All of you. I desire not to use my body, but only my mind. That would make this old descendant of Umar-Vaor most happy."

The servants dutifully complied.

As Vor-Vor watched the bovids pleasure themselves, they took the shapes of powerful people he had once lusted for—or rather, whose *influence* he had lusted for. He had never once been given the privilege of not participating in the events he attended; he had always been the center of attention. Now he could at last feel himself wholly satisfied.

Alaia sprawled on her back, entirely at ease. She smiled widely, feeling utter relaxation seep into her bones. After she had picked her pool, she had seen a familiar figure approach: Servant Speros had come to join her, and it was he who explained more about the Pink Caldera before the geysers erupted on the mountaintop.

Speros had lowered her onto the platform and now stood next to her, submerged to his hips. The erection he had grown from seeing her plain-skinned body was powerful, nearly painful, pulsating in and out of the water. He wished he had not eaten of the fruit of Themenn-Vaurvon, so that he too could experience the hallucinations. He wanted to let himself go, as he had done years back, when he had turned four times the sacred age.

He shook the thoughts away and chastised his own mind. He was not there for his own pleasure; he was there to serve.

"What does your body desire, Dark Princess?" he whispered in her ear.

Alaia quietly whispered her answer, utterly confident in her choice.

Speros looked stupefied. He was not expecting an answer like the one Alaia gave, yet it was only his first time as a servant. Unsure if her request was something commonplace or not, he asked for help from a wisent woman next to him, who leaned down and asked the question to Alaia once more, receiving the same answer.

The wisent woman shrugged. "We are here to serve, not to judge," she said, "so serve her in this way we must, no matter how unusual her request may be."

They picked Alaia up and turned her body over, revealing her thirteen spinal spurs. Alaia let her arms dangle into the water, relaxed her muscles, and closed her eyes.

"Well, I'm waiting," she said.

Sterjall could not tell how much time had passed. Too many bodies had taken their positions around him, inside him, always transforming before his eyes. He had noticed that servants had come and gone, although Rud was nearly always present. His rational mind was cognizant of the change in the light, noticing the mist turning darker over time, and eventually mingling with green-flamed lanterns that were lit all around the periphery of the caldera. Soon pink and green blended together everywhere he looked.

It's way past dusk, he thought. *We must have been at this for hours now. How am I still holding an erection?*

The pink steam was even denser now, completely overpowering his senses. He could do nothing but want and feel his wants met. But behind that urge, he had started to feel a lingering guilt.

He saw Servant Rud approach again, who had left briefly, right before the green flames were lit.

"Would you sit on me once more?" Sterjall asked Rud, a bit shyly.

The zebu straddling Sterjall heard the request and moved away. Rud was about to take the zebu's place when Sterjall stopped him.

"No," he said, "I want…" He breathed in more of the pink mist, letting it fill his lungs, his brain. "I want you… as Lune," he said. "I want to know what it's like to be with a woman."

Rud nodded. He put Trommosilv back on his face and let his anatomy change. Lune towered over Sterjall.

She too is magnificent, he thought, *just as she is. Scars and all.*

As the buffalo sat down on him, Sterjall did not try to picture her as someone else, but kept the image of Lune exactly as she was, feeling spellbound by her asymmetrical beauty. He saw her then, in her full muscular majesty, lifting and lowering herself rhythmically, her udders caressing his belly with each move as she worked to pleasure him. Lune smiled, and her green eyes sparkled with green flames.

Sterjall felt a thirst rise within him. Despite feeling more attracted to men, he had always wanted to try it all. He tightened his muscles, grabbed on to the buffalo's hips, and pushed his shaft and knot up, tying his body with Lune's, making her stop and clench tighter.

"You are seeing myself," she said.

"Yes," Sterjall admitted. "I think you are beautiful."

Lune smiled, then leaned down to kiss him. As if ignited by that kiss, Sterjall felt the pent-up energy from the last several hours boil within him. He closed his eyes and pictured all the hallucinations his mind had fabricated, recalled all the feelings his body had experienced. He felt the numerous bodies warming the space around him, reaching in to touch him all at once. He kissed Servant Lune feverishly, tying their tongues, and came deep within her.

His head was swimming, his heart pounding, his crotch throbbing. He briefly fell asleep, thoroughly spent, experiencing unimaginable bliss.

He awoke, feeling his cock pulling free, and saw Lune standing in the water next to him.

"It is time for your second cleansing, Sterjall of the Wolf. I hope we have served you well."

She turned to leave.

"Wait!" he said. "I…"

"Yes?"

"I don't… I don't know how to ask."

"You may ask whatever you want, as we are here to be of service to you."

"It's just… This is different. I don't want anyone else to know."

Lune dismissed the other servants, who disappeared into the green and pink mist.

Sterjall asked for Lune to lean closer, then whispered a secret desire in her ear. She understood then, and considered the request. She looked into Sterjall's eyes and, making sure he did not look away, said, "There is perhaps a danger in this, for both of us. Are you certain?"

"I… I need to try it."

"*Khumm,* I am here to serve. I will grant you this request, Sterjall of the Wolf. This will be our secret. Until you feel it is safe to reveal it."

CHAPTER FIFTY-THREE

THE MORNING AFTER

New servants took care of the guests' second cleansing, fully scrubbing their bodies as they floated in the warm pools. Once they had been guided out of the pink mists, they were sat in a room of white marble, where many padded, long seats ran from end to end. The room was dry and well lit, with no hint of steam breaking through the tightly closed doors. Covered in oversized towels of white and green, they were meticulously dried by the servants, then forced to gulp down a bitter drink made from the fruit of Themenn-Vaurvon.

It took them a long while to come back to their senses, with their inhibitions back in place, yet with a new understanding of themselves. They sat awkwardly near one another, too self-conscious to speak of what they had experienced, too embarrassed to ask what the others had gone through.

"Well, that was dee-lightful!" Hefra squawked, shattering the silence. "I fucked nearly every species I could imagine. I hope you all had as wild an experience as this stocky body here did, because I've *never* experienced nothing like it."

Siffo smiled sheepishly next to her, retreating further into his towel.

Alaia just looked confused.

Servant Lune and Servant Speros approached from a distant room, clad in their formal servant robes, hooves clicking on the marble floors. They sat with their guests.

"I hope we have served you well, *khum,*" Lune said. "Have you all recovered from the effects of the mists?"

"I think so?" Sterjall glanced around at the others uncertainly.

"My scalp still feels hot and strange," Kulak said. "Are you the real Lune?"

"I am the real one, Felid Lorr. All the visions should have faded from your minds by now. Your scalps will cool, and you will all feel more fully yourselves after a good night's sleep."

"What are they talking about?" Alaia whispered to Sterjall, but before he could answer, Vor-Vor asked a question.

"Servant Lune, what exactly happened at the pools? And I don't mean the details of the actions performed. I was joined in my experience by rulers who passed through the Sixth Gate long ago, and even demigods. Were their spirits summoned?"

"No spirits were involved, only bodies, empathy, and your own memories. The pinkness you breathed in had traces of a most precious and rare element in it. One of the waverers, the ones I heard you call the *aetheric* elements. *Nox* is the name of this element, and it was the reason for your visions."

Vor-Vor's eyes widened in recognition, but he said nothing in reply. Instead, it was Crysta who spoke. "Nox? Aetheric nitrogen? I've read about it before in a book of spritetales. No one in Zovaria considers its existence to be true, not even the most credulous alchemists at the institute."

"It is as real as Noss's heart is hot. We do not know much about nox, other than the effects it has on our minds. But we do know that keeping its existence a secret is paramount for maintaining the safety of our Four Blessings. Several times before have other realms tried to destroy this sacred caldera, claiming the pink mists were a curse, a pathway toward sin. Infiltrators also attempted to collect the substance for warfare or profit. We protected our homeland, as we have protected our strong culture—"

"Head strong!" Speros interjected.

"Head strong, Servant Speros. As we have protected our strong culture through millennia. You have been gifted with this knowledge. It is through these rites of initiation that we accept non-Tjardur into our family, and our family you are now."

"Thank you, Servants," Ambassador Vor-Vor said. "I am glad to know I am closer to you now than I was before, when only my thin Tjardur blood bound me to you. We will uphold utmost confidentiality in these matters."

"We are placing our trust in you," Lune said. "But now, it is time we feed you. I believe you must be starving, *khumm,* as it is close to midnight, and your bodies have been spent in ways they have never experienced before. You may dress yourselves now." As Lune finished speaking, a group of servants arrived, pushing rolling carts that held their clothes and belongings.

Sterjall dried his ears and dropped his towel to the ground. He picked up his blue tunic and stopped suddenly, realizing that despite there being no fog in this room, he cared not that his friends or the servants could see his naked body. He smiled, then continued dressing himself.

They were served a simple meal in a dining hall away from all the pools and steam. Lune and Speros sat with them, mingling and chatting but never eating. The guests recognized a few of the bovid faces bringing their dinner and drinks—all wearing robes now—who smiled kindly, feeling pride in having served them so well.

"So, are we going to talk about this or what?" Alaia asked. "Why is everyone so quiet? And what was all that talk about hallucinations?"

"Ain't something easy t'talk 'bout," Captain Siffo muttered, "not without revealing a bit too much 'bout ourselves."

"What do you mean?" Alaia persisted. "It was a bit awkward, with all of us being naked and such, but what's so serious about getting a back massage?"

They all stared at Alaia, uncertain whether she was joking.

Speros cleared his throat, making his dewlap wiggle. "Our Dark Princess, head strong she is, and knows herself too well. Too confident in her own self she is, and needs no servants to help her find other sides of her being. Her preference for a back massage was rather unique, but I hope we served her well."

"Your hoofy fingertips were a bit rough on my skin, to be honest," she admitted, "but it still felt really good. The mists and heat did make me feel lightheaded though."

"A rare find, that is," Servant Lune explained. "Very few are lucky enough to arrive at the Pink Caldera already certain of who they are, of who they want to be."

"What? What else did you all do?" Alaia glanced around at the others in confusion.

"We'll tell you later," Sterjall said. "In private. Maybe."

Utterly drained, the wayfarers fell asleep in the carriage while the longhorn bison pulled them down the mountain. Sunu, however, remained awake throughout the journey. The shaman had not spoken of their experience at the Pink Caldera, had not said so much as a word after leaving the pools. With their eyes unfocused, they recalled the moments of unbound pleasure they had experienced—pleasure of a kind they had never considered achievable for their own self. And now, eager to understand that pleasure, they were left with only guilt.

They could not even bring themself to wear their mask; the thought of their two penises sprouting from their slit, of the tongues wrapping around them, made them feel entirely ill at ease. They needed more time, more space to learn about themself, yet still the image of the Tjardur exploring their body was much too powerful to vanquish. The mists had allowed them to welcome other bodies into their own, to ask them to touch those forbidden parts. Yet even while under the mist's powerful influence, Lummukem had not mustered the courage to use their own hands to pleasure themself—the thought of that act was utterly appalling. And yet, they felt their slit warming and moistening, and fought to keep their penis from rising. They made sure their kilt was covering their legs properly, then crossed their arms, promising that they would never touch themself in that manner.

"Dragon Lerr!"

Sunu opened their eyes. They had fallen asleep after all, and now found that the carriage had arrived back at the ziggurat.

"Dragon Lerr, wake up!" the voice came again. It was Cort of the Pelorovis, shaking their shoulder. As Sunu struggled to regain full consciousness, they noticed their friends—all asleep—were being carried away, whereas they remained seated in the carriage.

"The children, they are missing," Cort said urgently.

Sunu immediately stood up, almost toppling over from lightheadedness.

"What happened? Tell us, at once." They put their mask on and quickly shapeshifted.

The gardeners led Lummukem down to the catacombs, showing the dragon the trail they had followed.

"We looked everywhere, *khumph*," one of the gardeners said, "but the catacombs are bigger than Bra'uur itself. This is where we lost their tracks."

While searching through a mossy cavern, Lummukem found a red hair on a rusty ladder. They climbed up, pushing through a trapdoor with a broken lock, and exited into the blackness of a yew forest.

Lummukem asked the gardeners and Cort to follow behind them. With their sensitive tongue licking the air, they stalked through the forest, tasting for any smells they could recognize. After an aimless walk in the dark, they felt it. Vanilla. Or not exactly vanilla, but they knew the fragrance. They followed their bifid tongue through tangles of branches until the sound of cascading water entered their ears. They found a creek and followed it upstream.

For a moment, they thought their tiredness was making them hallucinate, as if the pink mists were still churning in their lungs. In the middle of the creek they saw what to them looked like Kruwendrolom—same as they'd seen it while sailing on the Isdinnklad Sea, but in miniature. The reptilian dome reflected in the stream, its wisps streaking out shards of cold light from within its unruly form.

Lummukem hurried toward the glowing dome and saw it was made not of vines, but of gnarled branches and moss. They lifted it up. Underneath, peacefully asleep, was Pol in his long-eared chipmunk half-form. He was blanketed by Puuja's red hair, his twin using his soft hips as a pillow. So tired the children were that they did not stir at the sound of the branches of their den snapping.

Lago awoke in his and Aio's minimalistic room, rubbing his eyes. Aio yawned and stretched out next to him, like a cat.

"Is it morning?" Aio asked as he sat up.

With no windows to clue them in, neither of them had an inkling of the time of day. Lago shrugged, then said, "I can't believe we slept through the entire ride. I barely remember them carrying us in."

"My body has never felt more tired. Not even when we were at the scablands." Aio leaned on Lago's shoulder and began to rub his back. "So, what is it that you experienced?" he asked with a coy smile. "My scalp is very curious to find out."

"Wow. I mean. A lot," Lago fumbled. "Wh-why don't you tell me first?"

"As long as you do not become jealous."

"I don't think I could, not after all that. Though I have to admit, for a while I wished we could've been there together. I kept looking toward you but could see nearly nothing through the fog."

"My scalp felt the same, at first. But I will tell you what happened."

Aio described the ways the Tjardur servants had used his body, and how he had discovered that his own desires resided in helping others find themselves, in learning what made them feel pleasure, how *he* could make them feel pleasure. He graphically described all that he remembered save perhaps one detail, leaving Lago throbbing and dripping next to him by the time his story was over.

"So, you approve," Aio teased, pushing down on Lago's cock and releasing it like a spring. "Now is your turn. Tell me what you experienced."

Lago hesitated, trying to find a way to weave around some key subjects. "Well, I saw myself sitting on myself," he said to get started, "which was sort of odd. As a wolf, mostly, but once as my human self as well. And I saw you, in all your forms, and Banook too, seeing his half-form for the first time. That was the most intense part, him loving me through all of his forms, so real and so inconceivable. And I saw other people I once had sex with or fantasized about. There were so many bodies on top of me, so many familiar faces at once, that it's hard to describe. It's like every part of my body was used in the most pleasurable manner possible, all at the same time."

"This does not sound as much like a realization, as it sounds like you merely revisiting old friends. Was that all?"

"I mean, that's plenty, isn't it?"

Aio seemed doubtful.

"I'm more curious about what our friends experienced," Lago said to divert Aio's curiosity.

"That will perhaps not be a polite thing to ask. It can be too personal, like Siffo said last night. My scalp is curious as well, but I would prefer they not ask the same of me, so I will not ask it of them."

"Fair enough," Lago said, leaning down to pick up his trousers and mask. "Let's get breakfast. Or lunch. I'm starved."

As they exited their room, servants were cleaning their friends' chambers. *They are all up already?* Sterjall wondered. He noticed the brightness of the light down the corridor and realized it must be past noon in the dome. He heard laughter coming from the garth where breakfast was served. He shambled with Kulak in that direction, lured by the smell of fresh-baked goods.

"Again!" he heard Pol call out, followed by a brief applause.

They walked through the cloister and found the others at the table, all looking up. Sterjall's eyes followed their gazes, and up on a balcony he saw a long-eared lagomorph clad in leather armor. The hare jumped down fearlessly, landing on her long, powerful legs.

"Puuja!" Kulak exclaimed, hurrying to stroke the hare's long ears and soft fur.

"When did this happen?" Sterjall asked no one in particular.

They all partook of the midafternoon feast while Lummukem recounted the story once more, of how they'd found the twins in their glowing den in the middle of the night, and of how harshly they had admonished the children the moment they woke up, for disrespecting the resting place of the Tjardur.

"That is how we found them," the dragon finished, "sleeping atop the other. One as a human, another in a half-form. But..."—they hesitated—"it was not Puuja who we found in a half-form. It was Pollomekh."

There was a small gasp from someone, and also an "I knew it!" from Alaia.

Puuja handed the mask of glires to Pol, and he timidly took his new half-form, while Lummukem explained that the boy had been sharing the mask with his sister ever since Okridrolom was opened, telling them of the training the siblings had undergone together.

"Look!" Pol said from above them, happily demonstrating his abilities, climbing to the balcony his sister had moments ago reached with a somersault.

"He is so adorable," Crysta said.

"But why didn't you tell us sooner?" Sterjall complained to Lummukem, in between stuffing his muzzle with pastries.

"Pol's secret was his to hide or reveal. Seeing the Tjardur so freely sharing their Silv has given Pol comfort, knowing they would not admonish him like the Sehján might have at Okridrolom. We are happy seeing him so active, so open to the world."

And Pol did seem like an entirely different person. He was quick and snappy, curious and playful, no longer hiding behind his sister or keeping his body tense like a knot. He still had a hard time keeping eye contact or focusing much when others talked to him, but while in his half-form it was easy for him to shove those inconveniences to the side.

The chipmunk scampered down from the roof and sat back at the table, between Puuja and Sterjall. "Did you see that?" he asked the wolf. "I was much faster than Puuja, was I not?"

Sterjall was befuddled. Pol had never spoken to him directly, so he felt as if any answer could catastrophically upend what little rapport they had built with one another. He opened his muzzle and muttered an incomprehensible, "Yah, hum—ah…"

The chipmunk lost interest in the wolf and turned around to bother his sister.

CHAPTER FIFTY-FOUR

IRONCLAD

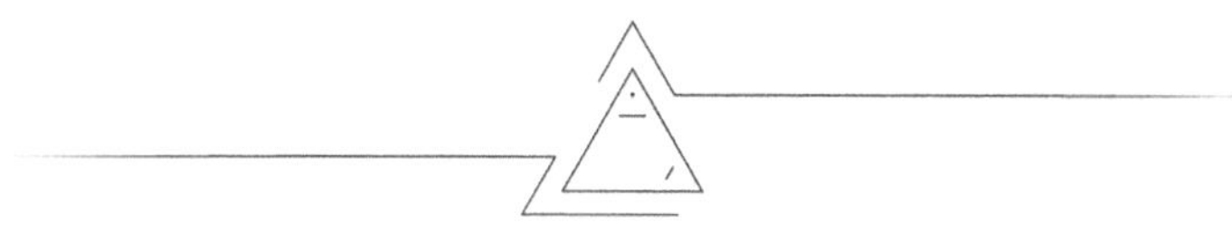

The wayfarers had only one day left at the Ashen Dome before they would set sail toward the Yenwu Peninsula, onward to their next adventure. They gathered in the Taur Citadel's garden that morning to meet with Chawól, the armorer.

The longhorn highlander had laid out the gear she had been painstakingly crafting for the past several weeks. For Sterjall, Kulak, Lummukem, and Siffo, Chawól had forged stylish Bra'uur steel helms, lighter than those crafted with traditional steel, and offering great visibility. The masterpieces looked powerful and regal, blending curves and sharp angles that drew inspiration from the Silvesh.

"Head strong we are," Chawól told them, "yet our strong heads we must protect. The most important part of any armor the helms are, *grrmmmph*. That's what my pop always said, and that's what I inscribed on his hide after his hooves marched through the Six Gates."

Chawól asked the three shapeshifters in the group to try on their helms. Seeing they fit well, she said, "Be sure to take the helms off before you turn back to your plain skins, as I did not shape them to fit your human heads and your Silvesh. I dare not think of what would happen if you attempted to shapeshift with the helms still on. Better cautious than dead, is what my mum always said, and that's what I inscribed on her hide after her hooves marched through the Six Gates."

Sterjall briefly wondered if he could even attempt to shapeshift while wearing his helmet. He tried to imagine whether it would crush his skull, or if the helm itself would break apart while Agnargsilv reformed inside of it. He decided it would be better not to experiment with such things and simply heeded Chawól's advice.

On Siffo's helm, Chawól had forged a kuba-like forehead horn—a last-moment request by the captain. Once he put it on, his single-horned helm radiantly sparkled, reflecting the light of his pharolith-capped tusks.

The armorer had brought a selection of full suits of armor that were not custom made, but that could fit Siffo, Lummukem, and Kulak. All three of them kindly refused: the Puqua captain because he did not think his job was to battle, but to move fast while commanding his ship, and the Laatu because they hated wearing anything that covered their chests.

Chawól was persuasive and insistent, and made Kulak and Lummukem agree to wear steel bracers and demi-gaunts to protect their forearms and wrists. The items were non-obtrusive and could easily deflect sword attacks without the need for a shield, if wielded properly.

With the aid of a dozen blacksmiths, Chawól had also reforged the missing parts of Lune's armor, including a new helm. While donning her full suit of armor, and leaning a new war hammer heavily over her shoulder, Lune had the air of a gladiator from ancient spritetales, and seemed ready to be cast in bronze to stand next to the Colossus of Thyra himself.

"Now what is aunt Chawól meant to do with these new creatures?" the armorer asked rhetorically, looking at Puuja and Pol. She had brought a perfectly tailored set of armor for each of the siblings, but not all the pieces would fit their half-form anatomies. She retrieved a measuring tape that was dangling from her left horn, took new measurements of the hare and chipmunk in turn, then frowned, long fur draped over her eyes.

"And it is tomorrow that you are leaving?" she inquired, looking toward Lummukem.

"That is so. In the evening we shall depart."

Her eyes returned to the two children. "*Grrmmmph.* Aunt Chawól will have to return to the forge and work all night. Could you not have found your half-forms with a bit more expediency?"

The twins didn't know what *expediency* meant, so they simply shrugged.

"I will carve ear holes into your helms and reshape them to fit your longer faces. Puuja, your new legs are too long, and Pol, yours are too short. I will find better-fitting parts that will not hinder your jumping or climbing. They won't be perfect, and they will need adjustment when you change forms, but they will fit better."

The long-horned cow ruffled Pol's red hair. He tightened up shyly.

"Either way," Chawól continued, "you will outgrow your armor in no time. Come see aunt Chawól when you find it too tight. I will know if you've been wearing it, because if you do, your bodies will grow strong, and you will come back to me as mighty and big as Drurum of the Gaur himself!" She clenched her fists and displayed her solid biceps.

Once done with the twins, Chawól showed Sterjall and Alaia the modifications she had made to their elytra armor. She had replaced parts of the joints with Bra'uur steel chainmail, which was comfortable and more durable. She had even replaced some of the leather stitches with Bra'uur steel rings and staples, which could endure much greater stress before breaking.

"I have also added splints on your sparking bracer," she said to Sterjall, showing him the long strips of steel running the length of his left forearm, which held the brime cubes much more sturdily. "The splints help dissipate the heat from these hot rocks you carry. No normal sword will buckle them, not unless swung by Ogóre herself. And if anyone is foolish enough to swing at you, when you block, they will be showered by sparks." She held up one of Sterjall's elytra pauldrons and added, "And I modified these to match your shoulder bracer, so that you can attach Agnargsilv to either side when you choose to be plain-skinned again."

Sterjall grinned in gratitude.

For Alaia, Chawól had made a special addition to the back of her ochre elytra suit. Where her thirteen sisters were—which had always poked a bit uncomfortably against her unmodified cuirass—Chawól had attached thirteen interlocking metal plates, which articulated to leave ample room for Alaia's spurs while keeping them heavily protected. The new steel plates protruded at threatening angles, like reptilian spines.

"That looks fantastic," Sterjall admitted, envy flashing in his eyes. "Makes me wish I had spurs too."

After Chawól left them, while the others were headed to lunch, Lummukem pulled Lune aside to ask her for permission to return to the catacombs. During the brief time they had explored the tunnels, they had done so hurriedly and while filled with anxiety, so they told Lune they wished to have one last chance to admire the sepulcher on their own terms. After a long moment of hesitation, Lune agreed to be their guide.

"I am glad you did not ask to bring the children," Lune said, leading them down a secret stairwell deep within the ziggurat. "As a servant, I could not refuse such a request, but given their recent… incursion, it is better if they take some time to ruminate about their behavior."

"It would serve them well if you were also to reprimand them," Lummukem suggested.

"That would be uncourteous of me. I could not do that to my guests."

Lummukem took off their new steel helm and gazed down at it while pondering. "Are the plans for tonight's ceremony still—"

"Yes, we shall be meeting after dinner."

"Then let us think about this some more. There might be a way to do this… politely."

They reached an antechamber to the catacombs—an ossuary built mostly of femurs. At its center, a row of gilded skulls was set on display atop elaborate pedestals. Lune walked slowly, explaining to Lummukem the history of the represented clans, pointing out the skulls of famous historians, warriors, traitors, and rulers. Lummukem observed it all absently as they walked, their tail leaving a sinuous wave in the dust behind them.

"Our capitals have mirrored counterparts," Servant Lune explained, leading them into a marble chamber carved as if it was the interior of a ribcage, the spaces between each rib embellished with stacked skulls. "Above ground are the cities for the living, while underground are the cities for the dead. The Bra'uur Catacombs is one of those mirror cities, as are the Vaults of Thyra, the mines of Taerám, the sunken temples of Phala, and the crystal caves of Shun-Ji."

She caressed one of the polished marble ribs, which seemed entirely out of place beside the dusty bones. "The old limestone that once formed our bedrock heated up with the coming of the Four Blessings, hardening into marble of kinds known nowhere else in Noss. As we dug the marble out to build our capitals, the tunnels our picks left behind became cities just as vast, inhabited only by memories, by echoes."

Lune quieted for a stretched moment, listening to the echoes of dripping water. It was only then that she realized Lummukem felt as distant from her as the stars beyond her dome. She placed a gentle hand on the dragon's shoulder and asked, "Are you feeling well, Lerr?"

"We apologize," Lummukem said. "These catacombs truly are magnificent. We do wish we had more time to explore them, but the truth is, we simply wanted an excuse to speak with you in private."

"What is this regarding? Is there more that happened with Puuja and Pollomekh?"

"No, this is regarding something else. We wish to speak to you about what happened at the Pink Caldera."

Lune waited, watching as the dragon nervously plucked shed skin from their scaled wrist.

Lummukem took a moment to think through their words, then said, "What you granted us at the caldera was an invaluable gift. Something we needed. Something we yearned for. But it has left us torn and struggling with guilt."

"Was the experience unpleasant? Did something go wrong with—"

"No. It was wonderful. But our cultures differ widely, Servant Lune. The Tjardur live their lives openly, so certain of themselves, but that is not the case with all the Laatu, particularly with allgenders. We are forbidden to partake in gifts such as the one you gave us."

"Forbidden? I do not understand."

"We know you do not. This is why we do not blame you. Yet we still blame ourself, even though we know that what we did was not wrong. Pleasures of the sexual kind are prohibited for us, as is conceiving children, and even entering marriage."

Lune was left aghast and wordless.

"Khuron Aio-Kulak has vowed to change these laws," Lummukem continued, "and we are thankful to him for this. But the Khuron cannot change what is already in our mind. That can only change with time. We always wanted to discover this side of ourself, but we wish we had done so under our own terms, although we do not know if we ever would have had the courage. Your aid, perhaps, was necessary."

"*Khumph...*" Lune grunted, her face distraught and contorting with shame. "I must apologize, Dragon Lerr. This is something I had not foreseen, that perhaps I could not even have conceived of. We are a stubborn people, set in our ways, protective of our culture and proud of it. We did not consider the customs of others."

"We wish not to shame you, only to bring this to your attention, and perhaps to speak more with you. We wish to understand how you manage to be so true to yourselves."

"We would be glad to serve in any way you wish, Lummukem of the Dragon. This also poses a new predicament to me. Do you know if others have felt the same pain as you did when we—no, it is not fair of me to ask you this. I must approach each of them individually and listen to their own voices, to make sure our cultural differences do not open a chasm between us. Again, I offer my apologies. Some of the clan leaders tried to persuade me not to reveal what lies in the caldera, although for different reasons. Perhaps I should have heeded their arguments with more openness."

Lummukem began to walk, headed deeper into the tunnels. "We are glad of what you chose, despite our feelings. The pink mist showed us that what is in our heart is magical, if still painful. And perhaps what you have done here, in this mirror world, is just the same. You dug deep into the crust of Noss, and from it carried ancient marble to expose its true nature to the light. Yet when doing so, you also left a hollowness underground, a deeper truth still beyond grasp. Someday, when we are ready, we wish to look deeper into ourself and understand this truth."

CHAPTER FIFTY-FIVE

LATIFRONS SKULL

"Where are we going?" Puuja groggily asked. "It's so late."

"You will soon see," Sunu answered.

With her long hare legs, Puuja easily kept up with Sunu's pace. Pol trotted to catch up—it was not his turn to wear the mask, for he had been wearing it most of the day.

"I don't like these robes," Puuja complained. "They are too loose."

"You only need to wear them for tonight. Servant Lune insisted, and we are her guests, so we should listen to her request."

"Then why are you not wearing robes?" Pol asked.

"We were not requested to," Sunu said. "And Olo does not like the fabrics," they added, glancing at the bird on their shoulder.

Pol's robes were too long for him, picking up dust at his feet. "Why did others not join us for dinner? Where did they go?" he asked, but Sunu did not answer.

The streets of Bra'uur were eerily empty. Many of the Tjardur had been leaving for the walls, ready to venture out into the New World.

"We are going to the round place again," Pol guessed.

"Are we having more boring meetings?" Puuja questioned.

"Yes," Sunu at last said. "So let us not be late."

The columns that surrounded the Loth Amphitheater each had cauldrons at their tops; the green fires within them illuminated the eight radial seating segments, which were empty of crowds. In the staging area at the center was the skull of a longhorn bison, turned upside down, with the hollow where a brain had once been now filled with pink-colored water. An orange bonfire crackled behind the skull, making the water sparkle.

Sunu and the twins walked down the steps and approached the stage.

"What is Lune doing?" Pol asked, spotting a single-horned figure tossing petals of white, purple-gray, black, and red into the skull.

"That is Rud," Sunu said, dodging the question. "Just like we are Sunu this evening, Lune is Rud. And Kulak is Aio, and Sterjall is Lago." They pointed to the front rows of seats at the end of each tier: all their friends were waiting there, sitting in the same seats that the clan leaders had taken during the Tjardur Council.

Other than the sound of the crackling cauldrons, the amphitheater was unnaturally silent.

Servant Rud turned and gestured for Sunu and the twins to join him by the skull.

"I'm scared…" Pol whispered, pulling on one of Puuja's long ears.

"It's alright Pol," Puuja said. "I'm here with you. They are just being weird."

The three of them made their way onto the stage and stopped in front of Servant Rud.

"Head strong," Rud greeted.

The twins blinked in response.

"Pollomekh and Puuja, we are glad you could attend, for this ceremony would be meaningless without you present. We have gathered here so that you may be properly exonerated for your recent actions. You have yet to show remorse for shattering the skull of one of the guardians of the Bra'uur Catacombs, and thus his spirit has been left restless."

"We didn't break it, Gwit did!" Puuja yelled.

Sunu shot an admonishing glare at her.

"And for entering the sacred grounds without permission," Rud added, to which the twins had no ready retort. "If the bovid ancestors absolve you, all your friends will be witnesses."

The siblings turned toward the seats, feeling the others' judgmental eyes pressing on them.

"But it is simple to appease the guardian's spirit," Rud continued. "All you need to do is ask for forgiveness from one of his ancestors." He waved an arm toward the massive skull at the center of the stage.

"But that's a longhorn bison," Puuja said. "The skull we bro—that Gwit broke was a pelorovis. You can tell by their horns."

"*Khumph*. They, uhm… They were ancestral friends, like a family."

"You must do as Rud requested," Sunu said. "Ask for forgiveness, and it shall be granted to you."

"But you left us all alone," Pol mumbled. "And you still haven't told us what you were doing there all day."

"That is a matter for adults," Sunu said. "Honor the ancient spirit now, or his soul will haunt you to your graves and beyond."

Pol shivered. He stared at the upside-down skull with the pink liquid instead of brains, and said, "We... I'm sorry. We didn't mean to break your friend."

Sunu's eyes moved to Puuja.

"I am sorry too," the hare said quietly. "And we won't do it again, we promise."

The cauldrons above the columns suddenly flared higher, the core of the green flames shifting to cyan and white.

"The spirits have heard you," Rud proclaimed, "and as witnessed by the eight clan leaders before you, your pardon is granted."

"That's it?" Puuja asked.

"Yes. No, actually," Rud said, squaring his shoulders. "Puuja and Pol-lomekh, daughter and son of Jessha and Tugrar of the Sehján, now that your sins have been forgiven, the spirits wish to honor you by granting you new names, *khummm.*"

The twins' faces lit up, although they still held a measure of cautious skepticism.

"We know not what tradition to follow," Rud went on, "as never have such young Silvfröash been named, and never have two at once needed naming. Sehján rituals we are unfamiliar with, so a Tjardur naming ceremony we will attempt, though one much different from any seen before, *khemkhummmph!*"

Sunu asked the siblings to stand in front of the longhorn bison skull, then said, "Follow Rud's instructions carefully. Worry not, we will be right in front of you." They headed to one of the clan leader seats.

Rud continued his speech, facing the eight spectators. "In our naming ceremony, our eight clans must offer their endorsement." He briefly turned to the twins. "Since the Tjardur leaders are now gathering their armies by the walls, we thought it appropriate to have your companions stand in their stead."

He pointed to the leftmost of the eight seats, and Sunu stood. "For the Four-Horned Clan, we call upon Sunu's blessing."

Servant Speros brought forth the Horn of Phalas, filled nearly to the brim with the bitterbroth, and held it toward Sunu. The shaman picked it up, took in a mouthful of the fetid liquid, and spat it back into the horn.

Speros carried the horn to the next seat, where Alaia waited.

"For the Yak Clan, we call upon Alaia's blessing."

Alaia stood. She had not needed to partake in the drinking last time, and she was none too pleased to be given the honor this time around, but she carried through with her duty and provided her own spittle. She gagged theatrically as she handed the horn back.

Aio was next.

"For the Gaur Clan, we call upon Aio's blessing."

During the council, the prince had been asked to swallow the liquid, but this time he merely had to spit it back out. Aio's face contorted as he swished and spat. Speros took the horn.

"For the Buffalo Clan, we call upon Siffo's blessing."

Siffo took a big gulp and handed the horn back.

"You must spit back into it, *hurff!*" Speros reproached him.

"I'm much sorry," the warthog captain said. He took the horn again, properly sharing his spit this time around. "Tastes mighty strong, like braaw left abandoned fur centuries in a shipwreck."

"For the Aurochs Clan, we call upon Vor-Vor's blessing. Would the descendant of Umar-Vaor please do us the honor?"

The old Jabrak-Tsing did what he was requested to do, without complaint, a sparkle of pride shining in his wrinkled eyes.

"For the Pelorovis Clan, we call upon Hefra's blessing."

Like Siffo, Hefra swallowed a gulp, then quickly took another and spat it into the horn. She thought it a bit bland—she had shared much more pungent drinks with the Khaar Du in the past.

"For the Wisent Clan, we call upon Crysta's blessing."

Crysta pinched her nose, closed her eyes, then took the smallest of sips.

"For the Spiral-Horned Clan, we call upon Lago's blessing."

Lago felt secretly happy about having been picked to represent the spiral-horned clan. He picked the horn up delicately, his painted fingernails sparkling with a silver lacquer that one of Rud-Lune's wives had let him borrow. He sipped from the horn and quickly spat the wretched fluid out without letting the flavor ruin his mood.

Speros then shared his own spittle while bringing the Horn of Phalas to Servant Rud, who spat eagerly into the receptacle before handing it to Puuja.

"Fermented since before Trommodrolom's birth is the bitterbroth you now share," Rud said with pride. "The saliva of our ancestors began the fermentation, *khum*, and that of honorable clan leaders kept it strong, head strong! Drink now, and be one with our ancestors, one with your friends."

Puuja timidly took the horn with her soft-furred paws and pretended to drink.

Rud leaned in and whispered, "You must drink it this time, *khummm*, not just pretend like you did last time." He gave her an encouraging wink.

Puuja took her time to muster enough courage. Once she sipped from the vile horn, her entire face puckered, whiskers bent forward near their breaking point. But she swallowed. Rud took the horn before the girl could drop it and asked her to hand Okrisilv to her brother. Puuja shapeshifted and handed over the mask, only to realize that, while in her human form, the flavor in her mouth was yet stronger. She kept herself from vomiting and stood as straight as she could.

Pol quickly shifted into his half-form and took the horn from Rud. "It's not so bad," he said, after taking a small sip. He then took another, and kept on drinking.

Rud's eyes widened, and he snatched the horn from the chipmunk; the brew was strong, and even a small amount could make an adult drunk. He made sure Speros carried the horn far away, then said, "Now you must cleanse yourselves, so that your new bodies are ready to receive their new names. Only in your half-forms must you enter the Latifrons Skull, so one at a time you will venture in. Will you go first, Pollomekh, or will you first return Okrisilv to your sister?"

Pol was uncertain. He looked toward Sunu, who nodded from the distance.

"Do I need to take these robes off?"

"Yes, Pollomekh," Rud said.

The Sehján were not self-conscious about nudity—living in the water, they often found the use of clothing obtrusive, so Pol handed his robes to Rud without worry. He stumbled, tipsy from the large gulps of bitterbroth he had ingested.

Rud caught the chipmunk before he toppled over. "I will help you," he said, offering a hand. Pol took it with a sharp-clawed handpaw and tiptoed onto the upside-down skull, balancing on the maxilla, taking short steps between the rows of molars, headed to the cavity where the brain had once been.

A fuzzy toe dipped in. The pink water in the cranial fossa was warm. Still holding on to Rud, Pol lowered his body into the water. His bushy tail floated among the colorful petals. The cranial pool was not deep, merely reaching his chest.

Rud walked behind the skull, standing between it and the bonfire. He grabbed on to Pol's head and dunked him without warning.

"Oxruk!" Pol cursed as he resurfaced.

Rud helped Pol climb out the same way he had walked in, then handed him his robe so that he could dry up.

"Khuron Pollomekh, son of Jessha and Tugrar," Rud spoke, loud and clear. "The clan leaders—apologies, *your friends* have chosen a name for your half-form, *khumm*. While Okrisilv grants you its essence, you shall be known as Dreldojak, which in Miscamish means *dart*, as you are fast and deadly as the darts that fly from your friends' blowguns. Do you accept this name, and vow to uphold the virtues entrusted to you by your ancestors?"

"Dart. Yes," Pol said. "I like it. Dart."

"The name is Dreldojak, which *translates* to *dart*."

"I prefer Dart."

The Tjardur had been using Common names for their half-forms for the last millennium, but since Pol came from a tribe still deeply rooted in Miscam traditions, Rud had thought it proper to uphold Miscam naming conventions. He looked toward Sunu for answers. The allgender shrugged, making Olo briefly adjust his footing on their shoulder.

The naming ceremony had already broken enough rules either way, so Rud gave in. "Then Dart it is. *Khum!* Dart of the Long-Eared Chipmunk, would you please let your sister have Okrisilv now?"

Rud repeated the steps with Puuja. He had to try three times to sink her properly into the pink water, as her long ears kept popping out, and Tjardur tradition dictated that she be fully submerged for the cleansing to take effect. Once she was back out and drying under her robes, the black-naped hare looked up to Rud.

The buffalo said, "Ierun Puuja, daughter of Jessha and Tugrar, your friends have also chosen a name for your half-form. While Okrisilv grants you its essence, you shall be known as Duërdivun, which in Miscamish means *gorget*, as you are your brother's defender, and the name echoes the black markings that protect your own furred neck. *Khummm…* Do you accept this name, and vow to uphold the virtues entrusted to you by your ancestors?"

"I also like the Common name better," Puuja said, wringing her long ears.

The buffalo looked up again; Sunu shrugged once more.

"Gorget. *Khum.* Then so be it," Rud defeatedly declared. "Gorget of the Black-Naped Hare, and Dart of the Long-Eared Chipmunk, your names are now bound to your essences. May they help you find yourselves fully, and grant you the wisdom to uphold the eight sacred virtues."

CHAPTER FIFTY-SIX

THE SOOTHSAYER

Ardof walked alongside the endless parade of bears. During the day, the sleuth always traveled at a trot, forcing the ranger to ride atop one of the polar bears, or sometimes atop Wadrook, one of the friendlier grizzlies. But in the evenings, the bears moved slower, letting some groups rush ahead to collect food for the others. At those times when the pace was appropriate for the legs of a human, Ardof took to his feet.

A splotchy brown dog and a black bear of cream-colored fur walked alongside him. The spirit bear lifted his pink nose and sniffed, scenting a familiar fragrance in the air. Then a growl mixed with a whine made him glance down—Bear had suddenly stopped. The mutt's head was tilted, one ear flipped over, his lolling tongue suspended in expectation.

The spirit bear grew into a dark smoke and took his human form. "Safís must be on her way back!" Banook reckoned. As soon as he'd said it, a wolf leapt on top of a pointed boulder, her white fur sparkling like fresh-fallen snow.

«Kerjaastórgnem, I see you have made good progress,» Safís mindspoke. She hopped off the boulder and joined the group, recounting her journey to Banook. After rescuing the dire wolves caged in the city of Umaagi, Safís had escorted her kindred to a forest where they could regain their health, breed with the other packs that had escaped the collapsing Heartpine Dome, and hopefully keep their species from falling into extinction.

«There is hope yet for the dire wolves, for my kind,» Safís said as they ambled together. «I asked the three we rescued why they had ventured so far from the lands of Agnargdrolom. They had been searching for someone, following her scent trail.»

"And who were they looking for, my moonlit lady?" Banook asked.

«A priestess who had been taken as a slave by the invaders. A Wutash survivor.»

"One of them yet lives?!"

"Who lives? What is she saying?" Ardof asked, feeling left out.

"I will interpret shortly, my friend."

Safís continued her tale. «The priestess lives. And she has been rescued and taken to a place of safety, guarded by my children. She thinks others of the tribe might have survived as well, but that might only be wishes of her heart, for no others has she seen in years.»

They made camp that evening in a half-collapsed barn. Despite the structure being abandoned, they found three baskets filled with fresh fruits and preserved meats at the barn's tilted entrance: a gift from the Negian farmers who lived in the valley. The wayfarers had grown accustomed to these offerings, which the locals left partly out of gratitude—they considered the migrating bears an omen of fertility and bountifulness—but also out of fear, for they did not wish to anger any sprites, gods, or netherbeasts.

As they dined on sausages and juicy plums, Banook told Ardof all he had learned from the white wolf.

"I've seen a few Wutash myself," Ardof said, "in Anglass. Back then, I had no idea they had come from Heartpine. Those poor souls were the first to be killed in the mines." He tossed a slice of sausage to Bear, then added, "What do you think this might mean? For Lago. For the mask."

"I do not know. In time, we will find out."

A few more days of travel elapsed, during which the sleuth marched southwest across the sandstone mesas of the Negian Empire. Arriving at a canyon's edge, they followed its ridgeline, searching for a way to the meadows below.

"I'm glad I saved this cured ham from the last offering," Ardof said to Banook as he chewed the savory meat. He handed a piece of ham to the polar bear he was riding, who had to crane her neck back to reach, then added, "I used to prepare the most sumptuous venison jerky. I even had my own little shop in Nargara! The secret is hickory from Yeredam for smoking it, plus cumin from Tsenhanuur to add that truly exotic flavor." The silence dragged on for too long after that, so Ardof continued, "You know, it gets awfully boring when I'm the only one doing the talking. This ridgeline is safe, there are no cities or farms for miles around. Your bears will warn us if you need to make yourself invisible."

The spirit bear walking by his side grew then, taking his primal form of an arctotherium that towered even higher than the polar bears. He huffed, blowing the ranger's hat off, leaving it dangling from its cord.

"Huffing doesn't count, big bear," Ardof berated his friend, to which Banook responded by transitioning from a four-legged walk to a two-legged trot while shifting to his human form.

"I still prefer pecan for smoking," Banook said. "It's more mellow. But I will have to try your recipe someday."

"Once this war is over, maybe I'll open my shop once more."

Their conversation was interrupted as they noticed the bears ahead of them slowing down. A kiuon leader approached in haste, mindspeaking to Banook.

"What's the matter?" Ardof asked once the kiuon seemed to be done.

"They found a path down from the mesa. An old switchback road. But there's a wagon there, stuck midway due to a rockslide."

"Only one wagon?"

"That is what she told me. Let us get a better view."

They approached the edge of a precipice that overlooked the switchback, getting a clear view of a roving merchant's wagon. Two oxen grazed by its side, yoke detached. A merchant was trying to move rocks out of the way, focusing on the smaller ones while not yet bothering to deal with the largest boulders—an effort that might take days if not weeks of work.

"We should offer our aid," Banook said. "I would rather not make my presence known, or that of my bears, but if we wish to clear the impediment, we will need some muscle."

"Ask your bears to stay up here so they won't be seen. Once we are done helping these folk, they can move ahead of us."

Banook agreed with the plan. He put on some clothes, then headed down the road, followed by Ardof. They walked past the two bored oxen, glanced at the canvas-covered wagon as they passed by it—only wares inside, no other people—then greeted the merchant who was trying to clear the rockslide.

"Moon lights, traveler!" Banook greeted them.

A sweat-drenched allgender turned around, frightened, but mostly just cautious. "Ushmahiel," they said, their feet well aligned as they performed a bow. "And may the heavens offer guidance on your journey," they added shakily, staring up at the imposing red-haired giant. Banook and Ardof stared back with matching bewilderment, for the person in front of them had skin the color of bluebells, of azurite, of lavender fields, and of volcanic rock, striped across their body as if they were carved out of layers of sandstone. Even their irises were turquoise, fringed with indigo.

"W–we seek no trouble," Banook said after having stared for much too long. "But we are traveling the same path, and perhaps could help you clear it."

"With no wagon behind you, you could easily scramble down that way," the blue merchant pointed out. "But I will not refuse an offer of aid." They bowed again, their unbuttoned jerkin draping down, then introduced themself. "Mildurilashten Sivar-Vok sar Ignaar ill Soman, but you may call me Mildur."

As they worked to remove the obstacle, which Banook handled mostly by himself, Mildur told them they were from the Quas Sejaar region of Bauram, and that their peculiarly pigmented skin was indeed related to the blue and purple sands of their remote homeland. "The colors you see represent the strata from the canyons I grew up in. One new color was tattooed on my skin each year, from the day I came of age, until my body was covered and my canyon's story was complete." And their body was indeed fully covered, from the gaps between their toes, to their labia, armpits, gums, and even eyelids. Each color traced a nearly perfect horizontal line across Mildur's body—some were striking in their contrast, such as the black-framed turquoise band at their neck, while others were subtle, like the cerulean transitions on their forehead. A few of the bands were scarified with faint bumps, as if encrusted with pebbles deposited by ancient rivers.

"It looks like a painful procedure," Ardof commented, kicking a small rock out of the way to pretend to be helping. "Why subject yourself to such agony?"

"It was excruciating, but it was my calling since the day I was born." They caressed a strand of yellow-white hair, following its length down to their bead-decorated goatee of the same refulgent color, and said, "I exited my mother's womb as white as the marbles of Ukhbria. A blank canvas, ready to be inscribed, and so my fate was sealed. And who am I to refuse the calling of fate? While each stratum was tattooed, the elders told me the tale of one epoch, and the pain helped me remember. This is the way we carry our story with us, as the stones that shelter us carry their own story, albeit one much grander than we can envision."

Banook heaved with all his might to dislodge the largest of the boulders, until it toppled down the cliffside and exploded at the bottom. He pushed off a few straggler rocks, wiped the sweat off his brow, and said, "This should suffice, Lerr Mildur. Once you ready your oxen, you may be on your way."

"I would offer you a ride in my wagon, but I don't presume you'd be very comfortable in the cramped space. I don't even see how you'd fit through the door. But I can slow my pace and offer you company as we travel down."

"Thank you, Lerr Mildur," Banook said, "but we are camping at the top of the mesa, and won't resume our march quite yet. You may ride ahead of us, and perhaps our paths will cross again in the future."

"Then I must at least offer repayment for your efforts," Mildur said, and before Banook could object, they waved a hand. "I know your selfless kind. Although I am a merchant, I carry no wares to sell, nor do I have enough Qupi to spare. I am a soothsayer, learned in the arts of aetheric divination, geomancy, and card reading. That is why I travel from sea to sea, making a living by reading people their fortunes." They noticed a cynical smile plastered on Ardof's face, so they offered to him, "Perhaps I could start with you? I promise it will change your perspective on my arts."

"Thank you kindly, Lerr, but I'll pass," Ardof replied. "I've had enough card readings done in my youth to satisfy all possible fates. I merely need to pick the right one now."

Mildur then glanced to Banook, who nodded to them with uncertainty and curiosity. The soothsayer briefly entered their wagon and returned holding a hexagonal box of inlaid cedarwood. "Please, sit," they said to Banook, and they both sat on the sand in the middle of the switchback road, while Ardof perched on a rock by their side, eyeing them skeptically.

The soothsayer unclasped the box and swung its lid open on its silver hinges, revealing a stack of hexagonal cards. "The Deck of Sands has changed much in the last few epochs," they intoned with their mellow voice. "But this deck holds only the original sixty-six cards that the oracles of Allathanathar used. Yet I am no oracle. I cannot predict the future, nor can I peek into the past. But I can help you glimpse truths within yourself."

Their blue eyes were locked on to Banook as they shuffled the cards. They blew on the deck, then handed it to Banook, who inspected it with his enormous hands. The back of each card had a design that alluded to blown sands, dunes, and distant realms. Their fronts were embellished with unique illustrations, glyphs, and names—some obvious, others confounding—and had edges matching the six colors of the moon's seasons.

"Shuffle it thoroughly," Mildur said, "and stop only when your heart tells you to."

Banook did as directed, then handed the deck back.

Mildur began to hum an enchanting melody, all the while drawing in the sand with a mauve-lacquered fingernail. They traced a hexagon just about as large as one of the cards, then surrounded it with six more hexagons. Once the drawing was finished, the soothsayer pulled seven cards from the top of the deck, placing them face down over the hexagons. They plucked a pinch of Baurami-blue sand from a pouch, then sprinkled the grains over the spread of cards while they sang an incantation:

Glim, glam, glom, gloom.

Glimmer of morning, glamour of noon,

Gloaming of evening, gloom of the moon.

The last word lingered like a howl, like a prayer.

"Flip two cards from the spread, any but the center one," Mildur instructed. Banook did so, choosing two cards that touched each other. He leaned in to stare at the figures, seeing one that held three flames, another with a shepherd holding a crook which had the crescent moon herself for its hooked end.

"The Three of Brime and the Moon Shepherd," Mildur said. "From your perspective, the Element card is upside down, but its home season is Summer, Sulphur, and since that edge of the card aligns to the central one, it is not inverted for the spread." Their striated fingers traced invisible connections over the cards as they spoke, enthralling Banook. "Brime speaks of passion, of movement, but it can also indicate anger. The Moon Shepherd is a Spirit card, so it has no suit, but here it is aligned to the core under Tourmaline, the opposite of the three flames. The two cards are joined by their Jade and Amethyst edges—one speaks of deception, but also wisdom. The other of time, of death."

"But what does it all mean?" Banook asked.

Mildur stared into Banook's honey-colored eyes and studied the fear within them. "I see a disconnect, a shattering between opposites, a departure. There is fervor, and a longing that will need time to settle."

"Does it have to do with… Will he—" Banook started, but kept himself from saying more.

"There is a loved one, someone left behind," Mildur ascertained. "Perhaps it has to do with him. Only your heart can know. Flip over two more."

This time, Banook chose two cards at opposite ends of the spread.

Mildur's fingers hovered over the new cards, casting a dancing shadow over them. "The Six of Magnium and the Hollow Moon. And you, at the core, are trapped within them. The Element card holds the highest number, so it speaks of great strength, and also of uncontainable attraction. But its home season of Pearl, of Thawing, points outside the spread. Yet still, its orientation matches that of the Moon Shepherd, so there is a connection between them."

"I don't think I see one," Banook commented.

"Magnium can be a shield to the Moon Shepherd, but also a cage," they said cryptically, then moved on to the other card. "All cards are imbued with opposite dualities. Here, the Hollow Moon is an end, but also a beginning. Being an Essence card, it represents not a quality or an individual, but a concept. It pulls opposite of power. And its Obsidian edge—that of life, of Spring—is mirrored by the edge of the Three of Brime. There is conflict, a war, and these sides are competing with one another." Mildur observed Banook's reaction, taking heed of his breathing pattern, of the way his knuckles tightened. "It might indicate that a new start is coming, but there will be struggles to face."

"That is as it has always been."

The soothsayer smiled with blue gums, then requested, "Two more cards, if you please."

Banook flipped the last two cards at the periphery, leaving the central one untouched.

"Aah," Mildur said. "One Essence and one Spirit. The Bezoar and the Root Mother. The Bezoar is something indigestible which must be expelled, yet it is said to cure any malady. Here it mirrors a cold Tourmaline edge with the Six of Magnium. A good omen, if ever I saw one, a powerful counter to illness. Yet the Root Mother is facing opposite of it. She shares an alignment with the Moon Shepherd, leaving your core card between the two. What was she like?"

"She? Who?" Banook asked, taken aback.

"Your mother. Did you inherit your… attributes from her, or from your father? Did she perhaps give birth to you in Summer, as the card here seems to indicate?"

"I… I do not know," Banook replied. "I never met my mother," he added, feeling unsure whether he was lying or not, for he did not even know if he had been birthed or had come to exist in some other manner.

"I see," Mildur said, fidgeting with the beads decorating their white goatee. "Then there is only one card that can reveal more to us." They placed a hand over the central card, covering it completely for a short moment, then added, "When I remove my hand, say the four words of the incantation, then flip the card over. You do not need to sing the words."

Banook nodded, and as soon as Mildur's blue hand left the spread, chanted, "Glim, glam, glom, gloom," then flipped the final card over. He flinched at the image as if slapped by it—the illustration was that of a furred gauntlet with five gilded claws stretching from the knuckles. The card was aligned to him, making its name easily readable: Golden Claw. He glanced at Mildur, but the soothsayer's expression was unreadable, like an unwritten book. With a broken voice, Banook asked, "What does it mean?"

"The Golden Claw is one of eighteen Essence cards that can sometimes stand for a Spirit card. It is a powerful weapon that is often pictured in coats of arms. A royal symbol, one of honor, one of legacy. But what it means on its own is less relevant than what it means in the context of the six cards that surround it, and how it aligns to your point of view. The Root Mother moves away from it, while the Moon Shepherd reaches up to find it. The only card with a mirroring season is the Three of Brime, touching Sulphur edges with the claw. There is untapped passion in here, a burning fire that keeps you alive, but that also must be controlled. The powerful suit of magnium, the enchantment of the Bezoar, the possibilities brought by the Hollow Moon—they all point to great strife ahead of you, but also indicate that you have the might of heart to overcome it."

Mildur began to sing once more, picking up one card at a time.

> Glimmer of morning, glamour of noon,
>
> Gloaming of evening, gloom of the moon.
>
> Glim, glam, glom, gloom.

As they erased the hexagons where the cards had been, the few grains of blue sand they'd cast upon them mixed with the ruddy soil of the road. They shuffled the seven cards into the deck, then rose to their feet.

"But wait," Banook said, standing up as well. "What is my fate then? You haven't yet told me."

"Your fate? How am I to know? As I said, I am no oracle, I'm merely a soothsayer. Fate is what you make of it. Unlike my skin, which is written with history that can no longer be changed, the rest of your story is yet unwritten, Ulv-Djar Zarienn. It is up to you to pick up the pen and write it."

Mildur placed the sixty-six cards back in the box and closed the lid with finality, then asked for Banook's aid once more, so he could lift the yoke over the necks of the oxen.

As the soothsayer departed down the cleared road, Ardof and Banook stood motionless for a while, watching them leave.

Once the wagon turned the next bend, Ardof said, "Like my aunt Ziima used to say, 'Just a bunch of glimglam.' What a waste of time."

"What do you mean?" Banook complained. "They perfectly read the cards. I am still in a bit of shock at how truthful all they said was."

"They weren't reading the cards, big fellow, they were reading you! Your expressions, your reactions, even your silence. They told you only what you wanted to hear."

"I'd give them a bit more credit than that. The cards I picked, that could not have been a coincidence. How they aligned, how it all made sense."

Ardof turned to head back uphill to where the bears were waiting. "They could've found meaning in any set of cards, it's just an old trick. If the cards spoke to you, it's simply because there was something you already wanted to hear."

Banook followed after the ranger, shuffling his steps as he pondered the reading. "But this does not explain the final card, Golden Claw. You know what that represents, its imagery was too specific."

"I'd say you look bearish, and your beard matched the gauntlet's color. That card was an easy pick for them to mesmerize you with."

"But it was I who picked it."

"You are wrong, friend. The entire time, one of Mildur's hands was luring your eyes while the other shuffled the deck on their lap. Did you see them place their hand over the spread before you turned the final card? They swapped the central card then. You didn't see them palm it, but from my view-point, I could see them do it. They were clever, but it doesn't mean they knew you to be the Nu'irg."

"Yet they did. They even knew my name."

"Your name?" Ardof asked, glancing over his shoulder.

"Once the reading ended, they called me *Ulv-Djar Zarienn*. It was a name given to me by Baurami nomads in times before the Downfall, mean-ing *citrine eyes*."

Ardof pondered, slowing his step. "Well… Maybe that one could be a co-incidence. They did come from Bauram, and your eyes do look like citrines."

"The skeptical ranger now believes in coincidences?" Banook retorted with good humor. "That sounds like a bunch of glimglam."

Ardof chuckled. "Well, maybe Mildur did realize who you are. But what I'm curious about now is if they knew all along, or if they read that from you while they pretended to read the cards. You can sometimes be an open book, my friend."

CHAPTER FIFTY-SEVEN

A WORTHY SACRIFICE

Sails furled, the Cabal ship cut through the waters of the Capricious Ocean at a speed unimaginable to even captains of the fastest Wastyrian galleys. The enormous Negórmea seals pulled the Silv-Thaars' ship using taut lines, carrying it toward the Alvforg Strait to meet Osef and the stolen Negian fleet at the Alommo Sea.

"How is your arm?" Silv-Thaar Daro asked Muriel.

Unable to face her chief, Muriel Clawwick faced the ocean. Her splinted arm dangled over the ship's railings, painful and useless. The strong winds flattened her spiky black hair, making her head feel cold and burning her ears.

"I asked you—"

"It's torn to fucking pieces, how do you think it is?" Muriel raged. "That rabid dog tore the tendons to shreds. I'll never…" Muriel trailed off, holding back tears. She spat at the ocean, but the wind pulled her spittle back onto the ship. "That dog took my brother. And he took Jovan, Salvina, Emma, Talled, Elian, Nikolina, and now Trevin too. And he fucking took my arm. I'll never shoot my bow again."

The ermine leaned closer to her friend, white fur flapping. She was lost in her thoughts, staring down at her sharp claws. "Remember that gal, what was her name? Beccai, from Fjarmallen. After she lost her arm to the Bayani, a bowyer in Hestfell crafted a one-handed crossbow for her, and she kept on shooting even—"

"A one-handed crossbow? Really, Chief?"

"It's better than nothing."

"Better than nothing would be to have that filthy mutt on a platter, while I use my one good arm to slice *his* tendons to ribbons." She spat again, harder. This time, her spittle made it to the ocean.

"Don't spit on my seals," Silv-Thaar Knivlar interjected, waddling her webbed feet toward the other two women.

"Fuck your seals," Muriel snapped. "They piss and shit in that water."

"Calm down, Muriel, I was only kidding. How is your—"

Daro lifted a hand to stop Knivlar before she finished the question. Knivlar was naked, as she always was nowadays, fully displaying the scarified patterns that dimpled her dense, spotted fur.

"How much longer?" Daro asked.

"Islav and Aness just returned," Knivlar replied, caressing the two magpies who perched awkwardly on her streamlined shoulders. "It didn't take them long, so we should be getting close to the strait. But they are antsy—they spotted something there. I wish I could hear their thoughts the same way I can hear my pinnipeds."

"I'm concerned. Osef hasn't sent a herald in days."

"Maybe he has?" the leopard seal suggested. "We've been traveling faster than most birds can fly, and far from shore. It's unlikely his heralds would be able to spot us. He's probably just as worried about us."

"What's the fucking point of any of this anyway?" Muriel said to no one.

"The point of what?" Daro asked.

"This fucking war. We've lost so much already, and for what? So you two can get fur coats?"

"Watch your tongue, Muriel." Daro straightened, her disfigured face tightening. "Do you think I wasn't there when they died? Do you think I wouldn't prefer to be back at the commons with our entire family?"

Muriel clenched her jaw. "Some days I just don't see the point of it all. We'll gather more of the masks, kill that dog and elk, and then what? Return to Hestfell to be Urcai's puppets just like Hallow is? Or perhaps we should stay in one of the domes and live naked like the savages."

Daro held a hand up again before Knivlar snapped back at the younger woman, then stepped closer, forcing Muriel to face her. "Hestfell can burn, for all I care. It's nothing but a nest for spineless sycophants. The Cabal was not formed to build over crumbling foundations. We will set our own rules, settle our own territories, build alliances that will benefit all our people. The masks are means to an end. If you wish to relinquish your claim to the next mask, which would've gone to either you or Trevin, you can do so now. And if you want to keep pretending we are doing this for selfish reasons, comparing us to Hallow and his ilk, then you are welcome to jump overboard and use your one good arm to swim all the way back to the wastes of Norviria."

Muriel stood taut as a drawn bowstring, saying nothing.

Daro's face transitioned from anger to disappointment. She took half a step back, then turned to face the ocean. "You and your brother showed so much ambition. So much promise. Whatever you do, don't do it for me, not even for the Cabal. Do it for Waldomar, for his memory."

Muriel wanted to slap Daro. She wanted to embrace her. But all she could do was hold still as her vision blurred from her tears.

"The choice is with you," Daro said as she walked away.

The ship sliced through the cold ocean. Silv-Thaar Daro made her way to the bow, trying to glimpse beyond the horizon. Stormy clouds were gathered in the distance, bulging in the direction of the Alommo Sea.

No, that is smoke, Daro realized. *Sapfire smoke.* She called for Silv-Thaar Knivlar.

"That must be Osef's handiwork," the leopard seal said. "But what is our fleet still doing in the strait?"

Soon enough, they had their answer.

Ahead of them they found the tail end of the Cabal fleet, wobbling idly on the water. The fire was still too far beyond the ships to be seen.

"What is happening? Where is the *Ballista*?" Daro asked as they slowed next to a war galley. Though the galley was meant to be used to deploy soldiers, it was mostly empty.

"Silv-Thaars!" the captain of the ship called out. "The Tsing have sent too many reinforcements. They deployed all their ships from Korolok, and we have no idea where the rest came from. We have not been able to make it through the strait. We are stuck here."

"Stuck? What of Afhora?" Daro asked.

"The kingdom has granted access to their ports at Cape Artok, but they do not have enough room for all of our ships. We are docking in shifts to resupply, guarding this end while Osef tries to make way for us. He's farther ahead in the flagship. Just follow the smoke."

Knivlar asked her seals to pull them forward once more, in the direction of the billowing fumes.

A formation of red-sailed Cabal ships was waiting on the southeast side of the strait, separated from a much larger enemy fleet by a wall of sickly yellow flames. The Tsing were blocking the passage where the strait was narrowest, at the only navigable portion that was not riddled with sand banks and sharp-edged islands. Although the water and some ships were still burning, there was no ongoing battle. The skirmish had occurred hours ago, and now the two fleets were simply waiting for the other side to make a bad move. Whoever tried to attack first would have to expose their flanks to the enemy while traversing a field of burning debris, forcing their own ships to slow to avoid crashing. No one wanted to be the first to sail, not even with a tailwind in their favor.

"There's Osef." Silv–Thaar Daro pointed out the *Ballista*, with the yellow-and-gray flag of the Cabal flying over its red sails. The ship was not at the frontlines, but moving east, approaching Afhoran shores.

Daro, Knivlar, and Muriel left their small vessel to board the flagship. Osef Windscar hurried to meet them.

"You are back sooner than expected," he said. "Did you not make it to the Ashen Dome?"

"We did, but we had to leave in a hurry," Silv–Thaar Daro replied. "A Lerevi frigate came chasing after us and—"

"Lerevi?"

"Long story. Either way, we made it back."

"What happened to your arm?" Osef asked Muriel, looking over Daro's shoulder. "Where's the bovid mask? And where's Trevin?"

Daro sighed.

Sitting inside Osef's quarters, they caught him up with all that had happened, then inquired about the situation with the fleet. Fjorna was taking a break from wearing Krostsilv, the mask resting on her lap. Since she only had a few jarv wolverines mindlocked, and they were all secured in cages, she was able to take her human form when she wished. Silv–Thaar Knivlar, however, did not have the same freedom, for she had amassed too great an army of pinnipeds to risk losing her mindlock on them.

"We are nearly out of sapfire," Osef brooded. "The Tsing are patient, they know they can wait us out. And twice they have sent small fleets to flank us from the gulf side. Their ships move fast and outmaneuver us, easily crossing back through the strait."

"And what of the Red Stag?" Fjorna asked.

"He's already at the Scoria Dome. We have no hope of beating him to it now. We're fucked, Chief. We have no way to make it into the Alommo Sea, our entire force is stuck. We used up nearly all the sapfire we have in our last attack, just to keep the Tsing fleet at bay. They assume we have more, but they'll smarten up sooner or later."

"But we have Urcai's formula," Knivlar said. "Why don't we make our own sapfire and scorch those fuckers sixteenfold?"

"Because of the bloody Graalman Horde," Osef snorted, "that's why. They've been patrolling the coast by the Scoria Dome and won't let us get our supply of sap into the Afhoran ships. Either way, those ships are stuck *inside* the sea, and we are stuck out here. Now our only choice is to transport the barrels by land. Sulphur and the other ingredients we have aplenty—it's just the sap that's holding us back."

"Get some from the Moonrise Dome, then," Muriel recommended. "Before the vines shrivel away."

"It's too bloody far, and we can't split our fleet in half just for that. The Tsing would tear us apart."

"How long until the supply of sap reaches us by land?" Fjorna asked.

Osef leaned over a map. The Scoria Dome was hundreds of miles away by land, over a path that required crossing nearly the entire Kingdom of Afhora. Although the road was wide and well maintained, it meandered too much, climbing and dropping constantly.

A drop of sweat landed on the map. Osef wiped his bald head and said, "A few weeks, if we are lucky. We can keep docking at Cape Artok and hold our bluff for longer. But I'm concerned… Even with fully replenished cannons, I don't know how we'll make it through the strait. We can't take them by surprise, and their fleet has only grown bigger." He nervously chewed on his fingers. "They have the upper hand here. We tried pushing once, and our ships were picked off like salmon rushing up a narrow stream." He spat out a piece of cuticle and shook his head.

"But next time we try, we'll have the help of my babies," Knivlar said. "I lured in thousands of small seals and hundreds of sea lions, walruses, and even some elephant seals. They can help push the hulls of the Tsing ships, keeping them from taking their positions."

"They fight with arrows and harpoons," Osef said dismissively. "And their ships are iron hulled and heavy. You'll need too many beasts to move a single one of their ships out of the way, they are nothing like the tiny vessel you all ventured off in. If we can't get close enough to use our sapfire on them—which takes careful maneuvering—we can't compete. It won't serve us to inconvenience a few dozen of their ships. We need them to burn."

Fjorna rose to her feet. She picked at the dirt under her nails with her white-hilted dagger. The mostly intact side of her face looked pensive, cunning. The disfigured half formed no expression; it simply was.

"I think I know what we can do," she said. "I'm not sure if this will work, but it's worth a try. Osef, do we have access to any artificers?"

"Plenty of smart ones at Cape Artok. The Afhorans are well known for their craft. This is where Urcai himself trained. What is it you are planning?"

"Let's set sail for Artok. I need a word with the shrewdest of their scholars."

Two weeks passed. During that time, Silv-Thaar Daro kept the Afhoran artificers working day and night, creating hundreds upon hundreds of copies of a very simple device—simple for the artificers to construct, but potentially deadly if used in the way she intended. The kingdom was glad to offer their support to the Cabal, having not only allied with them for the current campaign against the threat of the Red Stag, but also having negotiated vast land redistributions—particularly the territories of the Horde—that they were to control once the war was over.

The Tsing had once more sent a flanking fleet from the west, but the Cabal had been ready, taking shelter by the shores of the Afhoran Peninsula. The Tsing ships fled through the strait, unharmed, and joined their greater fleet. No more moves had been attempted, giving the Cabal time to prepare.

The shipment of sap at last arrived, hauled by a long caravan of wagons. The white blood was mixed with the secret ingredients until there was enough of the flammable liquid to resupply all the ships. After loading the items commissioned by Daro, the Cabal ships took to sea and formed a wall at the mouth of the strait, daring the Tsing to make a move. Well aware of the threat, the Tsing mobilized their entire fleet, blockading the strait as they had before.

"You sure this will work?" Muriel asked an artificer, holding one of the items they had crafted: a fist-sized sphere of blown glass. One half of the sphere was filled with a white powder, while the other had some sort of yellowish liquid in it. Two simple cork caps sealed the ends. It was nothing extraordinary, just a split container with two different reagents.

"It will work, Lurr Clawwick," the old artificer said, who had come along to supervise the deployment of the artifacts. "We ran extensive tests. Please, be careful with it."

"I'm not asking if your devices will work," Muriel clarified, "I'm asking if this strategy will work."

"We'll find out very soon," Daro said.

Silv-Thaar Knivlar stood near them with a pained expression, saying nothing. Daro took note of her demeanor and put a hand on her shoulder.

"This is for the greater good," she said. "With your help, the Cabal will finally enter the Alommo Sea. You will help us get our revenge on Lago, help us take down the Red Stag. You should be proud. Are you ready?"

Silv-Thaar Knivlar nodded weakly.

"Then speak to them," Daro said, "and tell them what to do."

Night had fallen by the time they were ready to make their move. The Cabal fleet worked only under the light of Sceres, whose pink crescent was soon to drop in the west; right before her light faded, they executed their plan. Knivlar directed her most agile seals to jump aboard their dromon ships, a few at a time. The barrels of sapfire were opened, but instead of being used to refill the cannons, mops were dipped in them, and then used to brush the sapfire onto the dense coats of the pinnipeds. The sapfire had been mixed with a thickening agent, taking on the consistency of hot tar. It clung to the fur of the seals, making them itch and want to jump back into the water. And soon they did.

The marine mammals seemed confused, pained, and scared. Silv-Thaar Knivlar understood their pain, but kept an impassive face as she watched her kindred swim away.

Each of the pinnipeds approached shallow skiffs from which soldiers were carefully lowering the glass containers into the water. The spheres floated like eggs from a dark sea creature. Each seal picked one up, holding it carefully in their jaws.

They swam. Thousands of them, coated in thick, sticky sapfire, moving as fast as the currents of the Tumultuous Ocean, cradling the glass artifacts between their sharpened teeth. Once they met the Tsing fleet, the seals picked up speed and launched themselves upward. As they landed on the decks of the enemy ships, they bit hard into the glass spheres. The powder and the liquid acid mixed and instantly burst into purple-tinted flames, making it look as if aquatic dragons had boarded the ships to spew fire from their mouths.

The thrashing seals soon caught the flames on their sapfire-coated fur. The purple blazing from their mouths exploded into pallid, greenish yellow. The animals writhed in pain, plastering the sticky, flammable substance all over the decks. They couldn't scream, but they could bark out their misery. Fire filled their throats and wrapped their bodies as they spread their pain and anguish to burn it all, to bring down the Tsing fleet with their last moments of agony.

The Tsing sailors tried to snuff out the flames, but every effort only further spread the viscous liquid. They quickly gave up and dove into the cold water, where the Negórmea seals, walruses, and sea lions met them with tusks and fangs.

From the safety of her ship, Silv-Thaar Daro gazed at the conflagration setting the horizon alight. The yellow flames reached the lines and sails, turning them orange as wood and canvas burned, masts toppling like timber.

"We did it. We fucking did it," Daro said with satisfaction, her white fur tinted by distant firelight. She turned around to celebrate with her friends. "Silv-Thaar Knivlar, this victory is all yours, you deserve—where is she?"

"She went belowdecks," Muriel said, nodding toward the steps that led into the hold.

Daro found Aurélien weeping in the compartment, with Gwonlesilv resting wordlessly by her knees. The hold was dark and chilly. Aurélien was cocooned in a white robe. Her short red hair was in disarray, plastered over her forehead. Her only company other than the judgmental mask were her two magpies, perched on a crate, watching without understanding.

"Their pain…" she sobbed, "their faces. They knew, they knew…"

"Aurélien, your mask," Daro gasped. "Your mindlock, your creatures, you can't—"

"Fuck you, Chief. So what if they go? There are plenty more where they came from."

Daro squatted next to her friend and, trying to sound encouraging, said, "It worked. It was not for naught. The Tsing fleet is burning. We'll move as soon as the flames clear up."

"I can't," Aurélien cried. "I can't do this, not like this. You didn't go through anything like this. You don't know! You didn't have to sacrifice thousands of your own kind to—"

"They are not your kind, Aurélien. *We* are your kind. Us, our squad, whatever is left of it, along with those who fight with us. The Cabal. Like you said, there are thousands more seals in the Alommo Sea, for Takh's sake. Once we sail in, you'll be able to—"

"You don't understand!" Aurélien screeched. "Don't you feel it? When they suffer, don't you feel it with them?"

"Of course I've felt it. When learning to wear them, we all felt it. And we also learned to control it."

The ermine sat on the cold floorboards. She thought about placing an arm on Aurélien's shoulders, but instead wrapped her arms around her own knees.

"You are not one of them," Daro said, more quietly. "The masks, they make you see things that aren't true. If you had worn a different mask, you'd feel differently. You'd think you were one of the bats, or horses, or whatever."

"It's not just about the pinnipeds," Aurélien said. "Before them, I felt… I have a different way of seeing things. I feel a stronger connection, like the one I have with Islav and Aness, but toward everything, toward everyone. Don't you feel it in those threads?"

"Like I said, you learn to push those feelings away. What's the point of feeling pain for everything? It'd make you useless. You'd let the mucks, the maggots, the spurs rule over you. You'd stop eating, stop fighting, stop working toward our common cause."

Aurélien did not respond.

Daro grabbed Gwonlesilv and examined its filigreed curves. "If it pains you so much, and you don't think you'll be able to send your soldiers out, we can see if Osef or Muriel—"

"Don't you fucking dare!" Aurélien snapped, snatching the mask from Daro. "Don't you dare take it from me. You know how it would feel."

The ermine lifted her handpaws in surrender, then stood up. "Stop being a hypocrite," she said, slowly walking away. "You've commanded thousands of human archers to fight and die before. You've killed hundreds of enemies with your own arrows. You're a killer. We all are. It's the reason we are still alive. Now put on your mask and come up to the deck. We'll sail through the strait shortly, and we might need the aid of your creatures."

"I'm not ready for—"

"I don't care if you are ready! Do your job, officer. This is not a game. These are not your pets. These are soldiers, and we have a war to win. Command them to fight, or relinquish your rank and your claim to the mask."

CHAPTER FIFTY-EIGHT

PURPLE LIGHTNING

It was the twilight before dawn when the Cabal ships sailed through the wreckage of the Tsing fleet. The Alvforg Strait was littered with uncountable shards of the destroyed ships, many still burning. The surviving pinnipeds who could still swim had fled as far from the red-sailed ships as they could, never to return to the horrors they had witnessed in these waters.

Aurélien was holding tight to her robe, with Gwonlesilv by her chest. She could have put the mask on to stop the cold with her fur, but she could not bring herself to do so. She didn't want to feel the lingering threads around her. The smoke smelled like grilled fish and burnt hair, sickening her.

"Put your mask on, Aurélien," Daro said, stepping behind her. She was polishing Whisper's stock, making the sandalwood of her crossbow shine like marble. "You need to start gathering soldiers again. We'll need them soon." She let her weapon drop, dangling it on her shoulder by the strap.

"The only ones left are too burned to be useful to you, Chief Daro," Aurélien hoarsely replied. "Leave me be."

Under the light of a sputtering fire, Aurélien saw a seal float by, scorched and pink. Eyes burnt and lidless, the seal flapped a hopeless flipper into the water.

Aurélien vomited onto the deck, then sat on a crate by the mainmast. Daro stared at her, as if waiting for an answer to an unasked question.

"I'll do what needs to be done," Aurélien said with bile in her voice. "I'll help us win this war. But after that, I want this to stop."

"This? Stop what?" Daro asked, standing in front of her. She felt something streak by her ear—a clump of ashes, perhaps. She ignored it.

"I want to stop this pointless killing. Once our new empire is established, I want Gwonlesilv to be used for good. I want to keep it, without conditions."

"We don't know what's coming after this. How could we ever promise something like that?"

"If we win, you'll have all the masks you could possibly want. Leave this one to me. Leave my kind alone. If we don't win, then there's no reason to argue either way."

"Fine, suit yourself." Daro tossed her arms into the air. "Go live on a fucking island. Go live under the ocean, if that suits you. Eat raw fish, piss where you sleep, whatever you want. But don't bail on me, because we need you right now."

"I'm not a traitor. I'm not a quitter. I'll do what needs to be done, but I'll trust that you'll follow through with your promise."

"Put your mask on," Daro quickly commanded.

"I'm not ready for—"

"Put the bloody mask on! Something is wrong."

Instead of brightening with the approach of dawn, the sky was darkening. Daro felt something fly past her again. Her keen ears sharpened toward a high-pitched sound, too quiet and yet too loud at the same time.

A cloud of bats slammed into their ship like a rain of volcanic rocks.

Aurélien felt something pull on her arm—a desmodus giant vampire bat, nearly as large as herself, had grabbed on to Gwonlesilv and was trying to fly away with it. Smaller bats slammed into her body, shattering their faces and wings, leaving red splatters on her white robes.

"Let go! Scorch you, piece of shit!" she screeched at the giant bat, but two more of the same kind arrived and dug their claws into the mask and into Aurélien's garments. The bats tried to fly away with her, but even three of them were not strong enough to lift an adult body.

Blood sprayed on Aurélien's face. The three bats toppled over, split in half. Silv-Thaar Daro stood there, holding a short sword streaked with red. She held it up, trying to use it as a shield to block the barrage of smaller wings.

"Put your mask on, now!" she commanded, but Aurélien could not hear her.

Daro grabbed Aurélien's arm and pulled at it, running in the same direction as the torrent of bats. She slammed her body over the deck's railings and dragged Aurélien down in a spiraling tumble.

They crashed hard into the cold water.

Aurélien sank in the blackness. The flames of burning flotsam told her which way was up. She saw Gwonlesilv floating there on the surface, out of reach. She swam for it, feeling useless without her flippers, cold without her fur, heavy with the robes around her body. A pair of shadowy wings blocked the light, landing atop the Silv.

Aurélien hurled herself up with one last push and wedged her fingers through the mask's eyeholes, pulling it down, bringing with it the enormous bat. They struggled under the water, a tangle of white cloth and black wings. Aurélien grabbed on to the slender limbs of the creature and snapped them like twigs, feeling the bat's fangs pierce her shoulder. She tugged hard on the mask until the bat's claws let go, then she placed it on her face and immediately took her leopard seal half-form. She bit hard on the bat's skull, cracking it like an egg, then swam up for air.

Daro was floating next to her, eyes on the sky.

"The fuck's happening?" Silv-Thaar Knivlar gasped.

"Get down!" Daro yelled. They both dove. Bats battered the surface of the water like hail.

Knivlar circled Daro, let her grab on to her neck, and swam far from the flagship before resurfacing.

The bats focused on swarming the ships, searching, littering the decks with their bodies as they collided against any humans they could find. Each of the formations of chiropterans trailed a red-painted leader, who was the first to sacrifice themselves before the others followed suit.

"Fucking Alvis Hallow," Daro swore. "That cocksucker sent his new toys after us."

"Shit, they've seen us!" Knivlar warned. "There's a bigger one coming."

They dove again. Knivlar took them away from the Cabal fleet, headed to the remnants of a Tsing carrack she hoped they would remain hidden behind.

"It's so cold," Daro said after they'd resurfaced, gulping for fresh air. "I won't be able to stay in this water for—"

"Is that Fjorna I'm hearing?" came a sneering voice from someone, something, perched at the top of a shattered, half-burnt hull. "You filthy traitor, it *is* you," the voice added. It sounded oddly familiar. Daro and Knivlar focused their Silvesh's sights toward the speaker and saw a distinct aura, shattered and obscure, like purple lightning.

"Korten?" Daro asked through chattering teeth.

"Silv-Thaar dus Fer, if you will," the spectacled flying fox replied. He was no more than a shadow wrapped within shadowy wings.

It was hard to see anything in the darkened sky, but Daro's ears offered her a warning. "Down!" she commanded, and they both sank again. As soon as they were underwater, a rain of bats pummeled the surface at full force, like a flock of gannets plunging for fish.

They swam away again, aiming for another wreck. This time, they surfaced underneath an upturned hull, peering through cracks in the wood. They could hear screeches all around—the bats had followed them.

"How did they see us underwater?" Daro asked.

"It's Korten," Knivlar said. "He can see our auras."

Silv-Thaar dus Fer hovered above them, directing his troops. Soon a cloud of bats landed on the hull and stuck there like toothy barnacles, pushing at the wreckage, slowly tipping it over.

"We'll have to go deeper to escape his sight," Knivlar said. "Hold tight," she added, and swam down, taking Daro with her.

They plunged deep. Deep enough that Daro felt her head would implode. She shook her arms and tried to scream, but she had little air to do so. Her lungs felt like they were collapsing. Knivlar pulled up again, having brought them near the safety of their fleet.

They could not spot the *Ballista*—it could have been anywhere in this darkness—but they agreed that any ship would do for protection. The cloud of bats was not so dense here, comprised only of confused stragglers who had survived the impacts, though the water was littered with twitching, membranous wings.

"Over here!" Daro called to the nearest ship. "Toss us a rope!"

"Chief?" a soldier called out, stupefied. "Stay right where you are!"

It was easier said than done, as the ships were all sailing forward. Knivlar swam alongside to keep up, leaving a wake of dead bats behind her.

"Shit, he's back!" Daro warned. Silv-Thaar dus Fer was flying toward them, sending forth red-painted leaders who were followed by deadly clouds.

A rope ladder splashed into the water. Knivlar grabbed it and began to climb, then looked down. Daro was holding on to the rope ladder, but not climbing it. She kept her arms below the water.

"What are you doing? Climb, now!" Knivlar urged, watching the cloud approach with dus Fer in the middle of it.

Silv-Thaar Daro lifted her arms above the water and aimed Whisper, a heavy bolt already nocked into its yak sinew drawstring. She pressed the trigger and felt the satisfactory *tch-clang!* as the bolt flew, leaving a trail of salty droplets behind it.

The bolt streaked through the darkness, exploding two small bats before slamming into Silv-Thaar dus Fer's left wing. The membranous tissue ripped violently, leaving a head-sized hole between his long, skeletal fingers. The spectacled flying fox tumbled and splashed into the water.

"The seals, send your seals!" Daro screamed toward Knivlar, but Knivlar could sense no pinnipeds to send toward dus Fer.

Daro ducked underwater to avoid the rain of bats, then resurfaced after their impact. She began to reload her crossbow, struggling with her cold-numbed fingers; all the while the creatures chewed on her neck like ticks. She heard a pathetic call for aid from dus Fer, who flapped hopelessly in the water while a tornado of bats gathered over his body.

Daro fitted a bolt into the flight groove. Her arms went up once more. As Whisper breached the water's surface, she saw dus Fer weakly rising into the air, aided by half a dozen of the giant bats, all struggling to find a place to sink their claws, to flap their wings, to pull the Silv-Thaar into the air.

Daro pressed the trigger. The bolt splattered through the whirling mass of chiropterans, impacting the ribs of one of the giants. The creature screeched a wet hiss and fell to the water, but five more pulled their cargo into the safety of the sky.

Dus Fer disappeared into the east, as if carried by a dark waterspout.

PART SIX

YENMAI

CHAPTER FIFTY-NINE

AN ELAND'S DEMANDS

The wayfarers were helping load *Fjummomurr*, carrying crates full of supplies while also slowly saying goodbye to many of the friends they'd made over the past several weeks. They were to leave that evening for the sovereign lands of the Yenwu, where before entering the Yenwu Dome, they first planned to pay a visit to Professor Lai-Nu.

Admiral Brannoa of the Wisent was also preparing her ship, the *Oakhoof*, a merchant knarr which had been retrofitted for battle. *Oakhoof* was to lead the way out of the dome, carrying the barrels of soot that would serve as payment to the Tsing Empire for the new lands the Tjardur would soon be resettling upon. Brannoa would join the wayfarers through the Gulf of Erjilm, to then part ways at the Bay of Hashmun, sailing the Stiss Galha and the Vardal Canal all the way to the capital. Most of the other Tjardur ships would follow toward Hashan soon after, once the vines were more fully opened, while the majority of the bovids—including the heavier companion species not suitable for ships— would travel by land.

"I wish Pamúnn could travel with us too," Sterjall said to Lune.

"The feral bovids will need him more than we will. And he is too proud and skittish to climb aboard a contraption like this one. Nelv, Gwit, and Ishke'ísuk will be with us for protection, do not worry."

Servant Speros arrived to say his farewells. "It has been my honor, *hurff!*" the eland said. He was already dressed for battle, even though it would likely take the Tjardur army months to reach the Tsing capital of Hashan—they still hoped to arrive before the Red Stag made his move.

Speros was one of several servants assigned to escort Pamúnn, who would also travel with the battalions of bovids. The Nu'irg's priority was not war, however, but helping the feral species spread as they marched east and north.

"Head strong you are, *khumm*," Servant Lune said to Speros. "In great company Pamúnn will be. Until our horns meet again!"

"Head strong!" Speros exclaimed. He clenched a fist under his chin, a gesture he had learned during his brief excursion to the Tsing Empire. He glanced toward Alaia. Instead of clenching his fist in front of her, Speros delicately grabbed her hand. "May your hides be inscribed with stories of truth, and may they be worthy of song," he said, and leaned down to plant a soft kiss on her knuckles.

"As long as my hides aren't turned into a pillow or a saddle, I think I'll be happy," she responded, failing to hide her sheepish grin.

Once all the supplies were loaded, Lune kissed her six husbands and nine wives farewell—they would remain at the Four Blessings with other servants and citizens who had chosen to protect their homeland from within rather than joining the war beyond.

"Let's go! I need to see Sunnokh again!" Dart belted out. "You seen him yet, Lune?" the chipmunk asked, overflowing with energy as he climbed the ratlines.

"No, child," Lune said. "The only time I was outside this dome, it was in the middle of the night, when I spent a large portion of my time bleeding and unconscious. But I did briefly glimpse Sceres's pink face."

"You have to see Sunnokh then!"

"Sceres is prettier," Puuja said. "And it's my turn to wear Okrisilv, you've had it all day."

"If you can catch me!" Dart said, climbing to the crow's nest in the blink of an eye.

Pollomekh-Dart had become a lot more outspoken since finding his half-form, though while in his human form he was still reserved and shy. Together with Puuja-Gorget, they tried to evenly split their time allotted to wear Okrisilv, though Sunu-Lummukem would often intervene, as the twins were still prone to the usual sibling scuffles and disagreements.

The brother and sister were wearing their new Bra'uur steel armor, which Chawól had speedily customized for their half-forms. The helms looked a bit odd on them while in their human forms, but a strap kept them in place. They both looked fierce, despite the way the heavy armor pulled down on their bodies.

"Ye better board yer asses, all of ye!" Captain Siffo called out. "Don't make me start a-singing!"

The stragglers followed Siffo's command and boarded *Fjummomurr*.

The Puqua sailors were in a great mood, singing shanties and some even dancing while they readied the ship. They had spent nearly a month mingling with the Tjardur at Sinsimbo, making lasting friendships while learning from one another. Though the Puqua were sad to leave the wonderful port town of green-and-black marble, they did not feel too sorrowful, as eight Tjardur sailors—one from each clan—had been chosen to join *Fjummomurr*'s crew. All of them were excited to see the New World.

Two laboring rowboats towed *Fjummomurr* clear of the docks, then the ship set its black sails to the wind. Captain Siffo directed the crew to follow Admiral Brannoa's knarr. The ships drifted between the enormous Horns of Valor.

"Head strong!" sailors in fishing skiffs around them called out.

"Head strong!" the Puqua bellowed passionately.

"And tusk strong!" a part-babirusa sailor added.

Fjummomurr and *Oakhoof* sailed into the Keldris Troméia, then made their way through the wall of vines.

Admiral Theggo Saurfall met them at the port of Ngau Tor.

"Where is your ship?" Sterjall asked Theggo, disembarking from *Fjummomurr*.

"Nice to see you too, Lorr Vaari. My fleet is too large for this port. We are anchored south of the city."

"Admiral, my eyes are happy to see you again!" Kulak said, trailing behind Sterjall. "We have much to tell you."

"And I have plenty to discuss with you." The fleet admiral flinched, moving out of the way of an armored chipmunk that was rushing down *Fjummomurr*'s ramp. "And I see Puuja at last found her half-form!"

"That is Dart, actually," Puuja said, trying to catch up to her brother, who was already climbing the overwater bungalows to reach their straw tops.

"Who in the Holy Scrolls is Dart?" Theggo asked.

The wayfarers made their way to a bungalow so they could sit down while debriefing Theggo.

"There's a great force of Tsing soldiers already gathered by the north end of the Ashen Dome," Theggo said. "They'll be there to escort the Tjardur, providing supplies, wagons, beasts of burden—"

Sterjall interrupted him, "Did you make sure—"

"Yes, I made sure. Only horses and caribou are pulling their wagons, no bison. A portion of the Tsing will show the Tjardur the safest route to Hashan, while the rest escort a group east to Mount Alvforg."

"Supplies for the long road are greatly appreciated," Lune said, "but we mostly have no need for animals to carry us, as we are just as fast and tireless as our feral bovids, *khum*. We hope your soldiers will be able to keep up with us."

"They are all mounted themselves, so they'll be able to keep up. Did your clan leaders accept the price for the lands?"

"We certainly did, Admiral Theggo of the Republic!" Admiral Brannoa interjected. "Two tons of soot are packed in my ship's hold, ready to be delivered, *grroomph!*"

"Two tons? Did the empress not request only half that much?"

"Call it proof of our commitment to the alliance," Brannoa said.

Ambassador Vor-Vor leaned his elbows on the table and addressed Theggo. "Fleet Admiral, I will need to travel with the Silvfröash to grant them access to the Yenmai Institute, so that they may speak with the professor there. My own ship and crew I'll need, as well as my shamans. You, on the other hand... Once we cross the gulf, I think it will be time for the Lerevi fleet to move ahead of us all, toward the capital, where we'll all meet next."

"Understood. Captain Mareesha is already there." He shifted his tone suddenly. "Regarding the Red Stag, last we heard, he had already left the Scoria Dome. No one could get close enough to his army, but he seems to be followed by a dark cloud now."

"He captured the mask," Sterjall grumbled.

"It would seem so," Theggo continued. "But he has a very long road ahead of him. If he wants to keep his troops supplied while on the move, it will take him at least a couple of months to reach the Nargara Bastion."

"By the time he gets to the bastion," Vor-Vor said, "we'll be waiting for him with an army of Tjardur, Lerevi, and perhaps Murtégo Miscam as well, if the Yenwu Dome inhabitants agree to join us. We will not allow the Negian army to step into our territories."

"What about Fjorna?" Sterjall asked.

"The Cabal still controls the stolen Negian fleet," Theggo said. "They've joined forces with Afhora, and used their seals to defeat the Tsing at the Alvforg Strait. They made it into the Alommo Sea."

"Seals to defeat the Tsing fleet?" Sterjall asked, incredulous. "How did they—"

"I will tell you later. It is too gruesome a tale for some present." He snuck a glance toward the twins. "But suffice to say, the Cabal are waiting at the

Afhoran shores. I'm not certain what Silv-Thaar Daro's next move will be, but they are too far away for us to worry about right now."

After their gathering concluded, while Theggo was untying Tinnomeg's reins in preparation for returning to his flagship, Servant Lune called for his attention.

"One-horned and proud," she said, stepping closer to the eland to caress the rough spot of his severed horn. "His breed is different from the feral elands we have in Trommodrolom. Smaller hump, darker neck fur."

"You know, I'm glad you came my way," Theggo began, "because I wanted to—"

"Yes, Sterjall of the Wolf has informed me. You once told him you'd like to say some words to this beautiful bovid, and as a servant, I would be happy to help you do so. What is the name you call him?"

"Tinnomeg," Theggo said. "And yes, I very much would like to—"

"Tinnomeg… He says he likes the name you gave him, but he wants you to learn his true name."

Tinnomeg lowered his head, then scratched the ground with his forefeet three times, making his knees click.

"*Khummm,*" Lune said. "He says his true name is"—she clicked her tongue three times in quick succession, mimicking the pattern the eland had produced.

"Those clicking sounds he makes when he walks are words? I thought elands just had bad knees." He tried repeating the pattern with his tongue, and Tinnomeg corrected him, clicking his knees once more.

Theggo bowed lightly. "I will do my best to call him by his true name from now on."

"What message did you want me to convey to him?" Lune asked.

"Simply… my gratitude," the admiral replied, bowing with a hand on his chest. "Tinnomeg has been with—sorry, I mean"—he clicked his tongue three times—"has been a trustworthy companion for well over a decade. I wish him to know that I treasure him, that I am thankful for his friendship, that I owe him greatly for having saved me during the battle with the new theocracy. And I want him to know I am sorry for the loss of his horn, that I wish I had parried the axe that claimed it."

"He says he will consider accepting your apology," Lune communicated, "although only under certain conditions."

Theggo straightened up. "Anything he wishes, of course."

Lune stared at him intently. "Lorr Saurfall, he wants you to know that he despises the metallic taste of his bridle. The bit stuck in his mouth is unbecoming and unnecessary, for he can sense you pulling on the reins well enough from the hornband alone. He also says he prefers it when you wear leather boots without the metallic greaves, and that the cinch of his saddle is more comfortable when farther up his chest, and that he prefers the deck of *Silverweave* to the stinking hold."

"I am terribly sorry, I never knew—"

"And he also says it is past his feeding time. And now that he can finally say so directly, he wants you to know he likes to browse as much as graze—he dislikes a diet of only grasses. He needs shrubs, leafy plants. He says you should try eating that dry dung you feed him, and see if you like it."

Theggo swallowed and nodded. "I had no idea. I-I feel like an utter fool. I will do my best to accommodate his request." He rubbed the bridge of his nose, unable to face the eland. "Servant Lune, do you think... Do you think he will be able to forgive me?"

"*Khumph.* Perhaps. Depending on what you find him for lunch, and how expediently you do so. Hurry now, Lorr Saurfall of the *Silverweave*, and make amends with your trusted friend. I am glad I was able to be of service to you."

CHAPTER SIXTY

AGAINST THE WIND

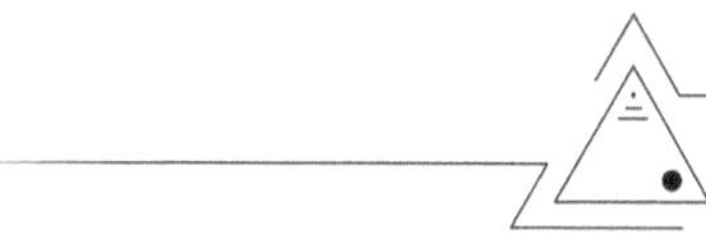

Fjummomurr and *Silverweave* sailed side by side, closely followed by *Oakhoof*, as well as by Vor-Vor's *Canvasback*, and a large portion of the Lerevi fleet. Against the wind they sailed, and though the gusts were not in their favor, still they progressed steadily through the Gulf of Erjilm.

"Watch it!" Sterjall barked at Pol, who had nearly bludgeoned him with his quarterstaff while he practiced with Gorget and Lummukem. The sounds of the twins training had woken the wolf up before dawn; he would have remained in bed, except that he had seen a big shadow headed up to the deck and had chosen to follow it.

Sterjall glanced around and did not find who he was looking for, but then tilted his head back, and up in *Fjummomurr*'s crow's nest spotted the bulky figure. He hesitated for a moment, then gripped the ratlines and climbed. He panted lightly as he made it to the top, then leaned playfully next to the buffalo. "They are getting so much better with that," he said, watching the twins practice. "Are you waiting for Sunnokh?"

Lune nodded nearly imperceptibly. The previous morning, Sunnokh had been obscured behind the dome. She was eagerly waiting to see her first sunrise today, from as high up as possible, but the star had not shown his face yet. She unglued her eyes from the eastern horizon and looked down for a moment. "The twins learn very quickly," she said. "I see they have picked up some moves from Ogóre. And Lummukem is a great teacher, *khumm*."

"We'd all be dead if it wasn't for their lessons. Without Agnargsilv, I'm not much of a fighter, though I'm trying my best."

Gorget somersaulted over Lummukem, trying to slam her quarterstaff down with a Bounding Frog maneuver, but the dragon easily parried with a Nacre Shroud, not even looking in her direction. Above them, Olo hovered in the breeze, as if studying the battle.

"Khest, Gorget can really jump," Sterjall said to Lune.

The two of them watched the twins for a bit longer. After a few more showy leaps, Puuja handed over Okrisilv, and Dart began to demonstrate his prowess. The twins had grown a small audience of Puqua and Tjardur sailors, so they worked hard to impress them. The chipmunk ran along the rigging and mast as if on flat ground, climbing and perching with ease, trying to attack Lummukem from all sides.

"Little Dart is as fast as a galloping tetracerus," Lune observed, "but also equally innocent."

Lummukem blocked all of Dart's attacks, even when Puuja tried to help her brother. The twins next tried a coordinated attack, and at last Puuja scored a hit, though it was merely on Lummukem's quaar tail armor.

"You must move faster," they heard Lummukem say, their voice carried by the wind.

"It's not fair," Puuja complained. "Our new armor is heavy!"

"Servant Lune wears armor ten times heavier, and she complains not. Try again, and grow stronger, grow faster."

The twins resumed their attacks with much more ferocity. Sooner or later, Lummukem would be hit hard, but they were ready for it.

"I wish Agnargsilv had given me abilities like that," Sterjall said. "I do feel more limber with my wolf legs, and the tail helps for balance, but I can't jump or climb like that."

"The greatest gift the Silvesh offer us is the chance to better understand ourselves," Lune replied gently. Her green eyes bounced between the twins and the beauty of the brightening sea around her. "What brings you up so high, Sterjall of the Wolf? It is quite early for you to be awake."

"I just noticed you like to come up here, and thought—"

"You thought this would be the best place to speak in private, *khumm.*"

"Yeah… I… I wanted to ask more about what happened that night, at the Pink Caldera, but—"

"But you do not want Aio-Kulak to find out more than what you have so far told him."

"Are you going to keep finishing my sentences? And how did you know I talked to him?"

"I apologize, *khumm*. And I simply assumed. Go on, Canid Lorr."

"You don't need to call me that. It's strange, you know. All we did, and you are still so formal with me sometimes."

"I am your servant. It is in my nature."

Sterjall looked up at her. The buffalo towered over him, even more when he focused on her single horn. "I know you are a servant, but that's not all you are," he softly protested.

"I am a friend, yes. But a servant nonetheless, and a proud one. What is it that you wanted to ask about?"

"Well, it's just a concern I didn't even have in mind that evening, but—"

"You are wondering if any of the guests or servants could have become pregnant from what we did."

"You are doing it again…"

"Apologies," Lune replied curtly but not unkindly. "It is a concern all your friends had as well, since none of you were familiar with our customs, so I've spoken with them in private to reassure them."

"You have? And what did you tell them? Since you took Rud's form after what we did, I guess that would not be a problem for you? But I haven't had the courage to ask Crysta and Hefra what their experiences were like, so I'm concerned about them."

"Each of them had the exact same question, and to each I answered in the same way I will answer you, *khummmph*." She put a hand on her belly, on her udders, and continued. "None of the servants nor guests can conceive children, not unless we perform the ceremony in a particular way. Remember the bitter drink you all took after leaving the sacred pools?"

Sterjall nodded.

"It's made from the fruit of Themenn-Vaurvon. It not only releases you from the pink mist's trance, but it prevents female-born guests from holding on to the seed of servants, or female-born servants from holding on to the seed of guests, *harkhumm*. If as servants we aim to conceive, as a favor to our guests, we also partake in the visions of desire you experienced, as the fruit of Themenn-Vaurvon is in those cases not within us—we do not eat it, nor do we drink its nectar."

"That… eases my worries, thank you. How do the pink mists work? I still don't fully understand what happened that night. It's so hard to even talk about it… And I haven't… I still can't find a way to tell Kulak about… you know."

Lune glanced down at him, but Sterjall couldn't tell if her expression was judgmental or simply concerned. After a long pause, she said, "Regarding your question—it is simple, though I am sure there are more complexities to the answer. Our artificers say that nox, what you call aetheric nitrogen, rushes to one's heart and brain and opens the floodgates of desire. Inhibitions are shattered, and the mind is left to see what it wants to see, without the pressure of expectations. Nox often reveals the subjects' half-forms, as well as other sides of themselves they might not have been aware of. This is why most Tjardur can easily share Trommosilv, as they already know themselves better."

"I can't imagine what it's like for you, having to share the mask with others all the time."

"That is not as hard as it may seem. Believe it or not, I envy you, Sterjall of the Wolf."

Sterjall waited for a clarification.

Lune slipped an arm around him and added, "It is easy for me to give Trommosilv up, to serve others. It is my calling, and it brings me joy. When Trommosilv leaves me, I can be Rud, and Rud and Lune are not that different from one another, even though I much prefer the female form. But one thing that I have not been, and I always have wanted to be, is a plain-skinned human. You, Lago-Sterjall, can be both, while I will never know what it is like to be like Lago."

"It's not that special, really. I like being a wolf a lot more."

"You say so, but do you mean it?"

Sterjall did not have to think too long about it. "No." He shook his head. "I feel like both forms are me, and each one gives me something different."

Lune nodded and put her arm back on the handrail.

A long moment passed as the horizon brightened. Lune held her breath in expectation. Then, in a piercing flare, Sunnokh blinked awake from his slumber and caressed Lune's single horn, then her glistening eyes. His touch was a welcome respite after the coldness of twilight.

Sterjall's whiskers lifted as he watched her smile. He leaned his shoulder on her for a moment, and then his handpaw reached for her thick arm, caressing it.

Lune had to look away from the brilliance of the star, her eyes pulsing with his refulgent image. She glanced down at Sterjall's trembling handpaw and said, "You may speak your mind with me, Sterjall of the Wolf."

He swallowed, feeling his paw pads sweating. "I was wondering if… if you'd be"—he clumsily cleared his throat—"willing to t-try it again. What we did at the Pink Caldera, after the other servants left."

Lune tried to catch the wolf's gaze, but his eyes were lost toward the sea, unfocused, unable or unwilling to face her.

"This was my fear that night, *khummmmmmmmm*," she said with the longest grunt she had yet released in his presence. "You must understand, what we did at the caldera was a gift from our kind to yours. They were illusions, truthful ones, but ones merely meant to awaken something within you, so that you may find your own paths without the need of servants in the future."

"What happened at that last moment wasn't an illusion."

"*Khumph.* I am a married woman, and a married man, Sterjall of the Wolf. If you ask me to serve you, I will serve you. If you ask me to love you, I already do. If you ask for more, I cannot provide that. Some Tjardur awakenings end with the same conundrum, when the guests lack experience and become overly attached. Some even ask for marriage. But you should know better."

"I wasn't asking for marriage."

"I know what you are asking for, Canid Lorr. I feel that it is not I who you must speak to. It is to Aio-Kulak, whom you have kept in the dark about what happened that night."

"And what will that accomplish? It'll just upset him."

"Perhaps. But you love each other, do you not? You must trust one another."

"So, you wouldn't—"

"No, I am sorry. I have served you well, and I admit that I enjoyed it myself, though we serve for others and not for our own pleasure. I apologize that I can't be of further assistance in that regard. You will one day understand."

She leaned down, kissed Sterjall on the lips, then climbed back down to the deck.

CHAPTER SIXTY-ONE

TWO CRESCENTS

The ships continued sailing north through the Gulf of Erjilm, the horizon to starboard extending endlessly as they passed the massive Bay of Hashmun. The breeze was as chill as the lights of the pharoliths illuminating *Fjummomurr*'s deck.

Sterjall leaned against the ship's foremast, hiding under its thick shadow. From his higher vantage point, he observed the motions on the main deck, but his mind was elsewhere. *I shouldn't have asked her,* he berated himself. *Why can't I be content with all I have?* His eyes drifted toward Aio, who was next to the cockboat, feeding Blu, Pichi, and Nelv a dinner of fresh munnji cakes—they had fully replenished their supply while at the Ashen Dome, finding a particular formulation of the paste that appealed to the felids. Sterjall saw Aio smile as Blu nearly choked on a big bite, and smiled with him. He shapeshifted, unaware that he'd been taking his human form whenever he saw Aio-Kulak do the same, then absently caressed the canid mask. *He deserves better than me.*

He heard laughter and leaned forward to get a better view over the forecastle's railing, spotting the twins sitting around a barrel they were using as a table to play a game of Qu. Alaia sat with them—she had taught them all the rules by now, but she was still working on teaching them proper strategies.

Lummukem passed by the three, tail swishing. "Should you not be in bed by now?" they asked, hovering over the board game. The breeze was steady that evening, the voices rising from the deck clear to Lago.

"Not yet. I'm winning this time," Puuja answered.

"Cheating…" Pol mumbled.

"You are the cheater, Pollomekh," she retorted.

"No one has been cheating this time around, not yet," Alaia clarified. "Nuh-uh," she added, stopping Pol from making an illegal move with his Horn. "You can't just take Puuja's Hex like that."

"But then she'll take my last chips," he whined, then made a weak play that only increased his disadvantage. He let go of the magnetic chip and winced when it clicked decisively onto the metallic board.

"Where is your mask?" Lummukem asked, suddenly aware of the absence.

"We left it in our hammock in the 'tween deck, so that Pol would stop cheating," Puuja said. "He keeps trying to feel where I'll move the next chip, that he does."

"And you tried to use it to ask Gwit for help," he parried, staring at the dormouse, who was curled up in a little nest Puuja had made with her braids.

"He doesn't even know the rules! He was just asking what the chips are for. Either way, you lost, brother." As she picked up her Hex to make the final move, Pol "accidentally" bumped the barrel, making it tilt unsteadily; despite his effort, the magnium in the chips held tightly to the board, allowing Puuja to land her finishing blow.

"I'll teach you more advanced strategies tomorrow," Alaia said, picking up the board and Qupi chips. "But now, listen to Lerr Lummukem and head to bed."

Lago shook his head as he watched the twins pretend to hurry down to their quarters, but scurry toward the stern of the ship instead. He attached his mask to his shoulder bracer and returned to being one with the darkness, sitting on the platform circling the foremast. He locked his eyes onto a dim nocturnal glow barely shining through the western clouds.

"Pol is getting better," Alaia said from behind him, startling Lago.

"Better?" he asked.

"You were watching our game, weren't you? I saw your shadow."

"Oh. Just caught a glimpse of it."

She sat next to him, handing him half of the chips so he'd help assemble one of the cubic puzzles. "You should play with them too, they'd enjoy it."

"They don't like me," he said dismissively, eyes still cast westward. "I'm not good with kids." He started to clink the chips together without looking at them.

"Is this about Lune?"

"Wh-what is?" he nearly choked.

"Whatever's had you in a mood since this morning."

"I'm not in a... How did you...?" He exhaled.

"How could I not notice you sulking around like this?"

"I wasn't sulking! I've just been… thinking."

"So it is about her…" she said with new certainty. "You've been avoiding her, and you put on this beaten puppy face when she's near you."

He huffed. "I really don't want to talk about it."

She leaned against his shoulder, then traded her completed Quggon for his jumble of magnetic chips and began to puzzle them together.

"You… You wouldn't understand," he added, as if prompting her.

Alaia wanted to be mad at the modest jab, but she simply smiled, grateful that Lago had been the one to push the conversation further.

"I may not have a mask," she said, "but that doesn't mean I'm unable to understand your feelings."

"It's not about that. It's about sex."

"About what happened at the Pink Caldera?"

Lago's back tensed up, his eyes briefly widening in unwilling confirmation.

"I know you don't wanna tell me all that happened there, and that's fine," she said, "I don't need all the dirty details. But it still surprises me that it bothers *you* so much." Her eyes darted around cautiously before she whispered, "Is Aio upset about it?"

Lago swallowed and looked away. "I haven't told him either."

Alaia's silence felt more disapproving than any words, so Lago broke it. "Sex is so… stupid, so complicated, so pointless sometimes. So irrational."

"I hear you there," she agreed brightly.

"I don't know how you do it. But it must be so liberating to not care about that, to simply ignore it all. I sometimes wish I could be like you."

She paused, head tilted, then said a touch reproachfully, "I don't simply 'ignore it all,' Gwoli. It's not easy for me either, it's not like it's my choice. Sex simply… doesn't do it for me. I'd been thinking about this for a while, trying to find a way to explain it… Remember Vikkor, that netherturd from Riftside who wouldn't let us borrow his 'precious' whetstone?"

"The one who stank like a bloated corpse?"

"Same one. Back at the mines they called him 'the smoosher.' He had this… thing. He liked to keep muskberries in his pockets and crush them, rolling the pulp in his fingertips, then he'd take his hand out and smell it."

"Disgusting!" Lago snorted. "Why would he even—"

"Who knows? But that was his thing, silently smooshing, then sniffing, always with that ominous grin on his face. I bet it made him magnium-hard too, but no one I know was ever foolish enough to corroborate that theory."

"I'm not sure where this is going."

"I'm getting there. What he did seems so silly and pointless, doesn't it? That's kind of how I see it. Sex, I mean. The handful of times I tried it, I only felt… disinterested, like I couldn't quite grasp the reason why it's so consequential to others. And it's not like I was grossed out—you know I love me some ripe muskberries—but it simply was not for me. And now imagine if most people out there were like Vikkor, and they all liked to smoosh and smoosh odorously around. What can you do but get used to the smell? And sometimes you have to pretend to enjoy it too, but the entire time you are flabbergasted as to why anyone takes pleasure in doing that."

"Smoosher," Lago said with a light chuckle, then composed himself. "That's how you see me?"

"You don't reek that bad. But a little, yes. Either way, what I'm trying to say is that I see where you are coming from, but to me it's the opposite. Sometimes I think it'd be easier to find pleasure in smooshing as well, but I don't think that'll happen for me. I'm really more interested in finding the right person—someone who cares for me, who understands what I like and who I truly am. And if sex does happen, maybe I'll be fine with it then, as long as they don't have that deranged grimace Vikkor had. You've been lucky. You've found your bear and your kitty, and they both understand you."

Lago remained silent as a moon shadow.

"I'm not gonna ask what happened between you and Lune, although I really think you should be talking to Aio about it." She stood up, holding the two Quggons in one hand, satisfied at how they snapped together. "But it's late, and we should all get some rest." She held a hand out, but Lago didn't take it.

"I'll be down there soon," he said.

Alaia nodded and left.

Lago paced around the bow, hands caressing a harpoon cannon. "Smoosher," he murmured with a head shake. The metallic contraption suddenly glistened, and his eyes immediately focused toward the west once more, spotting the source of the light.

"Aio! Over here!" he called immediately, not wanting to overthink things. He soon heard a scramble up the steps. Aio arrived followed by Blu, who was licking his chops to polish his saber-like teeth.

"What is it?" Aio asked.

But the light was gone once more, vanished as quickly as it had appeared.

"It's Sceres. She just went behind clouds again. She'll come back out, give her a moment."

Aio placed an arm around Lago's waist as they waited in the dark. Blu plopped onto the floorboards, purring like a saw. After a long moment chilled by the salty breeze, from behind the clouds appeared a dim but vibrant curve haloed by an iridescent veil. Thawing had begun in Noss, so Sceres was in her Pearl season now, shining with dozens of pastel colors, like a nacre pendant dangling in the sky.

"She is dressed in Pearl!" Aio whispered, pulling Lago tighter. "She looks like Mindreldrolom's sky, only more vibrant, more resplendent."

"You should see her when she's full. Then she *does* look like a real pearl, so round in the sky that you'd think you could reach up and pluck her straight out. But there you have it. I promised I'd show you all her dresses. You first saw her in Obsidian, then in Sulphur, Amethyst, Jade, Tourmaline, and now Pearl. You've seen her in all her glory."

"Nearly a year then," Aio murmured. "But like you say, I still need to see her full. She is too skinny right now, like Lune's horn."

"*Khumm*, my horn is not skinny," a deep voice behind them rumbled.

"Takh!" Lago cursed, his heart skipping a few beats. He avoided fully turning around, but his posture was tense now, and Aio could feel it. Lago tried to focus on the moon but all he could feel was the presence looming behind them.

"Sceres's crescent is much more beautiful than mine," Lune added in a reverential whisper. "She wears all hues at the same time. Perhaps she inhaled her own pink mists, has found herself in full, and has decided to show us all her colors, *khumm*. Seitho-Dovár would be proud to see her like this."

"She does this every year. It's a cycle," Lago said, shattering the magic with his logic.

"Just as we do then," Lune said. "We find new aspects of ourselves all the time, yet we are rarely as brave as Sceres is, who shows herself so openly. We are all so much more than the faces we let others see." She kissed Lago's curly hair, then Aio's bald scalp, right between the pigmented constellations of Lummukem and Kerjaastórgnem. She left then, as quietly as she had arrived.

"She acts a bit odd tonight," Aio observed.

"Yeah, she's odd sometimes," Lago replied evasively.

Sceres briefly blanketed herself with clouds again.

Lago paced around, scratched behind Blu's ears, and looked up toward the starless sky. "Do you think it's true? What she said?"

"Yes, my scalp thinks Sceres is more beautiful than her horn."

"Not that. I mean what she said about finding new aspects of ourselves. Do you think that those are things that have always been within us? Or are they new aspects we develop, or embrace, as we go along with our lives?"

"Your tongue is riddled with riddles. My heart knows you—when you speak vague words like this, you have thoughts that matter, but you know not how to say them."

"I don't know what I'm saying, really. That whole talk of the pink mists just reminded me of that night. Did you feel like you found a different person that evening? Or just a deeper version of the person you already knew?"

"My scalp realized that I like to see others become themselves, which is something I was somewhat aware of, yet never fully understood. I did not see myself as different people, in different half-forms, like Hefra so vividly described to us after. But perhaps finding those half-forms would be easier now, after that experience. Like finding jackal was easy, for I was close to you, to canid forms, and had enough time to think on it, to figure out who I was."

"It was harder for me to find the mountain lion," Lago whispered, "even though I knew all along. It was just hard to let myself go. What do you think you'd be? If you were to wear the other Silvesh. Say, Lune's mask, for example."

"That one is easy. My scalp thinks I would be an aurochs, like Bum-Vaor, with huge balls that dangle down to my knees."

Lago chuckled. "That would be very inconvenient, particularly when wearing a kilt."

"Yet something different would feel good. And you? Which bovid form do you think would fit you best?"

Lago's chest thumped so loudly that he took a step back, afraid Aio might hear his beating heart. "I… I was thinking. It's a bit of an odd one for me, but I thought I—"

Eeaaaarrrggggghhh! came a terrifying, muted wail.

Lago and Aio looked over the forecastle's railing and saw Lune rushing to the ship's lower deck, so they followed her. Deeper down they found a circle of sailors gathering around a thrashing figure.

"We can't get it uff!" one of them said.

The screams continued.

"It's gone!" came a high-pitched voice from the 'tween deck. "Someone stole it!"

Lago and Aio at last made it through the crates and ropes filling the hold and found Lune kneeling next to Hefra, who was rolling on the ground with a dark shape clenched to her face. The buffalo did her best to contain the movements of the stout woman so that she would stop scratching herself.

Lago froze at the sight, remembering the first time Agnargsilv had been stuck to his face, the pain he had felt, and how helpless his arms had been at detaching it. Before Lago had a chance to snap out of the memory, Aio had reached forward and removed Okrisilv from Hefra's face.

"Someone stole our mask!" Puuja cried, hurrying down into the hold, with Pol and Lummukem trailing behind her.

Siffo stomped down as well. "What's a-going un? Who stole what?"

Lune stood up, holding the unconscious woman in her thick arms. Her single horn poked the ceiling, so she ducked as she walked toward the steps. "She needs help," was all she said.

The others followed behind her. Aio saw Puuja and Pol crying, and was about to hand Okrisilv back to them, when Pol rushed to him.

"Give it back!" Pol screeched, thinking it had been Aio who'd taken their mask. "Give it back!" The boy punched at Aio's sides.

"Calm down, Pol," Lummukem said, using their tail to separate the two. "It was not Aio-Kulak who took it, but Lurr Boarmane. Let us help her now, for she is in much suffering."

"To mine quarters," Siffo said, hurrying in front of them. "Bring mour wood fur d'furnace."

They laid Hefra on Siffo's bed. She had scratches all over her neck and arms, and had fallen unconscious.

"How'd this a-happen?" Captain Siffo asked, staring at the woman he so desired lying on his bed, but not in any way he had envisioned since inhaling the pink mists.

Crysta had now joined them as well, nearly weeping with anxiety, unaware of what had happened. Lago pulled her to one side to explain the little they knew.

Hefra suddenly stirred and groaned. She placed her hands on her forehead and convulsed, then retched on the side of the bed.

Gorget was in her half-form now. Seeing Hefra partially awake, she rushed forward and began to beat her small handpaws against her. "Don't you ever take our—"

Lummukem pulled her back. "Not now. Stand back and let her recover."

Pol embraced his sister. They sulked in a corner to watch, their eyes incensed with anger. Gwit was observing as well, although he seemed unsurprised, or perhaps just indifferent.

"*Uuunnhgg…*" Hefra managed to voice. "I… What did… Where am…"

Now that Hefra was conscious, Lune and Lummukem were able to take some of her pain into themselves. The incapacitating agony left her, yet the throbbing numbness remained, leaving the naturalist drowsy and confused. She gradually sat up at the edge of the bed, cringing at the sight of the vomit by her feet. She looked up at the crowd her actions had summoned, then quickly tried to avert her eyes.

Crysta squatted beside her, using a towel to clean up the mess. "What in Takh's two names were you thinking?" she scolded her friend. "Stealing the mask from children? How low can you—"

"I wasn't stealing it!" Hefra nearly spat. "I… I…" she let a tear fall, perhaps one of pain, of shame, or both. "They left it there in the hammock. I just… wanted to know what it was like. I was going to put it back. Thought no one would find out…"

"It's not yours!" Gorget barked.

Lummukem lifted a claw to quiet her.

"This was so, so stupid of you," Crysta said. "And so disrespectful."

"I'm sorry, Crysta, alright?! I wasn't being myself. I was seeing… I kept seeing what I saw that night, at the caldera. I wanted to know if it was really that way, if it really could feel that good. I wasn't thinking. I was a brainless fuck, alright?"

Hefra looked toward the twins, her head waving out of sync with the bobbing of the vessel. "Sorry… Gorget, Pol… I don't expect you two to forgive me. I think I am… am going to…" She collapsed on the bed again and began to snore.

After a short discussion on what to do about Hefra, Siffo volunteered to watch over her through the rest of the night, saying he'd sleep on his couch once more. The others left his quarters.

Sceres was gone now, hiding below the horizon, but the deck was bright with the light of pharoliths, which cast spiderwebs of shadow from the rigging.

Lune looked pensive, leaning heavily on the mainmast. "I believe this might be my fault," she said.

No one answered; they just waited for her next words. Lune shifted into Rud and took off his mask, holding the two-horned figure in front of his single-horned face.

"Perhaps non-Tjardur are too susceptible to the power of the pink mists, *khumph*. Rather than learning something new about yourselves, and feeling content with the discovery, some of you are yearning too eagerly to re-experience it. It is good to want, to seek for the pleasure your bodies desire, but not at the expense of others, not by breaching trust."

"You won't even tell us what you did there," Gorget complained. "What happened at the caldera? Why won't you—"

Lummukem intervened. "We will explain when it is time. For now, please be more careful with Okrisilv."

"You leave Kruwensilv by your side when you sleep, sometimes," Gorget retorted. It was true, and Lummukem knew it to be true.

"We will be more careful as well," the varanus dragon allowed. "We hope Lurr Boarmane properly apologizes and recognizes her mistake, once her senses return to her. In the meantime, we hope you seek within your hearts for forgiveness."

Gorget grunted. Pol echoed the sentiment. They slowly made their way belowdecks to catch some sleep.

As they walked away, Aio put a hand on Lago's shoulder and said, "You never told me. We were talking about which forms we would take if wearing Trommosilv, when Hefra's scream pierced our ears. What was it you were going to say?"

"Oh, that? N-nothing, I mean… I'd probably be a pelorovis, or a longhorn bison. Big horns, I think that would be nice."

"Good. I like that. Big and strong, and hung like Rud," Aio said, and left it at that.

CHAPTER SIXTY-TWO

HEFRA'S DREAM

Siffo sprawled on the couch, finishing his second tankard of a strong braaw as he listened to Hefra's uneven snores. He heard her turning over in bed and peered at her. She seemed at peace, despite the uncomfortable position she was lying in. She was wearing a skirt, something odd for her, as she normally wore thick trousers. Siffo guessed that Hefra had been planning to find her half-form, and had chosen a skirt to make the transition easier in case she grew a tail.

The skirt was curled up, revealing her thighs and the crease where they merged with her buttocks.

The captain lowered his empty tankard, stood up quietly, and inched closer to the bed, tipping with the sway of the ship. He reached for the bedframe and regained his balance.

He gazed at Hefra's exposed legs and thighs and wondered what it would look like if he could only pull that skirt a bit higher. He swallowed, feeling the warmth of the alcohol in his face, the warmth of his blood in his crotch, contrasted against the chill from the glass windows over the bed. He reached forward and pinched the skirt between his thimble-like, hoofed fingertips. He pulled the skirt down, covering the woman, then spread a warm blanket over her.

Siffo threw a few more logs into the furnace, then dozed off on the uncomfortable couch.

Hefra dreamed.

She found herself lying face-up upon a cold table. She felt her arms and legs pinned down, and when she looked at them she saw they were indeed pinned, by enormous metal needles pierced right through her flesh and bone. She felt no pain, however, which allowed her to observe herself with an analytical mind.

Her naked body was splayed open upon the table, and though she knew she was naked, she could not see her skin, nor her fur. She could swear she had fur of some sort, but her eyes would not let her glimpse it. All she could see was her own viscera, drooping outward from between the layers of fat and muscle. Her sternum was cracked open, and her heart and lungs exposed. They breathed not; they pumped not.

She felt a pinch in her gut and flinched, twitching her tail, which she also could not see. Only then did she notice the enormous tweezers, pulling at her insides amid a tangle of blood and unknown tissues.

She saw her intestines extend into a dark sky. They grew so long, they reached so far, that they looked like threads in a loom. The intestines began to braid together and twitch in a helical motion. She recognized the pattern—it was the same motion ivies traced when growing, usually too slow to be detected by less patient observers.

The green tangle that was her insides grew denser, taller; far into the sky it splayed open in an umbellate form. For a heartbeat, in the expanding tendrils she saw the branches of a dragonblood tree, then a barnacle pulsing its feathered cirri outward, then the mycelium of a sprouting mushroom. The patterns grew in complexity until they became a fractal tangle so dense that their smallest details were lost.

She saw more. The dendritic pattern above was that of bronchioles in a lung, and they were breathing. No, they were a vascular system, iron-filled, oxygen-rich. That was wrong, too, or perhaps all answers were correct. It was a network of neurons. No, larger. Her viscera had formed into a spine—a lattice of entwined axons braiding a thick, sinewy nerve, which split above into the smaller tendrils of a complex nervous system.

The entire cladogram that was displayed above her kept shifting forms in her mind, binding, undoing, becoming. The tendrils expanded suddenly, not only outward, but inward, with a darkened circle growing smaller at the center.

She was looking at an enormous, domed iris, as if she was inside of it, looking out through the hole in the center. The pupil opened toward a field of endless stars.

With every saccadic motion of her eyes, the domed eye in the sky moved as well, looking out and looking in. She tried to direct her gaze, the eye's gaze, until it was aligned directly above her. The eye looked in both directions, so that Hefra saw herself, naked and cut open upon the cold table, while seeing the stars at the same time.

She was black as charcoal, just a lump of burnt organic matter. The only color came from her red, opened chest and belly. Her body fed the skies, and the skies fed back into her body.

Soot, she thought. *My body is not charcoal, but soot.*

Although lidless, the eye in the sky blinked. The blink brought forth not mere darkness, but the everlasting darkness of the Endfall itself.

Hefra swallowed a forced breath and woke herself up, choking on a snore. She felt her head pulsing, each throb invoking a circular afterimage at the center of her vision. The elusive circle in front of her was not perfect; its edges stretched into branches. The tentacles extended as if searching for answers, but before any answers were forthcoming, the afterimage had vanished, as had her memory of the dream.

"Yer up!" Siffo exclaimed from his seat by the oval table. He had a map of the Yenwu Peninsula spread open in front of him, next to an enamel pot that steamed alongside two mugs. "Coffee's a-ready, if ye wish t'partake."

Hefra nodded with a weak smile.

The day was painfully bright when Hefra exited Siffo's quarters. She shuffled to the bow and leaned on one of the whaling harpoons, watching a few small islands pass by. The winds were still against them, but the ships kept on masterfully tacking against the elements, forcing the pressure on their keels to drive them forward.

Her eyes drifted up, as if expecting to find the blue sky be nothing but a branching iris with a dark pupil at its center. She didn't know why she thought that. Either way, she found no darkness there, merely blues with scattered clouds.

"Weird dreams?" Sterjall asked from behind her.

Hefra jolted backward, making the harpoon turn and screech. She grabbed the heavily ornamented piece of metal and rotated it back to how she had found it.

"You could say that, whiskers."

Sterjall moved to lean on the other harpoon and stared at the self-conscious woman. "The Silvesh tend to do that. They change something in our minds, but they also prevent us from seeing too much. I think it's some means of protection, the same way the pain is intended to safeguard the masks from those who should not wear them."

"I know, I'm sorry," she began, taking the hint. "I'm going to apologize properly as soon as everyone's awake."

"Just… be glad. Be glad you did not take it to the next level."

"How so? What do you mean?"

"I wore Agnargsilv for the first time when I was just twelve, and I had those strange dreams right after. The mask did something to me, but not quite the same as what it did to me when I truly began to wear it, six years later. During those in-between years, I merely felt a light curiosity about trying it on again. But after that…" Sterjall moved farther toward the bow, leaning over the narwhal figurehead.

"After that, once Agnargsilv truly got a hold of me, it changed me. Deeply. I don't have the strength of the Tjardur—I don't think any of us do. If my mask were to be taken from me, it would feel like someone was ripping me in half. I am not Lago, nor Sterjall, I am both. If you had found yourself transformed by the mask, you would've lived the rest of your life unhappy, unable to experience that other side of yourself again. Unless you truly took the mask away from the twins, and let the two of them be the ones to suffer."

"I wasn't thinking of doing that, I swear."

"I know. You weren't thinking at all, that's the problem." Sterjall kept his tone harsh and resolute. "Be more careful next time," he added as he turned and walked away. "But don't worry too much, I think the twins will learn to forgive you."

CHAPTER SIXTY-THREE

GULLS A-CALLING

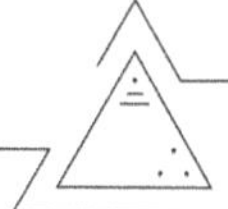

Fjummomurr sailed swift as a cormorant due northwest, following Vor-Vor's yellow-sailed *Canvasback* into the waters of the Yenwu Peninsula. Earlier that day, after stopping at Fel Sha-Met to finalize their plans with Theggo, they had watched *Silverweave* depart at full speed toward Hashan, the capital of the Tsing Empire. The admiral's many-sailed flagship was followed by his fleet and by *Oakhoof*, which was carrying the Tjardur's cargo of soot.

Before departing, Theggo had gifted *Fjummomurr*'s crew with a barrel of strong brandywine. The Puqua sailors quickly downed Theggo's offering, as a gifted drink was to be immediately drunk, even if that meant a barrelful.

Drunken and flush-faced, Captain Siffo led his crew in a riotous and raunchy shanty their new Tjardur crewmates were particularly fond of. The intoxicated bovids and suids sang:

> Gulls a-calling mine dear, mine rock,
>
> Winds a–blowing mine
>
> > *hardened cock*!
>
> Sails unfurling fur mine dear hogs.
>
> > *Away we steer frum home! Hoi!*

Lights a–flashing mine eyes awestruck,

Lightning clashes we're doomed,

we're fucked!

Brave boars stricken by damndest luck.

We'll brave d'fucking storm! Hah!

Darkness fallen like raging squalls,

Anchors dropping like

iron balls!

Braaw pints flowing fur me, fur all.

We'll piss away a storm! Yo!

Dome's a–lighting mine dear, mine tusk,

Winds a–blowing mine

arse's musk!

Home we leeward sail 'fore d'dusk!

We'll fart our sails till home! Har!

Siffo signaled to his lead shantywoman to take over the singing, then asked his boatswain to open up the pharolith lamps, as Sunnokh had set and darkness was falling.

The warthog captain stumbled toward his quarters. He wanted to once more refill his tankard, but when he tried to reach the barrel of brandywine it rolled away from his hooves, rolling empty on the deck while spilling out its last few aromatic drops. He dropped his tankard next to the mainmast and shambled onward. He froze midstride when he spotted Hefra Boarmane by the steps of the quarterdeck—she was in the middle of a conversation with an aurochs Tjardur recruit.

"That bull better not be a-trying to…" Siffo began to mutter aloud, but didn't quite finish the sentence, nor even the thought. He jostled his way between the two of them. "'Scuse mine tusks," he said, then opened the door to the captain's quarters. His body's momentum carried him through the portal, and a convenient bob of the ship helped him swing the door closed.

Siffo came to a halt. He searched deep within his gut and found the energy and balance needed to stand straight and reopen the door.

"Say, Lurr Boarmane," he said to Hefra, not even knowing where his tongue was taking him. "Why don't ye join me fur a moment. I think I thought uf sumethin' fur yer 'speriments ye might've likened to know."

"Muffin, I don't think there's much of a thought going 'round your head at this moment. Your brain is mush."

"I swearsth, let d'Cap show ye. Smart as Alaia's fancy tricks ye'll a-find it."

Hefra decided to humor the warthog and followed him into his quarters.

Siffo swallowed, then forced his intoxicated brain to somehow concoct a hurried plan. He closed the door behind Hefra and tried to reach the oval table at the center of the room, but a tilt of the ship made him stagger.

Hefra caught his thick arm before he toppled over and said, "I think what you need is someone to take you to your bed, Cap'n."

"Well if ye put it like that… I mean. I did, I do, mine mind is sharp as a… as a… I did have a greatest idea that'd get ye intreresterd, I think."

"You can tell me all about it in the morning," she said, guiding the inebriated captain to the bed in the corner. She let him fall tusks first onto the aged mattress, then partially opened up the pharolith lamp next to the bed. She had slept there only a few nights ago, and she already missed that bed; it was much warmer and more comfortable than the bunks and hammocks for the rest of the crew.

She turned to leave. "Moon lights, Cap'n. Think hard through your dreams and see if you can figure out what—"

"I rembendered!" Siffo grunted, his voice muffled by the comforter. He had spent the last few heartbeats fully unconscious—heartbeats during which a thought had slithered up his spine and manifested itself in his skull.

He sat up at the edge of the bed.

"Them furs ye like ter'study… Alaia was smart with them fiery shows. I think I thought uf a trick yet a-smarter." He pointed his hoofed fingers toward his chest—they aimed unsteadily. "See, Cap'n Siffo is aaall ye need. I'm a-half warthog un top, yet plain as a narwhal's buttocks down in… down below. Ye can easily cumpare."

"Narwhals don't have buttocks. And I don't think that's how it works, truffle bun. You aren't a Silvfröa, you aren't wearing a Silv. Your fur will seem—" she trailed off as Siffo dropped his tailcoat on the bed and opened up his shirt, revealing the bristly red fur covering his chest and the soft transition to a smooth black belly underneath.

"Like I've a-told ye, th-them-there's a bit uf everythingst ter study."

"On the contrary, Cap'n, there's plenty on top to study, nothing below."

"There's mour below, m'dear Boarmane," Siffo said coyly as he forced his body up, towering over the stocky woman and somehow keeping his balance, all while struggling to unbuckle his belt. "If ye'd jis' take a look, I do promise, there's mour." His breeches dropped, revealing his semi-hard cock, which was glowing brightly from the pharolith ring pierced through the glans.

Hefra eyed the glowing, growing erection, then looked up to the four pharolith-decorated tusks above her, then her eyes searched for the door. "Stay right there, Cap'n," she said quietly, backing away toward the exit. "I think I forgot to lock the door."

"There you are," Crysta said to Hefra the next morning—she had found her friend alone atop the quarterdeck. "I didn't see you last night. Did you sleep in the 'tween deck with the sailors again? I don't know how you can stand the smell in there."

"Something like that," Hefra murmured, staring into the distance.

Crysta's eyes followed her friend's. "Is that—"

"It is. The top of the Yenwu Dome." Far on the horizon they could see the snowy summit of the dome, like the upper edge of a persistent lenticular cloud.

"I wonder how much it has changed since I was last here," Crysta said.

"It's probably still the same," Hefra said. "But we are bringing change with us, that's for sure."

Siffo trotted up the steps wearing his new Bra'uur steel helm. The helm's single forehead horn was glowing fiercely now, circled by a row of pharolith rings, with a pharolith cap at the tip.

"Look, Lurr Boarmane!" he said proudly. "I fit in one mour ring. It's a-glowing like a shard uf Sceres now."

"More like a pigheaded anglerfish," Hefra replied, tapping a nail on the horn, "but it's getting there. I don't know why Chawól made your helm look like a narwhal, muffin, it's a bit odd."

"It's no narwhal tusk!" Siffo complained. "It's a kuba's horn!" He stepped closer and gave Hefra a little peck on the lips. Crysta nearly toppled over the railing as she backed away from the unexpected display of affection, but her mouth found no words to speak, not yet.

"It's not a true horn," Hefra lectured. "Kubas don't have true horns. Besides, you are a warthog."

"If ye think suids have no horns, then I don't know how ye call yerself a naturalist, fur them kubas' horns are them most majestic horns there are, covered in velvet, long and powerful."

"I have to admit, I have yet to see a kubanochoerus in person, but from the bones we studied, and the descriptions you gave me, those little corners over their brows are merely warts like your own, while the forehead 'horn' is nothing but a bone protrusion."

Siffo rubbed his crotch on Hefra's hip and said, "Ye had no problem with mine bone protrusion last night." He earned a hard punch in the gut as a reply. He winced as he backed off and said, "I shell take that as a compliment."

"Foreign lands ahead, Cap'n!" a loud Puqua barrelwoman shouted from the crow's nest.

"Crew's a-calling, mine dear, mine rock." He caressed Hefra's cheek and sauntered away with a shining, four-tusked smile.

"Hefra!" Crysta snapped. "What in the Six Gates was he talking about?"

"Beats me, he should know that not all bone protrusions count as horns."

"Hefra! He kissed you!"

"Did he? I guess I didn't notice."

"Don't play coy with me!"

"Then don't get jealous, sweet plum, there are plenty more suids aboard. Bovids too, if that's more your thing."

"It is *not* 'my thing.' I can't believe you are playing him like this. This is beneath you."

"Playing him? The Cap'n? What are you going on about?"

"You, trying on the masks, collecting specimens, this is going a bit too far."

Hefra cackled. "No, no, no, my innocent friend, you have it all wrong. I didn't spill a single drop, there was nothing left for a specimen vial."

"Hefra!"

She waved Crysta off and went down to join the others, who were gathering at the deck to witness the first sighting of the enormous peninsula.

"This is just the beginning of the Dhul-Kar Archipelago," Ambassador Vor-Vor yelled from *Canvasback*. "Please follow directly behind me, as the passages can be treacherous. We will enter Mandible Bay after passing a labyrinth of rocks, and that will take us directly into the harbor of Yenmai. In the morrow, we should make it to the city."

This mouth of the Ophidian which emptied into the great gulf was littered with dozens of islets sprinkled in unpredictable patterns. They weaved around the obstacles of rock throughout the rest of the day, then dropped anchors overnight, as the seascape was too treacherous to navigate in the dark. Before they set sail the next morning, Vor-Vor warned them, "Once we reach the harbor, do not approach the docks until we have permission from the sovereigns. I will sail on my own first, but you must wait for a Yenwu ship to escort you in."

They entered Mandible Bay and followed it toward the great city of Yenmai. At the far end of the bay, an uplift of rocky blades rose in its saw-toothed splendor—the Razor Summits. Its tallest peak, Mount Haya, pierced so high it seemed as tall as the dome behind it.

"What a beautiful mountain," Alaia said, eyeing the shining peak. The summit where the Mount Haya Observatory resided was obeying the commands of the Thawing season, striating its sides with countless steamy waterfalls, punctuated by sudden avalanches of dislodged ice.

"That's where my studies truly began," Crysta said, "up in the Mount Haya Observatory. You can't really see wisps from so close to the dome, but the night sky looked magical. The air up there is always so clear, and the stars shine bright as snow upon black velvet."

Sterjall aimed his binoculars toward the summit. "Is that little dot on top the observatory?" he asked.

"Yes, you should be able to see it now, though my eyes alone can't make it out. It's enormous—an entire fortress dedicated to housing the biggest telescope in all the realms."

"Biggest we know of," Sterjall corrected, still hopeful they might find an even bigger telescope within the Yenwu Dome.

Crysta's eyes suddenly unfocused, her thoughts traveling elsewhere. "I can't believe all that I worked for is… well… meaningless now," she lamented quietly. "All those numbers I crunched, all the hypotheses we concocted—they amounted to nothing, really, not now that we know what's actually inside the domes."

"Nothing? You got funding, sweet plum," Hefra said. "That's a lot more than I could claim. I had to pay for most of my outings."

"Well sure, it paid well… kind of. I had Artificer Grissem sponsor me for my early studies, but… Well, I guess it's not a secret now—most of the funding for the Mesa Observatory came from the military. We got paid to spy on the Negians, then used what was left to fund our research."

"Figured," Hefra said, not a bit surprised, which in turn surprised Crysta. "If the army could've found a way to turn moths into weapons, I would've been rich as the dukes of Bauram by now."

CHAPTER SIXTY-FOUR

A CITY BETWEEN BLADES

It was an early Spring afternoon, on the twenty-first day of Mudfront, when *Fjummomurr* at last arrived at the harbor of the city of Yenmai. The city itself was not yet visible, hiding beyond a strait that worked as a natural gateway to control naval traffic. Two rocky spires framed the portal, draped with monumental banners portraying a bold purple-gray cross with an abstracted symbol at the top that represented the two continents, the Gulf of Erjilm, and the Yenwu Peninsula at the center. Vor-Vor's *Canvasback* sailed directly through the towers of rock, while *Fjummomurr* dropped its anchors.

"I thought Vor-Vor had it all figured out with the empress already," Sterjall said as they waited, tightening his oilskin coat to protect himself from the drizzle. It had rained on and off, despite the sun's constant glow.

"Only for our visit with Professor Lai-Nu," Crysta said. "She's not Yenwu, she's Tsing, so the empress has jurisdiction over her. But the Yenwu are very strict about ruling their land by their own laws. You either obey their rules, or you don't set foot on Yenwu territory."

"How can you have jurisdiction over a person?" Sterjall wondered out loud.

"You better not voice strong opinions on these issues, whiskers," Hefra interjected. "The Yenwu have their ways, and they won't tolerate any discourse or take suggestions on how to run their state. Their scholars get to work on the most innovative projects, yet they are all basically slaves. Some slaves are traded, others borrowed, but they are the property of their institutes."

"Also, do be careful with how you treat the professor," Crysta added. "From what I've heard, her behavior can be… unsettling, so we should avoid unsettling her further."

Hours later, a ship arrived to inform the foreigners that they had been cleared to dock. A Yenwu envoy asked the Puqua ship to follow them past the strait.

Once they crossed into the Yenmai harbor, the sovereign capital at last revealed itself. Tucked between grassy farmlands and jagged peaks was a rocky formation that mimicked the Razor Summits behind it, but at a smaller scale. Here Yenmai had been constructed, its dwellings packed between the vertical slabs of rock like letters filling the pages of a book. The drizzle, aided by Sunnokh's lowering gaze, birthed sporadic rainbows over the scholarly city of the Yenwu, as if pointing them toward their destination.

Fjummomurr docked next to *Canvasback*. A squadron of Yenwu elite soldiers took up formation at the docks, unfazed by the wolf, dragon, caracal, and other strange faces that stared at them from the ship. The soldiers' faces were stern like those of inexpressive statues, their rehearsed postures sharp as their war scythes. They wore armor emblazoned with the purple-grays, pale yellows, and cyans of the Yenwu.

Vor-Vor climbed up the Puqua ship's gangplank, followed by a woman with a face long and hard as an anvil. He began by introducing the woman as Shui, a regent who had already discussed terms with him. She spoke only in the Yenwu tongue; no one seemed to speak any other language in the city, or if they did, they did not do so in public.

"We've been cleared to visit Professor Lai-Nu," the Jabrak-Tsing ambassador said, "but Yenwu soldiers will be with us at all times to supervise us, as well as to protect us while we are in the city. The regent has imposed strict rules regarding our visit with the professor. She will give us as much time as needed, but access will be restricted based on the professor's own schedule."

"I don't foresee us needing too much time with her," Sterjall said. "We should be on our way soon enough. Is there easy access to the dome from the city?"

"About two days' journey by foot, or one if mounted," Vor-Vor said. "The regent wishes you to know that she is fully informed of the situation. She demands that the Murtégo Miscam agree to the requests of the Yenwu Sovereign Territories before the dome is opened."

"What are those requests?" Lummukem asked.

"They demand this land be kept to the Yenwu alone, Lerr Lummukem, as it has always been, and must forever remain. The Murtégo may keep their current territories, but when they migrate from the dome, they must do so away from the Yenwu Peninsula, either across the Ophidian, or into the Jerjan mainland, where the Tsing Empire might welcome them. We believe the migration might not be as complicated as the ones from the other domes, as birds should reach far and wide with much more ease."

"The Murtégo do not know these lands," Kulak said. "They will need help."

Vor-Vor spoke with Shui, then interpreted for the others.

"If they wish to go north, or west into the Free Tribelands, then the Tsing Empire will provide help with their fleet, unless the Murtégo have ships of their own. If they wish to go east, they will be allowed passage over the Land-bridge of Shash. Either way, the Miscam must agree to these terms before their dome is opened."

"It sounds like a fair request, but it will be up to them to agree or not," Sterjall said. "For now, we should speak with Lai-Nu."

Kulak looked to Siffo. "Captain, can you take care of Blu and Pichi? We will come back for them once we are ready to head to the dome."

"Fret not. Puqua, Tjardur, n'kitties will be a-waiting. Go find that prufessor."

They all gathered the little gear they thought necessary, then walked down the ramp to be met by the vacant faces of a dozen Yenwu elites. With machine-like precision, the soldiers opened up their formation, then marched alongside them.

Hefra was the last to leave the ship, having mysteriously disappeared for a moment, along with the captain. She finally emerged to join the rest, hauling her monstrous backpack. Crysta was about to admonish her for the delay when she noticed something peculiar. "And what is that upon your finger?" she inquired.

Hefra lifted her hand, displaying a ring glowing with cold light. "It's one of Cap's tusk rings. Do you like it?"

"Did you steal it?"

"Calm your judgmental tits, Crysta, I didn't steal a thing. He gave it to me, so that I don't 'furget' him while we are away."

"It's… It's just too strange. You and him? For real? He's a warthog!"

"Quarter warthog, if being generous. And a more pleasant warthog than he I have never met! Have you?"

"Well… No, but—"

"Then let us enjoy it. He's a sweet potato of a man, that's what he is. He took good care of me after my… incident."

The glowing ring was quite alluring in its simplicity, yet Crysta sneered at it while shaking her head. "You know that glow is going to fade, sooner or later."

"Khest, love, you are trying really hard to be a downer, aren't you? I don't understand what your issue is. Suids, humans, bovids—we are all the same. And it's not like you haven't fucked a bovid before, or are you going to keep pretending nothing happened at the Pink Caldera?"

"Hefra! Don't you dare—"

"What are we talking about?" Sterjall interrupted, slowing his pace to walk next to the two women.

"Crysta was just about to tell me her story from the Pink Caldera," Hefra said.

"I wanna hear!" Alaia belted out, joining them as well. "I'm still shocked at how dull mine was in comparison to those of you who *have* told me about your adventures," she said, glaring at Sterjall for having been particularly evasive thus far.

Crysta wordlessly quickened her step.

Past the harbor, the rocky blades of Yenmai loomed in their perfect verticality. The jagged structures rose at the core of the capital, but the greater portion of the city sprawled over the green hills to either side and down by river-fed canyons. Yenmai looked immense—as big as Zovaria.

Rather than attempting to hide their presence, the wayfarers were paraded through the city as if in a royal procession. The Tsing Empire wanted to ensure that the Yenwu State would offer their full support in the coming war, and showcasing power and confidence was key to convincing the Yenwu people to support the cause. Servant Lune suggested that The Nu'irgesh should walk in front of the group, taking some of their largest forms to make sure their presence was unmistakable and inspirational, and Vor-Vor agreed with the proposition.

Many tales of the heroes had already reached the ears of the locals, and rumors of their visit had spread throughout the city. Onlookers filled the streets, but they were quiet and disciplined, even the children, watching from afar while leaving ample room for the newcomers and their elite guard.

The parallel walls of rock separated the city into strips with different functions, but plentiful tunnels connected these otherwise isolated neighborhoods. Complex, multilevel structures were branched between the slabs, oftentimes accessible by stairs carved right into the rock. At the summits, tarps with the colors of the Yenwu flag spread out, diverting rainwater into canals that funneled toward a lagoon at the widest, centermost strip.

"The flow of water is very important in this city," Vor-Vor explained to the others. "Each strip is like a slot canyon, which would normally be easily flooded, but the Yenwu have many methods to control rain and meltwater— there hasn't been a major flood since the mid-Reconstitution Epoch."

They traversed multiple tunnels, first entering the Merchant's Strip, then the Historic Strip, the Immigrants Strip, and the Scholar's Strip, until they arrived at the central lagoon. Heavily transited stone bridges connected to the next six strips on the opposite side, which were home to the Yenmai Institute.

They strode across the widest of the bridges, always escorted by the Yenwu elites. To their left, the central lagoon placidly reflected the unwelcoming sharpness of the Razor Summits. To their right, beyond a dam and a flowing river, they could see *Fjummomurr*'s black sails in the harbor.

"Where are we going?" Crysta asked six strips later, once they passed the area designated for the institute. "Shouldn't Professor Lai-Nu be at the institute?"

"Not exactly," Vor-Vor said. "The professor is being housed elsewhere."

They were taken through a tunnel with much tighter security, teeming with guards and suspicious eyes. The space narrowed, forcing the Nu'irgesh to return to their primal forms. Three consecutive portcullises lifted to grant them passage.

"This looks more like a prison than a research institute," Alaia said.

"It is," Vor-Vor replied quietly.

CHAPTER SIXTY-FIVE

SCHOLARLY PRISON

Long they waited in a tightly guarded room, with the elite guard standing so still that they seemed not to be breathing. Even Vor-Vor was growing impatient.

Suddenly, the soldiers lifted their war scythes and slammed their blunt ends on the ground. A sharply dressed bureaucrat came in and addressed Vor-Vor, inviting him to sign a ledger and requesting to see Empress Pian-Thi's brooch, which certified him as an official ambassador. Only after all the formalities were conducted did the gates to the prison open.

Instead of leading, this time the Yenwu elites followed behind the wayfarers.

"I don't know about this," Sterjall whispered to Kulak. "It feels as if we're being led straight into a trap. We don't even know where they are taking us."

"Nothing to do but keep going now," Kulak replied.

The hallway opened into a brightly lit laboratory, with thick glass ceilings filtering the light that fell between the two rising blades of rock that framed the building. The lab was any artificer's dream; the walls were lined with books, the tables covered in flasks full of alchemical reagents, optical paraphernalia, and dozens upon dozens of relics, most made of quaar. At a quick glance, Sterjall spotted a shield strikingly similar to the one Ockam had once used to protect him—and which the Red Stag now wielded—as well as quaar armor pieces, mechanical artifacts for unknowable purposes, and even textiles made out of quaar filaments.

It reminds me of Khopto's laboratory, he thought. *That, mixed with Balstei's lab. But all these instruments look much more advanced.*

The space was large enough for dozens of workers, yet only one scholar occupied it, who was busy at work on a brass apparatus, not even bothering to glance toward the newly arrived strangers.

Professor Lai-Nu looked nothing like the scholars of Zovaria. Her locs of hair were unkempt, her Tsing-style robes tied with precarious, unruly knots. She was barefoot, toenails grown curled as if trying to escape her feet. The only indication the woman gave of being involved in any sort of research was her white gloves, dirtied black at the fingertips.

The first person she perceived approach was Vor-Vor. Professor Lai-Nu seemed ready to provide a vociferous objection to the presence of so many intruders in her personal space, when she noticed the half-forms following behind the ambassador.

"*Ban-ho quo bensun, soe halov wun, hal-halien!*" she yelled in the Yenwu tongue. Her gloved hands went up to her mouth, smearing her dry lips with soot. She partially cowered behind a worktable even as she leaned forward, trying to get a closer look at the new arrivals.

"I am Tsing Ambassador Vor-Vor Lai dush Tieng," the ambassador greeted her in the common tongue. "Empress Pian-Thi has granted us permission to visit you, Professor, for my colleagues have many questions they wish to ask of you." He then waved a hand toward Sterjall, who happened to be closest to him.

Sterjall struggled to figure out what to say. "P-professor Lai-Nu?" he tried.

"And who else would I be!?" she snapped like a viper. "What are you? I do not believe in the nethervoids, so where did you come from, half-beasts? Is this to be part of my punishment?"

"Punishment?" Sterjall asked, taking one measured step forward. "I don't—"

"Stand back! I swear, I've done all I could! The answers are not down here, but up there," she implored, weakly pointing a finger toward the glass ceiling. "Spare my life, tell the empress to—"

"We are not here to hurt you, all we want is—"

"Please, you must let me go. I do not deserve your ire, wolf beast, I have done you no harm…"

"I'm not a…" Sterjall began to say, then simply shapeshifted and took off his mask, holding it out in his hands. "We came to ask you about quaar, about soot. Do you know what the Silvesh are?"

Lai-Nu squinted her singed eyelashes. She reached toward her chest, where a crystalline pendant hung, and brought the verdant-blue crystal to her right eye, using it as a monocle. From a safe distance, she gazed upon the black visage of Agnargsilv. Then her bespectacled eye scanned those who stood behind Lago, particularly the other Silvfröash and the three Nu'irgesh. The professor released an exaggerated gasp, dropped the crystal back to her chest, then fainted.

"I did not believe… I did not believe…" Lai-Nu admonished herself in a mumbling invocation. She took another sip of warm tea, her face safely caged behind her unkempt locs. The wayfarers had brought her back to consciousness and tried telling their story to her, but no one could tell if she was listening to them or only hearing the voices in her head.

"I am afraid the professor has been kept in the dark regarding the events of the past few years," Vor-Vor explained to his friends. "Empress Pian-Thi has granted me permission to update her on these matters, to see if she may somehow aid us in the coming war."

"We are at war?" Lai-Nu asked, her head snapping up as if on a spring. "Have the Yenwu at last given up their ludicrous claims of sovereignty? Is the empress here to take her rightful lands?"

"Not that, Lurr," Vor-Vor said. "The Tsing and Yenwu, as well as many other realms, are at war with the Negian Empire."

The professor cackled. "At war with that weakling's crumbling empire? Has that utter failure of an emperor sent a hole-ridden canoe to attack our mighty continent? How exactly does he plan to conquer us?"

"Emperor Uvon dus Grei has been dead for nearly a year and a half," Vor-Vor clarified. "It is not him who we fear."

Over the next several hours, the professor was briefed regarding the threat raging outside her prison and the battle that would soon befall the greatest of empires. A Tsing witness was always present to make sure that what was said was on the record, and to reassure the professor that she was no longer under any duress to keep her findings a secret—not from the current visitors, at least.

"But… why?" Lai-Nu asked when they were done speaking. She had been inspecting Agnargsilv through her crystal monocle, which seemed to shimmer with a strange light. "Why does Empress Pian-Thi suddenly not care for the secrecy of my research? For five years she kept me caged like a rat, and suddenly she wants me to reveal everything to a horde of Miscam savages?"

Kulak bristled at the comment, but Lago put a hand on his forearm, and the caracal let it slide.

Vor-Vor answered, "The reason is that soot, or ustlas as our Miscam *allies* call it, will soon no longer be of as much value as the empress had expected. We have found nearly inexhaustible sources of it in each of the domes that have opened. Your theories on where to find the substance are no longer as critical to the Empire as they once were. Your maps have provided a great boost to our economy, however, so the empress wishes to express her gratitude for all you have done. But now, more pressing matters are, well, pressing."

"I told her countless times, but she wouldn't believe me. I told her that… No." She looked up at them with bitterness in her eyes. "Why should I tell you what I believe? Will I be locked in here again, perhaps for fifty more years? I can't manufacture quaar, it's not within our current technological capabilities. We need a paradigm shift! I need to be at Mount Haya, not down here in this putrid Void of Khest. I need to see the stars! I have the theories in my mind, but I need to be certain, and the answers are up there."

"Whatever you know might help us, and it might help Noss themself," Lago said.

"And who helps me? Tell me, wolf boy. Who helps me get out of this prison?"

"Perhaps we could make a deal with the empress, *khumm,*" Lune suggested, glancing toward Vor-Vor, who nodded cautiously, then exchanged looks with the Tsing witness.

Lune shapeshifted into Rud. He took off his mask and placed it on the table. "We will let you study our Silvesh, but in exchange, we ask you to tell us all you can about them, and about quaar."

"Let me think!" Lai-Nu screamed, then clawed at her locs. "Let me think!"

The Tsing witness, who was closely familiar with Lai-Nu's erratic behavior, asked the others to back into a corner of the room. They complied, waiting while Lai-Nu paced around mumbling obscenities to herself.

After hurling a sextant at a wall, Lai-Nu downed the rest of her tea and approached the cornered group. "Fine!" she barked. "I will analyze your relics. But first, I have requests." She faced the witness directly. "Get your quill ready, lowly scribe, and do not skip a single word I say."

In extensive detail, while looking over the witness's shoulder, Lai-Nu requested, no, *demanded,* to be released from her Yenmai prison and stationed at the Mount Haya Observatory. She also insisted that her tools, books, and artifacts be hauled up the mountain, so that she could continue her research unhindered by the requests of the Tsing Empire or the Yenwu State.

She agreed to begin studying the Silvesh immediately, but would say not a word about her discoveries until after she received a signed and stamped letter from the empress herself, with a copy flown to a contact in Wastyr who would need to corroborate her receipt as well.

She agreed to reveal her findings to the empress, including those from her upcoming work at Mount Haya, which she promised would be much more consequential than the maps of soot veins she had been forced to draft for the past several years. However, she made no promises regarding the production of quaar, which the empress was greatly invested in, but which Lai-Nu believed would remain beyond her ability to provide.

"Your demands seem reasonable, Professor," Ambassador Vor-Vor said at last. "I will expedite the documents to the empress. A cormorant shall be flown at once, and a contract drafted by the empress's scribes to be sent to—"

"No, the contract will be drafted here, by me, and sent to her. *My* words will be on the page, not hers."

"This is a most atypical—"

"To Khest with propriety, you ball-less oxtail." She swung an arm, sweeping a bunch of invaluable quaar artifacts off the table. "Bring me parchments the right size for your cormorants to carry, and I will have the contract ready within the hour." Her head snapped toward the witness. "Now!"

The witness obeyed. The others waited uncomfortably for Lai-Nu to finish writing, standing as far from her as possible.

"She is feisty," Lummukem said.

"What is feisty?" Pol whispered in Gorget's long ears.

Gorget had picked up the meaning of the word by sensing with Okrisilv. "It's like nervous," she said, "but small, and... aggressive... Like Dart!"

"Feisty," Pol repeated to himself.

Once the contract and duplicate had been drafted and handed to Vor-Vor, Lai-Nu stood in front of the Silvfröash and said, "We will begin in the morning. I need time to think. Get out of my laboratory. Get out!" Even the Yenwu elites winced at the last screech.

The group was directed to the humble quarters in which they were to be hosted for the time being—one of the soldiers' barracks, outfitted with few comforts. The twenty bunk beds could host a squad of forty, enough for the dozen guards plus all their guests.

"She's wrathful as a rabid goose," Hefra muttered as they were getting ready for bed, "but I like her. She's got some guts, demanding stuff from the empress like that."

"We won't hear from the empress for a day or two," Vor-Vor told them right before he left the barracks—he had more luxurious quarters waiting for him. "So, make yourselves comfortable and help the professor do her work."

CHAPTER SIXTY-SIX

LUSTER LIGHT

The laboratory, or prison, was spotless the next morning. Lai-Nu had been busy rearranging things and jotting down notes. When the group arrived to meet her, she began spitting out her requests.

"You, the cat, you haven't shown me your Silv yet."

"I am a caracal," Kulak said, half-lidded.

"If you want to argue with a naturalist, that fat lady there will do, because I don't give a Jabrak's tail. Hand it to me, I need to see it."

Hefra was ready to punch the professor, but Crysta held her back. Aio begrudgingly handed over his mask.

"Be quiet. I'm not going to put it on," Lai-Nu said before Aio could warn her. She spun Mindrelsilv in her hands as if trying to solve a puzzle box, once again staring with her peculiar monocle, which to Aio seemed to shimmer more green than blue now. Lai-Nu's nose wrinkled as she studied the connections in the glossy reflections, in the filaments that made up the complex forms of the felid mask. She let her monocle drop to dangle from her neck, then looked up, pondering.

"A star map?" she said, noticing the pigments on Aio's scalp. She put a hand on his shoulder and forced him to sit down. "I see the main constellations, with a bias toward the old spirits. I thought you had no stars in your domes."

"They don't have stars," Crysta jumped in. "I painted that for him. Well, with some help from Lago."

"You are the cosmologist? It shows."

"Thank you, I—"

"It shows you were trained in Zovaria and not in Yenmai. This cluster is out of place, these two stars should not be here, and Gara'ébra's Hourglass is entirely askew. Sloppy work. Do better for the young man next time."

Aio wasn't sure if he should take that as a compliment or an insult to his scalp. Crysta made sure to take it as an insult.

"We were also wondering," Sterjall mumbled, "if you know more—"

"Speak up, mutt," Lai-Nu croaked.

"We were wondering if you know more about the other aetheric elements. We carry more surprises with us." He pulled out the golden crystal of brime that Aio-Kulak had once gifted to him, smiling as he held it up, teasing the professor with the wonderful treasure.

"Brime?" she snorted with a soured face, then smacked Sterjall's handpaw away, making the cube land on the ground in a sparkling fury. "I'm not interested in hot rocks. Keep your cheap toy away from me."

She then held still, as if holding her breath and her thoughts, and said, "There is no secret to brime, to magnium." She glanced toward the Tsing witness, who stood attentively by their side and seemed to reply with a look of warning. Vor-Vor whispered something to the witness, then to the professor. Carefully, Lai-Nu went on. "Brime is beyond the scope of my studies, as are most other aetheric elements. My research deals with only two elements—soot, as you know, but also lustrum, or aetheric beryllium."

Sterjall dared open his muzzle. "We've never heard of lustru—"

"Of course you haven't!" she snapped. "I possess one of the few known specimens. Of soot I will tell you more once the signed documents arrive from Hashan. But lustrum..." She removed her pendant monocle and held the platinum-rimmed crystal over her gloved hand. "It is not so much that I study it, but that I use it to study with."

The wayfarers quieted, noticing the professor's demeanor had suddenly cooled, and not wanting to upset the sudden balance. "This specimen is an aquamarine," she said with a tiny smile that faded much too quickly. "Some brainless jeweler from the Segregation Epoch polished it into a lens and didn't consider saving the shavings." She dangled the monocle by its chain next to Mindrelsilv, and as it spun it seemed to turn a deeper green on the side not facing the mask, incandescing then darkening with each subtle revolution.

"Aetheric beryllium acts as a prism for aetheric light. Or the *luster light*, as was known in the pre-Downfall literature."

"Aetheric light?" Crysta ventured to inquire. "How come I've never seen this before, nor even heard of it?"

"Because your cheap institute doesn't own one of these, only the Tsing Empire does. Well, there is also Dathereol's chrysoberyl, but it's impure, it's nothing like this. Luster light is invisible to our eyes, but lustrum transmutes it into the visible spectrum. Each aetheric element shines with its own mix of colors, though some are quite dim and hard to spot." She placed the monocle over a quaar buckler, and the crystal immediately took on a muted, ruddy hue. "From what you've told me, I can hypothesize that your Silvesh contain some traces of lustrum, which might explain why you can see those colorful auras— either way, this crystal is my primary tool for studying soot."

She clutched the aquamarine once more, scrutinizing the faces around her, and seemed to decide it must be safest to hand it to Crysta. "You should know how to handle this delicately. Look through it, but be careful."

Crysta's palms immediately began to sweat, but she took the monocle by the chain and let it dangle in front of her left eye. "It's... dimmer than I expected," she said, turning around to inspect her friends. "But Ishke'ísuk is glowing!" she exclaimed, squinting at the lilac brightness of the basilisk's aura. "And Nelv and Gwit too." Glancing toward Sterjall, she added, "It's much dimmer on you."

Lai-Nu snatched the monocle away and wrapped the chain around her neck once more. "The spirits are pure aetheric creatures, while the half-forms are diluted, impure. There's not much more we know about lustrum, but this single property of it is exceedingly valuable."

"Because it helps find aetheric veins inside mines?" Alaia asked.

The professor sneered but did not dispute the claim. Seemingly ignoring Alaia's question, she said, "The aetheric elements are everywhere. We inhale them with every breath, swallow them with every meal, but only in minuscule amounts. If you were to look through this lens in a fully dark room, you'd see the air sparkle with particles of ignium, nox, and aether itself."

"What can you tell us about aether?" Sterjall asked. From Lai-Nu's reaction, his inquiry might as well have been a slap.

"Watch your filthy tongue!" the professor yapped. "Do you wish me locked in here for sixteen eternities? Artificer Hem-Virr would ask for my head on a stake."

"Let us be careful now," Ambassador Vor-Vor smoothly interjected. "We have come with one quest in mind, and I have not secured clearance for more. I will make some inquiries, and if it becomes critical for our mission, I shall arrange a proper meeting with a representative of the Tsing Academy who could explain more."

"Like the senescent ambassador said," Lai-Nu added, "of the other elements, I am not at liberty to speak, for I am not one of the scholars researching them. Soot is the only element I truly care about, and lustrum is only a means to an end. That is my focus, so stop badgering me about things beyond my discipline and let me work."

Throughout the rest of the day, Lai-Nu asked them all to demonstrate their shapeshifting abilities, investigating the refracting smoke and the threads that formed within it. "Can the bird change forms as well?" she inquired regarding Olo.

"He is an azure-hooded jay, not the Nu'irg ust Kroowin," Lummukem explained.

"Then keep his mite-infested feathers away from my equipment while I examine you instead." She shone a pharolith through Lummukem's tail so that she could study the flow of the threads mid-transformation. She peered with both her uncovered eye and the monocled one, comparing, drafting notes.

"Keep your tail still!" she yelled at the partially shifted dragon. "Whatever the Silvesh are doing, it seems they break apart, then reform. They become one with your bodies and infuse you with an aetheric matrix."

"And what does that mean?" Alaia asked.

"Mean? Don't ask stupid questions!" Lai-Nu chastised, then moved on to the next experiment.

She analyzed the quaar conduits and spheres from what had once been Momsúndodrolom, finding them peculiar but too complex to evaluate properly. She then demanded to study Hefra's sap and fiber samples collected from within the domes' walls, forcing Hefra to comply.

"The empress, she was obsessed with the white blood," Lai-Nu muttered, for once giving a bit of information instead of purely taking from them. "I discovered that the sap was dense with soot, that soot was somehow integral to the domes. Once the empress learned of this, she wanted to find a way to harvest it. But it's too hard to do—it does not burn cleanly, it takes too much energy. We'd have to burn lakes of sap to get a smidge out, polluting our lands for minimal returns. Not worth the effort. Mining for soot is simpler, cleaner."

She went silent again as she analyzed the Silvesh under a variety of devices. All of her notes she wrote in a runic script of her own invention—a system she had devised to keep secrets to herself.

She replicated the experiment Alaia had concocted of burning the Nu'irgesh fur, using a few samples from Hefra's collection while disregarding her protests.

"And you are the one who came up with this destructive way of analyzing the samples?" Lai-Nu asked Alaia while not quite looking at her directly.

"That's me," she proudly answered.

"Very smart," Lai-Nu said.

"Thank yo—"

"For a slave. I would've expected the actual scholars in the group to think of it first."

Alaia glared but held back. She should have seen it coming.

"Now show me that magic trick," she said to Servant Lune. "You said you can make the flames dance?"

Lune nodded. Instead of burning Nu'irgesh fur, Lai-Nu asked the buffalo to demonstrate with pure soot, placing an open flask of the powder in front of her. Lune picked up a pinch of the powder and released it into the air. The soot hovered, trapped in the invisible empathic channels she had conjured, taking the form of a bull's head that seemed made of a thin smoke.

Lai-Nu brought a candle to the floating powder, and the shape erupted in green flames, holding the bull's head figure for a heartbeat before turning to white smoke.

"Pretty, but not very original," she complained, though her tone almost betrayed her being impressed. "You said you can control the particles and imbue them into your steel. Does that mean you can craft quaar?"

"I do not control the particles," Lune said, "I merely open the channels, and the nearly weightless particles find it to their liking to align themselves to them. With time, I have learned to link them into filaments, similar to what is found in senstregalv, but nothing near the complexity of quaar."

"Useless party tricks, then," Lai-Nu groused, then continued with the next experiment, asking Lago for his dagger. Lago handed Leif to her reluctantly, hoping that the professor would cut herself while examining the obsidian blade.

Crysta was getting bored watching Lai-Nu taking measurements of the dagger, so her eyes began to wander around the room. "Balstei would've given both his arms to work in a lab like this one," she mumbled to Lago.

Lai-Nu overheard this and turned around. "Artificer Balstei Woodslav?" she asked. "I read his papers. Gathered some insight from them, though his methods are questionable. Zovaria-trained as well, quite clearly. Your sloppy scholars can't figure out the proper methods of citation."

"He's actually working on something more important than you are, believe it or not," Crysta retorted.

Lai-Nu smirked and lifted a taunting brow. "More important? Do tell."

"He's the one transcribing Mamóru's writings, the old Nu'irg Lago told you about. He will be the one to gather that past knowledge, the memory of tens of thousands of years."

"The past. That's charming. But I'm more interested in the future," Lai-Nu said. "You have no idea what I am working on. No. Not yet."

After a few days of the wayfarers being scrutinized, questioned, and insulted by the professor, a herald flew in from the east, and another from the southeast. The first carried the contract with the empress's stamp and her blood signature. The second herald had come from Wastyr, with a letter to confirm that Lai-Nu's representative had received a copy of the contract. A secret code had been appended to that letter, one which only Lai-Nu knew how to decipher, informing her that her friend had not been under duress, and that the contract's copy was in good hands. "There is no way for the empress to trick me now, to break her word," Lai-Nu muttered, examining the signatures and stamps under a loupe. "Not this time."

She stowed the papers in a folder and nodded to Vor-Vor. "Once I am done with my test subjects, I will be immediately transferred to the Mount Haya Observatory. Is that clear?" she squawked, loud as a grackle. Vor-Vor offered no disagreement—he'd be glad to be rid of the rude woman and to be on their way to the Yenwu Dome. The sooner the better.

"You have your contract, and you've probed us enough," Sterjall said to the professor. "Can you now tell us what you know? Please?"

"I can't simply tell you, I have to show you. Tomorrow, be back here exactly one hour before noon. Do not be late, as I will be packing my instruments and books. An hour to noon. Tomorrow. Now get out and let me think. Out!"

THE HEARTS OF STARS

"You daft lot are lucky the skies are clear," the professor said the next day as the group punctually arrived. "Now sit down. We need to talk."

She pushed the locs away from her face and suddenly shifted modes, as if an entirely different person now sat in front of them. She steepled her fingers, sitting across from them next to an instrument both Sterjall and Crysta recognized.

"Twelve years ago," she began with a calm voice, "I had been studying the similarities between the charted soot deposits, working with geomancers and alchemists to determine any possible connections. We found a link, one that would become the focus of my studies from that day forward. Do you even know what soot is?"

Crysta opened her mouth to answer, but Lai-Nu spoke over her. "It is an unusual kind of carbon. It shares all the same alchemical properties we know from common carbon, yet it creates stronger bonds, and its mass fluctuates in odd ways, like all other aetheric elements. It is found in high concentrations only in key locations, at certain depths, between specific layers of sediments. I spent years measuring the ages of the rocks around the soot seams, and the data matched, the ages were all the same. Other than in isolated carbuncles, we found no aetheric carbon in rocks below the soot boundary, only above."

Lai-Nu spread open a map, where the known locations of soot veins had been marked with directional vectors. All the thin lines converged toward two points. She pointed to the smaller of the two points, a location on the map they were all familiar with, but which only Hefra and Lai-Nu herself had ever visited.

"The Sajal Crater," she said. "The location of the impact that caused the Downfall. What you've told me, that the comet which caused it is the same one whose tailings we cross every fifteen years, makes sense to me now."

"In what way?" Crysta asked.

Lai-Nu glared at the stupidity of the question, but she answered. "I studied the Sajal Crater. Its ejecta contain high levels of soot, though not remotely enough to be profitable for mining. The Sajal boundary is too diluted. The comet must've burned in the atmosphere and created its own thin strata that is too dim, barely detectable. But the evidence is there, showing that whatever was carried in that comet was a source of soot for our planet. And the Quindecims meteor shower... Every fifteen years it burns in the same spectral yellow-green, just like soot does, because it came from the same source, the same comet. And it glows yet brighter if you know how to look," she added, holding her monocle up. "We've had the signs written in the skies for us, yet we chose to ignore them."

Her finger then drifted hundreds of miles south of the Sajal Crater. "But most of the soot striations," she continued, "they indicate a much larger source—they all point toward the Gulf of Erjilm."

"Another crater?" Sterjall blurted out. "The gulf is a massive crater?"

"Obviously!" she snapped, briskly shifting into her more irascible self. After taking a deep breath, she calmed down and continued. "We've suspected for millennia that it's a crater, it's plain as your feeble minds to see. But *I* gathered the key evidence. The Gulf of Erjilm was not always underwater. It sank long before the Gestation Epoch, unimaginable eons ago. Something came down from the heavens, a meteor impact, or perhaps a comet like the one that caused the Downfall, but one much, much greater in size, one so big that it would've vaporized the domes if they had existed at the time. And that fragment of the sky, it seems, was made entirely of soot. Or rather, of alchemical structures soot can naturally take, like coal, graphite, or diamond."

"Was this..." Sterjall hesitated, still thinking of what he wanted to ask. "Was this what brought life to Noss? This meteor?"

"Don't be foolish, dog boy. Life was around long before. The records are there, on the fossils from before the impact. But life back then was a lot less complex, not amounting to much. But after the impact that formed the gulf... That was when the true explosion of life occurred, life that would take much more convoluted patterns than any that came before." Lai-Nu looked up at the glass ceiling of her prison. A scraping beam of sunlight was penetrating between the two parallel blades of rock that housed the complex.

"But before we get too far into this explanation, it is time to show you. It is time for you to see for yourselves."

She stood up and grabbed the instrument she had been sitting next to. It was a prismatic sunnograph, like the one Crysta had used at the Mesa Observatory to secretly send messages to Zovaria. This one, however, looked much more intricate, and included a unique set of prisms very different from the ones Crysta was familiar with. Lai-Nu gestured to a guard who had been waiting by the door, and the guard left in a hurry. Soon enough, a team of a few dozen servants appeared above the thick glass ceiling and began to cover it with an enormous, opaque tarp, leaving only one small opening through which a beam of sunlight fell.

The laboratory went dark. The only light came from the tiny aperture and from Hefra's pharolith ring. The professor approached her and smacked her hand. "Away with that!" she demanded. Hefra tucked the ring away and traded it for a scowl.

"I wish I could demonstrate this at night," Lai-Nu said, "because then… *Then* you would truly understand. But pay attention now."

She placed the sunnograph below the beam of light, not quite touching it, while aiming the signaling mirror and prism toward a blank wall. "I once noticed a strange pattern when sending messages across the Ophidian. Professor Holt, I'm sure you are familiar with how sunnographs work, as I don't believe your simplistic studies on wisps could've funded the telescope Yenmai built for your… monastery."

"We use a prismatic sunnograph as well," Crysta answered non-confrontationally. "I know very well how—"

"What you *don't* know is that with a special kind of prism, in some parts of the spectrum, the light dims. This is what I discovered, and this is the basis for my research."

Lai-Nu positioned the device to let it catch the light in its receptor mirror. A blinding beam of pure red light shone from the sunnograph, directed toward the blank wall.

Lai-Nu carefully tweaked knobs, shifting the prisms, making the red shift to orange, then yellow, then green, and all the way across the spectrum. Then she flipped a lever, and the beam refocused so that instead of a single color, a thick band was drawn on the wall, showing every color of the rainbow, from red to a piercing violet.

"Look closely at this image," she said. "Do you see it now? It is not perfect, but missing a few pieces." The spectrum was indeed slightly darkened in certain spots, although it was barely perceptible. Lai-Nu lit a gas burner that was mounted in front of the sunnograph's beam, and as soon as the fire picked up, some of the darker lines in the spectrum became more prominent.

"You are seeing the absorption spectrum of the gas that burns beneath the light," she explained, and then carefully repositioned the device to follow the sunbeam, which had been shifting slowly. She unscrewed the cap from a glass jar, and with a tiny spoon reached in to grab a sampling of a black powder.

"It's not soot," she said before they asked. "This is normal carbon." She set the carbon to ignite under the burner. A clear line of black appeared in the spectrum, right where the most vibrant orange hues were. A few other lines turned visible too, although none as thick and obvious as the core absorption line.

"Carbon's fingerprints are easy to spot," she said, "as are the traces of many other elements. And soot is no different from normal carbon." She took a sample from a different jar and set it under the burner. This time, the flame burned green, but the dark lines cast on the wall were no different.

"However, we can further filter this light, enhancing its luster component." She detached her lustrum monocle from its chain, then inserted it into a slot of the sunnograph. It clicked in solidly, and as soon as it did so, the entire spectrum took on a cooler hue from the aquamarine colors of the crystal. The spectrum lines had drastically changed; now there were six lines spread across the image, all equally wide, all equally spaced.

"If carbon's fingerprints were easy to spot, soot leaves not just fingerprints, but crater-sized hoof prints. Clear as the emptiness of space they are. This, too, is how I found that the blood of the domes was filled with soot. The color in which the sap burns was just a clue, but not proof—many substances burn green, for different reasons." Clearly unconcerned with the cost of her demonstration, she burned another spoonful of soot, making the six spectral lines reappear. "Years back, a Negian fleet attacked the city of Hai, and the smoke from their sapfire cannons clouded the Ophidian. When I received transmissions from the Stelm Sajal, I noticed a particular dimming of the light through the white smoke, but only while wearing my monocle. I found a way to combine this crystal with the sunnograph, then mapped the spectrum and found it matched with that of soot."

The bladed rocks above the prison began to cast a shadow onto the opening, making the spectrum dim. Lai-Nu turned the burner off and angrily yelled a Yenwu curse at the guard standing by. The guard rushed out, and soon the ceiling tarp was removed, and the room was once again filled with blinding light.

"Do you see now? The seams of soot Empress Pian-Thi is so obsessed with, they mean nothing in context. They are smears, debris from something much greater. They are minuscule compared to what's out there!"

Sterjall glanced around. "Out there where—"

"In the skies! In the stars! There is much more in the cosmos, so much more, and some of the clues left to us are as bright as the light of day."

"You mean that Sunnokh is filled with—"

"Not Sunnokh!" Lai-Nu yelled again, fully returning to her short-tempered self. "Sunnokh's gases are nothing like soot. I'm talking about Sceres!" She angrily shuffled through papers and pulled out a large sheet scored by a bunch of lines. They were spectral fingerprints, like the one they had just seen projected on the wall, although these ink diagrams on a yellow-white paper lacked color. Notes were scribbled alongside each set of lines, all of them in Lai-Nu's own undecipherable code.

"See this? These are the lines cast by Sceres herself, when the Ilaadrid Shard shines in her waxing gibbous phase. The shard. The shard!"

"The shard has soot in it?" Sterjall asked.

"No! Well… Yes, in a way. It's a diamond. The shard is a *diamond*, made entirely of aetheric carbon. An enormous. Crystal. Of it. Do you understand?"

Sterjall swallowed. "I do… yet… I don't—"

"The shard is only a part of this. What I believe, what I aim to prove, is that there is another shard, a piece of the one we see on the moon, one that is sunken at the center of the Gulf of Erjilm."

"A mountain of diamond? Beneath the sea?" Vor-Vor asked now, contemplating the possibilities.

"Yes, you greedy-tailed eunuch. A diamond shard of our own, too far underwater for us to reach, at least with our current technology. And Sceres… I am certain there *is* life up there, but that urine-smelling empress took me away from the observatory just before I could begin to properly study our moon. I need that telescope. I need to get back. And I need to pack, as I am to leave on the morrow."

"But wait," Kulak said. "Quaar, the Silvesh, what can you tell us about them?"

She waved him off. "They are beyond my understanding, beyond anyone's. I have no solid theories, only hypotheses." She clenched her jaw and seemed crestfallen at her own admission.

"Hypotheses will be good enough for us," Alaia said.

Lai-Nu paced around a table, mulling over something that seemed to be nagging at her. She dug into a box and pulled out a lavish book—it was bound in purple leather, with the image of a heart gilded on the front cover. She flipped through what seemed like alchemical formulas, then said, "No, no, this is all speculation. Untested, unverifiable. I could lose it all... She would mess it up somehow, and I hate that cunt." She dropped the purple-and-gold volume back into the box, trading it for a stack of papers, the top page showing careful drawings of what seemed like interweaving threads knotting around each other into ever diminishing patterns, some of them twisting into curves that merged back into themselves.

"That... that looks exactly like the threads I see with Agnargsilv," Sterjall said. "Did you draw these?"

"Foolish question. Who else would have?"

"So, you see the threads too?"

"Of course I see them!"

"By means of soot?" Lummukem asked.

"No, you sexless skink! Soot burns my sinuses. I detest inhaling the powder. The numbers. They are there, behind the numbers. The lines are written in the numbers. These curves, they make up everything, they weave into everything." She flicked her fingers around while mouthing something unintelligible, as if manipulating an invisible abacus, then stood still. "You spoke of consciousness as separate from self-awareness," she said. "I think the key, the key lies there, somewhere."

"That's what Ulésse taught us," Sterjall said. "The Quajufröa, she said that consciousness is the most basic level of the threads. It is life itself. Self-awareness is when the threads bend inward, when they begin to see themselves."

Lai-Nu traced a blackened fingernail on one of the curves of the drawing, one that looped back into itself growing multiple new loops, smaller each time, looking somewhat like the leaf of a fern.

"Imperfections. That is where true beauty lies," she mumbled. The others waited for a clarification.

"Imperfections," she emphasized, annoyed by their ignorance. "Soot causes imperfections in the threads. Some of them lead to nowhere, but others make the threads bend out of shape. This, in turn, causes some threads to loop back and perceive themselves. Imperfections. That is where self-awareness begins, in the random pattern of noise the soot particles create in our consciousnesses."

She thought for a while longer, scratching at her locs, going quiet and pensive once more. "Quaar, your Silvesh, they are the opposite. Quaar is pure perfection, rational, deliberate, organized. It's a machine, a crystal, an assembly. The Acoapóshi knew too much, they were too far advanced, or perhaps it was not them but Noss themself who knew so much. What I see in that refractive smoke your bodies briefly take is the Silvesh themselves becoming a part of you, like a pupating caterpillar dissolving itself within its chrysalis and reassembling into a new being. True metamorphosis. The threads themselves become visible then, filled with the quaar filaments the Silvesh are made of. How that works will likely forever be beyond my understanding."

Lai-Nu grabbed one of the quaar conduits and one of the spheres, which the wayfarers had gifted to her so that she might study them. "These devices, they are much like your Silvesh," she said. "They were assembled with a purpose, and perform discrete functions. Your Silvesh are not alive, at least not in the way we understand life, but they are so complex that they create their own threads, alongside the auras you've described to me."

She stowed the quaar artifacts into a box and lowered her gaze, as if defeated. "I do not know how to help you, not with the war that is coming to you. But perhaps... Perhaps there is hope for later." She stepped closer to the sunnograph and aimlessly turned a knob. It did nothing, as the sunbeam had drifted too far from the receptor mirror, but the fiddling kept her mind busy.

"Any machine can be used for purposes for which it was not created. This sunnograph, it was meant to be a means of communication, of connecting people, yet it found a purpose in war, in strategy, in sending secret messages so that people other than those we call *us* might die. Yet deeper inside, I found a way for this same machine to teach me—for it to teach all of us—that the stars themselves had been conspiring to bring life to us, and that all we had to do was gaze into their light and search for the beauty of its imperfections."

Professor Lai-Nu resumed packing her papers. As she lowered a folder into a box, she briefly paused to stare at the gilded book she had picked up earlier. She covered it with the folder and said, "Your Silvesh. Perhaps they are imperfect too, after all. There must be much more to them than we understand."

She tapped her fingernails on the table, then slammed a hand down.

"Now go! Leave me be!" she screeched. "If you want to learn more, find me at the Mount Haya Observatory someday in the distant future. Perhaps I will have more answers for you by then. Out! Get out!"

WINDWARD

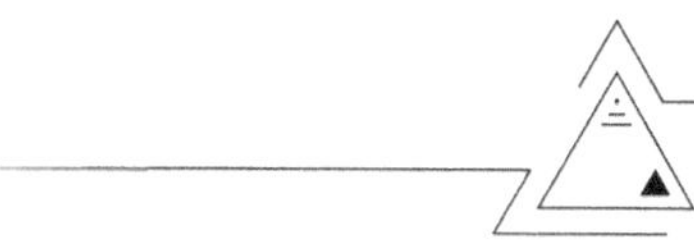

Once the wayfarers and their escort of soldiers exited into the streets of Yenmai, Alaia said, "Well, that was interesting, but not very helpful."

"Fuck her," Hefra snorted. "What are we waiting for anyway? Let's walk into that damnable dome already. It's right there."

"We'll fetch Blu and Pichi, then we can get going," Sterjall said.

"You hurry ahead of me," Vor-Vor said. "I have some business to attend to. And I will also procure us some horses to help with our trip."

Back on *Fjummomurr*, the group packed what they thought they might need, then dined with the Puqua and Tjardur crew while telling them of their findings. After Hefra said goodbye to Siffo in his private quarters, they mounted the smilodons—as well as four horses Vor-Vor brought back with him—and left the docks.

"I have some… peculiar news," Vor-Vor said, after they had reached a trail in the farmlands where no ears could eavesdrop on their conversation.

"What news?" Lummukem was the first to ask.

Vor-Vor adjusted his tail around the cantle of his saddle, then leaned in and said, "Professor Lai-Nu did have something that she feels might be of use to us, something related to soot. She was torn, unsure whether she was allowed to speak of it, thinking it could jeopardize her dealings with the empress. But I offered my reassurances to her, and she handed me a book along with instructions to send to the City of Bridges, where they will be reviewed by the Tsing Academy."

"How will that book help us?" Servant Lune asked. "What secrets hide between its pages?"

"It's… hard to tell. I do not understand her work, but Artificer Hem-Virr at the Academy might offer better insight. It relates to an alchemical formulation involving soot, but it also concerns other aetheric elements that I'm not at liberty to discuss. The formula dates to before the Downfall, but it is Lai-Nu's personal notes on it that might offer the most valuable aspect of all."

"But what does this formula do?" Kulak asked while Sterjall held on to his back, both of them sitting comfortably on Blu's saddle.

"We shall see, soon enough," Vor-Vor said. "Once we are done in the Yenwu Dome, I will make sure we hasten to the Tsing capital. Hopefully, by the time we arrive, the artificers there will have made progress with this concoction."

"I bet it is a gas that kills only elk," Dart hypothesized.

"Or a potion that makes you grow eighteenfold your size!" Puuja added.

"We shall see, we shall see," Vor-Vor said. "For now, we have something else to focus on." His aged eyes then drifted toward the Yenwu Dome, which was unmissable from anywhere in these lands—it waited for them almost too eagerly.

Sterjall tilted his head back to take in the full splendor of the dome and of the sharp rocks of the Razor Summits rising before it, but his mind drifted elsewhere. *I wish they could be here with us too,* he thought. At that moment, Banook, Bear, and Ardof were well on their way toward the lands of the Heartpine Dome, while Kitjári and Nalaníri were traversing the cold sierras north of the Tarpits Dome. *They feel so distant, like they were part of a separate life, or merely a dream.*

As the image of Banook lingered in his mind, Sterjall exhaled a shattered sigh, but his melancholy was dispelled when he felt a handpaw reaching back and closing around his. He leaned his head on Kulak's shoulder and smiled.

"What do your scalps think we will find in Kroowindrolom?" Kulak asked.

"The observatory!" Crysta replied, riding on a horse next to them. "There better be an observatory," she added, looking to Sterjall. "You promised."

"I didn't promise a thing! It's just what Mamóru mentioned. It might be there, might not."

"To the netherflames with your observatory," Alaia said. "What we'll find is birds. Thousands of them. Millions, even."

"That's my gal," Hefra said. "She knows where the good stuff is."

"We are certain Olo would be happy to see that too," Lummukem agreed, looking up at the jay hovering over them.

"Do you think they fly on giant birds?" Puuja asked.

"Yes!" Dart answered. "Like smilodons but with wings!"

"I wonder which species they would choose for that," Alaia said. "Do you think we'll get to ride on them too?"

"I guess we'll have to wait and see," Sterjall said, amber eyes looking forward.

A mellow, rain-scented wind blew toward their faces, calling them to places remote. They followed it with a latent craving, with a lust for the unknown, onward to their next adventure.

End of Book 4

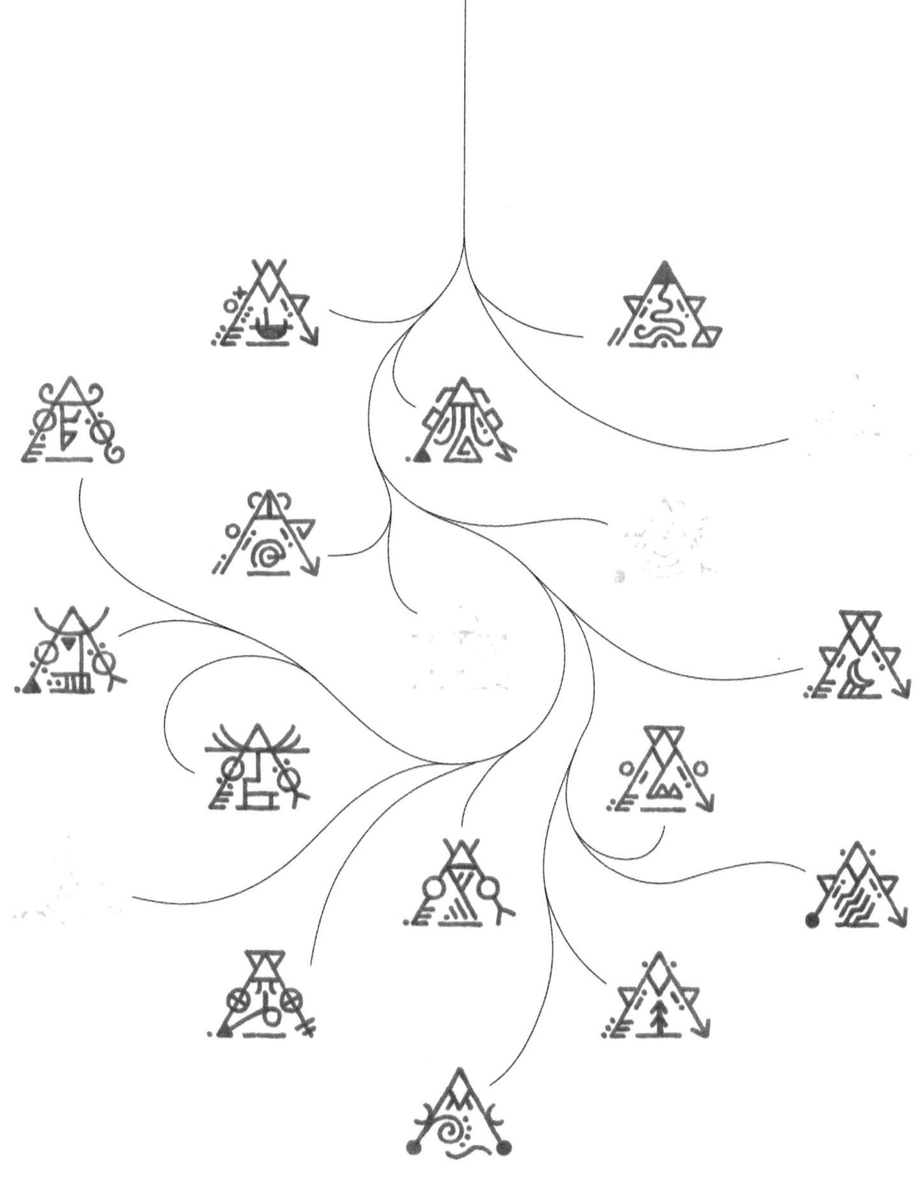

Appendices

All the materials found in these appendices can also be found online with much cleaner formatting and with additional goodies, such as a complete Mis-camish dictionary, full-resolution maps, and updated illustrations. They are included here for your convenience, but I recommend you check them out on the official website.

Scan this QR code or type in the
following URL to access the extras:

JoaquinBaldwin.com/book4/extras

To keep updated on new book releases and to gain access to unreleased illustrations, deleted chapters, tutorials, and lots more, sign up to my mailing list in the following link:

JoaquinBaldwin.com/list

Tjardur Clans, Tenets, and Virtues

Four-Horned Clan

Species: Tetracerus

Prophet: Rumah of the Tetracerus (F)

Clan leader: Maon-Javána of the Tetracerus (A)

Virtue: Altruism

Tenet: Strive to be of service to others, not because of what you may gain in return, but because being of service is the worthiest goal unto itself.

Yak Clan

Species: Domestic yak, grassland yak, mountain yak

Prophet: Au'óro of the Grassland Yak (M)

Clan leader: Mia-Mei of the Domestic Yak (F)

Virtue: Empathy

Tenet: Strive to feel as others feel, to understand circumstances from differing points of view, so that we may be one and be many. Be grateful for not just your wellbeing, but for the wellbeing of others.

GAUR CLAN

Species: Gaur, banteng, kouprey, gayal

Prophet: Drurum of the Gaur (A)

Clan leader: Dirvauk of the Gayal (M)

Virtue: Might

Tenet: Strive to take forms as mighty as the bovids of old, to protect our culture, to defend those weaker than us, to build for our future, to uphold our oaths to Noss.

BUFFALO CLAN

Species: Water buffalo, lowland anoa, mountain anoa, tamaraw, dwarf buffalo, savannah buffalo

Prophet: Naj'al'alás of the Mountain Anoa (A)

Clan leader: Ar of the Dwarf Buffalo (M)

Virtue: Cleanliness

Tenet: Strive to keep a clear mind and clean body. Find yourselves in the pink waters and learn your true calling.

AUROCHS CLAN

Species: Aurochs, zebu, taurine (including their multiple breeds, the ones referred to as "cattle" by non-Tjardur)

Prophet: Bum-Vaor of the Aurochs (M)

Clan leader: Buulin of the Zebu (F)

Virtue: Justice

Tenet: Strive for fairness with impartiality. Punish those who deserve it, but do so with compassion.

PELOROVIS CLAN

Species: Pelorovis

Prophet: Gweléshi of the Pelorovis (F)

Clan leader: Suháve of the Pelorovis (F)

Virtue: Perseverance

Tenet: Strive to be steadfast in your goals and the goals of the tribe. Work not for yourself, but for the generations to come. Persist with dedication, with mindfulness.

Wisent Clan

Species: Longhorn bison, plains bison, wood bison, wisent, steppe wisent

Prophet: Ejokk of the Steppe Wisent (M)

Clan leader: Seudi of the Wood Bison (M)

Virtue: Prescience

Tenet: Strive to have the foresight to anticipate the consequences of your own actions. Be cautious, and be ready for those outcomes hidden from your sight. Trust your intuition, but do so with skepticism, for you must trust the truth above all else.

Spiral-Horned Clan

Species: Giant eland, common eland, greater kudu, lesser kudu, nyala, balbok (mountain nyala), bongo, sitatunga, bushbuck

Prophet: Seitho-Dovár of the Nyala (F)

Clan leader: Topú'a of the Bongo (F)

Virtue: Authenticity

Tenet: Strive to explore all aspects of your true selves, to be closer to who you truly are and not to the person others expect you to be.

JOURNAL OF THE CUSTODIAN

Excerpt from *The Nambro Anthologies*, compiled and translated by Lerr Tyzra of the Klad Tenebra, first published in the year 27 B.D.

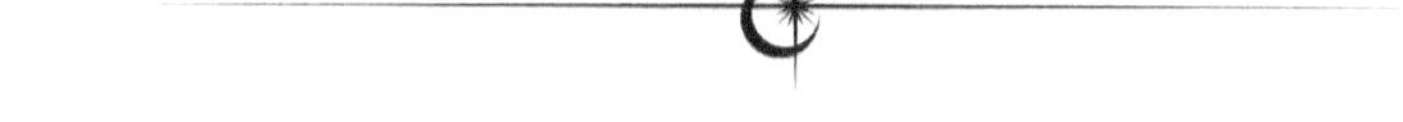

SEVENTH OF MUDFRONT

I have chosen to keep a journal of my search as a precaution in case my quest ends in failure. I hope others might find my notes useful, hope they might conclude my quest if my feet or heart fail me.

I have been searching for them for so long.

The only person who might have an answer has proven… elusive. I traded the last of the jewels the king provided me to buy useful information from a shaman, who revealed that they had seen [REDACTED] sleeping by the shadow of a sacred tree merely days ago, and that I might still find her there.

I quickly traveled to where the shaman pointed, hurrying seventy-two miles to the north, until I arrived at the gnarled branches of the Ancient One.

But she was already gone.

In her stead, tacked to the bark of the tree with a viper's fang, I found a rip of parchment with a most portentous augury. The note read, "I know of your quest, Custodian, and I can lead you to the answer you seek. Fifty-three miles south is a lake blue as starlight. At its shores you will find Tomut-Kich gur Hathar. He will take you to where you must travel to next."

TWENTY-THIRD OF CLOUDPOUR

It was a hard journey, taking me forty-six days, but at last I have reached the lake and found the gold-furred beast. At first I was afraid, but he minded not my presence. He also spoke not, nor did he seem to understand my words, yet he suddenly dropped to his belly and exposed his enormous shoulders to me, enticing me to climb onto his back. I did.

SEVENTH OF DUSTWIND

Time didn't seem to move at all as the beast traveled, but he took me up twenty-two mountains in just two and a half months! At that point, Tomut-Kich gur Hathar took the form of a curious, dog-like creature, then vanished into the sagebrushes.

I thought I was lost. That I had taken the wrong path once more.

But as I sat on the soil a snake poked his head out of the weeds. The snake then turned into an enormous saltwater crocodile. I nearly fainted, then realized the creature was asking that I climb onto his back. I did.

TWENTY-FIRST OF HARVESTLIGHT

I have been deceived.

Only four miles north of where I climbed onto this spirit, we came upon the sea, and the creature swam straight into the crashing waves. I nearly drowned, but held still to his back. Then he shrank under me, and I saw him bolting away over the waves as a lizard, as if he weighed nothing at all.

I tried to swim back to the shore, but the waves kept pulling me back. And then... Then I felt the sea sucking me in, and the light vanishing, and I was taken into the mouth of a giant beast.

???

It must have been forty days since I was swallowed, but I can't be certain of the date. Luckily, I have found sustenance among the entrails of this beast, and also was lucky enough to find a pharolith to guide my way. I climbed down nine of her stomachs, and there I found a sight most unexpected: a shipwreck.

I searched through the ship, and in the captain's quarters found a treasure chest. I broke through the gilded padlock and swung the lid open—the coffer exhaled a ghastly miasma, and inside was nothing but a piece of parchment, stuck to the bottom with a viper's fang. I immediately recognized her devious, sensuous script. It read, "Find the cave twenty-seven miles to the south."

That is all that the note said.

And then I felt the ship rattle, and a mighty wave took us. The ship was tossed about, and I was caught in the middle of it, and then there was an explosion as if a giant had sneezed, and I was up in the air among a flock of gulls, and then I hit the waves and lost consciousness.

When I awoke, I was on an unknown shore, where I'm writing these notes. I need to continue with my search. There is nothing else I can do. Tomorrow I will venture south to find the cave.

EIGHTH OF HOARTIDE

The arduous trip did end at a cave. I made my way through a winding canyon that reminded me of a giant snake, then encountered a foul-skinned pilgrim who confirmed the date to me, though I have to admit I was forced to hold my breath as he spoke. Then I crossed paths with a herd of behemoths, who ignored me as I ignored them, and at last I came upon the cave. It was no more than a nook, but in the nook was a small, burning candle, the wax nearly all melted, dripping over the rock upon which it sat.

As the last of the wick burned, I leaned over it and noticed the wax had dripped into triangular patterns… Miscamish runes. The runes read, "You are on the right path, Custodian. But now you must travel south, to the true south, until your nose tells you it's time to stop."

SIXTH OF MUDFRONT

It's been nearly two months since my last entry, and tomorrow will be one year since I began this journal. Twenty-nine miles into this stretch of the journey, my legs began to fail me. I was hungry, and could smell honey truffles nearby, and so I stopped to climb a hoodoo to fetch myself one. When I pulled the truffle from between rocks, its roots pulled a long string decorated with knots. I kept pulling at it, until the entire string was released.

I sat down to study it and recognized the patterns, for I am versed in Wastyrian knots. In the bumps, my fingers read, "Eight barrows you must climb until you are blessed by Her Shade."

To the north, I spotted conspicuously round hills. I am too tired to walk, and too hungry to think of anything but food, but the fear of failure keeps me moving. After I rest, I will venture in the direction of the barrows.

TWENTIETH OF CLOUDPOUR

For so many days I kept walking, crawling, agonizing as Sunnokh beat down hard upon me. I felt empty, and hollow, and weak, yet I crawled upon the crest of the first barrow, then the second, and all the way to the eighth, where I found a statue of a demigoddess. I am sitting by her feet now, feeling blessed by the coolness of her shade. But I fear I am nearing my end. I have no food, and my legs and arms can drag me nowhere else.

I've been fighting to keep my consciousness from leaving me, and writing these notes helps me a little, for I do not yet wish to cross into the Supernal Realms. But I am beginning to hear things, whispers. At first, I thought it was the demigoddess speaking. But no, I recognize that voice, it is [REDACTED]. I can even smell her breath, even if I cannot see her. "You must give yourself up to continue onward," rattles her voice.

Perhaps I should not argue with the spirits. Perhaps I should just close my eyes. Just for a moment…

TWENTIETH OF LUSTBLOOM

I gave in. I saw the red hand take me, and felt the barrow swallowing me whole.
I have died.
I have died, and without having found them.
I have failed.
When the barrow swallowed me, I entered not the Supernal Realms as I was expecting, but the Voids of Khest. Here, all was darkness, all but Sunnokh who shone in the distance like a languishing star, barely providing any light for me, but allowing me to count the days.

It has been a month since I died. And on this thirtieth day since my death, after having climbed down seven enormous canyons, I encountered a fennec fox caught in a giant spider's web. «I know the way out of the nether realms,» the fennec spoke in my mind, «and I can show it to you, if you would do me a kindness and set me free.» I should not have understood the language of his kind, yet I did, perhaps because I was no longer alive.

I gazed to the side and, deep in the canyon, spotted seven giant eyes shimmering at the center of the indigo-colored web. They were terrifying, but seemed to ignored me as I set the fennec free. Perhaps the spider saw only things that lived.

FOURTEENTH OF DUSTWIND

"We are going down, not up!" I complained to the fox, as he led me to deeper levels of the voids. But the fox seemed to know better, so I followed him. He showed me the way down sixteen more canyons until we came upon the tracks of an ungulate beast.

I was about to ask the fox if we should follow the tracks, but when I looked down the fox was no longer there. He left without saying goodbye.

I followed the tracks.

Ahead, I saw a light, and framed by that light was a massive caprid with threatening horns. He turned, huffed, and waited.

I carefully approached, blinded by the brightness of what I was sure must be daylight, when I noticed a piece of parchment pierced by the beast's left horn. I leaned in close. "Hold on tight," the runes read.

The beast swung his head at me, butting me in the chest, but I grabbed a hold of his left horn and held on tight.

The beast galloped away into the light.

I have crawled up to his neck by now, and was able to reach into my bag for my journal. He moves steadily, grazing and browsing and taking his time, allowing me to write.

TENTH OF HARVESTLIGHT

This beast can gallop down nearly vertical walls as if they are stairs! We exited at the top of a snowy peak, and for weeks we have traveled down eleven tall cliffs. When we at last reached the bottom of the mountain, the beast sat to rest in a meadow. I hopped down from his back and went to search for food.

I was not hungry, but I should've been hungry. I haven't been hungry since I fell into the voids. I've been wondering if, perhaps, I am still dead, even though I am no longer in the realm of the dead. At midday I found a creek and kneeled to drink from its glacial-cold waters. When I lifted my head, I spotted a striped creature drinking at the shore across from me. He noticed me, his back fur prickling, nostrils flaring.

I was not hungry, but I should've been hungry. My instincts told me to hunt the striped creature, for it was filled with meat, and I needed to eat if I was to be alive once more.

I've been keeping my eyes on him as I write this entry. He seems to be readying to cross the creek. If he does, if he gets close enough, I have a sharp stick next to me, and I will kill him. I want to feel alive once more.

EIGHTEENTH OF DEWREST

A fruitless endeavor, trying to catch such a nimble creature.

I hurled the stick at him but missed, then gave chase. After I lost track of his tracks, I came upon a warrior clad in armor made from shining scales. "I am a man of my word," said he, not even leaving time for introduction. "I promised her I would deliver her message to the man who is not dead nor alive. You seem like you travel between realms, lost pilgrim, and so I shall speak my message to you."

And then he spoke the message, but when he did so, his voice rattled like a snake. "A heart-to-heart you must have with the wolf of snow," said the warrior, then pointed to a white-capped peak, holding his armored arm up as still as a statue's. "Climb the peak, Custodian, for you are nearing the end of your journey."

He said no more, so I followed the direction his arm pointed in, always uphill for ten miles until I reached the top of the mountain.

But I found no wolf there. Or perhaps she was there, but, being as white as snow, I simply could not see her. I did, however, find tracks in the snow. My fingers are nearly frozen as I write this, and I do not want to wait any longer, so I will follow the tracks down the mountain.

TENTH OF HOARTIDE

I followed the tracks for six more miles. Only six miles, but it took me all of fifty-two days to traverse, for the southern side of the mountain is filled with treacherous vents and crags. Earlier today I was chilled to my marrow, so I walked to a steaming platform of sulphur with hot springs in the middle. As I dipped my toes into the egg-smelling, golden water, I spotted a macaque bathing there, her pink face shining like a hovering mask from within the whiteness. The simian rose, and as she rose she turned taller and curvaceous. I nearly wept with joy, for I thought that all my efforts had finally come to fruition.

"At last!" I cried out. "It is truly you! You are here before me, I have found you at last! Where are your—"

But I was pulled from my trance as the woman spoke, her voice not like the one I was expecting. "You have reached the end of your journey," said she, the parting mists revealing her true form, one unknown to me. Her olive skin glistened, and her perked nipples steamed like bread just leaving the oven.

"It isn't you," said I. The mists played tricks on my eyes, for in their obscureness the form of the woman before me seemed to change, sometimes letting me see who I sought, at other times turning back into the enchantress of the vapors.

"You have arrived to where you were meant to arrive," said the woman.

"Is this where I shall find them, then?" asked I. "Are they in this mountain?"

"No," answered the woman, her voice strained as if uncomfortable with the shapes her tongue was forced to take. "They are not here. Your journey is but a metaphor for something beyond your reach. But upon this path you traced is the answer you seek."

She left me then, vanishing into vapors.

I sat in the hot springs for hours.

I had failed. I was no longer dead, I was no longer alive, I was at the last step of my journey and I had not found them. I had failed, like I had failed them before.

As night settled upon me, I began to cry. As I pondered over my long travels and wept, through my distorted vision I finally saw the answer. I saw *them*.

I had found them! At last! And so I cried even harder.

THE DECK OF SANDS

The original Deck of Sands has three main types of cards: Elements, Essences, and Spirits. The Spirit and Essence cards are unique, while the Element cards each have variations numbered from one to six.

ELEMENT CARDS

- **Magnium**
  Glyph: Shield
  Color: White
  Seasons: Pearl, Thawing
  Forces: Power, attraction, strength, war

- **Pharos**
  Glyph: Moon
  Color: Green
  Seasons: Jade, Umbra
  Forces: Light, deception, divination, wisdom

- **Soot**
  Glyph: Twig
  Color: Black
  Seasons: Obsidian, Spring
  Forces: Empathy, nature, life, communication

- **Brime**
  Glyph: Flame
  Color: Yellow
  Seasons: Sulphur, Summer
  Forces: Heat, movement, passion, anger

- **Frisson**
  Glyph: Crystal
  Color: Pink
  Seasons: Tourmaline, Winter
  Forces: Cold, stillness, negation, darkness

- **Caesura**
  Glyph: Hourglass
  Color: Purple
  Seasons: Amethyst, Autumn
  Forces: Time, reversal, persuasion, death

ESSENCE CARDS

Of the twenty-four Essence cards, eighteen are considered Spirit-morphs, meaning they are primarily Essence cards but can stand for Spirit cards under some circumstances.

- **Ambergris**: Waxy, perfumed rock made of fossilized memories. By burning it and smelling its fumes, forgotten moments can be relived.

- **Anchor Tooth**: Cetacean Spirit-morph. A heavy anchor crafted from the tooth of a giant sea monster.

- **Antler Tree**: Cervid Spirit-morph. Tree made of skulls that grow antlers instead of branches and leaves, shedding them during each Hollow Moon.

- **Beard Pentacle**: Caprid Spirit-morph. Amulet braided from the bristly chin hairs of the Crone of Ukhagar.

- **Bezoar**: Indigestible, toxic pellet. Once expelled, it is said to cure any malady.

- **Black Roses**: Felid Spirit-morph. Crown of nightly flowers that allows the wearer to move in total silence while casting no shadow.

- **Bloodied Sock**: Primate Spirit-morph. Wool garment stuffed with the dismembered foot of the first human.

- **Bone Pyramid**: Perissodactyl Spirit-morph. Crypt under which the largest mammal to ever live is entombed.

- **Broken Stinger**: Musteloid Spirit-morph. Horn-sized stinger from a giant bee that endlessly drips the life-giving nectar of Eörel.

- **Diatom**: Microscopic, geometric dome that houses extinct giants from the depths, who wait until their time to return.

- **Feather Nebula**: Avian Spirit-morph. Feather that when fanned releases a cloud of sparkling pharos dust.

- **Fulgurite**: Galvanum-infused sand turned to a glowing crystal by sixteen thousand lightning strikes.

- **Gnawer Pickaxe**: Glires Spirit-morph. A mining pick made from two giant incisors that can cut through rock as if through butter.

- **Golden Claw**: Ursid Spirit-morph. Furred gauntlet with five gilded claws that can retract or extend at the wearer's will.

- **Granite Gonads**: Suid Spirit-morph. Two massive geodes carved into a temple of fertility.

- **Helix Foghorn**: Bovid Spirit-morph. Twin spiraling horns that when blown summon the mistdraft to cover everything in hoarfrost.

- **Hollow Moon**: The empty void of Sceres during her darkest phase. A sign of endings and beginnings.

- **Ivory Tower**: Proboscidean Spirit-morph. White lighthouse that shines with invisible light, housing the lustrum monolith.

- **Jade Caravel**: Reptilian Spirit-morph. Gemstone-cut ship that sails without ever touching the water.

- **Kelp Pennant:** Pinniped Spirit-morph. Portentous banner that blows leeward when a ship will survive a storm, and windward when it is about to meet its doom.

- **Leaf Skeleton:** Chiropteran Spirit-morph. Sprite of dead leaves, who carries Autumn in their wings.

- **Moonbeam Fang:** Canid Spirit-morph. Splinter of the Ilaadrid Shard that refracts light from the past.

- **Runic Gossamer:** Spider's web upon which, each morning, dew-drops gather in the shape of new auguring runes.

- **Striped Satchel:** Marsupial Spirit-morph. Bag that can hold as much as six tons without increasing its size or weight.

SPIRIT CARDS

- **The Star Weaver:** (F) Eight-legged seamstress who weaves the threads of the dead to the stars.

- **The Ore Binder:** (M) Blacksmith who crafts aetheric veins and hides them inside mountains.

- **The Tar Druid:** (A) Sage of shadows who crafts new life from the tarnished blood of the dead.

- **The Moon Shepherd:** (M) God of light and guidance, wielder of the Crook of Sceres.

- **The Root Mother:** (F) Goddess of empathy with a mycelium dress that connects all living creatures.

- **The Oracle:** (A) Reader of fate, harbinger of the Endfall. Their sixty-six eyes can each observe a different possible future.

GLOSSARY OF COMMONLY USED MISCAMISH WORDS

Parts of speech:

adj. adjective	*adv.* adverb	*art.* article
conj. conjunction	*det.* determiner	*interj.* interjection
nan. animate noun	*nina.* inanimate noun	*num.* numeral
prep. preposition	*pron.* pronoun	*v.* verb

Animate nouns, pronouns, and determiners come in six levels,
indicated by the numbers 1–6. An *s* is for singular, *p* for plural.

KEY

spelling – approx. pronunciation /IPA/ (part of speech) - **definition(s)**

agnarg AG-narg /ˈagnarg/ (nan4) - canid, canine

Agnargfröa ag-narg-FRO-ah /ˌagnargˈfro.a/ (nan5) - voice of the canids

Agnargsilv AG-narg-silv /ˈagnargsɪlv/ (nan5) - mask of canids

agnist AG-nist /ˈagnɪst/ (nan3) - fox

agnurf AG-noo-rf /ˈagnurf/ (nan3) - wolf

allastirg AH-last-irg /ˈallastɪrg/ (nina) - south

almel AL-mehl /ˈalmɛl/ (nan4) - perissodactyl, equine

amá'a ah-MAH-'ah /aˈmaʔa/ (nan4) - cetacean

ankrov ANKH-rohv /ˈankrov/ (adj) - rusty

arambukh AH-rahm-boo-kh /ˈarambuχ/ (nina) - money, coin

arudinn AH-roo-dihn /ˈarudɪnn/ (nan2) - seedlight

ash ash /aʃ/ (adj) - white, blank

baakiag BAA-key-ag /ˈbaːkɪag/ (adv) - please

balast BAH-last /ˈbalast/ (nan4) - chiropteran

bir beer /bɪr/ (nina) - home

braaw bra /braːw/ (nina) - mead

ca'éli kah-'EH-lee /kaʔˈɛlɪ/ (nan3) - pilgrim

dinn dihn /dɪnn/ (nan1) - light

drolom DROH-lom /ˈdrolom/ (nan5) - dome

drolv drolv /drolv/ (nan2) - wing

drolvis DROL-vis /ˈdrolvɪs/ (nina) - eternity

enwenn EN-when /ˈɛnwɛnn/ (nina) - graphite

ëovad EH-oh-vahd /ˈɛ.ovad/ (nan1) - fire

esht esht /ɛʃt/ (adj) - blue

far far /far/ (nan3) - pine, conifer

fel fell /fɛl/ (nina) - island

fröa FRO-ah /ˈfro.a/ (nan6) - voice

gralv grah-lv /gralv/ (adj) - purple

grest grest /grɛst/ (interj) - no

grin grin /grɪn/ (nina) - paint, color, hue

gwonle WON-leh /ˈgwonlɛ/ (nan4) - pinniped

gwur gwoor /gwur/ (nina) - province, territory

hed head /hɛd/ (nan3) - chief (allgender)

hod hohd /hod/ (nan3) - chief (male)

hoombu HOH-OHM-boo /ˈhoːmbu/ (nan4) - primate, ape, monkey

hud hood /hud/ (nan3) - chief (female)

idash EE-dash /ˈɪdaʃ/ (adj) - clear, transparent

ieren YEH-rehn /ˈjɛrɛn/ (nan3) - royal (allgender ruler)

ieron YEH-rohn /ˈjɛron/ (nan3) - king, emperor

ierun YEH-roon /ˈjɛrun/ (nan3) - queen

isdinn IS-dihn /ˈɪsdɪnn/ (nan1) - sea

Iskimesh IS-key-mesh /ˈɪskɪmɛʃ/ (nan6) - Enchantress, third planet from Sunnokh

jall jahl /dʒall/ (nan2) - heart

keldris KEHL-dris /ˈkɛldrɪs/ (nina) - bay, harbor, cove, port

Khumen KHOO-men /ˈχumɛn/ (nan6) - Dawn Pilgrim, first planet from Sunnokh

khuren KHOO-rehn /ˈχurɛn/ (nan3) - prince (allgender)

khuron KHOO-rohn /ˈχuron/ (nan3) - prince (male)

khurun KHOO-roon /ˈχurun/ (nan3) - princess

klad clad /klad/ (nan1) - lake

klannath KLA-nath /ˈklannath/ (nina) - north

kriss chris /krɪss/ (nina) - iron

kroovieth KROH-vee-eth /ˈkroːvɪɛθ/ (nan3) - starling

kroowin CROW-win /ˈkroːwɪn/ (nan4) - avian

krost crossed /krost/ (nan4) - musteloid, mustelid

kruwen CREW-when /ˈkɾuwɛn/ (nan4) - reptilian, reptile

kupógo coo-POH-goh /kuˈpogo/ (nan3) - snail

laaja LAH-jah /ˈlaːdʒa/ (nan1) - volcano

leif LAY-f /ˈlɛif/ (nan2) - fang

lerr LEH-rr /lɛrr/ (nan3) - liege (allgender honorific)

lerrkin LEH-rr-kin /ˈlɛrrkɪn/ (adj) - bisexual

loomdinn LOOM-dihn /ˈloːmdɪnn/ (nina) - east (birth-light)

lorr lore /lorr/ (nan3) - lord, sir, mister

lorrkin LORE-kin /ˈlorrkɪn/ (adj) - gay, attracted to men

lurr LOO-rr /lurr/ (nan3) - lady, madam, miss

lurrkin LOO-rr-kin /ˈlurrkɪn/ (adj) - lesbian, attracted to women

maarg mah-arg /maːrg/ (adj) - red

malpa MAHL-pah /ˈmalpa/ (adj) - great

mindahim MIHN-dah-him /ˈmɪndahɪm/ (nan3) - caracal

mindílli minh-DEE-lee /mɪnˈdɪllɪ/ (nan3) - sand cat

mindrégo mihn-DREH-goh /mɪnˈdrego/ (nan3) - saber-toothed cat, smilodon

mindrel MIHN-drehl /ˈmɪndrɛl/ (nan4) - felid, feline

mindu MIHN-doo /ˈmɪndu/ (nan3) - black panther

minnéllo mih-NEH-loh /mɪˈnnɛllo/ (nan1) - waterfall

minquoll MIHN-kwol /ˈmɪnkwoll/ (nina) - catball

Miscamish MISS-kah-mih-sh /ˈmɪskamɪʃ/ (nina) - Miscamish

momsúndo mom-SOON-doh /momˈsundo/ (nan4) - proboscidean

nagra NAH-grah /ˈnagra/ (nan4) - suid

ninn nihn /nɪnn/ (nina) - pass

nokh noh-kh /noχ/ (nan1) - sky

Noss noss /noss/ (nan6) - second planet from Sunnokh

nu'irg NOO-ʼee-rg /ˈnuʔɪrg/ (nan5) - ghost, spirit, soul

okri OH-kree /ˈokrɪ/ (nan4) - glires, rodent, lagomorph

okruwil OH-kroo-will /ˈokruwɪl/ (nan3) - pacarana

okruwom OH-kroo-wohm /ˈokruwom/ (nan3) - castoroides (giant beaver)

ommo OH-moh /ˈommo/ (nina) - temple, church

Ongumar ON-goo-mar /ˈongumar/ (nan6) - Amberlight, fifth planet from Sunnokh

quaar kwaar /ˈkwaːr/ (nina) - soot (crystalline, durable form)

quaju KWA-joo /ˈkwadʒu/ (nan4) - marsupial

quas kwas /kwas/ (nina) - **canyon**

rilg reel-g /rɪlg/ (nan4) - **caprid**

rilganesh REEL-gah-nesh /'rɪlganeʃ/ (nan3) - **sheep (big horned)**

rilgéreo reel-GEH-reh-oh /rɪl'gɛrɛo/ (nan3) - **goat**

sajal SAH-jahl /'sajal/ (adj) - **foreboding**

Sceres SEH-rehs /'ssɛrɛs/ (nan6) - **moon (the moon)**

senstregalv SENS-treh-gal-v /'sɛnstrɛgalv/ (nina) - **obsidian (special)**

Senstrell SENS-trell /'sɛnstrɛll/ (nan6) - **obsidian, fourth planet from Sunnokh**

shisendinn SHE-sen-dihn /'ʃɪsɛndɪnn/ (nina) - **west (death–light)**

shodog SHO-dog /'ʃodog/ (nina) - **jacket (open–chested)**

Silv silv /sɪlv/ (nan5) - **mask**

Silvfröa silv-FRO-ah /sɪlv'fro.a/ (nan5) - **voice of the mask**

stelm stelm /stɛlm/ (nina) - **mountain**

ster stare /stɛr/ (nan6) - **star**

stiss stiss /stɪss/ (nan1) - **river**

sulf soo-lf /sulf/ (nina) - **land**

sun soon /sun/ (nan1) - **flame**

Sunnokh SOO-noh-kh /'sunnoχ/ (nan6) - **sun (sky–flame)**

tago TAH-goh /'tago/ (adj) - **gray**

telm telm /tɛlm/ (nina) - **valley**

thaar tha-ar /'θaːr/ (nan3) - **vanguard**

trell trell /trɛll/ (adj) - **black**

trod troh-d /trod/ (nina) - **peak**

trommo TROM-moh /'trommo/ (nan4) - **bovid, bovine**

urg oorg /urg/ (nan4) - **cervid**

urgei OOr-gay /'urgɛɪ/ (nan3) - **elk**

urnaadi oor-NAH-dee /ur'naːdɪ/ (nan4) - **ursid, ursine, bear**

ust oo-st /ust/ (prep) - **of, of the**

ustlas OO-st-lahs /'ustlas/ (nan1) - **soot**

welkil WEHL-kihl /'wɛlkɪl/ (nan3) - **aphid (resin making beetle)**

wujann WOO-jan /'wudʒann/ (adj) - **icy**

CHARACTERS, GODS, ITEMS, TRIBES

Acoapóshi / *ah-kowa-POH-shee*
Miscam tribe in the Tarpits Dome. Stewards of Hoombusilv, the mask of primates.

Aio (M) *EYE-oh*
Kulak's human form. Prince of Mindreldrolom. Ierun Alúma's son.

Alaia (F) *ah-LAY-uh*
Lago's best friend. Worker at the Withervale coal mines.

Alampaari / *alam-PAH-ree*
Miscam tribe in the Archstone Dome. Stewards of Almelsilv, the mask of perissodactyls.

Allamónea (F) *ala-MOH-nea*
Cetacean Nu'irg. Sperm-whale primal form. Died in times before the Downfall.

Alúma-Farshálv (F) *ah-LOO-mah far-SHALL-v*
Queen of Mindreldrolom. Khuron Aio-Kulak's mother. Tigress half-form.

Alvis Hallow (M) *AHL-vis HAL-low*
Red Stag's human form. Monarch of the Negian Empire.

Aness (F) *AH-niss*
One of Aurélien's magpie heralds.

Ar of the Dwarf Buffalo (M) *are*
Tjardur leader for the Buffalo Clan. Short and pot-bellied.

Ardof Zaom-Zinemog (M) *ARD-of ZAH-om ZEE-neh-mog*
A ranger informant who frequents Brimstowne to gather information.

Ashaskem (M) *ASH-as-kem*
Kulak's brother who was killed as a baby for being born part tiger.

Au'óro of the Grassland Yak (A) *aw-'OH-ROH*
Tjardur prophet who embodies the virtue of empathy.

Aurélien Knivlar (F) *aw-REH-lee-en knee-VLAR*
Shaman in Fjorna's arbalister squad. Commands two magpie heralds,
Aness and Islav.

Bahimir (M) *bah-he-MERE*
Alaia's supervisor at the Withervale coal mines.

Balstei Woodslav (M) *BAHLL-stay WOOD-slav*
An artificer who studies the aetheric elements.

Banook (M) *bah-NOOK*
A mountain of a man who lives alone in the mountains.

Bear (M) *bear*
Lago's mostly-mutt, barely-shepherd dog.

Behler Broadleaf (M) *BEH-lehr BROAD-leaf*
General of the Fifth Legion of the Negian Empire. Snub-nosed.

Beiféren (M) *bay-FEH-ren*
Caprid Nu'irg. Bootherium (helmeted musk-ox) primal form.

Bikhéne / *bee-KHEH-neh*
Miscam tribe in the Scoria Dome. Stewards of Balastsilv, the mask of
chiropterans.

Blu (M) *blue*
Kulak's companion smilodon.

Brannoa of the Wisent (F) *BRA-noh-ah*
Tjardur admiral who welcomes the travelers to Sinsinbo.

Brovon (M) *BRO-vohn*
Scrollsinger. Representative for the Lavra Faithful at the Normouth Palace.

Buck Hallow (M) *buck HAL-low*
Son of the Red Stag and Ulle dus Grei. Future heir to the Negian throne.

Bum-Vaor of the Aurochs (M) *boom VAH-or*
Tjardur prophet who embodies the virtue of justice. Inscribed the
Trommo Hides.

Buujik (F) *BOO-jick*
Primate Nu'irg. Red-shanked douc primal form. Can take the form
of a woman.

Buulin of the Zebu (F) *BOO-linn*
Tjardur leader for the Auroch Clan. Enormous hump.

Cabal, The
Faction broken off from the Negian Empire, led by Fjorna Daro.

Chawól of the Longhorn Highlander (F) *chah-WOHL*
Tjardur head armorer.

Cort of the Pelorovis (M) *kort*
One of Lune's husbands. Smells like cabbage.

Crescu Valaran (M) *KREHS-coo VAH-lah-ran*
Arms-master in Fjorna's arbalister squad.

Crone of Ukhagar (F) *crone of OO-kha-gar*
Trickster character from spritetales.

Crysta Holt (F) *CHRIS-tuh holt*
Lago's professor. Works at the Mesa Observatory. Secretly works for the Zovarian military.

Däo-Varjak (F) *DAH-oh VAR-jack*
Pinniped Nu'irg. Ribbon-seal primal form.

Dart (M) *dart*
Translates to "dreldojak" in Miscamish.

Dedric (M) *DEAD-rick*
Captain in Theggo's flotilla.

Deon (M) *DEE-on*
Fat kid who goes to Lago's school. Dated Lago on and off.

Diduk of the Yak (M) *DEE-dook*
One of Lune's husbands. Murdered by The Cabal.

Dirvauk of the Gayal (M) *DEAR-vaw-k*
Tjardur leader for the Gaur Clan. Clad in inconveniently large pieces of steel armor.

Dorvauros / *door-VAH-ruhs*
Mysterious tribe who worshipped Sceres and Muri, and vanished without a trace.

Drolvisdinn / *DROLL-vis-dihn*
Ilsed's leaf-sailed ship with a hull of knotted roots.

Drurum of the Gaur (M) *DREW-room*
Tjardur prophet who embodies the virtue of might.

Dunokh Sull / *DOO-nokh sool*
"The Arc of the Night Sky." A legendary quaar bow. Also a constellation.

Ëalcor (M) *EH-al-core*
Marsupial Nu'irg. Thylacine primal form.

Eikra (F) *EY-krah*
Oldrin salt-miner who helps Kitjári and Nalaníri escape the Brinelaar salt mines.

Ejokk of the Steppe Wisent (M) *EH-jock*
Tjardur prophet who embodies the virtue of prescience.

Estriéggo (M) *ess-tree-EH-goh*
Perissodactyl Nu'irg. Woolly-rhinoceros primal form.

Fingrenn (A) *FIN-gren*
Laatu interpreter who tutors the travelers.

Fjorna Daro (F) *FYOR-nah DAHR-oh*
Chief Arbalister from a specialist squad of the Negian Empire.

Fjummomurr / *FEW-moh-murr*
Siffo's black-sailed whaling ship with a hull reinforced with kuba bones and a narwhal figurehead.

Fuuriseth (F) *FOO-ree-seth*
Chiropteran Nu'irg. White leaf-nosed bat primal form.

Gaõnir-Bijeor / *gah-OH-neer BEE-jeh-or*
"Shield of Creation." Takhísh's legendary shield.

Garvall Ferwillow (M) *GAR-vall FER-willow*
Cavalry general for the Republic of Lerev.

Gillean-Siroi (M) *GILL-eh-an SEE-roy*
Hoombufröa. One-eyed Acoapóshi prince. Ruffed lemur half-form.

Gino Baneras (M) *GEE-no bah-NEH-rahs*
General of the Fourth Legion of the Negian Empire. Longbowman.

Gorget (F) *GORE-jet*
Translates to "duërdivun" in Miscamish.

Grinn (M) *grinn*
Admiral of Zovaria's Centennial Fleet. Bashed in the head by Balstei.

Grunnel / *GRUN-el*
Square-shaped coins from the Graalman Horde.

Gweléshi of the Pelorovis (F) *weh-LEH-shee*
Tjardur prophet who embodies the virtue of perseverance.

Gwil (M) *gwill*
Chaplain at the Withervale chapter of the Havengall Congregation.

Gwit (M) *gWIT*
Glires (rodent & lagomorph) Nu'irg. Hazel dormouse primal form.

Gwoli (M) *WOH-lee*
"Younger brother" in Oldrin. Pet name Alaia has for Lago.

Havengall Congregation / *HEY-ven-gall*
Semi-religious sect of monks who specialize in reading the threads.

Hefra Boarmane (F) *HEH-fruh BOAR-main*
Naturalist who specializes in ornithology and entomology.

Ikhel / *EE-hell*
Miscam tribe in the Bighorn Dome. Stewards of Rilgsilv, the mask of caprids.

Ilaadrid Shard / *ee-LAH-drihd shard*
The beacon that shines on Sceres's face twice a month.

Isdinnuk / *IS-dih-nook*
Miscam tribe in the Seafaring Dome. Stewards of Amá'asilv, the mask of cetaceans.

Ishke'ísuk (M) *ish-keh-'EE-sook*
Reptilian Nu'irg. Double-crested basilisk primal form.

Iskimesh (F) *IS-key-mesh*
Enchantress. Third planet from Sunnokh.

Islav (M) *IZ-lahv*
One of Aurélien's magpie heralds.

Jabrak-Tsing / *jah-BRACK tsing*
Race from the southern Tsing Empire who have tufted tails.

Jaltovic (M) *YALL-toh-vick*
Graalman scout who leads the Red Stag into the Tarpits Dome.

Jessha (F) *JEH-sha*
Sehján queen who has never worn Okrisilv. Mother of Puuja and Pol.

Ji / *gee*
Miscam tribe in the Azurean Dome. Stewards of Quajusilv, the mask of marsupials.

Jiara Ascura (F) *gee-AH-rah as-COO-rah*
Kitjári's human form. Platoon commander in the Free Tribelands.

Jiu Zezi (F) *gee-oo ZEH-zee*
Yenwu cosmologist who discovered the comet that would cause the Downfall.

Jojek / *JOE-jeck*
Miscam tribe in the Lequa Dome. Stewards of Krostsilv, the mask of musteloids.

Kenzir stone / *KEN-sr*
Pharoliths. Glowing rocks made with the aetheric element of pharos.

Kerjaastórgnem (M) *ker-jah-STORE-gnem*
Ursid Nu'irg. Arctotherium primal form. Can take the form of a man. Also known as Banook.

Khardok / *KHAR-dock*
Miscam tribe in the Moonrise Dome. Stewards of Gwonlesilv, the mask of pinnipeds.

Khimbesum-Banvo (M) *KHIM-beh-soom BAN-voh*
Hoombufröa. One-eyed Acapóshi king. Spider monkey half-form.

Khopto (M) *KHOP-toh*
Havengall monk who works with soot and specializes in "seeing the threads."

Khumen (M) *KHOO-men*
Dawn Pilgrim. First planet from Sunnokh.

Kitjári (F) *kit-JAH-ree*
Urnaadifröa. Jiara's black-bear half-form. Platoon commander in the Free Tribelands.

Korten dus Fer (M) *COURT-en doos fair*
General of the Sixth Legion of the Negian Empire.

Krujel / *CROO-jill*
Sixteen-sided coins from the Negian Empire.

Kulak (M) *COO-lack*
Mindrelfröa. Khuron Aio's caracal half-form.

Laatu / *LAH-AH-too*
Miscam tribe in the Moordusk Dome. Stewards of Mindrelsilv, the mask of felids.

Lago Vaari (M) *LAH-goh VAH-ree*
Sterjall's human form. Young man from Withervale who by chance inherits Agnargsilv.

Lai-Nu (F) *lie noo*
Professor at the Yenmai Institute. Cosmologist focusing on quaar and soot.

Lakemother (F) *LAKE-mother*
Sehján deity of the waters and protection.

Leif / *LAY-f*
"Fang." Lago's dagger.

Luhásu (F) *loo-HA-soo*
Western Ikhel leader who allies with the Red Stag to obtain Rilgsilv.

Lummukem (A) *LOO-moo-kem*
Kruwenfröa. Sunu's varanus-dragon half-form. Laatu shaman warrior.

Lune of the Water Buffalo (F) *loon*
Trommofröa. Rud's wild-water-buffalo half-form. Servant of the Tjardur.

Macúsca (F) *mah-COOS-kah*
Jojek slave who helps start the revolt at the Lequa Dome.

Malazzari (M) *mah-lah-ZA-ree*
Graalman god of fertility. Hung horse. Also a constellation.

Mamóru (M) *mah-MOH-roo*
Proboscidean Nu'irg. Steppe mammoth primal form. Can take the form of a man.

Maon-Javána of the Tetracerus (A) *MAH-on jah-VAH-nah*
Tjardur leader for the Four-Horned Clan. Nearly plain-skinned but with four tiny horns.

Mareesha (F) *mah-REE-sha*
Captain in Theggo's flotilla.

Mia-Mei of the Domestic Yak (F) *MEE-ah may*
Tjardur leader for the Yak Clan. Wears no clothes other than her draping fur.

Mildur (A) *MILL-duhr*
Blue-skinned soothsayer from Bauram who travels as a roving merchant.

Mo'óto / *moh-'OH-toh*
Miscam tribe in the Varanus Dome. Stewards of Kruwensilv, the mask of reptilians.

Muri (M) *MOO-ree*
Musteloid Nu'irg. Honey-badger primal form.

Muriel Clawwick (F) *MEW-ree-el CLAW-wick*
Arbalister in Fjorna's squad. Waldomar's sister.

Murtégo / *moor-TEH-goh*
Miscam tribe in the Yenwu Dome. Stewards of Kroowinsilv, the mask of avians.

Naj'al'alás of the Mountain Anoa (A) *nash al ah-LAHs*
Tjardur prophet who embodies the virtue of cleanliness.

Nalaníri (F) *nah-lah-NEE-ree*
Nagrafröa. Prikka's boar half-form. Puqua chef.

Nelv (F) *nelv*
Felid Nu'irg. Clouded leopard primal form.

Noss / *noss*
Second planet from Sunnokh.

Oakhoof
Admiral Brannoa's merchant knarr retrofitted for battle.

Ockam Radiartis (M) *OCK-uhm ra-dee-AR-tiss*
Sylvan scout from the Free Tribelands. Bonmei's adoptive father.

Odask (M) *ODD-ask*
The father of Nalaníri's two children.

Ogóre of the Gaur (F) *oh-GORE-eh*
Tjardur captain built like a boulder.

Oldrin / *ALL-drin*
Race from the far east of the Jerjan Continent who grow bony protuberances called spurs.

Olo (M) *OH-loh*
Sunu's azure-hooded jay herald.

Ongumar (M) *ON-goo-mar*
Amberlight. Fifth planet from Sunnokh.

Osef Windscar (M) *OW-sehf WIND-scar*
Arbalister in Fjorna's squad.

Ouránama (F) *ow-RAH-nah-mah*
Ulésse's human form. Chief of Quajudrolom. Gardener, farmer, and botanist at Mikkagolm.

Oxruk / *OX-rook*
Pale race of underground dwellers in the Nisos Dome.

Pamúnn (M) *pah-MOON*
Bovid Nu'irg. Nyala primal form.

Pellámbri (F) *peh-LUHM-bree*
The Lodestar. A pink nebula at the heart of the Sword of Zeiheim.

Pian–Thi (F) *pee-an TEA*
Empress of the Tsing Empire.

Pichi (F) *PEE-chee*
Largest of smilodons, who usually carries all the gear.

Pliwe (F) *PLEA-weh*
Oldrin deity with three horns.

Pollomekh (Pol) (M) *POH-loh-mekh*
Prince of the Sehján. Puuja's twin brother.

Prikka (F) *PREE-kah*
Nalaníri's human form. Puqua chef.

Probo (M) *PROH-boh*
Suid Nu'irg. Javelina primal form.

Puqua / *POO-kwa*
Miscam tribe in the Fjordlands Dome. Stewards of Nagrasilv, the mask of suids.

Puuja (F) *POO-jah*
Princess of the Sehján. Pol's sister.

Qua (F) *kwa*
Feral tetracerus who follows Maon-Javána around.

Quggon / *KYOO-gone*
A cube made of nine chips that add up to a value of one hundred Qupi.

Quoda (F) *KWO-dah*
Chief of Gwur Pantuul in Mindreldrolom. Lives in Panjuul. Dreadlock wig.

Qupi / *KYOO-pee*
Chevron-shaped chips used as currency units.

Raushamitt (M) *RAW-sha-mitt*
Oldrin deity with a triple-split penis.

Red Stag (M) *red stag*
Alvis Hallow's elk half-form when wearing Urgsilv.

Rowan Holt (M) *ROW-uhn holt*
Crysta's husband.

Rud of the Savannah Buffalo (M) *rude*
Lune's natural half-form when not wearing Trommosilv. Servant of
the Tjardur.

Rumah of the Tetracerus (F) *ROO-mah*
Tjardur prophet who embodies the virtue of altruism.

Safís (F) *sah-FEES*
Canid Nu'irg. Tundra wolf primal form.

Sceres (F) *SEH-rehs*
Noss's moon.

Seera Ashbend (F) *SEE-ruh ASH-bend*
Infantry general for the Republic of Lerev.

Sehján / *seh-JAHN*
Miscam tribe in the Nisos Dome. Stewards of Okrisilv, the mask of glires.

Seitho-Dovár of the Nyala (F) *SAY-thoh doh-VAR*
Tjardur prophet who embodies the virtue of authenticity.

Senstrell (F) *SENS-trell*
"Obsidian." Fourth planet from Sunnokh.

Seshéni (F) *seh-SHEH-nee*
Dragoon leader of kudu-riding troop from Lerev.

Seudi of the Wood Bison (M) *SEU-dee*
Tjardur leader for the Wisent Clan. Long, braided goatee.

Siffo (M) *SEE-foh*
Puqua captain of *Fjummomurr*, the Tusked Whale. Quarter warthog.

Sijma Ascura (F) *SIJ-mah as-COO-rah*
Field Marshal in the Free Tribelands. Jiara's older sister.

Silv-Thaar Baneras (M) *silv-THAH-AR bah-NEH-rahs*
Gino's takhi (steppe wild horse) half-form when wearing Almelsilv.

Silv-Thaar Daro (F) *silv-THAH-AR DAHR-oh*
Fjorna's ermine half-form when wearing Krostsilv.

Silv-Thaar dus Fer (M) *silv-THAH-AR doos fair*
Korten's spectacled flying-fox half-form when wearing Balastsilv.

Silv-Thaar Knivlar (F) *silv-THAH-AR knee-VLAR*
Aurélien's leopard-seal half-form when wearing Gwonlesilv.

Silv-Thaar Markhor (F) *silv-THAH-AR MAR-core*
Luhásu's markhor half-form when wearing Rilgsilv.

Silv-Thaar Valaran (M) *silv-THAH-AR VAH-lah-ran*
Crescu's raccoon half-form when wearing Krostsilv.

Silverweave / *SILL-vr-weave*
Theggo's many-sailed frigate.

Skugge (A) *SKOO-geh*
Avian Nu'irg. Great-gray-owl primal form. Only all-gender Nu'irg.

Soroley (F) *SOH-roh-lay*
Sprite-queen from a spritetale. Also the name of a scrappy canoe.

Sovath (F) *SOH-vahth*
Cervid Nu'irg. Chital primal form; often seen as an antlerless megaloceros next to the Red Stag.

Speros of the Eland (M) *SPARE-ohs*
Tjardur gate guard who welcomes the travelers into the Ashen Dome.

Sterjall (M) *STARE-jahl*
Agnargfröa. Lago's timber-wolf half-form.

Suháve of the Pelorovis (F) *soo-HA-veh*
Tjardur leader for the Pelorovis Clan. Metal censers dangle from her horns.

Sunnokh (M) *SOO-noh-kh*
"Sky-flame." The sun.

Sunu (A) *SOO-noo*
Lummukem's human form. Laatu shaman-warrior trained in the arts of healing and battle.

Suux (F) *soo-ks*
Head chief of the Graalman Horde, ruler of the Duggor Veil.

Sword of Zeiheim / *ZEI-hime*
Legendary weapon crafted of lightning. Also a constellation.

Teldebran / *TELL-the-brahn*
Miscam tribe in the Anglass Dome. Stewards of Urgsilv, the mask of cervids.

Theggo Saurfall (M) *THEH-go SOUR-fall*
Fleet Admiral for a Lerevi flotilla of the Kilgane Naval Base.

Tinnomeg (M) *TEE-noh-meg*
Giant eland whom Theggo rides to battle.

Tjardur / *CHAR-dure*
Miscam tribe in the Ashen Dome. Stewards of Trommosilv, the mask of bovids.

Toldask / *TOLD-ask*
Miscam tribe in the Brasha'in Scablands. Stewards of Momsúndosilv, the mask of proboscideans.

Topú'a of the Bongo (F) *toh-POO-'ah*
Tjardur leader for the Spiral-Horned Clan. Striped robes.

Tor-Reveo / *tore REH-vee-oh*
"Spear of Undoing." Takhamún's legendary spear.

Tremor (M) *TREH-mr*
Jartadi steed the Red Stag rides. Black-velvet coat.

Trevin Gobbar (M) *TREH-vinn GOH-bar*
Arbalister in Fjorna's squad. Long nose.

Trommo Hides / *TROM-moh hides*
Keystone of Tjardur civilization. Hides inscribed by Bum-Vaor with the eight virtues and tenets.

Tsei (F) *t-SAY*
Sehján warrior who first finds the travelers inside the Nisos Dome.

Tupiel (M) *TOO-pee-el*
Western Ikhel survivor who helps infiltrate Ommo ust Rilg.

Ulésse (F) *oo-LEH-seh*
Quajufröa. Ouránama's wombat half-form. Gardener, farmer, and botanist at Mikkagolm.

Umar-Vaor (M) *OO-mar VAH-or*
Bum-Vaor's quarter-aurochs son.

Umiimi (F) *oo-MEE-mee*
Oldrin merchant who names Alaia's nub.

Urcai (M) *OOR-ky*
Crafty artificer from the Negian Empire.

Vor-Vor (M) *vore vore*
Tsing ambassador. Jabrak-Tsing eunuch who sails aboard *Canvasback*.

Vordeno (M) *vore-DAY-noh*
Princeps of Lerev. Democratically elected.

Wawumána (A) *wah-woo-MAH-nah*
Oldrin deity with three breasts.

Wutash, Northern / *WOO-tash*
Miscam tribe in the Da'áju Caldera. Stewards of Urnaadisilv, the mask of ursids.

Wutash, Southern / *WOO-tash*
Miscam tribe in the Heartpine Dome. Stewards of Agnargsilv, the mask of canids.

Yaumenn (A) *YAW-men*
Demigod whose red hands absorb life.

Yza (F) *IT-suh*
Demigoddess whose shade blesses all it touches.

LOCATIONS

Afhora, Kingdom of / *ah-FOR-uh*
One of the sixteen realms. Its capital is Sundhollow.

Agnargdrolom / *AG-narg-droh-lom*
Heartpine Dome. Located between the Free Tribelands and the
Negian Empire.

Ajacad / *AH-jah-cad*
Western Ikhel town by a silo in the Bighorn Dome.

Allathanathar / *ala-THA-na-thar*
Capital of the Kingdom of Bauram.

Almeldrolom / *AL-mehl-droh-lom*
Archstone Dome. Located between the Dorhond Tribes and the
Graalman Horde.

Alvforg Strait / *ALV-forg*
Narrow passage connecting the Alommo Sea to the Capricious Ocean.

Amá'adrolom / *ah-MAH-'ah-droh-lom*
Seafaring Dome. Located in the Capricious Ocean, locked to an atoll.

Anglass / *AN-glass*
Negian fortress on the south-east perimeter of the Anglass Dome.

Anglass Dome / *AN-glass*
Urgdrolom. Dome located in the Negian Empire, north of the Stiss Malpa.

Archstone Dome
Almeldrolom. Dome located between the Dorhond Tribes and the
Graalman Horde.

Arho / *AR-hoh*
Port city in the Fjordlands Dome.

Arjum / *AR-joom*
Capital of the Laatu Miscam, province of Gwur Ali, in Mindreldrolom, the
Moordusk Dome.

Arjum Promenade / *AR-joom*
Public walkway around Mindreldrolom's trunk, holding the stadium,
sculpture gardens, reliquary, etc.

Ashen Dome
Trommodrolom. Dome located in the southern Tsing Empire, with a top that constantly smokes.

Azash / *ah-ZAH-sh*
Capital of the Elmaren Queendom.

Azurean Dome / *ah-ZUR-ean*
Quajudrolom. Dome located in the Kingdom of Bauram, surrounded by blue sands.

Balastdrolom / *BAH-last-droh-lom*
Scoria Dome. Located between Afhoran, Tharman, and Graalman lands.

Bauram, Kingdom of / *bau-RAHM*
One of the sixteen realms. Its capital is Allathanathar.

Bay of Hashmun / *HASH-moon*
Wide bay opening east of the Gulf of Erjilm.

Bayanhong Tribes / *BAH-jann-hong*
One of the sixteen realms. Its capital is On Khurderen.

Bergsulf / *BERG-sulf*
Land of independent colonies in the Unclaimed Territories, north of the Fractured Range.

Bighorn Dome
Rilgdrolom. Dome located between the peaks of the Stelm Rilgéreo and Stelm Rilganesh.

Birsulf Allastirg / *BEER-sulf AH-las-teerg*
"Southern Homeland." Laatu settlement in the Udarbans Forest.

Bra'uur / *brah-OOR*
Capital of the Tjardur Miscam in Trommodrolom, the Ashen Dome.

Brasha'in Scablands / *brah-sha-'EEN*
Volcanic wasteland in the western Zovarian Union.

Brimstowne / *BRIMs-town*
Mining frontier town in an independent Bergsulfi colony by the Stelm Wujann.

Brinelaar / *BRINE-lar*
Salt mining town west of the Bighorn Dome.

Caerlye / *CARE-lie*
Potash mining town west of the Bighorn Dome.

Cape Artok / *AR-tok*
Afhoran port city on the east side of the Alvforg Strait.

Capricious Ocean
Southernmost of the four oceans, known for its unpredictable waters.

Colossus of Thyra / *THIGH-rah*
Massive black-marble sculpture of Bum–Vaor, holding the Trommo Hides crafted of Bra'uur steel.

Da'áju Caldera / *da-'AH-joo*
Vast, static cirque glacier in the Stelm Wujann.

Dathereol Princedom / *dah-THEE-ree-ol*
One of the sixteen realms. Its capital is Therimark.

Dhul–Kar Archipelago / *dool-CAR*
Islands on the northeast end of the Gulf of Erjilm, opening into the Ophidian Sea and Yenmai.

Doralghon / *DOH-ralg-hone*
Capital of the Graalman Horde.

Dorhond Tribes / *DOOR-hund*
One of the sixteen realms. Its capital is Oskirin.

Druhal / *droo-HAL*
Capital of the Wastyr Triumvirate. One of three.

Duam / *DOO-uhm*
Tsing port town in the Ophidian Sea.

Elanúbril / *ella-NOO-breel*
Capital of the Khaar Du Tribes.

Elmaren Queendom / *EL-ma-ren*
One of the sixteen realms. Its capital is Azash.

Emen Ruins / *EH-men*
Dorvauros ruins with hot springs resting within a lava tube.

Esduss Sea / *ES-doos*
Sea separating Fel Baubór from the Loorian mainland.

Fal–Aien Range / *fahl-EYE-en*
Southern half of the Tsing "Crescent Range."

Farjall / *FAR-jall*
Negian fortress on the south–east perimeter of the Heartpine Dome.

Farkhalum / *far-KHA-loom*
Capital of the Wastyr Triumvirate. One of three.

Farsulf Forest / *FAR-soolf*
"Pine Land." Forest north of the Heartpine Dome, south of the Stelm Ca'éli.

Fel Baubór / *fell bau-BORE*
Continent–sized island of blue sands, mostly belonging to the Kingdom of Bauram.

Fel Duyenhai / *fell DOO-yen-high*
Tsing island south of the Gulf of Erjilm.

Fel Mellanolv / *fell MEH-la-nohlv*
Bayani island on the far east.

Fel Nisos / *fell NY-sus*
Great island of the Republic of Lerev.

Fel Sha–Met / *fell sha-MET*
Island between the Gulf of Erjilm and the Bay of Hashmun.

Fel Varanus / *fell VAH-rah-noose*
Zovarian island on which the Varanus Dome spreads its tendrils.

Firefalls
"Minnelvad." Steaming waterfalls in the Stelm Wujann, northwest of Brimstowne.

Fjarmallen Peninsula / *fee-ar-MAH-lehn*
Loosely inhabited lands on the fast southwest of the Dathereol Princedom.

Fjordlands Dome
Nagradrolom. Dome located between the Zovarian Union and the Khaar Du Tribes.

Free Tribelands
One of the sixteen realms. Its capital is Klemes.

Graalman Horde / *GROWL-mahn*
One of the sixteen realms. Its capital is Doralghon.

Gulf of Erjilm / *ERR-juhlm*
Circular gulf at the split between the two great continents.

Gwonledrolom / *WON-leh-droh-lom*
Moonrise Dome. Located in the far east, in the Elmaren Queendom.

Hashan / *ha-SHUN*
Capital of the Tsing Empire. Also called the "City of Bridges."

Heartpine Dome
Agnargdrolom. Dome located between the Free Tribelands and the
Negian Empire.

Hestfell / *HEST-fell*
Capital of the Negian Empire.

Hoombudrolom / *HOH-OHM-boo-droh-lom*
Tarpits Dome. Located in the Tsing Empire, by the Khonn Tar Pits.

Humenath / *WHO-men-ath*
Capital of the province of Gwur Úrëath in the Moordusk Dome.

Illenev / *EE-leh-nehv*
Capital of the Wastyr Triumvirate. One of three.

Isdinnklad / *IS-dihn-clad*
"Sea Lake." Long, tapering sea splitting the Loorian Continent.

Istrilm / *IS-trilm*
An underground stream that runs from Enolv into the Istrilm Sanctum.

Jels Urosh / *gels OO-rosh*
"Four Blessings." The four sacred volcanoes of the Tjardur in the Ashen Dome.

Jels Urosh Rampart / *gels OO-rosh*
Central of the great Tjardur ramparts protecting their Four Blessings.

Jerjan Continent / *JER-jann*
Named after Laaja Jerja, tallest peak at 38,264 feet.

Kalford / *CAL-ford*
Negian town in the only Negian state in the Jerjan Continent.

Kayamur / *CAH-yah-moore*
Negian port city in the only Negian state in the Jerjan Continent.

Keldris Tromaag / *KEL-dris troh-MA-ahg*
Southern bay in the Ashen Dome.

Keldris Troméia / *KEL-dris troh-MEH-ya*
Western bay in the Ashen Dome.

Khaar Du Tribes / *khar doo*
One of the sixteen realms. Its capital is Elanúbril.

Kilkarag Peninsula / *KILL-cah-rahg*
Southwestern peninsula of the Jerjan Continent, attached to the Ashen Dome.

Klad Steio Ikhel / *clad STAY-oh EE-hell*
"New Ikhel Lake." Western lake in the Bighorn Dome.

Klemes / *CLEM-uhs*
Capital of the Free Tribelands, west of the Klad Senet.

Knife Point
Sharp peak cutting through the northwest walls of the Heartpine Dome.

Korolok / *COH-roh-lock*
Tsing port city controlling the Alvforg Strait into the Alommo Sea.

Kroowindrolom / *CROW-win-droh-lom*
Yenwu Dome. Located in the Yenwu Peninsula.

Krostdrolom / *CROSSED-droh-lom*
Lequa Dome. Located in the eastern Negian Empire, by Bayanhong settlements.

Krûn / *croon*
Capital of the Puqua Miscam in Nagradrolom, the Fjordlands Dome.

Kruwendrolom / *CREW-when-droh-lom*
Varanus Dome. Located in Fel Varanus, a far western island of the Zovarian Union.

Laaja Ash / *LA-AH-jah ash*
"White Volcano." One of the Tjardur's Four Blessings. Steams white, sometimes pink.

Laaja Ëovad / *LA-AH-jah EH-oh-vahd*
"Fire Volcano." One of the Tjardur's Four Blessings. Holds the Volcanic Forge and the Vaults of Thyra.

Laaja Jerja / *LA-AH-jah JIR-jah*
Volcano. Tallest peak of the Jerjan Continent at 38,264 feet.

Laaja Khem / *LA-AH-jah khem*
Volcano northwest of the Da'áju Caldera with old Dorvauros mines tunneling through it.

Laaja Kriss / *LA-AH-jah chris*
"Iron Volcano." One of the Tjardur's Four Blessings. From where they mine the ignium-rich iron.

Laaja Trell / *LA-AH-jah trell*
"Black Volcano." One of the Tjardur's Four Blessings. From where they mine soot.

Lawu / *LA-woo*
Tjardur city with a gate in the Nudoroth Rampart. On the southwest, by the Keldris Tromaag.

Lequa Dome / *LEH-kwa*
Krostdrolom. Dome located in the eastern Negian Empire, by Bayanhong settlements.

Lequa Sea / *LEH-kwa*
Northeastern sea that funnels into the Ophidian. Dome is named after it.

Lerev, Republic of / *luh-REHV*
One of the sixteen realms. Its capital is Normouth.

Loorian Continent / *LOO-ree-anne*
Named after Mount Loor, tallest peak at 35,167 feet.

Mandible Bay
Secluded bay with calm waters leading to Yenmai, the Yenwu capital.

Mindreldrolom / *MIHN-drehl-droh-lom*
Moordusk Dome. Located in the Zovarian Union, near Zovaria.

Minnelvad / *ME-nell-vahd*
"Firefalls." Steaming waterfalls in the Stelm Wujann, northwest of Brimstowne.

Mireinfield / *ME-reign-field*
Bayanhong settlement southeast of the Lequa Dome.

Moonrise Dome
Gwonledrolom. Dome located in the far east, in the Elmaren Queendom.

Moordusk Dome
Mindreldrolom. Dome located in the Zovarian Union, near Zovaria.

Mount Alvforg / *ALV-forg*
Prominent peak in the southern Tsing Empire, where the Jabrak–Tsing
originated.

Mount Loor / *lure*
Tallest peak of the Loorian Continent at 35,167 feet.

Nagradrolom / *NAH-grah-droh-lom*
Fjordlands Dome. Located between the Zovarian Union and the
Khaar Du Tribes.

Nannúr / *nah-NOOR*
Tjardur city with a gate in the Nudoroth Rampart. On the west, by the
Keldris Troméia.

Nargara / *nar-GAH-rah*
Tsing fortress city on the eastern borders, home of the Nargara Bastion.

Negian Empire / *NEE-jann*
One of the sixteen realms. Its capital is Hestfell.

Ngau Tor / *n-GAW tor*
Fishing town on the southwest of the Ashen Dome.

Ninn Tago / *nihn TAH-goh*
"Gray Pass." Old road cutting over the Stelm Ca'éli, connecting Withervale
to Knife Point.

Nisos / *NY-sus*
Lerevi port city. Used to be the capital of the old Kingdom of Nisos.

Nisos Dome / *NY-sus*
Okridrolom. Dome located in the Republic of Lerev, in the island of Fel Nisos.

Normouth / *NOR-muth*
Capital of the Republic of Lerev.

Nudoroth Rampart / *NOO-doh-roth*
Southwestern of the great Tjardur ramparts protecting their Four Blessings.

Okridrolom / *OH-kree-droh-lom*
Nisos Dome. Located in the Republic of Lerev, in the island of Fel Nisos.

Old Pilgrim's Road
Longest road in the Loorian Continent, running from Umarion to Wyrmwash.

On Khurderen / *on khur-DEH-rehn*
Capital of the Bayanhong Tribes.

Ophidian Sea
Snaking sea separating the Loorian and Jerjan continents.

Orhumbelen / *or-hoom-BEH-len*
Port in the Taring Peninsula, southwest of the Gulf of Erjilm.

Oskirin / *OSS-kih-ruhn*
Capital of the Dorhond Tribes.

Oxmaaga / *ox-MA-gah*
Capital of the Oxruk in the Nisos Dome, burrowing below the old Sehján Capital
of Kissumar.

Pink Caldera
Secret and sacred Tjardur temple at the top of Laaja Ash.

Quajudrolom / *KWA-joo-droh-lom*
Azurean Dome. Located in the Kingdom of Bauram, surrounded by blue sands.

Quiescent Ocean
Westernmost of the four oceans, known for its calm waters.

Ravine Road
Canyon road separating the Stelm Tai-Du and Stelm Rilganesh. Graalman trade
route.

Rilanhon Basin / *RYE-lan-hone*
Graalman territory on the eastern slopes of the Stelm Tai-Du, near the Tarpits Dome.

Rilgdrolom / *REEL-g-droh-lom*
Bighorn Dome. Located between the peaks of the Stelm Rilgéreo and
Stelm Rilganesh.

Runa / *ROO-nah*
Capital of the Ikhel Miscam in Rilgdrolom, the Bighorn Dome.

Sajal Crater / *SAH-jall*
Round crater in the volcanic lands of the Stelm Sajal. Known for its warm waters.

Scoria Dome
Balastdrolom. Dome located between Afhoran, Tharman, and Graalman lands.

Seaborr / *SEA-bore*
Negian port northwest of the Lequa Dome, in the Almoth Bay.

Seafaring Dome
Amá'adrolom. Dome located in the Capricious Ocean, locked to an atoll.

Shaderift
Negian city on the southwest of the Lequa Dome.

Sharr Helm / *shahr helm*
Capital of the Tharma Federation.

Sharzi / *SHAHR-zee*
Trading town connecting the Tsing Empire, Negian Empire, and Graalman Horde.

Shash / *shash*
Yenwu city by the Landbridge of Shash, which connects the peninsula to
the mainland.

Shusnukran / *SHOES-noo-cran*
Western Graalman city.

Sinsimbo / *SIN-sin-boh*
Fortified port in the Ashen Dome, where the Horns of Valor act as the gateway.

Snoring Mountain
Peak in the Stelm Wujann that tends to tremble unpredictably.

Stelm Mokvo / *stelm MOCK-voh*
"Broken Sierras." Mountains cracked by fault lines separating the Tsing and
Graalman lands.

Stelm Nedross / *stelm NED-ross*
"Bamboo Sierras." Mountains east of the Fjordlands Dome.

Stelm Rilganesh / *stelm REEL-gah-nesh*
"Bighorn Sheep Mountains." Range north of the Bighorn Dome.

Stelm Rilgéreo / *stelm reel-GEH-reh-oh*
"Goat Mountains." Range south of the Bighorn Dome.

Stelm Sajal / *stelm SAH-jall*
"Foreboding Mountains." Volcanic range east of the Brasha'in Scablands.

Stelm Shäerath / *stelm SHAH-eh-rath*
The Tricolored Mountain, central peak at the Fjordlands Dome from where the
trunk grows.

Stelm Tai-Du / *stelm tai-DOO*
"Night-Snow Mountains." Range north of the Tarpits Dome.

Stelm Wujann / *stelm WOO-jann*
"Icy Mountains." Vast sierras in the northern Loorian Continent.

Stiss Galha / *stiss GAL-hah*
Longest Tsing River, connected to the Stiss Vardal via the Vardal Canal.

Stiss Kikna / *stiss KICK-nah*
River that runs from Kalford, west of the Bighorn Dome, into the Ophidian Sea.

Stiss Malpa / *stiss MAHL-pah*
River that empties into the tip of the Isdinnklad Lake, right at Withervale.

Sundhollow / *SUHND-hollow*
Capital of the Kingdom of Afhora.

Taring / *TAH-ring*
Pre-Downfall ruins at the Taring Peninsula, southwest of the Gulf of Erjilm.

Tarpits Dome
Hoombudrolom. Dome located in the Tsing Empire, by the Khonn Tar Pits.

Tharma Federation / *THAHR-mah*
One of the sixteen realms. Its capital is Sharr Helm.

Therimark / *THEH-ree-mark*
Capital of the Dathereol Princedom.

Thirteen Peaks
Mountains separating the White Desert of Dorhond from the archlands of
the Horde.

Thornridge Lookout
Free Tribelands fortress protecting the perimeter road around the Heartpine Dome.

Topaz Beck
Wide river that enters the Heartpine Dome on the north and exits again
on the south.

Trommodrolom / *TROM-moh-droh-lom*
Ashen Dome. Located in the southern Tsing Empire, with a top that
constantly smokes.

Tsing Empire / *zing*
One of the sixteen realms. Its capital is Hashan.

Tsogi Rampart / *SO-gi*
Outermost of the great Tjardur ramparts protecting their Four Blessings.

Tumultuous Ocean
Easternmost of the four oceans, known for its rough waters.

Udarbans Forest / *OO-dar-bans*
Uninhabited forest southwest of the Brasha'in Scablands.

Uinin / *WE-neen*
Western Ikhel town by the Klad Steio Ikhel in the Bighorn Dome.

Ultad / *OOL-tad*
Negian port city in the only Negian state in the Jerjan Continent.

Unclaimed Territories
Areas not claimed by any of the sixteen realms.

Unthawing Ocean
Northernmost of the four oceans, known for its icesheets and icebergs.

Urgdrolom / *OORG-droh-lom*
Anglass Dome. Located in the Negian Empire, wrapped by the Stiss Malpa.

Varanus Dome / *VAH-rah-noose*
Kruwendrolom. Dome located in Fel Varanus, a far western island of the Zovarian Union.

Vardal / *VAR-dahl*
Tsing city at the Alommo Sea.

Vardal Canal / *VAR-dahl*
Waterway connecting the Alommo Sea to the Gulf of Erjilm.

Vaults of Thyra / *THIGH-rah*
Tjardur archive of ancestral hides in the depths of Laaja Ëovad.

Wastyr Triumvirate / *was-TIER*
One of the sixteen realms. Its capital is Illenev.

Welmouth / *WELL-muth*
Lerevi city west of the Nisos Dome.

White Desert
Expansive desert of white sands speckled with Dorhond temples.

Withervale
Easternmost Zovarian city, on the border with the Negian Empire.

Wuovad Kladesh / *WOE-vahd CLAD-esh*
"Fiery Lakes." Area southwest of the Sajal Crater known for its hot springs.

Wyrmwash
Negian port city at the mouth of the Stiss Negii.

Yenmai / *YEN-my*
Capital of the Yenwu State.

Yenwu Dome / *YEN-woo*
Kroowindrolom. Dome located in the Yenwu Peninsula.

Yenwu State / *YEN-woo*
One of the sixteen realms. Its capital is Yenmai.

Zovaria / *zoh-VAH-ree-uh*
Capital of the Zovarian Union.

Zovarian Union / *zoh-VAH-ree-uhn*
One of the sixteen realms. Its capital is Zovaria.

THE JOURNEY SO FAR
UNTHAWING OCEAN
Elanúbril
Khaar Du Tribes
TESLURKATH
Baysea Beyenaar
Tesz Bay
FJORDSULF
STELM NEDROSS
Klad Mahajaan
Dragonkeep Bay
STELM
Spine Bay
Fjordlands
Needlecove
Koroberg
Isdinnklad Sea
Zovaria
Isdinnklad Lake
Zovarian Union
Moordusk
STELM CA'ELY
Abrazion Bay
Muskeg
Nebush
Old Karst
Klemes
Klad Senet
Varanus
New Karst
QUIESCENT OCEAN
Pt Varanus
Free Tribelands
Yanan
STELM ANKROV
Del Paulia
Allathanathar
UKHBRIA RANGE
Brashayin Scablands
Sajal Crater
Dunewaar
STELM SAJAL
Yenwu
Unclaimed Territories
MOUNT LOOR
Yenmai
Lhambor Di
Yenwu State
Aksas Di
Esduss Sea
Azurean
Navar Mat
Bay of Hashmun
Kingdom of Bauram
Kizad
Banresht Sea
Gulf of Erjilm
Ashen
Ngau Tor
Taring
Nisos
Normouth
Republic of Terev
Nisos
Coorian Continent
Terjan Continent
CAPRICIOUS
NOSS

Khaar Du Wastes
Ash Sea
Dathereol Princedom
Therimark
Khaarkadesh
Unclaimed Territories
Bergsulf
Falbagrish Range
Loorian Continent
Jerjan Continent
Da'Aju Caldera
Stelm Khull
Brimstowne
Fractured Range
Lequa Sea
Wujann
Anglass
Lequa
Negian Empire
Withervale
Anglass
Shaderift
Wyrmwash
Ophidian Sea
Bayanhong Tribes
Hestfell
Heartpine
Ultad
Thornridge
Kayamur
Stelm Rilgéreo
Farjall
Montano
Caerlye
Kalford
Bighorn
On Khurderen
Brinelaar
Sharzi
Dorhond Tribes
Stelm Tai-Du
Stelm Rilganesh
Oskirin
Bay of Negórinea
White Desert
Azash
Tsing Empire
Tarpits
Archstone
Elmaren Queendom
Hashan
Stelm Mokyo
Shusnukran
Moonrise
Shash
Nargara
Graalman Horde
Doralghon
Sharr Helm
Alommo Sea
Tharma Federation
Scoria
Tumultuous Ocean
Mount Alvforg
Sundhollow
Korolok
Cape Artok
Kingdom of Athora
Ocean
Illenev
Austral Sea
Druhal
Wastyr Triumvirate
Farkhalum
Seafaring
0   100   200   300   400   500   Distance in Miles   1000

ACKNOWLEDGMENTS

I find it strange to write an acknowledgments section for Book 1 of a six-book series, knowing that it should also stand for the next five books I wrote simultaneously. Some names (such as those of my generous beta readers) will change from book to book, but most of the thanks I want to give are to the same people and groups. So let the core of these acknowledgments stand sixfold, for each of the volumes of the *Noss Saga*.

I was spoiled by my parents, Angélica Delgado and Juan Carlos Baldwin. They would let me buy any book I wanted, encouraging me to devour Bradbury, Sagan, Tolkien, Allende, Márquez, Vasconcelos, Gaiman, Asimov, Borges, and so much more. All my passions sprout from their unrelenting support—it is all their fault. Gracias, a él y ella.

Writing can be a lonesome endeavor, but I had my husband, Timothy, always here beside me, to whom I could blabber incoherent thoughts at random intervals, like a bouncing board for spittle and nonsense. Too many of the best ideas for this saga came from me spouting something massively stupid, only to hear him correct me or point out a different route I had not the foresight to envision.

Awfully prematurely, when I was merely in the planning stages of the first book, I had begun to envision the covers. Since the very start I knew I wanted Ilse Gort to lend her skillful hands for the illustrations. I was terrified to ask for her help. I was so happy when she said yes, and happier still when she proposed ideas that were much better than my own.

My editor, Andrew Corvin, was instrumental in fixing up my messes with a barrage of thoughtful suggestions. His notes were not just simple grammar and typo corrections, but offered insights on the characters' motivations, flow of sentences, word choice, and even broader story notes that truly helped focus the work and keep the voice consistent.

On the audiobook side, Magnus Carlssen did a fantastic job adding his own flavor to the narration, even getting all my tricky pronunciations right. I ran a poll among the beta readers to see which voice they preferred, and Magnus landed right at the top for a reason. And teaming him with Iain James Armour (Fox Amoore), who wrote the melodies for each of the lyrics, has been such a blessing—the first time I heard a work in progress of one of the songs, I squealed.

After so many last-minute tweaks, a final proofread was needed. Shiloh Skye joined in to help, not only offering meticulous corrections, but truly polishing and elevating the text. He is also an avid reader and a great advocate for indie authors, and has been helping the saga reach many new fans.

I had the luck to count with a thoughtful and diverse group of beta readers and friends who gave me a ton of notes to work with. Thank you for believing in me and for offering your help—this book is far better thanks to you, Abs M Rice, Alejandro Renteria, Alex Mui, Amanda Leigh, Angie Lee Camp, Arthur Huang, BirdsongChoir, Blackquill, Brian Jackson, Carlos A. Luna Aranguré, Charlie McGrew, Colleen Maloney, Conor Davitt, Cosmo, David "Professor Jefe" Jones, Edwin Herrell, Elliot D. Brown, Erik Tye, Fana, FFAT, Franz Anthony, Guephren, Ionuț Lala, Jack Sanderson, Jul, Kiko, Kyle Branch, Kyle Dolloff, Louis D.S, Marco Nowak, Marián Sulák, Marcus Rodriguez, Markus Lundberg, Marston Jones, Matt Morgan, Matthew Green, Max Sjöblom, Miguel Ángel García García, Mike Hillard, Miles Fox, Nora Rogers, North, Reverie Benedetto, Rosalea Barker, Ross Blocher, Rourkie, Ryan Tye, Sandra Malpica, Santi Rowe, Scurrow, Sean Wenzel, Shadow Worfu, Skiriki, Solomon H., Stormy-Sestleif, Streuhund, Ted Sawyer, Tiberius Rings, Timothy Dahlum, Victor Hugo Guadagnin, Zechariah Sanders, and a couple of anons.

One thing I never lacked during this process was encouragement. As an introvert, having an online community I can count on has been a true blessing. I truly appreciate everyone in social media who has been hitting little heart icons to trigger tiny releases of dopamine in my brain. In particular, thank you to my fervent furry following, who taught me to be courageous enough to be myself, to write a story that speaks my truth. You inspire me.

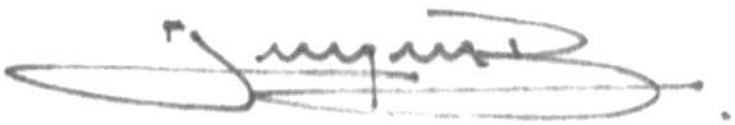

ABOUT THE AUTHOR

Joaquín Baldwin was born in Paraguay, where he first found his love of books by picking up every volume by Ray Bradbury he could get his hands on, and then by submerging himself into a single-bound copy of the Lord of the Rings trilogy—but it wasn't until much later that he'd acquire a taste for writing.

At age 19, he moved to the US to study film and animation, where he received a BFA from CCAD and an MFA from UCLA. He was the recipient of a full scholarship from the Jack Kent Cooke Foundation.

His short films have won over 100 awards and honors at festivals and competitions such as Cannes, the Student Academy Awards, Cinequest, and USA Film Festival. Soon after receiving his masters, he began working at the Walt Disney Animation Studios as a CG Layout Artist, and later as a Director of Cinematography, working on films such as Zootopia, Encanto, Wreck-It Ralph, Frozen, Raya, and Moana.

Never content with sticking to his lane, Joaquín has experience as a professional photographer, illustrator, comic artist, web designer, and 3D designer. His varied skillset came in handy when developing his fantasy saga, allowing him to create his own illustrations, maps, 3D models, book covers, website, and even his own language (phonetics, runes, and all).

Since the 2020 pandemic hit, he's been spending every second of his free time forging the complex world of Noss.

Sign up to Joaquín's mailing list:
JoaquinBaldwin.com/list

Connect with Joaquín on social media:
Search for @joabaldwin to find him on most sites, such as Bluesky, Mastodon, Facebook, Twitter, and Instagram.